KU-161-722

John Irving was born in Exeter, New Hampshire, in 1942. His first novel, *Setting Free the Bears*, was published in 1968, when he was twenty-six. He competed as a wrestler for twenty years, and coached wrestling until he was forty-seven.

John Irving has been nominated for a National Book Award three times – winning once, in 1980 for his novel *The World According to Garp*. He received an O. Henry Award in 1981 for his short story 'Interior Space'. In 2000, he won the Oscar for Best Adapted Screenplay for *The Cider House Rules*. In 2013 he won a Lambda Literary Award for his novel *In One Person*.

An international writer – his novels have been translated into more than thirty-five languages – John Irving lives in Toronto. His all-time best-selling novel, in every language, is *A Prayer for Owen Meany*. *Avenue of Mysteries* is his fourteenth novel.

For more information on John Irving and his books, see his website at www.john-irving.com

www.**penguin**.co.uk

THE NOVELS

Setting Free the Bears (1968)

'The most nourishing, satisfying novel I have read for years. I admire the hell out of it'
Kurt Vonnegut Jr.

The Water-Method Man (1972)

'Three or four times as funny as most novels'
The New Yorker

The 158-Pound Marriage (1973)

'Deft and hard-hitting'
New York Times

The World According to Garp (1978)

'Absolutely extraordinary . . . A rollercoaster ride that leaves one breathless'
Los Angeles Times

The Hotel New Hampshire (1981)

'A startlingly original family saga that combines macabre humour with Dickensian sentiment'
Time

The Cider House Rules (1985)

'Difficult to define, impossible not to admire'
Daily Telegraph

A Prayer for Owen Meany (1989)

'A work of genius'
Independent

A Son of the Circus (1994)

'A wide-ranging fiction of massive design that encapsulates our world'
Mail on Sunday

A Widow for One Year (1998)

'Grand farce, comic gusto and a deeply poetic sense of human vulnerability'
Time Out

The Fourth Hand (2001)

'A rich and deeply moving tale . . . Vintage Irving'
Washington Post

Until I Find You (2006)
'Superbly original . . . To be read and remembered'
The Times

Last Night in Twisted River (2009)

'A stately, sophisticated rumination on the nature of storytelling – and love'
Marie Claire

In One Person (2012)

'A sexual comedy that has both guts and heart . . . a hard novel to classify but an easy one to like'
Independent

Avenue of Mysteries (2015)

'Thoroughly modern, accessibly brainy, hilariously eccentric and beautifully human'
New York Times

The Short Stories

Trying to Save Piggy Snead (1993)

'Supple and energetic'
New York Times Book Review

The Non-Fiction

The Imaginary Girlfriend (1996)

'Rich, wonderful and diverse'
Denver Post

My Movie Business (1999)

'Instructive, delightful and riveting'
Boston Globe

JOHN

avenue of mysteries

IRVING

BLACK SWAN

TRANSWORLD PUBLISHERS
61–63 Uxbridge Road, London W5 5SA
www.penguin.co.uk

Transworld is part of the Penguin Random House group of
companies whose addresses can be found at global.
penguinrandomhouse.com

First published in the US in 2015 by Simon & Schuster

First published in Great Britain in 2015 by Doubleday
an imprint of Transworld Publishers
Black Swan edition published 2016

Copyright © Garp Enterprises Ltd 2015

John Irving has asserted his right under the Copyright, Designs
and Patents Act 1988 to be identified as the author of this work.

This book is a work of fiction and, except in the case of
historical fact, any resemblance to actual persons living or
dead, is purely coincidental.

Every effort has been made to obtain the necessary permissions
with reference to copyright material, both illustrative and quoted.
We apologize for any omissions in this respect and will be pleased
to make the appropriate acknowledgements in any future edition.

A CIP catalogue record for this book
is available from the British Library.

ISBN
9780552778640 (B format
9780552778657 (A format)

Typeset in 10.5/13.5pt Giovanni Book by
Falcon Oast Graphic Art Ltd.
Printed and bound in Great Britain by Clays Ltd, Bungay, Suffolk.

Penguin Random House is committed to a sustainable
future for our business, our readers and our planet. This book is
made from Forest Stewardship Council® certified paper.

1 3 5 7 9 10 8 6 4 2

For Martin Bell and
Mary Ellen Mark.
What we began together,
let us finish together.

Also for Minnie Domingo and
Rick Dancel, and their
daughter, Nicole Dancel,
for showing me the Philippines.

And for my son Everett,
my interpreter in Mexico,
and Karina Juárez,
our guide in Oaxaca
– dos abrazos muy fuertes.

Journeys end in lovers meeting.

– WILLIAM SHAKESPEARE, *Twelfth Night*

Chapters

• Chapters •

avenue of mysteries

• 1 •

Lost Children

Occasionally, Juan Diego would make a point of saying, 'I'm a Mexican – I was born in Mexico, I grew up there.' More recently, he was in the habit of saying, 'I'm an American – I've lived in the United States for forty years.' Or, in an effort to defuse the nationality issue, Juan Diego liked to say, 'I'm a midwesterner – in fact, I'm an Iowan.'

He never said he was a Mexican American. It wasn't only that Juan Diego disliked the label, though he thought of it as such and he *did* dislike it. What Juan Diego believed was that people were always seeking a commonality with the Mexican-American experience, and he could find no common ground in his own experience; more truthfully, he didn't look for it.

What Juan Diego said was that he'd had two lives – two separate and distinctly different lives. The Mexican experience was his first life, his childhood and early adolescence. After he left Mexico – he'd never gone back – he had a second life, the American or midwestern experience. (Or was he also saying that, relatively speaking, not a whole lot had happened to him in his second life?)

What Juan Diego always maintained was that, in his mind – in his memories, certainly, but also in his dreams – he lived and relived his two lives on 'parallel tracks.'

A dear friend of Juan Diego's – she was also his doctor – teased him about the so-called parallel tracks. She told him he was either a kid from Mexico or a grown-up from Iowa all the time. Juan Diego could be an argumentative person, but he agreed with her about that.

BEFORE THE BETA-BLOCKERS HAD disturbed his dreams, Juan Diego told his doctor friend that he used to wake up to the 'gentlest' of his recurrent nightmares. The nightmare he had in mind was really a memory of the formative morning he became a cripple. In truth, only the beginning of the nightmare or the memory was *gentle*, and the origin of this episode was something that happened in Oaxaca, Mexico – in the neighborhood of the city dump, in 1970 – when Juan Diego was fourteen.

In Oaxaca, he was what they called a dump kid (un niño de la basura); he lived in a shack in Guerrero, the colony for families who worked in the dump (el basurero). In 1970, there were only ten families living in Guerrero. At that time, about a hundred thousand people lived in the city of Oaxaca; many of them didn't know that the dump kids did most of the picking and sorting through stuff at the basurero.

The children had the job of separating the glass, aluminum, and copper.

People who knew what the dump kids did called them los pepenadores – 'the scavengers.' At fourteen, that was who Juan Diego was: a dump kid and a scavenger. But the boy was also a reader; the word got around that un niño de la basura had taught himself to read. Dump kids weren't the biggest readers, as a rule, and young readers of any origin or background are rarely self-taught. That was why the word got around, and how the Jesuits, who put such a high priority on education, heard about the boy from Guerrero. The two old Jesuit priests at the Temple of the Society of Jesus referred to Juan Diego as the 'dump reader.'

'Someone should bring the dump reader a good book or two – God knows what the boy finds to read in the basurero!' either Father Alfonso or Father Octavio said. Whenever one of these two old priests said 'someone should' do anything, Brother Pepe was always the one who did it. And Pepe was a big reader.

In the first place, Brother Pepe had a car, and, because he'd come from Mexico City, getting around Oaxaca was relatively easy for him. Pepe was a teacher at the Jesuit school; it had long been a successful school – everyone knew the Society of Jesus was good at running schools. On the other hand, the Jesuit orphanage was relatively new (it had been less than ten years since they'd remodeled the former convent as an orphanage), and not everyone was crazy about the orphanage's name – to some, Hogar de los Niños Perdidos was a long name that sounded a little severe.

But Brother Pepe had put his heart into the school *and* the orphanage; over time, most of those tender souls who objected to the *sound* of 'Home of the Lost Children' would certainly admit that the Jesuits ran a pretty good orphanage, too. Besides, everyone had already shortened the name of the place – 'Lost Children,' people called it. One of the nuns who looked after the children was more blunt about it; to be fair, Sister Gloria must have been referring to a couple of misbehaving kids, not to *all* the orphans, when she muttered, occasionally, 'los perdidos' – surely 'the lost ones' was a name the old nun intended for only a few of the more exasperating children.

Luckily, it was not Sister Gloria who brought the books to the basurero for the young dump reader; if Gloria had chosen the books and been their deliverer, Juan Diego's story might have ended before it began. But Brother Pepe put reading on a pedestal; he was a Jesuit because the Jesuits had made him a reader *and* introduced him to Jesus, not necessarily in that order. It was best not to ask Pepe if reading or Jesus had saved him, or which one had saved him more.

At forty-five, he was too fat – a 'cherubic-looking figure, if not a celestial being,' was how Brother Pepe described himself.

Pepe was the epitome of goodness. He embodied that mantra from Saint Teresa of Ávila: 'From silly devotions and sour-faced saints, good Lord, deliver us.' He made her holy utterance foremost among his daily prayers. No wonder children loved him.

But Brother Pepe had never been to the Oaxaca basurero before. In those days, they burned everything they could in the dump; there were fires everywhere. (Books were useful fire starters.) When Pepe stepped out of his VW Beetle, the smell of the basurero and the heat of the fires were what he'd imagined Hell would be like – only he hadn't imagined children working there.

There were some very good books in the backseat of the little Volkswagen; good books were the best protection from evil that Pepe had actually held in his hands – you could not hold faith in Jesus in your hands, not in quite the same way you could hold good books.

'I'm looking for the reader,' Pepe told the dump workers, both the adults and the children. Los pepenadores, the scavengers, gave Pepe a look full of contempt. It was evident that they did not value reading. One of the adults spoke first – a woman, perhaps Pepe's age or a little younger, probably the mother of one or more of the scavengers. She told Pepe to look for Juan Diego in Guerrero – in el jefe's shack.

Brother Pepe was confused; maybe he'd misunderstood her. El jefe was the dump boss – he was the head of the basurero. Was the reader el jefe's child? Pepe asked the woman worker.

Several dump kids laughed; then they turned away. The adults didn't think it was funny, and the woman said only: 'Not exactly.' She pointed in the direction of Guerrero, which was nestled into a hillside below the basurero. The shacks in the colony had been assembled from materials the workers had found in the dump, and el jefe's shack was the one at the periphery of the colony – at the edge nearest to the dump.

Black columns of smoke stood high above the basurero, pillars of blackness reaching into the sky. Vultures circled overhead, but Pepe saw that there were carrion eaters above *and* below; dogs were everywhere in the basurero, skirting the hellfires and grudgingly giving ground to the men in trucks but to almost no one else. The dogs were uneasy company around the children, because both were scavenging – if not for the same stuff. (The dogs weren't interested in glass or aluminum or copper.) The dump dogs were mostly strays, of course, and some were dying.

Pepe wouldn't be in the basurero long enough to spot the dead dogs, or to see what became of them – they were burned, but not always before the vultures found them.

Pepe found more dogs down the hill, in Guerrero. These dogs had been adopted by the families who worked in the basurero and lived in the colony. Pepe thought the dogs in Guerrero looked better fed, and they behaved more territorially than the dogs in the dump. They were more like the dogs in any neighborhood; they were edgier and more aggressive than the dump dogs, who tended to slink in an abject or furtive manner, though the dump dogs had a sly way of holding their ground.

You wouldn't want to be bitten by a dog in the basurero, or by one in Guerrero – Pepe was pretty sure about that. After all, most of the dogs in Guerrero originally came from the dump.

Brother Pepe took the sick kids from Lost Children to see Dr. Vargas at the Red Cross hospital on Armenta y López; Vargas made it his priority to treat the orphanage kids and the dump kids first. Dr. Vargas had told Pepe that those kids who were the scavengers in the basurero were in the greatest danger from the dogs and from the needles – there were lots of discarded syringes with used needles in the dump. Un niño de la basura could easily get pricked by an old needle.

'Hepatitis B or C, tetanus – not to mention any imaginable form of bacterial infection,' Dr. Vargas had told Pepe.

'And a dog at the basurero, or any dog in Guerrero, could have rabies, I suppose,' Brother Pepe had said.

'The dump kids simply must get the rabies shots, if one of those dogs bites them,' Vargas said. 'But the dump kids are more than usually afraid of needles. They're afraid of those old needles, which they *should* be afraid of, but this makes them afraid of getting shots! If dogs bite them, the dump kids are more afraid of the shots than they are of rabies, which is not good.' Vargas was a good man, in Pepe's opinion, though Vargas was a man of science, not a believer. (Pepe knew that Vargas could be a strain, spiritually speaking.)

Pepe was thinking about the rabies danger when

he got out of his VW Beetle and approached el jefe's shack in Guerrero; Pepe's arms were wrapped tightly around the good books he'd brought for the dump reader, and he was wary of all the barking and unfriendly-looking dogs. '¡Hola!' the plump Jesuit cried at the screen door to the shack. 'I have books for Juan Diego, the reader – *good* books!' He stepped back from the screen door when he heard the fierce growling from inside el jefe's shack.

That woman worker at the basurero had said something about the dump boss – el jefe himself. She'd called him by name. 'You won't have trouble recognizing Rivera,' the woman had told Pepe. 'He's the one with the scariest-looking dog.'

But Brother Pepe couldn't see the dog who was growling so fiercely behind the shack's screen door. He took a second step away from the door, which opened suddenly, revealing not Rivera or anyone resembling a dump boss; the small but scowling person in the doorway of el jefe's shack wasn't Juan Diego, either, but a dark-eyed, feral-looking girl – the dump reader's younger sister, Lupe, who was thirteen. Lupe's language was incomprehensible – what came out of her mouth didn't even sound like Spanish. Only Juan Diego could understand her; he was his sister's translator, her interpreter. And Lupe's strange speech was not the most mysterious thing about her; the girl was a mind reader. Lupe knew what you were thinking – occasionally, she knew more about you than that.

'It's a guy with a bunch of books!' Lupe shouted

into the shack, inspiring a cacophony of barking from the disagreeable-sounding but unseen dog. 'He's a Jesuit, and a teacher – one of the do-gooders from Lost Children.' Lupe paused, reading Brother Pepe's mind, which was in a state of mild confusion; Pepe hadn't understood a word she'd said. 'He thinks I'm retarded. He's worried that the orphanage won't accept me – the Jesuits would presume I'm *uneducable*!' Lupe called to Juan Diego.

'She's *not* retarded!' the boy cried out from somewhere inside the shack. 'She understands everything!'

'I guess I'm looking for your brother?' the Jesuit asked the girl. Pepe smiled at her, and she nodded; Lupe could see he was sweating in his herculean effort to hold all the books.

'The Jesuit is nice – he's just a little overweight,' the girl called to Juan Diego. She stepped back inside the shack, holding the screen door open for Brother Pepe, who entered cautiously; he was looking everywhere for the growling but invisible dog.

The boy, the dump reader himself, was barely more visible. The bookshelves surrounding him were better built than most, as was the shack itself – el jefe's work, Pepe guessed. The young reader didn't appear to be a likely carpenter. Juan Diego was a dreamy-looking boy, as many youthful but serious readers are; the boy looked a lot like his sister, too, and both of them reminded Pepe of someone. At the moment, the sweating Jesuit couldn't think who the *someone* was.

'We both look like our mother,' Lupe told him,

because she knew the visitor's thoughts. Juan Diego, who was lying on a deteriorated couch with an open book on his chest, did not translate for Lupe this time; the young reader chose to leave the Jesuit teacher in the dark about what his clairvoyant sister had said.

'What are you reading?' Brother Pepe asked the boy.

'Local history – *Church* history, you might call it,' Juan Diego said.

'It's boring,' Lupe said.

'Lupe says it's boring – I guess it's a *little* boring,' the boy agreed.

'Lupe reads, too?' Brother Pepe asked. There was a piece of ply-wood perfectly supported by two orange crates – a makeshift table, but a pretty good one – next to the couch. Pepe put his heavy armload of books there.

'I read aloud to her – everything,' Juan Diego told the teacher. The boy held up the book he was reading. 'It's a book about how you came third – you Jesuits,' Juan Diego explained. 'Both the Augustinians and the Dominicans came to Oaxaca before the Jesuits – you got to town third. Maybe that's why the Jesuits aren't such a big deal in Oaxaca,' the boy continued. (This sounded startlingly familiar to Brother Pepe.)

'And the Virgin Mary overshadows Our Lady of Guadalupe – Guadalupe gets shortchanged by Mary *and* by Our Lady of Solitude,' Lupe started babbling, incomprehensibly. 'La Virgen de la Soledad is such a local hero in Oaxaca – the Solitude Virgin and her stupid burro story! Nuestra Señora de la Soledad shortchanges Guadalupe, too. I'm a Guadalupe girl!' Lupe said, pointing to herself; she appeared to be angry about it.

Brother Pepe looked at Juan Diego, who seemed fed up with the virgin wars, but the boy translated all this.

'I know that book!' Pepe cried.

'Well, I'm not surprised – it's one of *yours*,' Juan Diego told him; he handed Pepe the book he'd been reading. The old book smelled strongly like the basurero, and some of the pages looked singed. It was one of those academic tomes – Catholic scholarship of the kind almost no one reads. The book had come from the Jesuits' own library at the former convent, now the Hogar de los Niños Perdidos. Many of the old and unreadable books had been sent to the dump when the convent was remodeled to accommodate the orphans, and to make more shelf space for the Jesuit school.

No doubt, Father Alfonso or Father Octavio had decided which books were bound for the basurero, and which were worth saving. The story of the Jesuits arriving third in Oaxaca might not have pleased the two old priests, Pepe thought; besides, the book had probably been written by an Augustinian or a Dominican – not by a Jesuit – and that alone might have condemned the book to the hellfires of the basurero. (The Jesuits did indeed put a priority on education, but no one ever said they weren't competitive.)

'I brought you some books that are more *readable*,'
Pepe said to Juan Diego. 'Some novels, good storytelling
– you know, *fiction*,' the teacher said encouragingly.

'I don't know what I think of *fiction*,' the thirteen-
year-old Lupe said suspiciously. 'Not all storytelling
is what it's cracked up to be.'

'Don't get started on that,' Juan Diego said to her.
'The dog story was just too grown-up for you.'

'*What* dog story?' Brother Pepe asked.

'Don't ask,' the boy told him, but it was too late;
Lupe was groping around, pawing through the books
on the shelves – there were books everywhere, saved
from burning.

'That Russian guy,' the intense-looking girl was
saying.

'Did she say "Russian" – you don't read *Russian*, do
you?' Pepe asked Juan Diego.

'No, no – she means the writer. The writer is a
Russian guy,' the boy explained.

'How do you understand her?' Pepe asked him.
'Sometimes I'm not sure if it's Spanish she's
speaking—'

'Of course it's Spanish!' the girl cried; she'd found
the book that had given her doubts about storytelling, about *fiction*. She handed the book to Brother
Pepe.

'Lupe's language is just a little different,' Juan
Diego was saying. 'I can understand it.'

'Oh, *that* Russian,' Pepe said. The book was a
collection of Chekhov's stories, *The Lady with the Dog
and Other Stories*.

'It's not about the dog at all,' Lupe complained. 'It's about people who aren't married to each other having sex.'

Juan Diego, of course, translated this. 'All she cares about is dogs,' the boy told Pepe. 'I told her the story was too grown-up for her.'

Pepe was having trouble remembering 'The Lady with the Dog'; naturally, he couldn't recall the dog at all. It was a story about an illicit relationship – that was all he could remember. 'I'm not sure this is age-appropriate for either of you,' the Jesuit teacher said, laughing uncomfortably.

That was when Pepe realized it was an English translation of Chekhov's stories, an American edition; it had been published in the 1940s. 'But this is in *English*!' Brother Pepe cried. 'You understand English?' he asked the wild-looking girl. 'You can read English, too?' the Jesuit asked the dump reader. Both the boy and his younger sister shrugged. Where have I seen that shrug before? Pepe thought to himself.

'From our mother,' Lupe answered him, but Pepe couldn't understand her.

'What about our mother?' Juan Diego asked his sister.

'He was wondering about the way we *shrug*,' Lupe answered him.

'You have taught yourself to read English, too,' Pepe said slowly to the boy; the girl suddenly gave him the shivers, for no known reason.

'English is just a little different – I can understand

it,' the boy told him, as if he were still talking about understanding his sister's strange language.

Pepe's mind was racing. They were extraordinary children – the boy could read anything; maybe there was nothing he couldn't understand. And the girl – well, she was different. Getting her to speak normally would be a challenge. Yet weren't they, these dump kids, precisely the kind of *gifted* students the Jesuit school was seeking? And didn't the woman worker at the basurero say that Rivera, el jefe, was 'not exactly' the young reader's father? Who was their father, and where was he? And there was no sign of a mother – not in this unkempt shack, Pepe was thinking. The carpentry was okay, but everything else was a wreck.

'Tell him we are not Lost Children – he found us, didn't he?' Lupe said suddenly to her talented brother. 'Tell him we're not orphanage material. I don't need to speak normally – you understand me just fine,' the girl told Juan Diego. 'Tell him we have a mother – he probably knows her!' Lupe cried. 'Tell him Rivera is *like* a father, only better. Tell him el jefe is *better* than any father!'

'Slow down, Lupe!' Juan Diego said. 'I can't tell him anything if you don't slow down.' It was quite a lot to tell Brother Pepe, beginning with the fact that Pepe probably knew the dump kids' mother – she worked nights on Zaragoza Street, but she also worked for the Jesuits; she was their principal cleaning woman.

That the dump kids' mother worked nights on

Zaragoza Street made her a likely prostitute, and Brother Pepe *did* know her. Esperanza was the Jesuits' best cleaning woman – no question where the children's dark eyes and their insouciant shrugs *came from*, though the origin of the boy's genius for reading was unclear.

Tellingly, the boy didn't use the 'not exactly' phrase when he spoke of Rivera, el jefe, as a potential father. The way Juan Diego put it was that the dump boss was 'probably not' his father, yet Rivera *could* be the boy's father – there was a 'maybe' involved; that was how Juan Diego expressed it. As for Lupe, el jefe was 'definitely not' her father. It was Lupe's impression that she had *many* fathers, 'too many fathers to name,' but the boy passed over this biological impossibility fairly quickly. He said simply that Rivera and their mother had 'no longer been together in that way' when Esperanza became pregnant with Lupe.

It was quite a lengthy but calm manner of storytelling – the way the dump reader presented his and Lupe's impressions of the dump boss as '*like* a father, only better,' and how the dump kids saw themselves as having a home. Juan Diego echoed Lupe that they were 'not orphanage material.' Embellishing, a little, the way Juan Diego put it was: 'We're not present *or* future Lost Children. We have a home here, in Guerrero. We have a *job* in the basurero!'

But, for Brother Pepe, this raised the question of why these children weren't working in the basurero alongside los pepenadores. Why weren't Lupe and

Juan Diego out there *scavenging* with the other dump kids? Were they treated better or worse than the children of the other families who worked in the basurero and lived in Guerrero?

'Better *and* worse,' Juan Diego told the Jesuit teacher, without hesitation. Brother Pepe recalled the *other* dump kids' contempt for reading, and only God knew what those little scavengers made of the wild-looking, unintelligible girl who gave Pepe the shivers.

'Rivera won't let us leave the shack unless he's with us,' Lupe explained. Juan Diego not only translated for her; he elaborated on this detail.

Rivera truly protected them, the boy told Pepe. El jefe was both *like* a father and *better* than a father because he provided for the dump kids and he watched over them. 'And he doesn't ever beat us,' Lupe interrupted him; Juan Diego dutifully translated this, too.

'I see,' Brother Pepe said. But he was only beginning to see what the brother and sister's situation was: indeed, it was better than the situation for many children who separated the stuff they picked through and sorted in the basurero. And it was worse for them, too – because Lupe and Juan Diego were resented by the scavengers and their families in Guerrero. These two dump kids may have had Rivera's protection (for which they were resented), but el jefe was *not exactly* their father. And their mother, who worked nights on Zaragoza Street, was a prostitute who didn't actually *live* in Guerrero.

There is a pecking order everywhere, Brother Pepe thought sadly to himself.

'What's a pecking order?' Lupe asked her brother. (Pepe was now beginning to understand that the girl knew what he was thinking.)

'A pecking order is how the *other* niños de la basura feel superior to us,' Juan Diego said to Lupe.

'Precisely,' Pepe said, a little uneasily. Here he'd come to meet the dump reader, the fabled boy from Guerrero, bringing him good books, as a good teacher would – only to discover that he, Pepe, the Jesuit himself, was the one with a lot to learn.

That was when the constantly complaining but unseen dog showed itself, if it was actually a dog. The weaselly little creature crawled out from under the couch – more rodential than canine, Pepe thought.

'His name is Dirty White – he's a dog, not a rat!' Lupe said indignantly to Brother Pepe.

Juan Diego explained this, but the boy added: 'Dirty White is a dirty little coward – an ungrateful one.'

'I saved him from death!' Lupe cried. Even as the skinny, hunched dog sidled toward the girl's outstretched arms, his lips involuntarily curled, baring his pointed teeth.

'He should be called Saved from Death, not Dirty White,' Juan Diego said, laughing. 'She found him with his head caught in a milk carton.'

'He's a puppy. He was starving,' Lupe protested.

'Dirty White is still starving for something,' Juan Diego said.

'Stop,' his sister told him; the puppy shivered in her arms.

Pepe tried to repress his thoughts, but this was harder than he'd imagined it would be; he decided it would be best to leave, even abruptly, rather than allow the clairvoyant girl to read his mind. Pepe didn't want the thirteen-year-old innocent to know what he was thinking.

He started his VW Beetle; there was no sign of Rivera, or el jefe's 'scariest-looking' dog, as the Jesuit teacher drove away from Guerrero. The spires of black smoke from the basurero were rising all around him, as were the good-hearted Jesuit's blackest thoughts.

Father Alfonso and Father Octavio looked upon Juan Diego and Lupe's mother – Esperanza, the prostitute – as the 'fallen.' In the minds of the two old priests, there were no fallen souls who had fallen further than prostitutes; there were no miserable creatures of the human kind as lost as these unfortunate women were. Esperanza was hired as a cleaning woman for the Jesuits in an allegedly holy effort to *save* her.

But don't these dump kids need saving, too? Pepe wondered. Aren't los niños de la basura among the 'fallen,' or aren't they in danger of *future* falling? Or of falling *further*?

When that boy from Guerrero was a grown-up, complaining to his doctor about the beta-blockers, he should have had Brother Pepe standing beside him; Pepe would have given testimony to Juan Diego's childhood memories *and* his fiercest dreams.

Even this dump reader's *nightmares* were worth preserving, Brother Pepe knew.

WHEN THESE DUMP KIDS were in their early teens, Juan Diego's most recurrent dream wasn't a nightmare. The boy often dreamed of flying – well, not exactly. It was an awkward-looking and peculiar kind of airborne activity, which bore little resemblance to 'flying.' The dream was always the same: people in a crowd looked up; they saw that Juan Diego was walking on the sky. From below – that is, from ground level – the boy appeared to be very carefully walking upside down in the heavens. (It also seemed that he was counting to himself.)

There was nothing spontaneous about Juan Diego's movement across the sky – he was not flying freely, as a bird flies; he lacked the powerful, straightforward thrust of an airplane. Yet, in that oft-repeated dream, Juan Diego knew he was where he belonged. From his upside-down perspective in the sky, he could see the anxious, upturned faces in the crowd.

When he described the dream to Lupe, the boy would also say to his strange sister: 'There comes a moment in every life when you must let go with your hands – with *both* hands.' Naturally, this made no sense to a thirteen-year-old – even to a *normal* thirteen-year-old. Lupe's reply was unintelligible, even to Juan Diego.

One time when he asked her what she thought of his dream about walking upside down in the heavens,

Lupe was typically mysterious, though Juan Diego could at least comprehend her exact words.

'It's a dream about the future,' the girl said.

'*Whose* future?' Juan Diego asked.

'Not yours, I hope,' his sister replied, more mysteriously.

'But I *love* this dream!' the boy had said.

'It's a death dream,' was all Lupe would say further.

But now, as an older man, since he'd been taking the beta-blockers, his childhood dream of walking on the sky was lost to him, and Juan Diego didn't get to relive the nightmare of that long-ago morning he was crippled in Guerrero. The dump reader missed that nightmare.

He'd complained to his doctor. 'The beta-blockers are blocking my *memories*!' Juan Diego cried. 'They are stealing my *childhood* – they are *robbing* my dreams!' To his doctor, all this hysteria meant was that Juan Diego missed the kick his adrenaline gave him. (Beta-blockers really do a number on your adrenaline.)

His doctor, a no-nonsense woman named Rosemary Stein, had been a close friend of Juan Diego's for twenty years; she was familiar with what she thought of as his hysterical overstatements.

Dr. Stein knew very well why she had prescribed the beta-blockers for Juan Diego; her dear friend was at risk of having a heart attack. He not only had very high blood pressure (170 over 100), but he was pretty sure his mother and one of his possible fathers had died of a heart attack – his mother, definitely, at a young age. Juan Diego had no shortage of adrenaline – the fight-or-flight hormone, which is released during moments of stress, fear, calamity, and performance anxiety, *and* during a heart attack. Adrenaline also shunts blood away from the gut and viscera – the blood goes to your muscles, so that you can run. (Maybe a dump reader has more need of adrenaline than most people.)

Beta-blockers do not prevent heart attacks, Dr. Stein had explained to Juan Diego, but these medications block the adrenaline receptors in the body and thus shield the heart from the potentially devastating effect of the adrenaline released during a heart attack.

'Where *are* my damn adrenaline receptors?' Juan Diego had asked Dr. Stein. ('Dr. *Rosemary*,' he called her – just to tease her.)

'In the lungs, blood vessels, heart – almost every-where,' she'd answered him. 'Adrenaline makes your heart beat faster. You breathe harder, the hair on your arms stands up, your pupils dilate, your blood vessels constrict – not good, if you're having a heart attack.'

'What could be *good*, if I'm having a heart attack?' Juan Diego had asked her. (Dump kids are persistent – they're stubborn types.)

'A quiet, relaxed heart – one that beats slowly, not faster and faster,' Dr. Stein said. 'A person on beta-blockers has a slow pulse; your pulse cannot increase, no matter what.'

There were consequences of lowering your blood

pressure; a person on beta-blockers should be a little careful not to drink too much alcohol, which raises your blood pressure, but Juan Diego didn't really drink. (Well, okay, he drank beer, but *only* beer – and not too much, he thought.) And beta-blockers reduce the circulation of blood to your extremities; your hands and feet feel cold. Yet Juan Diego didn't complain about this side effect – he'd even joked to his friend Rosemary that feeling cold was a luxury for a boy from Oaxaca.

Some patients on beta-blockers bemoan the accompanying lethargy, both a weariness and a reduced tolerance for physical exercise, but at his age – Juan Diego was now fifty-four – what did he care? He'd been a cripple since he was fourteen; *limping* was his exercise. He'd had forty years of sufficient limping. Juan Diego didn't want more *exercise*!

He did wish he felt more alive, not so 'diminished' – the word he used to describe how the beta-blockers made him feel, when he talked to Rosemary about his lack of sexual interest. (Juan Diego didn't say he was impotent; even to his doctor, the diminished word was where he began, and ended, the conversation.)

'I didn't know you were in a sexual relationship,' Dr. Stein said to him; in fact, she knew very well that he *wasn't* in one.

'My dear Dr. Rosemary,' Juan Diego said. 'If I were in a sexual relationship, I believe I *would* be diminished.'

She'd given him a prescription for Viagra – six tablets

a month, 100 milligrams – and told him to experiment.

'Don't wait till you meet someone,' Rosemary said.

He hadn't waited; he'd not met anyone, but he *had* experimented. Dr. Stein had refilled his prescription every month. 'Maybe *half* a tablet is sufficient,' Juan Diego told her, after his *experiments*. He hoarded the extra tablets. He'd not complained about any of the side effects from the Viagra. It allowed him to have an erection; he could have an orgasm. Why would he mind a stuffy nose?

Another side effect of beta-blockers is insomnia, but Juan Diego found nothing new or particularly upsetting about that; to lie awake in the dark with his demons was almost comforting. Many of Juan Diego's demons had been his childhood companions – he knew them so well, they were as familiar as friends.

An overdose of beta-blockers can cause dizziness, even fainting spells, but Juan Diego wasn't worried about dizziness or fainting. 'Cripples know how to fall – falling is no big deal to us,' he told Dr. Stein.

Yet, even more than the erectile dysfunction, it was his disjointed dreams that disturbed him; Juan Diego said that his memories and his dreams lacked a followable chronology. He hated the beta-blockers because, in disrupting his dreams, they had cut him off from his childhood, and his childhood mattered more to him than childhood mattered to other adults – to *most* other adults, Juan Diego thought. His childhood, and the people he'd encountered there – the ones who'd changed his life, or who'd been witnesses to what had happened to him at that crucial time – were what Juan Diego had instead of religion.

Close friend though she was, Dr. Rosemary Stein didn't know everything about Juan Diego; she knew very little about her friend's childhood. To Dr. Stein, it probably appeared to come out of nowhere when Juan Diego spoke with uncharacteristic sharpness to her, seemingly about the beta-blockers. 'Believe me, Rosemary, if the beta-blockers had taken my *religion* away, I would *not* complain to you about *that*! On the contrary, I would ask you to prescribe beta-blockers for *everyone*!'

This amounted to more of her passionate friend's hysterical overstatements, Dr. Stein thought. After all, he'd burned his hands saving books from burning – even books about Catholic history. But Rosemary Stein knew only bits and pieces about Juan Diego's life as a dump kid; she knew more about her friend when he was older. She didn't really know the boy from Guerrero.

• 2 •
The Mary Monster

On the day after Christmas, 2010, a snowstorm had swept through New York City. The next day, the unplowed streets of Manhattan were strewn with abandoned cars and cabs. A bus had burned on Madison Avenue, near East Sixty-second Street; spinning in the snow, its rear tires caught fire and ignited the bus. The blackened hulk had dotted the surrounding snow with ashes.

To the guests in those hotels along Central Park South, the view of the pristine whiteness of the park – and of those few brave families with young children, at play in the newly fallen snow – contrasted strangely with the absence of any vehicular traffic on the broad avenues and smaller streets. In the brightly whitened morning, even Columbus Circle was eerily quiet and empty; at a normally busy intersection, such as the corner of West Fifty-ninth Street and Seventh Avenue, not a single taxi was moving. The only cars in sight were stranded, half buried in the snow.

The virtual moonscape, which Manhattan was that Monday morning, prompted the concierge at

Juan Diego's hotel to seek special assistance for the handicapped man. This was not a day for a cripple to hail a cab, or risk riding in one. The concierge had prevailed upon a limousine company – not a very good one – to take Juan Diego to Queens, though there were conflicting reports regarding whether John F. Kennedy International Airport was open or not. On TV, they were saying that JFK was closed, yet Juan Diego's Cathay Pacific flight to Hong Kong was allegedly departing on time. As much as the concierge doubted this – he was certain that the flight would be delayed, if not canceled – he had nonetheless indulged the anxious and crippled guest. Juan Diego was agitated about getting to the airport on time – though no flights were departing, or had departed, in the aftermath of the storm.

It was not Hong Kong he cared about; that was a detour Juan Diego could do without, but a couple of his colleagues had persuaded him that he shouldn't go all the way to the Philippines without stopping to see Hong Kong en route. What was there to *see*? Juan Diego had wondered. While Juan Diego didn't understand what 'air miles' actually meant (or how they were calculated), he understood that his Cathay Pacific flight was free; his friends had also persuaded him that first class on Cathay Pacific was something he must experience – something else he was supposed to *see*, apparently.

Juan Diego thought that all this attention from his friends was because he was retiring from teaching; what else could explain why his colleagues had insisted on helping him organize this trip? But there were other reasons. Though he was young to retire, he was indeed 'handicapped' – and his close friends and colleagues knew he was taking medication for his heart.

'I'm not retiring from *writing*!' he'd assured them. (Juan Diego had come to New York for Christmas at the invitation of his publisher.) It was 'merely' the teaching he was leaving, Juan Diego said, though for years the writing and the teaching had been inseparable; together, they'd been his entire adult life. And one of his former writing students had become very involved with what Juan Diego now thought of as an aggressive takeover of his trip to the Philippines. This former student, Clark French, had made Juan Diego's mission in Manila – as Juan Diego had thought of it, for years – *Clark*'s mission. Clark's *writing* was as assertive, or forced, as he'd been about taking over his former teacher's trip to the Philippines – or so Juan Diego thought.

Yet Juan Diego had done nothing to resist his former student's well-intentioned assistance; he didn't want to hurt Clark's feelings. Besides, it wasn't easy for Juan Diego to travel, and he'd heard that the Philippines could be difficult – even dangerous. A little overplanning wouldn't hurt, he'd decided.

Before he knew it, a *tour* of the Philippines had materialized; his mission in Manila had given rise to side trips and distracting adventures. He worried that the purpose of his going to the Philippines had been compromised, though Clark French would have been quick to tell his former teacher that the zeal to assist him was borne of Clark's admiration for what a noble cause (for so long!) had inspired Juan Diego to take this trip in the first place.

As a very young teenager in Oaxaca, Juan Diego had met an American draft dodger; the young man had run away from the United States to evade the draft for the Vietnam War. The draft dodger's dad had been among the thousands of American soldiers who'd died in the Philippines in World War II – but not on the Bataan Death March, and not in the intense battle for Corregidor. (Juan Diego didn't always remember the exact details.)

The American draft dodger didn't want to die in Vietnam; before he died, the young man told Juan Diego, he wanted to visit the Manila American Cemetery and Memorial – to pay his respects to his slain father. But the draft dodger didn't survive the misadventure of his running away to Mexico; he had died in Oaxaca. Juan Diego had pledged to take the trip to the Philippines for the dead draft dodger; he would make the journey to Manila for him.

Yet Juan Diego had never known the young American's name; the antiwar boy had befriended Juan Diego and his seemingly retarded little sister, Lupe, but they knew him only as 'the good gringo.' The dump kids had met el gringo bueno before Juan Diego became a cripple. At first, the young American seemed too friendly to be doomed, though Rivera had called him a 'mescal hippie,' and the dump kids knew el jefe's opinion of the hippies who came to Oaxaca from the United States at that time.

The dump boss believed that the mushroom hippies were 'the stupid ones'; he meant they were seeking something they thought was profound – in el jefe's opinion, 'something as ridiculous as the interconnectedness of all things,' though the dump kids knew that el jefe himself was a Mary worshiper.

As for the *mescal* hippies, they were smarter, Rivera said, but they were 'the self-destructive ones.' And the mescal hippies were the ones who were also addicted to prostitutes, or so the dump boss believed. The good gringo was 'killing himself on Zaragoza Street,' el jefe said. The dump kids had hoped not; Lupe and Juan Diego adored el gringo bueno. They didn't want the darling boy to be destroyed by his sexual desires *or* the intoxicating drink distilled from the fermented juice of certain species of agave.

'It's all the same,' Rivera had told the dump kids, darkly. 'Believe me, you're not exactly uplifted by what you end up with. Those low women and too much mescal – you're left looking at that little worm!'

Juan Diego knew the dump boss meant the worm at the bottom of the mescal bottle, but Lupe said that el jefe had also been thinking about his penis – how it looked after he'd been with a prostitute.

'You believe all men are always thinking about their penises,' Juan Diego told his sister.

'All men *are* always thinking about their penises,' the mind reader said. To a degree, this was the point past which Lupe would no longer allow herself to adore the good gringo. The doomed American had crossed an imaginary line – the *penis* line, perhaps, though Lupe would never have put it that way.

One night, when the dump reader was reading aloud to Lupe, Rivera was with them in the shack in Guerrero, listening to the reading, too. The dump boss was probably building a new bookcase, or there was something wrong with the barbecue and Rivera was fixing it; maybe he had stopped by just to see if Dirty White (a.k.a. Saved from Death) had died.

The book Juan Diego was reading that night was another discarded academic tome, a mind-numbing exercise in scholarship, which had been designated for burning by one or the other of those two old Jesuit priests Father Alfonso and Father Octavio.

This particular work of unread academia had actually been written by a Jesuit, and its subject was both literary and historical – namely, an analysis of D. H. Lawrence's writing on Thomas Hardy. As the dump reader had not read anything by Lawrence or Hardy, a scholarly examination of Lawrence's writing on Hardy would have been mystifying – even in Spanish. And Juan Diego had selected this particular book because it was in English; he'd wanted more practice reading English, though his less-than-rapt audience (Lupe and Rivera and the disagreeable dog Dirty White) might have understood him better en español.

To add to the difficulty, several pages of the book had been consumed by fire, and a vile odor from the basurero still clung to the burned book; Dirty White wanted to sniff it, repeatedly.

The dump boss didn't like Lupe's saved-from-death dog any better than Juan Diego did. 'I think you should have left this one in the milk carton,' was all el jefe told her, but Lupe (as always) was indignant in Dirty White's defense.

And just then Juan Diego read aloud to them an unrepeatable passage, concerning someone's idea of the fundamental interrelatedness of all beings.

'Wait, wait, wait – stop right there,' Rivera interrupted the dump reader. '*Whose* idea is that?'

'It could be the one called Hardy – maybe it's his idea,' Lupe said. 'Or, more likely, the Lawrence guy – it sounds like him.'

When Juan Diego translated what Lupe said for Rivera, el jefe instantly agreed. 'Or the idea of the person writing the book – whoever that is,' the dump boss added. Lupe nodded that this was also true. The book was tedious while remaining unclear; it was seemingly nitpicking scrutiny of a subject that eluded any concrete description.

'*What* "fundamental interrelatedness of all beings" – *which* beings are supposedly *related*?' the dump boss cried. 'It sounds like something a mushroom hippie would say!'

That got a laugh out of Lupe, who rarely laughed. Soon she and Rivera were laughing together, which was even more rare. Juan Diego would always remember how happy he was to hear both his sister and el jefe laughing.

And now, so many years later – it had been *forty* years – Juan Diego was on his way to the Philippines, a trip he was taking in honor of the nameless good gringo. Yet not a single friend had asked Juan Diego how he intended to pay the dead draft dodger's respects to the slain soldier – like his lost son, the fallen father was without a name. Of course these friends all knew that Juan Diego was a novelist; maybe the fiction writer was taking a trip for el gringo bueno *symbolically*.

As a young writer, he'd been quite the traveler, and the dislocations of travel had been a repeated theme in his early novels – especially in that circus novel set in India, the one with the elephantine title. No one had been able to talk him out of that title, Juan Diego remembered fondly. *A Story Set in Motion by the Virgin Mary* – what a cumbersome title it was, and what a long and complicated story! Maybe my *most* complicated, Juan Diego was thinking – as the limo navigated the deserted, snowbound streets of Manhattan, making its determined way to the FDR Drive. It was an SUV, and the driver was contemptuous of other vehicles and other drivers. According to the limo driver, other vehicles in the city were ill equipped for snow, and the few cars that were 'almost correctly' equipped had the 'wrong tires'; as for the other drivers, they didn't know how to drive in snow.

'Where do you think we are – fuckin' *Florida*?' the driver yelled out his window to a stranded motorist who'd slid sideways and blocked a narrow crosstown street.

Out on the FDR Drive, a taxi had jumped the guardrail and was stuck in the waist-deep snow of the jogging path that ran alongside the East River; the cabbie was attempting to dig out his rear wheels, not with a shovel but a windshield scraper.

'Where are you from, you jerk-off – fuckin' *Mexico*?' the limo driver shouted to him.

'Actually,' Juan Diego said to the driver, '*I'm* from Mexico.'

'I didn't mean you, sir – you're gonna get to JFK on time. Your problem is, you're just gonna *wait* there,' the driver told him, not nicely. 'There's nothin' flyin' – in case you haven't noticed, sir.'

Indeed, Juan Diego hadn't noticed that no planes were flying; he just wanted to be at the airport, ready to leave, whenever his flight departed. The delay, if there was one, didn't matter to him. It was missing this trip that was unthinkable. 'Behind every journey is a reason,' he found himself considering – before he remembered that he'd already written this. It was something he'd stated most emphatically in *A Story Set in Motion by the Virgin Mary*. Now here I am, traveling again – there's *always* a reason, he thought.

'The past surrounded him like faces in a crowd. Among them, there was one he knew, but whose face was it?' For a moment, shrouded by the surrounding snow and intimidated by the vulgar limo driver, Juan Diego forgot that he'd already written this, too. He blamed the beta-blockers.

FROM THE SOUND OF him, Juan Diego's limo driver was a rough-spoken, hateful man, but he knew his way around Jamaica, Queens, where a wide street reminded the long-ago dump reader of Periférico – a street divided by train tracks in Oaxaca. Periférico was where el jefe used to take the dump kids shopping for food; the cheapest, closest-to-rotten produce was available in that market, in La Central – except in 1968, during the student revolts, when La Central was occupied by the military and the food market moved to the zócalo in the center of Oaxaca.

That was when Juan Diego and Lupe were twelve and eleven, and they first became familiar with the area of Oaxaca around the zócalo. The student revolts didn't last long; the market would move back to La Central, and Periférico (with that forlorn-looking footbridge over the train tracks). Yet the zócalo remained in the dump kids' hearts; it had become their favorite part of town. The kids spent as much time away from the dump, in the zócalo, as they could.

Why wouldn't a boy and girl from Guerrero be interested in the center of things? Why wouldn't two niños de la basura be curious to see all the tourists in town? The city dump wasn't on the tourist maps. What tourist ever went sightseeing in the basurero? One whiff of the dump, or the stinging in your eyes from the fires perpetually burning there, would send you running back to the zócalo; one look at the dump dogs (or the way those dogs looked at you) would do it.

Was it any wonder – around this time, during the student riots in 1968, when the military took over La Central and the dump kids started hanging around the zócalo – that Lupe, who was only eleven, began her crazy and conflicted obsessions with Oaxaca's various virgins? That her brother was the only one who could understand her babble cut Lupe off from any meaningful dialogue with adults. And of course these were *religious* virgins, *miraculous* virgins – of the kind who commanded a following, not only among eleven-year-old girls.

Wasn't it to be expected that Lupe would, at first, be drawn to these virgins? (Lupe could read minds; she knew no real-life counterpart who had her ability.) However, what dump kid wouldn't be a little suspicious of miracles? What were these competing virgins doing to prove themselves in the here and now? Had these miraculous virgins performed any miracles *lately*? Wasn't Lupe likely to be super-critical of these highly touted but nonperforming virgins?

There was a virgin shop in Oaxaca; the dump kids discovered it on one of their first outings in the area of the zócalo. This was Mexico: the country had been overrun by the Spanish conquistadors. Hadn't the ever-proselytizing Catholic Church been in the virgin-selling business for years? Oaxaca had once been central to the Mixtec and Zapotec civilizations. Hadn't the Spanish conquest been selling virgins to the indigenous population for centuries – beginning with the Augustinians and the Dominicans, and *thirdly* the Jesuits, all pushing their Virgin Mary?

There was more than Mary to deal with now – so Lupe had noticed from the many churches in Oaxaca – but nowhere in the city were the warring virgins on such tawdry display as you could find them (for sale) in the virgin shop on Independencia. There were life-size virgins and virgins who were larger than life-size. To name only three who were featured, in a variety of cheap and tacky replicas, throughout the shop: Mother Mary, of course, but also Our Lady of Guadalupe, and naturally Nuestra Señora de la Soledad. La Virgen de la Soledad was the virgin whom Lupe disparaged as merely a 'local hero' – the much-maligned Solitude Virgin and her 'stupid burro story.' (The burro, a small donkey, was probably blameless.)

The virgin shop also sold life-size (and larger than life-size) versions of Christ on the Cross; if you were strong enough, you could carry home a giant Bleeding Jesus, but the principal purpose of the virgin shop, which had been in business in Oaxaca since 1954, was providing for the Christmas parties (las posadas).

In fact, only the dump kids called the place on Independencia the virgin shop; everyone else referred to it as the Christmas-parties store – La Niña de las Posadas was the actual name of the ghoulish shop (literally, 'The Girl of the Christmas Parties'). The eponymous Girl was whatever virgin you chose to take home with you; obviously, one of the life-size virgins for sale could liven up your Christmas party – more than an agonizing Christ on the Cross ever could.

As serious as Lupe was about Oaxaca's virgins, the Christmas-parties place was a joke to Juan Diego and

Lupe. 'The Girl,' as the dump kids occasionally called the virgin shop, was where they went for a laugh. Those virgins for sale weren't half as realistic as the prostitutes on Zaragoza Street; the take-home virgins were more in the category of inflatable sex dolls. And the Bleeding Jesuses were simply grotesque.

There was also (as Brother Pepe would have put it) a *pecking order* of virgins on display in various Oaxaca churches – alas, this pecking order and *these* virgins affected Lupe deeply. The Catholic Church had its own virgin shops in Oaxaca; for Lupe, *these* virgins were no laughing matter.

Take the 'stupid burro story,' and how Lupe loathed la Virgen de la Soledad. The Basílica de Nuestra Señora de la Soledad was grandiose – a pompous eyesore between Morelos and Independencia – and the first time the dump kids visited it, their access to the altar was blocked by a caterwauling contingent of pilgrims, countryfolk (farmers or fruit pickers, Juan Diego had guessed), who not only prayed in cries and shouts but ostentatiously approached the radiant statue of Our Lady of Solitude on their knees, virtually crawling the length of the center aisle. The praying pilgrims put Lupe off, as did the local-hero aspect of the Solitude Virgin – she was occasionally called 'Oaxaca's patron saint.'

Had Brother Pepe been present, the kindly Jesuit teacher might have cautioned Lupe and Juan Diego against a pecking-order prejudice of their own: dump kids have to feel superior to *someone*; at the small colony in Guerrero, los niños de la basura believed that they were superior to countryfolk. By the behavior of the loudly praying pilgrims in the Solitude Virgin's basilica, and given their cloddishly rustic attire, Juan Diego and Lupe were left with little doubt: dump kids were definitely superior to these wailing and kneeling farmers or fruit pickers (whoever the uncouth country-folk were).

Lupe also had no love for how la Virgen de la Soledad was dressed; her severe, triangular-shaped robe was black, encrusted with gold. 'She looks like an evil queen,' Lupe said.

'She looks *rich*, you mean,' Juan Diego said.

'The Solitude Virgin is not one of us,' Lupe declared. She meant not indigenous. She meant Spanish, which meant *European*. (She meant *white*.)

The Solitude Virgin, Lupe said, was 'a white-faced pinhead in a fancy gown.' It further irked Lupe that Guadalupe got second-class treatment in the Basílica de Nuestra Señora de la Soledad; the Guadalupe altar was off to the left side of the center aisle – an unlit portrait of the dark-skinned virgin (not even a statue) was her sole recognition. And Our Lady of Guadalupe *was* indigenous; she was a native, an Indian; she was what Lupe meant by 'one of us.'

Brother Pepe would have been astonished at how much dump reading Juan Diego had done, and how closely Lupe had listened. Father Alfonso and Father Octavio believed they had purged the Jesuit library of the most extraneous and seditious reading matter, but the young dump reader had rescued many dangerous books from the hellfires of the basurero.

Those works that had chronicled the Catholic indoctrination of the indigenous population of Mexico had not gone unnoticed; the Jesuits had played a mind-game role in the Spanish conquests, and both Lupe and Juan Diego had learned a lot about the Jesuitical conquistadors of the Roman Catholic Church. While Juan Diego had at first become a dump reader for the purpose of teaching himself to read, Lupe had listened and learned – from the start, she'd been focused.

In the Solitude Virgin's basilica, there was a marble-floored chamber with paintings of the burro story: peasants were praying after they had met and were followed by a solitary, unaccompanied burro. On the little donkey's back was a long box – it looked like a coffin.

'What fool wouldn't have looked in the box right away?' Lupe always asked. Not these stupid peasants – their brains must have been deprived of oxygen by their sombreros. (Dumb countryfolk, in the dump kids' opinion.)

There was – there still exists – a controversy concerning what happened to the burro. Did it one day just stop walking and lie down, or did it drop dead? At the site where the little donkey either stopped in its tracks or just died, the Basílica de Nuestra Señora de la Soledad was erected. Because only then and there had the dumb peasants opened the burro's box. In it was a statue of the Solitude Virgin; disturbingly, a much smaller Jesus figure, naked except for a towel covering his crotch, was lying in the Solitude Virgin's lap.

'What is a shrunken Jesus doing *there*?' Lupe always asked. The discrepancy in the size of the figures was most disturbing: the larger Solitude Virgin with a Jesus half her size. And this was no Baby Jesus; this was Jesus with a *beard*, only he was unnaturally small and dressed in nothing but a towel.

In Lupe's opinion, the burro had been 'abused'; the larger Solitude Virgin with a smaller, half-naked Jesus in her lap spoke to Lupe of 'even worse abuse' – not to mention how 'stupid' the peasants were, for not having the brains to look in the box at the beginning.

Thus did the dump kids dismiss Oaxaca's patron saint and most fussed-over virgin as a hoax or a fraud – a 'cult virgin,' Lupe called la Virgen de la Soledad. As for the proximity of the virgin shop on Independencia to the Basílica de Nuestra Señora de la Soledad, all Lupe would say was: 'Fitting.'

Lupe had listened to a lot of grown-up (if not always well-written) books; her speech might have been incomprehensible to everyone except Juan Diego, but Lupe's exposure to language – and, because of the books in the basurero, to an educated vocabulary – was beyond her years and her experience.

In contrast to her feelings for the Solitude Virgin's basilica, Lupe called the Dominican church on Alcalá a 'beautiful extravagance.' Having complained about the gold-encrusted robe of the Solitude Virgin, Lupe loved the gilded ceiling in the Templo de Santo Domingo; she had no complaints about 'how very Spanish Baroque' Santo Domingo was – 'how very

European.' And Lupe liked the gold-encrusted shrine to Guadalupe, too – nor was Our Lady of Guadalupe overshadowed by the Virgin Mary in Santo Domingo.

As a self-described Guadalupe girl, Lupe was sensitive to Guadalupe being *overshadowed* by the 'Mary Monster.' Lupe not only meant that Mary was the most dominant of the Catholic Church's 'stable' of virgins; Lupe believed that the Virgin Mary was also 'a *domineering* virgin.'

And this was the grievance Lupe had with the Jesuits' Templo de la Compañía de Jesús on the corner of Magón and Trujano – the Temple of the Society of Jesus made the Virgin Mary the main attraction. As you entered, your attention was drawn to the fountain of holy water – agua de San Ignacio de Loyola – and a portrait of the formidable Saint Ignatius himself. (Loyola was looking to Heaven for guidance, as he is often depicted.)

In an inviting nook, after you passed the fountain of holy water, was a modest but attractive shrine to Guadalupe; special notice was paid to the dark-skinned virgin's most famous utterance, in large lettering easily viewed from the pews and kneeling pads.

'"¿No estoy aquí, que soy tu madre?"' Lupe would pray there, incessantly repeating this. '"Am I not here, for I am your mother?"'

Yes, you could say that this was an unnatural allegiance Lupe latched on to – to a mother *and* a virgin figure, which was a replacement for Lupe's actual mother, who was a prostitute (*and* a cleaning woman for the Jesuits), a woman who was not much of a mother to her children, an often absent mother, who lived apart from Lupe and Juan Diego. And Esperanza had left Lupe fatherless, save for the stand-in dump boss – and for Lupe's idea that she had a multitude of fathers.

But Lupe both genuinely worshiped Our Lady of Guadalupe and fiercely doubted her; Lupe's doubt was borne by the child's judgmental sense that Guadalupe had *submitted* to the Virgin Mary – that Guadalupe was *complicitous* in allowing Mother Mary to be in control.

Juan Diego could not recall a single dump-reading experience where Lupe might have learned this; as far as the dump reader could tell, Lupe both believed in and distrusted the dark-skinned virgin entirely on her own. No book from the basurero had led the mind reader down this tormented path.

And notwithstanding how tasteful and appropriate the adoration paid to Our Lady of Guadalupe was – the Jesuit temple in no way disrespected the dark-skinned virgin – the Virgin Mary unquestionably took center stage. The Virgin Mary *loomed*. The Holy Mother was enormous; the Mary altar was elevated; the statue of the Holy Virgin was towering. A relatively diminutive Jesus, already suffering on the cross, lay bleeding at Mother Mary's big feet.

'What is this shrunken-Jesus business?' Lupe always asked.

'At least *this* Jesus has some clothes on,' Juan Diego would say.

Where the Virgin Mary's big feet were firmly planted – on a three-tiered pedestal – the faces of angels appeared frozen in clouds. (Confusingly, the pedestal itself was composed of clouds and angels' faces.)

'What is it supposed to mean?' Lupe always asked. 'The Virgin Mary tramples angels – I can believe it!'

And to either side of the gigantic Holy Virgin were significantly smaller, time-darkened statues of two relative unknowns: the Virgin Mary's parents.

'She had *parents*?' Lupe always asked. 'Who even knows what they looked like? Who *cares*?'

Without question, the towering statue of the Virgin Mary in the Jesuit temple *was* the 'Mary Monster.' The dump kids' mother complained about the difficulty she had *cleaning* the oversize virgin. The ladder was too tall; there was no safe or 'proper' place to lean the ladder, except against the Virgin Mary herself. And Esperanza prayed endlessly to Mary; the Jesuits' best cleaning woman, who had a night job on Zaragoza Street, was an undoubting Virgin Mary fan.

Big bouquets of flowers – *seven* of them! – surrounded the Mother Mary altar, but even these bouquets were dwarfed by the giant virgin herself. She didn't just *tower* – she seemed to *menace* everyone and everything. Even Esperanza, who adored her, thought the Virgin Mary statue was 'too big.'

'Hence *domineering*,' Lupe would repeat.

'"¿No estoy aquí, que soy tu madre?"' Juan Diego found himself repeating in the backseat of the snow-surrounded limousine, now approaching the Cathay

Pacific terminal at JFK. The former dump reader murmured aloud, in both Spanish and English, this modest claim of Our Lady of Guadalupe – more modest than the penetrating stare of that overbearing giantess, the Jesuits' statue of the Virgin Mary. ' "Am I not here, for I am your mother?" ' Juan Diego repeated to himself.

His passenger's bilingual mutterings caused the contentious limo driver to look at Juan Diego in the rearview mirror.

It's a pity Lupe wasn't with her brother; she would have read the limo driver's mind – she could have told Juan Diego what the hateful man's thoughts were.

A successful wetback, the limo driver was thinking – that was his assessment of his Mexican-American passenger.

'We're almost at your terminal, pal,' the driver said: the way he'd said the *sir* word hadn't been any nicer. But Juan Diego was remembering Lupe, and their time together in Oaxaca. The dump reader was daydreaming; he didn't really hear his driver's disrespectful tone of voice. And without his dear sister, the mind reader, beside him, Juan Diego didn't know the bigot's thoughts.

It wasn't that Juan Diego had never encountered a commonality with the Mexican-American experience. It was more a matter of his mind, and where it wandered – his mind was often *elsewhere*.

Mother and Daughter

The handicapped man had not anticipated that he would be stranded at JFK for twenty-seven hours. Cathay Pacific sent him to the first-class lounge of British Airways. This was more comfortable than what the economy-fare passengers had to deal with – the concessionaires ran out of food, and the public toilets were not properly attended to – but the Cathay Pacific flight to Hong Kong, scheduled to depart at 9:15 A.M. on December 27, did not take off till noon of the following day, and Juan Diego had packed his beta-blockers with his toilet articles in his checked bag. The flight to Hong Kong was some sixteen hours. Juan Diego would have to do without his medication for more than forty-three hours; he would go without the beta-blockers for almost two days. (As a rule, dump kids don't panic.)

While Juan Diego considered calling Rosemary to ask her if he was at risk being without his medication for an unknown period of time, he didn't do it. He remembered what Dr. Stein had said: that if he ever had to go off the beta-blockers, for any reason, he should stop taking them *gradually*. (Inexplicably, the *gradually* part made him think there was nothing risky about stopping or restarting the beta-blockers.)

Juan Diego knew he would get scant sleep as he waited in the British Airways lounge at JFK; he looked forward to catching up on his sleep whenever he eventually boarded the sixteen-hour flight to Hong Kong. Juan Diego didn't call Dr. Stein because he was looking forward to having a break from the beta-blockers. With any luck, he might have one of his old dreams; his all-important childhood memories might come back to him – chronologically, he hoped. (As a novelist, he was a little fussy about chrono-logical order, a tad old-fashioned.)

British Airways did its best to make the crippled man comfortable; the other first-class passengers were aware of Juan Diego's limp and the misshapen, custom-made shoe on his damaged foot. Everyone was very understanding; though there were not enough chairs for all the stranded passengers in the first-class lounge, no one complained that Juan Diego had put two chairs together – he'd made a kind of couch for himself, so he could elevate that tragic-looking foot.

Yes, the limp made Juan Diego look older than he was – he looked at least *sixty*-four, not fifty-four. And there was something else: more than a hint of resig-nation gave him a faraway expression, as if the lion's share of excitement in Juan Diego's life had resided in his distant childhood and early adolescence. After all, he'd outlived everyone he'd loved – clearly, *this* had aged him.

His hair was still black; only if you were near him – and you had to look closely – could you see the intermittent flecks of gray. He'd not lost any hair, but it was long, which gave him the commingled appearance of a rebellious teenager and an aging hippie – that is, of someone who was unfashionable on purpose. His dark-brown eyes were almost as black as his hair; he was still a handsome man, and a slender one, yet he made an 'old' impression. Women – younger women, especially – offered him help he didn't necessarily need.

An aura of fate had marked him. He moved slowly; he often appeared to be lost in thought, or in his imagination – as if his future were predetermined, and he wasn't resisting it.

Juan Diego believed he was not so famous a writer that many of his readers recognized him, and strangers to his work never did. Only those who could be called his diehard fans found him. They were mostly women – older women, certainly, but many college girls were among his books' ardent readers.

Juan Diego didn't believe it was the subject of his novels that attracted women readers; he always said that women were the most enthusiastic readers of fiction, not men. He would offer no theory to explain this; he'd simply observed that this was true.

Juan Diego wasn't a theorizer; he was not big on speculation. He was even a little bit famous for what he'd said in an interview when a journalist had asked him to speculate on a certain shopworn subject.

'I don't speculate,' Juan Diego had said. 'I just observe; I only describe.' Naturally, the journalist – a persistent young fellow – had pressed the point. Journalists like speculation; they're always asking novelists if the novel is dead, or dying. Remember: Juan Diego had snatched the first novels he read from the hellfires of the basurero; he'd burned his hands saving books. You don't ask a dump reader if the novel is dead, or dying.

'Do you know any *women*?' Juan Diego had asked this young man. 'I mean women who *read*,' he said, his voice rising. 'You should talk to women – ask them what they read!' (By now, Juan Diego was shouting.) 'The day women stop reading – that's the day the novel dies!' the dump reader cried.

Writers who have any audience have more readers than they know. Juan Diego was more famous than he thought.

THIS TIME, IT WAS a mother and her daughter who discovered him – as only his most passionate readers did. 'I would have recognized you anywhere. You couldn't disguise yourself from me if you tried,' the rather aggressive mother said to Juan Diego. The way she spoke to him – well, it was almost as if he *had* tried to disguise himself. And where had he seen such a penetrating stare before? Without a doubt, that towering and most imposing statue of the Virgin Mary – *she* had such a stare. It was a way the Blessed

Virgin had of looking down at you, but Juan Diego could never tell if Mother Mary's expression was pitying or unforgiving. (He couldn't be sure in the case of this elegant-looking mother who was one of his readers, either.)

As for the daughter who was also his fan, Juan Diego thought she was somewhat easier to read. 'I would have recognized you in the dark – if you just spoke to me, even less than a complete sentence, I would have known who you were,' the daughter told him a little too earnestly. 'Your *voice*,' she said, shivering – as if she couldn't continue. She was young and dramatic, but pretty in a kind of peasant way; there was a thickness in her wrists and ankles, a sturdiness in her hips and low-slung breasts. Her skin was darker than her mother's; her facial features were more prominent, or less refined, and – especially in her manner of speaking – she was more blunt, more coarse.

'More like one of us,' Juan Diego could imagine his sister saying. (More indigenous-looking, Lupe would have thought.)

It unnerved Juan Diego that he suddenly imagined what tarted-up replications the virgin shop in Oaxaca might have made of this mother and her daughter. That Christmas-parties place would have exaggerated the slightly slipshod way the daughter dressed, but was it her clothes that looked a little slovenly or the careless way she wore them?

Juan Diego thought the virgin shop would have given the daughter's life-size mannequin a sluttish posture – a come-on appearance, as if the fullness of her hips couldn't possibly be contained. (Or was this Juan Diego's fantasizing about the daughter?)

That virgin shop, which the dump kids occasionally called The Girl, would have failed to come up with a mannequin to match the mother of this two-some. The mother had an air of sophistication and entitlement about her, and her beauty was the classical kind; the mother radiated expensiveness and superiority – her sense of privilege seemed inborn. If this mother, who was only momentarily delayed in a first-class lounge at JFK, had been the Virgin Mary, no one would have sent her to the manger; someone would have made room for her at the inn. That vulgar virgin shop on Independencia couldn't conceivably have replicated her; this mother was immune to being stereotyped – not even The Girl could have fabricated a sex-doll match for her. The mother was more 'one of a kind' than she was 'one of us.' There was no place for the mother in the Christmas-parties store, Juan Diego decided; she would never be for sale. And you wouldn't want to bring her home – at least not to entertain your guests or amuse the children. No, Juan Diego thought – you would want to keep her, all for yourself.

Somehow, without his *saying* to this mother and her daughter a word about his feelings for them, the two women seemed to know everything about Juan Diego. And this mother and daughter, despite their apparent differences, worked together; they were a team. They quickly inserted themselves into what they believed was the utter helplessness of Juan Diego's situation, if not his very existence. Juan Diego was tired; without hesitation, he blamed the beta-blockers. He didn't put up much of a fight. Basically, he let these women take charge of him. Besides, this had happened after they'd been waiting for twenty-four hours in the first-class lounge of British Airways.

Juan Diego's well-meaning colleagues, all close friends, had scheduled a two-day layover for him in Hong Kong; now it appeared that he would have only one night in Hong Kong before he had to catch an early-morning connection to Manila.

'Where are you staying in Hong Kong?' the mother, whose name was Miriam, asked him. She didn't beat around the bush; in keeping with her penetrating stare, she was very direct.

'Where *were* you staying?' the daughter, whose name was Dorothy, said. You could see little of her mother in her, Juan Diego had noticed; Dorothy was as aggressive as Miriam, but not nearly as beautiful.

What was it about Juan Diego that made more aggressive people feel they had to manage his business for him? Clark French, the former student, had inserted himself into Juan Diego's trip to the Philippines. Now two women – two strangers – were taking charge of the writer's arrangements in Hong Kong.

Juan Diego must have looked to this mother and her daughter like a novice traveler, because he had to consult his written itinerary to learn the name of his Hong Kong hotel. While he was still fumbling in the pocket of his jacket for his reading glasses, the mother snatched the itinerary out of his hands. 'Dear God – you don't want to be at the InterContinental Grand Stanford Hong Kong,' Miriam told him. 'It's an hour's drive from the airport.'

'It's actually in Kowloon,' Dorothy said.

'There's an adequate hotel at the airport,' Miriam said. 'You should stay there.'

'We *always* stay there,' Dorothy said, sighing.

Juan Diego started to say that he would need to cancel one reservation and make another – that was as far as he got.

'Done,' the daughter said; her fingers were flying over the keyboard of her laptop. It was a marvel to Juan Diego how young people always seemed to be using their laptops, which were never plugged in. Why don't their batteries run down? he was thinking. (And when they weren't glued to their laptops, they were madly texting on their cell phones, which never seemed to need recharging!)

'I thought it was a long way to bring my laptop,' Juan Diego said to the mother, who looked at him in a mostly pitying way. 'I left mine at home,' he said sheepishly to the hardworking daughter, who'd not once looked up from her constantly changing computer screen.

'I'm canceling your harbor-view room – two nights at the InterContinental Grand Stanford, *gone*. I don't like that place, anyway,' Dorothy said. 'And I'm getting you a king suite at the Regal Airport Hotel at Hong Kong International. It's not as totally tasteless as its name – all the Christmas shit notwithstanding.'

'*One* night, Dorothy,' her mother reminded the young woman.

'Got it,' Dorothy said. 'There's one thing about the Regal: the way you turn the lights on and off is weird,' she told Juan Diego.

'We'll show him, Dorothy,' the mother said. 'I've read everything of yours – every word you've written,' Miriam told him, putting her hand on his wrist.

'I've read *almost* everything,' Dorothy said.

'There's *two* you haven't read, Dorothy,' her mom said.

'*Two* – big deal,' Dorothy said. 'That's almost everything, isn't it?' the girl asked Juan Diego.

Of course he said, 'Yes – almost.' He couldn't tell if the young woman was flirting with him, or if her mother was; maybe neither of them was. The not-knowing part aged Juan Diego prematurely, too, but – to be fair – he'd been out of circulation for a while. It had been a long time since he'd dated anyone, not that he'd ever dated a lot, which two such worldly-looking travelers as this mother and daughter would have sized up about him.

Meeting him, did women think he looked wounded? Was he one of those men who'd lost the love of his life? What was it about Juan Diego that made women think he would never get over someone?

'I really like the sex in your novels,' Dorothy told him. 'I like how you do it.'

'I like it *better*,' Miriam said to him, giving her daughter an all-knowing look. 'I have the perspective to know what really bad sex is,' Dorothy's mom told her.

'Please, Mother – don't paint us a picture,' Dorothy said.

Miriam wasn't wearing a wedding ring, Juan Diego had noticed. She was a tall, trim woman, tense and impatient-looking, in a pearl-gray pantsuit, which she wore over a silvery T-shirt. Her beige-blond hair was certainly not its natural color, and she'd probably had a little work done on her face – either shortly after a divorce, or a somewhat longer time after she'd become a widow. (Juan Diego didn't intimately know about such things; he'd had no experience with women like Miriam, with the exception of his women readers or characters in novels.)

Dorothy, the daughter, who'd said she first read one of Juan Diego's novels when it had been 'assigned' to her – in college – looked as if she could still be of university age, or only a little older.

These women weren't on their way to Manila – 'not yet,' they'd told him – but Juan Diego didn't remember where they were going after Hong Kong, if they'd said. Miriam hadn't told him her full name, but her accent was European-sounding – the *foreign* part was what registered with Juan Diego. He wasn't an expert on accents, of course – Miriam *might* have been an American.

As for Dorothy, she would never be as beautiful as her mother, but the girl had a sullen, neglected prettiness – of the kind that a younger woman who's a little too heavy can get away with for a few more years. ('Voluptuous' wouldn't always be the word Dorothy brought to mind, Juan Diego knew – realizing, if only to himself, that he was *writing* about these efficient women, even as he allowed them to assist him.)

Whoever they were, and wherever they were going, this mother and daughter were veterans of traveling first class on Cathay Pacific. When Flight 841 to Hong Kong finally boarded, Miriam and Dorothy wouldn't let the doll-faced flight attendant show Juan Diego how to put on Cathay Pacific's one-piece pajamas or operate the cocoon-like sleeping capsule. Miriam marched him through the routine of how to put on the childish pajamas, and Dorothy – the technological wizard in the two-woman family – demonstrated the mechanics of the most comfortable bed Juan Diego had ever encountered on an airplane. The two women virtually tucked him in.

I think they were *both* flirting with me, Juan Diego mused as he was falling asleep – certainly the daughter was. Of course Dorothy reminded Juan Diego of students he'd known over the years; many of them, he knew, had only appeared to be flirting with him. There were young women that age – some solitary, tomboyish writers among them – who'd struck the older writer as knowing only two kinds of social behavior: they knew how to flirt, and they knew how to show irreversible contempt.

Juan Diego was almost asleep when he

remembered that he was taking an unplanned break from the beta-blockers; he was already beginning to dream when a mildly troubling thought occurred to him, albeit briefly, before it drifted away. The thought was: I don't really understand what *happens* when you stop and restart the beta-blockers. But the dream (or memory) was overtaking him, and he let it come.

• 4 •

The Broken Side-view Mirror

There was a gecko. It shrank from the first light of the sunrise, clinging to the mesh on the shack's screen door. In the blink of an eye, in that half-second before the boy could touch the screen, the gecko was gone. Quicker than turning on or off a light, the gecko's disappearance often began Juan Diego's dream – as the disappearing lizard had begun many of the boy's mornings in Guerrero.

Rivera had built the shack for himself, but he'd remodeled the interior for the kids; though he was probably not Juan Diego's father, and definitely not Lupe's, el jefe had made a deal with their mother. Even at fourteen, Juan Diego knew there was not much of a deal between those two now. Esperanza, notwithstanding that she'd been named for *hope*, had never been a source of hope to her own children, nor did she ever encourage Rivera – as far as Juan Diego had seen. Not that a fourteen-year-old boy would necessarily notice such things, and, at thirteen, Lupe wasn't a reliable witness to what might, or might not, have gone on between her mother and the dump boss.

As for 'reliable,' Rivera was the one person who could be counted on to look after these two dump kids – to the degree that anyone could protect los niños de la basura. Rivera had provided the only shelter for these two, and he'd sheltered Juan Diego and Lupe in other ways.

When el jefe went home at night – or wherever Rivera actually went – he left his truck and his dog with Juan Diego. The truck afforded the kids a second shelter, should they need it – unlike the shack, the cab of the truck could be locked – and no one but Juan Diego or Lupe would dare approach Rivera's dog. Even the dump boss was wary of that dog: an underfed-looking male, he was a terrier-hound mix.

According to el jefe, the dog was part pit bull, part bloodhound – hence he was predisposed to fight, and to track down things by their smell.

'Diablo is biologically inclined to be aggressive,' Rivera had said.

'I think you mean *genetically* inclined,' Juan Diego had corrected him.

It's hard to appreciate the degree that a dump kid could acquire such a sophisticated vocabulary; beyond the flattering attention paid to the unschooled boy by Brother Pepe at the Jesuit mission in Oaxaca, Juan Diego didn't have an education – yet the boy had managed to do more than teach himself to read. He also spoke exceedingly well. The dump kid even spoke English, though his only exposure to the spoken language came from the U.S. tourists. In Oaxaca, at that time, the American expatriates amounted to an arts-and-crafts crowd and the usual potheads. Increasingly, as the Vietnam War dragged on – past 1968, when Nixon had been elected on the promise that he would end it – there were those lost souls ('the young men searching for themselves,' Brother Pepe called them), who in many cases comprised the draft dodgers.

Juan Diego and Lupe had little luck communicating with the potheads. The mushroom hippies were too busy expanding their consciousness by hallucinogenic means; they didn't waste their time talking to children. The mescal hippies – if only when they were sober – enjoyed their conversations with the dump kids, and occasional readers could be found among them, although the mescal affected what these readers could remember. Quite a few of the draft dodgers were readers; they gave Juan Diego their paperback novels. These were mostly American novels, of course; they inspired Juan Diego to imagine living there.

And only seconds after the early-morning gecko had vanished, and the screen door of the shack slapped shut behind Juan Diego, a crow took flight from the hood of Rivera's truck, and all the dogs in Guerrero began to bark. The boy watched the crow in flight – any excuse to imagine flying captivated him – while Diablo, rousing himself from the flatbed of Rivera's pickup, commenced an ungodly baying that silenced all of the other dogs. Diablo's baying was the bloodhound gene in Rivera's scary dog; the pit-bull part, the fighter gene, was responsible for the missing lid of the dog's bloodshot and permanently open left eye. The pinkish scar, where the eyelid had been, gave Diablo a baleful stare. (A dogfight, perhaps, or a person with a knife; the dump boss hadn't witnessed the altercation, human or beast.)

As for the jagged-edged, triangular piece that had been less than surgically removed from one of the dog's long ears – well, that one was anyone's guess.

'*You* did it, Lupe,' Rivera once said, smiling at the girl. 'Diablo would let you do anything to him – even eat his ear.'

Lupe had made a perfect triangle with her index fingers and her thumbs. What she said required Juan Diego's translation, as always, or Rivera would not have understood her. 'No animal or human has the teeth to bite like that,' the girl incontrovertibly said.

Los niños de la basura never knew when (or from where) Rivera arrived every morning at the basurero, or by what means el jefe had come down the hill from the dump to Guerrero. The dump boss was usually found napping in the cab of his truck; either the pistol-shot slap of the closing screen door or the barking dogs woke him. Or Diablo's baying woke him, a half-second later – or earlier, that gecko, which almost no one saw.

'Buenos días, jefe,' Juan Diego usually said.

'It's a good day to do everything well, amigo,' Rivera often answered the boy. The dump boss would add: 'And where is the genius princess?'

'I am where I always am,' Lupe would answer him, the screen door slapping shut behind her. That second pistol shot reached as far as the hellfires in the basurero. More crows took flight. There was a disharmonious barking; the dump dogs *and* the dogs in Guerrero barked. Another menacing and all-silencing howl followed from Diablo, whose wet nose now touched the boy's bare knee below his tattered shorts.

The dump fires had long been burning – the smoldering mounds of piled-high garbage and pawed-through trash. Rivera must have lit the fires at first light; then he took a nap in the cab of his truck.

The Oaxaca basurero was a wasteland of burning; whether you were standing there or as far away as Guerrero, the towers of smoke from the fires rose as high into the sky as you could see. Juan Diego's eyes were already tearing when he came out that screen door. There was always a tear oozing from Diablo's lidless eye, even when the dog slept – with his left eye open but not seeing.

That morning, Rivera had found another water pistol in the basurero; he'd tossed the squirt gun into the flatbed of the pickup, where Diablo had briefly licked it before leaving it alone.

'I got one for you!' Rivera called to Lupe, who was eating a cornmeal tortilla with jam on it; there was jam on her chin, and on one cheek, and Lupe had invited Diablo to lick her face. She let Diablo have the rest of her tortilla, too.

There were two vultures hunched over a dead dog in the road, and two more vultures floated overhead; they were making those descending spirals in the sky.

In the basurero, there was usually at least one dead dog every morning; their carcasses did not remain intact for long. If the vultures failed to find a dead dog, or if the carrion eaters didn't quickly dispose of it, someone would burn it. There was always a fire.

The dead dogs in Guerrero were treated differently. Those dogs probably had belonged to somebody; you didn't burn someone else's dog – besides, there were rules about starting fires in Guerrero. (There were concerns that the little neighborhood might burn down.) You let a dead dog lie around in Guerrero – it didn't usually lie around for long. If the dead dog had an owner, the owner would get rid of it, or the carrion eaters would eventually do the job.

'I didn't know that dog – did you?' Lupe was saying to Diablo, as she examined the water pistol el jefe had found. Lupe meant the dead dog being attended to by the two vultures in the road, but Diablo didn't let on if he'd known the dog.

The dump kids could tell it was a copper day. El jefe had a load of copper in the flatbed of the pickup. There was a manufacturing plant that worked with copper near the airport; in the same area was another plant, which took aluminum.

'At least it isn't a glass day – I don't like glass days,' Lupe was saying to Diablo, or she was just talking to herself.

When Diablo was around, you never heard any growling from Dirty White – not even a whimper from the coward, Juan Diego was thinking. 'He's *not* a coward! He's a puppy!' Lupe shouted to her brother.

Then she went on and on (to herself) about the brand of water pistol Rivera had retrieved from the basurero – something about the 'feeble squirter mechanism.'

The dump boss and Juan Diego watched Lupe run into the shack; no doubt she was putting the new-found squirt gun with her collection.

El jefe had been checking the propane tank outside the kids' shack; he was always checking it to be sure it wasn't leaking, but this morning he was checking to see how full or near-empty the tank was. Rivera checked this by lifting the tank to see how heavy it was.

Juan Diego had often wondered on what basis the dump boss had decided that he was probably not Juan Diego's father. It was true they looked nothing alike, but – as in Lupe's case – Juan Diego looked so much like his mother that the boy doubted he could possibly resemble *any* father.

'Just hope that you resemble Rivera in his *kindness*,' Brother Pepe had told Juan Diego during the delivery of one bunch of books or another. (Juan Diego had been fishing for what Pepe might have known or heard about the boy's most likely father.)

Whenever Juan Diego had asked el jefe why he'd put himself in the probably-not category, the dump boss always smiled and said he was 'probably not smart enough' to be the dump reader's dad.

Juan Diego, who'd been watching Rivera lift the propane tank (a full tank was very heavy), suddenly said: 'One day, jefe, I'll be strong enough to lift the propane tank – even a full one.' (This was about as close as the dump reader could come to telling Rivera that he wished and hoped the dump boss was his father.)

'We should go,' was all Rivera said, climbing into the cab of his truck.

'You still haven't fixed your side-view mirror,' Juan Diego told el jefe.

Lupe was babbling about something as she ran to the truck, the shack's screen door slapping shut behind her. The pistol-shot sound of that closing screen door had no effect on the vultures hunched over the dead dog in the road; there were four vultures at work now, and not one of them flinched.

Rivera had learned not to tease Lupe by making vulgar jokes about the water pistols. One time, Rivera had said: 'You kids are so crazy about those squirt guns – people will think you're practicing artificial insemination.'

The phrase had long been used in medical circles, but the dump kids had first heard of it from a science fiction novel saved from burning. Lupe had been disgusted. When she heard el jefe mention artificial insemination, Lupe had erupted in a fury of preteen indignation; she was eleven or twelve at the time.

'Lupe says she knows what artificial insemination is – she thinks it's gross,' Juan Diego had translated for his sister.

'Lupe *doesn't* know what artificial insemination is,' the dump boss had insisted, but he looked anxiously at the indignant girl. Who knew what the dump reader might have read to her? el jefe thought. Even as a little girl, Lupe had been strongly opposed but attentive to everything indecent or obscene.

There was more moral outrage (of an unintelligible kind) expressed by Lupe. All Juan Diego said was: 'Yes, she does. Would you like her to describe artificial insemination to you?'

'No, no!' Rivera had cried. 'I was just kidding! Okay, the water pistols are nothing but squirt guns. Let's leave it at that.'

But Lupe wouldn't stop babbling. 'She says you're always thinking about sex,' Juan Diego had interpreted for Rivera.

'Not always!' Rivera had exclaimed. 'I try not to think about sex around you two.'

Lupe went on and on. She'd been stamping her feet – her boots were too big; she'd found them in the dump. Her stomping had turned into an impromptu dance – including a pirouette – as she berated Rivera.

'She says it's pathetic to disapprove of prostitutes while you still hang out with prostitutes,' Juan Diego was explaining.

'Okay, okay!' Rivera had shouted, throwing up his muscular arms. 'The water pistols, the squirt guns, are just *toys* – nobody's getting pregnant with them! Whatever you say.'

Lupe had stopped dancing; she kept pointing to her upper lip while she pouted at Rivera.

'What now? What is this – sign language?' Rivera had asked Juan Diego.

'Lupe says you'll never get a girlfriend who isn't a

prostitute – not with that stupid-looking mustache,' the boy had told him.

'Lupe says, Lupe says,' Rivera had muttered, but the dark-eyed girl continued to stare at him – all the while tracing the contours of a nonexistent mustache on her smooth upper lip.

Another time, Lupe had told Juan Diego: 'Rivera is too ugly to be your father.'

'El jefe isn't ugly *inside*,' the boy had answered her.

'He has mostly good thoughts, except about women,' Lupe said.

'Rivera loves us,' Juan Diego told his sister.

'Yes, el jefe loves us – *both* of us,' Lupe admitted. 'Even though I'm not his – and you're probably not his, either.'

'Rivera gave us his name – *both* of us,' the boy reminded her.

'I think it's more like a loan,' Lupe said.

'How can our names be a loan?' the boy had asked her; his sister shrugged their mother's shrug – a hard one to read. (A little bit always the same, a little bit different every time.)

'Maybe I'm Lupe Rivera, and always will be,' the girl had said, somewhat evasively. 'But you're someone else. You're not always going to be Juan Diego Rivera – that's not who you are,' was all Lupe would say about it.

ON THAT MORNING WHEN Juan Diego's life was about to change, Rivera made no vulgar squirt-gun jokes. El jefe sat distractedly at the wheel of his truck; the dump boss was ready to make his rounds, starting with the load of copper – a heavy load.

The distant airplane was slowing down; it must be landing, Juan Diego guessed to himself. He was still watching the sky for flying things. There was an airport (at the time, not much more than a landing strip) outside Oaxaca, and the boy loved watching the planes that flew over the basurero; he'd never flown.

In the dream, of course, was the devastating foreknowledge of who was on that airplane on that morning – thus, immediately upon the appearance of the plane in the sky, there came the simultaneous understanding of Juan Diego's future. In reality, on that morning, something fairly ordinary had diverted Juan Diego's attention from the far-off but descending plane. The boy had spotted what he thought was a feather – not from a crow or a vulture. A different-looking feather (but not *that* different-looking) was pinned under the left-rear wheel of the truck.

Lupe had already slipped into the cab beside Rivera.

Diablo, despite his lean appearance, was a well-fed dog – he was quite superior to the scavenging dump dogs, not only in this respect. Diablo was an aloof, macho-looking dog. (In Guerrero, they called him the 'male animal.')

With his forepaws on Rivera's toolbox, Diablo could extend his head and neck over the passenger side of the pickup; if he put his forepaws on el jefe's spare tire, Diablo's head would obstruct Rivera's vision of his side-view mirror – the broken one, on the driver's side. When the dump boss glanced in that broken mirror, he had a multifaceted view: a spiderweb of shards of glass reflected Diablo's four-eyed face. The dog suddenly had two mouths, two tongues.

'Where is your brother?' Rivera asked the girl.

'I'm not the only one who's crazy,' Lupe said, but the dump boss didn't understand her at all.

When el jefe had a nap in the cab of his truck, he often put the stick shift, which was on the floor of the cab, in reverse. If the gear shift was set in first gear, the knob could poke him in his ribs while he was trying to sleep.

Diablo's 'normal' face now appeared in the passenger-side mirror – the unbroken one – but when Rivera looked in the driver's-side mirror, in the spiderweb of broken glass, he never saw Juan Diego trying to retrieve the slightly unusual-looking, reddish-brown feather that was trapped under the left-rear wheel of the truck. The truck lurched backward in reverse, rolling over the boy's right foot. It's just a chicken feather, Juan Diego realized. In the same half-second, he acquired his lifelong limp – for a feather as common as dirt in Guerrero. On the outskirts of Oaxaca, lots of families kept chickens.

The small bump under the left-rear tire caused the Guadalupe doll on the dashboard to wobble her hips. 'Be careful you don't get yourself pregnant,' Lupe told the doll, but Rivera had no comprehension of what she'd said; el jefe could hear Juan Diego screaming. 'You've lost your touch for miracles – you've sold out,' Lupe was saying to the Guadalupe doll. Rivera had braked the truck; he climbed out of the cab, running to the injured boy. Diablo was barking crazily – he sounded like a different dog. All the dogs in Guerrero began to bark. '*Now* see what you've done,' Lupe admonished the doll on the dashboard, but the girl quickly climbed out of the cab and ran to her brother.

The boy's right foot had been crushed; flattened and bleeding, the maimed foot pointed away from his right ankle and shin in a two-o'clock position. His foot looked smaller, somehow. Rivera carried Juan Diego to the cab; the boy would have continued to scream, but the pain made him hold his breath, then gasp for air, then hold his breath again. His boot slipped off.

'Try to breathe normally, or you'll faint,' Rivera told him.

'Maybe now you'll fix that stupid mirror!' Lupe was screaming at the dump boss.

'What is she saying?' Rivera asked the boy. 'I hope it's not about my side-view mirror.'

'I'm trying to breathe normally,' Juan Diego told him.

Lupe got in the truck's cab first, so that her brother could put his head in her lap and stick his bad foot out the passenger-side window. 'Take him to Dr. Vargas!' the girl was screaming at Rivera, who understood the *Vargas* word.

'We'll try for a miracle first – then Vargas,' Rivera said.

'Expect no miracles,' Lupe said; she punched the Guadalupe doll on the dashboard, and the doll's hips started shaking again.

'Don't let the Jesuits have me,' Juan Diego said. 'Brother Pepe is the only one I like.'

'Perhaps I should be the one to explain this to your mother,' Rivera was saying to the kids; he drove slowly ahead, not wanting to kill any dogs in Guerrero, but once the truck was out on the highway, el jefe sped up.

The jostling in the cab made Juan Diego moan; his crushed foot, bleeding out the open window, had streaked the passenger side of the cab with blood. In the undamaged side-view mirror, Diablo's blood-flecked face appeared. In the rushing wind, a stream of the injured boy's blood ran to the rear of the cab, where Diablo was licking it up.

'Cannibalism!' Rivera shouted. 'You disloyal dog!'

'Cannibalism is not the right word,' Lupe declared, with her usual moral indignation. 'Dogs like blood – Diablo is a good dog.'

With his teeth clenched in pain, the effort to translate his sister's defense of the blood-licking dog was beyond Juan Diego, who thrashed his head from side to side in Lupe's lap.

When he could manage to hold his head still, Juan Diego believed he saw some menacing eye contact between the Guadalupe doll on Rivera's dashboard and his fervent sister. Lupe had been named after the Virgin of Guadalupe. Juan Diego was named for the Indian who'd encountered the dark-skinned virgin in 1531. Los niños de la basura were born to Indians in the New World, but they also had Spanish blood; this made them (in their eyes) the conquistadors' bastard children. Juan Diego and Lupe didn't feel that the Virgin of Guadalupe was necessarily looking out for them.

'You should pray to her, you ungrateful heathen – not punch her!' Rivera now said to the girl. 'Pray for your brother – ask for Guadalupe's help!'

Juan Diego had translated Lupe's invective on this religious subject too many times; he clenched his teeth, his lips tightly closed, not uttering a word.

'Guadalupe has been corrupted by the Catholics,' Lupe began. 'She was *our* Virgin, but the Catholics stole her; they made her the Virgin Mary's dark-skinned servant. They might as well have called her Mary's slave – maybe Mary's *cleaning woman*!'

'Blasphemy! Sacrilege! Unbeliever!' Rivera shouted. The dump boss didn't need Juan Diego to translate Lupe's diatribe – he'd heard Lupe sound off about the Guadalupe business before. It was no secret to Rivera that Lupe had a love-hate thing going with Our Lady of Guadalupe. El jefe also knew Lupe disliked Mother Mary. The Virgin Mary was an imposter, in the crazy child's opinion; the Virgin of Guadalupe had been the real deal, but those crafty Jesuits had stolen her for their Catholic agenda. In Lupe's opinion, the dark-skinned virgin had been compromised – hence 'corrupted.' The child believed that Our Lady of Guadalupe had once been miraculous but wasn't anymore.

This time, Lupe's left foot delivered a near-lethal kick to the Guadalupe doll, but the suction-cup base held fast to the dashboard while the doll shimmied and shook herself in a frankly less-than-virginal way.

In order to kick the dashboard doll, Lupe had done little more than arch her lap upward, toward the windshield, but even this much movement caused Juan Diego to scream.

'You *see*? Now you've hurt your brother!' Rivera cried, but Lupe bent over Juan Diego; she kissed his forehead, her smoke-smelling hair falling to either side of the injured boy's face.

'Remember this,' Lupe whispered to Juan Diego. '*We* are the miracle – you and me. Not them. Just us. We're the miraculous ones,' she said.

With his eyes tightly closed, Juan Diego heard the plane roar over them. At the time, he knew only that they were near the airport; he knew nothing about who was on that plane and coming closer. In the dream, of course, he knew everything – the future, too. (Some of it.)

'We're the miraculous ones,' Juan Diego whispered. He was asleep – he was still dreaming – though his lips were moving. No one heard him; no one hears a writer who's writing in his sleep.

Besides, Cathay Pacific 841 was still hurtling toward Hong Kong – on one side of the plane, the

Taiwan Strait, on the other, the South China Sea. But in Juan Diego's dream, he was only fourteen – a passenger, in pain, in Rivera's truck – and all the boy could do was repeat after his clairvoyant sister: 'We're the miraculous ones.'

Perhaps all the passengers on the plane were asleep, for not even the scarily sophisticated mother and her slightly-less-dangerous-looking daughter had heard him.

5

Yielding Under No Winds

The American who landed in Oaxaca that morning – to Juan Diego's future, he was the most important passenger on that incoming plane – was a scholastic in training to be a priest. He'd been hired to teach at the Jesuit school and orphanage; Brother Pepe had picked him out of a list of applicants. Father Alfonso and Father Octavio, the two old priests at the Templo de la Compañía de Jesús, had expressed their doubts regarding the young American's command of Spanish. Pepe's point was that the scholastic was overqualified; he'd been a whale of a student – surely his Spanish would catch up.

Everyone at the Hogar de los Niños Perdidos was expecting him. Except for Sister Gloria, the nuns who watched over the orphans at Lost Children had confided to Pepe that they liked the young teacher's photograph. Pepe didn't tell anyone, but he'd found the picture appealing, too. (If it was possible, in a photo, for someone to *look* zealous – well, this guy did.)

Father Alfonso and Father Octavio had sent Brother

Pepe to meet the new missionary's plane. From the photograph on the American teacher's dossier, Brother Pepe had been anticipating a bigger, more mature-looking man. It was not only that Edward Bonshaw had recently lost a lot of weight; the young American, who was not yet thirty, hadn't bought any new clothes since his weight loss. His clothes were huge on him, even clownish, which gave the deeply serious-looking scholastic an aura of childish haphazardness. Edward Bonshaw resembled the youngest kid in a big family – the one who wore the hand-me-downs discarded or outgrown by his older, larger siblings and cousins. The short sleeves of his Hawaiian shirt hung below his elbows; the untucked shirt (a parrots-in-palm-trees theme) drooped to his knees. Upon exiting the plane, young Bonshaw tripped on the cuffs of his sagging trousers.

As usual, the plane, upon landing, had struck one or more of the chickens that chaotically overran the runway. The reddish-brown feathers flew upward in the seemingly random funnels of wind; where the two chains of the Sierra Madre converge, it can be windy. But Edward Bonshaw did not notice that a chicken (or chickens) had been killed; he reacted to the feathers and the wind as if they were a warm greeting, expressly for him.

'Edward?' Brother Pepe started to say, but a chicken feather stuck to his lower lip and made him spit. He simultaneously thought that the young American looked insubstantial, out of place, and unprepared, but Pepe remembered his own insecurity at that age, and his heart went out to young Bonshaw – as if the new missionary were one of the orphans at Lost Children.

The three-year service in preparation for the priest-hood was called regency; thereafter, Edward Bonshaw would pursue theological studies for another three years. Ordination followed theology, Pepe was remind-ing himself as he assessed the young scholastic, who was attempting to wave the chicken feathers away. And after his ordination, Edward Bonshaw then faced a fourth year of theological study – not to mention that the poor guy had already completed a Ph.D. in English literature! (No wonder he's lost some weight, Brother Pepe considered.)

But Pepe had underestimated the zealous young man, who seemed to be making an unnatural effort to look like a conquering hero in a spiral cloud of chicken feathers. Indeed, Brother Pepe didn't know that Edward Bonshaw's ancestors had been a formid-able bunch, even by Jesuitical standards.

The Bonshaws had come from the Dumfries area of Scotland, near the English border. Edward's great-grandfather Andrew had immigrated to the Canadian Maritimes. Edward's grandfather Duncan had immigrated to the United States – albeit cautiously. (As Duncan Bonshaw had been fond of saying, 'Only to Maine, not to the rest of the United States.') Edward's father, Graham, had moved farther west – no farther west than Iowa, in fact. Edward Bonshaw was born in Iowa City; until he came to Mexico, he'd never left the Midwest.

As for how the Bonshaws became Catholics, only God and the great-grandfather knew. Like many Scots, Andrew Bonshaw had a Protestant upbringing; he'd sailed from Glasgow a Protestant, but when he disembarked in Halifax, Andrew Bonshaw was closely tied to Rome – he came ashore a Catholic.

A conversion, if not a miracle of a near-death kind, must have occurred onboard that ship; something miraculous had to have happened during the trans-atlantic crossing, but – even as an old man – Andrew never spoke of it. He took the miracle to his grave. All Andrew ever said about the voyage was that a nun had taught him how to play mah-jongg. *Something* must have happened during one of their games.

Edward Bonshaw was suspicious of most miracles; however, he was preternaturally interested in the miraculous. Yet Edward had not once questioned his Catholicism – nor even his great-grandfather's unexplained conversion. Naturally, all the Bonshaws had learned to play mah-jongg.

'It seems there is often a contradiction that can't be, or simply isn't, explained in the lives of the most ardent believers,' Juan Diego had written in his India novel, *A Story Set in Motion by the Virgin Mary*. Though that novel was about a fictional missionary, perhaps Juan Diego had specific qualities of Edward Bonshaw in mind.

'Edward?' Brother Pepe asked again – only slightly less tentatively than before. '*Eduardo?*' Pepe then tried. (Pepe lacked confidence in his English; he wondered if he'd mispronounced 'Edward' in some way.)

'*Aha!*' young Edward Bonshaw cried; for no apparent reason, the scholastic then resorted to Latin. 'Haud ullis labentia ventis!' he proclaimed to Pepe.

Brother Pepe's Latin was beginner-level. Pepe thought he'd heard the word for *wind*, or possibly the plural; he assumed that Edward Bonshaw was showing off his superior education, which included his mastery of Latin, and that he was probably *not* making a joke about the chicken feathers blowing in the wind. In fact, young Bonshaw was reciting his family crest – a *Scottish* thing. The Bonshaws had an identifying plaid – a *tartan* thing. The Latin words on this family crest were what Edward recited to himself when he felt nervous or insecure.

Haud ullis labentia ventis meant 'Yielding under no winds.'

My dear Lord, what have we here? Brother Pepe marveled; poor Pepe believed the content of the Latin was religious. Pepe had met those Jesuits who too fanatically patterned their behavior on the life of Saint Ignatius Loyola, the founder of the Jesuit order – the Society of Jesus. It was in Rome where Saint Ignatius had announced that he would sacrifice his life if he could prevent the sins of a single prostitute on a single night. Brother Pepe had lived in Mexico City and Oaxaca all his life; Pepe knew just how crazy Saint Ignatius Loyola must have been to ever propose such a thing as sacrificing his life to prevent the sins of a single prostitute on a single night.

Even a pilgrimage can be a fool's errand when

undertaken by a fool, Brother Pepe reminded himself as he stepped forward on the feather-strewn tarmac to greet the young American missionary.

'Edward – Edward Bonshaw,' Pepe said to the scholastic.

'I liked the *Eduardo*. It's new – I *love* it!' Edward Bonshaw said, startling Brother Pepe with a fierce embrace. Pepe was awfully pleased to be hugged; he liked how expressive the eager American was. And Edward (or Eduardo) immediately launched into an explanation of his Latin proclamation. Pepe was surprised to learn that 'Yielding under no winds' was a Scottish dictum, not a religious one – not unless it was of *Protestant* origin, Brother Pepe speculated.

The young midwesterner was definitely a positive person and an outgoing personality – a joyful presence, Brother Pepe decided. But what will the *others* think of him? Pepe was wondering to himself. In Pepe's opinion, the *others* were a joyless lot. He was thinking of Father Alfonso and Father Octavio, but also, perhaps especially, of Sister Gloria. Oh, how they will be unnerved by the *hugs* – not to mention the parrots-in-palm-trees theme of the hysterical Hawaiian shirt! Brother Pepe thought; he was happy about it.

Then Eduardo – as the Iowan preferred – wanted Pepe to see how his bags had been abused when he had passed through customs in Mexico City.

'Look what a mess they made of my things!' the excited American cried; he was opening his suitcases so that Pepe could see. It didn't matter to the passionate new teacher that the passersby at the Oaxaca airport could see his strewn belongings.

In Mexico City, the examining customs officer must have torn through the colorfully dressed missionary's bags with a vengeance – finding more of the same unsuitable and oversize clothes, Pepe observed.

'So understated – must be the new papal issue!' Brother Pepe had said to young Bonshaw, indicating (in a small, disheveled suitcase) more Hawaiian shirts.

'It's all the rage in Iowa City,' Edward Bonshaw said; maybe this was a joke.

'A possible monkey wrench in the ointment for Father Alfonso,' Pepe cautioned the scholastic. That didn't sound right; he'd meant a possible *fly* in the ointment, of course – or perhaps he *should* have said, 'Those shirts will look like monkey business to Father Alfonso.' Yet Edward Bonshaw had understood him.

'Father Alfonso is a little *conservative*, is he?' the young American asked.

'An underdescription,' Brother Pepe said.

'An understatement,' Edward Bonshaw corrected him.

'My English has rusted a small size,' Pepe admitted.

'I'll spare you my Spanish, for the moment,' Edward said.

Pepe was shown how the customs officer had found the first whip, then the second. 'Instruments of torture?' the officer had asked young Bonshaw – first in Spanish, then in English.

'Instruments of *devotion*,' Edward (or Eduardo) had answered. Brother Pepe was thinking, Oh, my merciful Lord – we have a poor soul who *flagellates* himself when what we wanted was an *English* teacher!

The second suitcase in upheaval was full of books. 'More instruments of torture,' the customs officer had continued, in Spanish and English.

'Of *further* devotion,' Edward Bonshaw had corrected the officer. (At least the flagellant reads, Pepe was thinking.)

'The sisters at the orphanage – among them, a few of your fellow teachers – were quite taken with your photograph,' Brother Pepe told the scholastic, who was struggling to repack his violated bags.

'*Aha!* But I've lost a lot of weight since then,' the young missionary said.

'Apparently – you've not been ill, I hope,' Pepe ventured.

'Denial, denial – denial is *good*,' Edward Bonshaw explained. 'I stopped smoking, I stopped drinking – I think the zero-alcohol factor has curtailed my appetite. I'm just not as *hungry* as I used to be,' the zealot said.

'*Aha!*' Brother Pepe said. (Now he has me saying it! Pepe marveled to himself.) He'd never had any alcohol – not a drop. The 'zero-alcohol factor' had not once *curtailed* Brother Pepe's appetite.

'Clothes, whips, reading material,' the customs

officer had summarized, in Spanish and English, to the young American.

'Just the bare essentials!' Edward Bonshaw had declared.

Merciful Lord, spare his soul! Pepe was thinking, as if the scholastic's remaining days on this mortal earth were already numbered.

The customs officer in Mexico City had also questioned the American's visa, which had a temporary delimitation.

'You're intending to stay for *how* long?' the officer had asked.

'If everything goes well, three years,' the young Iowan had replied.

The prospects of the pioneer before him struck Brother Pepe as poor. Edward Bonshaw seemed an unlikely survivor of a mere six months of the missionary life. The Iowan would need more clothes – ones that fit him. He would run out of books to read, and the two whips wouldn't suffice – not for the number of times the doomed zealot would feel inclined to flagellate himself.

'Brother Pepe, you drive a VW Beetle!' Edward Bonshaw exclaimed, as the two Jesuits made their way to the dusty red car in the parking lot.

'Just Pepe, please – the *Brother* part is not necessary,' Pepe said. He was wondering if all Americans made exclamations about the obvious, but he quite liked the young scholastic's enthusiasm for everything.

Who else would those smart Jesuits have chosen to run their school, if not a man like Pepe, who both embodied and admired *enthusiasm*? Who else would the Jesuits have put in charge of Niños Perdidos? You don't add an orphanage to a successful school, and call it 'Lost Children,' without a good-hearted worrier like Brother Pepe to oversee everything.

But worriers, including the good-hearted ones, can be distracted drivers. Perhaps Pepe was thinking about the dump reader; maybe Pepe was imagining that he was bringing more books to Guerrero. For whatever reason, Pepe turned the wrong way when he left the airport – instead of turning toward Oaxaca, and back to town, he headed to the basurero. By the time Brother Pepe realized his mistake, he was already in Guerrero.

Pepe wasn't all that familiar with the area. In looking for a safe place to turn around, he chose the dirt road to the dump. It was a wide road, and only those smelly trucks – moving slowly to or from the basurero – usually traveled there.

Naturally, once Pepe had stopped the little VW and managed to turn it around, the two Jesuits were enveloped in the black plumes of smoke from the dump; the mountains of smoldering garbage and trash towered above the road. Scavenging children could be seen; they scrambled up and down the reeking mounds. A driver had to be wary of the scavengers – both the ragamuffin children and the dump dogs. The smell, borne by the smoke, made the young American missionary gag.

'What is this place? A vision of Hades, with a matching odor! What terrible rite of passage do these poor children undertake here?' the dramatic young Bonshaw asked.

How will we endure this lovable lunatic? Brother Pepe asked himself; that the zealot was well meaning would not impress Oaxaca. But all Pepe said was: 'It's just the city dump. The smell comes from burning the dead dogs, among other things. Our mission has reached out to two children here – dos pepenadores, two scavengers.'

'Scavengers!' Edward Bonshaw cried.

'Los niños de la basura,' Pepe said softly, hoping to create some separation between the scavenging children and the scavenging dogs.

Just then, a begrimed boy of indeterminable age – definitely a dump kid; you could tell by his too-big boots – thrust a small, shivering dog in the passenger-side window of Brother Pepe's VW Beetle.

'No, thank you,' Edward Bonshaw politely said – more to the foul-smelling little dog than to the dump kid, who bluntly stated that the starving creature was free. (Dump kids weren't beggars.)

'You shouldn't touch that dog!' Pepe shouted at the dump kid in Spanish. 'You could be bitten!' Pepe told the urchin.

'I know about rabies!' the dirty kid cried; he withdrew the cringing dog from the window. 'I know about the shots!' the little scavenger yelled at Brother Pepe.

'What a beautiful language!' Edward Bonshaw remarked.

Dearest Lord – the scholastic doesn't understand

Spanish at all! Pepe surmised. A film of ash had coated the windshield of the VW Beetle, and Pepe discovered that the wipers only served to smear the ashes – further obscuring his view of the road out of the basurero. It was because he had to get out of his car to clean the windshield with an old cloth that Brother Pepe told the new missionary about Juan Diego, the dump reader; perhaps Pepe should have said a little more about the boy's younger sister – specifically, Lupe's apparent mind-reading ability *and* the girl's unintelligible speech. But, given the optimist and the enthusiast that he was, Brother Pepe tended to focus his attention on the positive and the uncomplicated.

The girl, Lupe, was somewhat disturbing, whereas the *boy* – well, Juan Diego was simply wonderful. There was nothing contradictory about a fourteen-year-old, born and raised in the basurero, who'd taught himself to read in two languages!

'Thank you, Jesus,' Edward Bonshaw said, when the two Jesuits were under way again – headed in the right direction, back to Oaxaca.

Thanks for *what*? Pepe was wondering when the young American continued his oh-so-earnest prayer. 'Thank you for my total immersion in where I am most needed,' the scholastic said.

'It's just the city dump,' Brother Pepe said, again. 'Dump kids are pretty well looked after. Trust me, Edward – you are not needed in the basurero.'

'Eduardo,' the young American corrected him.

'Sí, Eduardo,' was all Pepe managed to say. For

years, he'd stood alone against Father Alfonso and
Father Octavio; those priests were older and more
theologically informed than Brother Pepe. Father
Alfonso and Father Octavio could make Pepe feel as
if he were a betrayer of the Catholic faith – as if he
were a raving secular humanist, or worse. (Could
there be anyone worse, from a Jesuitical perspective?)
Father Alfonso and Father Octavio knew their
Catholic dogma by rote; while the two priests talked
circles around Brother Pepe, and they made Pepe feel
inadequate in his belief, they were irreparably
doctrinaire.

In Edward Bonshaw, perhaps Pepe had found a
worthy opponent for those two old Jesuit priests
– a crazy but daring combatant, one who might
challenge the very nature of the mission at Niños
Perdidos.

Had the young scholastic actually thanked the
dear Lord for what he called his 'total immersion' in
the need to save two dump kids? Did the American
really believe the dump kids were candidates for
salvation?

'I'm sorry for not properly welcoming you, Señor
Eduardo,' Brother Pepe now said. 'Lo siento – bienvenido,' Pepe added admiringly.

'¡Gracias!' the zealot cried. Through the ash-
bleared windshield, they could both discern a small
obstacle in the rotary ahead; the traffic was veering
away from something. 'Road kill?' Edward Bonshaw
asked.

A quarrelsome contingent of dogs and crows

competed over the unseen dead; as the red VW Beetle came closer, Brother Pepe blew his horn. The crows took flight; the dogs scattered. All that remained in the road was a smear of blood. The road kill, if that's what had spilled the blood, was gone.

'The dogs and the crows ate it,' Edward Bonshaw said. More exclamations about the obvious, Brother Pepe was thinking, but that was when Juan Diego spoke – instantly waking himself from his long sleep, his dream, which wasn't strictly a dream. (It was more like dreams manipulated by memories, or the other way around; it was what he'd been missing since the beta-blockers had stolen his childhood and his all-important early adolescence.)

'No – it's not road kill,' Juan Diego said. 'It's my blood. It dripped from Rivera's truck – Diablo didn't lick up every drop.'

'Were you *writing*?' Miriam, the imperious mother, asked Juan Diego.

'It sounds like a gruesome story,' the daughter, Dorothy, said.

Their two less-than-angelic faces peered down at him; he was aware that they'd both been to the lavatory and had brushed their teeth – their breath, but not his, was very fresh. The flight attendants were fussing about the first-class cabin.

Cathay Pacific 841 was descending to Hong Kong; a foreign but welcome smell was in the air, definitely *not* the Oaxaca basurero.

'We were about to wake you, when you woke up,' Miriam told him.

'You don't want to miss the green-tea muffins –
they're almost as good as sex,' Dorothy said.

'Sex, sex, sex – enough sex, Dorothy,' her mother
said.

Juan Diego, aware of how bad his breath must be,
gave the two women a tight-lipped smile. He was
slowly realizing where he was, and who these two
attractive women were. Oh, yes – I skipped the beta-
blockers, he was remembering. I was briefly back
where I *belong*! he was thinking; how his heart ached
to be back there.

And what was *this*? He had an erection in his
comical Cathay Pacific sleeping suit, his clownish
trans-Pacific pajamas. And he hadn't taken even half
of one Viagra – his gray-blue Viagra tablets, together
with the beta-blockers, were in his checked bag.

Juan Diego had slept for more than fifteen hours of
what was a flight lasting sixteen hours and ten minutes.
He limped off to the lavatory with noticeably quicker,
lighter steps. His self-appointed angels (if not quite in
the *guardian* category) watched him go; both mother
and daughter seemed to regard him fondly.

'He's *darling*, isn't he?' Miriam asked her daughter.

'He's cute, all right,' Dorothy said.

'Thank goodness we found him – he would be
utterly lost without us!' the mother remarked.

'Thank goodness,' Dorothy repeated; the goodness
word escaped somewhat unnaturally from the young
woman's overripe lips.

'He was *writing*, I think – imagine writing in your
sleep!' Miriam exclaimed.

'About blood dripping from a truck!' Dorothy said. 'Doesn't *diablo* mean "the devil"?' she asked her mom, who just shrugged.

'Honestly, Dorothy – you do go on and on about green-tea muffins. It's just a *muffin*, for Christ's sake,' Miriam told her daughter. 'Eating a muffin isn't remotely the same as having sex!'

Dorothy rolled her eyes and sighed; her body had a permanent aspect of slouching about it, whether she sat or stood. (One could best imagine her lying down.)

Juan Diego emerged from the lavatory, smiling to the oh-so-engaging mother and daughter. He'd managed to extricate himself from the crazy Cathay Pacific pajamas, which he handed to one of the flight attendants; he was looking forward to having a green-tea muffin, if not quite as much as Dorothy apparently did.

Juan Diego's erection had only slightly subsided, and he was very aware of it; after all, he'd missed having erections. Normally, he needed to take half a Viagra to have one – until now.

His maimed foot always throbbed a little after he'd been asleep and had just woken up, but the foot was throbbing in a new and different way – or so Juan Diego imagined. In his mind, he was fourteen again, and Rivera's truck had just flattened his right foot. He could feel the warmth of Lupe's lap against his neck and the back of his head. The Guadalupe doll, on Rivera's dashboard, jiggled this way and that – the way women often seemed to be promising something unspoken and unacknowledged, which was the way Miriam and her daughter, Dorothy, presented themselves to Juan Diego right now. (Not that their hips jiggled!)

But the writer could not speak; Juan Diego's teeth were clenched, his lips tightly sealed, as if he were still making an effort not to scream in pain and thrash his head from side to side in his long-departed sister's lap.

6

Sex and Faith

The elongated passageway to the Regal Airport Hotel at Hong Kong International was bedecked with an incomplete assortment of Christmas memorabilia – happy-faced reindeer and Santa's elf-laborer types, but no sleigh, no gifts, no Santa himself.

'Santa's getting laid – he probably called an escort service,' Dorothy explained to Juan Diego.

'Enough sex, Dorothy,' her mother cautioned the wayward-looking girl.

From the testiness that infiltrated their seemingly more than mother-daughter banter, Juan Diego would have guessed this mother and daughter had been traveling together for years – improbably, for centuries.

'Santa is definitely staying here,' Dorothy said to Juan Diego. 'The Christmas shit is year-round.'

'Dorothy, you're not *here* year-round,' Miriam said. 'You wouldn't know.'

'We're here *enough*,' the daughter sullenly said. 'It *feels like* we're here year-round,' she told Juan Diego.

They were on an ascending escalator, passing a

crèche. To Juan Diego, it seemed strange that they'd not once been outdoors – not since he'd arrived at JFK in all the snow. The crèche was surrounded by the usual cast of characters, humans and barn animals – only one exotic creature among the animals. And the miraculous Virgin Mary could not have been entirely human, Juan Diego had always believed; here in Hong Kong she smiled shyly, averting her eyes from her admirers. At the crèche moment, wasn't all the attention supposed to be paid to her precious son? Apparently not – the Virgin Mary was a scene-stealer. (Not only in Hong Kong, Juan Diego had always believed.)

There was Joseph – the poor fool, as Juan Diego thought of him. But if Mary truly was a virgin, Joseph appeared to be handling the childbirth episode as well as could be expected – no fiery glances or suspicious looks at the inquisitive kings or wise men and shepherds, or at the manger's other gawkers and hangers-on: a cow, a donkey, a rooster, a camel. (The camel, of course, was the one exotic creature.)

'I'll bet the father was one of the wise guys,' Dorothy offered.

'Enough sex, Dorothy,' her mother said.

Juan Diego wrongly surmised he was alone in noticing that the Christ Child was missing from the crèche – or buried, perhaps smothered, in the hay. 'The Baby Jesus—' he started to say.

'Someone kidnapped the Holy Infant years ago,' Dorothy explained. 'I don't think the Hong Kong Chinese care.'

'Maybe the Christ Child is getting a face-lift,' Miriam offered.

'Not everyone gets a face-lift, Mother,' Dorothy said.

'That Holy Infant is no kid, Dorothy,' her mother remarked. 'Believe me – Jesus has had a face-lift.'

'The Catholic Church has done more to cosmetically enhance itself than a face-lift,' Juan Diego said sharply – as if Christmas, and all the crèche promotion, were strictly a Roman Catholic affair. Both mother and daughter looked inquiringly at him, as if puzzled by his angry tone. But surely Miriam and Dorothy couldn't have been surprised by the sting in Juan Diego's voice – not if they'd read his novels, which they had. He had an ax to grind – not with people of faith, or believers of any kind, but with certain social and political policies of the Catholic Church.

Yet the occasional sharpness when he spoke surprised everyone about Juan Diego; he *looked* so mild-mannered, and – because of the maimed right foot – he moved so slowly. Juan Diego didn't resemble a risk-taker, except when it came to his imagination.

At the top of the escalator, the three travelers arrived at a baffling intersection of underground passages – signs pointing to Kowloon and Hong Kong Island, and to somewhere called the Sai Kung Peninsula.

'We're taking a train?' Juan Diego asked his lady admirers.

'Not now,' Miriam told him, seizing his arm. They

were connected to a train station, Juan Diego guessed, but there were confusing advertisements for tailor shops and restaurants and jewelry stores; for jewels, they were offering 'endless opals.'

'Why *endless*? What's so special about *opals*?' Juan Diego asked, but the women seemed strangely selective about listening.

'We'll check into the hotel first, just to freshen up,' Dorothy was telling him; she'd grabbed his other arm.

Juan Diego limped forward; he imagined he wasn't limping as much as he usually did. But why? Dorothy was rolling Juan Diego's checked bag and her own – effortlessly, the two bags with one hand. How can she manage to do that? Juan Diego was wondering when they came upon a large floor-length mirror; it was near the registration desk for their hotel. But when Juan Diego quickly assessed himself in the mirror, his two companions weren't visible alongside him; curiously, he did not see these two efficient women reflected in the mirror. Maybe he'd given the mirror too quick a look.

'We'll take the train to Kowloon – we'll see the skyscrapers on Hong Kong Island, their lights reflected in the water of the harbor. It's better to see it after dark,' Miriam was murmuring in Juan Diego's ear.

'We'll grab a bite to eat – maybe have a drink or two – then take the train back to the hotel,' Dorothy told him in his other ear. 'We'll be sleepy then.'

Something told Juan Diego that he had seen these two ladies before – but where, but *when*?

Was it in the taxi that had jumped the guardrail and got stuck in the waist-deep snow of the jogging path that ran alongside the East River? The cabbie was attempting to dig out his rear wheels – not with a snow shovel but with a windshield scraper.

'Where are you from, you jerk-off – fuckin' *Mexico*?' Juan Diego's limo driver had shouted.

The peering faces of two women were framed in the rear window of that taxi; they could have been a mother and her daughter, but it seemed highly unlikely to Juan Diego that those two frightened-looking women could have been Miriam and Dorothy. It was difficult for Juan Diego to imagine Miriam and Dorothy being *afraid*. Who or what would frighten them? Yet the thought remained: he'd seen these two formidable women before – he was sure of it.

'It's very *modern*,' was all Juan Diego could think of saying about the Regal Airport Hotel when he was riding on the elevator with Miriam and Dorothy. The mother and daughter had registered for him; he'd only had to show his passport. He didn't think he'd paid.

It was one of those hotel rooms where your room key was a kind of credit card; after you'd entered your room, you stuck the card in a slot that was mounted on the wall just inside the door.

'Otherwise, your lights won't work and your TV won't turn on,' Dorothy had explained.

'Call us if you have any trouble with the modern devices,' Miriam told Juan Diego.

'Not just trouble with the modern shit – *any* kind of trouble,' Dorothy had added. On Juan Diego's key-card folder, she'd written her room number – and her mom's.

They're not sharing a room? Juan Diego wondered when he was alone in his room.

In the shower, his erection returned; he knew he should take a beta-blocker – he was aware he was overdue. But his erection made him hesitate. What if Miriam, or Dorothy, made herself *available* to him – more unimaginable, what if *both* of them did?

Juan Diego removed the beta-blockers from his toilet kit; he put the tablets beside the water glass, next to his bathroom sink. They were Lopressor tablets – elliptical, a bluish gray. He took out his Viagra tablets and looked at them. The Viagra were not exactly elliptical; they were somewhat football-shaped, but four-sided. The closer similarity, between the Viagra and the Lopressor, was the color of the tablets – they were both a gray-blue color.

If such a miracle as Miriam or Dorothy making herself *available* to him were to happen, it would be too soon to take a Viagra now, Juan Diego knew. Even so, he removed his pill-cutting device from his toilet kit; he put it next to the Viagra tablets, on the same side of his bathroom sink – just to remind himself that *half* of one Viagra would suffice. (As a novelist, he was always looking ahead, too.)

I'm imagining things like a horny teenager! Juan Diego thought as he was getting dressed to rejoin the ladies. His own behavior surprised him. Under these

unusual circumstances, he took no medication; he
hated how the beta-blockers diminished him, and he
knew better than to take half of one Viagra tablet
prematurely. When he got back to the United States,
Juan Diego was thinking, he must remember to thank
Rosemary for telling him to experiment!

It's too bad that Juan Diego wasn't traveling with
his doctor friend. 'To thank Rosemary' (for her
instructions concerning Viagra usage) was *not* what
the writer needed to remember. Dr. Stein could have
reminded Juan Diego of the reason he was feeling
like a star-crossed Romeo, limping around in an older
writer's body: if you're taking beta-blockers and you
skip a dose, watch out! Your body has been starved
for adrenaline; your body suddenly makes *more*
adrenaline, and more adrenaline receptors. Those
misnamed dreams, which were really heightened,
high-definition memories of his childhood and early
adolescence, were as much the result of Juan Diego
not taking a single Lopressor tablet as was his
suddenly supercharged lust for two strangers – a
mother and her daughter, who seemed more familiar
to him than strangers ever should.

THE TRAIN, THE AIRPORT Express to Kowloon Station,
cost ninety Hong Kong dollars. Maybe his shyness
prevented Juan Diego from looking closely at Miriam
or Dorothy on the train; it's doubtful he was genuinely
interested in reading every word on both sides of his
round-trip ticket, twice. Juan Diego was a little
interested in comparing the Chinese characters to

the corresponding words in English. SAME DAY RETURN was in small capitals, but there seemed to be no equivalent to small capitals in the unvarying Chinese characters.

The writer in Juan Diego found fault with '1 single journey'; shouldn't the numeral 1 have been written out as a word? Didn't 'one single journey' look better? Almost like a title, Juan Diego thought. He wrote something on the ticket with his ever-present pen.

'What are you *doing*?' Miriam asked Juan Diego. 'What can be so fascinating about a train ticket?'

'He's *writing* again,' Dorothy said to her mother. 'He's always writing.'

'"Adult Ticket to City,"' Juan Diego said aloud; he was reading to the women from his train ticket, which he then put away in his shirt pocket. He really didn't know how to behave on a date; he'd never known how, but these two women were especially unnerving.

'Whenever I hear the *adult* word, I think of something pornographic,' Dorothy said, smiling at Juan Diego.

'*Enough*, Dorothy,' her mother said.

It was already dark when their train arrived at Kowloon Station; the Kowloon harborfront was crowded with tourists, many of them taking pictures of the skyscraper-lined view, but Miriam and Dorothy glided unnoticed through the crowds. It must have been a measure of Juan Diego's infatuation with this mother and daughter that he imagined he limped less when either Miriam or Dorothy held his arm or his hand; he even believed that he managed to *glide* as unnoticed as the two of them.

The snug, short-sleeved sweaters the women wore under their cardigans were revealing of their breasts, yet the sweaters were somehow conservative. Maybe the conservative part was what went *unnoticed* about Miriam and Dorothy, Juan Diego thought; or was it that the other tourists were mostly Asian, and seemingly uninterested in these two attractive women from the West? Miriam and Dorothy wore skirts with their sweaters – also revealing, meaning *tight*, or so Juan Diego would have said, but their skirts were not glaringly attention-getting.

Am I the only one who can't stop looking at these women? Juan Diego wondered. He wasn't aware of fashion; he couldn't be expected to understand how neutral colors worked. Juan Diego didn't notice that Miriam and Dorothy wore skirts and sweaters that were beige and brown, or silver and gray, nor did he notice the impeccable design of their clothes. As for the fabric, he may have thought it looked welcoming to touch, but what he *noticed* were Miriam's and Dorothy's breasts – and their hips, of course.

Juan Diego would remember next to nothing of the train ride to Kowloon Station, and not a bit of the busy Kowloon harborfront – not even the restaurant they ate their dinner in, except that he was unusually hungry, and he enjoyed himself in Miriam and Dorothy's company. In fact, he couldn't remember when he'd last enjoyed himself as much, although later – less than a week later – he couldn't recall what they'd talked about. His novels? His childhood?

When Juan Diego met his readers, he had to be careful not to talk too much about himself – because his readers tended to ask him about himself. He often tried to steer the conversation to his readers' lives; surely he would have asked Miriam and Dorothy to tell him about themselves. What about *their* childhood years, *their* adolescence? And Juan Diego must have asked these ladies, albeit discreetly, about the men in their lives; certainly he would have been-curious to know if they were attached. Yet he would remember nothing of their conversation in Kowloon – not a word beyond the absurd attention paid to the train ticket when they were en route to Kowloon Station on the Airport Express, and only a bit of bookish conversation on the train ride back to the Regal Airport Hotel.

There was one thing that stood out about their return trip – a moment of awkwardness in the sleek, sanitized underground of Kowloon Station, when Juan Diego was waiting with the two women on the train platform.

The glassy, gold-tinted interior of the station with its gleaming stainless-steel trash cans – standing like sentinels of cleanliness – gave the station platform the aura of a hospital corridor. Juan Diego couldn't find a camera or photo icon on his cell phone's so-called menu – he wanted to take a photo of Miriam and Dorothy – when the all-knowing mother took the cell phone from him.

'Dorothy and I don't do pictures – we can't stand the way we look in photographs – but let me take *your* photo,' Miriam said to him.

They were almost alone on the platform, except for a young Chinese couple (kids, Juan Diego thought) holding hands. The young man had been watching Dorothy, who'd grabbed Juan Diego's cell phone out of her mother's hands.

'Here, let *me* do it,' Dorothy had said to her mom. 'You take terrible pictures.'

But the young Chinese man took the cell phone from Dorothy. 'If I do it, I can get one of *all* of you,' the boy said.

'Oh, yes – thank you!' Juan Diego told him.

Miriam gave her daughter one of those looks that said: If you'd just let me do it, Dorothy, this wouldn't be happening.

They could all hear the train coming, and the young Chinese woman said something to her boy-friend – no doubt, given the train, that he should hurry up.

He did. The photo caught Juan Diego, and Miriam and Dorothy, by surprise. The Chinese couple seemed to think it was a disappointing picture – perhaps out of focus? – but then the train was there. It was Miriam who snatched the cell phone away from the couple, and Dorothy who – even more quickly – took it from her mom. Juan Diego was already seated on the Airport Express when Dorothy gave him back his phone; it was no longer in the camera mode.

'We don't photograph well,' was all Miriam

said – to the Chinese couple, who seemed unduly disturbed by the incident. (Perhaps the pictures they took usually turned out better.)

Juan Diego was once more searching the menu on his cell phone, which was a maze of mysteries to him. What did the Media Center icon do? *Nothing I want*, Juan Diego was thinking, when Miriam covered his hands with hers; she leaned close to him, as if it were a noisy train (it wasn't), and spoke to him as if they were alone, though Dorothy was very much with them and clearly heard her – every word.

'This *isn't* about sex, Juan Diego, but I have a question for you,' Miriam said. Dorothy laughed harshly – loudly enough to get the attention of the young Chinese couple, who'd been whispering to each other in a nearby seat of the train. (The girl, though she sat in the boy's lap, seemed to be upset with him for some reason.) 'It truly isn't, Dorothy,' Miriam snapped.

'We'll see,' the scornful daughter replied.

'In *A Story Set in Motion by the Virgin Mary*, there's a part where your missionary – I forget his name,' Miriam interrupted herself.

'Martin,' Dorothy quietly said.

'Yes, *Martin*,' Miriam quickly said. 'I guess you've read that one,' she added to her daughter. 'Martin admires Ignatius Loyola, doesn't he?' Miriam asked Juan Diego, but before the novelist could answer her, she hurried on. 'I'm thinking about the saint's encounter with that Moor on a mule, and their ensuing discussion of the Virgin Mary,' Miriam said.

'Both the Moor *and* Saint Ignatius were riding mules,' Dorothy interrupted her mom.

'I *know*, Dorothy,' Miriam dismissively said. 'And the Moor says he can believe that Mother Mary has conceived without a man, but he does not believe that she remains a virgin after she gives birth.'

'That part is about sex, you know,' Dorothy said.

'It *isn't*, Dorothy,' her mother snapped.

'And after the Moor rides on, young Ignatius thinks he should go after the Muslim and *kill* him, right?' Dorothy asked Juan Diego.

'Right,' Juan Diego managed to say, but he wasn't thinking about that long-ago novel or the missionary he'd named Martin, who admired Saint Ignatius Loyola. Juan Diego was thinking about Edward Bonshaw, and that life-changing day he arrived in Oaxaca.

As Rivera was driving the injured Juan Diego to the Templo de la Compañía de Jesús, when the boy was grimacing in pain with his head held in Lupe's lap, Edward Bonshaw was also on his way to the Jesuit temple. While Rivera was hoping for a miracle, of a kind the dump boss imagined the Virgin Mary could perform, it was the new American missionary who was about to become the most credible miracle in Juan Diego's life – a miracle of a *man*, not a saint, and a mixture of human frailties, if there ever was one.

Oh, how he missed Señor Eduardo! Juan Diego thought, his eyes blurring with tears.

'"It was extraordinary that Saint Ignatius felt so

strongly about defending Mother Mary's virginity,"'
Miriam was saying, but her voice trailed off when she
saw that Juan Diego was about to cry.

'"The defaming of the Virgin Mary's postbirth
vaginal condition was inappropriate and unacceptable
behavior,"' Dorothy chimed in.

At that moment, fighting back his tears, Juan Diego
realized that this mother and her daughter were
quoting the passage he'd written in *A Story Set in
Motion by the Virgin Mary*. But how could they so
closely remember the passage from his novel, almost
verbatim? How could any reader do that?

'Oh, don't cry – you dear man!' Miriam suddenly
told him; she touched his face. 'I simply *love* that
passage!'

'*You* made him cry,' Dorothy told her mom.

'No, no – it's not what you think,' Juan Diego
started to say.

'Your missionary,' Miriam went on.

'Martin,' Dorothy reminded her.

'I *know*, Dorothy!' Miriam said. 'It's just so touching, so *sweet*, that Martin finds Ignatius admirable,'
Miriam continued. 'I mean, Saint Ignatius sounds
completely insane!'

'He wants to kill some stranger on a mule – just for
doubting the Virgin Mary's postbirth vaginal condition. That's *nuts*!' Dorothy declared.

'But, as always,' Juan Diego reminded them,
'Ignatius seeks God's will on the matter.'

'*Spare me* God's will!' Miriam and Dorothy
spontaneously cried out – as if they were in the habit

of saying this, either alone or together. (*That* got the young Chinese couple's attention.)

'"And where the road parted, Ignatius let his own mule's reins go slack; if the animal followed the Moor, Ignatius would kill the infidel,"' Juan Diego said. He could have told the story with his eyes closed. It's not so unusual that a novelist can remember what he's written, almost word for word, Juan Diego was thinking. Yet for *readers* to retain the actual words – well, *that* was unusual, wasn't it?

'"But the mule chose the other road,"' mother and daughter said in unison; to Juan Diego, they seemed to have the omniscient authority of a Greek chorus.

'"But Saint Ignatius was crazy – he must have been a madman,"' Juan Diego said; he wasn't sure they understood that part.

'Yes,' Miriam said. 'You're very brave to say so – even in a novel.'

'The subject of someone's postbirth vaginal condition is sexual,' Dorothy said.

'It is *not* – it's about *faith*,' Miriam said.

'It's about sex and faith,' Juan Diego mumbled; he wasn't being diplomatic – he meant it. The two women could tell he did.

'Did you know someone like that missionary who admired Saint Ignatius?' Miriam asked him.

'Martin,' Dorothy repeated softly.

I think I need a beta-blocker – Juan Diego didn't *say* it, but this was what he thought.

'She means, Was Martin *real*?' Dorothy asked him; she'd seen the writer stiffen at her mother's question, so noticeably that Miriam had let go of his hands.

Juan Diego's heart was racing – his adrenaline receptors were receiving like crazy, but he couldn't speak. 'I've lost so many *people*,' Juan Diego tried to say, but the *people* word was unintelligible – like something Lupe might have said.

'I guess he was real,' Dorothy told her mom.

Now they both put their hands on Juan Diego, who was shaking in his seat.

'The missionary I knew was *not* Martin,' Juan Diego blurted out.

'Dorothy, the dear man has lost loved ones – we both read that interview, you know,' Miriam told her daughter.

'I *know*,' Dorothy replied. 'But you were asking about the Martin character,' the daughter said to her mom.

All Juan Diego could do was shake his head; then his tears came, lots of tears. He couldn't have explained to these women why (and for whom) he was crying – well, at least not on the Airport Express.

'¡Señor Eduardo!' Juan Diego cried out. '¡Querido Eduardo!'

That was when the Chinese girl, who was still sitting in her boyfriend's lap – she was still upset about something, too – had an apparent fit. She began to hit her boyfriend, more in frustration than out of anger, and almost playfully (as opposed to anything approaching actual violence).

'I *told* him it was you!' the girl said suddenly to

Juan Diego. 'I *knew* it was you, but he didn't believe me!'

She meant that she'd recognized the writer, perhaps from the start, but her boyfriend hadn't agreed – or he wasn't a reader. To Juan Diego, the Chinese boy didn't look like a reader, and it couldn't have surprised the writer that the boy's girlfriend *was*. Wasn't this the point Juan Diego had made repeatedly? Women readers kept fiction alive – here was another one. When Juan Diego had used Spanish in crying out the scholastic's name, the Chinese girl knew she'd been right about who he was.

It was just another writer-recognition moment, Juan Diego realized. He wished he could stop sobbing. He waved to the Chinese girl, and tried to smile; if he'd noticed the way Miriam and Dorothy looked at the young Chinese couple, he might have asked himself how safe he was in the company of this unknown mother and her daughter, but Juan Diego didn't see how Miriam and Dorothy utterly silenced his Chinese reader with a withering look – no, it was more of a *threatening* look. (It was actually a look that said: We found him first, you slimy little twat. Go find your own favorite writer – he's *ours*!)

Why was it that Edward Bonshaw was always quoting from Thomas à Kempis? Señor Eduardo liked to make a little gentle fun of that bit from *The Imitation of Christ*: 'Be rarely with young people and strangers.'

Ah, well – it was too late to warn Juan Diego about Miriam and Dorothy *now*. You don't skip a dose of your beta-blockers and *ignore* a couple of women like this mom and her daughter.

Dorothy had hugged Juan Diego to her chest; she rocked him in her surprisingly strong arms, where he went on sobbing. He'd no doubt noticed how the young woman was wearing one of those bras that let her nipples show – you could see her nipples through her bra *and* through the sweater Dorothy wore under her open cardigan.

It must have been Miriam (Juan Diego thought) who now massaged the back of his neck; she had once more leaned close to him as she whispered in his ear. 'You darling man, of course it hurts to be you! The things you *feel*! Most men don't feel what you feel,' Miriam said. 'That poor mother in *A Story Set in Motion by the Virgin Mary* – my God! When I think about what *happens* to her—'

'*Don't*,' Dorothy warned her mother.

'A statue of the Virgin Mary falls from a pedestal and crushes her! She is killed on the spot,' Miriam continued.

Dorothy could feel Juan Diego shudder against her breasts. 'Now you've done it, Mother,' the disapproving daughter said. 'Are you trying to make him *more* unhappy?'

'You miss the point, Dorothy,' her mom quickly said. 'As the story says: "At least she was happy. It is not every Christian who is fortunate enough to be instantly killed by the Blessed Virgin." It's a *funny* scene, for Christ's sake!'

But Juan Diego was shaking his head (again), this

time against young Dorothy's breasts. 'That wasn't *your* mom – that wasn't what happened to *her*, was it?' Dorothy asked him.

'That's enough with the autobiographical insinuations, Dorothy,' her mother said.

'Like *you* should talk,' Dorothy said to Miriam.

No doubt, Juan Diego had noticed that Miriam's breasts were also attractive, though her nipples were not visible through her sweater. Not such a *contemporary* kind of bra, Juan Diego was thinking as he struggled to answer Dorothy's question about *his* mother, who *hadn't* been crushed to death by a falling statue of the Virgin Mary – not exactly.

Yet, again, Juan Diego couldn't speak. He was emotionally and sexually overcharged; there was so much adrenaline surging through his body, he couldn't contain his lust *or* his tears. He was missing everyone he ever knew; he was desiring both Miriam and Dorothy, to the degree that he could not have articulated which of these women he wanted more.

'Poor baby,' Miriam whispered in Juan Diego's ear; he felt her kiss the back of his neck.

All Dorothy did was inhale. Juan Diego could feel her chest expand against his face.

What was it Edward Bonshaw used to say in those moments when the zealot felt that the world of human frailties must yield to God's will – when all we mere mortals could do was *listen* to whatever God's will was, and then *do* it? Juan Diego could still hear Señor Eduardo saying this: 'Ad majorem Dei gloriam – to the greater glory of God.'

Under the circumstances – cuddled against Dorothy's bosom, kissed by her mother – wasn't that all Juan Diego could do? Just *listen* to whatever God's will was, and then *do* it? Of course, there was a contradiction in this: Juan Diego wasn't exactly in the company of a couple of *God's-will* kind of women. (Miriam and Dorothy were *'Spare me* God's will!' kind of women.)

'Ad majorem Dei gloriam,' the novelist murmured.

'It must be Spanish,' Dorothy told her mom.

'For Christ's sake, Dorothy,' Miriam said. 'It's fucking *Latin.*'

Juan Diego could feel Dorothy shrug. 'Whatever it is,' the rebellious daughter said, 'it's about sex – I know it is.'

7

Two Virgins

There was a panel of push-buttons on the night table in Juan Diego's hotel room. Confusingly, these buttons dimmed – or turned on and off – the lights in Juan Diego's bedroom and bathroom, but the buttons had a bewildering effect on the radio and TV.

The sadistic maid had left the radio on – this perverse behavior, often below levels of early detection, must be ingrained in hotel maids the world over – yet Juan Diego managed to mute the volume on the radio, if not turn it off. Lights had indeed dimmed; yet these same lights faintly endured, despite Juan Diego's efforts to turn them off. The TV had flourished, briefly, but was once more dark and quiet. His last resort, Juan Diego knew, would be to extract the credit card (actually, his room key) from the slot by the door to his room; then, as Dorothy had warned him, everything electrical would be extinguished, and he would be left to grope around in the pitch-dark.

I can live with *dim*, the writer thought. He couldn't

understand how he'd slept for fifteen hours on the plane and was already tired again. Perhaps the push-button panel was at fault, or was it his newfound lust? And the cruel maid had rearranged the items in his bathroom. The pill-cutting device was on the opposite side of the sink from where he'd so carefully placed his beta-blockers (with his Viagra).

Yes, he was aware that he was now long overdue for a beta-blocker; even so, he didn't take one of the gray-blue Lopressor pills. He'd held the elliptical tablet in his hand but then had returned it to the prescription container. Juan Diego had taken a Viagra instead – a *whole* one. He'd not forgotten that half a pill was sufficient; he was imagining that he would need more than half a Viagra if Dorothy called him or knocked on his door.

As he lay awake, but barely, in the dimly lit hotel room, Juan Diego imagined that a visit from Miriam might also require him to have a whole Viagra. And because he was accustomed to only half a Viagra – 50 milligrams, instead of 100 – he was aware that his nose was stuffier than usual and his throat was dry, and he sensed the beginnings of a headache. Always deliberate, he'd drunk a lot of water with the Viagra; water seemed to lessen the side effects. And the water would make him get up in the night to pee, if the beer didn't suffice. That way, if Dorothy or Miriam never made an appearance, he wouldn't have to wait till the morning to take a *diminishing* Lopressor pill; it had been so long since he'd had a beta-blocker, maybe he should take *two* Lopressor pills, Juan Diego considered. But his confounding, adrenaline-driven desires had commingled with his tiredness, and with his eternal self-doubt. Why would either of those desirable women want to sleep with me? the novelist asked himself. By then, of course, he was asleep. There was no one to notice, but, even asleep, he had an erection.

IF THE RUSH OF adrenaline had stimulated his desire for women – for a mother *and* her daughter, no less – Juan Diego should have anticipated that his dreams (the reenactment of his most formative adolescent experiences) might suffer a surge of detail.

In his dream at the Regal Airport Hotel, Juan Diego almost failed to recognize Rivera's truck. Streaks of the boy's blood laced the exterior of the windswept cab; barely more recognizable was the blood-flecked face of Diablo, el jefe's dog. The gore-glazed truck, which was parked at the Templo de la Compañía de Jesús, got the attention of those tourists and worshipers who'd come to the temple. It was hard not to notice the blood-spattered dog.

Diablo, who'd been left in the flatbed of Rivera's pickup, was fiercely territorial; he would not permit the bystanders to approach the truck too closely, though one bold boy had touched a drying streak of blood on the passenger-side door – long enough to ascertain that it was still sticky and, indeed, was blood.

'¡Sangre!' the brave boy said.

Someone else murmured it first: 'Una matanza.'

(This means 'a bloodbath' or 'a massacre.') Oh, the conclusions a crowd will come to!

From a little blood spilled on an old truck, and a bloodstained dog, this crowd was leaping to conclusions – one after another. A splinter group of the crowd rushed inside the temple; there was talk that the victim of an apparent gang-style shooting had been deposited at the feet of the big Virgin Mary. (Who would want to miss seeing *that*?)

It was on the heels of this rampant speculation, and the partial but sudden shift in the crowd – a mad dash leaving the scene of the crime (the truck at the curb) for the drama taking place inside the temple – that Brother Pepe found a parking place for his dusty red VW Beetle, next to the blood-smeared vehicle and the murderous-looking Diablo.

Brother Pepe had recognized el jefe's truck; he saw the blood and assumed that the poor children, who were (Pepe knew) in Rivera's care, might have come to some unmentionable harm.

'Uh-oh – los niños,' Pepe said. To Edward Bonshaw, Pepe said quickly: 'Leave your things; there appears to be some *trouble*.'

'*Trouble?*' the zealot repeated, in his eager way. Someone in the crowd had uttered the *perro* word, and Edward Bonshaw – hurrying after the waddling Brother Pepe – got a glimpse of the terrifying Diablo. 'What about the dog?' Edward asked Brother Pepe.

'El perro ensangrentado,' Pepe repeated. 'The bloodstained dog.'

'Well, I can *see* that!' Edward Bonshaw said, somewhat peevishly.

The Jesuit temple was thronged with stupefied onlookers. '¡Un milagro!' one of the gawkers shouted.

Edward Bonshaw's Spanish was more selective than just plain bad; he knew the *milagro* word – it sparked in him an abiding interest.

'A *miracle*?' Edward asked Pepe, who was pushing his way toward the altar. '*What* miracle?'

'I don't know – I just got here!' Brother Pepe panted. We wanted an English teacher and we have un milagrero, poor Pepe was thinking – 'a miracle monger.'

It was Rivera who'd been audibly praying for a miracle, and the crowd of idiots – or some idiots in the crowd – had doubtless overheard him. Now the *miracle* word was on everyone's lips.

El jefe had carefully placed Juan Diego before the altar, but the boy was screaming nonetheless. (In his dreams, Juan Diego downplayed the pain.) Rivera kept crossing himself and genuflecting to the overbearing statue of the Virgin Mary, all the while looking over his shoulder for the appearance of the dump kids' mother; it was unclear if Rivera was praying for Juan Diego to be cured as much as the dump boss was hoping for a miracle to save himself from Esperanza's wrath – namely, her blaming Rivera (as she surely would) for the accident.

'The screaming isn't good,' Edward Bonshaw was muttering. He'd not yet seen the boy, but the sound of a child screaming in pain lacked miracle potential.

'A case of hopeful wishing,' Brother Pepe gasped; he knew his words weren't quite right. He asked Lupe what had happened, but Pepe couldn't understand what the crazed child said.

'What language is she speaking?' Edward eagerly asked. 'It sounds a little like *Latin*.'

'It's gibberish, though she seems very intelligent – even prescient,' Brother Pepe whispered in the newcomer's ear. 'No one can understand her – just the boy.' The screaming was unbearable.

That was when Edward Bonshaw saw Juan Diego, prostrate and bleeding before the towering Virgin Mary. 'Merciful Mother! Save the poor child!' the Iowan cried, silencing the murmuring mob but not the screaming boy.

Juan Diego hadn't noticed the other people in the temple, except for what appeared to be two mourners; they knelt in the foremost pew. Two women, all in black – they wore veils, their heads completely covered. Strangely, it comforted the crying child to see the two women mourners. When Juan Diego saw them, his pain abated.

This was not exactly a miracle, but the sudden reduction of his pain made Juan Diego wonder if the two women were mourning *him* – if *he* were the one who'd died, or if he was going to die. When the boy looked for them again, he saw that the silent mourners had not moved; the two women in black, their heads bowed, were as motionless as statues.

Pain or no pain, it was no surprise to Juan Diego
that the Virgin Mary hadn't healed his foot; the boy
wasn't holding his breath for an ensuing miracle from
Our Lady of Guadalupe, either.

'The lazy virgins aren't working today, or they don't
want to help you,' Lupe told her brother. 'Who's the
funny-looking gringo? What's he want?'

'What did she say?' Edward Bonshaw asked the
injured boy.

'The Virgin Mary is a fraud,' the boy replied;
instantly, he felt his pain returning.

'A *fraud* – not our Mary!' Edward Bonshaw
exclaimed.

'This is the dump kid I was telling you about, un
niño de la basura,' Brother Pepe was trying to explain.
'He's a smart one—'

'Who are you? What do you want?' Juan Diego
asked the gringo in the funny-looking Hawaiian
shirt.

'He's our new teacher, Juan Diego – be nice,'
Brother Pepe warned the boy. 'He's one of us, Mr.
Edward Bon—'

'Eduardo,' the Iowan insisted, interrupting Pepe.

'Father Eduardo? *Brother* Eduardo?' Juan Diego
asked.

'*Señor* Eduardo,' Lupe suddenly said. Even the
Iowan had understood her.

'Actually, just Eduardo is okay,' Edward modestly
said.

'Señor Eduardo,' Juan Diego repeated; for no
known reason, the injured dump reader liked the

sound of this. The boy looked for the two women mourners in the foremost pew, not finding them. How they could have just disappeared struck Juan Diego as unlikely as the fluctuations in his pain; it had briefly relented but was now (once again) relentless. As for those two women, well – maybe those two were always just appearing, or disappearing. Who knows what just appears, or disappears, to a boy in this much pain?

'Why is the Virgin Mary a fraud?' Edward Bonshaw asked the boy, who lay unmoving at the Holy Mother's feet.

'Don't ask – not now. There isn't time,' Brother Pepe started to say, but Lupe was already babbling unintelligibly – pointing first to Mother Mary, then to the smaller, dark-skinned virgin, who was often unnoticed in her more modest shrine.

'Is that Our Lady of Guadalupe?' the new missionary asked. From where they were, at the Mary Monster altar, the Guadalupe portrait was small and off to one side of the temple – almost out of sight, purposely tucked away.

'¡Sí!' Lupe cried, stamping her foot; she suddenly spat on the floor, almost perfectly between the two virgins.

'Another probable fraud,' Juan Diego said, to explain his sister's spontaneous spitting. 'But Guadalupe isn't entirely bad; she's just a little corrupted.'

'Is the girl—' Edward Bonshaw started to say, but Brother Pepe put a cautionary hand on the Iowan's shoulder.

'Don't say it,' Pepe warned the young American.

'No, she's *not*,' Juan Diego answered. The unspoken *retarded* word hovered there in the temple, as if one of the miraculous virgins had communicated it. (Naturally, Lupe had read the new missionary's mind; she knew what he'd been thinking.)

'The boy's foot isn't right – it's flattened, and it's pointing the wrong way,' Edward said to Brother Pepe. 'Shouldn't he see a *doctor*?'

'¡Sí!' Juan Diego cried. 'Take me to Dr. Vargas. Only the boss man was hoping for a miracle.'

'The boss man?' Señor Eduardo asked, as if this were a religious reference to the Almighty.

'Not *that* boss man,' Brother Pepe said.

'*What* boss man?' the Iowan asked.

'El jefe,' Juan Diego said, pointing to the anxious, guilt-stricken Rivera.

'*Aha!* The boy's father?' Edward asked Pepe.

'No, probably not – he's the *dump* boss,' Brother Pepe said.

'He was driving the truck! He's too lazy to get his side-view mirror fixed! And look at his stupid mustache! No woman who isn't a prostitute will ever want him with that hairy caterpillar on his lip!' Lupe raved.

'Goodness – she has her own language, doesn't she?' Edward Bonshaw asked Brother Pepe.

'This is Rivera. He was driving the truck that backed over me, but he's like a father to us – *better* than a father. He doesn't leave,' Juan Diego told the new missionary. 'And he never beats us.'

'Aha,' Edward said, with uncharacteristic caution. 'And your *mother*? Where is—'

As if summoned by those do-nothing virgins, who were taking the day off, Esperanza rushed to her son at the altar; she was a ravishingly beautiful young woman who made an entrance of herself wherever and whenever she appeared. Not only did she *not* look like a cleaning woman for the Jesuits; to the Iowan, she most certainly didn't look like anyone's *mother*.

What is it about women with *chests* like that? Brother Pepe was wondering to himself. Why are their chests always *heaving*?

'Always late, usually hysterical,' Lupe said sullenly. The girl's looks at the Virgin Mary and Our Lady of Guadalupe had been disbelieving – in her mother's case, Lupe simply looked away.

'Surely she isn't the boy's—' Señor Eduardo began.

'Yes, she is – the girl's, too,' was all Pepe said.

Esperanza was raving incoherently; it seemed she was beseeching the Virgin Mary, rather than be so mundane as to ask Juan Diego what had happened to him. Her incantations sounded to Brother Pepe like Lupe's gibberish – possibly genetic, Pepe thought – and Lupe (of course) chimed in, adding *her* incoherence to the babble. Naturally, Lupe was pointing to the dump boss as she reenacted the saga of the multifaceted mirror and the foot-flattening truck in reverse; there was no pity for the caterpillar-lipped Rivera, who seemed ready to throw himself at the

Virgin Mary's feet – or repeatedly bash his head against the pedestal where the Holy Mother so dispassionately stood. But was she dispassionate?

It was then that Juan Diego looked upward at the Virgin Mary's usually unemotional face. Did the boy's pain affect his vision, or did Mother Mary indeed *glower* at Esperanza – she who'd brought so little hope, her name notwithstanding, into her son's life? And what exactly did the Holy Mother disapprove of ? What had made the Virgin Mary glare so angrily at the children's mother?

The low-cut neckline of Esperanza's revealing blouse certainly showed a lot of the implausible cleaning woman's cleavage, and from the Virgin Mary's elevated position on her pedestal, the Holy Mother looked down upon Esperanza's décolletage from an all-encompassing height.

Esperanza herself was oblivious to the towering statue's implacable disapproval. Juan Diego was surprised that his mom understood what her vehement daughter was babbling about. Juan Diego was used to being Lupe's interpreter – even for Esperanza – but not this time.

Esperanza had stopped wringing her hands imploringly in the area of the Virgin Mary's toes; the sensual-looking cleaning woman was no longer beseeching the unresponsive statue. Juan Diego always underestimated his mother's capacity for blame – that is, for blaming *others*. In this case, Rivera – el jefe, with his unrepaired side-view mirror, he who slept in the cab of his truck with his gear shift in reverse – was the recipient of Esperanza's animated blame. She beat the dump boss with both her hands, in tightly clenched fists; she kicked his shins; she yanked his hair, her bracelets scratching his face.

'You have to help Rivera,' Juan Diego said to Brother Pepe, 'or he'll need to see Dr. Vargas, too.' The injured boy then spoke to his sister: 'Did you see how the Virgin Mary looked at our mother?' But the seemingly all-knowing child simply shrugged.

'The Virgin Mary disapproves of everyone,' Lupe said. 'No one is good enough for that big bitch.'

'What did she say?' Edward Bonshaw asked.

'God knows,' Brother Pepe said. (Juan Diego didn't offer a translation.)

'If you want to worry about something,' Lupe said to her brother, 'you ought to worry about how Guadalupe was looking at *you*.'

'How?' Juan Diego asked the girl. It hurt his foot to turn his head to look at the less noticed of the two virgins.

'Like she's still making up her mind about you,' Lupe said. 'Guadalupe hasn't *decided* about you,' the clairvoyant child told him.

'Get me out of here,' Juan Diego said to Brother Pepe. 'Señor Eduardo, you have to help me,' the injured boy added, grasping the new missionary's hand. 'Rivera can carry me,' Juan Diego continued. 'You just have to rescue Rivera first.'

'Esperanza, *please*,' Brother Pepe said to the cleaning woman; he had reached out and caught her slender wrists. 'We have to take Juan Diego to Dr. Vargas – we need Rivera, and his truck.'

'His truck!' the histrionic mother cried.

'You should pray,' Edward Bonshaw said to Esperanza; inexplicably, he knew how to say this in Spanish – he said it perfectly.

'*Pray?*' Esperanza asked him. 'Who is he?' she suddenly asked Pepe, who was staring at his bleeding thumb; one of Esperanza's bracelets had cut him.

'Our new teacher – the one we've all been waiting for,' Brother Pepe said, as if suddenly inspired. 'Señor Eduardo is from *Iowa*,' Pepe intoned. He made *Iowa* sound as if it were Rome.

'*Iowa*,' Esperanza repeated, in her enthralled way – her chest heaving. 'Señor Eduardo,' she repeated, bowing to the Iowan with an awkward but cleavage-revealing curtsy. 'Pray *where*? Pray *here*? Pray *now*?' she asked the new missionary in the riotous, parrot-covered shirt.

'Sí,' Señor Eduardo told her; he was trying to look everywhere except at her breasts.

You have to hand it to this guy; he's got a way about him, Brother Pepe was thinking.

Rivera had already lifted Juan Diego from the altar where the Virgin Mary imposingly stood. The boy had cried out in pain, albeit briefly – just enough to quiet the murmuring crowd.

'Look at him,' Lupe was telling her brother.

'Look at—' Juan Diego started to ask her.

'At *him*, at the gringo – the parrot man!' Lupe said.

'*He's* the miracle man. Don't you see? It's him. He came for us – for *you*, anyway,' Lupe said.

'What do you mean: "He came for us" – what's that supposed to mean?' Juan Diego asked his sister.

'For you, anyway,' Lupe said again, turning away; she was almost indifferent, as if she'd lost interest in what she was saying or she no longer believed in herself. 'Now that I think of it, I guess the gringo isn't my miracle – just yours,' the girl said, disheartened.

'The parrot man!' Juan Diego repeated, laughing; yet, as Rivera carried him, the boy could see that Lupe wasn't smiling. Serious as ever, she appeared to be scanning the crowd, as if looking for who *her* miracle might be, and not finding him.

'You Catholics,' Juan Diego said, wincing as Rivera shouldered his way through the congested entrance-way to the Jesuit temple; it was unclear to Brother Pepe and Edward Bonshaw if the boy had spoken to them. 'You Catholics' could have meant the gawking crowd, including the shrill but unsuccessful praying of the dump kids' mother – Esperanza always prayed out loud, like Lupe, and in Lupe's language. And now, also like Lupe, Esperanza had stopped beseeching the Virgin Mary; it was the smaller, dark-skinned virgin who received the pretty cleaning woman's earnest attention.

'Oh, you who were once disbelieved – you who were doubted, you who were asked to prove who you were,' Esperanza was praying to the child-size portrait of Our Lady of Guadalupe.

'You Catholics,' Juan Diego began again. Diablo

saw the dump kids coming and began to wag his tail, but this time the injured boy had clutched a handful of parrots on the new missionary's overlarge Hawaiian shirt. 'You Catholics stole our virgin,' Juan Diego said to Edward Bonshaw. 'Guadalupe was *ours*, and you took her – you *used* her, you made her merely an acolyte to your Virgin Mary.'

'An *acolyte*!' the Iowan repeated. 'This boy speaks English remarkably well!' Edward said to Brother Pepe.

'Sí, *remarkably*,' Pepe answered.

'But perhaps the pain has made him delirious,' the new missionary suggested. Brother Pepe didn't think Juan Diego's pain had anything to do with it; Pepe had heard the boy's Guadalupe rant before.

'For a dump kid, he is *milagroso*,' was how Brother Pepe put it – *miraculous*. 'He reads better than our students, and remember – he's self-taught.'

'Yes, I know – that's amazing. *Self-taught*!' Señor Eduardo cried.

'And God knows how and where he learned his English – not only in the basurero,' Pepe said. 'The boy's been hanging out with hippies and draft dodgers – an enterprising boy!'

'But everything ends up in the basurero,' Juan Diego managed to say, between waves of pain. 'Even books in English.' He'd stopped looking for those two women mourners; Juan Diego thought his pain meant he wouldn't see them, because he wasn't dying.

'I'm not riding with caterpillar lip,' Lupe was saying. 'I want to ride with the parrot man.'

'We want to ride in the pickup part, with Diablo,' Juan Diego told Rivera.

'Sí,' the dump boss said, sighing; he knew when he'd been rejected.

'Is the dog friendly?' Señor Eduardo asked Brother Pepe.

'I'll follow you, in the VW,' Pepe replied. 'If you are torn to pieces, I can be a witness – make recommendations to the higher-ups, on behalf of your eventual sainthood.'

'I was being serious,' said Edward Bonshaw.

'So was I, Edward – sorry, *Eduardo* – so was I,' Pepe replied.

Just as Rivera had settled the injured boy in Lupe's lap, in the bed of the pickup, the two old priests arrived on the scene. Edward Bonshaw had braced himself against the truck's spare tire – the children between him and Diablo, who viewed the new missionary with suspicion, a perpetual tear oozing from the dog's lidless left eye.

'What is happening here, Pepe?' Father Octavio asked. 'Did someone faint or have a heart attack?'

'It's those dump kids,' Father Alfonso said, frowning. 'One could smell that garbage truck from the Hereafter.'

'What is Esperanza praying for *now*?' Father Octavio asked Pepe, because the cleaning woman's keening voice could be heard from the Hereafter, too – or at least from as far away as the sidewalk in front of the Jesuit temple.

'Juan Diego was run over by Rivera's truck,' Brother

Pepe began. 'The boy was brought here for a miracle, but our two virgins failed to deliver.'

'They're on their way to Dr. Vargas, I presume,' Father Alfonso said, 'but why is there a gringo with them?' The two priests were wrinkling their unusually sensitive and frequently condemning noses – not only at the garbage truck, but at the gringo with the Polynesian parrots on his tasteless tent of a shirt.

'Don't tell me Rivera ran over a tourist, too,' Father Octavio said.

'That's the man we've all been waiting for,' Brother Pepe told the priests, with an impish smile. 'That is Edward Bonshaw, from Iowa – our new teacher.' It was on the tip of Pepe's tongue to tell them that Señor Eduardo was un milagrero – a miracle monger – but Pepe restrained himself as best he could. Brother Pepe wanted Father Octavio and Father Alfonso to discover Edward Bonshaw for themselves. The way Pepe put it was calculated to provoke these two oh-so-conservative priests, but he was careful to mention the *miracle* subject in only the most offhand manner. 'Señor Eduardo es bastante milagroso,' was how Pepe put it. 'Señor Eduardo is somewhat miraculous.'

'Señor Eduardo,' Father Octavio repeated.

'*Miraculous!*' Father Alfonso exclaimed, with distaste. These two old priests did not use the *milagroso* word lightly.

'Oh, you'll see – you'll see,' Brother Pepe said innocently.

'Does the American have other shirts, Pepe?' Father Octavio asked.

'Ones that fit him?' Father Alfonso added.

'Sí, *lots* more shirts – all Hawaiian!' Pepe replied. 'And I think they're all a little big for him, because he's lost a lot of weight.'

'Why? Is he dying?' Father Octavio asked. The losing-weight part was no more appealing to Father Octavio and Father Alfonso than the hideous Hawaiian shirt; the two old priests were almost as overweight as Brother Pepe.

'*Is* he – that is, *dying*?' Father Alfonso asked Brother Pepe.

'Not that I know of,' Pepe replied, trying to repress his impish smile a little. 'In fact, Edward seems very healthy – and most eager to be of use.'

'*Of use*,' Father Octavio repeated, as if this were a death sentence.

'How utilitarian.'

'Mercy,' Father Alfonso said.

'I'm following them,' Brother Pepe told the priests; he was waddling hurriedly to his dusty red VW Beetle. 'In case anything happens.'

'Mercy,' Father Octavio echoed.

'Leave it to the Americans, to make themselves *of use*,' Father Alfonso said.

Rivera's truck was pulling away from the curb, and Brother Pepe followed it into the traffic. Ahead of him, he could see Juan Diego's little face, held protectively in his strange sister's small hands. Diablo had once again put his forepaws on the pickup's toolbox; the wind blew the dog's unmatched ears away from his face – both the normal one and the ear that was missing a jagged-edged, triangular piece. But it was Edward Bonshaw who captured and held Brother Pepe's attention.

'Look at him,' Lupe had said to Juan Diego. 'At *him*, at the gringo – the parrot man!'

What Brother Pepe saw in Edward Bonshaw was a man who looked like he *belonged* – like a man who had never felt at home, but who'd suddenly found his place in the scheme of things.

Brother Pepe didn't know if he was excited or afraid, or both; he saw now that Señor Eduardo was truly a man with a purpose.

It was the way Juan Diego felt in his dream – the way you feel when you know everything has changed, and that this moment heralds the rest of your life.

'Hello?' a young woman's voice was saying on the phone, which Juan Diego only now realized he held in his hand.

'Hello,' the writer, who'd been fast asleep, said; only now was he aware of his throbbing erection.

'Hi, it's *me* – it's *Dorothy*,' the young woman said. 'You're alone, aren't you? My mother isn't with you, is she?'

8

Two Condoms

What can you believe about a fiction writer's dreams? In his dreams, obviously, Juan Diego felt free to imagine what Brother Pepe was thinking and feeling. But in whose point of view were Juan Diego's dreams? (Not in Pepe's.)

Juan Diego would have been happy to talk about this, and about other aspects of his resurgent dream life, though it seemed to him that now was not the time. Dorothy was playing with his penis; as the novelist had observed, the young woman brought to this postcoital play the same unwavering scrutiny she tended to bring to her cell phone and laptop. And Juan Diego wasn't much inclined to male fantasies, not even as a fiction writer.

'I think you can do it again,' the naked girl was saying. 'Okay – maybe not immediately, but pretty soon. Just *look* at this guy!' she exclaimed. She'd not been shy the first time, either.

At his age, Juan Diego didn't do a lot of looking at his penis, but Dorothy had – from the start.

What happened to foreplay? Juan Diego had

wondered. (Not that he'd had much experience with foreplay *or* afterplay.) He'd been trying to explain to Dorothy the Mexican glorification of Our Lady of Guadalupe. They'd been cuddled together in Juan Diego's dimly lit bed, where they were barely able to hear the muted radio – as if from a faraway planet – when the brazen girl had pulled back the covers and taken a look at his adrenaline-charged, Viagra-enhanced erection.

'The problem began with Cortés, who conquered the Aztec Empire in 1521 – Cortés was *very* Catholic,' Juan Diego was saying to the young woman. Dorothy lay with her warm face against his stomach, staring at his penis. 'Cortés came from Extremadura; the Extremadura Guadalupe, I mean a *statue* of the virgin, was supposedly carved by Saint Luke, the evangelist. It was discovered in the fourteenth century,' Juan Diego continued, 'when the virgin pulled one of her tricky apparitions – you know, an appearance before a humble-shepherd type. She commanded him to dig at the site of her apparition; the shepherd found the icon on the spot.'

'This is *not* an old man's penis – this is one alert-looking guy you have here,' Dorothy said, not remotely apropos of the Guadalupe subject. Thus she'd begun; Dorothy didn't waste time.

Juan Diego did his best to ignore her. 'The Guadalupe of Extremadura was dark-skinned, not unlike most Mexicans,' Juan Diego pointed out to Dorothy, although it disconcerted him to be speaking to the back of the dark-haired young woman's head. 'Thus the Extremadura Guadalupe was the perfect proselytizing tool for those missionaries who followed Cortés to Mexico; Guadalupe became the ideal icon to convert the natives to Christianity.'

'Uh-huh,' Dorothy replied, slipping Juan Diego's penis into her mouth.

Juan Diego was not, and had never been, a sexually confident man; lately, discounting his solo experiments with Viagra, he'd had no sexual relationships at all. Yet Juan Diego managed a cavalier response to Dorothy's going down on him – he kept talking. It must have been the novelist in him: he could concentrate on the long haul; he'd never been much of a short-story writer.

'It was ten years after the Spanish conquest, on a hill outside Mexico City—' Juan Diego said to the young woman sucking his penis.

'Tepeyac,' Dorothy briefly interrupted herself; she pronounced the word perfectly before she slipped his cock back in her mouth. Juan Diego was nonplussed that such an unscholarly-looking girl knew the name of the place, but he tried to be as nonchalant about that as he was pretending to be about the blow job.

'It was an early morning in December 1531—' Juan Diego began again.

He felt a sharp nick from Dorothy's teeth when the impulsive girl spoke quickly, not pausing to take his penis out of her mouth: 'In the Spanish Empire, this particular morning was the Feast of the Immaculate Conception – no coincidence, huh?'

'Yes, however—' Juan Diego started to say, but he

stopped himself. Dorothy was now sucking him in a way that suggested the young woman would not bother to interject her points of clarification again. The novelist struggled ahead. 'The peasant Juan Diego, for whom I was named, saw a vision of a girl. She was surrounded by light; she was only fifteen or sixteen, but when she spoke to him, this *peasant* Juan Diego allegedly understood – from her words, or so we're expected to believe – that this girl either *was* the Virgin Mary or was, somehow, *like* the Virgin Mary. And what she wanted was a church – a whole church, in her honor – to be built on the site where she appeared to him.'

To which, in probable disbelief, Dorothy grunted – or she made a similarly noncommittal sound, subject to interpretation. If Juan Diego had to guess, Dorothy knew the story, and, regarding the prospect of the Virgin Mary (or someone *like* her) appearing as a young teenager and expecting a hapless peasant to build a whole church for her, Dorothy's nonverbal utterance conveyed more than a hint of sarcasm.

'What was the poor peasant to do?' Juan Diego asked – a rhetorical question if Dorothy had ever heard one, to judge by the young woman's sudden snort. This rude snorting sound made Juan Diego – *not* the peasant, the *other* Juan Diego – flinch. The novelist no doubt feared another sharp nick from the busy girl's teeth, but he was spared further pain – at least for the moment.

'Well, the peasant told his hard-to-believe story to the Spanish archbishop—' the novelist persevered.

'Zumárraga!' Dorothy managed to blurt out before she made a quickly passing gagging sound.

What an unusually well-informed young woman – she even knew the name of the doubting archbishop! Juan Diego was amazed.

Dorothy's apparent grasp of these specific details momentarily deterred Juan Diego from continuing his version of Guadalupe's history; he stopped short of the *miraculous* part of the story, either daunted by Dorothy's knowledge of a subject that had long obsessed him or (at last!) distracted by the blow job.

'And what did that doubting archbishop do?' Juan Diego asked. He was testing Dorothy, and the gifted young woman didn't disappoint him – except that she stopped sucking his cock. Her mouth released his penis with an audible *pop*, once more making him flinch.

'The asshole bishop told the peasant to prove it, as if that were the peasant's job,' Dorothy said with disdain. She moved up Juan Diego's body, sliding his penis between her breasts.

'And the poor peasant went back to the virgin and asked her for a sign, to prove her identity,' Juan Diego went on.

'As if that were *her* fucking job,' Dorothy said; she was all the while kissing his neck and nibbling the lobes of his ears.

At that point, it became confusing – that is, it's impossible to delineate who said what to whom. After all, they both knew the story, and they were in a rush to move past the storytelling process. The virgin told Juan Diego (the peasant) to gather flowers; that there were flowers growing in December possibly stretches the boundaries of credibility – that the flowers the peasant found were Castilian roses, not native to Mexico, is more of a stretch.

But this was a *miracle* story, and by the time Dorothy or Juan Diego (the novelist) got to the part of the narrative where the peasant showed the flowers to the bishop – the virgin had arranged the roses in the peasant's humble cloak – Dorothy had already produced a small marvel of her own. The enterprising young woman had brought forth her own condom, which she'd managed to put on Juan Diego while the two of them were talking; the girl was a multitasker, a quality the novelist had noticed and much admired in the young people he'd known in his life as a teacher.

The small circle of Juan Diego's sexual contacts did not include a woman who carried her own condoms and was an expert at putting them on; nor had he ever encountered a girl who assumed the superior position with as much familiarity and assertiveness as Dorothy did.

Juan Diego's inexperience with women – especially with young women of Dorothy's aggressiveness and sexual sophistication – had left him at a loss for words. It's doubtful that Juan Diego could have completed this essential part of the Guadalupe story – namely, what happened when the poor peasant opened his cape of roses for Bishop Zumárraga.

Dorothy, even as she settled herself so solidly on

Juan Diego's penis – her breasts, falling forward, brushed the novelist's face – was the one who reiterated that part of the tale. When the flowers fell out of the cloak, there in their place, imprinted on the fabric of the poor peasant's rustic cape, was the very image of the Virgin of Guadalupe, her hands clasped in prayer, her eyes modestly downcast.

'It wasn't so much that the image of Guadalupe was imprinted on the stupid cloak,' the young woman, who was rocking back and forth on top of Juan Diego, was saying. 'It was the virgin herself – I mean, the way she *looked*. That must have impressed the bishop.'

'What do you mean?' Juan Diego managed to say breathlessly. 'How did Guadalupe *look*?'

Dorothy threw back her head and shook her hair; her breasts wobbled over him, and Juan Diego held his breath at the sight of a rivulet of sweat that ran between them.

'I mean her *demeanor*!' Dorothy panted. 'Her hands were held in such a way that you couldn't even see her boobs, if she actually had boobs; her eyes looked down, but you could still see a spooky light in her eyes. I don't mean in the dark part—'

'The iris—' Juan Diego started to say.

'*Not* in her irises – in her *pupils*!' Dorothy gasped. 'I mean in the *center* part – there was a creepy light in her eyes.'

'Yes!' Juan Diego grunted; he'd always thought so – he'd just not met anyone who agreed with him until now. 'But Guadalupe was different – not just her dark skin,' he struggled to say; it was becoming harder and harder to breathe, with Dorothy bouncing on him. 'She spoke Nahuatl, the local language – she was an *Indian*, not Spanish. If she was a virgin, she was an *Aztec* virgin.'

'What did the dipshit bishop care about that?' Dorothy asked him. 'Guadalupe's demeanor was so fucking *modest*, so *Mary*-like!' the hardworking young woman cried.

'*¡Sí!*' Juan Diego shouted. 'Those manipulative Catholics—' he'd scarcely started to say, when Dorothy grabbed his shoulders with what felt like supernatural strength. She pulled his head and shoulders entirely off the bed – she rolled him over, on top of her.

Yet in that instant when she was still on top of him, and Juan Diego was looking up at her – into her eyes – he'd seen how Dorothy was regarding him.

What was it Lupe had said, so long ago? 'If you want to worry about something, you ought to worry about how Guadalupe was looking at *you*. Like she's still making up her mind about you. Guadalupe hasn't *decided* about you,' the clairvoyant child had told him.

Wasn't *that* how Dorothy was looking at Juan Diego in the half-second before she wrestled him over and pulled him on top of her? It had been, albeit briefly, a scary look. And now, beneath him, Dorothy resembled a woman possessed. Her head thrashed from side to side; her hips thrust against him with such a powerful, upward force that Juan Diego clung to her like a man in fear of falling. But falling where? The bed was huge; there was no danger of falling off it.

At first, he imagined that his nearness to an orgasm was responsible for how acute his hearing had become. Was that the muted radio he heard? The unknown language was both disturbing and strangely familiar. Don't they speak Mandarin here? Juan Diego wondered, but there was nothing Chinese about the woman's voice on the radio – nor was this voice *muted*. In the violence of their lovemaking, had one of Dorothy's flailing hands – or her arm, or a leg – struck the panel of push-buttons on the night table? The woman on the radio, in whatever foreign language she was speaking, was – in fact – *screaming*.

This was when Juan Diego realized that the screaming woman was Dorothy. The radio had remained as muted as before; it was Dorothy's orgasm that was amplified, above any expectation and beyond all reason.

There was an unwelcome confluence of Juan Diego's next two thoughts: coincident to his strictly physical awareness that he was coming, in a more sensational manner than he'd ever done so before, was the conviction that he should definitely take two beta-blockers – at the earliest opportunity. But this unexamined idea had a brother (or a sister). Juan Diego thought he knew what language Dorothy was speaking, although it had been many years since he'd last heard someone speak it. What Dorothy was screaming, just before she came, sounded like

Nahuatl – the language Our Lady of Guadalupe spoke, the language of the Aztecs. But Nahuatl belonged to a group of languages of central and southern Mexico and Central America. Why would – how could – Dorothy speak it?

'Aren't you going to answer your phone?' Dorothy was calmly asking him in English. She'd arched her back, with both hands held behind her head on the pillow, to make it easier for Juan Diego to reach over her for the phone on the night table. Was it the dimness of the light that made Dorothy's skin appear darker than it really was? Or was she truly more dark-skinned than Juan Diego had noticed until now?

He had to stretch to reach the ringing phone; first his chest, then his stomach, touched Dorothy's breasts.

'It's my mother, you know,' the languid young woman told him. 'Knowing her, she called my room first.'

Maybe *three* beta-blockers, Juan Diego was thinking. 'Hello?' he said sheepishly into the phone.

'Your ears must be ringing,' Miriam told him. 'I'm surprised you could hear the phone.'

'I can hear you,' Juan Diego said, more loudly than he'd intended; his ears were *still* ringing.

'The entire floor, if not the whole hotel, must have heard Dorothy,' Miriam added. Juan Diego couldn't think of what to say. 'If my daughter has recovered her faculties of speech, I would like to speak with her. Or I could give *you* the message,' Miriam continued, 'and you could tell Dorothy – when she is once again *herself.*'

'She is herself,' Juan Diego said, with an absurdly

misplaced and exaggerated dignity. What a ridiculous thing this was to say about anyone! Why wouldn't Dorothy be *herself*? Who else would the young woman in bed with him be? Juan Diego wondered, handing Dorothy the phone.

'What a surprise, Mother,' the young woman said laconically. Juan Diego couldn't hear what Miriam was saying to her daughter, but he was aware that Dorothy didn't say much.

Juan Diego thought this mother-daughter conversation might be an opportune moment for him to discreetly remove the condom, but when he rolled off Dorothy, and lay on his side with his back turned to her, he discovered – to his surprise – that the condom had already been removed.

It must be a generational thing – these young people today! Juan Diego marveled. Not only are they able to make a condom appear out of nowhere; they can, as quickly, make a condom *dis*appear. But where *is* it? Juan Diego wondered. When he turned toward Dorothy, the girl wrapped one of her strong arms around him – hugging him to her breasts. He could see the foil wrapper on the night table – he'd not noticed it before – but the condom itself was nowhere to be seen.

Juan Diego, who'd once referred to himself as a 'keeper of details' (he meant *as a novelist*), wondered where the used condom was: perhaps tucked under Dorothy's pillow, or carelessly discarded in the disheveled bed. Possibly, disposing of a condom in this fashion was a generational thing, too.

'I *am* aware that he has an early-morning flight, Mother,' Dorothy was saying. 'Yes, I *know* that's why we're staying here.'

I have to pee, Juan Diego was thinking, and I mustn't forget to take two Lopressor pills the next time I'm in the bathroom. But when he tried to slip away from the dimly lit bed, Dorothy's strong arm tightened around the back of his neck; his face was pressed against her nearest breast.

'But when is *our* flight?' he heard Dorothy ask her mother. '*We* aren't going to Manila next, are we?' Either the prospect of Dorothy and Miriam being with him in Manila, or the feeling of Dorothy's breast against his face, had given Juan Diego an erection. And then he heard Dorothy say: 'You're kidding, right? Since when are you "expected in" Manila?'

Uh-oh, Juan Diego thought – but if my heart can handle being with a young woman like Dorothy, surely I can survive being in Manila with Miriam. (Or so he thought.)

'Well, he's a *gentleman*, Mother – of course he didn't call me,' Dorothy said, taking Juan Diego's hand and holding it against her far breast. 'Yes, I called him. Don't tell me you didn't think about it,' the caustic young woman said.

With one breast pressed into his face and another held fast in his inadequate hand, Juan Diego was reminded of something Lupe liked to say – often inappropriately. 'No es buen momento para un terremoto,' Lupe used to say. 'It's not a good moment for an earthquake.'

'Fuck you, too,' Dorothy said, hanging up the phone. It may not have been a good moment for an earthquake, but it also wouldn't have been an appropriate time for Juan Diego to go to the bathroom.

'There's a dream I have,' he started to say, but Dorothy sat up suddenly, pushing him to his back.

'You don't want to hear what I dream about – believe me,' she told him. She'd curled up, with her face on his belly but turned away from him; once again, Juan Diego was looking at the back of Dorothy's dark-haired head. When Dorothy began playing with his penis, the novelist wondered what the right words were for this – *this postcoital play*, he imagined.

'I think you can do it again,' the naked girl was saying. 'Okay – maybe not immediately, but pretty soon. Just *look* at this guy!' she exclaimed. He was as hard as the first time; the young woman didn't hesitate to mount him.

Uh-oh, Juan Diego thought again. He was thinking only about how much he had to pee – he wasn't speaking symbolically – when he said, 'It's not a good moment for an earthquake.'

'I'll show you an earthquake,' Dorothy said.

THE NOVELIST AWOKE WITH the certain feeling that he had died and gone to Hell; he'd long suspected that if Hell existed (which he doubted), there would be bad music playing constantly – in the loudest possible competition with the news in a foreign language. When he woke up, that was the case, but Juan Diego was still in bed – in his brightly lit and blaring room at the Regal Airport Hotel. Every light in his room was on, at the brightest possible setting; the music on his radio and the news on his TV were cranked to the highest possible volume.

Had Dorothy done this as she was leaving? The young woman was gone, but had she bequeathed to Juan Diego her idea of an amusing wake-up call? Or perhaps the girl had left in a huff. Juan Diego couldn't remember. He felt he'd been more soundly asleep than he'd ever been before, but for no longer than five minutes.

He hit the panel of push-buttons on his night table, hurting the heel of his right hand. The volume on the radio and TV were muted sufficiently for him to hear, and answer, the ringing phone: it was someone yelling at him in an Asian-sounding language (whatever 'Asian-sounding' sounds like).

'I'm sorry – I don't understand you,' Juan Diego replied in English. 'Lo siento—' he started to say in Spanish, but the caller didn't wait.

'You   asswheel!'   the   Asian-sounding   person shouted.

'I think you mean ass*hole*—' the writer answered, but the angry caller had hung up. Only then did Juan Diego notice that the foil wrappers for his first and second condom were missing from his night table; Dorothy must have taken them with her, or thrown them in a wastebasket.

Juan Diego saw that the second condom was still on his penis; in fact, it was the only evidence he had that he'd once more 'performed.' He had no memory past that moment when Dorothy had mounted him for another try. The earthquake she'd promised to show him was lost in time; if the young woman had again broken the sound barrier in a language that sounded like Nahuatl (but it couldn't have been), that moment hadn't been captured in memory or in a dream.

The novelist knew only that he'd been asleep and *hadn't* dreamed – not even a nightmare. Juan Diego got out of bed and limped to the bathroom; that he didn't have to pee forewarned him that he already had. He hoped he hadn't peed in the bed, or in the condom, or on Dorothy, but he could see – when he got to the bathroom – that the cap on his Lopressor prescription was off. He must have taken one (or two) of the beta-blockers when he'd gotten up to pee.

But how long ago was that? Was it before or after Dorothy left? And had he taken only one Lopressor, as he'd been prescribed, or the two he'd imagined that he *should have* taken? Actually, of course, he should not have taken two. A double dose of beta-blockers wasn't recommended as a remedy for missing a dose.

There was already a gray light outside, not to mention the blazing light in his hotel room; Juan Diego knew he had an early-morning flight. He'd not unpacked much, so he didn't have a lot to do. He was, however, meticulous about *how* he packed the articles in his toilet kit; this time, he would put the Lopressor prescription (and the Viagra) in his carry-on.

He flushed the second condom down the toilet but

was disconcerted that he couldn't find the first. And when had he peed? At any moment, he imagined, Miriam would be calling him or knocking on his door, telling him it was time to go; hence he pulled back the top sheet and looked under the pillows, hoping to find the first condom. The damn thing was not in any of the wastebaskets – neither were the foil wrappers.

Juan Diego was standing under the shower when he saw the missing condom circling the drain at the bottom of the bathtub. It had unrolled itself and resembled a drowned slug; the only explanation had to be that the first condom he'd used with Dorothy had been stuck to his back, or his ass, or the back of one leg.

How embarrassing! He hoped Dorothy hadn't seen it. If he'd skipped taking a shower, he might have boarded his flight to Manila with the used condom attached to him.

Unfortunately, he was still in the shower when the telephone rang. To men his age, Juan Diego knew – and surely the odds were worse for *crippled* men his age – bad accidents happened in bathtubs. Juan Diego turned off the shower and almost daintily stepped out of the tub. He was dripping wet and aware of how slippery the tiles on the bathroom floor could be, but when he grabbed a towel, the towel rod was reluctant to release it; Juan Diego tugged at the towel harder than he should have. The aluminum towel rod pulled free of the bathroom wall, bringing the porcelain mounting with it. The porcelain shattered on the floor, scattering the wet tiles with translucent ceramic chips; the aluminum rod hit Juan Diego in the face, cutting his forehead above one eyebrow. He limped, dripping, into the bedroom, holding the towel to his bleeding head.

'Hello!' he cried into the phone.

'Well, you're awake – that's a start,' Miriam told him. 'Don't let Dorothy go back to sleep.'

'Dorothy isn't here,' Juan Diego said.

'She's not answering her phone – she must be in the shower or something,' her mother said. 'Are you ready to leave?'

'How about ten minutes?' Juan Diego asked.

'Make it eight, but shoot for five – I'll come get you,' Miriam told him. 'We'll get Dorothy last – girls her age are the last to be ready,' her mother explained.

'I'll be ready,' Juan Diego told her.

'Are you all right?' Miriam asked him.

'Yes, of course,' he replied.

'You sound different,' she told him, then hung up.

Different? Juan Diego wondered. He saw he'd bled on the exposed bedsheets; the water had dripped from his hair and diluted the blood from the cut on his forehead. The water had turned the blood a pinker color, and there was more blood than there should have been; it was a small cut, but it kept bleeding.

Yes, facial cuts bleed a lot – and he'd just stepped out of a hot shower. Juan Diego tried to wipe the blood off the bed with his towel, but the towel was bloodier than the bedsheets; he managed to make more of a mess. The side of the bed nearest the night table looked like the site of a ritualistic-sex slaying.

Juan Diego went back in the bathroom, where there was more blood and water – and the scattered ceramic chips from the shattered porcelain mounting. He put cold water on his face – on his forehead, especially, to try to stop the stupid cut from bleeding. Naturally, he had a virtual lifetime supply of Viagra, and his despised beta-blockers – and don't forget the fussy pill-cutting device – but no Band-Aids. He stuck a wad of toilet paper on the profusely bleeding but tiny cut, temporarily stanching the flow of blood.

When Miriam knocked on his door, and he let her in, he was ready to go – except for putting the custom-made shoe on his crippled foot. That was always a little tricky; it could also be time-consuming.

'Here,' Miriam said, pushing him to the bed, 'let me help you.' He sat at the foot of the bed while she put the special shoe on him; to his surprise, she seemed to know how to do it. In fact, she did it so expertly, and in such an offhand manner, that she was able to take a long look at the bloodstained bed while she secured the shoe on Juan Diego's bad foot.

'Not a case of lost virginity, or a murder,' Miriam said, with a nod to all the blood and water on the horrifying bedsheets. 'I guess it doesn't matter what the maids will think.'

'I cut myself,' Juan Diego said. No doubt Miriam had noticed the blood-soaked toilet paper stuck to Juan Diego's forehead, above his eyebrow.

'In all likelihood, not a shaving injury,' she said. He watched her walk from the bed to the closet, peering inside; then she opened and closed the drawers where there might have been forgotten clothes. 'I always sweep a hotel room before I go – *every* hotel room,' she told him.

He couldn't stop her from having a look in the bathroom, too. Juan Diego knew he'd not left any of his toilet articles there – certainly not his Viagra, or the Lopressor pills, which he'd transferred to his carry-on. As for the first condom, he remembered only now that he'd left it in the bathtub, where it would have been lying forlornly against the drain – as if signifying an act of pitiful lewdness.

'Hello, little condom,' he heard Miriam say, from the bathroom; Juan Diego was still sitting at the foot of the bloodstained bed. 'I guess it doesn't matter what the maids will think,' Miriam repeated, when she returned to the bedroom, 'but don't most people flush those things down the toilet?'

'Sí,' was all Juan Diego could say. Not much inclined to male fantasies, Juan Diego certainly wouldn't have had this one.

I must have taken two Lopressor pills, he thought; he was feeling more diminished than usual. Maybe I can sleep on the plane, he thought; he knew it was too soon to speculate what might happen to his dreams. Juan Diego was so tired that he hoped his dream life might be momentarily curtailed by the beta-blockers.

*　*　*

'DID MY MOTHER HIT you?' Dorothy asked him when Juan Diego and Miriam got to the younger woman's hotel room.

'I did *not*, Dorothy,' her mother said. Miriam had already begun her sweep of her daughter's room. Dorothy was half dressed – a skirt, but only a bra, no blouse or sweater. Her open suitcase was on her bed. (The bag was big enough to hold a large dog.)

'A bathroom accident,' was all Juan Diego said, pointing to the toilet paper stuck to his forehead.

'I think it's stopped bleeding,' Dorothy told him. She stood in her bra in front of him, picking at the toilet paper; when Dorothy plucked the paper off his forehead, the little cut began to bleed again – but not so much that she couldn't stop the bleeding by wetting one index finger and pressing it above his eyebrow. 'Just hold still,' the young woman said, while Juan Diego tried not to look at her fetching bra.

'For Christ's sake, Dorothy – just get dressed,' her mother told her.

'And where are we going – I mean *all* of us?' the young woman asked her mom, not so innocently.

'First get dressed, then I'll tell you,' Miriam said. 'Oh, I almost forgot,' she said suddenly to Juan Diego. 'I have your itinerary – you should have it back.' Juan Diego remembered that Miriam had taken his itinerary from him when they were still at JFK; he'd not noticed that she hadn't returned it. Now Miriam handed it to him. 'I made some notes on it – about where you *should* stay in Manila. Not this time – you're not staying there long enough this first time for it to matter where you stay. But, trust me, you won't like where you're staying. When you come back to Manila – I mean the second time, when you're there a little longer – I made some suggestions regarding where you should stay. And I made a copy of your itinerary for *us*,' Miriam told him, 'so we can check on you.'

'For *us*?' Dorothy repeated suspiciously. 'Or for *you*, do you mean?'

'For *us* – I said "we," Dorothy,' Miriam told her daughter.

'I'm going to see you again, I hope,' Juan Diego said suddenly. '*Both* of you,' he added – awkwardly, because he'd been looking only at Dorothy. The girl had put on a blouse, which she hadn't begun to button; she was looking at her navel, then picking at it.

'Oh, you'll see us again – definitely,' Miriam was saying to him, as she walked into the bathroom, continuing her sweep.

'Yeah, *definitely*,' Dorothy said, still attending to her belly button – she was still unbuttoned.

'Button it, Dorothy – the blouse has buttons, for Christ's sake!' her mother was shouting from the bathroom.

'I haven't left anything behind, Mother,' Dorothy called into the bathroom. The young woman had already buttoned herself up when she quickly kissed Juan Diego on his mouth. He saw she had a small envelope in her hand; it looked like the hotel stationery – it was that kind of envelope. Dorothy slipped the envelope into his jacket pocket. 'Don't read it now – read it later. It's a love letter!' the girl whispered; her tongue darted between his lips.

'I'm surprised at you, Dorothy,' Miriam was saying, as she came back into the bedroom. 'Juan Diego made more of a mess of his bathroom than you did of yours.'

'I live to surprise you, Mother,' the girl said.

Juan Diego smiled uncertainly at the two of them. He'd always imagined that his trip to the Philippines was a kind of sentimental journey – in the sense that it wasn't a trip he was taking for himself. In truth, he'd long thought of it as a trip he was taking for someone else – a dead friend who'd wanted to make this journey but had died before he was able to go.

Yet the journey Juan Diego found himself taking was one that seemed inseparable from Miriam and Dorothy, and what was *that* trip but one he was taking solely for himself?

'And you – you *two* – are going exactly *where*?' Juan Diego ventured to ask this mother and her daughter, who were veteran world travelers (clearly).

'Oh, boy – have we got shit to do!' Dorothy said darkly.

'*Obligations*, Dorothy – your generation overuses the *shit* word,' Miriam told her.

'We'll see you sooner than you think,' Dorothy told Juan Diego. 'We *end up* in Manila, but not today,' the young woman said enigmatically.

'We'll see you in Manila *eventually*,' Miriam

explained to him a little impatiently. She added: 'If not sooner.'

'If not sooner,' Dorothy repeated. 'Yeah, yeah!'

The young woman abruptly lifted her suitcase off the bed before Juan Diego could help her; it was such a big, heavy-looking bag, but Dorothy lifted it as if it weighed nothing at all. It gave Juan Diego a pang to remember how the young woman had lifted *him* – his head and shoulders, entirely off the bed – before she'd rolled him over on top of her.

What a strong girl! was all Juan Diego thought about it. He turned to reach for his suitcase, *not* his carry-on, and was surprised to see that Miriam had taken it – together with her own big bag. What a strong *mother*! Juan Diego was thinking. He limped out into the hallway of the hotel, hurrying to keep up with the two women; he almost didn't notice that he scarcely limped at all.

THIS WAS PECULIAR: IN the middle of a conversation he couldn't remember, Juan Diego became separated from Miriam and Dorothy as they were going through the security check at Hong Kong International. He stepped toward the metal-detection device, looking back at Miriam, who was removing her shoes; he saw that her toenails were painted the same color as Dorothy's. Then he passed through the metal-screening machine, and when he looked for the women again, both Miriam and Dorothy were gone; they had simply (or not so simply) disappeared.

Juan Diego asked one of the security guards about

the two women he'd been traveling with. Where had they gone? But the security guard was an impatient young fellow, and he was distracted by an apparent problem with the metal-detection device.

'*What* women? *Which* women? I've seen an entire civilization of women – they must have moved on!' the guard told him.

Juan Diego thought he would try to text or call the women on his cell phone, but he'd forgotten to get their cell-phone numbers. He scrolled through his contacts, looking in vain for their nonexistent names. Nor had Miriam written her cell-phone number, or Dorothy's, among the notes she'd made on his itinerary. Juan Diego saw just the names and addresses of alternative Manila hotels.

What a big deal Miriam had made about 'the second time' he would be in Manila, Juan Diego was thinking, but he stopped thinking about it and made his slow way to the gate for his flight to the Philippines – his *first time* in Manila, he was thinking to himself (*if* he was thinking about it at all). He was preternaturally tired.

It must be the beta-blockers, Juan Diego was pondering. I guess I shouldn't have taken two – if I did.

Even the green-tea muffin on the Cathay Pacific flight – it was a much smaller plane this time – was a little disappointing. It wasn't such a heightened experience as eating that *first* green-tea muffin, when he and Miriam and Dorothy were arriving in Hong Kong.

Juan Diego was in the air when he remembered

the love letter Dorothy had put in his jacket pocket. He took out the envelope and opened it.

'See you soon!' Dorothy had written on the Regal Airport Hotel stationery. She had pressed her lips – apparently, with fresh lipstick – to the page, leaving him the impression of her lips in intimate contact with the *soon* word. Her lipstick, he only now noticed, was the same color as her toenail polish – and her mother's. Magenta, Juan Diego guessed he would call it.

He couldn't miss seeing what was also in the envelope with the so-called love letter: the two empty foil wrappers, where the first and second condom had been. Maybe there *was* something wrong with the metal-screening machine at Hong Kong International, Juan Diego considered; the device hadn't detected the foil condom wrappers. Definitely, Juan Diego was thinking, this wasn't quite the *sentimental* journey he'd been expecting, but he was long on his way and there was no turning back now.

9

In Case You Were Wondering

Edward Bonshaw had an L-shaped scar on his forehead – from a childhood fall. He'd tripped over a sleeping dog when he was running with a mah-jongg tile clutched in his little hand. The tiny game block was made of ivory and bamboo; a corner of the pretty tile had been driven into Edward's pale forehead above the bridge of his nose, where it made a perfect check mark between his blond eyebrows.

He'd sat up but had felt too dizzy to stand. Blood streamed down between his eyes and dripped from the end of his nose. The dog, now awake, had wagged her tail and licked the bleeding boy's face.

Edward found the dog's affectionate attention soothing. The boy was seven; his father had labeled him a 'mama's boy,' for no better reason than that Edward had expressed his dislike of hunting.

'Why shoot things that are alive?' he'd asked his father.

The dog didn't like hunting, either. A Labrador retriever, she'd blundered into a neighbor's swimming pool when she was still a puppy, and had almost drowned; thereafter, she was afraid of water – not normal for a Lab. Also 'not normal,' in the unwavering opinion of Edward's dictatorial father, was the dog's disposition not to retrieve. (Neither a ball nor a stick – certainly not a dead bird.)

'What happened to the *retriever* part? Isn't she supposed to be a Labrador *retriever*?' Edward's cruel uncle Ian always said.

But Edward loved the nonretrieving, never-swimming Lab, and the sweet dog doted on the boy; they were both 'cowardly,' in the harsh judgment of Edward's father, Graham. To young Edward, his father's brother – the bullying uncle Ian – was an unkind dolt.

This is all the background necessary to understand what happened next. Edward's father and Uncle Ian were hunting pheasants; they returned with a couple of the murdered birds, barging into the kitchen by the door to the garage.

This was the house in Coralville – at the time, a distant-seeming suburb of Iowa City – and Edward, bloody-faced, was sitting on the kitchen floor, where the nonretrieving, never-swimming Lab appeared to be eating the boy head-first. The men burst into the kitchen with Uncle Ian's Chesapeake Bay retriever, a thoughtless male gundog of Ian's own aggressive disposition and lack of discernible character.

'Fucking *Beatrice*!' Edward's father shouted.

Graham Bonshaw had named the Lab *Beatrice*, the most derisively female name he could imagine; it was a name suitable for a dog that Uncle Ian said should be spayed – 'so she won't reproduce herself and further dilute a noble breed.'

The two hunters left Edward sitting on the kitchen floor while they took Beatrice outside and shot her in the driveway.

This was not quite the story you were expecting when Edward Bonshaw, in his later life, pointed to the L-shaped scar on his forehead and began, with disarming indifference, 'In case you were wondering about my scar—' thereby leading you to the brutal killing of Beatrice, a dog young Edward had adored, a dog with the sweetest disposition imaginable.

And for all those years, Juan Diego remembered, Señor Eduardo had kept that pretty little mah-jongg tile – the block that had permanently checkmarked his fair forehead.

Was it the inconsequential cut from the towel rod on Juan Diego's forehead, which had finally stopped bleeding, that triggered this nightmarish memory of Edward Bonshaw, who'd been so dearly beloved in Juan Diego's life? Was it too short a flight, from Hong Kong to Manila, for Juan Diego to sleep soundly? It was not as short a flight as he'd imagined, but he was restless and half awake the entire two hours, and his dreams were disjointed; Juan Diego's fitful sleep and the narrative disorder of his dreams were further evidence to him that he'd taken a double dose of beta-blockers.

He would dream intermittently all the way to Manila – foremost, the horrible history of Edward Bonshaw's scar. That is exactly what taking *two*

Lopressor pills will get you! Yet, tired though he was, Juan Diego was grateful to have dreamed at all, even disjointedly. The past was where he lived most confidently, and with the surest sense of knowing who he was – not only as a novelist.

THERE IS OFTEN TOO much dialogue in disjointed dreams, and things happen violently and without warning. The doctors' offices in Cruz Roja, the Red Cross hospital in Oaxaca, were confusingly close to the emergency entrance – either a bad idea or by design, or both. A girl who'd been bitten by one of Oaxaca's rooftop dogs was brought to the orthopedic office of Dr. Vargas instead of the ER; though her hands and forearms had been mangled while she was trying to protect her face, the girl did not present any obvious orthopedic problems. Dr. Vargas was an orthopedist – though he did treat circus people (mainly child performers), dump kids, and the orphans at Lost Children, not just for orthopedics.

Vargas was irked that the dog-bite victim had been brought to him. 'You're going to be *fine*,' he kept telling the crying girl. 'She should be in the ER – not with me,' Vargas repeatedly said to the girl's hysterical mother. Everyone in the waiting room was upset to see the mauled girl – including Edward Bonshaw, who had only recently arrived in town.

'What is a rooftop dog?' Señor Eduardo asked Brother Pepe. 'Not a *breed* of dog, I trust!' They were following Dr. Vargas to the examining room. Juan Diego was being wheeled on a gurney.

Lupe babbled something, which her injured brother was disinclined to translate. Lupe said some of the rooftop dogs were spirits – actual ghosts of dogs who'd been willfully tortured and killed. The ghost dogs haunted the rooftops of the city, attacking innocent people – because the dogs (in their innocence) had been attacked, and they were seeking revenge. The dogs lived on rooftops because they could fly; because they were ghost dogs, no one could harm them – not anymore.

'*That's* a long answer!' Edward Bonshaw confided to Juan Diego. 'What did she say?'

'You're right, *not* a breed,' was all Juan Diego told the new missionary.

'They're mostly mongrels. There are many stray dogs in Oaxaca; some are feral. They just hang out on the rooftops – no one knows how the dogs get there,' Brother Pepe explained.

'They *don't* fly,' Juan Diego added, but Lupe went on babbling. They were now in the examining room with Dr. Vargas.

'And what has happened to *you*?' Dr. Vargas asked the incomprehensible girl. 'Just calm down and tell me slowly, so I can understand you.'

'*I'm* the patient – she's just my sister,' Juan Diego said to the young doctor. Maybe Vargas hadn't noticed the gurney.

Brother Pepe had already explained to Dr. Vargas that he'd examined these dump kids before, but Vargas saw too many patients – he had trouble keeping the kids straight. And Juan Diego's pain had quieted down; for the moment, he'd stopped screaming.

Dr. Vargas was young and handsome; an aura of intemperate nobility, which can occasionally come from success, emanated from him. He was used to being right. Vargas was easily perturbed by the incompetence of others, though the impressive young man was too quickly inclined to judge people he was meeting for the first time. Everyone knew that Dr. Vargas was the foremost orthopedic surgeon in Oaxaca; crippled children were his specialty – and who didn't care about crippled children? Yet Vargas rubbed everyone the wrong way. Children resented him because Vargas couldn't remember them; adults thought he was arrogant.

'So *you're* the patient,' Dr. Vargas said to Juan Diego. 'Tell me about yourself. *Not* the dump-kid part. I can smell you; I know about the basurero. I mean your foot – just tell me about that part.'

'The part about my foot *is* a dump-kid part,' Juan Diego told the doctor. 'A truck in Guerrero backed over my foot, with a load of copper from the basurero – a heavy load.'

Sometimes Lupe spoke in lists; this was one of those times. 'One: this doctor is a sad jerk,' the all-seeing girl began. 'Two: he is ashamed to be alive. Three: he thinks he should have died. Four: he's going to say you need X-rays, but he's just stalling – he already knows he can't fix your foot.'

'That sounds a little like Zapoteco or Mixteco, but it isn't,' Dr. Vargas declared; he wasn't asking Juan

Diego what his sister had said, but (like everyone else) Juan Diego was not fond of the young doctor, and he decided to tell him everything Lupe had proclaimed. 'She said all *that*?' Vargas asked.

'She's usually right about the past,' Juan Diego told him. 'She doesn't do the future as accurately.'

'You *do* need X-rays; I probably can't fix your foot, but I have to see the X-rays before I know what to tell you,' Dr. Vargas said to Juan Diego. 'Did you bring our Jesuit friend for divine assistance?' the doctor asked the boy, nodding to Brother Pepe. (In Oaxaca, everyone knew Pepe; almost as many people had heard of Dr. Vargas.)

'My mom is a cleaning woman for the Jesuits,' Juan Diego told Vargas. The boy then nodded to Rivera. 'But *he's* the one who looks after us. El jefe—' the boy started to say, but Rivera interrupted him.

'I was driving the truck,' the dump boss said guiltily.

Lupe launched into her routine about the broken side-view mirror, but Juan Diego didn't bother to translate. Besides, Lupe had already moved on; there was more detail concerning *why* Dr. Vargas was such a sad jerk.

'Vargas got drunk; he overslept. He missed his plane – a family trip. The stupid plane crashed. His parents were onboard – his sister, too, with her husband and their two children. All gone!' Lupe cried. 'While Vargas was sleeping it off,' she added.

'Such a strained voice,' Vargas said to Juan Diego. 'I

should have a look at her throat. Maybe her vocal cords.'

Juan Diego told Dr. Vargas he was sorry about the plane crash that had killed the young doctor's entire family.

'She told you *that*?' Vargas asked the boy.

Lupe wouldn't stop babbling: Vargas had inherited his parents' house, and all their things. His parents had been 'very religious'; it had long been a source of family friction that Vargas was 'not religious.' Now the young doctor was '*less* religious,' Lupe said.

'How can he be "*less* religious" than he used to be when he was "not religious" to begin with, Lupe?' Juan Diego asked his sister, but the girl just shrugged. She knew certain things; messages came to her, usually without any explanations.

'I'm just telling you what I know,' Lupe was always saying. 'Don't ask me what it means.'

'Wait, wait, *wait*!' Edward Bonshaw interjected, in English. '*Who* was "not religious" and has become "*less* religious"? I know about this syndrome,' Edward said to Juan Diego.

In English, Juan Diego told Señor Eduardo everything Lupe had told him about Dr. Vargas; not even Brother Pepe had known the whole story. All the while, Vargas went on examining the boy's crushed and twisted foot. Juan Diego was beginning to like Dr. Vargas a little better; Lupe's irritating ability to divine a stranger's past (and, to a lesser degree, that person's future) was serving as a distraction from Juan Diego's pain, and the boy appreciated how

Vargas had taken advantage of the distraction to examine him.

'Where does a dump kid learn English?' Dr. Vargas asked Brother Pepe in English. '*Your* English isn't this good, Pepe, but I presume you had a hand in teaching the boy.'

'He taught himself, Vargas – he speaks, he understands, he *reads*,' Pepe replied.

'This is a gift to be nurtured, Juan Diego,' Edward Bonshaw told the boy. 'I'm so sorry for your family tragedy, Dr. Vargas,' Señor Eduardo added. 'I know a little something about family *adversities*—'

'Who's the gringo?' Vargas rudely asked Juan Diego in Spanish.

'El hombre papagayo,' Lupe said. ('The parrot man.')

Juan Diego deciphered this for Vargas.

'Edward is our new teacher,' Brother Pepe told Dr. Vargas. 'From *Iowa*,' Pepe added.

'Eduardo,' Edward Bonshaw said; the Iowan extended his hand before he regarded the rubber gloves Dr. Vargas was wearing – the gloves were spotted with blood from the boy's grotesquely flattened foot.

'You're sure he's not from *Hawaii*, Pepe?' Vargas asked. (It was impossible to overlook the clamorous parrots on the new missionary's Hawaiian shirt.)

'Like you, Dr. Vargas,' Edward Bonshaw began, as he wisely changed his mind about shaking the young doctor's hand, 'I have had my faith assailed by doubts.'

'I never had any faith, hence no doubts,' Vargas replied; his English was clipped but correct – there was nothing doubtful about it. 'Here's what I like about X-rays, Juan Diego,' Dr. Vargas continued in his no-nonsense English. 'X-rays are not spiritual – in fact, they are wholly less ambiguous than a lot of elements I can think of at the moment. You come to me, injured, and with two Jesuits. You bring your visionary sister, who – as you say yourself – is more right about the past than she is about the future. Your esteemed jefe comes along – your dump boss, who looks after you *and* runs over you.' (It was fortunate, for Rivera's sake, that Vargas's assessment was made in English, not Spanish, because Rivera was already feeling badly enough about the accident.) 'And what the X-rays will show us are the *limitations* of what can be done for your foot. I'm speaking *medically*, Edward,' Vargas interrupted himself, looking not only at Edward Bonshaw but also at Brother Pepe. 'As for *divine* assistance – well, I leave that to you Jesuits.'

'Eduardo,' Edward Bonshaw corrected Dr. Vargas. Señor Eduardo's father, Graham (the dog-killer), had the middle name *Edward*; this was ample reason for Edward Bonshaw to prefer *Eduardo*, which Juan Diego had also taken a shine to.

Vargas delivered an impromptu outburst to Brother Pepe – this time in Spanish. 'These dump kids live in Guerrero and their mother is *cleaning* the Templo de la Compañía de Jesús – how *Jesuitical*! And I suppose she's cleaning Niños Perdidos, too?'

'Sí – the orphanage, too,' Pepe replied.

Juan Diego was on the verge of telling Vargas that Esperanza, his mother, wasn't only a cleaning woman, but what else Esperanza did was *ambiguous* (at best), and the boy knew what a low opinion the young doctor had of ambiguity.

'Where is your mother now?' Dr. Vargas asked the boy. 'She's not cleaning at this moment, surely.'

'She's in the temple, praying for me,' Juan Diego told him.

'Let's do the X-rays – let's move on,' Dr. Vargas duly said; it was apparent that he'd had to restrain himself from making a disparaging comment on the powers of prayer.

'Thank you, Vargas,' Brother Pepe said; he spoke with such uncharacteristic insincerity that everyone looked at him – even Edward Bonshaw, who'd met him only recently. 'Thank you for making such an effort to spare us your constant atheism,' Pepe said, more to the point.

'I *am* sparing you, Pepe,' Vargas answered him.

'Surely your absence of belief is your own business, Dr. Vargas,' Edward Bonshaw said. 'But perhaps now is not the best time for it – for the *boy's* sake,' the new missionary added, making absence of belief his business.

'It's okay, Señor Eduardo,' Juan Diego told the Iowan in his near-perfect English. 'I'm not much of a believer, either – I'm not much more of a believer than Dr. Vargas.' But Juan Diego was more of a believer than he let on. He had his doubts about the Church – the local virgin politics, as he thought of them, included – yet the miracles intrigued him. He was open to miracles.

'Don't say that, Juan Diego – you're too young to cut yourself off from belief,' Edward said.

'For the *boy's* sake,' Vargas said in his abrupt-sounding English, 'perhaps now is a better time for reality than for *belief*.'

'Personally, I don't know *what* to believe,' Lupe started in, heedless of who could (and couldn't) understand her. 'I want to believe in Guadalupe, but look how she lets herself be used – look how the Virgin Mary *manipulates* her! How can you trust Guadalupe when she lets the Mary Monster be the boss?'

'Guadalupe lets Mary walk all over her, Lupe,' Juan Diego said.

'Whoa! Stop! Don't say *that*!' Edward Bonshaw told the boy. 'You're entirely too young to be *cynical*.' (When the subject was religious, the new missionary's grasp of Spanish was better than you first thought.)

'Let's do the X-rays, *Eduardo*,' Dr. Vargas said. 'Let's move on. These kids live in Guerrero and work in the dump, while their mother cleans for you. Is that not *cynical*?'

'Let's move on, Vargas,' Brother Pepe said. 'Let's do the X-rays.'

'It's a *nice* dump!' Lupe insisted. 'Tell Vargas we *love* the dump, Juan Diego. Between Vargas and the parrot man, we'll end up living in Lost Children!' Lupe screamed, but Juan Diego translated nothing; he was silent.

'Let's do the X-rays,' the boy said. He just wanted to know about his foot.

'Vargas is thinking there's no point in operating on your foot,' Lupe told him. 'Vargas believes that, if the blood supply is compromised, he'll have to *amputate*! He thinks you can't live in Guerrero with only one foot, *or* with a limp! In all likelihood, Vargas believes, your foot will heal by itself in a right-angle position – permanently. You'll walk again, but not for a couple of months. You'll never walk without a limp – that's what he's thinking. Vargas is wondering why the parrot man is here and not our mother. Tell him I know his thoughts!' Lupe screamed at her brother.

Juan Diego began: 'I'll tell you what she says you're thinking.' He told Vargas what Lupe had said, pausing dramatically to explain everything in English to Edward Bonshaw.

Vargas spoke to Brother Pepe as if the two men were alone: 'Your dump kid is bilingual and his sister is a mind reader. They could do better for themselves in the circus, Pepe. They don't have to live in Guerrero and work in the basurero.'

'Circus?' Edward Bonshaw said. 'Did he say *circus*, Pepe? They're *children*! They're not *animals*! Surely Lost Children will care for them? A *crippled* boy! A girl who can't *speak*!'

'Lupe speaks a *lot*! She says too much,' Juan Diego said.

'They're not *animals*!' Señor Eduardo repeated; perhaps it was the *animals* word (even in English) that made Lupe look more closely at the parrot man.

Uh-oh, Brother Pepe was thinking. God help us if the crazy girl reads his mind!

'The circus takes care of its kids, usually,' Dr. Vargas said in English to the Iowan, giving a passing look at the guilt-stricken Rivera. 'These kids could be a sideshow—'

'A *sideshow*!' Señor Eduardo cried, wringing his hands; maybe the way he was wringing his hands gave Lupe a vision of Edward Bonshaw as a seven-year-old boy. The girl began to cry.

'Oh, *no!*' Lupe blubbered; she covered her eyes with both hands.

'More mind reading?' Vargas asked, with seeming indifference.

'Is the girl really a mind reader, Pepe?' Edward asked.

Oh, I hope not *now*, Pepe was thinking, but all he said was: 'The boy has taught himself to read in two languages. We can help the boy – think about *him*, Edward. We can't help the girl,' Pepe added softly in English, though Lupe wouldn't have heard him if he'd said it en español. The girl was screaming again.

'Oh, no! They shot his *dog*! His father and his uncle – they killed the parrot man's poor *dog*!' Lupe wailed in her husky falsetto. Juan Diego knew how much his sister loved dogs; she either couldn't or wouldn't say more – she was sobbing inconsolably.

'What is it now?' the Iowan asked Juan Diego.

'You had a dog?' the boy asked Señor Eduardo.

Edward Bonshaw fell to his knees. 'Merciful Mary,

Mother of Christ – thank you for bringing me where I belong!' the new missionary cried.

'I guess he did have a dog,' Dr. Vargas said in Spanish to Juan Diego.

'The dog died – someone shot it,' the boy told Vargas, as quietly as possible. The way Lupe was weeping, and with the Iowan's exclamatory praise of the Virgin Mary, it's unlikely that anyone heard this brief doctor-patient exchange – or what followed between them.

'Do you know someone in the circus?' Juan Diego asked Dr. Vargas.

'I know the person you should know, when the time comes,' Vargas told the boy. 'We'll need to get your mother involved—' Here Vargas saw Juan Diego instinctively shut his eyes. 'Or Pepe, perhaps – we'll need Pepe's approval, in lieu of your mom's being sympathetic to the idea.'

'El hombre papagayo—' Juan Diego started to say.

'I'm not the best choice for a constructive conversation with the parrot man,' Dr. Vargas interrupted his patient.

'His *dog*! They shot his dog! Poor *Beatrice*!' Lupe was blubbering.

Notwithstanding the strained and unintelligible way Lupe spoke, Edward Bonshaw could make out the *Beatrice* word.

'Clairvoyance is a gift from God, Pepe,' Edward said to his colleague. 'Is the girl truly *prescient*? You said that word.'

'Forget about the girl, Señor Eduardo,' Brother

Pepe quietly said – again, in English. 'Think about the boy – we can save him, or help him to save himself. The boy is *salvageable*.'

'But the girl *knows* things—' the Iowan started to say.

'Not things that will help her,' Pepe quickly said.

'The orphanage will take these kids, won't they?' Señor Eduardo asked Brother Pepe.

Pepe was worried about the nuns at Lost Children; it was not necessarily the dump kids the nuns didn't like – the preexisting problem was Esperanza, their cleaning-lady-with-a-night-job mother. But all Pepe said to the Iowan was: 'Sí – Niños Perdidos will take the kids.' And here Pepe paused; he was wondering what to say next, and if he should say it – he had doubts.

None of them had noticed when Lupe stopped crying. 'El circo,' the clairvoyant girl said, pointing at Brother Pepe. 'The circus.'

'What about the circus?' Juan Diego asked his sister.

'Brother Pepe thinks it's a good idea,' Lupe told him.

'Pepe thinks the circus is a good idea,' Juan Diego told them all, in English *and* in Spanish. But Pepe didn't look so sure.

That ended their conversation for a while. The X-rays took a lot of time, mostly the part when they were waiting for the radiologist's opinion; as it turned out, the waiting went on so long that there was little doubt among them concerning what they would hear. (Vargas had already thought it, and Lupe had already told them his thoughts.)

While they were waiting to hear from the radiologist, Juan Diego decided that he actually *liked* Dr. Vargas. Lupe had come to a slightly different conclusion: the girl adored Señor Eduardo – chiefly, but not only, because of what had happened to the seven-year-old's dog. The girl had fallen asleep with her head in Edward Bonshaw's lap. That the all-seeing child had bonded with him gave the new teacher added zeal; the Iowan kept looking at Brother Pepe, as if to say: And *you* believe we can't save her? Of *course* we can!

Oh, Lord, Pepe prayed – what a perilous road lies ahead of us, in both lunatic and unknown hands! Please guide us!

It was then that Dr. Vargas sat beside Edward Bonshaw and Brother Pepe. Vargas lightly touched the sleeping girl's head. 'I want a look at her throat,' the young doctor reminded them. He told them he'd asked his nurse to contact a colleague whose office was also in the Cruz Roja hospital. Dr. Gomez was an ear, nose, and throat specialist – it would be ideal if *she* were available to have a look at Lupe's larynx. But if Dr. Gomez couldn't have a look for herself, Vargas knew she would at least lend him the necessary instruments. There was a special light, and a little mirror that you held at the back of the throat.

'Nuestra madre,' Lupe said in her sleep. 'Our mother. Let them look in her throat.'

'She's not awake – Lupe always talks in her sleep,' Rivera said.

'What is she saying, Juan Diego?' Brother Pepe asked the boy.

'It's about our mother,' Juan Diego said. 'Lupe can read your mind while she's asleep,' the boy warned Vargas.

'Tell me more about Lupe's mother, Pepe,' Vargas said.

'Her mother sounds the same but different – no one can understand her when she gets excited, or when she's praying. But Esperanza is *older*, of course,' Pepe tried to explain – without really saying what he meant. He was struggling to express himself, both in English *and* in Spanish. 'Esperanza can make herself comprehensible – she's not *always* impossible to understand. Esperanza is, from time to time, a *prostitute!*' Pepe blurted out, after checking to be sure that Lupe was still asleep. 'Whereas this child, this *innocent* girl – well, she can't manage to communicate what she means, except to her brother.'

Dr. Vargas looked at Juan Diego, who simply nodded; Rivera was nodding, too – the dump boss was both nodding and crying. Vargas asked Rivera: 'When she was an infant, and when she was a small child, did Lupe have any *respiratory distress* – anything you can recall?'

'She had *croup* – she coughed and coughed,' Rivera said, sobbing.

When Brother Pepe explained Lupe's history of

croup to Edward Bonshaw, the Iowan asked: 'Don't lots of kids get croup?'

'It's her hoarseness that is distinctive – the audible evidence of vocal strain,' Dr. Vargas said slowly. 'I still want to have a look at Lupe's throat, her larynx, her vocal cords.'

Edward Bonshaw, with the clairvoyant girl asleep on his lap, sat as if frozen. The enormity of his vows seemed to assail him and give him strength in the same riotous millisecond: his devotion to Saint Ignatius Loyola, for the insane reason of the saint's announcement that he would sacrifice his life if he could prevent the sins of a single prostitute on a single night; the two gifted dump kids on the threshold of either danger or salvation – perhaps *both*; and now the atheistic young man of science Dr. Vargas, who could think only of examining the child psychic's throat, her larynx, her *vocal cords* – oh, what an opportunity, and what a collision course, this was!

That was when Lupe woke up, or – if she'd been awake for a while – when she opened her eyes.

'What is my larynx?' the little girl asked her brother. 'I don't want Vargas looking at it.'

'She wants to know what her larynx is,' Juan Diego translated for Dr. Vargas.

'It's the upper part of her trachea – where her vocal cords are,' Vargas explained.

'Nobody's getting near my trachea. What is it?' Lupe asked.

'Now she's concerned about her trachea,' Juan Diego reported.

'Her trachea is the main trunk of a system of tubes; air passes through these tubes, to and from Lupe's lungs,' Dr. Vargas told Juan Diego.

'There are tubes in my throat?' Lupe asked.

'There are tubes in all our throats, Lupe,' Juan Diego said.

'Whoever Dr. Gomez is, Vargas wants to have sex with her,' Lupe told her brother. 'Dr. Gomez is married, she has children, she's a lot older than he is, but Vargas still wants to have sex with her.'

'Dr. Gomez is an ear, nose, and throat specialist, Lupe,' Juan Diego said to his unusual sister.

'Dr. Gomez can look at my larynx, but Vargas can't – he's disgusting!' Lupe said. 'I don't like the idea of a mirror at the back of my throat – this hasn't been a good day for mirrors!'

'Lupe's a little worried about the mirror,' was all Juan Diego said to Dr. Vargas.

'Tell her the mirror doesn't hurt,' Vargas said.

'Ask him if what he wants to do to Dr. Gomez *hurts*!' Lupe cried.

'Either Dr. Gomez or I will hold Lupe's tongue with a gauze pad – just to keep her tongue away from the back of her throat—' Vargas was explaining, but Lupe wouldn't let him continue.

'The Gomez woman can hold my tongue – not Vargas,' Lupe said.

'Lupe is looking forward to meeting Dr. Gomez,' was all Juan Diego said.

'Dr. Vargas,' Edward Bonshaw said, after he'd drawn a deep breath, 'at a mutually convenient time – I mean some *other* time, of course – I think you and I should talk about our *beliefs*.'

With the hand that had so gently touched the sleeping girl, Dr. Vargas – with a more forceful step – closed his fingers tightly around the new missionary's wrist. 'Here's what I think, Edward – or *Eduardo*, or whatever your name is,' Vargas said. 'I think the girl has got something going on in her *throat*; perhaps the problem is her larynx, affecting her vocal cords. And this boy is going to *limp* for the rest of his life, whether he keeps that foot or loses it. That's what we have to *deal with* – I mean here, on this earth,' Dr. Vargas said.

When Edward Bonshaw smiled, his fair skin seemed to shine; the idea that an inner light had been suddenly switched on was eerily plausible. When Señor Eduardo smiled, a wrinkle as precise and striking as a lightning bolt crossed the bright-white tissue of that perfect check mark on the zealot's forehead – smack between his blond eyebrows. 'In case you were wondering about my scar,' Edward Bonshaw began, as he *always* began, his story.

10

No Middle Ground

'We'll see you sooner than you think,' Dorothy had told Juan Diego. 'We *end up* in Manila,' the young woman had said enigmatically.

In a moment of hysteria, Lupe had told Juan Diego that they would *end up* living in Lost Children – a half-truth, as it turned out. The dump kids – like everyone else, the nuns called them 'los niños de la basura' – moved their things from Guerrero to the Jesuit orphanage. Life at the orphanage was different from life at the dump, where only Rivera and Diablo had protected them. The nuns at Niños Perdidos – together with Brother Pepe and Señor Eduardo – would look after Lupe and Juan Diego more closely.

It was heartbreaking to Rivera that he'd been replaced, but he was on Esperanza's shit list for running over her only son, and Lupe was unforgiving on the subject of the unrepaired side-view mirror. Lupe said it was only Diablo and Dirty White she would miss, but she would miss the other dogs in Guerrero *and* the dump dogs – even the dead ones.

With Rivera's help or Juan Diego's, Lupe had been in the habit of burning the dead dogs at the basurero. (And of course Rivera would be missed – both Juan Diego *and* Lupe would miss el jefe, despite what Lupe had said.)

Brother Pepe was right about the nuns at Lost Children: they could accept the kids, albeit grudgingly; it was their mother, Esperanza, who gave the nuns fits. But Esperanza gave *everyone* fits – including Dr. Gomez, the ENT specialist, who was a very nice woman. It wasn't *her* fault that Dr. Vargas wanted to have sex with her.

Lupe had liked Dr. Gomez – even while the doctor was having a look at Lupe's larynx, with Vargas hovering uncomfortably nearby. Dr. Gomez had a daughter Lupe's age; the ENT specialist knew how to talk to young girls.

'Do you know what's different about a duck's feet?' Dr. Gomez, whose first name was Marisol, asked Lupe.

'Ducks swim better than they walk,' Lupe answered. 'A flat thing grows over their toes, uniting them.'

When Juan Diego translated what Lupe had said, Dr. Gomez replied: 'Ducks are web-footed. A membrane grows over their toes – it's called a web. You have a web, Lupe – it's called a congenital laryngeal web. *Congenital* means you were born with it; you have a web, a kind of membrane, across your larynx. It's pretty rare, which means *special*,' Dr. Gomez told Lupe. 'Only one in ten thousand births – that's how special you are, Lupe.'

Lupe shrugged. 'That web isn't what's special about me,' Lupe said, untranslatably. 'I know stuff I'm not supposed to know.'

'Lupe can be psychic about things. She's usually right about the past,' Juan Diego tried to explain to Dr. Gomez. 'She doesn't do the future as accurately.'

'What does Juan Diego mean?' Dr. Gomez asked Dr. Vargas.

'Don't ask *Vargas* – he wants to have sex with you!' Lupe cried. 'He *knows* you're married, he *knows* you have kids – and you're much too old for him – but he still thinks about doing it with you. Vargas is *always* thinking about having sex with you!' Lupe said.

'Tell me what that's about, Juan Diego,' Dr. Gomez said. What the hell, Juan Diego thought. He told her – every word.

'The girl *is* a mind reader,' Vargas said, when Juan Diego had finished. 'I was thinking of a way to tell you, Marisol, but more privately than this way – that is, if I ever got up the nerve to tell you.'

'Lupe knew what happened to his dog!' Brother Pepe said to Marisol Gomez, pointing at Edward Bonshaw. (Obviously, Pepe was trying to change the subject.)

'Lupe knows what's happened to almost everyone, and what almost everybody is thinking,' Juan Diego told Dr. Gomez.

'Even if Lupe is asleep when you're thinking it,' Vargas said. 'I don't think the laryngeal web has anything to do with this,' he added.

'The child is completely incomprehensible,' Dr.

Gomez said. 'A laryngeal web explains the *pitch* of her voice – her hoarseness, and the strain in her voice – but not that no one can understand her. Except *you*,' Dr. Gomez added to Juan Diego.

'Marisol is a nice name – tell her about our retarded mother,' Lupe said to Juan Diego. 'Tell Dr. Gomez to have a look at our mother's throat; there's more wrong with her than there is with me!' Lupe said. '*Tell* Dr. Gomez!' Juan Diego did.

'There's nothing *wrong* with you, Lupe,' Dr. Gomez said to the girl, after Juan Diego had told the doctor about Esperanza. 'A congenital laryngeal web isn't *retarded* – it's *special*.'

'Some of the things I know aren't good things to know,' Lupe said, but Juan Diego left that untranslated.

'Ten percent of children with webs have associated congenital anomalies,' Dr. Gomez said to Dr. Vargas, but she wouldn't look in his eyes when she spoke to him.

'Explain the *anomalies* word,' Lupe said.

'Lupe wants to know what *anomalies* are,' Juan Diego translated.

'Deviating from a general rule – irregularities,' Dr. Gomez said.

'Abnormalities,' Dr. Vargas said to Lupe.

'I'm not as abnormal as *you* are!' Lupe told him.

'I'm guessing I don't need to know what *that's* about,' Vargas said to Juan Diego.

'I'll have a look at the mother's throat,' Dr. Gomez said, not to Vargas but to Brother Pepe. 'I should talk to the mother anyway. There are some options concerning Lupe's web—'

Marisol Gomez, a pretty and young-looking mother, got no further; Lupe interrupted her. 'It's *my* web!' the girl cried. 'Nobody touches my *abnormalities*,' Lupe said, glaring at Vargas.

When Juan Diego repeated this verbatim, Dr. Gomez said: 'That's one option. And I'll have a look at the mother's throat,' she repeated. 'I'm not expecting her to have a web,' Dr. Gomez added.

Brother Pepe left Dr. Vargas's office to look for Esperanza. Vargas had said he would also need to talk to Juan Diego's mother about the boy's situation. As the X-rays would confirm, there weren't many options for Juan Diego's foot, which was inoperable. It would heal as it was: crushed, but with a sufficient supply of blood, and twisted to one side. That was how it would be forever. No weight-bearing for a while, was how Vargas put it. First a wheelchair, then the crutches – last, the limp. (A cripple's life is one of watching others do what he can't do, not the worst option for a future novelist.)

As for Esperanza's throat – well, that was a different story. Esperanza didn't have a laryngeal web, but a throat culture tested positive for gonorrhea. Dr. Gomez explained to her that 90 percent of pharyngeal gonorrhea infections were undetectable – no symptoms.

Esperanza had wondered where and what her *pharynx* was. 'The space, way back in your mouth, into which your nostrils, your esophagus, and your trachea open,' Dr. Gomez had told her.

Lupe was not present for this conversation, but Brother Pepe had permitted Juan Diego to be there; Pepe knew that if Esperanza became agitated or hysterical, only Juan Diego could understand her. But, in the beginning, Esperanza had been blasé about it; she'd had gonorrhea before, though she hadn't known she had it in her throat. 'Señor Clap,' Esperanza called it, shrugging; it was easy to see where Lupe's shrug came from, though there was little else of Esperanza in Lupe – or so Brother Pepe hoped.

'Here's the thing about fellatio,' Dr. Gomez said to Esperanza. 'The tip of the urethra comes in contact with the pharynx; that's asking for trouble.'

'Fellatio? Urethra?' Juan Diego asked Dr. Gomez, who shook her head.

'A blow job, the stupid hole in your penis,' Esperanza impatiently explained to her son. Brother Pepe was glad Lupe wasn't there; the girl and the new missionary were waiting in another room. Pepe was also relieved that Edward Bonshaw wasn't hearing this conversation, even in Spanish, though both Brother Pepe *and* Juan Diego would make sure that Señor Eduardo had a complete account of the details pertaining to Esperanza's throat.

'*You* try getting a guy to wear a condom for a blow job,' Esperanza was saying to Dr. Gomez.

'A condom?' Juan Diego asked.

'A rubber!' Esperanza cried in exasperation. 'What can your nuns possibly teach him?' she asked Pepe. 'The kid knows nothing!'

'He can *read*, Esperanza. He'll soon know everything,' Brother Pepe told her. Pepe knew that Esperanza couldn't read.

'I can give you an antibiotic,' Dr. Gomez told Juan Diego's mother, 'but you'll be infected again in no time.'

'Just give me the antibiotic,' Esperanza said. 'Of course I'll be infected *again*! I'm a prostitute.'

'Does Lupe read *your* mind?' Dr. Gomez asked Esperanza, who became agitated and hysterical, but Juan Diego said nothing. The boy liked Dr. Gomez; he wouldn't tell her what unintelligible filth and vilification his mother was spewing.

'Tell the cunt doctor what I said!' Esperanza was screaming at her son.

'I'm sorry,' Juan Diego said to Dr. Gomez, 'but I can't understand my mom – she's a raving, foul-mouthed lunatic.'

'*Tell* her, you little bastard!' Esperanza cried. She started to hit Juan Diego, but Brother Pepe got between them.

'Don't touch me,' Juan Diego told his mother. 'Don't come anywhere near me – you're infected. You're *infected*!' the boy repeated.

This may have been the word that woke Juan Diego from his disjointed dream – either the *infected* word or the sound of the landing gear descending from the plane, because his Cathay Pacific flight was also descending. He saw he was about to land in Manila, where his real life – well, if not entirely *real*, at least what passed as his *present* life – awaited him.

As much as Juan Diego liked to dream, whenever he dreamed about his mother, he was not sorry to wake up. If the beta-blockers didn't disjoint him, she did. Esperanza was not the kind of mother who should have been named for hope. '*Des*esperanza,' the nuns called her, albeit behind her back. 'Hopelessness,' the sisters had named her, or they referred to her as despair itself – 'Desesperación' – when that word made more sense. Even as a fourteen-year-old, Juan Diego felt he was the adult in the family – he and Lupe, too, who was an insightful thirteen. Esperanza was a child, not least in her children's eyes – except sexually. And what mother would want to be the sexual presence in her children's eyes that Esperanza was?

Esperanza never wore a cleaning woman's clothes; she was always dressed for her other line of work. When she cleaned, Esperanza was dressed for Zaragoza Street and the Hotel Somega – the 'whore hotel,' Rivera called it. The way Esperanza dressed was childish, or childlike, except for the sexually obvious part.

Esperanza was also a child when it came to money. The orphans at Lost Children weren't allowed to have money, but Juan Diego and Lupe still hoarded it. (You cannot take the scavenging out of scavengers; los pepenadores carry their picking and sorting with them, long after they've stopped looking for aluminum or copper or glass.) The dump kids were very skillful at hiding their money in their room at Niños Perdidos; the nuns never found it.

But Esperanza could find their money, and she stole from them when she needed to. Esperanza did repay the kids, in her fashion. Occasionally, after a successful night, Esperanza would put money under Lupe's or Juan Diego's pillow. The kids were lucky that they could *smell* the money their mother left them before the nuns found it. Esperanza's perfume gave her (*and* the money) away.

'Lo siento, madre,' Juan Diego said softly to himself, as his plane was landing in Manila. 'I'm sorry, Mother.' As a fourteen-year-old, he'd not been old enough to have sympathy for her – for either the child *or* the adult that she was.

THE CHARITY WORD WAS a big one with the Jesuits – with Father Alfonso and Father Octavio, especially. It was out of charity that they'd hired a prostitute to clean for them; the priests referred to this act of kindness as giving Esperanza a 'second chance.' (Brother Pepe and Edward Bonshaw would stay up late one night, discussing what kind of *first* chance Esperanza had been given – that is, before she'd become a prostitute and the Jesuits' cleaning woman.)

Yes, it was clearly out of Jesuitical *charity* that los niños de la basura had been afforded the status of orphans; after all, they had a mother – irrespective of how fit or unfit (as a mother) Esperanza was. No doubt, Father Alfonso and Father Octavio believed they'd been exceptionally *charitable* in allowing Juan Diego and Lupe to have their own bedroom and bathroom – irrespective of how dependent the girl was on her brother. (That would be another late-night discussion between Brother Pepe and Señor Eduardo: namely, how Father Alfonso and Father Octavio imagined Lupe might have functioned without Juan Diego translating for her.)

The other orphans, including siblings, were divided by gender. The boys slept in a dormitory setting on one floor of Niños Perdidos, the girls on another floor; there was a communal bathroom for the boys, and a similar arrangement (but with better mirrors) for the girls. If the children had parents, or other relatives, these adults weren't permitted to visit the children in their dormitories, but Esperanza was allowed to visit Juan Diego and Lupe in the dump kids' bedroom, which had formerly been a small library, a so-called reading room for visiting scholars. (Most of the books were still on the shelves, which Esperanza regularly dusted; as everyone repeated, ad nauseam, she was actually a good cleaning woman.)

Of course it would have been awkward to keep Esperanza away from her own kids; she also had a bedroom at Lost Children, but in the servants' quarters. Only female servants stayed in the orphanage, possibly to protect the children, though the servants themselves – Esperanza was the most vocal among them, not least on this subject – fervently imagined it was chiefly the priests ('those celibate weirdos,' Esperanza called them) whom the children needed protection from.

No one, not even Esperanza, would have accused Father Alfonso or Father Octavio of this particular, much-documented perversion among priests; no one believed the orphans at Niños Perdidos were in this particular danger. The conversation among the female servants concerning those children who were the sexual victims of allegedly celibate priests was very general; the talk was more about the 'unnaturalness' of celibacy for men. As for the nuns – well, that was different. Celibacy was more imaginable for women; no one ever said it was 'natural,' but not a few of the female servants expressed the feeling that the nuns were lucky not to have sex.

Only Esperanza said: 'Well, just *look* at the nuns. Who would want to have sex with them?' But this was unkind, and – like much of what Esperanza said – not necessarily true. (Yes, the subject of celibacy and its *unnaturalness*, or not, was another of those late-night discussions between Brother Pepe and Edward Bonshaw – as you might imagine.)

Because he whipped himself, Señor Eduardo would try to joke to Juan Diego about it; the flagellating Iowan said it was a good thing he had his own bedroom in the orphanage. But Juan Diego knew the flagellant shared a bathroom with Brother Pepe; the boy used to wonder if poor Pepe found traces of Edward Bonshaw's blood in the bathtub or on the towels. While Pepe was disinclined to mortifications of the body, he was amused that Father Alfonso and Father Octavio, who thought they were so superior to the Iowan in other ways, praised Edward Bonshaw for his painful self-castigations.

'How very twelfth-century!' Father Alfonso exclaimed admiringly.

'A rite worth maintaining,' Father Octavio said. (Whatever else they thought of Edward Bonshaw, both priests found his whipping himself brave.) And while these two *twelfth-century* admirers continued to criticize Señor Eduardo's Hawaiian shirts, Brother Pepe was also amused that the two old priests never connected Edward Bonshaw's flagellations with the Polynesian parrots and jungles on his overlarge shirts. Pepe knew that Señor Eduardo was always oozing blood; he whipped himself *hard*. The riotous colors and overall confusion of the zealot's Hawaiian shirts concealed the bleeding.

The bathroom they shared, and the close proximity of their separate bedrooms, made unlikely room-mates out of Pepe and the Iowan, and their rooms were on the same floor of the orphanage as the former reading room the dump kids shared. No doubt Pepe and the Iowan were aware of Esperanza – she passed by in the late hours of the night, or in the wee hours of the morning, as if she were more the ghost of the dump niños' mom than an actual mother. Because Esperanza was an *actual* woman, she might have been a disconcerting presence to these two celibate men; she must have occasionally heard Edward Bonshaw beating himself, too.

Esperanza knew how clean the floors were in Lost Children; after all, she had cleaned them. She was barefoot when she came to visit her children; she could be more silent that way, and – given the hours she kept during her time *not* spent as a cleaning woman – almost everyone else in Niños Perdidos was asleep when Esperanza was creeping around. Yes, she came to kiss her niños when they were sleeping – in this single respect, Esperanza resembled other moms – but she also came to steal from them, or to leave them a little perfumed money under their pillows. Most of all, Esperanza made these silent visits in order to use the bathroom Juan Diego and Lupe shared. She must have wanted some privacy; either in the Hotel Somega or in the servants' quarters of the orphanage, Esperanza probably had no privacy. She must have wanted, at least once a day, to bathe alone. And who knows how the other female servants at Lost Children treated Esperanza? Did those other women like sharing their communal bathroom with a prostitute?

Because Rivera had left his stick shift in reverse, he backed over Juan Diego's foot; because of a broken side-view mirror, the dump kids slept in a small library, a former reading room, in the Jesuit orphanage. And because their mother was a cleaning woman for the Jesuits (*because* she was also a prostitute), Esperanza haunted the same floor of Niños Perdidos where the new American missionary lived.

Wasn't this an arrangement that might have endured? Doesn't the deal they all had sound compatible enough to have worked? Why wouldn't the dump kids have preferred, eventually, their life at Lost Children to their shack in Guerrero? As for the perishable beauty, which Esperanza surely was, and the perpetually bleeding Edward Bonshaw, who so tirelessly whipped himself – well, is it absurd to imagine they might have taught each other something?

Edward Bonshaw might have benefited from hearing Esperanza's thoughts about celibacy and self-flagellation, and it's certain she would have had something to say to him on the subject of sacrificing his life to prevent the sins of a single prostitute on a single night.

In turn, Señor Eduardo might have asked Esperanza why she was *still* working as a prostitute. Didn't she already have a job and a safe place to sleep? Was it her vanity, perhaps? Was she so vain that being *wanted* was somehow better than being loved?

Weren't both Edward Bonshaw and Esperanza going to extremes? Wouldn't some middle ground have worked as well?

In one of their many late-night conversations, here is how Brother Pepe put it to Señor Eduardo: 'Merciful Lord, there must be some middle ground where it is possible *not* to sacrifice your life and still prevent the sins of a single prostitute on a single night!' But they would not resolve this; Edward Bonshaw would never explore that middle ground.

They would not, all of them, live together long enough to learn what *might have* happened. It was Vargas who first said the *circus* word; the undying idea of the circus came from him.

Blame it on the atheist. Hold the secular humanist

(the everlasting enemy of Catholicism) accountable for what happened next. It might not have been a bad life: to be slightly less than actual orphans, or to be orphans with unusual privileges, at Lost Children. It could have turned out all right.

But Vargas had planted the circus seed. What children don't love the circus, or imagine that they do?

Spontaneous Bleeding

When the dump niños vacated the shack in Guerrero for Lost Children, they brought almost as many water pistols with them as they had clothes. Of course the nuns were going to confiscate the squirt guns, but Lupe let them find only the ones that didn't work. The nuns never knew what the water pistols were for.

Juan Diego and Lupe had practiced on Rivera; if they could fool the dump boss with the stigmata trick, they thought they could make it work on anyone. They didn't fool him for long. Rivera could tell real blood from fake, and Rivera bought the beets – Lupe was always asking el jefe to buy her beets.

The dump kids would fill a water pistol with a mixture of beet juice and water. Juan Diego liked to add a little of his own saliva to the mixture. He said his spit gave the beet juice a 'bloodier texture.'

'Explain *texture*,' Lupe had said.

The way the trick worked was that Juan Diego would conceal the loaded squirt gun under the waistband of his pants, beneath an untucked shirt. The safest target was someone's shoe; the victims couldn't feel the fake blood when it was squirted on their shoes. Sandals were a problem; you could feel the gunk against your bare toes.

With women, Juan Diego liked to squirt them from behind, on a bare calf. Before the woman could turn her head to look, the boy had time to hide the water pistol. That was when Lupe started babbling. She pointed first to the area of spontaneous bleeding, then to the sky; if the blood were Heaven-sent, surely the source was the everlasting abode of God (and of the blessed dead). 'She says the blood is a miracle,' Juan Diego would translate for his sister.

Sometimes Lupe would equivocate, incomprehensibly. 'No, sorry – it's either a miracle or ordinary bleeding,' Juan Diego would then say. Lupe was already bending down, the rag in her small hand; she would wipe the blood, miraculous or not, off the shoe (or the woman's bare calf) before the victim had time to react. If the money for this service was immediately forthcoming, the dump kids were prepared to protest; they always refused to accept payment for pointing out a miracle, or for wiping the holy (or unholy) blood away. Well, at least they refused the money *at first*; dump kids weren't beggars.

After the accident with Rivera's truck, Juan Diego found that the wheelchair helped; he was usually the one to hold out his palm and reluctantly accept compensation, and the wheelchair offered more options for concealing the squirt gun. The crutches were a bit awkward – that is, letting go of one of them in order to extend his hand. When Juan Diego was on crutches, Lupe was usually the one who hesitantly took the money – never, of course, with the hand that had wiped the blood away.

In the jerkily limping stage of Juan Diego's recovery – the category of limp that would endure, the one that was not a phase – the dump niños made more impromptu decisions. Generally, Lupe (in her disinclined way) yielded to the men who insisted on rewarding her. With the women victims of the stigmata trick, the limping Juan Diego discovered that a crippled boy was more persuasively sympathetic than an angry-looking girl. Or was it that the women sensed Lupe was reading their minds?

The dump kids reserved the actual *stigmata* word for those high-risk occasions when Juan Diego dared to aim for a direct hit on the potential customer's hand; this was always a from-behind shot with the water pistol. When people allow their hands to rest at their sides, whether they are standing or walking, their palms face behind them.

When a sudden splash of diluted, beet-red blood appears in the palm of your hand – and there's a girl kneeling at your feet, smearing her rapturous face with the blood in your palm – well, you might be more than usually vulnerable to religious belief. And that was when the crippled boy began screaming the *stigmata* word. With the tourists in the zócalo, Juan Diego would resort to bilingual screaming – both *estigmas* and *stigmata*.

The one time the dump kids fooled Rivera, they got him with the shoe shot. The dump boss had glanced at the sky, but he wasn't looking for Heavenly evidence. 'Maybe a bird is bleeding,' was all Rivera had said; nor did el jefe offer to tip the dump kids.

Another time, the direct hit on Rivera's hand didn't work. While Lupe was smearing her face with the blood from el jefe's palm, Rivera had calmly taken his hand away from the enraptured girl. While Juan Diego was screaming the *estigmas* word, the dump boss licked the 'blood' in his palm.

'Los betabeles,' el jefe said, smiling at Lupe. The beets.

THE PLANE HAD LANDED in the Philippines. Juan Diego wrapped part of a green-tea muffin in a paper napkin, putting it in his coat pocket. The passengers were standing, gathering their things – an awkward moment for a crippled older man. But Juan Diego's mind was not in the moment; in his mind, he and Lupe were barely teenagers. They were scouting the zócalo, in the heart of Oaxaca, on the lookout for unsuspecting tourists and hapless locals who appeared capable of believing that a phantom God had singled them out – from an unseen height – for spontaneous bleeding.

As always, and anywhere – even in Manila – it was a woman who took pity on the older man's limp. 'May I help you?' the young mother asked. She was traveling with her small children, a little girl and an even smaller son. She was a woman with her hands full, in more ways than one, but such was the effect of Juan Diego's limp (on women, especially).

'Oh, no – I can manage. But thank you!' Juan Diego immediately said. The young mother smiled – she looked relieved, in fact. Her children continued to stare at Juan Diego's misdirected right foot; kids were always fascinated by that two-o'clock angle.

In Oaxaca, Juan Diego was remembering, the dump niños had learned to be wary in the zócalo, which was closed to traffic but overrun by beggars and hawkers. The beggars could be territorial, and one of the hawkers, the balloon man, had observed the stigmata trick. The dump kids didn't know he'd been watching them, but one day the man gave Lupe a balloon; he was looking at Juan Diego when he spoke. 'I like her style, blood boy, but you're too obvious,' the balloon man said. He had a sweat-stained rawhide shoelace around his neck, a crude necklace, to which a crow's foot was attached, and he fingered the crow's foot while he talked, as if the remnant of the bird were a talisman. 'I've seen *real* blood in the zócalo – I mean accidents can happen, blood boy,' he went on. 'You don't want the wrong people to know your game. The wrong people wouldn't want you, but they'll take *her*,' he said, pointing the crow's foot at Lupe.

'He knows where we're from; he shot the crow who had that foot at the basurero,' Lupe told Juan Diego. 'There's a pinprick in the balloon. It's losing air. He can't sell it. It won't be a balloon tomorrow.'

'I like her style,' the balloon man said again to Juan

Diego. He looked at Lupe, giving her another balloon. 'No pinprick; this one isn't losing air. But who knows about *tomorrow*? I've shot more than crows at the basurero, little sister,' the balloon man told her. The dump kids were freaked out that the creepy hawker had understood Lupe without the benefit of a translation.

'He kills dogs, he has shot *dogs* at the basurero – *many* dogs!' Lupe cried. She let go of both balloons. Soon they were drifting high above the zócalo, even the one with the pinprick. After that, the zócalo would never be the same for the dump kids. They became wary of everyone.

There was a waiter at the outdoor café at the most popular tourist hotel, the Marqués del Valle. The waiter knew who the dump niños were; he'd seen the stigmata trick, or the balloon man had told him about it. The waiter slyly warned the kids that he 'might tell' the nuns at Niños Perdidos. 'Don't you two have something to confess to Father Alfonso or Father Octavio?' was how the waiter put it.

'What do you mean that you *might tell* the nuns?' Juan Diego asked him.

'I mean the fake blood – that's what you've got to confess,' the waiter said.

'You said *might tell*,' Juan Diego insisted. 'Are you telling the nuns or aren't you?'

'I live on tips,' was how the waiter put it. Thus was the best place to squirt beet juice on tourists lost to the dump kids; they had to stay away from the outdoor café at the Marqués del Valle, where there was an opportunistic waiter who wanted a cut.

Lupe said she was superstitious about going to the Marqués del Valle, anyway; one of the tourists they'd nailed with the water pistol dived off a fifth-floor balcony into the zócalo. This suicide happened shortly after the unhappy-looking tourist had rewarded Lupe, very generously, for wiping the blood off his shoe. He was one of those sensitive souls who hadn't listened to the dump kids' claim that they weren't begging; he'd spontaneously handed Lupe quite a lot of money.

'Lupe, the guy didn't kill himself *because* his shoe started bleeding,' Juan Diego had explained to her, but Lupe didn't feel right about it.

'I knew he was sad about something,' Lupe said. 'I could tell he was having a bad life.'

Juan Diego didn't mind avoiding the Marqués del Valle; he'd hated the hotel before he and Lupe had encountered the money-grubbing waiter. The hotel was named for the title Cortés took for himself (Marqués del Valle de Oaxaca), and Juan Diego was suspicious of everything to do with the Spanish conquest – Catholicism included. Oaxaca had once been central to the Zapotec civilization. Juan Diego thought of himself and Lupe as Zapotecs. The dump kids hated Cortés; they were Benito Juárez people, not Cortés people, Lupe liked to say – they were *indigenous* people, Juan Diego and Lupe believed.

TWO MOUNTAIN CHAINS OF the Sierra Madre converge and meld into a single range in the state of Oaxaca;

the city of Oaxaca is the capital. But, beyond the predictable interference of the ever-proselytizing Catholic Church, the Spanish weren't all that interested in the state of Oaxaca – with the exception of growing coffee in the mountains. And, as if summoned by Zapotec gods, two earthquakes would destroy the city of Oaxaca – one in 1854, and another in 1931.

This history caused Lupe to obsess about earthquakes. Not only would she say, often inappropriately, 'No es buen momento para un terremoto' – that is, 'It's not a good moment for an earthquake' – but she would illogically wish for a third earthquake to destroy Oaxaca and its one hundred thousand inhabitants, for no better reason than the sadness of the suicidal guest at the Marqués del Valle or the abominable behavior of the balloon man, that unrepentant dog-killer. A person who killed dogs deserved to die, in Lupe's judgment.

'But an *earthquake*, Lupe?' Juan Diego used to ask his sister. 'What about the *rest* of us? Do we *all* deserve to die?'

'We better get out of Oaxaca – well, *you* better, anyway,' was Lupe's answer. 'A third earthquake is definitely *due*,' was how she put it. 'You better get out of *Mexico*,' she added.

'But not you? How come you're staying behind?' Juan Diego always asked her.

'I just do. I stay in Oaxaca. I just do,' Juan Diego remembered his sister repeating.

In this state of reflection did Juan Diego Guerrero,

the novelist, arrive for the first time in Manila; he was both distracted *and* disoriented. The young mother of those two small children had been right to offer him her help; Juan Diego had been mistaken to tell her he could 'manage.' The same thoughtful woman was waiting by the baggage carousel with her kids. There were too many bags on the moving belt, and people were aimlessly milling around – including, it seemed, people who had no business being there. Juan Diego was oblivious to how overwhelmed he appeared in crowds, but the young mother must have noticed what was painfully evident to everyone else. The distinguished-looking man with the limp looked lost.

'It's a chaotic airport. Is someone meeting you?' the young woman asked him; she was Filipino, but her English was excellent. He'd heard her children speaking only Tagalog, but they seemed to understand what their mom said to the cripple.

'Is someone meeting me?' Juan Diego repeated. (How is it possible he doesn't *know*? the young mother must have been thinking.) Juan Diego was unzipping a compartment of his carry-on bag where he'd put his itinerary; next would come the requisite fumbling in the pocket of his jacket for his reading glasses – as he'd been doing in the first-class lounge of British Airways, back at JFK, when Miriam had snatched the itinerary out of his hands. Here he was again, looking like a novice traveler. It was a wonder he didn't say to the Filipino woman (as he'd said to Miriam), 'I thought it was a long way to bring my laptop.' What a ridiculous thing to have said, he now thought – as if long distances *mattered* to a laptop!

His most assertive former student, Clark French, had made the arrangements in the Philippines for him; without consulting his itinerary, Juan Diego couldn't remember what his plans were – except that Miriam had found fault with where he was staying in Manila. Naturally, Miriam had made some suggestions regarding where he should stay – 'the second time,' she'd said. As for *this* time, what Juan Diego remembered was the all-knowing way Miriam had used the *trust me* expression. ('But, trust me, you won't like where you're staying' – that was how she'd put it.) As he searched his itinerary for the Manila arrangements, Juan Diego tried to account for the fact that he *didn't* trust Miriam; yet he desired her.

He saw he was staying at the Makati Shangri-La in Makati City; he was alarmed, at first, because Juan Diego didn't know that Makati City was considered part of metropolitan Manila. And because he was leaving Manila the next day for Bohol, no one he knew was meeting his plane – not even one of Clark French's relatives. Juan Diego's itinerary informed him that he was to be met at the airport by a professional driver. 'Just a driver' was the way Clark had written it on the itinerary.

'Just a driver is meeting me,' Juan Diego finally answered the young Filipino woman.

The mother said something in Tagalog to her children. She pointed to a large, unwieldy-looking piece of luggage on the carousel; the big bag rounded a corner on the moving belt, pushing other bags off the carousel. The children laughed at the bloated bag. You could have packed two Labrador retrievers in that stupid bag, Juan Diego was thinking; it was his bag, of course – he was embarrassed by it. A bag that huge and ugly also marked him as a novice traveler. It was orange – the unnatural orange that hunters wear, so they won't be mistaken for anything resembling an animal; the eye-catching orange of those traffic cones indicating road construction. The saleswoman who'd sold Juan Diego the bag had persuaded him by saying that his fellow travelers would never mistake his bag for theirs. No one else had a bag like it.

And just then – as the realization was dawning on the Filipino mother and her laughing kids that the garish albatross of all luggage belonged to the crippled man – Juan Diego thought of Señor Eduardo: how his Lab had been shot when he was at such a formative age. Tears came to Juan Diego's eyes at the awful idea of his hideous bag being big enough to contain *two* of Edward Bonshaw's beloved Beatrices.

It often happens with grown-ups that their tears are misunderstood. (Who can know which time in their lives they are reliving?) The well-meaning mother and her children must have imagined that the limping man was crying because they'd made fun of his checked bag. The confusion wouldn't end there. It was chaos in that area of the airport where friends and family members *and* professional drivers waited to meet arriving passengers. The young

Filipino mother rolled Juan Diego's coffin for two dogs; he struggled with her bag and his carry-on; the children wore backpacks and toted their mom's carry-on between them. Of course it was necessary for Juan Diego to tell the helpful young woman his name; that way, they could both look for the right driver – the one holding up the sign with the *Juan Diego Guerrero* name. But the sign said SEÑOR GUERRERO. Juan Diego was confused; the young Filipino mother knew it was his driver right away.

'That's *you*, isn't it?' the patient young woman asked him.

There was no easy answer regarding why he'd been confused by his own name – only a story – but Juan Diego did comprehend the context of the moment: he'd not been *born* Señor Guerrero, but he was now the Guerrero the driver was looking for. 'You're the *writer* – you're *that* Juan Diego Guerrero, right?' the handsome young driver had asked him.

'Yes, I am,' Juan Diego told him. He didn't want the young Filipino mother to feel the least bit bad about not knowing who he was (the *writer*), but when Juan Diego looked for her, she and her kids were gone; she had slipped away, never knowing he was *that* Juan Diego Guerrero. Just as well – she'd done her good deed for the year, Juan Diego imagined.

'I was named for a writer,' the young driver was saying; he strained to lift the gross orange bag into the trunk of his limo. 'Bienvenido Santos – have you ever read him?' the driver asked.

'No, but I've heard of him,' Juan Diego answered.

(I would *hate* to hear anyone say that about *me*! Juan Diego was thinking.)

'You can call me Ben,' the driver said. 'Some people are puzzled by the Bienvenido.'

'I *like* Bienvenido,' Juan Diego told the young man.

'I'll be your driver everywhere you go in Manila – not just this trip,' Bienvenido said. 'Your former student asked for me – that's the person who said you were a writer,' the driver explained. 'I'm sorry I haven't read your books. I don't know if you're famous—'

'I'm not famous,' Juan Diego quickly said.

'Bienvenido Santos is famous – he was famous *here*, anyway,' the driver said. 'He's dead now. I've read all his books. They're pretty good. But I think it's a mistake to name your kid after a writer. I grew up knowing I had to read Mr. Santos's books; there were a lot of them. What if I'd *hated* them? What if I didn't like to read? There's a *burden* attached to it – that's all I'm saying,' Bienvenido said.

'I understand you,' Juan Diego told him.

'Do you have any kids?' the driver asked.

'No, I don't,' Juan Diego said, but there was no easy answer to this question – that was another story, and Juan Diego didn't like to think about it. 'If I *do* have any children, I won't name them after writers,' was all he said.

'I already know one of your destinations while you're here,' his driver was saying. 'I understand you want to go to the Manila American Cemetery and Memorial—'

'Not this trip,' Juan Diego interrupted him. 'My time in Manila is too short this trip, but when I come back—'

'Whenever you want to go there, it's fine with me, Señor Guerrero,' Bienvenido quickly said.

'Please call me Juan Diego—'

'Sure, if that's what you like,' the driver rejoined. 'My point is, Juan Diego, everything's been taken care of – it's all been arranged. Whatever you want, at whatever time—'

'I may change hotels – not this time, but when I come back,' Juan Diego blurted out.

'Whatever you say,' Bienvenido told him.

'I've heard bad things about this hotel,' Juan Diego said.

'In my job, I hear lots of bad things. About *every* hotel!' the young driver said.

'What have you heard about the Makati Shangri-La?' Juan Diego asked him.

The traffic was at a standstill; the hubbub in the congested street had the sort of chaotic atmosphere Juan Diego associated with a bus station, not an airport. The sky was a dirty beige, the air damp and fetid, but the air-conditioning in the limo was too cold.

'It's a matter of what you can believe, you know,' Bienvenido answered. 'You hear everything.'

'That was my problem with the novel – believing it,' Juan Diego said.

'*What* novel?' Bienvenido asked.

'Shangri-La is an imaginary land in a novel called

Lost Horizon. I think it was written in the thirties – I forget who wrote it,' Juan Diego said. (Imagine hearing someone say that about a book of *mine*! he was thinking; it would be like hearing you had died, Juan Diego thought.) He was wondering why the conversation with the limo driver was so exhausting, but just then there was an opening in the traffic, and the car moved swiftly ahead.

Even bad air is better than air-conditioning, Juan Diego decided. He opened a window, and the dirty-beige air blew on his face. The haze of smog suddenly reminded him of Mexico City, which he didn't want to be reminded of. And the traffic-choked, bus-terminal atmosphere of the airport summoned Juan Diego's boyhood memory of the buses in Oaxaca; proximity to the buses seemed contaminating. But, in his adolescent memories, those streets south of the zócalo *were* contaminated – Zaragoza Street particularly, but even those streets on the way to Zaragoza Street from Lost Children and the zócalo. (After the nuns were asleep, Juan Diego and Lupe used to look for Esperanza on Zaragoza Street.)

'Maybe one of the things I've heard about the Makati Shangri-La is imaginary,' Bienvenido ventured to say.

'What would that be?' Juan Diego asked the driver.

Cooking smells blew in the open window of the moving car. They were passing a kind of shantytown, where the traffic slowed; bicycles were weaving between the cars – children, barefoot and shirtless, darted into the street. The dirt-cheap jeepneys were packed with people; the jeepneys cruised with their headlights turned off, or the headlights were burned out, and the passengers sat close together on benches like church pews. Perhaps Juan Diego thought of church pews because the jeepneys were adorned with religious slogans.

GOD IS GOOD! one proclaimed. GOD'S CARE FOR YOU IS APPARENT, another said. He'd just arrived in Manila, but Juan Diego was already zeroing in on a sore subject: the Spanish conquerors and the Catholic Church had been to the Philippines before him; they'd left their mark. (He had a limo driver named Bienvenido, and the jeepneys – the lowest of low-income transportation – were plastered with advertisements for *God*!)

'There's something wrong with the dogs,' Bienvenido said.

'The dogs? *What* dogs?' Juan Diego asked.

'At the Makati Shangri-La – the bomb-sniffing dogs,' the young driver explained.

'The hotel has been *bombed*?' Juan Diego asked.

'Not that I know of,' Bienvenido replied. 'There are bomb-sniffing dogs at all the hotels. At the Shangri-La, people say the dogs don't know what they're sniffing for – they just like to sniff *everything*.'

'That doesn't sound so bad,' Juan Diego said. He liked dogs; he was always defending them. (Maybe the bomb-sniffing dogs at the Shangri-La were just being extra careful.)

'People say the dogs at the Shangri-La are untrained,' Bienvenido was saying.

But Juan Diego couldn't focus on this conversation. Manila was reminding him of Mexico; he'd been unprepared for that, and now the talk had turned to dogs.

At Lost Children, he and Lupe had missed the dump dogs. When a litter of puppies was born in the basurero, the kids had tried to take care of the puppies; when a puppy died, Juan Diego and Lupe tried to find it before the vultures did. The dump kids had helped Rivera burn the dead dogs – burning them was a way to love the dogs, too.

At night, when they went looking for their mother on Zaragoza Street, Juan Diego and Lupe tried not to think about the rooftop dogs; those dogs were different – they were scary. They were mostly mongrels, as Brother Pepe had said, but Pepe was wrong to say that only *some* of the rooftop dogs were feral – *most* of them were. Dr. Gomez said she knew how the dogs ended up on the roofs, although Brother Pepe believed that no one knew how the dogs got there.

A lot of Dr. Gomez's patients had been bitten by the rooftop dogs; after all, she was an ear, nose, and throat specialist, and that's where the dogs tried to bite you. The dogs attacked your face, Dr. Gomez said. Years ago, in the top-floor apartments of those buildings south of the zócalo, people had let their pets run free on the roofs. But the pet dogs had run away, or they'd been scared away by wild dogs; many of those buildings were so close together that the dogs could run from roof to roof. People stopped letting their pet dogs up on the roofs; soon almost all the rooftop dogs were wild. But how had the first wild dogs ended up on the roofs?

At night, on Zaragoza Street, the headlights of passing cars were reflected in the eyes of the rooftop dogs. No wonder Lupe thought these dogs were ghosts. The dogs ran along the rooftops, as if they were hunting people in the street below. If you didn't talk, or you weren't listening to music, you could hear the dogs panting as they ran. Sometimes, when the dogs were jumping from roof to roof, a dog fell. The falling dogs were killed, of course, unless one landed on a person in the street below. The person passing by served to break the dog's fall. Those lucky dogs usually *didn't* die, but if they were injured from the fall, this made the dogs more likely to bite the people they'd fallen on.

'I guess you like dogs,' Bienvenido was saying.

'I do – I *do* like dogs,' Juan Diego said, but he was distracted by his thoughts of those ghost dogs in Oaxaca (if the rooftop dogs, or some of them, were truly ghosts).

'Those dogs aren't the only ghosts in town – Oaxaca is full of ghosts,' Lupe had said, in her know-it-all way.

'I haven't seen them,' was Juan Diego's first response.

'You will,' was all Lupe would say.

Now, in Manila, Juan Diego was also distracted by an overloaded jeepney with one of the same religious slogans he'd already seen; evidently, it was a popular message: GOD'S CARE FOR YOU IS APPARENT. A contrasting sticker in the rear window of a taxi then caught Juan Diego's eye. CHILD-SEX TOURISTS, the taxi sticker said. DON'T TURN AWAY. TURN THEM IN.

Well, yes – turn the fuckers in! Juan Diego thought. But for those children who were recruited to have sex with tourists, Juan Diego believed, God's care for *them* wasn't all that *apparent*.

'I'll be interested to see what you think of the bomb-sniffers,' Bienvenido was saying, but when he glanced in the rearview mirror, he saw that his client was asleep. Or *dead*, the driver might have thought, except that Juan Diego's lips were moving. Maybe the limo driver imagined that the not-so-famous novelist was composing dialogue in his sleep. The way Juan Diego's lips were moving, he appeared to be having a conversation with himself – the way writers do, Bienvenido supposed. The young Filipino driver couldn't have known the actual argument the older man was remembering, nor could Bienvenido have guessed where Juan Diego's dreams would transport him next.

12

Zaragoza Street

'Listen to me, Mr. Missionary – these two should stick together,' Vargas was saying. 'The circus will buy them clothes, the circus will pay for any medicine – plus three meals a day, *plus* a bed to sleep in, and there's a family to look after them.'

'*What* family? It's a *circus*! They sleep in *tents*!' Edward Bonshaw cried.

'La Maravilla is a kind of family, Eduardo,' Brother Pepe told the Iowan. 'Circus children aren't in need,' Pepe said, more doubtfully.

The name of Oaxaca's little circus, like Lost Children, had not escaped criticism. It could be confusing – Circo de La Maravilla. The *L* in *La* was uppercase because The Wonder herself was an actual person, a performer. (The act itself, the alleged marvel, was confusingly called la maravilla – a lowercase wonder or marvel.) And there were people in Oaxaca who thought Circus of The Wonder misleadingly advertised itself. The other acts were ordinary, not so marvelous; the animals weren't special. And there were rumors.

All anyone in town ever talked about was La Maravilla herself. (Like Lost Children, the circus's name was usually shortened; people said they were going to el circo or to La Maravilla.) The Wonder herself was always a young girl; there had been many. It was a breathtaking act, not always death-defying; several previous performers had been killed. And the survivors didn't continue to be The Wonder for very long. There was a lot of turnover among the performers; the stress probably got to these young girls. After all, they were risking their lives at that time when they were coming of age. Maybe the stress *and* their hormones got to them. Wasn't it truly wondrous that these young girls were doing something that could kill them *while* they were having their first periods and watching their breasts get bigger? Wasn't their coming of age the real danger, the actual marvel?

Some of the older dump kids who lived in Guerrero had sneaked into the circus; they'd told Lupe and Juan Diego about La Maravilla. But Rivera would never have tolerated such shenanigans. In those days when La Maravilla was in town, the circus set up shop in Cinco Señores; the circus grounds in Cinco Señores were closer to the zócalo and the center of Oaxaca than to Guerrero.

What drew the crowds to Circo de La Maravilla? Was it the prospect of seeing an innocent girl die? Yet Brother Pepe wasn't wrong to say that La Maravilla, or any circus, was a kind of family. (Of course, there are good and bad families.)

'But what can La Maravilla do with a *cripple*?' Esperanza asked.

'Please! Not when the boy is right here!' Señor Eduardo cried.

'It's okay. I *am* a cripple,' Juan Diego had said.

'La Maravilla will take you because you're *necessary*, Juan Diego,' Dr. Vargas said. 'Lupe requires translation,' Vargas said to Esperanza. 'You can't have a fortune-teller you don't understand; Lupe needs an interpreter.'

'I'm not a fortune-teller!' Lupe said, but Juan Diego didn't translate this.

'The woman you want is Soledad,' Vargas said to Edward Bonshaw.

'*What* woman? I don't want a *woman*!' the new missionary cried; he'd imagined that Dr. Vargas had misunderstood what a vow of celibacy entailed.

'Not a woman for *you*, Mr. Celibacy,' Vargas said. 'I mean the woman you need to talk to, on behalf of the kids. Soledad is the woman who looks after the kids at the circus – she's the lion tamer's wife.'

'Not the most reassuring name for the wife of a lion tamer,' Brother Pepe said. '*Solitude* doesn't bode well – widowhood awaits her, one might conclude.'

'For Christ's sake, Pepe – it's just her *name*,' Vargas said.

'You are an antichrist – you know that, don't you?' Señor Eduardo said, pointing to Vargas. 'These kids can live at Lost Children, where they will receive a Jesuit education, and you want to put them in harm's way! Is it their education you're frightened of, Dr. Vargas? Are you such a convinced atheist that you're afraid we might manage to turn these kids into believers?'

'These kids are in harm's way in *Oaxaca*!' Vargas cried. 'I don't care what they believe.'

'He's an antichrist,' the Iowan said, this time to Brother Pepe.

'Are there dogs at the circus?' Lupe asked. Juan Diego translated this.

'Yes, there are – *trained* dogs. There are acts with dogs. Soledad trains the new acrobats, including the flyers, but the dogs have their own troupe tent. Do you like dogs, Lupe?' Vargas asked the girl; she shrugged. Juan Diego could tell that Lupe liked the *idea* of La Maravilla as much as he did; she just didn't like Vargas.

'Promise me something,' Lupe said to Juan Diego, holding his hand.

'Sure. What?' Juan Diego said.

'If I die, I want you to burn me at the basurero – like the dogs,' Lupe told her brother. 'Just you and Rivera – nobody else. Promise me.'

'Jesus!' Juan Diego shouted.

'No Jesus,' Lupe told him. 'Just you and Rivera.'

'Okay,' Juan Diego said. 'I promise.'

'How well do you know this Soledad woman?' Edward Bonshaw asked Dr. Vargas.

'She's my patient,' Vargas replied. 'Soledad is a former acrobat – a trapeze artist. Lots of stress on the joints – hands and wrists and elbows, especially. All that grabbing and holding tight, not to mention the falls,' Vargas said.

'Isn't there a net for the aerialists?' Señor Eduardo asked.

'Not in most Mexican circuses,' Vargas told him.

'Merciful God!' the Iowan cried. 'And you're telling me that these children are in harm's way in *Oaxaca*!'

'Not a lot of falls in fortune-telling – no stress on the joints,' Vargas replied.

'I don't know what's on everybody's mind – it's not clear to me what everyone is thinking. I just know what *some* people are thinking,' Lupe said. Juan Diego waited. 'What about those people with minds I can't read?' Lupe asked. 'What does a fortune-teller say to those people?'

'We need to know more about how the sideshow works. We need to think about it.' (That was how Juan Diego interpreted his sister.)

'That's not what I said,' Lupe told her brother.

'We need to think about it,' Juan Diego repeated.

'What about the lion tamer?' Brother Pepe asked Vargas.

'What about him?' Vargas said.

'I hear Soledad has trouble with him,' Pepe said.

'Well, lion tamers are probably difficult to live with – I suppose there's no small amount of testosterone involved in taming lions,' Vargas said, shrugging. Lupe imitated his shrug.

'So the lion tamer is a macho guy?' Pepe asked Vargas.

'That's what I hear,' Vargas told him. 'He's not my patient.'

'Not a lot of falls in lion-taming – no stress on the joints,' Edward Bonshaw commented.

'Okay, we'll think about it,' Lupe said.

'What did she say?' Vargas asked Juan Diego.

'We're going to think about it,' Juan Diego told him.

'You can always come to Lost Children – you could visit me,' Señor Eduardo said to Juan Diego. 'I'll tell you what to read, we can talk about books, you could show me your writing—'

'This kid is *writing*?' Vargas asked.

'He wants to, yes – he wants an *education*, Vargas; he clearly has a gift for *language*. This boy has a future in some kind of higher learning,' Edward Bonshaw said.

'You can always come to the circus,' Juan Diego said to Señor Eduardo. 'You could visit me, bring me books—'

'Yes, of course you could,' Vargas told Edward Bonshaw. 'You can practically *walk* to Cinco Señores, and La Maravilla also travels. There are occasional road trips; the kids will get to see Mexico City. Maybe you can go with them. Travel is a kind of *education*, isn't it?' Dr. Vargas asked the Iowan; without waiting for an answer, Vargas turned his attention to the dump niños. 'What is it you miss about the basurero?' he asked them. (Everyone who knew the niños knew how much Lupe missed the dogs, and not only Dirty White and Diablo. Brother Pepe knew it was a *long* walk from Lost Children to Cinco Señores.)

Lupe didn't answer Vargas, and Juan Diego silently counted to himself – adding up the things he missed about Guerrero and the dump. The lightning-fast gecko on the shack's screen door; the vast expanse of waste; the various ways to wake up Rivera when he was sleeping in the cab of his truck; the way Diablo could silence the barking of the other dogs; the solemn dignity of the dogs' funeral fires in the basurero.

'Lupe misses the dogs,' Edward Bonshaw said – Lupe knew it was what Vargas had wanted the Iowan to say.

'You know what?' Vargas suddenly said, as if he'd just thought of it. 'I'll bet Soledad would let these kids *sleep* in the tent with the dogs. I could ask her. It wouldn't suprise me if Soledad thought the dogs would like that, too – then everyone would be happy! Small world, sometimes,' Vargas said, shrugging again. Once more, Lupe imitated his shrug. 'Does Lupe think I don't know what she's doing?' Vargas asked Juan Diego; both the boy and his sister shrugged.

'Children sharing a tent with dogs!' Edward Bonshaw exclaimed.

'We'll see what Soledad says,' Vargas said to Señor Eduardo.

'I like most animals better than most people,' Lupe remarked.

'Let me guess: Lupe likes animals better than people,' Vargas told Juan Diego.

'I said *most*,' Lupe corrected him.

'I know Lupe hates me,' Vargas said to Juan Diego.

Listening to Lupe and Vargas bitch about each other, or to each other, Juan Diego was reminded of the mariachi bands that forced themselves on tourists in the zócalo. On weekends, there were always bands in the zócalo – including the miserable high school bands, with cheerleaders. Lupe liked pushing Juan Diego in his wheelchair through the crowds. Everyone made way for them, even the cheerleaders. 'It's like we're famous,' Lupe said to Juan Diego.

The dump kids *were* famous for haunting Zaragoza Street; they became regulars there. No stupid stigmata tricks on Zaragoza Street – no one would have tipped the niños for wiping up any blood. Too much blood was routinely spilled on Zaragoza Street; wiping it up would have been a waste of time.

Along Zaragoza Street, there were always prostitutes, and the men cruising for prostitutes; in the courtyard of the Hotel Somega, Juan Diego and Lupe could watch the prostitutes and their customers come and go, but the kids never saw their mother on Zaragoza Street or in the hotel courtyard. There was no verification that Esperanza was working the street, and there may have been other guests at the Somega – people who were neither prostitutes nor their clients. Yet Rivera was not the only one the kids had heard call the Somega the 'whore hotel,' and all the coming and going certainly made the hotel appear that way.

One night, when Juan Diego was wheelchair-bound, he and Lupe had followed a prostitute named

Flor on Zaragoza Street; they knew the prostitute wasn't their mother, but Flor looked a little like Esperanza from behind – Flor *walked* like Esperanza.

Lupe liked to make the wheelchair go fast; she would come up close to people who had their backs turned to her – they never knew the wheelchair was there until it bumped them. Juan Diego was always afraid that these people would fall backward into his lap; he would lean forward and try to touch them with his hand before the speeding wheelchair made contact. That was how he first touched Flor; he'd meant to touch one of her hands, but Flor swung her arms back and forth when she walked, and Juan Diego unintentionally touched her swaying bottom.

'Jesus Mary Joseph!' Flor exclaimed, spinning around. She was very tall; she'd been prepared to throw a punch at head level, but she found herself looking down at the boy in a wheelchair.

'It's just me and my sister,' Juan Diego said, cringing. 'We're looking for our mother.'

'Do I look like your mother?' Flor asked. She was a transvestite prostitute. There weren't so many transvestite prostitutes in Oaxaca in those days; Flor really stood out, and not only because she was tall. She was almost beautiful; what was beautiful about her truly *wasn't* affected by the softest-looking trace of a mustache on her upper lip, though Lupe noticed it.

'You look like our mom, a little,' Juan Diego answered Flor. 'You're both very pretty.'

'Flor's a lot bigger, and there's the you-know-what,'

Lupe said, passing her finger over her upper lip. There was no need for Juan Diego to translate this.

'You kids shouldn't be here,' Flor told them. 'You should be in bed.'

'Our mother's name is Esperanza,' Juan Diego said. 'Maybe you've seen her here – maybe you *know* her.'

'I know Esperanza,' Flor told them. 'But I don't see her around here. I see *you* around here, all the time,' she told the kids.

'Maybe our mom is the most popular of all the prostitutes,' Lupe said. 'Maybe she never leaves the Hotel Somega – the men just come to her.' But Juan Diego didn't translate this.

'Whatever she's babbling about, I can tell you one true thing,' Flor said. 'Everybody who's ever been here has been *seen* – I can promise you that. Maybe your mother hasn't been here at all; maybe you kids should just go to *sleep*.'

'Flor knows a lot about the circus – it's on her mind,' Lupe said. 'Go on – ask her about it.'

'We have an offer from La Maravilla – just a side-show act,' Juan Diego said. 'We would have our own tent, but we would share it with the dogs – they're *trained* dogs, very smart. I don't suppose you see any circus people, do you?' the boy asked.

'I don't do dwarfs. You have to draw the line somewhere,' Flor told them. 'The dwarfs have an unreasonable interest in me – they're all over me,' she said.

'I won't be able to sleep tonight,' Lupe told Juan Diego. 'The thought of dwarfs all over Flor will keep me awake.'

'You told me to ask her. I won't be able to sleep, either,' Juan Diego said to his sister.

'Ask Flor if she knows Soledad,' Lupe said.

'Maybe we don't want to know,' Juan Diego said, but he asked Flor what she knew about the lion tamer's wife.

'She's a lonely, unhappy woman,' Flor answered. 'Her husband is a pig. In his case, I'm on the lions' side,' she said.

'I guess you don't do lion tamers, either,' Juan Diego said.

'Not that one, chico,' Flor said. 'Aren't you Niños Perdidos kids? Doesn't your mother work there? Why would you move into a tent with dogs if you don't *have* to?'

Lupe began to recite a list of reasons. 'One: love of dogs,' she started. 'Two: to be stars – in a circus, we might be famous. Three: because the parrot man will come visit us, and our future—' She stopped for a second. '*His* future, anyway,' Lupe said, pointing to her brother. 'His future is in the parrot man's hands – I just know it is, circus or no circus.'

'I don't know the parrot man – I've never met him,' Flor told the kids, after Juan Diego had struggled to translate Lupe's list.

'The parrot man doesn't want a woman,' Lupe reported, which Juan Diego also translated. (Lupe had heard Señor Eduardo say this.)

'I know *lots* of parrot men!' the transvestite prostitute said.

'Lupe means that the parrot man has taken a vow

of celibacy,' Juan Diego tried to explain to Flor, but she wouldn't let him finish what he was going to say.

'Oh, no – I don't know *any* men like that,' Flor said. 'Does the parrot man have a sideshow act at La Maravilla?'

'He's the new missionary at the Templo de la Compañía de Jesús – he's a Jesuit from Iowa,' Juan Diego told her.

'Jesus Mary Joseph!' Flor exclaimed again. '*That* kind of parrot man.'

'His dog was killed – it probably changed his life,' Lupe said, but Juan Diego left this untranslated.

Their attention was then diverted by a fight in front of the Hotel Somega; the altercation must have started in the hotel, but it had progressed from the courtyard into Zaragoza Street.

'Shit, it's the good gringo – that kid is a liability to himself,' Flor said. 'He might have been safer in Vietnam.'

There were more and more of the American hippie boys in Oaxaca; some of them came with girlfriends, but the girlfriends never stayed long. Most of the draft-age boys were alone, or they ended up alone. They were running away from the war in Vietnam, or from what their country had become, Edward Bonshaw said. The Iowan reached out to them – he tried to help them – but most of the hippie boys weren't religious types. Like the rooftop dogs, they were lost souls – they were running wild, or they drifted around town like ghosts.

Flor had reached out to the young American draft

dodgers, too; all the lost boys knew her. Maybe they liked her because she was a transvestite – like them, she was still a boy – but the lost Americans also liked Flor because her English was excellent. Flor had lived in Texas, but she'd come back to Mexico. Flor never changed the way she told that story. 'Let's just say my only way out of Oaxaca took me to Houston,' she would always begin. 'Have you ever been to Houston? Let's just say I had to get out of Houston.'

Lupe and Juan Diego had seen the good gringo around Zaragoza Street before. One morning Brother Pepe had found him sleeping in a pew of the Jesuit temple. El gringo bueno was singing 'Streets of Laredo,' the cowboy song, in his sleep – just the first verse, over and over again, Pepe had said.

As I walked out in the streets of Laredo
As I walked out in Laredo one day,
I spied a young cowboy, all wrapped in white
    linen,
Wrapped up in white linen and cold as the
    clay.

The hippie boy was always friendly to the dump kids. As for the fracas that had started in the Hotel Somega, it appeared that el gringo bueno hadn't been given time to get dressed. He lay curled on the sidewalk in a fetal position, to protect himself from being kicked; he wore just a pair of jeans. He was carrying his sandals and a dirty long-sleeved shirt, the only shirt the dump kids had seen him wear. But Lupe and

Juan Diego had not seen the boy's big tattoo before. It was a Christ on the Cross; the bleeding face of Jesus, crowned with thorns, filled the slender hippie's bare chest. Christ's torso, including the pierced part, covered the hippie's bare belly. Christ's outstretched arms (Jesus's sorely abused wrists and hands) were tattooed over the hippie boy's upper arms and fore-arms. It was as if the upper body of Christ had been violently affixed to the upper body of the good gringo. Both the crucified Christ and the hippie boy needed to shave, and their long hair was similarly matted.

There were two thugs standing over the boy on Zaragoza Street. The dump kids knew Garza – the tall, bearded one. Either he let you in the lobby of the Somega or he didn't; he was usually the one who told the kids to get lost. Garza had a territorial attitude concerning the hotel courtyard. The other thug – the young, fat one – was Garza's slave boy, César. (Garza fucked everything.)

'Is this how you get your rocks off?' Flor asked the two thugs.

There was another prostitute on the sidewalk of Zaragoza Street, one of the younger ones; she had badly pockmarked skin, and she wasn't wearing much more than the good gringo was. Her name was Alba, which means 'dawn,' and Juan Diego thought she looked like a girl you might meet for a moment as short-lived as a sunrise.

'He didn't pay me enough,' Alba told Flor.

'It was more than she told me it was going to be,' el

gringo bueno said. 'I paid her what she first told me.'

'Take the gringo with you,' Flor said to Juan Diego. 'If you can sneak out of Lost Children, you can sneak in – right?'

'The nuns will find him in the morning – or Brother Pepe or Señor Eduardo or our mother will find him,' Lupe said.

Juan Diego tried to explain this to Flor. He and Lupe shared a bedroom and a bathroom; their mother, unannounced, came to use the bathroom, and so on. But Flor wanted the dump niños to get the good gringo off the street. Niños Perdidos was *safe*; the kids should take the hippie boy with them – no one at the orphanage would beat him. 'Tell the nuns you found him on the sidewalk, and you were just doing the *charitable* thing,' Flor said to Juan Diego. 'Tell them the boy didn't have a tattoo, but when you woke up in the morning, the Crucified Christ was all over the good gringo's body.'

'And we heard him singing in his sleep – that cowboy song – for *hours*, but we couldn't see in the dark,' Lupe improvised. 'El gringo bueno must have been getting that tattoo in the dark all night!'

As if on cue, the half-naked hippie boy had begun to sing; he was not asleep now. He must have been singing 'Streets of Laredo' to taunt the two thugs who'd been harassing him – just the second verse, this time.

'I see, by your outfit, that you are a cowboy.'
These words he did say as I slowly walked by.

'Come sit down beside me and hear my sad
  story,
Got shot in the breast, and I know I must die.'

'Jesus Mary Joseph,' was all Juan Diego said softly.

'Hey, how's it going, man on wheels?' the good
gringo asked Juan Diego, as if he'd just noticed the
boy in his wheelchair. 'Hey, fast-drivin' little sister!
You got any speedin' tickets yet?' (Lupe had bumped
the good gringo with the wheelchair before.)

Flor was helping the hippie boy into his clothes. 'If
you touch him again, Garza,' Flor was saying, 'I'll cut
your cock and balls off while you're asleep.'

'You got the same junk between your legs,' Garza
told the transvestite prostitute.

'No, my junk is a lot bigger than yours,' Flor told
him.

César, Garza's slave boy, started to laugh, but the
way both Garza and Flor looked at him made him
stop.

'You ought to say what you're worth the first time,
Alba,' Flor said to the young prostitute with the bad
skin. 'You shouldn't change your mind about what
you're worth.'

'You can't tell me what to do, Flor,' Alba said, but
the girl had waited until she'd slunk back inside the
courtyard of the Hotel Somega before she said it.

Flor walked with the dump kids and the good
gringo as far as the zócalo. 'I owe you!' the young
American called to her, after she left them. 'I owe you
niños, too,' the hippie boy told the dump kids.

'I'm going to get you a present for this,' he told them.

'How are we supposed to keep him hidden?' Lupe asked her brother. 'We can sneak him into Lost Children tonight – no problem – but we can't sneak him out in the morning.'

'I'm working on the story that his Bleeding Christ tattoo is a miracle,' Juan Diego told her. (This was definitely an idea that would appeal to a dump reader.)

'It *is* a miracle, kind of,' el gringo bueno started to tell them. 'I got the idea for this tattoo—'

Lupe wouldn't let the lost young man tell his story, not then. 'Promise me something,' she said to Juan Diego.

'Another promise—'

'Just promise me!' Lupe cried. 'If I end up on Zaragoza Street, kill me – just kill me. Let me hear you say it.'

'Jesus Mary Joseph!' Juan Diego said; he was trying to exclaim this the way Flor had done it.

The hippie had forgotten what he was saying; he struggled with a verse of 'Streets of Laredo,' as if he were writing the inspired lyrics for the first time.

'Get six jolly cowboys to carry my coffin,
Get six pretty maidens to bear up my pall.
Put bunches of roses all over my coffin,
Roses to deaden the clods as they fall.'

'Say it!' Lupe yelled at the dump reader.

'Okay, I'll kill you. There, I said it,' Juan Diego told her.

'Whoa! Man on wheels, little sister – nobody's *killin'* anyone, right?' the good gringo asked them. 'We're all friends, *right?*'

The good gringo had mescal breath, which Lupe called 'worm breath' because of the dead worm in the bottom of the mescal bottle. Rivera called mescal the poor man's tequila; the dump boss said you drank mescal and tequila the same way, with a lick of salt and a little lime juice. The good gringo smelled like lime juice and beer; the night the dump kids sneaked him into Lost Children, the young American's lips were crusty with salt, and there was more salt in the V-shaped patch of beard the boy had left unshaven beneath his lower lip. The niños let the good gringo sleep in Lupe's bed; they had to help him undress, and he was already asleep – on his back, and snoring – before Lupe and Juan Diego could get themselves ready for bed.

Through his snores, the guttural-sounding verse of 'Streets of Laredo' seemed to emanate from el gringo bueno – like his smell.

'Oh, beat the drum slowly and play the fife
   lowly,
Play the dead march as you carry me along;
Take me to the valley, and lay the sod o'er me,
For I'm a young cowboy and I know I've done
   wrong.'

Lupe wet a washcloth and wiped the salty crust off the hippie boy's lips and face. She meant to cover him with his shirt; she didn't want to see his Bleeding Jesus in the middle of the night. But when Lupe smelled the gringo's shirt, she said it smelled like mescal or beer puke, or like the dead worm – she just pulled the sheet up to the young American's chin and made some effort to tuck him in.

The hippie boy was tall and thin, and his long arms – with Christ's mangled wrists and hands imprinted on them – lay at his sides, outside the bedsheet. 'What if he dies in the room with us?' Lupe asked Juan Diego. 'What happens to your soul if you die in some-one else's room in a foreign country? How can the gringo's soul get back home?'

'Jesus,' Juan Diego said.

'Leave Jesus out of it. We're the ones who are responsible for him. What do we do if the hippie boy dies?' Lupe asked.

'Burn him at the basurero. Rivera will help us,' Juan Diego said. He didn't really mean it – he was just trying to get Lupe to go to bed. 'The good gringo's soul will escape with the smoke.'

'Okay, we have a plan,' Lupe said. When she got into Juan Diego's bed, she was wearing more clothes than she usually slept in. Lupe said she wanted to be 'modestly dressed' with the hippie boy in their bed-room. She wanted Juan Diego to sleep on the side of the bed nearest the gringo; Lupe didn't want the sight of the Agonizing Christ to startle her in the night. 'I hope you're working on the miracle story,' she said to her brother, turning her back to him in the narrow bed. 'Nobody's going to believe that tattoo is a milagro.'

Juan Diego would be awake half the night, rehearsing how he would present the lost American's Bleeding Christ tattoo as an overnight miracle. Just before he finally fell sleep, Juan Diego realized that Lupe was still awake, too. 'I would marry this hippie boy, if he smelled better and stopped singing that cowboy song,' Lupe said.

'You're thirteen,' Juan Diego reminded his little sister.

In his mescal stupor, el gringo bueno could manage no more than the first two lines of the first verse of 'Streets of Laredo'; the way the song just petered out almost made the dump kids wish the good gringo would keep singing.

As I walked out in the streets of Laredo
As I walked out in Laredo one day—

'You're *thirteen*, Lupe,' Juan Diego repeated, more insistently.

'I mean later, when I'm older – *if* I get older,' Lupe said. 'I am beginning to have breasts, but they're very small. I know they're supposed to get bigger.'

'What do you mean, *if* you get older?' Juan Diego asked his sister. They lay in the dark with their backs turned to each other, but Juan Diego could feel Lupe shrug beside him.

'I don't think the good gringo and I get much older,' she told him.

'You don't *know* that, Lupe,' Juan Diego said.

'I know my breasts don't get any bigger,' Lupe told him.

Juan Diego would be awake a little longer, just thinking about this. He knew Lupe was usually right about the past; he fell asleep with the half-comforting knowledge that his sister didn't do the future as accurately.

13

Now and Forever

What happened to Juan Diego with the bomb-sniffing dogs at the Makati Shangri-La can be calmly and rationally explained, though what transpired developed quickly, and in the panic-stricken eyes of the hotel doorman and the Shangri-La security guards – the latter instantly lost control of the two dogs – there was nothing calm or rational attending the arrival of the Distinguished Guest. Such was the lofty-sounding designation attached to Juan Diego Guerrero's name at the hotel registration desk: *Distinguished Guest*. Oh, that Clark French – Juan Diego's former student had been busy, asserting himself.

There'd been an upgrade to the Mexican-American novelist's room; special amenities, one of which was unusual, had been arranged. And the hotel management had been warned not to call Mr. Guerrero a Mexican American. Yet you wouldn't have known that the natty hotel manager himself was hovering around the registration desk, waiting to confer celebrity status on the weary Juan Diego – that is, not if you witnessed the writer's rude reception at the driveway entrance to the Shangri-La. Alas, Clark wasn't on hand to welcome his former teacher.

As they pulled into the driveway, Bienvenido could see in the rearview mirror that his esteemed client was asleep; the driver tried to wave off the doorman, who was hurrying to open the rear door of the limo. Bienvenido saw that Juan Diego was slumped against this same rear door; the driver quickly opened his own door and stepped into the hotel entranceway, waving both arms.

Who knew that bomb-sniffing dogs were agitated by arm-waving? The two dogs lunged at Bienvenido, who raised both arms above his head, as if the security guards held him at gunpoint. And when the hotel doorman opened the limo's rear door, Juan Diego, who appeared to be dead, began to fall out of the car. A falling dead man further excited the bomb-sniffing dogs; both of them bounded into the limo's backseat, wresting the leather handles of their dog harnesses from the security guards' hands.

The seat belt kept Juan Diego from falling entirely out of the car; he was suddenly jerked awake, his head lolling in and out of the limo. There was a dog in his lap, licking his face; it was a medium-size dog, a small male Labrador or a female Lab, actually a Lab mix, with a Lab's soft, floppy ears and warm, wide-apart eyes.

'Beatrice!' Juan Diego cried. One can only imagine what he'd been dreaming about, but when Juan Diego cried out a woman's name, a female name, the Lab mix, who was male, looked puzzled – his name was James. And Juan Diego's crying out 'Beatrice!' utterly unnerved the doorman, who'd presumed the arriving guest was dead. The doorman screamed.

Evidently, the bomb-sniffing dogs were predisposed to become aggressive when there was screaming. James (who was in Juan Diego's lap) sought to protect Juan Diego by growling at the doorman, but Juan Diego had not noticed the *other* dog; he didn't know there was a second dog seated next to him. This was one of those nervous-looking dogs with perky, stand-up ears and a shaggy, bristling coat; it was not a purebred German shepherd but a shepherd mix, and when this savage-sounding dog began to bark (in Juan Diego's ear), the writer must have imagined he was sitting beside a *rooftop* dog, and that Lupe might have been right: some rooftop dogs were ghosts. The shepherd mix had one wonky eye; it was a greenish yellow, and the wonky eye's unsteady focus was not aligned with the dog's good eye. The mismatched eye was further evidence to Juan Diego that the trembling dog next to him was a rooftop dog *and* a ghost; the crippled writer unbuckled his seat belt and tried to get out of the car – a difficult task with James (the Lab mix) in his lap.

And, just then, both dogs thrust their muzzles into the general vicinity of Juan Diego's crotch; they pinned him to his seat – they were intently *sniffing*. Since the dogs were allegedly trained to sniff *bombs*, this got the attention of the security guards. 'Hold it right there,' one of them said ambiguously – to either Juan Diego or the dogs.

'Dogs love me,' Juan Diego proudly announced. 'I was a dump kid – un niño de la basura,' he tried to explain to the security guards; the two of them were fixated on the unsteady-looking man's custom-made shoe. What the handicapped gentleman was saying made no sense to the guards. ('My sister and I tried to look after the dogs in the basurero. If the dogs died, we tried to burn them before the vultures got to them.')

And here was the problem with the only two ways Juan Diego could limp: either he led with the lame foot at that crazy two-o'clock angle, in which case the jolt of his limp was the first thing you saw, or he started out on his good foot and dragged the bad one behind – in either case, the two-o'clock foot and that misshapen shoe drew your attention.

'Hold it right there!' the first security guard commanded again; both the way he raised his voice and how he pointed at Juan Diego made it clear he wasn't speaking to the dogs. Juan Diego froze, mid-limp.

Who knew that bomb-sniffing dogs didn't like it when people did that freezing thing and held themselves unnaturally still? The bomb-sniffers, both James and the shepherd mix, their noses now prodding Juan Diego in the area of his hip – more specifically, at the coat pocket of his sport jacket, where he'd put the paper napkin with the uneaten remains of his green-tea muffin – suddenly stiffened.

Juan Diego was trying to remember a recent terrorist incident – where was it, in Mindanao?

Wasn't that the southernmost island of the Philippines, the one nearest Indonesia? Wasn't there a sizable Muslim population in Mindanao? Hadn't there been a suicide bomber who'd strapped explosives to one of his legs? Before the explosion, all anyone had noticed was the bomber's limp.

This doesn't look good, Bienvenido was thinking. The driver left the orange albatross of a bag with the cowardly doorman, who was still recovering from the conviction that Juan Diego was a dead person come back to life with a zombie-like limp and calling out a woman's name. The young limo driver went inside the hotel to the registration desk, where he told them they were about to shoot their Distinguished Guest.

'Call off the untrained dogs,' Bienvenido told the hotel manager. 'Your security guards are poised to kill a crippled writer.'

The misunderstanding was soon sorted out; Clark French had even prepared the hotel for Juan Diego's early arrival. Most important to Juan Diego was that the dogs be forgiven; the green-tea muffin had misled the bomb-sniffers. 'Don't blame the dogs,' was how Juan Diego put it to the hotel manager. 'They are perfect dogs – promise me they won't be mistreated.'

'Mistreated? No, sir – never mistreated!' the manager declared. It's unlikely that a Distinguished Guest of the Makati Shangri-La had been such an advocate of the bomb-sniffing dogs before. The manager himself showed Juan Diego to his room. The amenities provided by the hotel included a fruit basket and the standard platter of crackers and cheese; the ice bucket with four bottles of beer (instead of the usual Champagne) had been the idea of Juan Diego's devoted former student, who knew that his beloved teacher drank only beer.

Clark French was also one of Juan Diego's doting readers, though Clark was surely better known in Manila as an American writer who'd married a Filipino woman. At a glance, Juan Diego knew, the giant aquarium had been Clark's idea. Clark French loved to give his former teacher gifts that demonstrated the younger writer's zeal for commemorating highlights from Juan Diego's novels. In one of Juan Diego's earliest efforts – a novel almost no one had read – the main character is a man with a defective urinary tract. His girlfriend has a huge fish tank in her bedroom; the sights and sounds of the exotic underwater life have an unsettling effect on the man, whose urethra is described as 'a narrow, winding road.'

Juan Diego had an enduring fondness for Clark French, a diehard reader who retained the most specific details – details of the kind writers generally remembered only in their own work. Yet Clark didn't always recall how these same details were intended to affect the reader. In Juan Diego's urinary-tract novel, the main character is greatly disturbed by the underwater dramas forever unfolding in his girlfriend's bedside aquarium; the fish keep him awake.

The hotel manager explained that the overnight loan of the lighted, gurgling fish tank was the gift of

Clark French's Filipino family; an aunt of Clark's wife owned a store for exotic pets in Makati City. The aquarium had been too heavy for any table in the hotel room, so it stood immovably on the floor of the bedroom, beside the bed. The tank was half as tall as the bed, an imposing rectangle of sinister-looking activity. A welcoming note from Clark had accompanied the aquarium: *Familiar details will help you sleep!*

'They are all creatures from our own South China Sea,' the hotel manager remarked warily. 'Don't feed them. For one night, they can go without eating – so I'm told.'

'I see,' Juan Diego said. He didn't see, at all, how Clark – or the Filipino aunt who owned the store for exotic pets – could have imagined anyone would find the aquarium *restful*. It held over sixty gallons of water, the aunt had said; after dark, the green under-water light would surely seem greener (not to mention, brighter). Small fish, too fast to describe, darted furtively in the upper reaches of the water. Something larger lurked in the darkest corner at the bottom of the tank: a pair of eyes glowed; there was a wavy undulation of gills.

'Is that an eel?' Juan Diego asked.

The hotel manager was a small, neatly dressed man with a painstakingly trimmed mustache. 'Maybe a moray,' the manager said. 'Better not stick your finger in the water.'

'No, of course not – that's definitely an eel,' Juan Diego replied.

* * *

JUAN DIEGO HAD AT first regretted that he'd agreed to let Bienvenido drive him to a restaurant that evening. No tourists, mostly families – 'a well-kept secret,' the driver had said to persuade him. Juan Diego had imagined he might be happier to have room service in his hotel room, and to go to bed early. Yet he now felt relieved that Bienvenido was taking him away from the Shangri-La; the unfamiliar fish and the evil-looking eel would await his return. (He would rather have slept with the bomb-sniffing Lab mix James!)

The P.S. to Clark French's welcoming note read as follows: *You are in good hands with Bienvenido! Everyone excited to see you in Bohol! My whole family can't wait to meet you! Auntie Carmen says the moray's name is Morales – no touching!*

As a graduate student, Clark French had needed defending, and Juan Diego had defended him. The young writer was unfashionably ebullient, an ever-optimistic presence; it wasn't only his writing that suffered from an overuse of exclamation points.

'That's definitely a moray,' Juan Diego told the hotel manager. 'Name of Morales.'

'Ironic name for a biting eel – "Morals," the moray,' the manager said. 'The pet store sent a team to assemble the aquarium: two luggage carts to carry the jugs of seawater; the underwater thermometer is most delicate; the system that circulates the water had a water-bubble problem; the rubber bags with the individual creatures had to be carried by hand – an impressive production for a one-night visit. Maybe the moray was sedated for such a stressful trip.'

'I see,' Juan Diego repeated. Señor Morales did not appear to be under the influence of sedation at the moment; the eel was menacingly coiled in the farthest corner of the tank, calmly breathing, the yellowish eyes unblinking.

As a student at the Iowa Writers' Workshop – and later, as a published novelist – Clark French eschewed an ironic touch. Clark was unstintingly earnest and sincere; naming a moray eel Morales was not his style. The irony must have been entirely Auntie Carmen's, from the Filipino side of Clark's family. It made Juan Diego anxious that all of them were waiting to meet him in Bohol; yet he was happy for Clark French – the seemingly friendless young writer had found a family. Clark French's fellow students (would-be writers, all) had found him hopelessly naïve. What young writer is attracted to a sunny disposition? Clark was improbably positive; he had an actor's handsome face, an athletic body, and he was as badly but conservatively dressed as a door-to-door Jehovah's Witness.

Clark's actual religious convictions (Clark was very Catholic) must have reminded Juan Diego of a young Edward Bonshaw. In fact, Clark French had met his Filipino wife – and her 'whole family,' as he'd enthusiastically described them – during a Catholic do-gooder mission in the Philippines. Juan Diego couldn't remember the exact circumstances. A Catholic charity, of one kind or another? Orphaned children and unwed mothers might have been involved.

Even Clark French's novels exerted a tenacious and combative goodwill: his main characters, lost souls and serial sinners, always found redemption; the act of redeeming usually followed a moral low point; the novels predictably ended in a crescendo of benevolence. Quite understandably, these novels were critically attacked. Clark had a tendency to preach; he evangelized. Juan Diego thought it was sad that Clark French's novels were scorned – in the same manner poor Clark himself had been mocked by his fellow students. Juan Diego truly liked Clark French's writing; Clark was a craftsman. But it was Clark's curse to be annoyingly *nice*. Juan Diego knew Clark meant it – the young optimist was genuine. But Clark was also a proselytizer – he couldn't help it.

Crescendos of benevolence following moral low points – formulaic, but does this work with religious readers? Was Clark to be scorned for having readers? Could Clark help it that he was uplifting? ('*Terminally* uplifting,' a fellow grad student at Iowa had said.)

Yet the aquarium for one night was too much; this was more Clark than Clark – this was going too far. Or am I just too tired from all the traveling to appreciate the gesture? Juan Diego wondered. He hated to blame Clark for being Clark – or for having an eternal goodness. Juan Diego was sincerely fond of Clark French; yet his fondness for the young writer tormented him. Clark was *obdurately* Catholic.

A wild thrashing sent a sudden spray of warm sea-water from the aquarium, startling Juan Diego and the hotel manager. Had an unlucky fish been eaten or killed? The strikingly clear, green-lit water revealed no traces of blood or body parts; the ever-watchful eel gave no outward indication of wrongdoing. 'It's a violent world,' the hotel manager remarked; it was a sentence, eschewing irony, one would find at a moral low point in a Clark French novel.

'Yes,' was all Juan Diego said. He'd been born a guttersnipe; he hated himself when he looked down on other people, especially when they were *good* people, like Clark, and Juan Diego was looking down on him the way every superior and condescending person in the literary world looked down on Clark French – for being *uplifting*.

After the manager left him alone, Juan Diego wished he'd asked about the air-conditioning; it was too cold in the room, and the thermostat on the wall presented the tired traveler with a labyrinthine choice of arrows and numbers – what Juan Diego imagined he might encounter in the cockpit of a fighter plane. Why was he so *tired*? Juan Diego wondered. Why is it that all I want to do is sleep and dream, or see Miriam and Dorothy *again*?

He had another impromptu nap; he sat at the desk and fell asleep in the chair. He woke up shivering.

There was no point in unpacking his huge orange bag for a one-night stay. Juan Diego displayed his beta-blockers on the bathroom sink, to remind himself to take the usual dose – the *right* dose, not a double one. He put the clothes he'd been wearing on the bed; he showered and shaved. His traveling life without Miriam and Dorothy was very much like his *normal* life; yet it suddenly seemed empty and purposeless without them. And why was that? he wondered, along with wondering about his tiredness.

Juan Diego watched the news on TV in his hotel bathrobe; the chill of cold air was no less cold, but he'd fiddled with the thermostat and had managed to reduce the speed of the fan. The air-conditioning was no warmer – it just blasted less. (Weren't those poor fish used to warm seas, the moray included?)

On the TV, there was an unclear video, captured on a surveillance camera, of the suicide bomber in Mindanao. The terrorist was not recognizable, but his limp bore a disquieting resemblance to Juan Diego's. Juan Diego had been scrutinizing the slight differences – it was the same leg that was affected, the right one – when the explosion obliterated every-thing. There was a click, and the TV screen showed a scratchy-sounding blackness. The video clip left Juan Diego with the upsetting feeling that he'd seen his own suicide.

He noted that there was enough ice in the bucket to keep the beer cold long after his dinner – not that the frigid air-conditioning wouldn't suffice. Juan Diego dressed himself in the greenish glow cast from the aquarium. 'Lo siento, Señor Morales,' he said, as he was leaving the hotel room. 'I'm sorry if it's not warm enough for you and your friends.' The moray appeared to be watching him as the writer stood uncertainly in the doorway; the eel's stare was so steadfast that Juan Diego waved to the unresponsive creature before he closed the hotel-room door.

At the family restaurant Bienvenido drove him to – 'a well-kept secret' to some, perhaps – there was a screaming child at every table, and the families all seemed to know one another; they shouted from table to table, passing platters of food back and forth.

The decor defied Juan Diego's understanding: a dragon, with an elephant's trunk, was trampling soldiers; a Virgin Mary, with an angry-looking Christ Child in her arms, guarded the restaurant's entrance. She was a menacing Mary – a Mary with a bouncer's attitude, Juan Diego decided. (Leave it to Juan Diego to find fault with the Virgin Mary's attitude. Didn't that dragon with the elephant's trunk, the one trampling the soldiers, have an attitude problem, too?)

'Isn't San Miguel a Spanish beer?' Juan Diego asked Bienvenido in the limo; they were driving back to the hotel. Juan Diego must have had a few beers.

'Well, it's a Spanish brewery,' Bienvenido said, 'but their parent company is in the Philippines.'

Any version of colonialism – Spanish colonialism, in particular – was certain to set off Juan Diego. And then there was *Catholic* colonialism, as Juan Diego thought of it. 'Colonialism, I suppose,' was all the writer said; in the rearview mirror, he could see the limo driver thinking this over. Poor Bienvenido: he'd imagined they were talking about beer.

'I suppose,' was all Bienvenido said.

* * *

IT MUST HAVE BEEN a saint's day – which one, Juan Diego didn't remember. The responsive prayer, beginning in the chapel, didn't exist only in Juan Diego's dream; the prayer had drifted upstairs on the morning the dump kids woke up with el gringo bueno in their room at Niños Perdidos.

'¡Madre!' one of the nuns called; it sounded like Sister Gloria's voice. 'Ahora y siempre, serás mi guía.'

'Mother!' the orphans in the kindergarten responded. 'Now and forever, you will be my guide.'

The kindergartners were in the chapel, one floor below Juan Diego and Lupe's bedroom. On saints' days, the responsive prayers drifted upstairs before the kindergartners began their morning march. Lupe, either awake or half asleep, would murmur her own prayer in response to the kindergartners' ode to the Virgin Mary.

'Dulce madre mía de Guadalupe, por tu justicia, presente en nuestros corazones, reine la paz en el mundo,' Lupe prayed – somewhat sarcastically. 'My sweet mother Guadalupe, in your righteousness, present in our hearts, let peace reign in the world.'

But this morning, when Juan Diego was barely awake, with his eyes still closed, Lupe said, '*There's* a miracle for you: our mother has managed to pass through our room – she's taking a bath – without ever seeing the good gringo.'

Juan Diego opened his eyes. Either el gringo bueno had died in his sleep or he'd not moved; yet the bedsheet no longer covered him. The hippie and his

Crucified Christ lay still and exposed – a tableau of an untimely death, of youth struck down – while the dump kids could hear Esperanza singing some secular ditty in the bathtub. 'He's a beautiful boy, isn't he?' Lupe asked her brother.

'He smells like beer piss,' Juan Diego noted, bending over the young American to be sure he was breathing.

'We should get him out on the street – at least get him dressed,' Lupe said. Esperanza had already pulled the plug; the niños could hear the sound the tub made when it was draining. Esperanza's singing was muffled – she was probably towel-drying her hair.

In the chapel, one floor below them, or perhaps in the poetic license taken in Juan Diego's dream, the nun who sounded like Sister Gloria once more exhorted the children to repeat after her: '¡Madre! Ahora y siempre—'

'"I want my arms and legs around you!"' Esperanza sang. '"I want my tongue touching your tongue, too!"'

'"I spied a young cowboy, all wrapped in white linen,"' the dead-asleep gringo was singing. '"Wrapped up in white linen and cold as the clay."'

'Whatever this mess is, it isn't a miracle,' Lupe said; she got out of bed to help Juan Diego dress the helpless gringo.

'Whoa!' the hippie boy moaned; he was still asleep, or he'd completely passed out. 'We're all friends, *right*?' he kept asking. 'You smell great, and you're so beautiful!' he told Lupe, as she was trying to button his dirty shirt. But the good gringo's eyes never opened; he couldn't see Lupe. He was too hung over to wake up.

'I'll marry him only if he stops drinking,' Lupe said to Juan Diego.

The good gringo's breath smelled worse than all the rest of him, and Juan Diego tried to distract himself from the bad smell by thinking about what present the friendly hippie might give the dump kids – last night, when he'd been more lucid, the young draft dodger had promised them a present.

Naturally, Lupe knew what her brother was thinking. 'I don't believe the dear boy can afford to give us very extravagant presents,' Lupe said. 'One day, in about five to seven years, a simple gold wedding band might be nice, but I wouldn't count on anything special now – not when the hippie is spending his money on alcohol and prostitutes.'

As if summoned by the *prostitutes* word, Esperanza came out of the bathroom; she was wearing her customary two towels (her hair bound in one, her body scarcely covered by the other) and carrying her Zaragoza Street clothes.

'Look at him, Mom!' Juan Diego cried; he began unbuttoning the good gringo's shirt, faster than Lupe had buttoned it up. 'We found him on the street last night – he didn't have a mark on him. But this morning, *look* at him!' Juan Diego pulled open the hippie boy's shirt to reveal the Bleeding Jesus. 'It's a *miracle*!' Juan Diego cried.

'It's el gringo bueno – he's no miracle,' Esperanza said.

'Oh, let me die – she *knows* him! They've been naked together – she's done *everything* to him!' Lupe cried.

Esperanza rolled the gringo over on his stomach; she pulled down his underpants. 'You call *this* a miracle?' she asked her children. On the dear boy's bare ass was a tattoo of the American flag, but the flag was purposely ripped in half; the crack of the hippie's ass divided the flag. It was pretty much the opposite of a patriotic picture.

'Whoa!' the unconscious gringo said in a strangled voice; he was lying facedown on the bed, where he appeared in danger of suffocating.

'He smells like upchuck,' Esperanza said. 'Help me get him into the bathtub – the water will bring him back to life.'

'The gringo put his thing in her mouth,' Lupe was babbling. 'She put his thing in her—'

'Stop it, Lupe,' Juan Diego said.

'Forget what I said about marrying him,' Lupe said. 'Not in five years *or* in seven – not *ever*!'

'You'll meet someone else,' Juan Diego told his sister.

'Who has Lupe met? Who has upset her?' Esperanza asked. She held the naked hippie under his arms; Juan Diego took hold of the boy's ankles, and they carried him into the bathroom.

'*You* have upset her,' Juan Diego told his mother. 'Just the thought of you with the good gringo has upset her.'

'Nonsense,' Esperanza said. 'Every girl loves the gringo kid, and he loves us. It would break your heart to be his mother, but the gringo kid makes all the other women in the world very happy.'

'The gringo kid has broken *my* heart!' Lupe was wailing.

'What is the matter with her – did she get her period or something?' Esperanza asked Juan Diego. 'I'd already had my first period by the time I was her age.'

'No, I didn't get my period – I'm *never* getting my period!' Lupe screamed. 'I'm *retarded*, remember? My period is retarded!'

Juan Diego and his mom hit the hippie's head on the hot-water faucet when they were sliding him into the bathtub, but the boy didn't flinch or open his eyes; his only response was to hold his penis.

'Isn't that sweet?' Esperanza asked Juan Diego. 'He's a darling guy, isn't he?'

'"I see, by your outfit, that you are a cowboy,"' the sleeping gringo sang.

Lupe wanted to be the one who turned the water on, but when she saw that el gringo bueno was holding his penis, she got upset all over again. 'What is he doing to himself ? He's thinking about sex – I know he is!' she said to Juan Diego.

'He's singing – he's *not* thinking about sex, Lupe,' Juan Diego said.

'Sure he is – the gringo kid thinks about sex all the time. That's why he's so young-looking,' Esperanza told them, turning on the tub; she opened both faucets all the way.

'Whoa!' cried the good gringo, opening his eyes. He saw the three of them peering down at him in the bathtub. He'd probably not seen Esperanza looking quite this way – in a tight white towel with her damp, tousled hair fallen forward, to either side of her pretty face. She had taken the second towel off her head; the towel for her hair was a little wet, but she wanted to leave it for the hippie boy to use. It would take her a while to get herself dressed, and to bring a couple of clean towels to the kids' bathroom.

'You drink too much, kid,' Esperanza told the good gringo. 'You don't have a big enough body to handle the alcohol.'

'What are *you* doing here?' the dear boy asked her; he had a wonderful smile, the Dying Christ on his scrawny chest notwithstanding.

'She's our *mother*! You're fucking our *mother*!' Lupe yelled.

'Yikes, little sister—' the gringo started to say. Naturally, he hadn't understood her.

'This is our mother,' Juan Diego told the hippie, as the tub was filling.

'Oh, wow. We're all friends, *right*? Amigos, aren't we?' the boy asked, but Lupe turned away from the bathtub; she went back into the bedroom.

They could all hear Sister Gloria and the kinder-gartners coming up the stairs from the chapel, because Esperanza had left the door to the hall open, and Lupe had left the bathroom door open. Sister Gloria called the enforced march for the kinder-gartners their 'constitutional'; the children tramped upstairs, chanting the responsive '¡Madre!' prayer. They marched around the hall, praying – they did this daily, not only on saints' days. Sister Gloria said she made the children march for the 'additional benefit' of the good effect this had on Brother Pepe and Edward Bonshaw, who loved to see and hear the kindergartners repeating the 'now and forever' business.

But Sister Gloria had a punitive streak in her. Sister Gloria probably wanted to punish Esperanza, catching her – as it usually happened – in the two towels, fresh from her bath. Sister Gloria must have imagined that the endearing holiness of the chanting kindergartners burned in Esperanza's sinning heart like a heated sword. Possibly, Sister Gloria deluded herself even further: she might have thought that the 'you will be my guide' kindergartners had a cleansing effect on the prostitute's wayward brats, those dump kids who'd been given special privileges at Lost Children. A room of their own and their own bathroom, too! – this was *not* how Sister Gloria would have treated los niños de la basura. This was no way to run an orphanage – not in Sister Gloria's opinion. You didn't give special privileges to smoke-smelling scavengers from the basurero!

But on the morning when Lupe learned that her mother and the good gringo had been lovers, Lupe was not in the mood to hear Sister Gloria and the kindergartners reciting the '¡Madre!' prayer.

'Mother!' Sister Gloria arduously repeated; she had paused at the open door to the dump kids' bedroom, where the nun could see Lupe sitting on one of the unmade beds. The kindergartners stopped marching ahead in the hall; they stood, shuffling in place, staring into the bedroom. Lupe was sobbing, which was not entirely new.

'Now and forever, you will be my guide,' the children were repeating – for what must have seemed, at least to Lupe, the hundredth (or the thousandth) time.

'Mother Mary is a *fake!*' Lupe screamed at them. 'Let the Virgin Mary show me a miracle – just the tiniest miracle, *please!* – and I might believe, for a minute, that your Mother Mary has actually *done* something, except steal Mexico from our Guadalupe. What did the Virgin Mary ever actually *do*? She didn't even get herself *pregnant!*'

But Sister Gloria and the chanting kindergartners were used to incomprehensible outbursts from the presumed-to-be-retarded vagabond. ('La vagabunda,' Sister Gloria called Lupe.)

'¡Madre!' Sister Gloria simply said, again, and the children once more repeated the incessant prayer.

Esperanza's emergence from the bathroom came as a ghostly apparition to the kindergartners – they halted their responsive praying in midsentence. 'Ahora y siempre –' the children were saying when they suddenly stopped, the 'now and forever' incantation just ending. Esperanza was wearing only one towel, the one that scantily covered her body. Her wild, freshly shampooed hair momentarily made the kindergartners think she was not the orphanage's fallen cleaning woman; Esperanza now appeared to the children as a different, more confident being.

'Oh, get over it, Lupe!' Esperanza said. 'He's not the last naked boy who will break your heart!' (This was sufficient to make Sister Gloria stop praying, too.)

'Yes he is – the first and last naked boy!' Lupe cried. (Of course the kindergartners and Sister Gloria didn't get this last bit.)

'Pay no attention to Lupe, children,' Esperanza told the kindergartners, as she walked barefoot into the hall. 'A vision of the Crucified Christ has disturbed her. She thought the Dying Jesus was in her bathtub – the crown of thorns, the excessive bleeding, the whole nailed-to-the-cross thing! Who wouldn't get upset to wake up to *that*?' Esperanza asked Sister Gloria, who was speechless. 'Good morning to you, too, Sister,' Esperanza said, sashaying her way down the hall – such as it was possible to *sashay* in a skimpy, tight towel. In fact, the tightness of the towel caused Esperanza to stride ahead with small, mincing steps – yet she managed to walk fairly fast.

'*What* naked boy?' Sister Gloria asked Lupe. The little vagabond sat stone-faced on the bed; Lupe pointed to the open bathroom door.

'"Come sit down beside me and hear my sad story,"' someone was singing. '"Got shot in the breast, and I know I must die."'

Sister Gloria hesitated; upon the cessation of the '¡Madre!' prayer and Esperanza's scantily covered exit, the hatchet-faced nun could hear what she

thought were voices coming from the dump kids'
bathroom. At first, Sister Gloria might have imagined
she'd heard Juan Diego talking (or singing) to himself. But now, rising above the splashing sounds and
the running water, the nun knew she'd been listening to two voices: that chatterbox of a boy from the
Oaxaca basurero, Juan Diego (Brother Pepe's prize
pupil), and what struck Sister Gloria as the voice of a
much older boy or young *man*. What Esperanza had
called a naked *boy* sounded very much to Sister Gloria
like a grown *man* – that was why the nun had hesitated.

The kindergartners, however, had been indoctrinated; the kindergartners were trained to *march*, and
march they did. The kindergartners tramped forward, through the dump kids' bedroom and into the
bathroom.

What else could Sister Gloria *do*? If there were a
young man who, in any fashion, resembled the
Crucified Christ – a Dying Jesus in the dump kids'
bathtub, as Esperanza had described him – wasn't it
Sister Gloria's duty to protect the orphans from what
Lupe had misinterpreted as a *vision* (one that had,
apparently, upset her so)?

As for Lupe herself, she didn't wait around; she
headed for the hallway. '¡Madre!' Sister Gloria
exclaimed, hurrying into the bathroom after the
kindergartners.

'Now and forever, you will be our guide,' the
kindergartners were chanting in the bathroom –
before all the screaming started. Lupe just kept
walking down the hall.

The conversation Juan Diego had been having with the good gringo was very interesting, but – given what happened when the kindergartners marched into the bathroom – it's understandable why Juan Diego (especially, in his later years) had trouble keeping the details straight.

'I don't know why your mom keeps callin' me "kid" – I'm not as young as I look,' el gringo bueno had begun. (Of course he didn't look like a *kid* to Juan Diego, who was only fourteen – Juan Diego *was* a kid – but Juan Diego just nodded.) 'My dad died in the Philippines, in the war – *lots* of Americans died there, but not when my dad did,' the draft dodger continued. 'My dad was *really* unlucky. That kind of luck can run in the family, you know. That was *part* of the reason I didn't think I should go to Vietnam – the bad luck runnin' in the family part – but also I always wanted to go to the Philippines, to see where my dad is buried and to pay my respects, just to say how sorry I was that I never got to meet him, you know.'

Of course Juan Diego just nodded; he was beginning to notice that the tub kept filling, but the water level never changed. Juan Diego realized that the tub was draining and filling in equal amounts; the hippie had probably knocked out the plug – he kept slipping and sliding around on his tattooed bare ass. He also kept putting more and more shampoo in his hair, until the shampoo was all gone, and the suds from the shampoo rose all around the slippery gringo; the Crucified Christ had completely disappeared.

'Corregidor, May 1942 – that was the culmination

of a battle in the Philippines,' the hippie was saying. 'The Americans got wiped out. A month before had been the Bataan Death March – sixty-five fuckin' miles after the U.S. surrender. A lot of American prisoners didn't make it. This is why there's such a big American cemetery and memorial in the Philippines – it's in Manila. That's where I gotta go and tell my dad I love him. I can't go to Vietnam, and die there, before I can visit my dad,' the young American said.

'I see,' was all Juan Diego said.

'I thought I could convince them I was a pacifist,' the good gringo went on; he was completely covered in shampoo, the spade-shaped patch of beard under his lower lip excepted. This tuft of dark hair seemed to be the only place where the boy's beard grew; he looked too young to need to shave the rest of his face, but he'd been running away from the draft for three years. He told Juan Diego he was twenty-six; they'd tried to draft him after he finished college, when he'd been twenty-three. That was when he got the Agonizing Christ tattoo: to convince the U.S. Army that he was a pacifist. Naturally, the religious tattoo didn't work.

In an expression of anti-patriotic hostility, the good gringo then got his ass tattooed – the American flag, apparently ripped in two by the crack in his ass – and fled to Mexico.

'This is what pretendin' to be a pacifist will get you – three years on the lam,' the gringo was saying. 'But just look what happened to my poor dad: he was younger than I am when they sent him to the

Philippines. The war was almost over, but he was among the amphibious troops who recaptured Corregidor – February 1945. You can die when you're *winnin'* a war, you know – same as you can die when you're losin'. But is that bad luck, or what?'

'It's bad luck,' Juan Diego agreed.

'I'll say it is – I was born in '44, just a few months before my dad was killed. He never saw me,' the good gringo said. 'My mom doesn't even know if he saw my baby pictures.'

'I'm sorry,' Juan Diego said. He was kneeling on the bathroom floor, beside the bathtub. Juan Diego was as impressionable as most fourteen-year-olds; he thought the American hippie was the most fascinating young man he'd ever met.

'Man on wheels,' the gringo said, touching Juan Diego's hand with his shampoo-covered fingers. 'Promise me somethin', man on wheels.'

'Sure,' Juan Diego said; after all, he'd just made a couple of absurd promises to Lupe.

'If anythin' happens to me, you gotta go to the Philippines for me – you gotta tell my dad I'm sorry,' el gringo bueno said.

'Sure – yes, I will,' Juan Diego said.

For the first time, the hippie looked surprised. 'You *will*?' he asked Juan Diego.

'Yes, I will,' the dump reader repeated.

'Whoa! Man on wheels! I guess I need more friends like you,' the gringo told him. At that point, he slid entirely under the water and the shampoo suds; the hippie and his Bleeding Jesus had completely disappeared when the kindergartners, followed by the outraged Sister Gloria, marched into the bathroom, to the relentless chanting of '¡Madre!' and 'Now and forever—' not to mention the 'you will be my guide' inanity.

'Well, where is he?' Sister Gloria asked Juan Diego. 'There's no naked boy here. *What* naked boy?' the nun repeated; she didn't notice the bubbles under the bathwater (not with all the shampoo suds), but one of the kindergartners pointed to the bubbles, and Sister Gloria suddenly looked where the alert child was pointing.

That was when the sea monster rose from the frothy water. One can only guess that this is what the tattooed hippie and the Crucified Christ (or a shampoo-covered convergence of the two) looked like to the indoctrinated kindergartners: a *religious* sea monster. And, in all probability, the good gringo thought that his emergence from the bathwater should be of some entertainment value; after he'd just told Juan Diego such a heavy-hearted story, maybe the draft dodger sought to change the mood of the moment. We'll never know what the crazy hippie had intended by *flinging* himself upward from the bottom of the bathtub, spouting water like a whale and extending his arms to either side of the tub – as if *he* were as nailed-to-the-cross, and dying, as the Bleeding Jesus tattooed on the naked boy's heaving chest. And what possessed the tall boy – what made him decide to stand up in the bathtub, so that he towered over everyone and made his nakedness all the more apparent? Well, we'll never know what el gringo bueno was thinking, or even *if* he was thinking. (The young American runaway was not known on Zaragoza Street for *rational* behavior.)

To be fair: the hippie had submerged himself when he and Juan Diego were alone in the bathroom; the good gringo had no idea, when he rose out of the water, that he was emerging to a multitude – not to mention that most of them were five-year-olds who believed in Jesus. The fact that the little children were there was not this Jesus's fault.

'Whoa!' cried the Crucified Christ – he looked more like the *Drowned* Christ at the moment, and the *whoa* word was a foreign-sounding one to the Spanish-speaking kindergartners.

Four or five of the terrified children instantly wet their pants; one little girl shrieked so loudly that several girls and boys bit their tongues. Those kinder-gartners nearest the door to the bedroom bolted through the bedroom, screaming, and raced into the hall. Those children who must have believed there was no escape from the gringo Christ fell to their knees, peeing and crying, and covered their heads with their hands; one little boy hugged a little girl so hard that she bit him in the face.

Sister Gloria had swooned, catching her balance by putting one hand on the bathtub, but the hippie Jesus, who feared that the nun was falling, wrapped his wet arms around her. 'Whoa, Sister—' was all the young man managed to say, before Sister Gloria beat against the naked boy's chest with both her fists. She landed several blows on the Heaven-beseeching and tortured face of the Jesus tattoo, but when she saw (with horror) what she was doing, Sister Gloria threw up her arms and lifted her eyes in her own most Heaven-beseeching manner.

'¡Madre!' Sister Gloria once more cried, as if Mother Mary were the nun's single savior and confidante – truly, as the nun's responsive prayer maintained, her one and only guide.

That was when el gringo bueno slipped and fell forward into the bathtub; the soapy water sloshed over the sides of the tub, drenching the bathroom floor. The hippie, now on his hands and knees, had enough presence of mind to turn off the running water. The tub, at last, could drain, but as the water quickly receded, those kindergartners still in the bathroom – for the most part, they'd been too afraid to run away – saw the emerging American flag (torn in two) on the gringo Christ's bare ass.

Sister Gloria saw the flag, too – a tattoo of such secular certainty that it clashed with the tattoo of the Agonizing Jesus. To the instinctively disapproving nun, a satanic discord seemed to emanate from the naked boy in the emptying tub.

Juan Diego had not moved. He knelt on the bathroom floor, the spilled bathwater touching his thighs. Around him, the cringing kindergartners lay curled in wet balls. It must have been the future writer developing in him, but Juan Diego thought of the amphibious troops killed in recapturing Corregidor, some of them not much older than children. He thought of the wild promise he'd made to the good gringo, and he was thrilled – the way, at fourteen, you can be thrilled by an utterly unrealistic vision of the future.

'Ahora y siempre – now and forever,' one of the soaking-wet kindergartners was whimpering.

'Now and forever,' Juan Diego said, more confidently. He knew this was a promise to himself – to seize every opportunity that looked like the future, from this moment forward.

14

Nada

In the corridor outside Edward Bonshaw's classroom at Niños Perdidos was a bust of the Virgin Mary with a tear on her cheek. The bust stood on a pedestal in a corner of the second-floor balcony. There was often a beet-red smudge on Mary's other cheek; it looked like blood to Esperanza – every week she wiped it off, but the next week it was back. 'Maybe it *is* blood,' she'd told Brother Pepe.

'It can't be,' Pepe told her. 'There have been no reported stigmata cases at Lost Children.'

On the landing between the first and second floors was the suffer-the-little-children statue of San Vicente de Paul with two infants in his arms. Esperanza reported to Brother Pepe that she'd also wiped blood off the hem of the saint's cloak. 'Every week I wipe it off, but it comes back!' Esperanza had said. 'It must be *miraculous* blood.'

'It can't be blood, Esperanza,' was all Pepe would say about it.

'You don't know what I see, Pepe!' Esperanza said, pointing to her fiery eyes. 'And whatever it is, it leaves a stain.'

They were both right. It was not blood, but every week it came back *and* it left a stain. The dump kids had had to lie low with the beet juice after the episode with the good gringo in their bathtub; they'd had to cut back on their nighttime visits to Zaragoza Street, too. Señor Eduardo and Brother Pepe – not to mention that witch Sister Gloria and the other nuns – were keeping a close eye on them. And Lupe was right about the gifts el gringo bueno could afford for them: they were less than outstanding presents.

The hippie had no doubt haggled over the cheap religious figures he'd bought from the Christmas-parties place, the virgin shop on Independencia. One was a small totem, in the category of a statuette – more of a figurine than a lifelike figure – but the Guadalupe virgin was life-size.

The Guadalupe virgin was actually a little bigger than Juan Diego. She was his present. Her blue-green mantle – a kind of cloak or cape – was traditional. Her belt, or what looked like a black girdle, would one day give rise to the speculation that Guadalupe was pregnant. Long after the fact, in 1999, Pope John Paul II invoked Our Lady of Guadalupe as Patroness of the Americas and Protectress of Unborn Children. ('That Polish pope,' Juan Diego would later rail against him – and his unborn business.)

The virgin-shop Guadalupe didn't look pregnant, but this Guadalupe mannequin appeared to be about fifteen or sixteen – and she had breasts. The boobs made her seem not religious at all. 'She's a sex doll!' Lupe immediately said.

Of course, that wasn't strictly true; there was, however, a sex-doll aspect to the Guadalupe figure, though Juan Diego could not undress her and she didn't have movable limbs (or recognizable reproductive parts).

'What's *my* present?' Lupe asked the hippie boy.

The good gringo asked Lupe if she forgave him for sleeping with her mother. 'Yes,' Lupe said, 'but we can't ever get married.'

'That sounds pretty final,' the hippie said, when Juan Diego translated Lupe's answer to the forgiveness question.

'Show me the present,' was all Lupe said.

It was a Coatlicue figurine, as ugly as any replica of the goddess. Juan Diego thought it was a blessing that the hideous statuette was small – it was even smaller than Dirty White. El gringo bueno had no clue how to pronounce the name of the Aztec goddess; Lupe, in her hard-to-follow fashion, couldn't manage to help him say it.

'Your mom said you *admired* this weird mother goddess,' the good gringo explained to Lupe; he didn't sound so sure.

'I *love* her,' Lupe told him.

Juan Diego had always found it hard to believe that one goddess could have so many contradictory attributes attached to her, but it was easy for him to see why Lupe loved her. Coatlicue was an extremist – a goddess of childbirth *and* of sexual impurity and wrongful behavior. Several creation myths were connected to her; in one, she was impregnated by a ball of feathers that fell on her while she was sweeping a temple – enough to piss anyone off, Juan Diego thought, but Lupe said this was the kind of thing she could imagine happening to their mother, Esperanza.

Unlike Esperanza, Coatlicue wore a skirt of serpents. She was basically dressed in writhing snakes; she wore a necklace of human hearts and hands and skulls. Coatlicue's hands and feet had claws; her breasts were flaccid. In the figurine the good gringo gave to Lupe, Coatlicue's nipples were made of rattlesnake rattles. ('Too much nursing, maybe,' Lupe observed.)

'But what do you *like* about her, Lupe?' Juan Diego had asked his sister.

'Some of her own children vowed to kill her,' Lupe had answered him. 'Una mujer difícil.' A difficult woman.

'Coatlicue is a devouring mother; the womb and the grave coexist in her,' Juan Diego explained to the hippie boy.

'I can see that,' the good gringo said. 'She looks *deadly*, man on wheels,' the hippie more confidently stated.

'Nobody messes with her!' Lupe proclaimed.

Even Edward Bonshaw (always looking on the bright side) found Lupe's Coatlicue figurine frightening. 'I understand there are repercussions that come from the ball-of-feathers mishap, but this goddess is not very sympathetic-looking,' Señor Eduardo said to Lupe, as respectfully as anyone possibly could.

'Coatlicue didn't ask to be born who she was,' Lupe answered the Iowan. 'She was sacrificed – supposedly to do with creation. Her face was formed by two serpents – after her head was cut off and the blood spurted from her neck in the form of two gigantic snakes. Some of us,' Lupe told the new missionary, pausing for Juan Diego's translation to catch up, 'don't have a choice about who we are.'

'But—' Edward Bonshaw began.

'I am who I am,' Lupe said; Juan Diego rolled his eyes when he repeated this to Señor Eduardo. Lupe pressed the grotesque Coatlicue totem to her cheek; it was apparent that she didn't just love the goddess because the good gringo had given her the statuette.

As for his gift from the gringo, Juan Diego would occasionally masturbate with the Guadalupe doll lying next to him on his bed, her enraptured face on the pillow alongside his face. The slight swell of Guadalupe's breasts sufficed.

The impassive mannequin was made of a light but hard plastic, unyielding to the touch. Although the Guadalupe virgin was a couple of inches taller than Juan Diego, she was hollow – she weighed so little that Juan Diego could carry her under one arm.

There was a twofold awkwardness attached to Juan Diego's attempts to have sex with the life-size Guadalupe doll – better said, the awkwardness of Juan Diego's *imagining* he was having sex with the plastic virgin. In the first place, it was necessary for Juan Diego to be alone in the bedroom he shared with his little sister – not to mention that Lupe knew her brother *thought* about having sex with the Guadalupe doll; Lupe had read his mind.

The second problem was the pedestal. The fetching feet of the Guadalupe virgin were affixed to a pedestal of chartreuse-colored grass, which was the circumference of an automobile tire. The pedestal was an impediment to Juan Diego's desire to *snuggle* with the plastic virgin when he was lying next to her.

Juan Diego had thought about sawing off the pedestal, but this meant removing the virgin's pretty feet at her ankles, which would mean the statue couldn't stand. Naturally, Lupe had known her brother's thoughts.

'I don't ever want to see Our Lady of Guadalupe lying down,' Lupe told Juan Diego, '*or* leaning up against our bedroom wall. Don't even *think about* standing her on her head in a corner, with the stumps of her amputated feet sticking up!'

'*Look* at her, Lupe!' Juan Diego cried. He pointed to the Guadalupe figure, standing by one of the bookshelves in the former reading room; the Guadalupe mannequin looked a little like a misplaced literary character, a woman who'd escaped from a novel – one who couldn't find her way back to the book where she belonged. '*Look* at her,' Juan Diego repeated. 'Does Guadalupe strike you as being even slightly interested in lying down?'

As luck would have it, Sister Gloria was passing by the dump kids' bedroom; the nun peered into their room from the hall. Sister Gloria had objected to the life-size Guadalupe doll's presence in the niños' bedroom – more unmerited *privileges*, the sister had presumed – but Brother Pepe had defended the dump kids. How could the disapproving nun disapprove of a *religious* statue? Sister Gloria believed Juan Diego's Guadalupe figure more closely resembled a dressmaker's dummy – 'a suggestive one,' was the way the nun put it to Pepe.

'I don't want to hear another word about Our Lady of Guadalupe *lying down*,' Sister Gloria said to Juan Diego. The virgins from La Niña de las Posadas were not *proper* virgins, Sister Gloria was thinking. The proprietors of The Girl of the Christmas Parties and Sister Gloria did not see eye to eye concerning what Our Lady of Guadalupe looked like – not like a sexual temptation, Sister Gloria thought, not like a *seductress*!

IT WAS, ALAS, *THIS* memory – among all the others – that woke Juan Diego from his dream in the suddenly stifling heat of his hotel room at the Makati Shangri-La. But how was it possible for that refrigerator of a hotel room to be *hot*?

The dead fish floated on the surface of the green-lit water in the becalmed aquarium; the previously upright-swimming sea horse was no longer vertical, its lifeless prehensile tail signifying that it had joined (forever) those lost members of its family of pipefish. Had the aquarium's water-bubble problem returned? Or had one of the dead fish clogged the water-circulation system? The fish tank had ceased gurgling; the water was unmoving and murky, yet a pair of yellowish eyes stared at Juan Diego from the clouded bottom of the aquarium. The moray – his gills gulping in the remaining oxygen – appeared to be the sole survivor of the disaster.

Uh-oh, Juan Diego was remembering: he'd returned from dinner to a freezing-cold hotel room; the air-conditioning was once more blasting. The hotel maid must have cranked it up – she'd also left the radio on. Juan Diego couldn't figure out how to turn the relentless music off; he'd been forced to unplug the clock radio to kill the throbbing sound.

And the maid wasn't easily satisfied: she'd seen how he'd prepared his beta-blockers for his proper dose; the maid had laid out *all* his medications (his Viagra, too) *and* the pill cutter. This both irritated and distracted Juan Diego – it didn't help that he discovered the maid's interfering attention to his toilet articles and his pills only after he'd unplugged the clock radio and had drunk one of the four *Spanish* beers in the ice bucket. Was San Miguel ubiquitous in Manila?

In the harsh light of the aquarium calamity, Juan Diego saw there was only *one* beer bobbing in the tepid water in the ice bucket. Did he drink *three* beers after dinner? And when had he turned the air-conditioning completely *off*? Maybe he'd woken up with his teeth chattering, and (half frozen to death, and half asleep) he'd shivered his way to the thermostat on the bedroom wall.

Keeping a watchful eye on Señor Morales, Juan Diego quickly dipped an index finger in and out of the aquarium; the South China Sea was never this warm. The water in the fish tank was nearly as hot as a slowly simmering bouillabaisse.

Oh, dear – what have I done? Juan Diego wondered. And such vivid dreams! Not usual – not with the right dose of the beta-blockers.

Uh-oh, he was remembering – uh-oh, uh-oh! He limped to the bathroom. The power of suggestion would reveal itself there. He'd apparently used the pill-cutting device to cut a Lopressor tablet in half; he'd taken *half* the right dose. (At least he'd not taken half a Viagra instead!) A double dose of the beta-blockers the night before, and only a half-dose last night – what would Dr. Rosemary Stein have said to her friend about that?

'Not good, not good,' Juan Diego was muttering to himself when he walked back into the overheated bedroom.

The three empty bottles of San Miguel confronted him; they resembled small but inflexible bodyguards on the TV table, as if they were defending the remote. Oh, yes, Juan Diego remembered; he'd sat stupefied (for how long, after dinner?) watching the obliteration-to-blackness of the limping terrorist in Mindanao. By the time he'd gone to bed, after the three ice-cold beers and the air-conditioning, his *brain* must have been refrigerated; half a Lopressor tablet was no match for Juan Diego's dreams.

He remembered how hot and humid it had been outside on the street when Bienvenido drove him back to the Makati Shangri-La from the restaurant;

Juan Diego's shirt had stuck to his back. The bomb-sniffing dogs had been panting in the hotel entranceway. It upset Juan Diego that the night-shift bomb-sniffers weren't the dogs he knew; the security guards were different, too.

The hotel manager had described the aquarium's underwater thermometer as 'most delicate'; maybe he'd meant to say *thermostat*? In an air-conditioned hotel room, wasn't it the underwater thermostat's job to keep the seawater warm enough for those former residents of the South China Sea? When Juan Diego had turned off the air-conditioning, the thermostat's job had changed. Juan Diego had cooked an aquarium of Auntie Carmen's exotic pets; only the angry-looking moray eel was clinging to life among his dead and floating friends. Couldn't the thermostat also keep the seawater *cool* enough?

'Lo siento, Señor Morales,' Juan Diego said again. The eel's overworked gills weren't merely undulating – they were flapping.

Juan Diego called the hotel manager to report the massacre; Auntie Carmen's store for exotic pets in Makati City had to be alerted. Maybe Morales could be saved, if the pet-store crew came quickly enough – if they disassembled the aquarium and revived the moray in fresh seawater.

'Maybe the moray needs to be sedated for traveling,' the hotel manager suggested. (From the way Señor Morales was staring at him, Juan Diego thought the moray would not take kindly to sedation.)

Juan Diego turned on the air-conditioning before

he left his hotel room in search of breakfast. At the doorway to his room, he took what he hoped would be a last look at the loaned aquarium – the fish tank of death. Mr. Morals watched Juan Diego leave, as if the moray couldn't wait to see the writer again – preferably, when Juan Diego was on his deathbed.

'Lo siento, Señor Morales,' Juan Diego said once more, letting the door close softly behind him. But when he found himself alone in the stifling stink-box of an elevator – naturally, there was no air-conditioning there – Juan Diego shouted as loudly as he could. '*Fuck* Clark French!' he cried. 'And fuck *you*, Auntie Carmen – whoever the fuck you are!' Juan Diego yelled.

He stopped shouting when he saw that the sur-veillance camera was pointed right at him; the camera was mounted above the bank of the elevator buttons, but Juan Diego didn't know if the surveillance camera also recorded *sound*. With or without his actual words, the writer could imagine the hotel security guards watching the lunatic cripple – alone and screaming in the descending elevator.

The hotel manager found the Distinguished Guest as he was finishing breakfast. 'Those unfortunate fish, sir – they've been taken care of. The pet-store team, come and gone – they wore surgical masks,' the man-ager confided to Juan Diego, lowering his voice at the *surgical-masks* part. (No need to alarm the other guests; talk of surgical masks might imply a contagion.)

'Perhaps you heard if the moray—' Juan Diego started to say.

'The eel survived. Hard to kill, I imagine,' the manager said. 'But very *agitated*.'

'*How* agitated?' Juan Diego asked.

'There was a biting, sir – not serious, I'm told, but
there was a bite. It drew blood,' the manager confided,
again lowering his voice.

'A bite *where*?' Juan Diego asked.

'A cheek.'

'A *cheek*!'

'Not serious, sir. I saw the man's face. It will heal
– not a bad scar, just *unfortunate*.'

'Yes – *unfortunate*,' was all Juan Diego could say. He
didn't dare ask if Auntie Carmen had come and gone
with the pet-store team. With any luck, she'd left
Manila for Bohol – she might be in Bohol, waiting to
meet him (with the Filipino side of Clark French's
whole family). Naturally, word of the slain fish would
reach Auntie Carmen in Bohol – including the report
on the *agitated* Señor Morales, and the *unfortunate*
pet-store worker's bitten cheek.

What is happening to me? Juan Diego wondered,
upon returning to his hotel room. He saw there was a
towel on the floor by the bed – doubtless where some
of the seawater from the aquarium had spilled. (Juan
Diego imagined the moray thrashing his tail and
attacking the face of his frightened handler, but there
was no blood on the towel.)

The writer was about to use the toilet when he
spotted the tiny sea horse on the bathroom floor; the
sea horse was so small that it must have escaped
the attention of the pet-store team, at that moment

when the little creature's fellow fish were flushed away. The sea horse's round and startled eyes still seemed alive; in its miniature and prehistoric face, the fierce eyes expressed an indignation at all human-kind – like the eyes of a hunted dragon.

'Lo siento, caballo marino,' Juan Diego said, before he flushed the sea horse down the toilet.

Then he was angry – angry at himself, at the Makati Shangri-La, at the servile wheedling of the hotel manager. The fashion plate with his fussy mustache had given Juan Diego a brochure of the Manila American Cemetery and Memorial, a publication of the American Battle Monuments Commission, Juan Diego had learned (in a cursory reading of the little brochure, on the elevator after breakfast).

Who had told the busybody hotel manager that Juan Diego had a personal interest in the Manila American Cemetery and Memorial? Even Bienvenido knew Juan Diego intended to visit the graves of those Americans lost to 'operations' in the Pacific.

Had Clark French (or his Filipino wife) told *everyone* about Juan Diego's intentions to pay his respects to the good gringo's hero father? Juan Diego had, for years, possessed a *private* reason for coming to Manila. Leave it to the well-meaning Clark French, in his devoted way, to make Juan Diego's mission in Manila a matter of public knowledge!

Naturally, Juan Diego was angry at Clark French. Juan Diego had no desire to go to Bohol; he barely understood what or where Bohol was. But Clark had insisted that his revered mentor couldn't be alone in Manila for New Year's Eve.

'For God's sake, Clark – I've been alone in Iowa City for most of my *life*!' Juan Diego had said. 'Once *you* were alone in Iowa City!'

Ah, well – perhaps the well-meaning Clark hoped Juan Diego might meet a future *wife* in the Philippines. Just look what had happened to Clark! Hadn't *he* met someone? Wasn't Clark French (possibly *because of* his Filipino wife) insanely happy? Truthfully, Clark had been insanely happy when he was alone in Iowa City. Clark was *religiously* happy, Juan Diego suspected.

It might have been the wife's Filipino family – maybe *they* had made a big deal of inviting Juan Diego to Bohol. But in Juan Diego's opinion, Clark was capable of making a big deal out of the invitation all by himself.

Every year, Clark French's Filipino family occupied a seaside resort at a beach near Panglao Bay; they took over the whole hotel for a few days following Christmas, through New Year's Day and the day after.

'Every room in the hotel is *ours* – no strangers!' Clark had told Juan Diego.

I'm a stranger, you idiot! Juan Diego had thought. Clark French would be the only person he knew. Naturally, Juan Diego's image as a murderer of precious underwater life would precede him to Bohol. Auntie Carmen would know everything; Juan Diego didn't doubt that the exotic-pet person would (somehow) have *communicated* with the moray. If Señor Morales had been *agitated*, there was no telling what

Juan Diego should expect for *agitation* from Auntie Carmen – a likely *Mrs.* Morals.

As for his rising anger, Juan Diego knew what his beloved physician and dear friend, Dr. Rosemary Stein, would say. She would surely have pointed out to him that anger of the kind he'd vented in the elevator, and was still experiencing now, was an indication that half a Lopressor tablet wasn't enough.

Was not the level of anger he was feeling a sure sign that his body was making more adrenaline, and more adrenaline receptors? Yes. And, yes, there was a lethargy that came with the right dose of the beta-blockers – and the reduced blood circulation to the extremities gave Juan Diego cold hands and feet. And, yes, a Lopressor pill (the *whole* pill, not a half) could potentially give him as disturbed and vivid dreams as he'd had when he went off the beta-blockers altogether. This was truly confusing.

Yet he not only had very high blood pressure (170 over 100). Hadn't one of Juan Diego's *possible* fathers died of a heart attack at a young age – if Juan Diego's mother could be believed?

And then there was what had happened to Esperanza – I hope *not* my next disturbing dream! Juan Diego thought, knowing that the idea would lodge in his mind, making it all the more likely to be the case. Besides, what had happened to Esperanza – in Juan Diego's dreams *and* in his memory – was recurrent.

'No stopping it,' Juan Diego said aloud. He was

still in the bathroom, still recovering from the flushed-away sea horse, when he saw the untaken half of the Lopressor tablet and swallowed it quickly, with a glass of water.

Was Juan Diego consciously welcoming a diminished feeling for the rest of the day? And if he took a full dose of his beta-blockers later tonight in Bohol, wouldn't Juan Diego once more experience the ennui, the inertia, the sheer sluggishness, he'd so often complained about to Dr. Stein?

I should call Rosemary right away, Juan Diego thought. He knew he'd tampered with the dosage of his beta-blockers; he may even have known he was inclined to keep altering the dose, in an on-and-off fashion, because of his temptation to manipulate the results. He knew perfectly well he was *supposed* to block the adrenaline, but he missed the adrenaline in his life, and – he also knew – he wanted *more* of it. There was no good reason why Juan Diego *didn't* call Dr. Stein.

What was really going on here is that Juan Diego understood, very well, what Dr. Rosemary Stein would say to him about *playing* with his adrenaline and adrenaline receptors. (He just didn't want to hear it.) And because Juan Diego understood, very well, that Clark French was one of those people who knew everything – Clark was either all-knowing or poised to find out about anything – Juan Diego made an effort to memorize the most conspicuous inform-ation in the tourist brochure about the Manila American Cemetery and Memorial. Anyone would have thought that Juan Diego had already visited the place.

In fact, in the limo with Bienvenido, Juan Diego was tempted to say he'd been there. (*There was a World War II veteran staying at the hotel – I went with him. He'd come ashore with MacArthur – you know, when the general returned in October 1944. MacArthur landed at Leyte,* Juan Diego almost told Bienvenido.) But instead he said: 'I'll go see the cemetery another time. I want to take a look at a couple of hotels – places to stay when I come back. A friend recommended them.'

'Sure – you're the boss,' Bienvenido told him.

In the brochure about the Manila American Cemetery and Memorial, there'd been a photo of General Douglas MacArthur striding ashore at Leyte in the knee-deep water.

There were more than seventeen thousand head-stones in the cemetery; Juan Diego had committed this figure to memory – not to mention more than thirty-six thousand 'missing in action' but fewer than four thousand 'unknowns.' Juan Diego was dying to tell someone what he knew, but he restrained himself from telling Bienvenido.

More than one thousand U.S. military were killed in the Battle of Manila – at about the same time those amphibious troops were recapturing Corregidor Island, the good gringo's lost dad among the fallen heroes – but what if one or more of Bienvenido's relatives had been killed in the month-long Battle of Manila, when one hundred thousand Filipino civilians died?

Juan Diego did ask Bienvenido what he knew about
the headstone locations in the vast cemetery – more
than 150 acres! Juan Diego wondered if there was a
specific area for the U.S. soldiers killed at Corregidor,
either in '42 or '45. The brochure made mention of a
specific memorial for the servicemen who lost their
lives at Guadalcanal, and Juan Diego knew there
were as many as eleven burial plots. (However, not
knowing the good gringo's name – or the name of his
slain father – was a problem.)

'I think you tell them the soldier's name, and they
tell you which plot, which row, which grave,'
Bienvenido answered. 'You just tell them the name
– that's how it works.'

'I see,' was all Juan Diego said. The driver kept
glancing at the tired-looking writer in the rearview
mirror. Maybe he thought Juan Diego looked like
he'd had a bad night's sleep. But Bienvenido didn't
know about the aquarium murders, and the youthful
driver didn't understand that the slumped-over way
Juan Diego was sitting in the limo's rear seat was just
an indication that the second half of the Lopressor
pill was beginning to take effect.

THE SOFITEL, WHERE BIENVENIDO drove him, was in
the Pasay City part of Manila – even from his
slumped-over position in the limo's rear seat, Juan
Diego noticed the bomb-sniffing dogs.

'It's the buffet you have to worry about,' Bienvenido
told him. 'That's what I hear about the Sofitel.'

'What about the buffet?' Juan Diego asked. The

prospect of food poisoning seemed to perk him up. But that wasn't it: Juan Diego knew he could learn a lot from limo drivers; trips to those foreign-language countries where he was published had taught him to pay attention to his drivers.

'I know where every men's room in the vicinity of every hotel lobby or hotel restaurant is,' Bienvenido was saying. 'If you're a professional driver, you have to know these things.'

'Where to take a leak, you mean,' Juan Diego said; he'd heard this from other drivers. 'What about the buffet?'

'If there's a choice, the men's room the hotel restaurant-goers use is a better men's room than the one in the area of the hotel lobby – *usually*,' Bienvenido explained. 'Not here.'

'The buffet,' Juan Diego repeated.

'I've seen people barfing in the urinals; I've heard them shitting their brains out in the toilet stalls,' Bienvenido warned him.

'Here? At the Sofitel? And you're sure it's the buffet?' Juan Diego asked.

'Maybe the food sits out forever. Who knows how long the shrimp has been lying around at room temperature? I'll bet it's the buffet!' Bienvenido exclaimed.

'I see,' was all Juan Diego said. Too bad, he thought – the Sofitel looked as if it might be nice. Miriam must have liked the hotel for some reason; maybe she'd never tried the buffet. Maybe Bienvenido was wrong.

They drove away from the Sofitel without Juan
Diego setting foot inside the place. The other hotel
Miriam had suggested was the Ascott.

'You should have mentioned the Ascott first,'
Bienvenido said, sighing. 'It's on Glorietta, back in
Makati City. The Ayala Center is right there – you can
get anything there,' Bienvenido told him.

'What do you mean?' Juan Diego asked.

'Miles and miles of shopping – it's a shopping mall.
There are escalators and elevators – there's every kind
of restaurant,' Bienvenido was saying.

Cripples aren't crazy about shopping malls, Juan
Diego was thinking, but all he said was: 'And the
hotel itself, the Ascott? No reported deaths by
buffet?'

'The Ascott is fine – you should have stayed there
the first time,' Bienvenido told him.

'Don't get me started on *should* have, Bienvenido,'
Juan Diego said; his novels had been called *should-
have* and *what-if* propositions.

'Next time, then,' Bienvenido said.

They drove back to Makati City, so that Juan Diego
could make an in-person reservation at the Ascott for
his return trip to Manila. Juan Diego would ask Clark
French to cancel his reservation at the Makati
Shangri-La for him; after the aquarium Armageddon,
all parties would doubtless be relieved by the return-
trip cancellation.

You took an elevator from the street-level entrance
of the Ascott to the hotel lobby, which was on an
upper floor. At the elevators, both at street level and

in the lobby, there were a couple of anxious-looking security guards with two bomb-sniffing dogs.

He didn't tell Bienvenido, but Juan Diego adored the dogs. As he made his reservation, Juan Diego could imagine Miriam checking in at the Ascott. It was a long walk to the registration desk from where the elevators opened into the lobby; Juan Diego knew that the security guards would be watching Miriam the whole way. You had to be blind, or a bomb-sniffing dog, not to watch Miriam walk away from you – you would be compelled to watch her every step of the way.

What is happening to me? Juan Diego wondered again. His thoughts, his memories – what he imagined, what he dreamed – were all jumbled up. And he was obsessed with Miriam and Dorothy.

Juan Diego sank into the rear seat of the limo like a stone into an unseen pond.

'We *end up* in Manila,' Dorothy had said; Juan Diego wondered if she had somehow meant every-one. Maybe all of us *end up* in Manila, Juan Diego was thinking.

One Single Journey. It sounded like a title. Was it something he'd written, or something he intended to write? The dump reader couldn't remember.

'I would marry this hippie boy, if he smelled better and stopped singing that cowboy song,' Lupe had said. ('Oh, let me die!' she'd also said.)

How he cursed the names the nuns at Niños Perdidos had called his mother! Juan Diego regretted that he'd called her names, too. '*Des*esperanza' –

'Hopelessness,' the nuns had called Esperanza. 'Desesperación' – 'Desperation,' they'd called her.

'Lo siento, madre,' Juan Diego said softly to himself in the rear seat of the limo – so softly that Bienvenido didn't hear him.

Bienvenido couldn't tell if Juan Diego was awake or asleep. The driver had said something about the airport for domestic flights in Manila – how the check-in lines arbitrarily closed, then spontaneously reopened, and there were extra fees for everything. But Juan Diego didn't respond.

Whether he was awake or asleep, the poor guy seemed out of it, and Bienvenido decided he would walk Juan Diego through the check-in process, despite the hassle he would have to go through with the car.

'It's too cold!' Juan Diego suddenly cried. 'Fresh air, please! No more air-conditioning!'

'Sure – you're the boss,' Bienvenido told him; he shut off the AC and automatically opened the limo's windows. They were near the airport, passing through another shantytown, when Bienvenido stopped the car at a red light.

Before Bienvenido could warn him, Juan Diego found himself beseeched by begging children – their skinny arms, palms up, were suddenly thrust inside the open rear windows of the stopped limo.

'Hello, children,' Juan Diego said, as if he'd been expecting them. (You cannot take the scavenging out of scavengers; los pepenadores carry their picking and sorting with them, long after they've stopped looking for aluminum or copper or glass.)

Before Bienvenido could stop him, Juan Diego was fumbling around with his wallet.

'No, no – give them nothing,' Bienvenido said. 'I mean, not anything. Sir, Juan Diego, please – it will never stop!'

What was this funny currency, anyway? It was like *play* money, Juan Diego thought. He had no change, and only two small bills. He gave the twenty-piso note to the first outstretched hand; he had nothing smaller than a fifty for the second small hand.

'Dalawampung piso!' the first kid cried.

'Limampung piso!' shouted the second child. Was that Tagalog they were speaking? Juan Diego wondered.

Bienvenido stopped him from handing out the one-thousand-piso bill, but one of the beseeching children saw the amount before Bienvenido could block the young beggar's hand.

'Sir, please – that's too much,' the driver told Juan Diego.

'Sanlibong piso!' one of the beseeching children cried.

The other kids quickly took up the cry. 'Sanlibong piso! Sanlibong piso!'

The light turned green, and Bienvenido slowly accelerated; the beggar children withdrew their skinny arms from the car.

'There's no such thing as *too much* for those children, Bienvenido – there's only *not enough* for them,' Juan Diego said. 'I'm a dump kid,' he told the driver. 'I should know.'

'A dump kid, sir?' Bienvenido asked.

'I was a dump kid, Bienvenido,' Juan Diego told him. 'My sister and I – we were niños de la basura. We grew up in the basurero – we virtually lived there. We should never have left – it's been all downhill since!' the dump reader declared.

'Sir—' Bienvenido started to say, but he stopped when he saw that Juan Diego was crying. The bad air of the polluted city was blowing in the open windows of the car; the cooking smells assailed him; the children were begging in the streets; the women, who looked exhausted, wore sleeveless dresses, or shorts with halter tops; the men loitered in doorways, smoking or just talking to one another, as if they didn't have anything to do.

'It's a *slum*!' Juan Diego cried. 'It's a sickening, polluted slum! *Millions* of people who have nothing or not enough to do – yet the Catholics want more and more *babies* to be born!'

He meant Mexico City – at that moment, Manila was forcefully reminding him of Mexico City. 'And just look at the stupid *pilgrims*!' Juan Diego cried. 'They walk on their bleeding knees – they *whip* themselves, to show their devotion!'

Naturally, Bienvenido was confused. He thought Juan Diego meant Manila. *What* pilgrims? the limousine driver was thinking. But all he said was: 'Sir, it's just a small shantytown – it's not exactly a slum. I will admit the pollution is a problem—'

'Watch out!' Juan Diego cried, but Bienvenido was a good driver. He'd seen the boy fall out of the overfull and moving jeepney; the jeepney driver never noticed – he just kept going – but the boy rolled (or he was pushed) off one of the rear rows of seats. He fell into the street; Bienvenido had to swerve the car not to run over him.

The boy was a dirty-faced urchin with what appeared to be a ratty-looking stole (or a fur boa) draped over his neck and shoulders; the shabby-looking garment was like something an old woman in a cold climate might wrap around her neck. But when the boy fell, both Bienvenido and Juan Diego could see that the furry scarf was actually a small dog, and the dog, not the boy, was the one injured in the fall. The dog yelped; the dog could not put weight on one of its forepaws, which it tremblingly held off the ground. The boy had skinned one of his bare knees, which was bleeding, but he seemed otherwise unhurt – he was chiefly concerned for the dog.

GOD IS GOOD! the sticker on the jeepney had said. Not to this boy, or his dog, Juan Diego thought.

'Stop – we must stop,' Juan Diego said, but Bienvenido just kept going.

'Not here, sir – not now,' the young driver said. 'The checking-in part at the airport – it takes longer than your flight.'

'God *isn't* good,' Juan Diego told him. 'God is indifferent. Ask that boy. Speak to his dog.'

'*What* pilgrims?' Bienvenido asked him. 'You said *pilgrims*, sir,' the driver reminded him.

'In Mexico City, there is a street—' Juan Diego began. He closed his eyes, then quickly opened them, as if he didn't want to see this street in Mexico City. 'The pilgrims go there – the street is their approach to a shrine,' Juan Diego continued, but his speech slowed, as if the approach to this shrine was difficult, at least for him.

'What shrine, sir? Which street?' Bienvenido asked him, but now Juan Diego's eyes were closed; he may not have heard the young driver. 'Juan Diego?' the driver asked.

'Avenida de los Misterios,' Juan Diego said, with his eyes closed; the tears were streaming down his face. 'Avenue of Mysteries.'

'It's okay, sir – you don't have to tell me,' Bienvenido said, but Juan Diego had already stopped talking. The crazy old man was somewhere else, Bienvenido could tell – somewhere far away or long ago, or both.

It was a sunny day in Manila; even with his eyes closed, the darkness Juan Diego saw was streaked with light. It was like looking deep underwater. For a moment, he imagined he saw a pair of yellowish eyes staring at him, but there was nothing discernible in the light-streaked darkness.

This is how it will be when I die, Juan Diego was thinking – only darker, pitch-black. No God. No goodness *or* evil. No Señor Morales, in other words. Not a caring God. Not a Mr. Morals, either. Not even a moray eel, struggling to breathe. Just nothing.

'Nada,' Juan Diego said; his eyes were still closed.

Bienvenido didn't say anything; he just drove. But by the way the young driver nodded his head, and in the manifest sympathy with which he regarded his dozing passenger in the rearview mirror, it was obvious that Bienvenido knew the *nothing* word – if not the whole story.

15

The Nose

'I'm not much of a believer,' Juan Diego had once told Edward Bonshaw.

But that had been a fourteen-year-old talking; at first, it was easier for the dump kid to say he wasn't much of a believer than it would have been for him to articulate his distrust of the Catholic Church – especially to as likable a scholastic (in training to be a priest!) as Señor Eduardo.

'Don't say that, Juan Diego – you're too young to cut yourself off from belief,' Edward Bonshaw had said.

In truth, it was not *belief* that Juan Diego lacked. Most dump kids are seekers of miracles. At least Juan Diego wanted to believe in the miraculous, in all sorts of inexplicable mysteries, even if he doubted the miracles the Church wanted everyone to believe – those preexisting miracles, the ones dulled by time.

What the dump reader doubted was the Church: its politics, its social interventions, its manipulations of history and sexual behavior – which would have been difficult for the fourteen-year-old Juan Diego to say in Dr. Vargas's office, where the atheist doctor and the Iowa missionary were squaring off against each other.

Most dump kids are believers; maybe you have to believe in something when you see so many discarded things. And Juan Diego knew what every dump kid (and every orphan) knows: every last thing thrown away, every person or thing that isn't wanted, may have been wanted once – or, in different circumstances, *might* have been wanted.

The dump reader had saved books from burning, *and* he'd actually read the books. Don't ever think a dump reader is incapable of belief. It takes an eternity to read some books, even (or especially) some books saved from burning.

The flight time from Manila to Tagbilaran City, Bohol, was only a little more than an hour, but dreams can seem an eternity. At fourteen, Juan Diego's transition from the wheelchair to walking on crutches, and (eventually) to walking with a limp – well, in reality, this transition had taken an eternity, too, and the boy's memory of that time was jumbled up. All that remained in the dream was the developing rapport between the crippled boy and Edward Bonshaw – their give-and-take, theologically speaking. The boy had backtracked about not being much of a believer, but he'd dug in his heels concerning his disbelief in the Church.

Juan Diego recalled saying, when he was still on the crutches: 'Our Virgin of Guadalupe was not Mary.

Your Virgin Mary was not Guadalupe. This is Catholic mumbo jumbo; this is papal hocus-pocus!' (The two of them had been down this road before.)

'I get your point,' Edward Bonshaw had said, in his seemingly reasonable Jesuitical way. 'I admit there was a delay; a lot of time passed before Pope Benedict the Fourteenth saw a copy of Guadalupe's image on the Indian's cloak and declared that *your* Guadalupe was Mary. That is your point, isn't it?'

'Two hundred years after the fact!' Juan Diego declared, poking Señor Eduardo's foot with one of the crutches. 'Your evangelists from Spain got naked with the Indians, and the next thing you know – well, that's where Lupe and I come from. We're *Zapotecs*, if we're anything. We're *not* Catholics! Guadalupe *isn't* Mary – that imposter.'

'And you're still burning dogs at the dump – Pepe told me,' Señor Eduardo said. 'I don't understand why you think burning the dead is of any *assistance* to them.'

'It's you Catholics who are opposed to cremation,' Juan Diego would point out to the Iowan. On and on they bickered, before and after Brother Pepe drove the dump kids to and from the dump to partake in the eternal dog-burning. (And all the while the circus beckoned the kids away from Niños Perdidos.)

'Look what you did to Christmas – you Catholics,' Juan Diego would say. 'You chose December twenty-fifth as Christ's date of birth, simply to co-opt a pagan feast day. This is my point: you Catholics *co-opt* things.

And did you know there might have been an *actual* Star of Bethlehem? The Chinese reported a nova, an exploding star, in 5 B.C.'

'Where does the boy read this, Pepe?' Edward Bonshaw would repeatedly ask.

'In our library at Lost Children,' Brother Pepe replied. 'Are we supposed to stop him from reading? We *want* him to read, don't we?'

'And there's another thing,' Juan Diego remembered saying – not necessarily in his dream. The crutches were gone; he was just limping. They were somewhere in the zócalo; Lupe was running ahead of them, and Brother Pepe was struggling to keep up with them. Even with the limp, Juan Diego could walk faster than Pepe. 'What is so appealing about celibacy? Why do priests care about being celibate? Aren't priests always telling us what to do and think – I mean *sexually*?' Juan Diego asked. 'Well, how can they have any authority on sexual matters if they don't ever have sex?'

'Are you telling me, Pepe, the boy has learned to question the sexual authority of a celibate clergy from our library at the mission?' Señor Eduardo asked Brother Pepe.

'I think about some stuff I don't read,' Juan Diego remembered saying. 'It just occurs to me, all by myself.' His limp was relatively new; he remembered the newness of it, too.

The limp was still new on the morning Esperanza was dusting the giant Virgin Mary in the Templo de la Compañía de Jesús. Esperanza couldn't come close

to reaching the statue's face without using a ladder.
Usually, Juan Diego or Lupe held the ladder. Not this
morning.

The good gringo had fallen on hard times; Flor had
told the dump kids that el gringo bueno had run out
of money, or he was spending what he had left on
alcohol (not on prostitutes). The prostitutes rarely
saw him anymore. They couldn't look after someone
they hardly saw.

Lupe had said that, somehow, Esperanza was
'responsible' for the hippie boy's deteriorating situation; at least this was how Juan Diego had translated
his sister's words.

'The war in Vietnam is responsible for him,'
Esperanza said; she may or may not have believed
this. Esperanza accepted and repeated as gospel
whatever she'd heard on Zaragoza Street – what the
draft dodgers were saying in defense of themselves,
or what the prostitutes said about those lost young
men from America.

Esperanza had leaned the ladder against the Virgin
Mary. The pedestal was elevated so that Esperanza
stood at eye level with the Mary Monster's enormous
feet. The Virgin, who was *much* larger than life-size,
towered over Esperanza.

'El gringo bueno is fighting his own war now,' Lupe
mysteriously whispered. Then she looked at the
ladder leaning against the towering Virgin. 'Mary
doesn't like the ladder,' was all Lupe said. Juan Diego
translated this, but not the bit about the good gringo
fighting his own war.

'Just hold the ladder so I can dust her,' Esperanza said.

'Better not dust the Mary Monster now – something's bugging the big Virgin today,' Lupe said, but Juan Diego left this untranslated.

'I don't have all day, you know,' Esperanza was saying as she climbed the ladder. Juan Diego was reaching to hold the ladder when Lupe started screaming.

'Her eyes! Look at the giant's eyes!' Lupe screamed, but Esperanza couldn't understand; besides, the cleaning woman was flicking the tip of the Virgin Mary's nose with the feather duster.

That was when Juan Diego saw the Virgin Mary's eyes – they were angry-looking, and they darted from Esperanza's pretty face to her décolletage. Maybe, in the giant Virgin's estimation, Esperanza was showing a little too much cleavage.

'Madre – not her nose, perhaps,' was all Juan Diego managed to say; he'd been reaching for the ladder but he suddenly stopped reaching. The big Virgin's angry eyes darted only once in his direction – enough to freeze him. The Virgin Mary quickly returned her condemning glare to Esperanza's cleavage.

Did Esperanza lose her balance, and attempt to throw her arms around the Mary Monster to stop herself from falling? Had Esperanza then looked into Mary's burning eyes, and let go – more afraid of the giant Virgin's anger than of falling? Esperanza did not fall that hard; she didn't even hit her head. The ladder itself did not fall – Esperanza appeared to push herself (or she was shoved) away from the ladder.

'She died before she fell,' Lupe always said. 'The fall had nothing to do with it.'

Had the big statue itself ever moved? Did the Virgin Mary totter on her pedestal? No and no, the dump kids would say to anyone who asked. But how, exactly, was the Virgin Mary's nose broken off? How had the Holy Mother been rendered noseless? As she was falling, maybe Esperanza hit Mary in the face? Had Esperanza whacked the giant Virgin with the wooden handle of the feather duster? No and no, the dump kids said – not that they'd seen. Talk about someone's nose being 'out of joint'; the Virgin Mary's nose had *broken off*! Juan Diego was looking all around for it. How could such a big nose just disappear?

The big Virgin's eyes were once again opaque and unmoving. No anger remained, only the usual obscurity – an opacity bordering on the bland. And now that the towering statue was without a nose, the giant's unseeing eyes were all the more lifeless.

The dump kids couldn't help but notice that there was more life in Esperanza's wide-open eyes, though the kids certainly knew their mother was dead. They'd known it the instant Esperanza had dropped off the ladder – 'the way a leaf falls from a tree,' Juan Diego would later describe it to that man of science Dr. Vargas.

It was Vargas who explained the findings of Esperanza's autopsy to the dump kids. 'The most likely way to die from fright would be through an arrhythmia,' Vargas began.

'You know she was frightened to death?' Edward Bonshaw had interjected.

'She was definitely frightened to death,' Juan Diego told the Iowan.

'Definitely,' Lupe repeated; even Señor Eduardo and Dr. Vargas understood her one-word utterance.

'If the conduction system of the heart is over-whelmed with adrenaline,' Vargas continued, 'the heart's rhythm will become abnormal – no blood gets pumped, in other words. The name of this most dangerous type of arrhythmia is "ventricular fibrillation"; the muscle cells just twitch – there's no pumping action at all.'

'Then you drop dead, right?' Juan Diego asked.

'Then you drop dead,' Vargas said.

'And this can happen to someone as *young* as Esperanza – someone with a *normal* heart?' Señor Eduardo asked.

'Being young doesn't necessarily help your heart,' Vargas replied. 'I'm sure Esperanza *didn't* have a "normal" heart. Her blood pressure was abnormally high—'

'Her lifestyle, perhaps—' Edward Bonshaw suggested.

'No evidence that prostitution causes heart attacks, except to Catholics,' Vargas said, in that scientific-sounding way he had. 'Esperanza didn't have a "normal" heart. And you kids,' Vargas said, 'will have to watch *your* hearts. At least *you* will, Juan Diego.'

The doctor paused; he was sorting out the business of Juan Diego's *possible* fathers, a seemingly manageable number, as opposed to a purportedly different and vastly greater cast of characters who numbered among *Lupe's* possible fathers. It was, even for an atheist, a delicate pause.

Vargas looked at Edward Bonshaw. '*One* of Juan Diego's possible fathers – I mean, maybe his *most likely* biological father – died of a heart attack,' Vargas said. 'Juan Diego's *possible* dad was very young at the time, or so Esperanza told me,' Vargas added. 'What do you know about this?' Vargas asked the dump kids.

'No more than you know,' Juan Diego told him.

'Rivera knows something – he's just not saying,' Lupe said.

Juan Diego couldn't explain what Lupe said much better. Rivera had told the dump kids that Juan Diego's 'most likely' father died of a *broken* heart.

'A heart attack, right?' Juan Diego had asked el jefe – because that's what Esperanza had told her children, and everyone else.

'If that's what you call a heart that's permanently broken,' was all Rivera had ever said to the kids.

As for the Virgin Mary's nose – ah, well. Juan Diego had spotted la nariz; it was lying near the kneeling pad for the second row of pews. He'd had some difficulty fitting the big nose in his pocket. Lupe's screams would soon bring Father Alfonso and Father Octavio on the run to the Temple of the Society of Jesus. Father Alfonso was already praying over Esperanza by the time that bitch Sister Gloria showed up. Brother Pepe, out of breath, was not far behind the forever-disapproving nun, who seemed irritated by the attention-getting way Esperanza had died – not to mention, even in death, the display of the cleaning woman's cleavage, of which the giant Virgin had been most dramatically condemning.

The dump kids just stood around, waiting to see how long it would take the priests – or Brother Pepe, or Sister Gloria – to notice that the monster Holy Mother was missing her big nose. For the longest time, they didn't notice.

Guess who noticed the missing nose? He came running along the aisle toward the altar, not pausing to genuflect – his untucked Hawaiian shirt resembling a jailbreak of monkeys and tropical birds released from a rain forest by a lightning bolt.

'Bad Mary did it!' Lupe cried to Señor Eduardo. 'Your big Virgin killed our mother! Bad Mary frightened our mother to death!' Juan Diego didn't hesitate to translate this.

'Next thing you know, she'll be calling this accident a *miracle*,' Sister Gloria said to Father Octavio.

'Do not say the *miracle* word to me, Sister,' Father Octavio said.

Father Alfonso was just finishing with the prayers he was saying over Esperanza; it was something about her being freed from her sins.

'Did you say un milagro?' Edward Bonshaw asked Father Octavio.

'¡Milagroso!' Lupe shouted. Señor Eduardo had no trouble understanding the *miraculous* word.

'Esperanza fell off the ladder, Edward,' Father Octavio told the Iowan.

'She was struck dead before she fell!' Lupe was babbling, but Juan Diego left the struck-dead drama untranslated; darting eyes don't kill you, unless you're scared to death.

'Where's Mary's nose?' Edward Bonshaw asked, pointing at the noseless giant Virgin.

'Gone! Vanished in a puff of smoke!' Lupe was raving. 'Keep your eye on Bad Mary – her other parts may start to disappear.'

'Lupe, tell the truth,' Juan Diego said.

But Edward Bonshaw, who hadn't understood a word Lupe said, couldn't take his eyes from the maimed Mary.

'It's just her nose, Eduardo,' Brother Pepe tried to tell the zealot. 'It means nothing – it's probably lying around somewhere.'

'How can it mean *nothing*, Pepe?' the Iowan asked. 'How can the Virgin Mary's nose not be there?'

Father Alfonso and Father Octavio were down on all fours; they weren't praying – they were looking for the Mary Monster's missing nose under the first few rows of pews.

'You wouldn't know anything about la nariz, I suppose?' Brother Pepe asked Juan Diego.

'Nada,' Juan Diego said.

'Bad Mary's eyes moved – she looked alive,' Lupe was saying.

'They'll never believe you, Lupe,' Juan Diego told his sister.

'The parrot man will,' Lupe said, pointing to Señor Eduardo. 'He needs to believe more than he does – he'll believe anything.'

'What won't we believe?' Brother Pepe asked Juan Diego.

'I *thought* that's what he said! What do you mean, Juan Diego?' Edward Bonshaw asked.

'Tell him! Bad Mary moved her eyes – the giant Virgin was looking all around!' Lupe cried.

Juan Diego crammed his hand in his crowded pocket; he was actually holding the Virgin Mary's nose when he told them about the giant Virgin's angry-looking eyes, how they kept darting everywhere but always came back to Esperanza's cleavage.

'It's a miracle,' the Iowan said matter-of-factly.

'Let's get the man of science involved,' Father Alfonso said sarcastically.

'Yes, Vargas can arrange an autopsy,' Father Octavio said.

'You want to autopsy a miracle?' Brother Pepe asked, both innocently and mischievously.

'She was frightened to death – that's all you'll find in an autopsy,' Juan Diego told them, squeezing the Holy Mother's broken nose.

'Bad Mary did it – that's all I know,' Lupe said. True enough, Juan Diego decided; he translated the Bad Mary bit.

'Bad Mary!' Sister Gloria repeated. All of them looked at the noseless Virgin, as if expecting more damage – of one kind or another. But Brother Pepe noticed something about Edward Bonshaw: only the

Iowan was looking at the Virgin Mary's eyes – just her eyes.

Un milagrero, Brother Pepe was thinking as he watched Señor Eduardo – the Iowan is a miracle monger, if I've ever seen one!

Juan Diego wasn't thinking at all. He had a grip on the Virgin Mary's nose, as if he would never let go.

DREAMS EDIT THEMSELVES; DREAMS are ruthless with details. Common sense does not dictate what remains, or is not included, in a dream. A two-minute dream can feel like forever.

Dr. Vargas didn't hold back; he told Juan Diego much more about adrenaline, but not everything Vargas said found its way into Juan Diego's dream. According to Vargas, adrenaline was toxic in large amounts, such as would be released in a situation of sudden fear.

Juan Diego had even asked the man of science about other emotional states. What else, besides fear, could lead to an arrhythmia? If you had the wrong kind of heart, what else could give you these fatal heart rhythms?

'Any strong emotion, positive or negative, such as happiness or sadness,' Vargas had told the boy, but this answer wasn't in Juan Diego's dream. 'People have died during sexual intercourse,' Vargas told him. Turning to Edward Bonshaw, Dr. Vargas said: 'Even in religious passion.'

'What about whipping yourself?' Brother Pepe had asked in his half-innocent, half-mischievous way.

'Not documented,' the man of science slyly said.

Golfers had died hitting holes-in-one. An unusually high number of Germans suffered sudden cardiac deaths whenever the German soccer team was competing for the World Cup. Men, only a day or two after their wives have died; women who've lost their husbands, not only to death; parents who've lost children. They have all died of sadness, suddenly. These examples of emotional states leading to fatal heart rhythms were missing from Juan Diego's dream.

Yet the sound of Rivera's truck – that special whine the reverse gear made when Rivera was backing up – made its insidious way into Juan Diego's dream, no doubt at the moment the landing gear was dropping down from his plane, which was about to arrive in Bohol. Dreams do this: like the Roman Catholic Church, dreams *co-opt* things; dreams appropriate things that are not truly their own.

To a dream, it's all the same: the grinding sound of the landing gear for Philippine Airlines 177, the whine that Rivera's truck made in reverse. As for how the tainted smell of the Oaxaca morgue managed to infiltrate Juan Diego's dream on his short flight from Manila to Bohol – well, not everything can be explained.

Rivera knew where the loading platform was at the morgue; he knew the autopsy guy, too – the forensic surgeon who cut open the bodies in the anfiteatro de disección. As far as the dump kids were concerned, there'd never been any need to perform an autopsy on Esperanza. The Virgin Mary had scared her to death, and – what's more – the Mary Monster had meant to do it.

Rivera did his best to prepare Lupe for what Esperanza's cadaver would *look* like – the stitched autopsy scar (neck to groin), running straight down her sternum. But Lupe was unprepared for the pile of unclaimed corpses awaiting autopsies, or for the post-op body of el gringo bueno, whose outstretched white arms (as if he'd just been removed from the cross, where he'd been crucified) stood in stark relief against the more brown-skinned cadavers.

The good gringo's autopsy gash was fresh, newly stitched, and there'd been some cutting in the area of his head – more damage than a crown of thorns would have caused. The good gringo's war was over. It was a shock to Lupe and Juan Diego to see the hippie boy's cast-aside cadaver. El gringo bueno's Christlike face was at last at rest, though the Christ tattooed on the beautiful boy's pale body had also suffered from the forensic surgeon's dissection.

It was not lost on Lupe that her mother and the good gringo were the most beautiful bodies on display in the amphitheater of dissection, though they'd both looked a lot better when they were alive.

'We take el gringo bueno, too – you promised me we would burn him,' Lupe said to Juan Diego. 'We'll burn him with Mother.'

Rivera had talked the autopsy guy into giving him and the dump kids Esperanza's body, but when Juan Diego translated Lupe's request – how she wanted the dead hippie, too – the forensic surgeon had a fit.

The American runaway was part of a crime investi-gation. Someone in the Hotel Somega told the police that the hippie had succumbed to alcohol poisoning – a prostitute claimed the kid had 'just died' on top of her. But the autopsy guy had learned otherwise. El gringo bueno had been beaten to death; he'd been drunk, but the alcohol wasn't what killed him.

'His soul has to fly back home,' Lupe kept saying. '"As I walked out in the streets of Laredo,"' she suddenly sang. '"As I walked out in Laredo one day—"'

'What language is that kid singing?' the forensic surgeon asked Rivera.

'The police aren't going to *do* anything,' Rivera told him. 'They're not even going to say the hippie was beaten to death. They'll say it was alcohol poisoning.'

The forensic surgeon shrugged. 'Yeah, that's what they're already saying,' the surgeon said. 'I told them the tattoo kid had been beaten, but the cops told me to keep it to myself.'

'It's alcohol poisoning – that's how they're going to handle it,' Rivera said.

'The only thing that matters now is the good gringo's *soul*,' Lupe insisted. Juan Diego decided he should translate this.

'But what if his mother wants his body back?' Juan Diego added, after he told them what Lupe said about el gringo bueno's *soul*.

'The mom has asked for his ashes. That's not what

we usually do, not even with foreigners,' the surgeon replied. 'We certainly don't burn the bodies at the basurero.'

Rivera shrugged. 'We'll get you some ashes,' Rivera told him.

'There are two bodies, and we'll keep half the ashes for ourselves,' Juan Diego said.

'We'll take the ashes to Mexico City – we'll scatter them at the Basílica de Nuestra Señora de Guadalupe, at the feet of *our* Virgin,' Lupe said. 'We're not bringing their ashes anywhere near Bad Mary without a nose!' Lupe cried.

'That girl doesn't sound like anyone else,' the forensic surgeon said, but Juan Diego didn't translate Lupe's craziness about scattering the good gringo's *and* Esperanza's ashes at the feet of Our Lady of Guadalupe in Mexico City.

Rivera, probably because there was a young girl present, insisted that Esperanza and el gringo bueno be put in separate body bags; Juan Diego and Rivera helped the forensic surgeon do that. During this funereal moment, Lupe looked at the other cadavers, both the dissected ones and the ones waiting for dissection – the corpses that didn't matter to her, in other words. Juan Diego could hear Diablo barking and howling from the back of Rivera's truck; the dog could tell that the air around the morgue was tainted. There was a cold-meat smell in the anfiteatro de disección.

'How could his mother not want to see his body first? How could any mom want the dear boy's ashes *instead*?' Lupe was saying. She wasn't expecting an answer – after all, she believed in burning.

Esperanza may not have wanted to be cremated, but the dump kids were doing it anyway. Considering her Catholic zeal (Esperanza had *loved* confession), she might not have chosen a funeral pyre at the dump, but if the deceased doesn't leave prior instructions (Esperanza didn't), the disposal of the dead is for the children to decide.

'The Catholics are crazy not to believe in cremation,' Lupe was babbling. 'There's no better place to burn things than at the dump – the black smoke rising as far as you can see, the vultures drifting across the landscape.' Lupe had closed her eyes in the amphitheater of dissection, clutching the hideous Coatlicue earth goddess to her not-yet-noticeably-emerging breasts. 'You have the nose, don't you?' Lupe asked her brother, opening her eyes.

'Yes, of course I have it,' Juan Diego said; his pocket bulged.

'The nose goes in the fire, too – just to be sure,' Lupe said.

'Sure of *what*?' Juan Diego asked. 'Why burn the nose?'

'Just in case the imposter Mary has any power – just to be *safe*,' Lupe said.

'La nariz?' Rivera asked; he had a body bag slung over each big shoulder. '*What* nose?'

'Say nothing about Mary's nose. Rivera is too superstitious. Let him figure it out. He'll see the noseless monster Virgin the next time he goes to

Mass, or to confess his sins. I keep telling him, but he doesn't listen – his *mustache* is a sin,' Lupe babbled. She saw that Rivera was listening to her closely; la nariz had gotten el jefe's attention – he was trying to figure out what the dump kids had been saying about a *nose*.

'"Get six jolly cowboys to carry my coffin,"' Lupe started singing. '"Get six pretty maidens to bear up my pall."' It was the right moment for the cowboy dirge – Rivera was toting two bodies to his truck. '"Put bunches of roses all over my coffin,"' Lupe kept singing. '"Roses to deaden the clods as they fall."'

'The girl is a marvel,' the forensic surgeon said to the dump boss. 'She could be a rock star.'

'How could *she* be a rock star?' Rivera asked him. 'No one but her brother can understand her!'

'Nobody knows what rock stars are singing. Who can understand the lyrics?' the surgeon asked.

'There's a reason the idiot autopsy guy spends his whole life with dead people,' Lupe was babbling. But the rock-star business made Rivera forget about the nose. El jefe carried the body bags outside to the loading platform, and then put them gently on the flatbed of his truck, where Diablo immediately sniffed the bodies.

'Don't let Diablo *roll* on the bodies,' Rivera told Juan Diego; the dump kids and Rivera knew how much the dog liked rolling on dead things. Juan Diego would ride to the basurero in the flatbed of the truck with Esperanza and el gringo bueno and, of course, Diablo.

Lupe rode in the cab of the truck with Rivera.

'The Jesuits will come here, you know,' the forensic surgeon was saying to the dump boss. 'They come to collect their *flock* – they'll be here for Esperanza.'

'The children are in charge of their mother – tell the Jesuits that the dump kids are Esperanza's *flock*,' Rivera told the autopsy guy.

'That little girl could be in the *circus*, you know,' the forensic surgeon said, pointing to Lupe in the cab.

'Doing *what*?' Rivera asked him.

'People would pay just to hear her talk!' the autopsy guy said. 'She wouldn't even have to sing.'

It would haunt Juan Diego, later, how this surgeon with his rubber gloves, tainted with death and dissection, had brought the *circus* into the conversation at the Oaxaca morgue.

'Drive on!' Juan Diego cried to Rivera; the boy pounded on the truck's cab, and Rivera drove away from the loading platform. It was a cloudless day with a perfect bright-blue sky. 'Don't roll on them – no rolling!' Juan Diego shouted at Diablo, but the dog just sat in the flatbed, watching the live boy, not even sniffing the bodies.

Soon the wind dried the tears on Juan Diego's face, but the wind did not permit him to hear what Lupe was saying inside the truck's cab to Rivera. Juan Diego could hear only his sister's prophesying voice, not her words; she was going on and on about something. Juan Diego thought she was babbling about Dirty White. Rivera had given the runt to a family in

Guerrero, but the rodent-size dog kept returning to el jefe's shack – no doubt looking for Lupe.

Now Dirty White was missing; naturally, Lupe had harangued Rivera without mercy. She said she knew where Dirty White would go – she meant where the little dog would go to die. ('The puppy place,' she'd called it.)

From the flatbed of the pickup, Juan Diego could hear only bits and pieces of what the dump boss was saying. 'If you say so,' el jefe would interject from time to time, or: 'I couldn't have said it better myself, Lupe' – all the way to Guerrero, from where Juan Diego could see the isolated plumes of smoke; there were already a few fires burning in the not-too-distant dump.

Overhearing, inexactly, Lupe's not-a-conversation with Rivera reminded Juan Diego of studying literature with Edward Bonshaw in one of the sound-proof reading rooms in the library of Niños Perdidos. What Señor Eduardo meant by *studying literature* was a reading-aloud process: the Iowan would begin by reading what he called a 'grown-up novel' to Juan Diego; in this way, they could determine together whether or not the book was age-appropriate for the boy. Naturally, there would be differences of opinion between them regarding the aforementioned appropriateness or lack thereof.

'What if I'm really liking it? What if I know that, if I were *allowed* to read this book, I would never stop reading it?' Juan Diego asked.

'That's not the same as whether or not the book

is *suitable*,' Edward Bonshaw would answer the fourteen-year-old. Or Señor Eduardo would pause in his reading aloud, tipping off Juan Diego that the missionary was attempting to skip over some sexual content.

'You're censoring a sex scene,' the boy would say.

'I'm not sure this is *appropriate*,' the Iowan would reply.

The two of them had settled on Graham Greene; matters of faith and doubt were clearly at the forefront of Edward Bonshaw's mind, if not the sole motivation for his whipping himself, and Juan Diego liked Greene's sexual subjects, though the author tended to render the sex offstage or in an understated manner.

The way the studying worked was that Edward Bonshaw would begin a Greene novel by reading it aloud to Juan Diego; then Juan Diego would read the rest of the novel to himself; last, the grown man and the boy would discuss the story. In the discussion part, Señor Eduardo was very keen about citing specific passages and asking Juan Diego what Graham Greene had *meant*.

One sentence in *The Power and the Glory* had prompted a lengthy and ongoing discussion regarding its meaning. The student and the teacher had contrasting ideas about the sentence, which was: 'There is always one moment in childhood when the door opens and lets the future in.'

'What do you make of that, Juan Diego?' Edward Bonshaw had asked the boy. 'Is Greene saying that our future *begins* in childhood, and we should pay attention to—'

'Well, of course the future *begins* in childhood – where *else* would it begin?' Juan Diego asked the Iowan. 'But I think it's bullshit to say there is *one* moment when *the* door to the future opens. Why can't there be *many* moments? And is Greene saying there's only *one* door? He says *the* door, like there's only one.'

'Graham Greene isn't *bullshit*, Juan Diego!' Señor Eduardo had cried; the zealot was clutching something small in one hand.

'I know about your mah-jongg tile – you don't have to show it to me again,' Juan Diego told the scholastic. 'I know, I know – you fell, the little piece of ivory and bamboo cut your face. You bled, Beatrice licked you – that's how your dog died, shot and killed. I know, I know! But did that *one* moment make you want to be a priest? Did the door to no sex for the rest of your life open *only* because Beatrice got shot? There must have been *other* moments in your childhood; you could have opened *other* doors. You still could open a *different* door, right? That mah-jongg tile didn't have to be your childhood *and* your future!'

Resignation: that was what Juan Diego had seen on Edward Bonshaw's face. The missionary seemed resigned to his fate: celibacy, self-flagellation, the priesthood – all this was caused by a fall with a mah-jongg tile in his little hand? A life of beating himself and sexual denial because his beloved dog was cruelly shot and killed?

It was also resignation that Juan Diego saw on Rivera's face now, as el jefe backed up the truck to the shack they had shared as a family in Guerrero. Juan Diego knew what it was like to have a not-a-conversation with Lupe – just to *listen* to her, whether you understood her or not.

Lupe always knew more than you did; Lupe, though incomprehensible much of the time, knew stuff no one else knew. Lupe was a child, but she argued like a grown-up. She said things even she didn't understand; she said the words 'just came' to her, often before she had any awareness of their meaning.

Burn el gringo bueno with Mother; burn the Virgin Mary's nose with them. Just do it. Scatter their ashes in Mexico City. Just do it.

And there had been the zealous Edward Bonshaw spouting Graham Greene (another Catholic, clearly tortured by faith *and* doubt), claiming there was only *one* moment when *the* door – a single fucking door! – opened and let the fucking future in.

'Jesus Christ,' Juan Diego was muttering when he climbed out of the flatbed of Rivera's truck. (Neither Lupe nor the dump boss thought the boy was praying.)

'Just a minute,' Lupe told them. She walked purposefully away from them, disappearing behind the shack the dump kids had once called home. She has to take a leak, Juan Diego was thinking.

'No, I *don't* have to take a leak!' Lupe called. 'I'm looking for Dirty White!'

'Is she peeing, or do you need more water pistols?' Rivera asked. Juan Diego shrugged. 'We should start burning the bodies – before the Jesuits get to the basurero,' el jefe said.

Lupe came back carrying a dead dog – it was a puppy, and Lupe was crying. 'I always find them in the same place, or nearly the same place,' she was blubbering. The dead puppy was Dirty White.

'We're going to burn Dirty White with your mother and the hippie?' Rivera asked.

'If you burned me, I would want to be burned with a puppy!' Lupe cried. Juan Diego thought this was worth translating, and he did. Rivera paid no attention to the dead puppy; el jefe had hated Dirty White. The dump boss was doubtless relieved that the disagreeable runt wasn't rabid, and hadn't bitten Lupe.

'I'm sorry the dog adoption didn't work,' Rivera said to Lupe when the little girl had reseated herself in the cab of el jefe's truck, the dead puppy lying stiffly in her lap.

When Juan Diego was once more with Diablo and the body bags in the flatbed of the pickup, Rivera drove to the basurero; once there, he backed up the truck to the fire that burned brightest among the smoldering piles.

Rivera was rushing a little when he took the two body bags out of the flatbed and doused them with gasoline.

'Dirty White looks soaking wet,' Juan Diego said to Lupe.

'He is,' she said, laying the puppy on the ground beside the body bags. Rivera respectfully poured some gasoline on the dead dog.

The dump kids turned away from the fire when el jefe threw the body bags on the coals, into the low flames; suddenly the flames shot higher. When the fire was a towering conflagration, but Lupe's back was still turned to the blaze, Rivera tossed the little puppy into the inferno.

'I better move the truck,' the dump boss said. The kids had already noticed that the side-view mirror remained broken. Rivera claimed he would never repair it; he said he wanted to torture himself with the memory.

Like a good Catholic, Juan Diego thought, watching el jefe move the truck away from the sudden heat of the funeral pyre.

'*Who's* a good Catholic?' Lupe asked her brother.

'Stop reading my mind!' Juan Diego snapped at her.

'I can't help it,' she told him. When Rivera was still in the truck, Lupe said: 'Now's a good time to put the monster nose in the fire.'

'I don't see the point of it,' Juan Diego said, but he threw the Virgin Mary's broken nose into the conflagration.

'Here they come – right on time,' Rivera said, joining the kids where they stood at some distance from the fire; it was very hot. They could see Brother Pepe's dusty red VW racing into the basurero.

Later, Juan Diego thought that the Jesuits tumbling

out of the little VW Beetle resembled a clown act at the circus. Brother Pepe, the two outraged priests – Father Alfonso *and* Father Octavio – and, of course, the dumbstruck Edward Bonshaw.

The funeral pyre spoke for the dump kids, who said nothing, but Lupe decided that singing was okay. '"Oh, beat the drum slowly and play the fife lowly,"' she sang. '"Play the dead march as you carry me along—"'

'Esperanza wouldn't have wanted a *fire*—' Father Alfonso started to say, but the dump boss interrupted him.

'It was what her children wanted, Father – that's how it goes,' Rivera said.

'It's what we do with what we love,' Juan Diego said.

Lupe was smiling serenely; she was watching the ascending columns of smoke drifting far away, and the ever-hovering vultures.

'"Take me to the valley, and lay the sod o'er me,"' Lupe sang. '"For I'm a young cowboy and I know I've done wrong."'

'These children are orphans now,' Señor Eduardo was saying. 'They are surely our responsibility, more than they ever were. Aren't they?'

Brother Pepe didn't immediately answer the Iowan, and the two old priests just looked at each other.

'What would Graham Greene say?' Juan Diego asked Edward Bonshaw.

'Graham Greene!' Father Alfonso exclaimed. 'Don't tell me, Edward, that this boy has been reading *Greene*—'

'How unsuitable!' Father Octavio said.

'Greene is hardly age-appropriate—' Father Alfonso began, but Señor Eduardo wouldn't hear of it.

'Greene is a Catholic!' the Iowan cried.

'Not a good one, Edward,' Father Octavio said.

'Is this what Greene means by *one* moment?' Juan Diego asked Señor Eduardo. 'Is this *the* door opening to the future – Lupe's and mine?'

'This door opens to the circus,' Lupe said. 'That's what comes next – that's where we're going.'

Juan Diego translated this, of course, before he asked Edward Bonshaw: 'Is this our *only* moment? Is this the *one* door to the future? Is this what Greene *meant*? Is this how childhood ends?' The Iowan was thinking hard – as hard as he ever had, and Edward Bonshaw was a deeply thoughtful man.

'Yes, you're right! That's exactly right!' Lupe suddenly said to the Iowan; the little girl touched Señor Eduardo's hand.

'She says you're right – whatever you're thinking,' Juan Diego said to Edward Bonshaw, who kept staring into the raging flames.

'He's thinking that the poor draft dodger's ashes will be returned to his homeland, and to his grieving mother, with the ashes of a prostitute,' Lupe said. Juan Diego translated this, too.

Suddenly there was a harsh spitting sound from the funeral pyre, and a thin blue flame shot up among the vivid oranges and yellows, as if something chemical had caught fire, or perhaps a puddle of gasoline had ignited.

'Maybe it's the puppy – it was so wet,' Rivera said, as they all stared at the intense blue flame.

'The puppy!' Edward Bonshaw cried. 'You burned a dog with your mother and that dear hippie child? You burned another dog in their fire!'

'Everyone should be so lucky as to be burned with a puppy,' Juan Diego told the Iowan.

The hissing blue flame had everyone's attention, but Lupe reached up her arms and pulled her brother's face down to her lips. Juan Diego thought she was going to kiss him, but Lupe wanted to whisper in his ear, although no one else could have understood her, not even if they'd heard.

'It's definitely the wet puppy,' Rivera was saying.

'La nariz,' Lupe whispered in her brother's ear, touching his nose. The second she spoke, the hissing sound stopped – the blue flame disappeared. The flaming blue hiss was the nose, all right, Juan Diego was thinking.

The jolt of Philippine Airlines 177 landing in Bohol didn't even wake him up, as if there were nothing that could wake Juan Diego from the dream of when his future started.

16

King of Beasts

Several passengers paused at the cockpit exit for Philippine Airlines 177, telling the flight attendant of their concerns about the older-looking, brown-skinned gentleman who was slumped over in a window seat. 'He's either dead to the world or just dead,' one of the passengers told the flight attendant, in a confounding combination of the vernacular and the laconic.

Juan Diego definitely looked dead, but his thoughts were far away, on high, in the spires of smoke funneling above the Oaxaca basurero; if only in his mind, he had a vulture's view of the city limits – of Cinco Señores, where the circus grounds were, and the distant but brightly colored tents of Circo de La Maravilla.

The paramedics were notified from the cockpit; before all the passengers had left the plane, the rescuers rushed on. Various lifesaving methods were seconds away from being performed when one of the lifesavers realized that Juan Diego was very much alive, but by then the supposedly stricken passenger's carry-on had been searched. The prescription drugs drew the most immediate attention. The beta-blockers signified there was a heart problem; the Viagra, with the printed warning not to take the stuff with nitrates, prompted one of the paramedics to ask Juan Diego, with no little urgency, if he'd been taking nitrates.

Juan Diego not only didn't know what nitrates were; his mind was in Oaxaca, forty years ago, and Lupe was whispering in his ear.

'La nariz,' Juan Diego whispered to the anxious paramedic; she was a young woman, and she understood a little Spanish.

'Your nose?' the young paramedic asked; to make herself clear, she touched her own nose when she spoke.

'You can't breathe? You're having trouble breathing?' another of the paramedics asked; he also touched his nose, doubtless to signify breathing.

'Viagra can make you stuffy,' a third paramedic said.

'No, not *my* nose,' Juan Diego said, laughing. 'I was dreaming about the Virgin Mary's nose,' he told the team of paramedics.

This was not helpful; the insanity of mentioning the Virgin Mary's nose distracted the medical personnel from the line of questioning they should have pursued – namely, if Juan Diego had been manipulating the dosage of his Lopressor prescription. Yet, to the team of paramedics, the passenger's life signs were okay; that he'd managed to sleep through a turbulent landing (crying children, screaming women) was not a medical matter.

'He looked dead,' the flight attendant kept saying to anyone who would listen to her. But Juan Diego had been oblivious to the rocky landing, the sobbing children, the wails of the women who'd been certain they were going to die. The miracle (or not) of the Virgin Mary's nose had completely captured Juan Diego's attention, as it had so many years ago; all he'd heard was the hissing blue flame, which had disappeared as suddenly as it first appeared.

The paramedics didn't linger with Juan Diego; they weren't needed. Meawhile, the nose-dreamer's friend and former student kept sending text messages, inquiring if his old teacher was all right.

Juan Diego didn't know it, but Clark French was a famous writer – at least in the Philippines. It is too simplistic to say this was *because* the Philippines had a lot of Catholic readers, and uplifting novels of faith and belief were received in a more welcoming fashion there than such novels were greeted in the United States or in Europe. Partly true, yes, but Clark French had married a Filipino woman from a venerable Manila family – Quintana was a distinguished name in the medical community. This helped make Clark a more widely read author in the Philippines than he was in his own country.

As Clark's onetime teacher, Juan Diego still saw his former student as needing protection; the condescending reviews Clark had received in the United States amounted to all that Juan Diego knew of the younger writer's reputation. And Juan Diego and Clark corresponded by email, which gave Juan Diego only a general idea of where Clark French lived – namely, somewhere in the Philippines.

Clark lived in Manila; his wife, Dr. Josefa Quintana, was what Clark called a 'baby doctor.' Juan Diego knew that Dr. Quintana was a higher-up at the Cardinal Santos Medical Center – 'one of the leading hospitals in the Philippines,' Clark was fond of saying. A *private* hospital, Bienvenido had told Juan Diego – to distinguish Cardinal Santos from what Bienvenido disparagingly called 'the dirty government hospitals.' A *Catholic* hospital was what registered with Juan Diego – the Catholic factor mingled with his annoyance at not knowing if a 'baby doctor' meant that Clark's wife was a pediatrician or an OB-GYN.

Because Juan Diego had spent his entire adult life in the same university town, and his life as a writer in Iowa City had (until now) been inseparable from that as a teacher at a single university, he hadn't realized that Clark French was one of those *other* writers – the ones who can live anywhere, or everywhere.

Juan Diego did know that Clark was one of those writers who appeared to be at every authors' festival; he seemed to like, or excel at, the nonwriting part of being a writer – the talking-about-it part, which Juan Diego didn't like or do well. In fact, increasingly, as he grew older, the writing (the *doing-it* part) was the only aspect of being a writer that Juan Diego enjoyed.

Clark French traveled all over the world, but Manila was Clark's home – his home base, anyway. Clark and his wife had no children. Because he traveled? Because she was a 'baby doctor,' and she saw enough children? Or, if Josefa Quintana was the *other* kind of 'baby doctor,' perhaps she'd seen too many terrible complications of an obstetrical and gynecological kind.

Whatever the reason for the no-children situation, Clark French was one of those writers who could and did write everywhere, and there wasn't an important authors' festival or writers' conference that he hadn't traveled to; the public part of being a writer did not confine him to the Philippines. Clark came 'home' to Manila because his wife was there; she was the one with an actual job.

Probably because she was a doctor, and one from such a distinguished family of doctors – most medical people in the Philippines had heard of her – the paramedics who'd examined Juan Diego on the plane were somewhat indiscreet. They gave Dr. Josefa Quintana a full account of their medical (and non-medical) findings. And Clark French was standing right beside his wife, listening in.

The sleeping passenger had an out-of-it appearance; he'd laughingly dismissed the dead-to-the-world episode on the grounds of having been engrossed in a dream about the Virgin Mary.

'Juan Diego was dreaming about *Mary*?' Clark French interjected.

'Just her nose,' one of the medics said.

'The Virgin's *nose*!' Clark exclaimed. He'd told his wife to be prepared for Juan Diego's anti-Catholicism, but a tasteless joke about Mother Mary's nose denoted to Clark that his former teacher had descended to a lower level of Catholic bashing.

The paramedics wanted Dr. Quintana to know about the Viagra and Lopressor prescriptions. Josefa had to tell Clark, in detail, about the way beta-blockers worked; she was completely correct to add that, due to common side effects of the Lopressor tablets, the Viagra might have been 'necessary.'

'There was a novel in his carry-on, too – at least I think it was a novel,' one of the paramedics said.

'*What* novel?' Clark asked eagerly.

'*The Passion* by Jeanette Winterson,' the medic said. 'It sounds religious.'

The young-woman paramedic spoke cautiously. (Maybe she was trying to connect the novel to the Viagra.) 'It sounds pornographic,' she said.

'No, no – Winterson is *literary*,' Clark French said. 'A lesbian, but literary,' he added. Clark didn't know the novel, but he assumed it had something to do with lesbians – he wondered if Winterson had written a novel about an order of lesbian nuns.

When the paramedics moved on, Clark and his wife were left alone; they were still waiting for Juan Diego, though it had been a while, and Clark was worried about his former teacher.

'To my knowledge, he lives alone – he has *always* lived alone. What's he doing with the Viagra?' Clark asked his wife.

Josefa was an OB-GYN (she was *that* kind of 'baby doctor'); she knew a lot about Viagra. Many of her patients had asked her about Viagra; their husbands or boyfriends were taking it, or they thought they wanted to try it, and the women wanted Dr. Quintana to tell them how the Viagra would affect the men in their lives. Would the women be raped in the middle of the night, or mounted when they were just trying to make coffee in the morning – humped against the unyielding car, when they'd merely been bending over to lift the groceries out of the trunk?

Dr. Josefa Quintana said to her husband: 'Look, Clark, your former teacher might not live with anybody, but he probably *likes* getting an erection – right?'

That was when Juan Diego limped into sight; Josefa saw him first – she recognized him from his book-jacket photos, and Clark had prepared her for the limp. (Naturally, Clark French had exaggerated the limp – the way writers do.)

'What for?' Juan Diego heard Clark ask his wife, the doctor. She looked a little embarrassed, Juan Diego thought, but she waved to him and smiled. She seemed very nice; it was a sincere smile.

Clark turned and saw him. There was Clark's boyish grin, which was confused by a concurrent expression of guilt, as if Clark had been caught in the act of doing or saying something. (In this case, by responding to his wife's professional opinion that his former teacher probably *liked* getting an erection with a doltish 'What for?')

'What *for*?' Josefa quietly repeated to her husband, before she reached to shake Juan Diego's hand.

Clark couldn't stop grinning; now he was pointing to Juan Diego's giant orange albatross of a bag. 'Look, Josefa – I told you Juan Diego did a lot of research for his novels. He brought all of it with him!'

The same old Clark, a lovable but embarrassing guy, Juan Diego was thinking; he then steeled himself, knowing he was about to be crushed in Clark's athletic embrace.

In addition to the Winterson novel, there was a lined notebook in Juan Diego's carry-on. It contained notes for the novel Juan Diego was writing – he was always writing a novel. He'd been writing his next novel since he took a translation trip to Lithuania in February 2008. The novel-in-progress was now more than two years old; Juan Diego would have guessed he had another two or three years to go.

The trip to Vilnius was his first time in Lithuania, but not the first of his translations to be published there. He'd gone to the Vilnius Book Fair with his publisher and his translator. Juan Diego was interviewed onstage by a Lithuanian actress. After a few excellent questions of her own, the actress invited the audience to ask questions; there were a thousand people, many of them young students. It was a larger and more informed audience than Juan Diego usually encountered at comparable events in the United States.

After the book fair, he'd gone with his publisher and translator to sign books at a bookstore in the old

town. The Lithuanian names were a problem – but
not the first names, usually. So it was decided that
Juan Diego would inscribe only his readers' first
names. For example, the actress who'd interviewed
him at the book fair was a Dalia – that was easy
enough, but her last name was much more challenging. His publisher was a Rasa, his translator a Daiva,
but their last names were not English- or Spanish-
sounding.

Everyone was most sympathetic, including the
young bookseller; his English was a struggle, but he'd
read everything Juan Diego had written (in
Lithuanian) and he couldn't stop talking to his
favorite author.

'Lithuania is a birth-again country – we are your
newborn readers!' he cried. (Daiva, the translator,
explained what the young bookseller meant: since
the Soviets had left, people were free to read more
books – especially foreign novels.)

'We have awakened to find someone like you pre-
existed us!' the young man exclaimed, wringing his
hands. Juan Diego was very moved.

At one point, Daiva and Rasa must have gone to
the women's room – or they just needed a break from
the enthusiastic young bookseller. His first name was
not so easy. (It was something like Gintaras, or maybe
it was Arvydas.)

Juan Diego was looking at a bulletin board in the
bookstore. There were photographs of women with
what looked like lists of authors' names next to them.
There were numbers that looked like the women's

phone numbers, too. Were these women in a book club? Juan Diego recognized many of the authors' names, his own among them. They were all fiction writers. Of course it was a book club, Juan Diego thought – no men were pictured.

'These women – they read novels. They're in a book club?' Juan Diego asked the hovering bookseller.

The young man looked stricken – he may not have understood, or he didn't know the English for what he wanted to say.

'All despairing readers – seeking to meet other readers for a coffee or a beer!' Gintaras or Arvydas shouted; surely the *despairing* word was not what he'd meant.

'Do you mean a *date*?' Juan Diego had asked. It was the most touching thing: women who wanted to meet men to talk about the books they'd read! He'd never heard of such a thing. 'A kind of dating service?' Imagine matchmaking on the basis of what novels you liked! Juan Diego thought. But would these poor women find any men who read novels? (Juan Diego didn't think so.)

'Mail-order brides!' the young bookseller said dismissively; with a gesture toward the bulletin board, he expressed how these women were beneath his consideration.

Juan Diego's publisher and translator were back at his side, but not before Juan Diego looked longingly at one of the women's photographs – it was someone who'd put Juan Diego's name at the top of her list. She was pretty, but not too pretty; she looked a little unhappy. There were dark circles under her haunting eyes; her hair looked somewhat neglected. There was no one in her life to talk to about the wonderful novels she'd read. Her first name was Odeta; her last name must have been fifteen letters long.

'Mail-order brides?' Juan Diego asked Gintaras or Arvydas. 'Surely they can't be—'

'Pathetic ladies with no lifes, coupling with characters in novels instead of meeting real mens!' the bookseller shouted.

That was it – the spark of a new novel. Mail-order brides advertising themselves by the novels they'd read – in a bookstore, of all places! The idea was born with a title: *One Chance to Leave Lithuania*. Oh, no, Juan Diego thought. (This was what he always thought when he thought of a new novel – it always struck him, at first, as a terrible idea.)

And, naturally, it was all a mistake – just a language confusion. Gintaras or Arvydas couldn't express himself in English. Juan Diego's publisher and translator were laughing as they explained the bookseller's error.

'It's just a bunch of readers – all women,' Daiva told Juan Diego.

'They meet one another, other women, for coffee or beer, just to talk about the novelists they like,' Rasa explained.

'Kind of an impromptu book club,' Daiva told him.

'There are no mail-order brides in Lithuania,' Rasa stated.

'There must be *some* mail-order brides,' Juan Diego suggested.

The next morning, at his unpronounceable hotel, the Stikliai, Juan Diego was introduced to a police-woman from Interpol in Vilnius; Daiva and Rasa had found her and brought her to the hotel. 'There are no mail-order brides in Lithuania,' the policewoman told him. She didn't stay to have a coffee; Juan Diego didn't catch her name. The policewoman's grittiness could not be disguised by her hair, which was dyed a surfer-blond color, tinged with sunset-orange streaks. No amount or hue of dye could conceal what she was: not a good-time girl but a no-nonsense cop. No novels about mail-order brides in Lithuania, please; that was the stern policewoman's message. Yet *One Chance to Leave Lithuania* had endured.

'What about adoption?' Juan Diego had asked Daiva and Rasa. 'What about orphanages or adoption agencies – there must be state services for adoptions, maybe state services for children's rights? What about women who want or need to put their children up for adoption? Lithuania is a Catholic country, isn't it?'

Daiva, the translator of many of his novels, under-stood Juan Diego very well. 'Women who put their children up for adoption don't advertise themselves in a *bookstore*,' she said, smiling at him.

'That was just the start of something,' he explained. 'Novels begin somewhere; novels undergo revision.' He'd not forgotten Odeta's face on the bookstore bulletin board, but *One Chance to Leave Lithuania* was a different novel now. The woman who was putting up a child for adoption was also a reader; she was seeking to meet other readers. She didn't just love novels and the characters in them for themselves; she sought to leave her life in the past behind, her child included. She wasn't thinking about meeting a man.

But *whose* one chance to leave Lithuania was it? Hers, or her child's? Things can go wrong during the adoption process, Juan Diego knew – not only in novels.

As for Jeanette Winterson's *The Passion*, Juan Diego loved that novel; he'd read it two or three times – he kept returning to it. It wasn't about an order of lesbian nuns. It was about history and magic, including Napoleon's eating habits and a girl with webbed feet – she was a crossdresser, too. It was a novel about unfulfilled love and sadness. It was not uplifting enough for Clark French to have written it.

And Juan Diego had highlighted a favorite sentence in the middle of *The Passion*: 'Religion is somewhere between fear and sex.' That sentence would have provoked poor Clark.

It was almost five in the afternoon on New Year's Eve in Bohol when Juan Diego limped out of the ramshackle airport and into the mayhem of Tagbilaran City, which struck him as a squalid metropolis of motorcycles and mopeds. There were so many difficult names for places in the Philippines, Juan Diego couldn't keep them straight – the islands had names, and the cities, not to mention the names of the neighborhoods in the cities. It was confusing.

And in Tagbilaran City, there were also plenty of the now-familiar *religious* jeepneys, but these were intermixed with homemade vehicles that resembled rebuilt lawnmowers or supercharged golf carts; there were lots of bicycles, too, not to mention the masses of people on foot.

Clark French had manfully lifted Juan Diego's enormous bag above his head – out of consideration for the women and small children who didn't come up to his chest. That orange albatross was a woman-and-child crusher; it could roll right over them. Yet Clark didn't hesitate to knife like a running back through the men in the mob – the smaller brown bodies got out of his way, or Clark muscled through them. Clark was a bull.

Dr. Josefa Quintana knew how to follow her husband through a crowd. She kept one of her small hands flat against Clark's broad back; with the other, she held tightly to Juan Diego. 'Don't worry – we have a driver, somewhere,' she told him. 'Clark, notwithstanding his opinion to the contrary, doesn't have to do *everything*.' Juan Diego was charmed by her; she was genuine, and she struck him as both the brains and the common sense in the family. Clark was the instinctual one – both an asset and a liability.

The beach resort had provided the driver, a feral-faced boy who looked too young to drive – but he was eager to do so. Once they were out of the city, there were smaller mobs of people walking along the road, although the vehicular traffic now careened at highway speeds. There were goats and cows tethered at the roadside, but their tethers were too long; occasionally, a cow's head (or a goat's) would reach into the road, causing the assorted vehicles to veer.

Dogs were chained near the shacks, or in the cluttered yards of those homesteads along the roadside; when the dogs' chains were too long, the dogs would attack the pedestrians passing by – hence people, not only the heads of cows and goats, would materialize in the road. The boy driving the resort's SUV relied heavily on his horn.

Such chaos reminded Juan Diego of Mexico – people spilling into the road, and the animals! To Juan Diego, the presence of improperly-cared-for animals was a telltale indication of overpopulation. So far, Bohol had made him think about birth control.

To be fair: Juan Diego's birth-control awareness was keener around Clark. They'd exchanged combative emails on the subject of fetal pain, inspired by a fairly recent Nebraska law preventing abortions after twenty weeks' gestation. And they'd fought about the use of the 1995 papal encyclical in Latin America, an effort by conservative Catholics to attack contraception as part of 'the culture of death' – this was how John Paul II preferred to refer to abortion. (That Polish pope was a sore subject between them.) Did Clark French have a cork up his ass about sexuality – a Catholic cork?

But Juan Diego thought it was hard to say what kind of cork it was. Clark was one of those socially liberal Catholics. He said he was 'personally opposed' to abortion – 'it's distasteful,' Juan Diego had heard Clark say – but Clark was politically liberal; he believed women should be able to choose an abortion, if that was what they wanted.

Clark had always supported gay rights, too; yet he defended the entrenched position of his revered Catholic Church – he found the Church's position on abortion, and on traditional marriage (that is, between a man and a woman), 'consistent and to be expected.' Clark had even said he believed the Church 'should uphold' its views on abortion and marriage; Clark saw no inconsistency to his having personal views on 'social subjects' that differed from the views upheld by his beloved Church. This exasperated Juan Diego no end.

But now, in the darkening twilight, as their boy driver dodged fleetingly appearing and instantly vanishing obstacles in the road, there was no talk of birth control. Clark French, befitting his self-sacrificing zeal, rode in the suicide seat – the one beside the boy driver – while Juan Diego and Josefa had buckled themselves into the seeming fortress that was the SUV's rear seat.

The resort hotel on Panglao Island was called the Encantador; to get there, they drove through a small fishing village on Panglao Bay. It grew darker there. The glimmer of lights on the water and the briny smell in the heavy air were the only hints that the sea was near. And reflected in the headlights, at every curve of the winding road, were the watchful, face-less eyes of dogs or goats; the taller pairs of eyes were cows or people, Juan Diego guessed. There were lots of eyes out there in the darkness. If you were that boy driver, you would have driven fast, too.

'This writer is the master of the collision course,' Clark French, ever the expert on Juan Diego's novels, was saying to his wife. 'It is a fated world; the inevitable looms ahead—'

'It's true that even your accidents are not coincidental – they're planned,' Dr. Quintana said to Juan Diego, interrupting her husband. 'I think the world is scheming against your poor characters,' she added.

'This writer is the *doom* master!' Clark French held forth in the speeding car.

It irritated Juan Diego how Clark, albeit know-ledgeably, often spoke of him in the third person while delivering a dissertation on his work – à la *this writer* – notwithstanding that Juan Diego was present (in this case, in the car).

The boy driver suddenly veered the SUV away from a shadowy form – with startled-looking eyes, with multiple arms and legs – but Clark was carrying on as if they were in a classroom.

'Just don't ask Juan Diego about anything *autobiographical*, Josefa – or the lack thereof,' Clark continued.

'I wasn't going to!' his wife protested.

'India is not Mexico. What happens to those children in the circus novel is *not* what happened to Juan Diego and his sister in *their* circus,' Clark went on. 'Right?' Clark suddenly asked his former teacher.

'That's right, Clark,' Juan Diego said.

He'd also heard Clark hold forth on the 'abortion novel' – as many critics had called another of Juan Diego's novels. 'A compelling argument for a woman's right to an abortion,' Juan Diego had heard Clark describe that novel. 'Yet it's a complicated argument, coming from a former Catholic,' Clark always added.

'I'm *not* a former Catholic. I never *was* a Catholic,' Juan Diego not once failed to point out. 'I was *taken in* by the Jesuits, which was neither my choice nor against my will. What choice *or* will do you have when you're fourteen?'

'What I'm trying to say is,' Clark went on in the swerving SUV – on the dark, narrow road that was everywhere dotted with bright, unblinking eyes – 'in Juan Diego's world, you always know the collision is coming. Exactly what the collision is – well, this may come as a surprise. But you definitely know there's going to be one. In the abortion novel, from the moment that orphan is taught what a D and C is, you know the kid is going to end up being a doctor who *does* one – right, Josefa?'

'Right,' Dr. Quintana answered in the backseat of the car. She gave Juan Diego a difficult-to-read smile – or a faintly apologetic one. It was dark in the back of the jouncing SUV; Juan Diego couldn't tell if Dr. Quintana was apologizing for her husband's assertiveness, his literary bullying, or if she was smiling a little sheepishly in lieu of admitting she knew more about a dilation and curettage than anyone in the collision-daring car.

'I do not write about myself,' Juan Diego had said in interview after interview, *and* to Clark French. He'd also explained to Clark, who adored Jesuitical disputation, that (as a former dump kid) he had greatly benefited from the Jesuits in his young life; he'd *loved* Edward Bonshaw and Brother Pepe. Juan Diego even wished, at times, he could engage in conversation with Father Alfonso and Father Octavio – now that the dump reader was an adult, and somewhat better equipped to argue with such formidably conservative priests. And the nuns at Lost Children had done him and Lupe no harm – notwithstanding what a bitch Sister Gloria had been. (Most of the other nuns had been okay to the dump kids.) In the case of Sister Gloria, Esperanza had been the disapproving nun's principal provocateur.

Yet Juan Diego had anticipated that a part of being with Clark – devoted student though he was – would be once more to find himself under scrutiny for the anti-Catholicism charge. What got under Clark's oh-so-Catholic skin, Juan Diego knew, wasn't that his former teacher was an unbeliever. Juan Diego was not an atheist – he simply had issues with the Church. Clark French was frustrated by this conundrum; Clark could more easily dismiss or ignore an unbeliever.

Clark's casual-sounding D&C remark – not the most relaxing subject for a practicing OB-GYN, Juan Diego imagined – seemed to turn Dr. Quintana away from further discussion of a literary kind. Josefa clearly sought to change the subject – much to Juan Diego's relief, if not to her husband's.

'Where we're staying, I'm afraid, is all about my family – it's a family *tradition*,' Josefa said, smiling more uncertainly than apologetically. 'I can vouch for the *place* – I'm sure you'll like the Encantador – but I can't begin to be an advocate for every member of my family,' she continued warily. 'Who's married to whom, who never should have married – their many, *many* children,' she said, her small voice trailing off.

'Josefa, there's no need to apologize for anyone in your family,' Clark chimed in from the suicide seat. 'What we can't vouch for is the mystery guest – there's an uninvited guest. We don't know who it is,' he added, disassociating himself from the unknown person.

'My family generally takes over the whole place – every room at the Encantador is ours,' Dr. Quintana explained. 'But this year, the hotel booked one room to *someone else*.'

Juan Diego, his heart beating faster than he was used to – enough so he noticed it, in other words – stared out the window of the hurtling car at the myriad eyes bobbing along the roadside, staring back at him. Oh, God! he prayed. Let it be Miriam or Dorothy, please!

'Oh, you'll see us again – definitely,' Miriam had said to him.

'Yeah, *definitely*,' Dorothy had said.

In the same conversation, Miriam had told him: 'We'll see you in Manila *eventually*. If not sooner.'

'If not sooner,' Dorothy had repeated.

Let it be Miriam – *just* Miriam! Juan Diego was thinking, as if an enticing pair of eyes aglow in the darkness could possibly be *hers*.

'I suppose,' Juan Diego said slowly, to Dr. Quintana, 'this *uninvited* guest must have booked a room *before* your family made your usual reservations?'

'No! That's just it! That's *not* what happened!' Clark French exclaimed.

'Clark, we don't know exactly what happened—' Josefa started to say.

'Your family books the whole place every *year*!' Clark cried. 'This person *knew* it was a private party. She booked a room anyway, and the Encantador took her reservation – even *knowing* all the rooms were fully booked! What kind of person wants to crash a private party? She *knew* she would be entirely isolated! She *knew* she would be absolutely alone!'

'*She*,' was all Juan Diego said, once again feeling his heart race. Outside, in the darkness, there were no eyes now. The road had narrowed, and turned to gravel, then to dirt. Perhaps the Encantador was a secluded place, but *she* would not be entirely isolated there. *She*, Juan Diego hoped, would be with *him*. If Miriam was the uninvited guest, she absolutely wouldn't be alone for long.

That was when the boy driver must have noticed something odd in the rearview mirror. He spoke quickly in Tagalog to Dr. Quintana. Clark French only partially understood the driver, but there was an element of alarm in the boy's tone; Clark turned and peered into the rear seat, where he could see that his wife had unbuckled her seat belt and was looking closely at Juan Diego.

'Is something wrong, Josefa?' Clark asked his wife.

'Give me a second, Clark – I think he's just asleep,' Dr. Quintana told her husband.

'Stop the car – stop it!' Clark told the boy driver, but Josefa spoke sharply in Tagalog to the boy, and the kid kept driving.

'We're almost there, Clark – it's not necessary to stop here,' Josefa said. 'I'm sure your old friend is sleeping – *dreaming*, if I had to guess, but I'm sure he's just asleep.'

FLOR DROVE THE DUMP kids to Circo de La Maravilla, because Brother Pepe was already beginning to blame himself for los niños taking such a risk; Pepe was too upset to go with them, although el circo had been his idea – his and Vargas's. Flor drove Pepe's VW Beetle, with Edward Bonshaw in the passenger seat and the kids in the back.

Lupe had delivered a tearful challenge to the nose-less statue of the Virgin Mary; this was seconds before they'd driven away from the Templo de la Compañía de Jesús. 'Show me a *real* miracle – anyone can scare a superstitious cleaning woman to death!' Lupe had shouted at the towering Virgin. '*Do* something to make me believe in you – I think you're just a big bully! Look at you! All you do is stand there! You don't even have a nose!'

'You're not going to offer some prayers, too?' Señor

Eduardo asked Juan Diego, who was disinclined to translate his sister's outburst for the Iowan – nor did the limping boy dare to tell the missionary his most dire fears. If anything happened to Juan Diego at La Maravilla – or if, for any reason, he and Lupe were ever separated – there would be no future for Lupe, because no one but her brother could understand her. Not even the Jesuits would keep her and care for her; Lupe would be put in the institution for retarded children, where she would be forgotten. Even the name of the place for retarded children was unknown or had been forgotten, and no one seemed to know where it was – or no one would say exactly where it was, nothing more than 'out of town' or 'up in the mountains.'

At that time, when Lost Children was relatively new in town, there was only one other orphanage in Oaxaca, and it was a little bit 'out of town' and 'up in the mountains.' It was in Viguera, and everyone knew its name – Ciudad de los Niños, 'City of Children.'

'City of *Boys*' was what Lupe called it; they didn't take girls. Most of the boys were ages six to ten; twelve was the cut-off, so they wouldn't have taken Juan Diego.

City of Children had opened in 1958; it had been around longer than Niños Perdidos, and the all-boys' orphanage would outlast Lost Children, too.

Brother Pepe would not speak ill of Ciudad de los Niños; perhaps Pepe believed all orphanages were a godsend. Father Alfonso and Father Octavio said only that education was not a priority at City of Children. (The dump kids had merely observed that the boys were bused to school – their school was near the Solitude Virgin's basilica – and Lupe had said, with her characteristic shrug, that the buses themselves were as beat to shit as you would expect for buses accustomed to transporting *boys*.)

One of the orphans at Lost Children had been at Ciudad de los Niños as a younger boy. He didn't bad-mouth the all-boys' orphanage; he never said he was mistreated there. Juan Diego would remember that this boy said there were shoe boxes stacked in the dining hall (this was said without any explanation), and that all the boys – twenty or so – slept in one room. The mattresses were unsheeted, and the blankets and stuffed animals had earlier belonged to other boys. There were stones in the soccer field, this boy said – you didn't want to fall down – and the meat was cooked on an outdoor wood fire.

These observations were not offered as criticisms; they simply contributed to Juan Diego and Lupe's impression that City of *Boys* would not have been an option for them – even if Lupe had been the right sex for that place, and even if both kids hadn't been too old.

If the dump kids went crazy at Lost Children, they would go back to the basurero before they would submit to the institution for the retarded, where Lupe had heard the children were 'head-bangers,' and some of the head-bangers had their hands tied behind their backs. This prevented them from gouging out the eyes of other kids, or their own eyes. Lupe would not tell Juan Diego her source.

There's no explaining why the dump kids thought it was perfectly logical that Circo de La Maravilla was a fortunate option, and the only acceptable alternative to their returning to Guerrero. Rivera would have welcomed the Guerrero choice, but he was notably absent when Flor drove the dump kids and Señor Eduardo to La Maravilla. And it would have been a tight fit for the dump boss, had he tried to squeeze into Brother Pepe's VW Beetle. To the dump kids, it also seemed perfectly logical that they were driven to the circus by a transvestite prostitute.

Flor was smoking as she drove, holding her cigarette out the driver's-side window, and Edward Bonshaw, who was nervous – he knew Flor was a prostitute; he *didn't* know she was a transvestite – said, as casually as he could, 'I used to smoke. I kicked the habit.'

'You think celibacy isn't a *habit*?' Flor asked him. Señor Eduardo was surprised that Flor's English was so good. He knew nothing of the unmentionable Houston experience in her life, and no one had told him that Flor had been born a boy (or that she still had a penis).

Flor navigated her way through a wedding party that had exited a church into the street: the bride and groom, the guests, a nonstop mariachi band – 'the usual imbeciles,' Flor called them.

'I'm worried about los niños at the circus,' Edward Bonshaw confided to the transvestite, choosing not to engage the celibacy subject, or tactfully allowing it to wait.

'Los niños de la basura are almost old enough to be getting married,' Flor said, as she made threatening gestures out the driver's-side window to anyone (even children) in the wedding party, the cigarette now dangling from her lips. 'If these kids were getting married, I would be worried about them,' Flor carried on. 'At the circus, the worst that can go wrong is a lion kills you. There's a lot more that can go wrong with a marriage.'

'Well, if that's how you feel about marriage, I suppose celibacy isn't such a bad idea,' Edward Bonshaw said, in his Jesuitical way.

'There's only one actual lion at the circus,' Juan Diego interposed from the backseat. 'All the rest are lionesses.'

'So that asshole Ignacio is a *lioness* tamer – is that what you're saying?' Flor asked the boy.

She'd just managed to get around, or through, the wedding party, when Flor and the VW Beetle encountered a tilted burro cart. The cart was overloaded with melons, but all the melons had rolled to the rear end of the cart, hoisting the burro by its harness into the air; the melons outweighed the little donkey, whose hooves were flailing. The front end of the burro cart was also suspended in the air.

'Another dangling donkey,' Flor said. With surprising delicacy, she gave the finger to the burro-cart driver – using the same long-fingered hand that once again held her cigarette (between her thumb and index finger). About a dozen melons had rolled into the street, and the burro-cart driver had abandoned the dangling donkey because some street kids were stealing his melons.

'I know that guy,' Flor said, in her by-the-way fashion; no one in the little VW knew if she meant *as a client* or in another way.

When Flor drove into the circus grounds at Cinco Señores, the crowd for the matinee performance had gone home. The parking lot was almost empty; the audience for the evening show hadn't begun to arrive.

'Watch out for the elephant shit,' Flor warned them, when they were carrying the dump kids' stuff down the avenue of troupe tents. Edward Bonshaw promptly stepped in a fresh pile of it; the elephant shit covered his whole foot, up to his ankle.

'There's no saving your sandals from elephant shit, honey,' Flor told him. 'You'll be better off barefoot, once we find you a hose.'

'Merciful God,' Señor Eduardo said. The missionary walked on, but with a limp; it was not as exaggerated a limp as Juan Diego's, but enough of one to make the Iowan aware of the comparison. 'Now everyone will think we're related,' Edward Bonshaw good-naturedly told the boy.

'I wish we *were* related,' Juan Diego told him; he had blurted it out, too sincerely to have any hope of stopping himself.

'You *will* be related – all the rest of your lives,' Lupe said, but Juan Diego was suddenly unable to translate this; his eyes had welled with tears and he couldn't speak, nor could he understand that, in this case, Lupe was being accurate about the future.

Edward Bonshaw had difficulty speaking, too. 'That's a very sweet thing to say to me, Juan Diego,' the Iowan haltingly said. 'I would be proud to be related to you,' Señor Eduardo told the boy.

'Well, isn't that great? You're both very sweet,' Flor said. 'Except that priests can't have children – one of the downsides of celibacy, I suppose.'

It was twilight at Circo de La Maravilla, and the various performers were between shows. The new-comers were an odd foursome: a Jesuit scholastic who flagellated himself, a transvestite prostitute who'd had an unspeakable life in Houston, and two dump kids. Where the flaps of the troupe tents were open, the kids could see some of the performers fussing with their makeup or their costumes – among them, a transvestite dwarf. She was standing in front of a full-length mirror, putting on her lipstick.

'¡Hola, Flor!' the stout dwarf called, wiggling her hips and blowing Flor a kiss.

'Saludos, Paco,' Flor said, with a wave of her long-fingered hand.

'I didn't know Paco could be a girl's name,' Edward Bonshaw said politely to Flor.

'It isn't,' Flor told him. 'Paco is a guy's name – Paco is a guy, like me,' Flor said.

'But you're not—'

'Yes, I am,' Flor said, cutting him off. 'I'm just more *passable* than Paco, honey,' she told the Iowan.

'Paco isn't trying to be passable – Paco is a *clown*.'

They went on; they were expected at the lion tamer's tent. Edward Bonshaw kept looking at Flor, saying nothing.

'Flor has a *thing*, like a *boy's* thing,' Lupe said helpfully. 'Does the parrot man get it that Flor has a penis?' Lupe asked Juan Diego, who didn't translate her helpful tip to Señor Eduardo, although he knew his sister had trouble reading the parrot man's mind.

'El hombre papagayo – that's me, isn't it?' the Iowan asked Juan Diego. 'Lupe is talking about me, isn't she?'

'I think you're a very nice parrot man,' Flor said to him; she saw that the Iowan was blushing, and this had encouraged her to be more flirtatious with him.

'Thank you,' Edward Bonshaw said to the transvestite; he was limping more. Like clay, the elephant shit was hardening on his ruined sandal and between his toes, but something else was weighing him down. Señor Eduardo seemed to be bearing a burden; whatever it was, it appeared to be heavier than elephant shit – no amount of whipping would lessen the load. Whatever cross the Iowan had borne, and for how long, he couldn't carry it a step farther. He was struggling, not only to walk. 'I don't think I can do this,' Señor Eduardo said.

'Do *what*?' Flor asked him, but the missionary merely shook his head; his limp looked more like staggering than limping.

The circus band was playing somewhere – just the start of a piece of music, which stopped shortly after it began and then started up again. The band couldn't overcome a hard part; the band was struggling, too.

There was a good-looking Argentinian couple standing in the open flap of their tent. They were aerialists, checking over each other's safety harnesses, testing the strength of the metal grommets where the guy wires would be attached to them. The aerialists wore tight, gold-spangled singlets, and they couldn't stop fondling each other while they checked out their safety gear.

'I hear they have sex all the time, even though they're already married – they keep people in the nearby tents awake,' Flor said to Edward Bonshaw. 'Maybe having sex all the time is an Argentinian thing,' Flor said. 'I don't think it's a *married* thing,' she added.

There was a girl about Lupe's age standing outside one of the troupe tents. The girl was wearing a blue-green singlet and a mask with a bird's beak on it; she was practicing with a hula hoop. Some older girls, improbably costumed as flamingos, ran past the dump kids in the avenue between the tents; the girls wore pink tutus, and they were carrying their flamingo heads, which had long, rigid necks. Their silver anklets chimed.

'Los niños de la basura,' Juan Diego and Lupe heard one of the headless flamingos say. The dump kids hadn't known they would be recognized at the circus, but Oaxaca was a small city.

'Cunt-brained, half-dressed flamingos,' Flor

observed, saying nothing more; Flor, of course, had been called worse names.

In the seventies, there was a gay bar on Bustamante, in the neighborhood of Zaragoza Street. The bar was called La China, after someone with curly hair. (The name was changed about thirty years ago, but the bar on Bustamante is still there – and still gay.)

Flor felt at ease; she could be herself at La China, but even there they called her La Loca – 'The Crazy Lady.' It was not all that common, in those days, for transvestites to be themselves – to cross-dress everywhere they went, the way Flor did. And in the parlance of the crowd at La China, their calling Flor 'La Loca' had a gay connotation – it amounted to calling her 'The Queen.'

There was a special bar for the cross-dressers, even in the seventies. La Coronita – 'The Little Crown' – was on the corner of Bustamante and Xóchitl. It was a party place – the clientele was mostly gay. The transvestites all dressed up – they cross-dressed like crazy, and everyone had a good time – but La Coronita was not a place for prostitution, and when the transvestites arrived at the bar, they were dressed as men; they didn't cross-dress until they were safely inside The Little Crown.

Not Flor; she was always a woman, everywhere she went – whether she was working on Zaragoza Street or just partying on Bustamante, Flor was always herself. That was why she was called The Queen; she was La Loca everywhere she went.

They even knew her at La Maravilla; the circus

knew who the real stars were – they were the ones who were stars all the time.

Edward Bonshaw was only now discovering who Flor was, as he tramped through elephant shit at Circus of The Wonder. (To Señor Eduardo, 'The Wonder' was Flor.)

A juggler was practicing outside one of the troupe tents, and the contortionist called Pajama Man was limbering up. He was called Pajama Man because he was as loose and floppy as a pair of pajamas without a body; he moved like something you might see hanging on a clothesline.

Maybe the circus isn't such a good place for a cripple, Juan Diego was thinking.

'Remember, Juan Diego – you are a reader,' Señor Eduardo said to the worried-looking boy. 'There is a life in books, and in the world of your imagination; there is more than the physical world, even here.'

'I should have met you when I was a kid,' Flor told the missionary. 'We might have helped each other get through some shit.'

They made way in the avenue of troupe tents for the elephant trainer and two of his elephants; distracted by the actual elephants, Edward Bonshaw stepped in another enormous mound of elephant shit, this time with his good foot and the one clean sandal.

'Merciful God,' the Iowan said again.

'It's a good thing *you're* not moving to the circus,' Flor told him.

'The elephant shit isn't small,' Lupe was babbling.

'How does the parrot man manage not to see it?'

'My name again – I know you're talking about me,' Señor Eduardo said cheerfully to Lupe. '"El hombre papagayo" has a nice ring to it, doesn't it?'

'You not only need a wife,' Flor told the Iowan. 'It would take an entire family to look after you properly.'

They came to the cage for the three lionesses. One of the lady lions eyed them languidly – the other two were asleep.

'You see how the females get along together?' Flor was saying; it was increasingly clear that she knew her way around La Maravilla. 'But not *this* guy,' Flor said, stopping at the solitary lion's cage; the alleged king of beasts was in a cage by himself, and he looked disgruntled about it. 'Hola, Hombre,' Flor said to the lion. 'His name is Hombre,' Flor explained. 'Check out his balls – big ones, aren't they?'

'Lord, have mercy,' Edward Bonshaw said.

Lupe was indignant. 'It's not the poor lion's fault – he didn't have a choice about his balls,' she said. 'Hombre doesn't like it if you make fun of him,' she added.

'You can read the lion's mind, I suppose,' Juan Diego said to his sister.

'Anyone can read Hombre's mind,' Lupe answered. She was staring at the lion, at his huge face and heavy mane – not at his balls. The lion seemed suddenly agitated by her. Perhaps sensing Hombre's agitation, the two sleeping lionesses woke up; all three of the lionesses were watching Lupe, as if she were a rival for Hombre's affection. Juan Diego had the feeling that Lupe and the lionesses felt sorry for the lion – they seemed almost as sorry for him as they feared him.

'Hombre,' Lupe said softly to the lion, 'it'll be all right. Nothing's your fault.'

'What are you talking about?' Juan Diego asked her.

'Come on, niños,' Flor was saying, 'you have an appointment with the lion tamer and his wife – you don't have any business with the lions.'

By the transfixed way Lupe was staring at Hombre, and the restless way the lion paced in his cage as he stared back at her, you would have thought that Lupe's business at Circo de La Maravilla was entirely with that lone male lion. 'It'll be all right,' she repeated to Hombre, like a promise.

'*What* will be all right?' Juan Diego asked his sister.

'Hombre is the last dog. He's the last one,' Lupe told her brother. Naturally, this made no sense – Hombre was a lion, not a dog. But Lupe had distinctly said 'el último perro'; *the last one*, she'd repeated, to be clear – 'el último.'

'What do you mean, Lupe?' Juan Diego asked impatiently; he was sick of her endlessly prophetic pronouncements.

'That Hombre – he's the *top* rooftop dog *and* the last one,' was all she said, shrugging. It irritated Juan Diego when Lupe couldn't be bothered to explain herself.

Finally, the circus band had found its way beyond the beginning of the repeated piece of music. Darkness was falling; lights were turned on in the troupe tents. In the avenue ahead of them, the dump kids could see Ignacio, the lion tamer; he was coiling his long whip.

'I hear you like whips,' Flor said quietly to the hobbling missionary.

'You earlier mentioned a hose,' Edward Bonshaw replied, somewhat stiffly. 'Right now, I would like a hose.'

'Tell the parrot man to check out the lion tamer's whip – it's a big one,' Lupe was babbling.

Ignacio was watching them approach in the calmly calculating way he might have measured the courage and reliability of new lions. The lion tamer's tight pants were like a matador's; he wore nothing but a fitted V-necked vest on his torso, to show off his muscles. The vest was white, not only to accentuate Ignacio's dark-brown skin; if he were ever attacked by a lion in the ring, Ignacio wanted the crowd to see how red his blood was – blood shows up the brightest against a white background. Even when dying, Ignacio would be vain.

'Forget his whip – look at *him*,' Flor whispered to the beshitted Iowan. 'Ignacio is a born crowd-pleaser.'

'*And* a womanizer!' Lupe babbled. It didn't matter if she failed to hear what you whispered, because she already knew what you were thinking. Yet the parrot man's mind, like Rivera's, was a hard one for Lupe to read. 'Ignacio likes the lionesses – he likes *all* the ladies,' Lupe was saying, but by now the dump kids were at the lion tamer's tent, and Soledad, Ignacio's wife, had come out of the troupe tent to stand beside her preening, powerful-looking husband.

'If you think you just saw the king of beasts,' Flor was still whispering to Edward Bonshaw, 'think again. You're about to meet him now,' the transvestite whispered to the missionary. 'Ignacio is the king of beasts.'

'The king of *pigs*,' Lupe said suddenly, but of course Juan Diego was the only one who understood her. And he would never understand everything about her.

17

New Year's Eve at the Encantador

Maybe it was nothing more than the melancholy of that moment when the dump kids arrived at La Maravilla, or else the unattached eyes in the darkness – those disembodied eyes surrounding the car speeding toward the beach resort with the bewitching name of Encantador. Who knows what made Juan Diego suddenly nod off? It might have been that moment when the road narrowed and the car slowed down, and the intriguing eyes vanished. (When the dump kids moved to the circus, there were more eyes watching them than they'd been used to.)

'At first, I thought he was daydreaming – he seemed to be in a kind of trance,' Dr. Quintana was saying.

'Is he all right?' Clark French asked his wife, the doctor.

'He's just asleep, Clark – he fell sound asleep,' Josefa said. 'It may be the jet lag, or what a bad night's sleep your ill-advised aquarium caused him.'

'Josefa, he fell asleep when we were talking – in the middle of a conversation!' Clark cried. 'Does he have narcolepsy?'

'Don't shake him!' Juan Diego heard Clark's wife say, but he kept his eyes closed.

'I've never heard of a narcoleptic writer,' Clark French was saying. 'What about the drugs he's taking?'

'The beta-blockers can affect your sleep,' Dr. Quintana told her husband.

'I was thinking of the Viagra—'

'The Viagra does only one thing, Clark.'

Juan Diego thought this was a good moment to open his eyes. 'Are we here?' he asked them. Josefa was still sitting beside him in the backseat; Clark had opened the rear door and was peering into the SUV at his former teacher. 'Is this the Encantador?' Juan Diego asked innocently. 'Has the mystery guest arrived?'

She had, but no one had seen her. Perhaps she'd traveled a long way and was resting in her room. She seemed to know the room – that is, she had requested it. It was near the library, on the second floor of the main building; either she'd stayed at the Encantador before or she assumed that a room near the library would be quiet.

'Personally, I never nap,' Clark was saying; he had wrestled Juan Diego's mammoth orange bag away from the boy driver and was now lugging it along an outdoor balcony of the pretty hotel, which was a magical but rambling assemblage of adjoining buildings on a hillside overlooking the sea. The palm trees obscured any view of the beach – even from the perspective of the second- and third-floor rooms

– but the sea was visible. 'A good night's sleep is all I need,' Clark carried on.

'There were fish in my room last night, and an eel,' Juan Diego reminded his former student. Here he would have a second-floor room, on the same floor as the uninvited guest – in an adjacent building that was easily reached by the outdoor balcony.

'About the fish – pay no attention to Auntie Carmen,' Clark was saying. 'Your room is some distance from the swimming pool. The children in the pool, in the early morning, shouldn't wake you up.'

'Auntie Carmen is a pet person,' Clark's wife interjected. 'She cares more about fish than she does about people.'

'Thank God the moray survived,' Clark joined in. 'I believe Morales *lives* with Auntie Carmen.'

'It's a pity no one else does,' Josefa said. 'No one else *would*,' the doctor added.

Below them, children were playing in the pool. 'Lots of teenagers in this family – therefore, lots of free nannies for the little ones,' Clark pointed out.

'Lots of children, period, in this family,' the OB-GYN observed. 'We're not all like Auntie Carmen.'

'I'm taking a medication – it plays games with how I sleep,' Juan Diego told them. 'I'm taking beta-blockers,' he said to Dr. Quintana. 'As you probably know,' he said to the doctor, 'beta-blockers can have a depressing effect, or a diminishing one, on your real life – whereas the effect they have on your *dream* life is a little unpredictable.'

Juan Diego *didn't* tell the doctor that he'd been playing games with the dosage of his Lopressor prescription. Probably he came across as being completely candid – that is, as far as Dr. Quintana and Clark French could tell.

Juan Diego's room was delightful; the sea-view windows had screens, and there was a ceiling fan – no air-conditioning would be necessary. The big bathroom was charming, and it had an outdoor shower with a pagoda-shaped bamboo roof over it.

'Take your time to freshen up before dinner,' Josefa said to Juan Diego. 'The jet lag – you know, the time difference – could also be influencing how the beta-blockers affect you,' she told him.

'After the bigger kids take the little kids to bed, the *real* dinner-table conversation can get started,' Clark was saying, squeezing his former teacher's shoulder.

Was this a warning not to bring up adult subjects around the children and the teenagers? Juan Diego was wondering. Juan Diego realized that Clark French, despite his bluff heartiness, was still uptight – a forty-something prude. Clark's fellow MFA students at Iowa, if they could meet him now, would *still* be teasing him.

Abortion, Juan Diego knew, was illegal in the Philippines; he was curious to know what Dr. Quintana, the OB-GYN, thought about *that*. (And did she and her husband – Clark, the oh-so-good Catholic – feel the *same* about that?) Surely *that* was a dinner-table conversation he and Clark couldn't (or shouldn't) have before the children and the teenagers had trotted off to bed. Juan Diego hoped he might have this conversation with Dr. Quintana after *Clark* had trotted off to bed.

Juan Diego became so agitated thinking about this that he almost forgot about Miriam. Of course he hadn't entirely forgotten about her – not for a minute. He resisted taking an outdoor shower, not only because it was dark outside (there would be insects galore in the outdoor shower after nightfall) but because he might not hear the phone. He couldn't call Miriam – he didn't even know her last name! – nor could he call the front desk and ask to be connected to the 'uninvited' woman. But if Miriam was the mystery woman, wouldn't she call him?

He elected to take a bath – no insects, and he could keep the door to the bedroom open; if she called, he could hear the phone. Naturally, he rushed his bath and there was no call. Juan Diego tried to remain calm; he plotted his next move with his medications. Not to confuse the issue, he returned the pill-cutting device to his toilet kit. The Viagra and the Lopressor prescriptions stood side by side on the counter, next to the bathroom sink.

No half-doses for me, Juan Diego decided. After dinner, he would take one whole Lopressor pill – the right amount, in other words – but *not* if he was with Miriam. Skipping a dose hadn't hurt him before, and a surge of adrenaline could be beneficial – even necessary – with Miriam.

The Viagra, he thought, presented him with a more complicated decision. For his rendezvous with Dorothy, Juan Diego had traded his usual half-dose for a whole one; for Miriam, he imagined, a half-dose wouldn't suffice. The complicated part was when to take it. The Viagra needed nearly an hour to work. And how long would one Viagra – a whole one, the full 100 milligrams – last?

And it was New Year's Eve! Juan Diego suddenly remembered. Certainly the teenagers would be up past midnight, if not the little children. Wouldn't most of the adults also stay up to herald the coming year?

Suppose Miriam invited him to *her* room? Should he bring the Viagra with him to dinner? (It was too soon to take one now.)

He dressed slowly, trying to imagine what Miriam would want him to wear. He'd written about more long-lasting, more complex, and more diverse relationships than he'd ever had. His readers – that is, the ones who'd never met him – might have imagined that he'd lived a sophisticated sexual life; in his novels, there were homosexual and bisexual experiences, and plenty of the plain-old heterosexual ones. Juan Diego made a political point of being sexually explicit in his writing; yet he'd never even lived with anyone, and the *plain-old* part of being a heterosexual was the kind of heterosexual he was.

Juan Diego suspected he was probably pretty boring as a lover. He would have been the first to admit that what passed for his sex life existed almost entirely in his imagination – like now, he thought ruefully. All he was doing was *imagining* Miriam; he didn't even know if she was the mystery guest who'd checked into the Encantador.

The conviction that he chiefly had an *imaginary* sex life depressed him, and he'd taken only *half* a Lopressor pill today; this time, he couldn't entirely blame the beta-blockers for making him feel diminished. Juan Diego decided to put one Viagra tablet in his right-front pants pocket. This way, he'd be prepared – Miriam or no Miriam.

He often put his hand in his right-front pocket; Juan Diego didn't need to see that pretty mah-jongg tile, but he liked the feel of it – so smooth. The game block had made a perfect check mark on Edward Bonshaw's pale forehead; Señor Eduardo had carried the tile with him as a keepsake. When the dear man was dying – when Señor Eduardo was not only no longer dressing himself, but wasn't wearing clothes with pockets – he'd given the mah-jongg tile to Juan Diego. The game block, once imbedded between Edward Bonshaw's blond eyebrows, would become Juan Diego's talisman.

The four-sided gray-blue Viagra tablet was not as smooth as the bamboo-and-ivory mah-jongg tile; the game block was twice the size of the Viagra pill – his *rescue* pill, as Juan Diego thought of it. And if Miriam was the uninvited guest in the second-floor room near the Encantador library, the Viagra tablet in Juan Diego's right-front pants pocket was a second talisman he carried with him.

Naturally, the knock on his hotel-room door filled him with false expectations. It was only Clark, coming to take him to dinner. When Juan Diego was turning out the lights in his bathroom and bedroom, Clark advised him to turn on the ceiling fan and leave it on.

'See the gecko?' Clark said, pointing to the ceiling. A gecko, smaller than a pinky finger, was poised on the ceiling above the headboard of the bed. There wasn't much Juan Diego missed about Mexico – hence he'd never been back – but he did miss the geckos. The little one above the bed darted on its adhesive toes across the ceiling at the exact instant Juan Diego turned on the fan.

'Once the fan has been on awhile, the geckos will settle down,' Clark said. 'You don't want them racing around when you're trying to go to sleep.'

Juan Diego was disappointed in himself for not seeing the geckos until Clark pointed one out; as he was closing his hotel-room door, he spotted a second gecko scurrying over the bathroom wall – it was lightning-fast and quickly disappeared behind the bathroom mirror.

'I miss the geckos,' Juan Diego admitted to Clark. Outside, on the balcony, they could hear music coming from a noisy club for locals on the beach.

'Why don't you go back to Mexico – I mean, just to *visit*?' Clark asked him.

It was always like this with Clark, Juan Diego remembered. Clark wanted Juan Diego's 'issues' with childhood and early adolescence to be over; Clark wanted all grievances to end in an uplifting manner, as in Clark's novels. Everyone should be saved, Clark believed; everything could be forgiven, he imagined. Clark made goodness seem tedious.

But what *hadn't* Juan Diego and Clark French fought about?

There'd been no end to their to and fro about the late Pope John Paul II, who'd died in 2005. He'd been a young cardinal from Poland when he was elected pope, and he became a very popular pope, but John Paul's efforts to 'restore normality' in Poland – this meant making abortion illegal again – drove Juan Diego crazy.

Clark French had expressed his fondness for the Polish pope's 'culture of life' idea – John Paul II's name for his stance against abortion *and* contraception, which amounted to protecting 'defenseless' fetuses from the 'culture of death' idea.

'Why would you – you of all people, given what *happened* to you – choose a death idea over a life idea?' Clark had asked his former teacher. And now Clark was suggesting (again) that Juan Diego should go back to Mexico – just to *visit*!

'You know why I won't go back, Clark,' Juan Diego once more answered, limping along the second-floor balcony. (Another time, when he'd had too much beer, Juan Diego had said to Clark: 'Mexico is in the hands of criminals and the Catholic Church.')

'Don't tell me you blame the Church for AIDS – you're not saying safe sex is the answer to *everything*, are you?' Clark now asked his former teacher. This was not a very skillfully veiled reference, Juan Diego knew – not that Clark was necessarily trying to *veil* his references.

Juan Diego remembered how Clark had called condom use 'propaganda.' Clark was probably paraphrasing Pope Benedict XVI. Hadn't Benedict said something to the effect that condoms 'only exacerbate' the AIDS problem? Or was that what *Clark* had said?

And now, because Juan Diego hadn't answered Clark's question about safe sex solving *everything*, Clark kept pressing the Benedict point: '*Benedict's* position – namely, that the only efficient way to combat an epidemic is by *spiritual renovation*—'

'Clark!' Juan Diego cried. 'All "spiritual renovation" means is more of the same old family values – meaning heterosexual marriage, meaning nothing but sexual abstinence before marriage—'

'Sounds to me like *one* way to slow down an epidemic,' Clark said slyly. He was as doctrinaire as ever!

'Between your Church's unfollowable rules and human nature, I'll bet on human nature,' Juan Diego said. 'Take celibacy—' he began.

'Maybe after the children and the teenagers have gone to bed,' Clark reminded his former teacher.

They were alone on the balcony, and it was New Year's Eve; Juan Diego was pretty sure that the teenagers would be up later than the adults, but all he said was: 'Think about pedophilia, Clark.'

'I knew it! I knew that was next!' Clark said excitedly.

In his Christmas address in Rome – not even two weeks ago – Pope Benedict XVI had said that pedophilia was considered *normal* as recently as the 1970s. Clark knew that would have made Juan Diego hot under the collar. Now, naturally, his former teacher was up to his old tricks, quoting the pope as if the entire realm of Catholic theology were to blame for Benedict's suggesting there was no such thing as evil in itself or good in itself.

'Clark, Benedict *said* there is only a "better than" and a "worse than" – that's what your pope said,' Clark's former teacher was telling him.

'May I remind you that the statistics on pedophilia *outside* the Church, in the general population, are exactly the same as the statistics *inside* the Church?' Clark French said to Juan Diego.

'Benedict said: "Nothing is good or bad in itself." He said *nothing*, Clark,' Juan Diego told his former student. 'Pedophilia isn't nothing; surely pedophilia is "bad in itself," Clark.'

'After the children have—'

'There are no children here, Clark!' Juan Diego shouted. 'We're alone, on a balcony!' he cried.

'Well—' Clark French said cautiously, looking all around; they could hear the voices of children somewhere, but no children (not even teenagers, or other adults) were anywhere in sight.

'The Catholic hierarchy believes kissing leads to sin,' Juan Diego whispered. 'Your Church is against birth control, against abortion, against gay marriage – your Church is against *kissing*, Clark!'

Suddenly, a swarm of small children ran past them on the balcony; their flip-flops made a slapping sound and their wet hair gleamed.

'After the little ones have gone to bed—' Clark French began again; conversation was a competition with him, akin to a combat sport. Clark would have made an indefatigable missionary. Clark had that Jesuitical 'I know everything' way about him – always the emphasis on learning and evangelizing. The mere thought of his own martyrdom probably motivated Clark. He would happily suffer, just to make an impossible point; if you abused him, he would smile and thrive.

'Are you all right?' Clark was asking Juan Diego.

'I'm just a little out of breath – I'm not used to limping this fast,' Juan Diego told him. 'Or limping and talking, together.'

They slowed their pace as they descended the stairs and made their way to the main lobby of the Encantador, where the dining room was. There was an overhanging roof to the hotel restaurant, and a rolled-up bamboo curtain that could be lowered as a barrier against wind and rain. The openness to the palm trees and the view of the sea gave the dining room the feeling of a spacious veranda. There were paper party hats at all the tables.

What a big family Clark French had married into! Juan Diego was thinking. Dr. Josefa Quintana must have had thirty or forty relatives, and more than half of them were children or young people.

'No one expects you to remember everyone's name,' Clark whispered to Juan Diego.

'About the mystery guest,' Juan Diego said suddenly. 'She should sit next to me.'

'Next to *you*?' Clark asked him.

'Certainly. All of you hate her. At least I'm neutral,' Juan Diego told Clark.

'I don't *hate* her – no one *knows* her! She's inserted herself into a *family*—'

'I know, Clark – I know,' Juan Diego said. 'She should sit next to me. We're both strangers. All of you know one another.'

'I was thinking of putting her at one of the children's tables,' Clark told him. 'Maybe at the table with the most obstreperous children.'

'You see? You *do* hate her,' Juan Diego said to him.

'I was kidding. Maybe a table of teenagers – the most sullen ones,' Clark continued.

'You definitely hate her. I'm *neutral*,' Juan Diego reminded him. (Miriam could corrupt the teenagers, Juan Diego was thinking.)

'Uncle Clark!' A small, round-faced boy tugged on Clark's hand.

'Yes, Pedro. What is it?' Clark asked the little boy.

'It's the big gecko behind the painting in the library. It came out from behind the painting!' Pedro told him.

'Not the *giant* gecko – not *that* one!' Clark cried, feigning alarm.

'Yes! The giant one!' the little boy exclaimed.

'Well, it just so happens, Pedro, that *this* man knows all about geckos – he's a gecko expert. He not only loves geckos; he *misses* geckos,' Clark told the child. 'This is Mr. Guerrero,' Clark added, slipping away and leaving Juan Diego with Pedro. The boy instantly clutched the older man's hand.

'You *love* them?' the boy asked, but before Juan Diego could answer him, Pedro said: 'Why do you miss geckos, Mister?'

'Ah, well—' Juan Diego started and then stopped, stalling for time. When he began to limp in the direction of the stairs to the library, his limp drew a dozen children to him; they were five-year-olds, or only a little older, like Pedro.

'He knows all about geckos – he loves them,' Pedro was telling the other kids. 'He *misses* geckos. *Why?*' Pedro asked Juan Diego again.

'What happened to your foot, Mister?' one of the other children, a little girl with pigtails, asked him.

'I was a dump kid. I lived in a shack near the Oaxaca basurero – *basurero* means 'dump'; Oaxaca is in Mexico,' Juan Diego told them. 'The shack my sister and I lived in had only one door. Every morning, when I got up, there was a gecko on that screen door. The gecko was so fast, it could disappear in the blink of an eye,' Juan Diego told the children, clapping his hands for effect. He was limping more as he went up the stairs. 'One morning, a truck backed over my right foot. The driver's side-view mirror was broken; the driver couldn't see me. It wasn't his fault; he was a good man. He's dead now, and I miss him. I miss the dump, and the geckos,' Juan Diego told the children. He was not aware that some adults were also following him upstairs to the library. Clark French was following his former teacher, too; it was, of course, Juan Diego's *story* that they were following.

Had the man with the limp really said he missed the *dump*? a few of the children were asking one another.

'If I'd lived in the basurero, I don't think I would *miss* it,' the little girl with pigtails told Pedro. 'Maybe he misses his *sister*,' she said.

'I can understand missing *geckos*,' Pedro told her.

'Geckos are mostly nocturnal – they're more active at night, when there are more insects. They eat insects; geckos don't hurt you,' Juan Diego was saying.

'Where is your sister?' the little girl with the pigtails asked Juan Diego.

'She's dead,' Juan Diego answered her; he was about to say *how* Lupe had died, but he didn't want to give the little ones nightmares.

'Look!' Pedro said. He pointed at a big painting; it hung over a comfortable-looking couch in the Encantador library. The gecko was enough of a giant to be almost as visible, even from a distance, as the painting. The gecko clung to the wall beside the painting; as Juan Diego and the children approached, the gecko climbed higher. The big lizard waited, watching them, about halfway between the painting and the ceiling. It really was a big gecko, almost the size of a house cat.

'The man in the painting is a saint,' Juan Diego was telling the children. 'He was once a student at the University of Paris; he'd been a soldier, too – he was a Basque soldier, and he was wounded.'

'Wounded *how*?' Pedro asked.

'By a cannonball,' Juan Diego told him.

'Wouldn't a cannonball kill you?' Pedro asked.

'I guess not if you're going to be a saint,' Juan Diego answered.

'What was his name?' the little girl with pigtails asked; she was full of questions. 'Who was the saint?'

'Your uncle Clark knows who he was,' Juan Diego answered her. He was aware of Clark French watching him, and listening to him – ever the devoted student. (Clark looked like someone who might survive being shot with a cannonball.)

'Uncle Clark!' the children were calling.

'What was the saint's *name*?' the little girl with pigtails kept asking.

'Saint Ignatius Loyola,' Juan Diego heard Clark French tell the children.

The giant gecko moved as fast as a small one. Maybe Clark's voice had been too confident, or just too loud. It was amazing how the big lizard could flatten itself out – how it managed to fit behind the painting, although it had moved the painting slightly. The painting now hung a little crookedly on the wall, but it was as if the gecko had never been there. Saint Ignatius himself had not seen the lizard, nor was Loyola even looking at the children and adults.

From all the portraits of Loyola that Juan Diego had seen – in the Templo de la Compañía de Jesús, at Lost Children, and elsewhere in Oaxaca (and in Mexico City) – he couldn't recall the bald but bearded saint ever looking back at him. Saint Ignatius's eyes looked *above*; Loyola was looking, ever-beseechingly, toward Heaven. The Jesuits' founder was seeking a higher authority – Loyola wasn't inclined to make eye contact with mere bystanders.

'Dinner is served!' an adult's voice was calling.

'Thank you for the story, Mister,' Pedro said to Juan Diego. 'I'm sorry about all the stuff you miss,' the little boy added.

Both Pedro and the little girl with pigtails wanted to hold Juan Diego's hands when all three of them got back to the top of the stairs, but the stairs were too narrow; it wouldn't have been safe for a crippled man to go down those stairs holding hands with two little children. Juan Diego knew he should hold the railing instead.

Besides, he saw Clark French waiting for him at the bottom of the stairs – no doubt the new seating plan had given a few of the most senior family members fits. Juan Diego imagined there were women of a certain age who'd wanted to sit next to him; these older women were his most avid readers – at least they were usually the ones who weren't shy about speaking to him.

All Clark enthusiastically said to him was: 'I just love listening to how you tell a story.'

Maybe you wouldn't love listening to my Virgin

Mary story, Juan Diego was thinking, but he felt inordinately tired – especially for someone who'd slept on the plane *and* had a nap in the car. Young Pedro was right to feel sorry about 'all the stuff' Juan Diego missed. Just thinking about all the stuff he missed made Juan Diego miss everyone *more* – he'd hardly scratched the surface with that dump story for the children.

The seating plan had been very carefully worked out; the children's tables were at the perimeters of the dining room, the adults clustered together at the center tables. Josefa, Clark's wife, would be seated to one side of Juan Diego, who saw that the other seat beside him was empty. Clark took a seat diagonally across the table from his former teacher. No one wore a party hat – not yet.

Juan Diego wasn't surprised to see that the middle of his table was, for the most part, composed of those 'women of a certain age' – the ones he'd been thinking about. They smiled knowingly at him, the way women who've read your novels (and assume they know everything about you) do; only one of these older women wasn't smiling.

You know what they say about people who look like their pets. Before Clark commenced making a ringing sound with a spoon against his water glass, before Clark's garrulous introduction of his former teacher to his wife's family, Juan Diego saw in an instant who Auntie Carmen was. There was no one else in sight who even slightly resembled a brightly colored, sharp-toothed, voracious eel. And, in the flattering light at the dinner table, Auntie Carmen's jowls might have been mistaken for a moray's quivering gills. Like a moray, too, Auntie Carmen radiated distance and distrust – her aloofness disguising the biting eel's renowned ability to launch a lethal strike from afar.

'I have something I want to say to *you two*,' Dr. Quintana said to her husband and Juan Diego, when their table had quieted down – Clark had *finally* stopped talking; the first course, a ceviche, had been served. 'No religion, no Church politics, not a word about abortion or birth control – not while we're eating,' Josefa said.

'Not while the children and teenagers are—' Clark started to say.

'Not while the *adults* are here, Clark – no talking about any of it unless you two are *alone*,' his wife told him.

'And no *sex*,' Auntie Carmen said; she was looking at Juan Diego. He was the one who wrote about sex – Clark didn't. And the way the eel woman had said 'no *sex*' – as if it left a bad taste in her wizened mouth – implied both talking about it *and* doing it.

'I guess that leaves literature,' Clark said truculently.

'That depends on *which* literature,' Juan Diego said. As soon as he'd sat down, he felt a little light-headed; his vision had blurred. This happened with Viagra – usually, the feeling soon passed. But when Juan Diego felt his right-front pocket, he was reminded that he hadn't taken the Viagra; he could feel the tablet and the mah-jongg tile through the fabric of his trousers.

There was, of course, some seafood in the ceviche – what looked like shrimp, or perhaps a kind of crayfish. And wedges of mango, Juan Diego noticed; he'd slightly touched the marinade with the tines of his salad fork. Citrus, certainly – probably lime, Juan Diego thought.

Auntie Carmen saw him sneaking a taste; she brandished her salad fork, as if to demonstrate that she'd restrained herself long enough.

'I see no reason why we should wait for *her*,' Auntie Carmen said, pointing her fork at the empty chair next to Juan Diego. 'She's not *family*,' the eel woman added.

Juan Diego felt something or someone touch his ankles; he saw a small face looking up at him from under the table. The little girl with pigtails sat at his feet. 'Hi, Mister,' she said. 'The lady told me to tell you – she's coming.'

'What lady?' Juan Diego asked the little girl; to everyone at the table, except for Clark's wife, he must have looked like he was talking to his lap.

'Consuelo,' Josefa said to the little girl. 'You're supposed to be at your table – please go there.'

'Yes,' Consuelo said.

'*What* lady?' Juan Diego asked Consuelo again. The little girl had crawled out from under the table and now endured Auntie Carmen's cruel stare.

'The lady who just appears,' Consuelo said; she tugged on both her pigtails, making her head bob up and down. She ran off. The waiters were pouring wine – one of them was the boy driver who'd brought Juan Diego from the airport in Tagbilaran City.

'You must have driven the mystery lady from the airport,' Juan Diego said to him, waving the wine away, but the boy seemed not to understand. Josefa spoke to him in Tagalog; even then, the boy driver looked confused. He gave Dr. Quintana what sounded like an overlong answer.

'He says he didn't drive her – he says she just appeared in the driveway. No one saw her car or driver,' Josefa said.

'The plot thickens!' Clark French declared. 'No wine for him – he drinks only beer,' Clark was telling the boy driver, who was a lot less confident as a waiter than he'd been behind the wheel.

'Yes, sir,' the boy said.

'You shouldn't have provided your former teacher with all that *beer*,' Auntie Carmen said suddenly to Clark. 'Were you *drunk*?' Auntie Carmen asked Juan Diego. 'Whatever possessed you to turn off the air-conditioning? No one turns off the air-conditioning in Manila!'

'That's enough, Carmen,' Dr. Quintana told her aunt. 'Your precious aquarium is not dinner-table conversation. You say "no *sex*," I say "no *fish*." Got it?'

'It was *my* fault, Auntie,' Clark started in. 'The aquarium was *my* idea—'

'I was freezing cold,' Juan Diego explained to the eel woman. 'I *hate* air-conditioning,' he told every-one. 'I probably *did* have too much beer—'

'Don't apologize,' Josefa said to him. 'They were just fish.'

'*Just* fish!' Auntie Carmen cried.

Dr. Quintana leaned across the table, touching Auntie Carmen's leathery hand. 'Do you want to hear how many vaginas I've seen in the last week – in the last *month*?' she asked her aunt.

'Josefa!' Clark cried.

'No fish, no sex,' Dr. Quintana told the eel woman. 'You want to talk about *fish*, Carmen? Just watch out.'

'I hope Morales is okay,' Juan Diego said to Auntie Carmen, in an effort to be pacifying.

'Morales is different – the experience *changed* him,' Auntie Carmen said haughtily.

'No eels, either, Carmen,' Josefa said. 'You just watch out.'

Women doctors – how Juan Diego loved them! He'd adored Dr. Marisol Gomez; he was devoted to his dear friend Dr. Rosemary Stein. And here was the wonderful Dr. Josefa Quintana! Juan Diego was fond of Clark, but did Clark *deserve* a wife like this?

She 'just appears,' the little girl with pigtails had said about the mystery lady. And hadn't the boy driver confirmed that the lady *just appeared*?

Yet the aquarium conversation had been intense; no one, not even Juan Diego, was thinking about the uninvited guest – not at that moment when the little gecko fell (or dropped) from the ceiling. The gecko landed in the untouched ceviche next to Juan Diego; it was as if the tiny creature knew this was an

unguarded salad plate. The gecko appeared to drop
into the conversation at the only empty seat.

The lizard was as slender as a ballpoint pen, and
only half as long. Two women shrieked; one was a
well-dressed woman seated directly opposite the
mystery guest's unoccupied seat – she had her eyeglasses spattered with the citrus marinade. A wedge
of mango slipped off the salad plate in the direction
of the older man who'd been introduced to Juan
Diego as a retired surgeon. (He and Juan Diego sat on
either side of the empty seat.) The surgeon's wife, one
of those readers of 'a certain age,' had shrieked more
loudly than the well-dressed woman, who was now
calm and wiping her eyeglasses.

'*Damn* those things,' the well-dressed woman said.

'Just who invited *you*?' the retired surgeon asked
the little gecko, who now crouched (unmoving)
in the unfamiliar ceviche. Everyone but Auntie
Carmen laughed; the anxious-looking little gecko
was no laughing matter to her, apparently. The
gecko looked ready to spring, but where?

Later everyone would say that the gecko had distracted all of them from the slender woman in the
beige silk dress. She had *just appeared*, they would all
think later; no one saw her approaching the table,
though she was very watchable in that perfectly fitted,
sleeveless dress. She seemed to glide unnoticed to the
chair that was waiting for her – not even the gecko
saw her coming, and geckos are acutely alert. (If
you're a gecko and you want to stay alive, you'd better
be alert.)

Juan Diego would remember seeing only the briefest flash of the woman's slim wrist; he never saw the salad fork in her hand, not until she'd stabbed the gecko through its twig-size spine – pinning it to a wedge of mango on her plate.

'Got you,' Miriam said.

This time, only Auntie Carmen cried out – as if *she'd* been stabbed. You can always count on the children to see everything; maybe the kids had seen Miriam coming, and they'd had the good sense to watch her.

'I didn't think human beings could be as fast as geckos,' Pedro would say to Juan Diego another day. (They were in the second-floor library, staring at the Saint Ignatius Loyola painting, waiting for the *giant* gecko to make an appearance, but that big gecko was never seen again.)

'Geckos are really, *really* fast – you can't catch one,' Juan Diego would tell the little boy.

'But that lady—' Pedro started to say; he just stopped.

'Yes, she was fast,' was all Juan Diego would say.

In the hushed dining room, Miriam held the salad fork between her thumb and index finger, reminding Juan Diego of the way Flor used to hold a cigarette – as if it were a joint. 'Waiter,' Miriam was saying. The lifeless gecko hung limply from the glistening tines of the little fork. The boy driver, who was a clumsy waiter, rushed to take the murder weapon from Miriam. 'I'll need a new ceviche, too,' she told him, taking her seat.

'Don't get up, darling,' she said, putting her hand on Juan Diego's shoulder. 'I know it hasn't been long, but I've missed you terribly,' she added. Everyone in the dining room had heard her; no one was talking.

'I've missed *you*,' Juan Diego said to her.

'Well, I'm here now,' Miriam told him.

So they *knew* each other, everyone was thinking; she wasn't quite the mystery guest they'd been expecting. Suddenly, she didn't look *uninvited*. And Juan Diego didn't seem exactly *neutral*.

'This is *Miriam*,' Juan Diego announced. 'And this is Clark – Clark French, the writer. My former student,' Juan Diego said.

'Oh, yes,' Miriam said, smiling demurely.

'And Clark's wife, Josefa – Dr. Quintana,' Juan Diego went on.

'I'm so glad there's a doctor here,' Miriam told Josefa. 'It makes the Encantador seem less *remote*.'

A chorus of shouts greeted her – other doctors, raising their hands. (Mostly men, of course, but even the female doctors put up their hands.)

'Oh, wonderful – a *family* of doctors,' Miriam said, smiling to everyone. Only Auntie Carmen remained less than charmed; no doubt, she'd taken the gecko's side – she was a pet person, after all.

And what about the children? Juan Diego was wondering. What did they make of the mystery guest?

He felt Miriam's hand graze his lap; she rested it on his thigh. 'Happy New Year, darling,' she whispered to him. Juan Diego thought he also felt her foot touch his calf, then his knee.

'Hi, Mister,' Consuelo said, from under the table. This time, the little girl in pigtails was not alone; Pedro had crawled under the table with her. Juan Diego peered at them.

Josefa had not seen the children – she was leaning across the table, involved in some unreadable sign language with Clark.

Miriam looked under the table; she saw the two children peering up at them.

'I guess the lady doesn't love geckos, Mister,' Pedro was saying.

'I don't think she *misses* geckos,' Consuelo said.

'I don't love geckos in my ceviche,' Miriam told the children. 'I don't miss geckos in my *salad*,' she added.

'What do *you* think, Mister?' the little girl in pigtails asked Juan Diego. 'What would your sister think?' she asked him.

'Yeah, what would—' Pedro started to say, but Miriam leaned down to them; her face, under the table, was suddenly very close to the kids.

'Listen, you two,' Miriam told them. 'Don't ask him what his sister thinks – his sister was killed by a lion.'

That sent the kids away; they crawled off in a hurry.

I didn't want to give them nightmares, Juan Diego was trying to tell Miriam, but he couldn't speak. I didn't want to *frighten* them! he tried to tell her, but the words wouldn't come. It was as if he'd seen Lupe's face under the table, although the girl with pigtails, Consuelo, was much younger than Lupe had been when she died.

His vision suddenly blurred again; this time, Juan Diego knew it wasn't the Viagra.

'Just tears,' he said to Miriam. 'I'm fine – there's nothing wrong. I'm just crying,' he tried to explain to Josefa. (Dr. Quintana had taken his arm.)

'Are you all right?' Clark asked his former teacher.

'I'm fine, Clark – there's nothing wrong. I'm just *crying*,' Juan Diego repeated.

'Of course you are, darling – of course you are,' Miriam told him, taking his other arm; she kissed his hand.

'Where is that lovely child with the pigtails? Get her,' Miriam said to Dr. Quintana.

'Consuelo!' Josefa called. The little girl ran up to them at the table; Pedro was right behind her.

'There you are, you two!' Miriam cried; she let go of Juan Diego's arm, hugging the children to her. 'Don't be frightened,' she told them. 'Mr. Guerrero is sad about his sister – he's always thinking about her. Wouldn't you cry if you never forgot how *your* sister was killed by a lion?' Miriam asked the children.

'Yes!' Consuelo cried.

'I guess so,' Pedro told her; he actually looked like he might forget about it.

'Well, that's how Mr. Guerrero feels – he just *misses* her,' Miriam told the kids.

'I miss her – her name was Lupe,' Juan Diego

managed to tell the children. The boy driver, now a waiter, had brought him a beer; the awkward boy stood there, not knowing what to do with the beer.

'Just put it down!' Miriam told him, and he did.

Consuelo had climbed into Juan Diego's lap. 'It'll be okay,' the little girl was saying; she was tugging on her pigtails – it made him cry and cry. 'It'll be okay, Mister,' Consuelo kept saying to him.

Miriam picked up Pedro and held him in her lap; the boy seemed somewhat uncertain about her, but Miriam quickly solved that. 'What do you imagine *you* might miss, Pedro?' Miriam asked him. 'I mean, one day – what would you miss, if you lost it? *Who* would you miss? Who do you love?'

Who *is* this woman? Where did she *come from*? all the adults were thinking – Juan Diego was thinking this, too. He desired Miriam; he was thrilled to see her. But who *was* she, and what was she doing here? And why were they all riveted by her? Even the children, despite the fact that she'd frightened them.

'Well,' Pedro started to say, frowning seriously, 'I would miss my father. I *will* miss him – one day.'

'Yes, of course you will – that's very good. That's exactly what I mean,' Miriam told the boy. A kind of melancholy seemed to descend on little Pedro; he leaned back against Miriam, who cradled him against her breast. 'Smart boy,' she whispered to him. He closed his eyes; he sighed. It was almost obscene how Pedro looked *seduced*.

The table – the entire dining room – seemed

hushed. 'I'm sorry about your sister, Mister,' Consuelo said to Juan Diego.

'I'll be okay,' he told the little girl. He felt too tired to go on – too tired to change anything.

It was the boy driver, the unsure-of-himself waiter, who said something in Tagalog to Dr. Quintana.

'Yes, naturally – serve the main course. What a question – serve it!' Josefa said to him. (Not a single person had put on one of the party hats. It was still not party time.)

'Look at Pedro!' Consuelo said; the little girl was laughing. 'He's fallen asleep.'

'Oh, isn't that sweet?' Miriam said, smiling at Juan Diego. The little boy was sound asleep in Miriam's lap, his head against her breast. How unlikely that a boy his age could just drop off to sleep in the lap of a total stranger – and she was such a scary one!

Who *is* she? Juan Diego wondered again, but he couldn't stop smiling back at her. Maybe all of them were wondering who Miriam was, but no one said anything or did the slightest thing to stop her.

18

Lust Has a Way

For years after he'd left Oaxaca, Juan Diego would stay in touch with Brother Pepe. What Juan Diego knew about Oaxaca since the early seventies was largely due to Pepe's faithful correspondence.

The problem was that Juan Diego couldn't always remember *when* Pepe had passed along this or that important piece of information; to Pepe, every new thing was 'important' – each change mattered, as did those things that hadn't changed (and never would).

It was during the AIDS epidemic when Brother Pepe wrote to Juan Diego about that gay bar on Bustamante, but whether this was in the late eighties or early nineties – well, this was the kind of specificity that eluded Juan Diego. 'Yes, that bar is still there – and it's still gay,' Pepe had written; Juan Diego must have asked about it. 'But it's not La China anymore – it's called Chinampa now.'

And, around that time, Pepe had written that Dr. Vargas was feeling the 'hopelessness of the medical community.' AIDS had made Vargas feel it was 'irrelevant' to be an orthopedist. 'No doctor is trained to watch people die; we're not in the holding-hands business,' Vargas had told Pepe, and Vargas wasn't even dealing with infectious disease.

That sounded like Vargas, all right – still feeling left out because he'd missed the family plane crash.

Pepe's letter about La Coronita came in the nineties, if Juan Diego remembered correctly. The transvestite 'party place' had closed down; the owner, who was gay, had died. When The Little Crown reopened, it had expanded; there was a second floor, and it was now a place for transvestite prostitutes and their clients. There was no more waiting to dress up until you got to the bar; the cross-dressers were who they were when they arrived. They were women when they got there, or so Pepe implied.

Brother Pepe was doing hospice work in the nineties; unlike Vargas, Pepe was suited for the hand-holding business, and Lost Children was long gone by then.

Hogar de la Niña, 'Home of the Girl,' had opened in 1979. It was an all-girls' answer to City of Children – what Lupe had called City of *Boys*. Pepe had worked at Home of the Girl through the eighties and into the early nineties.

Pepe would never disparage an orphanage. Hogar de la Niña was not all that far from Viguera, where its all-boys' counterpart, Ciudad de los Niños, was still open for business. Home of the Girl was in the neighborhood of Cuauhtémoc.

Pepe had found the girls unruly; he'd complained to Juan Diego that they could be cruel to one another.

And Pepe hadn't liked the girls' adoration of *The Little Mermaid*, the 1989 Disney animated film. There were life-size decals of the Little Mermaid herself in the sleeping room – 'larger than the portrait of Our Lady of Guadalupe,' Pepe had complained. (As Lupe doubtless would have complained, Juan Diego thought.)

Pepe had sent a picture of some of the girls in their old-fashioned, hand-me-down dresses – the kind that buttoned up the back. In the photo, Juan Diego couldn't see that the girls hadn't bothered to button up the backs of their dresses, but Brother Pepe had complained about that, too; apparently, leaving themselves unbuttoned was just one of the 'unruly' things those girls did.

Brother Pepe (notwithstanding his small complaints) would go on being 'one of Christ's soldiers,' as Señor Eduardo had been fond of calling himself and his Jesuit brethren. But, in truth, Pepe was a servant of children; that had been his calling.

More orphanages had come to town; when Lost Children was gone, there were replacements – maybe not with the *educational* priorities that had once mattered to Father Alfonso and Father Octavio, but they were orphanages nonetheless. Oaxaca, one day, would have several.

In the late nineties, Brother Pepe went to work at the Albergue Josefino in Santa Lucía del Camino. The orphanage had opened in 1993, and the nuns looked after both boys and girls, though the boys weren't allowed to stay past the age of twelve. Juan Diego didn't understand who the nuns were, and Brother

Pepe didn't bother to explain. Madres de los Desamparados – 'Mothers of the Forsaken,' Juan Diego would have translated this. (He thought *forsaken* sounded better than *abandoned*.) But Pepe called the nuns 'mothers of those who are without a place.' Of all the orphanages, Pepe believed the Albergue Josefino was the nicest. 'The children hold your hands,' he wrote to Juan Diego.

There was a Guadalupe in the chapel, and another one in the schoolroom; there was even a Guadalupe *clock*, Pepe said. The girls could stay until they wanted to leave; a few girls were in their twenties before they left. But it wouldn't have worked for Lupe and Juan Diego, since Juan Diego would have been too old.

'Don't ever die,' Juan Diego had written to Brother Pepe from Iowa City. What Juan Diego meant was that he would die if he lost Pepe.

THAT NEW YEAR'S EVE, how many doctors must have been staying at the Encantador seaside resort? Ten or twelve? Perhaps more. Clark French's Filipino family was full of doctors. Not one of these doctors – not Clark's wife, Dr. Josefa Quintana, certainly – would have encouraged Juan Diego to skip another dose of the beta-blockers.

Maybe the *men* among those doctors – the ones who'd seen Miriam, especially the ones who'd witnessed her lightning-fast skewering of the gecko with a salad fork – would have agreed that the 100-milligram tablet of Viagra was advisable.

But as for alternating no doses with double doses (or half-doses) of a Lopressor prescription – absolutely not! Not even the men among those doctors celebrating New Year's Eve at the Encantador would have approved of *that*.

When Miriam, albeit briefly, made Lupe's death dinner-table conversation, Juan Diego had thought of Lupe – the way she'd scolded the noseless statue of the Virgin Mary.

'Show me a *real* miracle,' Lupe had challenged the giantess. '*Do* something to make me believe in you – I think you're just a big bully!'

Was *that* what triggered in Juan Diego his growing awareness of a puzzling similarity between the towering Virgin Mary in the Templo de la Compañía de Jesús and Miriam?

At this unresolved moment, Miriam touched him under the table – his thigh, the small lumps in his right-front pants pocket. 'What's here?' Miriam whispered to him. He quickly showed her the mah-jongg tile, the historic game block, but before he could begin the elaborate explanation, Miriam murmured, 'Oh, not *that* – I know about the all-inspiring keepsake you carry with you. I mean what *else* is in your pocket?'

Had Miriam read about the mah-jongg tile in an interview with the author? Had Juan Diego piddled away the story of such a treasured memento to the ever-trivializing media? And Miriam seemed to know about the Viagra tablet without his telling her what it was. Had Dorothy told her mother that Juan Diego took Viagra? Surely, he hadn't talked about taking Viagra in an interview – or had he?

His not knowing what Miriam knew (or didn't) about the Viagra made Juan Diego remember the quickly passing dialogue upon his arrival at the circus – when Edward Bonshaw, who knew Flor was a prostitute, learned she was a transvestite.

It was an accident – through the open flaps of a troupe tent they'd seen Paco, the transvestite dwarf, and Flor had told the Iowan, 'I'm just more *passable* than Paco, honey.'

'Does the parrot man get it that Flor has a penis?' Lupe (untranslated) had asked. It became clear that el hombre papagayo was thinking about Flor's penis. Flor, who knew what Señor Eduardo was thinking, stepped up her flirting with the Iowan.

Fate is everything, Juan Diego was considering – he thought of the little girl in pigtails, Consuelo, and how she'd said 'Hi, Mister.' How she reminded him of Lupe!

The way Lupe had repeated to Hombre, 'It'll be all right.'

'I hear you like whips,' Flor had said quietly to the hobbling missionary, who had elephant shit all over his sandals.

'The king of *pigs*,' Lupe had suddenly said, when she saw Ignacio, the lion tamer.

Juan Diego wondered why it was coming back to him now; it couldn't only be because Consuelo, that little girl in pigtails, had said 'Hi, Mister.' What had Consuelo called Miriam? 'The lady who just appears.'

'Wouldn't you cry if you never forgot how *your* sister was killed by a lion?' Miriam had asked the children. And then Pedro had fallen asleep with his head against Miriam's breast. It was as if the boy had been bewitched, Juan Diego was considering.

Juan Diego had been staring at his lap – at Miriam's hand, which was pressing the Viagra tablet against his right thigh – but when he looked up at the dinner table (at all the dinner tables), he realized he'd missed the moment when everyone had put on a party hat. He saw that even Miriam wore a paper party hat, like a king's or a queen's crown – hers was pink, however. The party hats were all pastel colors. Juan Diego touched the top of his head and felt the party hat – a paper crown, ringing his hair.

'Mine is—' he started to say.

'Powder blue,' Miriam told him, and when he patted his right-front pants pocket, he felt the mah-jongg tile but not the Viagra tablet. He also felt Miriam's hand cover his.

'You took it,' she whispered.

'I did?'

The dinner dishes had been cleared, though Juan Diego couldn't remember eating – not even the ceviche.

'You look tired,' Miriam was telling him.

If he'd had more experience with women, wouldn't Juan Diego have known that there was something strange, or a little 'off,' about Miriam? What Juan Diego knew of women mostly came from fiction, from reading novels and writing them. The women in fiction were often alluring and mysterious; in Juan Diego's novels, the women were intimidating, too. And wasn't it normal – or not unusual, surely – for women in fiction to be a little bit dangerous?

If the women in Juan Diego's real life lagged behind those women he'd met only in his imagination – well, that might explain why women like Miriam and Dorothy, who were far beyond Juan Diego's experience with *actual* women, seemed so attractive and familiar to him. (Maybe he'd met them in his imagination many times. Was that where he'd seen them before?)

If the paper party hats had suddenly materialized on the heads of the New Year's Eve revelers at the Encantador, there was a similar lack of explanation for the equally spontaneous appearance of the band, beginning with three scruffy-looking young men with intermittent facial hair and starvation-symptom physiques. The lead guitarist had a neck tattoo that resembled a scalding injury, a burn-scar facsimile. The harmonica player and the drummer liked the tank-top look, which revealed their tattooed arms; the drummer fancied an insect theme, whereas the harmonica player preferred reptiles – nothing but scaly vertebrates, snakes and lizards could crawl on his bare arms.

Miriam's comment on the young men was withering: 'Lots of testosterone but few prospects.' Juan Diego could tell that Clark French heard this, but Clark had his back turned to the boys in the band

– Clark's slightly startled expression revealed that he thought Miriam had meant *him*.

'Those boys, behind you – the *band*, Clark,' Dr. Quintana told her husband.

They were called (everyone knew) the Nocturnal Monkeys. The group's reputation, which was strictly local, rested on the bony bare shoulders of the lead singer – a skeletal waif in a strapless dress. Her breasts were not substantial enough to keep her dress from slipping down, and her lank black hair, savagely chopped at earlobe level, stood in stark contrast to her cadaverous pallor. There was an unnatural white-ness to her skin – not very Filipino, Juan Diego was thinking. That the lead singer looked like a freshly unearthed corpse made Juan Diego wonder if a tattoo or two might have helped – even an insect or a reptile, if not the grotesque damage done to the lead guitarist's neck.

As for the band's name, the Nocturnal Monkeys, naturally Clark had an explanation. The nearby Chocolate Hills were a local landmark. There were monkeys in the Chocolate Hills.

'No doubt the monkeys are nocturnal,' Miriam said.

'Exactly,' Clark answered her uncertainly. 'If you're interested, and if it's not raining, a day trip to the Chocolate Hills can be arranged – a group of us go every year,' Clark said.

'But we wouldn't see the monkeys in the daytime – not if they're nocturnal,' Miriam pointed out.

'That's true – we never see the monkeys,' Clark

mumbled. He had trouble looking at Miriam, Juan Diego noticed.

'I guess these monkeys are the best we can do,' Miriam said; she languidly waved her bare arm in the general direction of the hapless-looking band. They looked like Nocturnal Monkeys, all right.

'One night, every year, a group of us go on a river-boat cruise,' Clark ventured, more cautiously than before. Miriam made him nervous; she just waited for him to continue. 'We take a bus to the river. There are docks by the river, places to eat,' Clark rambled on. 'After dinner, we take a sightseeing boat up the river.'

'In the dark,' Miriam said flatly. 'What's there to see in the dark?' she asked Clark.

'Fireflies – there must be thousands. The fireflies are spectacular,' Clark said.

'What do the fireflies do – besides blink?' Miriam asked.

'The fireflies blink *spectacularly*,' Clark insisted.

Miriam shrugged. 'Blinking is what those beetles do for courtship,' Miriam said. 'Imagine if the only way we could come on to one another was to *blink*!' Whereupon she started blinking at Juan Diego, who blinked back at her; they both began to laugh.

Dr. Josefa Quintana also laughed; she blinked across the dinner table at her husband, but Clark French was not in a blinking mood. 'The fireflies are spectacular,' he repeated, in the manner of a school-teacher who has lost control of the class.

The way Miriam was blinking her eyes at Juan

Diego gave him a hard-on. He remembered (thanks to Miriam) that he'd taken the Viagra, and Miriam's hand on his thigh, under the table, might have contributed. Juan Diego found it disconcerting that he had the distinct impression someone was breathing on his knee – very near to where Miriam's hand rested on his thigh – and when he looked under the table, there was the little girl in pigtails, Consuelo, staring up at him. 'Good night, Mister – I'm supposed to go to bed,' Consuelo said.

'Good night, Consuelo,' Juan Diego said. Both Josefa and Miriam looked under the table at the little girl.

'My mother usually unbraids my pigtails before I go to bed,' the child explained. 'But tonight a *teenager* is putting me to bed – I have to sleep in my pigtails.'

'Your hair will not die overnight, Consuelo,' Dr. Quintana told the little girl. 'Your pigtails can survive one night.'

'My hair will be all *twisted*,' Consuelo complained.

'Come here,' Miriam told her. 'I know how to unbraid pigtails.'

Consuelo was reluctant to go to Miriam, but Miriam smiled and held out her arms to the little girl, who climbed into Miriam's lap. She sat there with her back very straight and her hands clasped tightly together. 'You're supposed to brush it, too, but you don't have a brush,' Consuelo was saying nervously.

'I know what to do with pigtails with my fingers,'

Miriam told the little girl. 'I can brush your hair with my fingers.'

'Please don't make me fall asleep, like Pedro,' Consuelo said.

'I'll try not to,' Miriam said in her deadpan, no-promises fashion.

When Miriam was unbraiding Consuelo's pigtails, Juan Diego looked under the table for Pedro, but the boy had slipped unseen into Dr. Quintana's chair. (Juan Diego also hadn't noticed when Dr. Quintana had left her seat, but he saw now that the doctor was standing next to Clark, diagonally across the table.) Many of the adults had left their chairs at the tables in the center of the dining room; those tables were being carried away – the center of the dining-room area would become the dance floor. Juan Diego didn't like to watch people dance; dancing doesn't work for cripples, not even vicariously.

The little children were being taken to bed; the older children, the teenagers, had also left the tables at the perimeter of the dance floor. Some adults had already seated themselves at those perimeter tables. When the music started, no doubt the teenagers would be back, Juan Diego was thinking, but they had disappeared for the moment – doing whatever teenagers do.

'What do you suppose has happened to the big gecko behind that painting, Mister?' Pedro quietly asked Juan Diego.

'Well—' Juan Diego began.

'It's gone. I looked. Nothing there,' Pedro whispered.

'The big gecko must be off on a hunting expedition,' Juan Diego suggested.

'It's gone,' Pedro repeated. 'Maybe the lady stabbed the big gecko, too,' Pedro whispered.

'No – I don't think so, Pedro,' Juan Diego said, but the boy looked convinced that the big gecko was gone for good.

Miriam had unbraided Consuelo's pigtails and was expertly running her fingers through the little girl's thick black hair. 'You have beautiful hair, Consuelo,' Miriam told the girl, who was sitting only slightly less rigidly in Miriam's lap than before. Consuelo was fighting off sleep, suppressing a yawn.

'Yes, I *do* have nice hair,' Consuelo said. 'If I were ever kidnapped, the kidnappers would cut off my hair and sell it.'

'Don't think about that – it isn't going to happen,' Miriam told her.

'Do you know everything that's going to happen?' Consuelo asked Miriam.

For some reason, Juan Diego held his breath; he was waiting intently for Miriam's answer – he didn't want to miss a word.

'I think the lady *does* know everything,' Pedro whispered to Juan Diego, who shared the fearful-looking boy's premonition about Miriam. Juan Diego had stopped breathing because he believed that Miriam *did* know the future, though Juan Diego doubted Pedro's conviction that Miriam had done away with the big gecko. (She would have needed a more formidable murder weapon than a salad fork.)

And the whole time, while Juan Diego wasn't breathing, both he and Pedro were watching Miriam massage Consuelo's scalp. Not a single kink remained in the little girl's luxuriant hair, and Consuelo herself was slumped against Miriam in a succumbed state; the drowsy-looking little girl had half-closed her eyes – she seemed to have forgotten that she'd ever asked Miriam an unanswered question.

Pedro hadn't forgotten. 'Go on, Mister – you better ask her,' the boy whispered. 'She's putting Consuelo to sleep – maybe that's what she did to the big gecko,' Pedro suggested.

'*Do* you—' Juan Diego started to say, but his tongue felt funny in his mouth and his speech was slurred. Do you know everything that's going to happen? he'd meant to ask Miriam, but Miriam held a finger to her lips and silenced him.

'*Shhh* – the poor child should be in bed,' Miriam whispered.

'But *you*—' Pedro began. That was as far as he got.

Juan Diego saw the gecko fall or drop from the ceiling; it was another small one. This one landed on Pedro's head, in his hair. The startled-looking gecko had landed perfectly on top of the boy's head, inside the open crown of the paper party hat, which in Pedro's case was a sea-green color – not that different from the little lizard's coloring. When Pedro felt the gecko in his hair, the boy began to scream; this retrieved Consuelo from her trance – the little girl started screaming, too.

Juan Diego would realize only later why two

Filipino kids would scream about a gecko. It wasn't the gecko that made Pedro and Consuelo scream. They were screaming because they must have imagined that Miriam was going to stab the gecko, pinning the little lizard to the top of Pedro's head.

Juan Diego was reaching for the gecko in Pedro's hair when the panic-stricken boy swatted the little lizard into the area of the dance floor, where his party hat also ended up. It was the drummer (the guy with the insect tattoos on his bare arms) who stomped on the gecko; he spattered some of the lizard's innards on his tight jeans.

'Oh, man – that's harsh,' the harmonica player said; he was the one in the other tank top, the musician with the snakes and lizards tattooed on his arms.

The lead guitarist with the burn-scar tattoo on his neck didn't notice the spattered gecko; he was diddling with the amplifier and the speaker boxes, tweaking the sound.

But Consuelo and Pedro had seen what happened to the little gecko; their screams had turned to wails of protestation, not relieved by the teenagers who were taking them off to bed. (Screaming and wailing had brought the teenagers back to the dining room, where they'd perhaps mistaken the cries of the children for the band's first number.)

More philosophical than some lead singers, the waif of a corpse-colored girl stared at the ceiling above the dance floor – as if she were expecting more falling geckos. 'I hate those fuckin' things,' she said to no one in particular. She also saw that the drummer was trying to wipe the lizard's spattered innards off his jeans. '*Gross*,' the lead singer said matter-of-factly; the way she said it made 'Gross' sound like the title of her best-known song.

'I'm betting my bedroom is closer to the dance floor than yours,' Miriam was saying to Juan Diego, as the freaked-out children were being carried away. 'What I mean, darling, is that the choice of where we sleep might best be guided by how much of these Nocturnal Monkeys we want to hear.'

'Yes,' was all Juan Diego could manage to say. He saw that Auntie Carmen was no longer among the remaining adults in the vicinity of the newly emerging dance floor; either she'd been carried away with the dinner tables or she'd slipped off to bed before the little children. *These* Nocturnal Monkeys must not have won over Auntie Carmen with their charms. As for the *actual* nocturnal monkeys, the ones in the Chocolate Hills, Juan Diego imagined that Auntie Carmen might have liked them – if only to feed one to her pet moray.

'Yes,' Juan Diego repeated. It was definitely time to slip away. He stood up from the table as if he didn't limp – as if he'd never limped – and because Miriam took immediate hold of his arm, Juan Diego almost didn't limp as he began to walk with her.

'Not staying to welcome in the New Year?' Clark French called to his former teacher.

'Oh, we're going to welcome it in, all right,' Miriam

called to him, once more with a languid wave of one bare arm.

'Leave them alone, Clark – let them go,' Josefa said.

Juan Diego must have looked a little foolish, touching the top of his head as he limped (just slightly) away; he was wondering where his party hat had gone, not recalling how Miriam had removed it from his head with as little wasted motion as she'd expended in taking off hers.

By the time Juan Diego had climbed the stairs to the second floor, he and Miriam could hear the karaoke music from the beach club; the music was faintly audible from the outdoor balcony of the Encantador, but not for long. The distant karaoke music couldn't compete with the eviscerating sound of the Nocturnal Monkeys – the suddenly throbbing drum, the angrily combative guitar, the harmonica's piteous wail (an expression of feline pain).

Juan Diego and Miriam were still outside, on the balcony – he was opening the door to his hotel room – when the lead singer, that girl from the grave, began her lament. As the couple came inside the room and Juan Diego closed the door behind them, the sounds of the Nocturnal Monkeys were muted by the soft whir of the ceiling fan. There was another concealing sound: through the open windows – the breeze through the screens was offshore – the insipid karaoke song from the beach club was (mercifully) the only music that they could hear.

'That poor girl,' Miriam said; she meant the lead

singer for the Nocturnal Monkeys. 'Someone should call an ambulance – she's either giving birth or being disemboweled.'

These were exactly the words Juan Diego was going to say before Miriam said them. How was that possible? Was she a writer, too? (If so, surely not the *same* writer.) Whatever the reason, it seemed unimportant. Lust has a way of distracting you from mysteries.

Miriam had slipped her hand into Juan Diego's right-front pants pocket. She knew he'd already taken the Viagra tablet, and she wasn't interested in holding his mah-jongg tile; that pretty little game block wasn't *her* lucky charm.

'Darling,' Miriam began, as if no one had ever used that old-fashioned endearment before – as if no one had ever touched a man's penis from inside his pants pocket.

In Juan Diego's case, in fact, no one had touched *his* penis in this way, though he'd written a scene where such a thing happened; it unnerved him, a little, that he'd already imagined it exactly this way.

It also unnerved him that he'd forgotten the context of a conversation he'd been having with Clark. Juan Diego couldn't remember if this had happened after or before Miriam's gecko-stabbing arrival at their dinner table. Clark had been elaborating about a recent writing student – she sounded to Juan Diego like a protégée-in-progress, though he could tell Josefa was skeptical about her. The writing student was a 'poor Leslie' – a young woman who'd suffered, somehow, and of course there was a *Catholic* context. But lust has a way of distracting you, and suddenly Juan Diego was with Miriam.

· 19 ·

Boy Wonder

Across the top of the troupe tent for the young-women acrobats was a ladder bolted horizontally to two parallel two-by-fours. The rungs were loops of rope; eighteen loops ran the length of the ladder. This was where the skywalkers practiced, because the ceiling of the acrobats' troupe tent was only twelve feet high. Even if you were hanging by your feet from the loops of rope, head down, you couldn't kill yourself if you fell off the ladder in the troupe tent.

In the main tent, where the circus acts were performed – well, that was another matter. The exact same ladder with the eighteen rope rungs was bolted across the top of the main tent, but if you fell from that ladder, you would fall eighty feet – without a net, you would die. There was no net for the skywalk at Circo de La Maravilla.

Whether you called it Circus of The Wonder or just The Wonder, an important part of the marvel was the no-net part. Whether you meant the circus (the *whole* circus) when you said La Maravilla, or if you meant the actual *performer* when you said The Wonder

– meaning La Maravilla herself – what made *her* so special had a lot to do with the no-net part.

This was on purpose, and entirely Ignacio's doing. As a young man, the lion tamer had traveled to India and had first seen the skywalk at a circus there. That is where the lion tamer also got the idea of using children as acrobats. Ignacio acquired the no-net idea from a circus he saw in Junagadh, and from one he'd seen in Rajkot. No net, child performers, a high-risk act – the skywalk proved itself to be a real crowd-pleaser in Mexico, too. And because Juan Diego *hated* Ignacio, he had traveled to India – he wanted to see what the lion tamer had seen; he needed to know where Ignacio's ideas came from.

The *came-from* part was a major aspect of Juan Diego's life as a writer. *A Story Set in Motion by the Virgin Mary*, his India novel, had been about where everything 'comes from' – in that novel, as in much of Juan Diego's childhood and adolescence, a lot came from the Jesuits or the circus. Yet no novel by Juan Diego Guerrero was set in Mexico; there were no Mexican (or Mexican-American) characters in his fiction. 'Real life is too sloppy a model for good fiction,' Juan Diego had said. 'The good characters in novels are more fully formed than most of the people we know in our lives,' he would add. 'Characters in novels are more understandable, more consistent, more predictable. No good novel is a mess; many so-called real lives are messy. In a good novel, everything important to the story comes from something or somewhere.'

Yes, his novels *came from* his childhood and adolescence – that was where his fears came from, and his imagination came from everything he feared. This *didn't* mean he wrote about himself, or about what happened to him as a child and adolescent – he didn't. As a writer, Juan Diego Guerrero had imagined what he feared. You could not ever know enough about where real people *came from*.

Take Ignacio, the lion tamer – his depravity, in particular. He could not be blamed on India. No doubt he'd acquired his lion-taming skills at the Indian circuses, but taming lions wasn't an athletic ability – it definitely wasn't acrobatic. (Lion-taming is a matter of domination; this appears to be true in the case of male and female lion tamers.) Ignacio had mastered how to look intimidating, or he had that quality before he ever went to India. With lions, of course, the intimidation part was an illusion. And whether or not the domination worked – well, that depended on the individual lion. Or the individual lionesses, in Ignacio's case – the *female* factor.

The skywalk itself was mostly a matter of technique; for skywalkers, this entailed mastering a specific system. There was a way to do it. Ignacio had seen it, but the lion tamer wasn't an acrobat – he'd only married one. Ignacio's wife, Soledad, was the acrobat – or *former* acrobat. She'd been a trapeze artist, a flyer; physically, Soledad could do anything.

Ignacio had merely described how the skywalk *looked*; Soledad was the one who taught the young-women acrobats how to do it. Soledad had taught herself to skywalk on that safe ladder in the troupe tent; when she'd mastered it without falling, Soledad knew she could teach the girl acrobats how to do it.

At Circus of The Wonder, only young women – just the girl acrobats, of a certain age – were trained to be skywalkers (The Wonders themselves). This was also on purpose, and entirely Ignacio's doing. The lion tamer liked young women; he thought that pre-pubescent girls were the best skywalkers. Ignacio believed that if you were in the audience, you wanted to be worried about the girls falling, not thinking about them sexually; once women were old enough for you to have sexual thoughts about them – well, at least in the lion tamer's opinion, you weren't so worried about them dying if you could imagine having sex with them.

Naturally, Lupe had known this about the lion tamer from the moment she'd met him – Lupe could read Ignacio's mind. That first meeting, upon the dump kids' arrival at La Maravilla, had been Lupe's introduction to the lion tamer's thoughts. Lupe had never read a mind as terrible as Ignacio's mind before.

'This is Lupe – the new fortune-teller,' Soledad was saying, introducing Lupe to the young women in the troupe tent. Lupe knew she was in foreign territory.

'Lupe prefers "mind reader" to "fortune-teller" – she usually knows what you're thinking, not necessarily what happens next,' Juan Diego explained. He felt insecure, adrift.

'And this is Lupe's brother, Juan Diego – he's the

only one who can understand what she says,' Soledad continued.

Juan Diego was in a tent full of girls close to his age; a few were as young as (or younger than) Lupe, only ten or twelve, and there were a couple of fifteen- or sixteen-year-olds, but most of the girl acrobats were thirteen or fourteen. Juan Diego had never felt as self-conscious. He was not used to being around athletic girls.

A young woman hung upside down from the sky-walking ladder at the apex of the troupe tent; the tops of her raw-looking bare feet, inserted in the first two rope rungs, were flexed at rigidly held right angles to her bare shins. She swung back and forth, her forward momentum never changing, as she stepped out of one rope rung, rhythmically moving ahead to the next – and, never losing her rhythm, to the next. There were sixteen steps in the skywalk, start to finish; at eighty feet, without a net, one of those sixteen steps could be your last. But the skywalker in the acrobats' troupe tent seemed unconcerned; an insouciance attended her – she looked as relaxed as her untucked T-shirt, which she held to her chest (her wrists were crossed on her small breasts). 'And *this*,' Soledad was saying, as she pointed to the upside-down skywalker, 'is Dolores.' Juan Diego stared at her.

Dolores was La Maravilla of the moment; she was The Wonder in Circus of The Wonder, if only for a fleeting half-second – Dolores would not be pre-pubescent for long. Juan Diego held his breath.

The young woman, who was named for 'pain' and

'suffering,' just kept skywalking. Her loose gym shorts revealed her long legs; her bare belly was wet with sweat. Juan Diego adored her.

'Dolores is fourteen,' Soledad said. (Fourteen going on twenty-one, as Juan Diego would long remember her.) Dolores was beautiful but bored; she seemed indifferent to the risk she was taking, or to – more dangerously – any risk. Lupe already hated her.

But the lion tamer's thoughts were what Lupe was reciting. 'The pig thinks Dolores should be fucking, not skywalking,' Lupe babbled.

'Who should she be—' Juan Diego started to ask, but Lupe wouldn't stop babbling. She stared at Ignacio.

'*Him*. The pig wants her to fuck him – he thinks she's done with skywalking. There's just no other girl who's good enough to replace her – not yet,' Lupe said. She went on to say that Ignacio believed it was a *conflict* if The Wonder gave him a hard-on; the lion tamer found it impossible to fear for a girl's life if he also wanted to fuck her.

'Ideally, as soon as a girl gets her period, she shouldn't be a skywalker,' Lupe elaborated. Ignacio had told all the girls that the lions knew when the girls got their periods. (Whether this was true or not, the girl acrobats believed it.) Ignacio knew when the girls had their periods because they became anxious around the lions or avoided the lions altogether.

'The pig can't wait to fuck this girl – he thinks she's *ready*,' Lupe said, nodding to the serene, upside-down Dolores.

'What does the skywalker think?' Juan Diego whispered to Lupe.

'I'm not reading her mind – La Maravilla has no thoughts right now,' Lupe said dismissively. 'But you're wishing you could have sex with her, too – aren't you?' Lupe asked her brother. 'Sick!' she said, before Juan Diego could answer her.

'What does the lion tamer's wife—' Juan Diego whispered.

'Soledad knows the pig fucks the girl acrobats, when they're "old enough" – she's just sad about it,' Lupe told him.

When Dolores got to the end of the skywalk, she reached up for the ladder with both hands and allowed her long legs to hang down; her scarred bare feet were not many inches above the ground when she let go of the ladder and dropped to the dirt floor of the tent.

'Remind me,' Dolores said to Soledad. 'What does the cripple do? Something not with his feet, probably,' the superior young woman said – a goddess of bitchery, Juan Diego thought.

'Mouse tits, spoiled cunt – let the lion tamer knock her up! That's her only future!' Lupe said. Vulgarity to this extreme was uncharacteristic of Lupe, but she was reading the minds of the other girl acrobats; Lupe's language would coarsen at the circus. (Juan Diego didn't translate this outburst, of course – he was smitten by Dolores.)

'Juan Diego is a translator – the brother is his sister's interpreter,' Soledad told the proud girl. Dolores shrugged.

'Die in childbirth, monkey twat!' Lupe said to Dolores. (More mind reading – the other girl acrobats hated Dolores.)

'What did she say?' Dolores asked Juan Diego.

'Lupe was wondering if the rope rungs hurt the tops of your feet,' Juan Diego said haltingly to the skywalker. (The raw-looking scars on the tops of Dolores's feet were obvious to anyone.)

'At first,' Dolores answered, 'but you get used to it.'

'It's good that they're talking to each other, isn't it?' Edward Bonshaw asked Flor. No one in the troupe tent wanted to stand next to Flor. Ignacio stood as far away from Flor as he could get – the transvestite was a lot taller and broader in the shoulders than the lion tamer.

'I guess so,' Flor said to the missionary. No one wanted to stand next to Señor Eduardo, either, but that was only because of the elephant shit on his sandals.

Flor said something to the lion tamer, and received the shortest possible reply; this brief exchange happened so quickly that Edward Bonshaw didn't understand.

'What?' the Iowan asked Flor.

'I was asking where we might find a hose,' Flor told him.

'Señor Eduardo is still thinking about Flor having a penis,' Lupe said to Juan Diego. 'He can't stop thinking about her penis.'

'Jesus,' Juan Diego said. Too many things were happening too fast.

'The mind reader is talking about Jesus?' Dolores asked.

'She said you walk on the sky the way Jesus could walk on water,' Juan Diego lied to the stuck-up fourteen-year-old.

'What a liar!' Lupe exclaimed, with disgust.

'She wonders about how you support your weight, upside down, by the tops of your feet. It must take a while to develop the muscles that hold your feet in that right-angle position, so your feet don't slip out of the ropes. Tell me about that part,' Juan Diego said to the pretty skywalker. He finally got his breathing under control.

'Your sister is very observant,' Dolores said to the cripple. 'That's the hardest part.'

'It would be only half as hard for *me* to skywalk,' Juan Diego told Dolores. He kicked off his special shoe and showed her his twisted foot; yes, it was a little out of alignment with his shin – the foot pointed off in a two-o'clock direction – but the crushed foot was permanently frozen at a right angle. There was no muscle that needed to be developed in the crippled boy's right foot. That foot wouldn't bend; it *couldn't* bend. His maimed right foot was locked in the perfect position for skywalking. 'You see?' Juan Diego said to Dolores. 'I would have to train only *one* foot – the left one. Wouldn't that make skywalking easier for me?'

Soledad, who trained the skywalkers, knelt on the dirt floor of the troupe tent, feeling Juan Diego's crippled foot. Juan Diego would always remember this moment: it was the first time anyone had handled that foot since it had healed, in its fashion – not to mention this being the first time anyone would touch that foot appreciatively.

'The boy's right, Ignacio,' Soledad said to her husband. 'The skywalk is half as hard for Juan Diego to learn. This foot is a hook – this foot already knows how to skywalk.'

'Only girls can be skywalkers,' the lion tamer said. 'La Maravilla is always a girl.' (The man was a male machine, a penile robot.)

'The dirty pig isn't interested in *your* puberty,' Lupe explained to Juan Diego, but she was angrier with Juan Diego than she was disgusted by Ignacio. 'You can't be The Wonder – you'll *die* skywalking! You're supposed to leave Mexico with Señor Eduardo,' Lupe said to her brother. 'You don't *stay* at the circus. La Maravilla isn't permanent – not for *you*!' Lupe said to him. 'You're not an acrobat, you're no athlete – you can't even walk without a limp!' Lupe cried.

'No limp upside down – I can walk fine up there,' Juan Diego told her; he pointed to the horizontal ladder on the ceiling of the troupe tent.

'Maybe the cripple should have a look at the ladder in the *big* tent,' Dolores said, to no one in particular. 'It takes balls to be The Wonder on *that* ladder,' the superior girl said to Juan Diego. 'Anyone can be a skywalker in the *practice* tent.'

'I have balls,' the boy told her. The girl acrobats laughed at this, not only Dolores. Ignacio laughed, too, but not his wife.

Soledad had kept her hand on the cripple's bad foot. 'We'll see if he has the balls for it,' Soledad said. 'This foot gives him an *advantage* – that's all the boy and I are saying.'

'No boy can be La Maravilla,' Ignacio said; he was coiling and uncoiling his whip – more in a nervous than a threatening fashion.

'Why not?' his wife asked. 'I'm the one who trains the skywalkers, aren't I?' (Not all the lionesses were tamed, either.)

'I don't like the sound of this,' Edward Bonshaw said to Flor. 'They're not serious about Juan Diego going anywhere near that ladder trick, are they? The *boy* isn't serious, is he?' the Iowan asked Flor.

'The kid has balls, doesn't he?' Flor asked the missionary.

'No, no – no skywalking!' Lupe cried. 'You have *another* future!' the girl told her brother. 'We should go back to Lost Children. No more circus!' Lupe cried. 'Too much mind reading,' the girl said. She was suddenly looking at how the lion tamer was looking at *her*; Juan Diego saw Ignacio looking at Lupe, too.

'What?' Juan Diego asked his little sister. 'What's the pig thinking *now*?' he whispered to her.

Lupe couldn't look at the lion tamer. 'He's thinking he would like to fuck me, when I'm *ready*,' Lupe told Juan Diego. 'He's wondering what it would be like to fuck a retarded girl – a girl who can be understood only by her crippled brother.'

'You know what I've been thinking?' Ignacio suddenly said. The lion tamer was looking at an undesignated location, perfectly between Lupe and Juan Diego, and Juan Diego wondered if this was a tactic Ignacio used with the lions – namely, not to make eye contact with an individual lion but to make the lions think he was looking at all of them. Definitely, too many things were happening at once.

'Lupe knows what you've been thinking,' Juan Diego told the lion tamer. 'She's *not* retarded.'

'What I was *going to* say,' Ignacio said, still looking at neither Juan Diego nor Lupe, but at a spot somewhere between them, 'is that most mind readers or fortune-tellers, or whatever they call themselves, are fakes. The ones who can do it on demand are definitely fakes. The real ones can read *some* people's minds, but not everyone's. The real ones find most people's minds uninteresting. The real ones pick up from people's minds only the stuff that stands out.'

'Mostly terrible stuff,' Lupe said.

'She says the stuff that stands out is mostly terrible,' Juan Diego told the lion tamer. Things were definitely going too fast.

'She must be one of the real ones,' Ignacio said; he looked at Lupe then – only at her, at no one else. 'Have you ever read an animal's mind?' the lion tamer asked her. 'I'm wondering if you could tell what a *lion* was thinking.'

'It depends on the individual lion, or *lioness*,' Lupe said. Juan Diego repeated this exactly as Lupe had said it. The way the girl acrobats retreated from Ignacio, upon hearing the *lioness* word, let the dump kids know that the lion tamer was sensitive about being thought of as a *lioness* tamer.

'But you might be able to pick up the stuff that an *individual* lion, or lioness, was thinking?' Ignacio asked; his eyes were unfocused again, darting about in the general area between the clairvoyant girl and her brother.

'Mostly terrible stuff,' Lupe repeated; this time, Juan Diego translated her literally.

'Interesting,' was all the lion tamer said, but everyone in the troupe tent could tell that he knew Lupe was one of the real ones, and that she'd read his mind accurately. 'The cripple can try skywalking – we'll see if he has the balls for it,' Ignacio said, as he was leaving. He'd allowed his whip to completely uncoil, and he dragged it, at full length, behind him, as he left the troupe tent. The whip trailed after him as if it were a pet snake, following its master. The girl acrobats were all looking at Lupe; even Dolores, the superstar skywalker, was looking at Lupe.

'They all want to know what Ignacio thinks about fucking them – if he thinks they're *ready*,' Lupe told Juan Diego. The lion tamer's wife (and everyone else, even the missionary) had heard the *Ignacio* word.

'What about Ignacio?' Soledad asked; she didn't bother to ask Lupe – she spoke directly to Juan Diego.

'Yes, Ignacio thinks about fucking all of us – with every young woman, he thinks about doing it,' Lupe said. 'But you know that already – you don't need *me* to tell you,' Lupe said, straight to Soledad. '*All* of you know that already,' Lupe told them; she looked at each of the girl acrobats when she said it – at Dolores the longest.

No one was surprised by Juan Diego's verbatim translation of what his sister said. Flor looked the least surprised. Not even Edward Bonshaw was surprised, but of course he hadn't understood most of the conversation – including Juan Diego's translation.

'There's an evening performance,' Soledad was explaining to the newcomers. 'The girls have to put on their costumes.'

Soledad showed the dump kids to the troupe tent where they would be living. It was the dogs' troupe tent, as promised; there were two collapsible cots for the kids, who also had their own wardrobe closet, and there was a tall standing mirror.

The dog beds and water bowls were arranged in an orderly fashion, and the coat rack for the dogs' costumes was small and not in the way. The dog trainer was happy to meet the dump kids; she was an old woman who dressed as if she were still young, and still pretty. She was dressing the dogs for the evening performance when the dump kids got to the tent. Her name was Estrella, the word for 'star.' She told the niños she needed a break from sleeping with the dogs, though it was clear to the kids, as they watched Estrella dress the dogs, that the old woman genuinely loved the dogs, and that she took good care of them.

Estrella's refusal to dress or behave her age made

her more of a child than the dump kids; both Lupe
and Juan Diego liked her, as did the dogs. Lupe had
always disapproved of her mother's sluttish appearance, but the low-cut blouses Estrella wore were more
comical than tawdry; her withered breasts often
slipped into view, but they were small and shrunken
– there was nothing of a come-on in Estrella's revealing them. And her once-tight skirts were clownish
now; Estrella was a scarecrow – her clothes didn't
cling to her, not the way they once had (or as she may
have imagined they still did).

Estrella was bald; she hadn't liked the way her hair
had thinned, or how it had lost its crow-black luster.
She shaved her head – or she persuaded someone else
to shave it for her, because she was prone to cutting
herself – and she wore wigs (she had more wigs than
dogs). The wigs were way too young for her.

At night, Estrella slept in a baseball cap; she complained that the visor forced her to sleep on her back.
It was not her fault that she snored – she blamed the
baseball cap. And the headband of the cap left a
permanent indentation on her forehead, below where
she wore her wigs.

When Estrella was tired, there would be days when
she failed to exchange the baseball cap for one wig or
another. If La Maravilla wasn't performing, Estrella
dressed like a bald stick figure of a prostitute in a
baseball cap.

She was a generous person; Estrella was not
possessive about her wigs. She would let Lupe try
them on, and both Estrella and Lupe liked trying one

wig or another on the dogs. Today Estrella wasn't having one of her baseball-cap days; she wore the 'flaming-redhead' wig, which arguably would have looked better on one of the dogs – it definitely would have looked better on Lupe.

Anyone could see why the dump kids and the dogs adored Estrella. But her generosity notwithstanding, she was not as welcoming to Flor and Señor Eduardo as she was to the niños de la basura. Estrella wasn't a sexual bigot; she was not hostile to having a transvestite prostitute in the dogs' troupe tent. But the dog trainer had made a point of scolding the dogs if they ever crapped in the troupe tent. Estrella didn't want the beshitted Iowan to give the dogs any bad ideas, so she wasn't welcoming to the Jesuit.

Near the outdoor showers, which were behind the men's latrine tent, there was a faucet with a long hose; now Flor took Edward Bonshaw there to do something about the elephant shit that had hardened on the missionary's sandals – and, more uncomfortably, between the toes of his bare feet.

Because Estrella was telling Lupe the names of the dogs and how much to feed each one, Soledad seized this moment of privacy; in a life lived in troupe tents, Juan Diego would soon realize, there were not many private moments – not unlike life at the orphanage.

'Your sister is very special,' Soledad began quietly. 'But why doesn't she want you to try to become The Wonder? The skywalkers are the stars of this circus.' The concept of being a star stunned him.

'Lupe believes I have a different future – not

skywalking,' Juan Diego said. He felt caught off-guard.

'Lupe knows the future, too?' Soledad asked the crippled boy.

'Only some of it,' Juan Diego answered her; in truth, he didn't know how much (or how little) Lupe knew. 'Because Lupe doesn't see skywalking in my future, she thinks I'll die trying it – *if* I try it.'

'And what do *you* think, Juan Diego?' the lion tamer's wife asked him. She was an unfamiliar kind of adult to a dump kid.

'I just know I wouldn't limp if I were skywalking,' the boy told her. He saw the decision, looming ahead of him.

'The dachshund is a male called Baby,' he heard Lupe repeating to herself; Juan Diego knew this was the way she memorized things. He could see the dachshund: the little dog was wearing a baby bonnet tied under his chin and was sitting up straight in a child's stroller.

'Ignacio wanted a mind reader for the *lions*,' Soledad said suddenly to Juan Diego. 'What kind of sideshow is a mind reader at a circus? You said yourself that your sister isn't a fortune-teller,' Soledad continued softly. This wasn't going as expected.

'The sheepdog is a female called Pastora,' Juan Diego heard Lupe saying. (The noun *pastora* means 'shepherdess.') Pastora was a sheepdog of the border-collie type; she was wearing a girl's dress. When the dog walked on all fours, she tripped on the dress, but when she stood on her hind legs, pushing the child's stroller with Baby (the dachshund) in it, the dress fit her correctly.

'What would Lupe tell people in a sideshow? What woman wants to hear someone say what her husband is thinking? What guy is going to be happy hearing what's on his wife's mind?' Soledad was asking Juan Diego. 'Won't kids be embarrassed if their friends know what they're thinking? Just think about it,' Soledad said. 'All Ignacio cares about is what that old lion and those lionesses are thinking. If your sister can't read the lions' minds, she's of no use to Ignacio. And once she *has* read what's on the lions' minds – then she's no longer of use, is she? Or do lions change their minds?' Soledad asked Juan Diego.

'I don't know,' the boy admitted. He felt frightened.

'I don't know, either,' Soledad told him. 'I just know you've got better odds of *staying* at the circus if you're a skywalker – especially if you're a *boy* sky-walker. You understand what I'm saying, Boy Wonder?' Soledad asked him. It all felt too abrupt.

'Yes, I do,' he told her, but the abruptness scared him. It was hard for him to imagine that she'd ever been pretty, but Juan Diego knew Soledad was a clear thinker; she understood her husband, perhaps well enough to survive him. Soledad understood that the lion tamer was a man who made mostly selfish decisions – his interest in Lupe as a mind reader was a matter of self-preservation. One thing was obvious about Soledad: she was a strong woman.

There'd been stress on her joints, no doubt, as Dr. Vargas had observed of the former trapeze artist.

Damage to her fingers, her wrists, her elbows – these joint injuries notwithstanding, Soledad was still strong. As a flyer, she'd ended her career as a catcher. In trapeze work, men are usually the catchers, but Soledad had strong enough arms, and a strong enough grip, to be a catcher.

'The mongrel is male. I don't think it's *fair* that he's called Perro Mestizo – 'Mongrel' shouldn't be the poor dog's *name!*' Lupe was saying. The mongrel, poor Perro Mestizo, wasn't wearing a costume. In the act for the dogs, Mongrel was a baby-stealer. Perro Mestizo tries to run off with the stroller with Baby in it – with the dachshund in the baby bonnet barking like a lunatic, of course. 'Perro Mestizo is always the bad guy,' Lupe was saying. 'That's not fair, either!' (Juan Diego knew what Lupe was going to say next because it was an oft-repeated theme with his sister.) 'Perro Mestizo didn't ask to be born a mongrel,' Lupe said. (Naturally, Estrella, the dog trainer, hadn't the slightest idea what Lupe was saying.)

'I guess Ignacio is a little afraid of the lions,' Juan Diego said cautiously to Soledad. It wasn't a question; he was stalling.

'Ignacio *should* be afraid of the lions – he should be a *lot* afraid,' the lion tamer's wife said.

'The German shepherd, who is female, is called Alemania,' Lupe was babbling. Juan Diego thought it was a cop-out to name a German shepherd 'Germany'; it was also a stereotype to dress a German shepherd in a police uniform. But Alemania was supposed to be a policía – a policewoman. Naturally, Lupe was babbling about how 'humiliating' it was for Perro Mestizo, who was male, to be apprehended by a *female* German shepherd. In the circus act, Perro Mestizo is caught stealing the baby in the stroller; the undressed mongrel is dragged out of the ring by the scruff of his neck by Alemania in her police uniform. Baby (the dachshund) and his mother (Pastora, the sheepdog) are reunited.

It was at this moment of realization – the dump kids' slim chances of success at Circo de La Maravilla, the fate of a crippled skywalker juxtaposed with the unlikelihood of Lupe becoming a mind reader of lions – when the barefoot Edward Bonshaw hobbled into the dogs' troupe tent. The tender-footed way the Iowan was walking must have set off the dogs, or perhaps it was the sheer ungainliness of the smaller Señor Eduardo clinging to the bigger transvestite for support.

Baby barked first; the little dachshund in the baby bonnet leapt out of the stroller. This was so off-script, so not the circus act, that poor Perro Mestizo became agitated and bit one of Edward Bonshaw's bare feet. Baby quickly lifted one leg, as most male dogs do, and peed on Señor Eduardo's other bare foot – the unbitten one. Flor kicked the dachshund and the mongrel.

Alemania, the police dog, disapproved of kicking; there was a tense standoff between the German shepherd and the transvestite – growls from the big dog, a no-retreat policy from Flor, who would never back down from a fight. Estrella, her flaming-redhead wig askew, tried to calm the dogs down.

Lupe was so upset to read (in an instant) what was on Juan Diego's mind that she paid no attention to the dogs. 'I'm a mind reader for *lions*? That's *it*?' the girl asked her brother.

'I trust Soledad – don't you?' was all Juan Diego said.

'We're indispensable if you're a skywalker – otherwise, we're dispensable. That's it?' Lupe asked Juan Diego again. 'Oh, I get it – you like the sound of being a Boy Wonder, don't you?'

'Soledad and I don't know if lions change their minds – assuming you can read what the lions are thinking,' Juan Diego said; he was trying to be dignified, but the Boy Wonder idea had tempted him.

'I know what's on Hombre's mind,' was all Lupe would tell him.

'I say we just try it,' Juan Diego said. 'We give it a week, just see how it goes—'

'A week!' Lupe cried. 'You're no Boy Wonder – believe me.'

'Okay, okay – we'll give it just a couple of *days*,' Juan Diego pleaded. 'Let's just *try* it, Lupe – you don't know *everything*,' he added. What cripple doesn't dream of walking without a limp? And what if a cripple could walk *spectacularly*? Skywalkers were applauded, admired, even adored – just for *walking*, only sixteen steps.

'It's a leave-or-die-here situation,' Lupe said. 'A couple of days or a week won't matter.' It all felt too abrupt – to Lupe, too.

'You're so dramatic!' Juan Diego told her.

'Who wants to be The Wonder? Who's being *dramatic*?' Lupe asked him. 'Boy Wonder.'

Where were the responsible adults?

It was hard to imagine anything more happening to Edward Bonshaw's feet, but the barefoot Iowan was thinking about something else; the dogs had failed to distract him from his thoughts, and Señor Eduardo could not have been expected to understand the dump kids' plight. Not even Flor, in her continuing flirtation with the Iowan, should be blamed for missing the leave-or-die-here decision the dump kids faced. The available adults were thinking about themselves.

'Do you really have breasts *and* a penis?' Edward Bonshaw blurted out in English to Flor, whose unspoken Houston experience had given her a good grasp of the language. Señor Eduardo had counted on Flor's understanding him, of course; he just hadn't realized that Juan Diego and Lupe, who'd been arguing with each other, would hear and understand him. And no one in the dogs' troupe tent could have guessed that Estrella, the old dog trainer – not to mention Soledad, the lion tamer's wife – also understood English.

Naturally, when Señor Eduardo asked Flor if she had breasts *and* a penis, the crazy dogs had stopped barking. Truly *everyone* in the dogs' troupe tent heard and appeared to understand the question. The dump kids were not the subject of this question.

'Jesus,' Juan Diego said. The kids were on their own.

Lupe had clutched her Coatlicue totem to her too-small-to-notice breasts. The terrifying goddess with the rattlesnake rattles for nipples seemed to understand the breasts-and-penis question.

'Well, I'm not showing you the penis – not *here*,' Flor said to the Iowan. She was unbuttoning her blouse and untucking it from her skirt. Children on their own make abrupt decisions.

'Don't you see?' Lupe said to Juan Diego. 'She's the one – the one for *him*! Flor and Señor Eduardo – they're the ones who adopt you. They can take you away with them only if they're *together*!'

Flor had taken her blouse completely off. It was not necessary for her to remove her bra. She had small breasts – what she would later describe as 'the best the hormones could do'; Flor said she was 'not a surgery person.' But, just to be sure, Flor took off her bra, too; small as they were, she wanted Edward Bonshaw to have no doubt that she indeed had breasts.

'Not rattlesnake rattles, are they?' Flor asked Lupe, when everyone in the dogs' troupe tent could see her breasts *and* the nipples.

'It's a leave-or-die-here situation,' Lupe repeated. 'Señor Eduardo and Flor are your ride *out*,' the little girl told Juan Diego.

'For now, you'll just have to believe me about the penis,' Flor was saying to the Iowan; she'd put her bra back on and was buttoning her blouse when Ignacio walked in. Tent or no tent, the dump kids got the feeling that the lion tamer would never knock before entering.

'Come meet the lions,' Ignacio said to Lupe. 'I guess you have to come, too,' the lion tamer said to the cripple – to the *would-be* Boy Wonder.

There was no question that the dump kids understood the terms: the mind-reading job was all about the lions. And whether the lions changed their minds or not, it would also be Lupe's job to make the lion tamer believe the lions might change their minds.

But what must the barefoot, bitten, and pissed-on missionary have been thinking? Edward Bonshaw's vows were unhinged; Flor's breasts-and-penis combination had made him reconsider celibacy in ways no amount of whipping would dispel.

'One of Christ's soldiers,' Señor Eduardo had called himself and his Jesuit brethren, but his certainty was shaken. And the two old priests clearly didn't want the dump kids to stay at Lost Children; their half-hearted questioning about the safety of the circus had been more a matter of priestly protocol than of genuine concern or conviction.

'Those children are so wild – I suppose they could be eaten by wild animals!' Father Alfonso had said, throwing up his hands – as if such a fate would be fitting for dump kids.

'They do lack restraint – they could fall off those *swinging* things!' Father Octavio had chimed in.

'Trapezes,' Pepe had said helpfully.

'Yes! Trapezes!' Father Octavio had cried, almost as if the idea appealed to him.

'The boy won't be swinging from anything,' Edward Bonshaw had assured the priests. 'He'll be a *translator* – at least he won't be a dump-scrounger!'

'And the girl will be reading minds, telling fortunes – no swinging from anything for her. At least she won't end up a prostitute,' Brother Pepe had told the two priests; Pepe knew the priests so well – the *prostitute* word was the clincher.

'Better to be eaten by wild animals,' Father Alfonso had said.

'Better to fall off the trapezes,' Father Octavio had of course concurred.

'I knew you would understand,' Señor Eduardo had told the two old priests. Yet, even then, the Iowan looked uncertain about which side he should be on. He looked like he wondered what he'd been arguing *for*. Why was the circus *ever* such a good idea?

And now – once more navigating the avenue of troupe tents, on the lookout for elephant shit – Edward Bonshaw hobbled uncertainly on his tender bare feet. The Iowan was slumped against Flor, clinging to the bigger, stronger transvestite for support; the short distance to the lions' cages, only two minutes away, must have seemed an eternity for Edward Bonshaw – meeting Flor, and merely thinking about her breasts and her penis, had altered the trajectory of his life.

That walk to the lions' cages was a skywalk for Señor Eduardo; to the missionary, this short distance amounted to *his* walk at eighty feet without a net – however much the Iowan hobbled, these were *his* life-changing steps.

Señor Eduardo slipped his small hand into Flor's

much bigger palm; the missionary almost fell when she squeezed his hand in hers. 'The truth is,' the Iowan struggled to say, 'I am falling for you.' Tears were streaming down his face; the life he had long sought, the one he'd flagellated himself for, was over.

'You don't sound too happy about it,' Flor pointed out to him.

'No, no – I *am*, I'm truly very happy!' Edward Bonshaw told her; he began telling Flor how Saint Ignatius Loyola had founded an asylum for fallen women. 'It was in Rome, where the saint announced he would sacrifice his life if he could prevent the sins of a single prostitute on a single night,' Señor Eduardo was blubbering.

'I don't want you to sacrifice your life, you idiot,' the transvestite prostitute told him. 'I don't want you to *save* me,' she said. 'I think you should start by *fucking* me,' Flor told the Iowan. 'Let's just start with that, and see what happens,' Flor told him.

'Okay,' Edward Bonshaw said, almost falling again; he was staggering, but lust has a way.

The girl acrobats ran by them in the avenue of troupe tents; the green and blue spangles on their singlets glimmered in the lantern lights. Also passing them, but not running, was Dolores; she was walking fast, but she saved her running for the training beneficial to a superstar skywalker. The spangles on her singlet were silver and gold, and her anklets had silver chimes; as Dolores walked past them, her anklets were chiming. 'Noise-making, attention-seeking slut!'

Lupe called after the pretty skywalker. '*Not* your future – forget about it,' was all Lupe said to Juan Diego.

Ahead of them were the lion cages. The lions were awake now – all four of them. The eyes of the three lionesses were alertly following the pedestrian traffic in the avenue of troupe tents. The sullen male, Hombre, had his narrowed eyes fixed on the approaching lion tamer.

To the passersby in the busy avenue, it might have seemed that the crippled boy stumbled, and that his little sister caught hold of his arm before he could fall; someone watching the dump kids more closely might have imagined that the limping boy simply bent over to kiss his sister in the area of one of her temples.

What actually happened was that Juan Diego whispered in Lupe's ear. 'If you really can tell what the lions are thinking, Lupe—' Juan Diego started to say.

'I can tell what *you're* thinking,' Lupe interrupted him.

'For Christ's sake, just be careful what you *say* the lions are thinking!' Juan Diego whispered to her harshly.

'*You're* the one who has to be careful,' Lupe told him. 'Nobody knows what I'm saying unless you tell them,' she reminded him.

'Just remember this: I'm not your rescue project,' Flor was telling the Iowan, who was dissolved in tears – tears of happiness, conflicted tears, or just plain tears. Inconsolable crying, in other words – sometimes lust has a way of doing that to you, too.

Their small entourage had stopped in front of the lion cages.

'Hola, Hombre,' Lupe said to the lion. There was no question that the big male cat was looking at Lupe – *only* at Lupe, not at Ignacio.

Maybe Juan Diego was summoning the necessary courage to be a skywalker; perhaps this was the moment when he believed he had the *balls* for it. Actually *being* a Boy Wonder seemed possible.

'Any lingering thoughts on your mind about her being *retarded*?' the crippled boy asked the lion tamer. 'You can see that Hombre knows she's a mind reader, can't you?' Juan Diego asked Ignacio. 'A *real* one,' the boy added. He wasn't half as confident as he sounded.

'Just don't try to fuck with me, *ceiling*-walker,' Ignacio told Juan Diego. 'Don't ever lie to me about what your sister says. I'll know if you're lying, *practice*-tent-walker. I can read what's on your mind – a little,' the lion tamer said.

When Juan Diego looked at Lupe, she made no comment – she didn't even shrug. The girl was concentrating on the lion. To even the most casual passerby in the avenue of troupe tents, Lupe and Hombre were completely attuned to each other's thoughts. The old male lion and the girl weren't paying attention to anyone else.

20

Casa Vargas

In Juan Diego's dream, it was impossible to tell where the music came from. It did not have the hard-sell sound of a mariachi band, working its way among the outdoor café tables at the Marqués del Valle – one of those annoying bands that might have been playing anywhere in the zócalo. And although the circus band at La Maravilla had its own brass-and-drum version of 'Streets of Laredo,' this was not their moribund and dirgelike distortion of the cowboy's lament.

For one thing, Juan Diego heard a voice singing; in his dream, he heard the lyrics – if not as sweetly as the good gringo used to sing them. Oh, how el gringo bueno had loved 'Streets of Laredo' – the dear boy could sing that ballad in his sleep! Even Lupe sang that song sweetly. Though her voice was strained and difficult to understand, Lupe did have a girl's voice – an innocent-sounding voice.

The amateur vocalizing from the beach club had ceased, so it couldn't have been the shopworn karaoke music that Juan Diego heard; the New Year's Eve celebrants at the Panglao Island beach club had gone to bed, or they'd drowned taking a night swim. And no one was still ringing in the New Year at the Encantador – even the Nocturnal Monkeys were mercifully silent.

It was pitch-dark in Juan Diego's hotel room; he held his breath because he could not hear Miriam breathing – only the mournful cowboy song in a voice Juan Diego didn't recognize. Or did he? It was strange to hear 'Streets of Laredo' sung by an older woman; it didn't sound right. But wasn't the voice itself borderline recognizable? It was just the wrong voice for that song.

'"I see, by your outfit, that you are a cowboy,"' the woman was singing in a low, husky voice. '"These words he did say as I slowly walked by."'

Was it Miriam's voice? Juan Diego wondered. How could she be singing when he couldn't hear her breathing? In the darkness, Juan Diego wasn't sure she was really there.

'Miriam?' he whispered. Then he said her name again, a little louder.

There was no singing now – 'Streets of Laredo' had stopped. There was no detectable breathing, either; Juan Diego held his breath. He was listening for the slightest sound from Miriam; maybe she'd returned to her own room. He might have been snoring, or talking in his sleep – occasionally, Juan Diego talked when he dreamed.

I should touch her – just to feel if she's there or not, Juan Diego was thinking, but he was afraid to find out. He touched his penis; he smelled his fingers. The sex smell shouldn't have startled him – surely he remembered having sex with Miriam. But he didn't, not exactly. He had definitely said something – about the way she felt, how it felt to be inside her. He'd said 'silky' or 'silken'; this was all he could recall, only the language.

And Miriam had said: 'You're funny – you need to have a word for everything.'

Then a rooster crowed – in total darkness! Were roosters crazy in the Philippines? Was this stupid rooster disoriented by the karaoke music? Had the dumb bird mistaken the Nocturnal Monkeys for nocturnal *hens*?

'Someone should kill that rooster,' Miriam said in her low, husky voice; he felt her bare breasts touch his chest and his upper arm – the fingers of her hand closed around his penis. Maybe Miriam could see in the dark. 'There you are, darling,' she told him, as if he'd needed assurance that *he* existed – that he was really there, with her – when all the while he'd been wondering if *she* were real, if she actually *existed*. (That was what he'd been afraid to find out.)

The crazy rooster crowed again in the darkness.

'I learned to swim in Iowa,' he told Miriam in the dark – a funny thing to say to someone holding your penis, but this was how time happened to Juan Diego (not only in his dreams). Time jumped ahead or back; time seemed more associative than linear, but it wasn't exclusively associative, either.

'Iowa,' Miriam murmured. 'Not what comes to mind when I think of swimming.'

'I don't limp in the water,' Juan Diego told her. Miriam was making him hard again. When he wasn't in Iowa City, Juan Diego didn't meet many people who were interested in Iowa. 'You've probably never been in the Midwest,' Juan Diego said to Miriam.

'Oh, I've been everywhere,' Miriam demurred, in that laconic way she had.

Everywhere? Juan Diego wondered. No one's been everywhere, he thought. But in regard to a sense of place, one's individual perspective matters, doesn't it? Not every fourteen-year-old, upon encountering Iowa City for the first time, would have found the move from Mexico exhilarating; for Juan Diego, Iowa was an adventure. He was a boy who'd never emulated the young people he saw around him; suddenly there were students everywhere. Iowa City was a college town, a Big Ten town – the campus was downtown, the city and the university were one and the same. Why wouldn't a dump reader find a college town fascinating?

Granted, it would soon strike any fourteen-year-old boy that the Iowa campus heroes were its sports stars. Yet this was consistent with what Juan Diego had imagined about the United States – from a Mexican kid's perspective, movie stars and sports heroes seemed to be the zenith of American culture. As Dr. Rosemary Stein had told Juan Diego, he was either a kid from Mexico or a grown-up from Iowa all the time.

For Flor, the transition to Iowa City from Oaxaca must have been more difficult – if not the magnitude of misadventure Houston had represented for her. In a Big Ten university town, what opportunities existed for a transvestite and former prostitute? She'd already made a mistake in Houston; Flor was disinclined to take any chances in Iowa City. Meekness, keeping a low profile – well, it wasn't in Flor's nature to be tentative. Flor had always asserted herself.

When the deranged rooster crowed a third time, his crowing was cut off mid-squawk. 'There, that does it,' Miriam said. 'No more heralding of a false dawn, no more untruthful messengers.'

While Juan Diego tried to comprehend exactly what Miriam had meant – she sounded so authoritative – one dog began to bark; soon other dogs were barking. 'Don't hurt the dogs – nothing is their fault,' Juan Diego told Miriam. It was what he imagined Lupe would have said. (Here was another New Year, and Juan Diego was still missing his dear sister.)

'No harm will come to the dogs, darling,' Miriam murmured.

Now a breeze could be felt through the open seaward windows; Juan Diego thought he could smell the salt water, but he couldn't hear the waves – if there were waves. He only then realized that he could *swim* in Bohol; there was a beach and a pool at the Encantador. (The good gringo, the inspiration for Juan Diego's trip to the Philippines, had not inspired thoughts of swimming.)

'Tell me how you learned to swim in *Iowa*,' Miriam whispered in his ear; she was straddling him, and he felt himself enter her again. A feeling of such smoothness surrounded him – it was almost like swimming, he thought, before it crossed his mind that Miriam had known what he was thinking.

Yes, it had been a long time ago, but, because of Lupe, Juan Diego knew what it was like to be around a mind reader.

'I swam in an indoor pool, at the University of Iowa,' Juan Diego began, a little breathlessly.

'I meant *who*, darling – I meant who taught you, who took you to the swimming pool,' Miriam said softly.

'Oh.'

Juan Diego couldn't say their names, not even in the dark.

Señor Eduardo had taught him to swim – this was in the swimming pool in the old Iowa Field House, next to the university hospitals and clinics. Edward Bonshaw, who had left academia to pursue the priesthood, was welcomed back to the English Department at the University of Iowa – 'from whence he'd come,' Flor was fond of saying, exaggerating her Mexican accent with the *whence* word.

Flor wasn't a swimmer, but after Juan Diego had learned to swim, she occasionally took him to the pool – it was used by the university faculty and staff, and by their children, and also popular with townies. Señor Eduardo and Juan Diego had loved the old Field House – in the early seventies, before the

Carver-Hawkeye Arena was built, most of Iowa's indoor sports took place in the Field House. In addition to swimming there, Edward Bonshaw and Juan Diego went to see the basketball games and the wrestling matches.

Flor had liked the pool but not the old Field House; there were too many jocks running around, she said. Women took their kids to the pool – women were uneasy around Flor, but they didn't stare at her. Young men couldn't help themselves, Flor always said – young men just stared. Flor was tall and broad-shouldered – six-two and 170 pounds – and although she was small-breasted, she was both very attractive (in a womanly way) and very masculine-looking.

At the pool, Flor wore a one-piece bathing suit, but she was only viewable above her waist. She always wrapped a big towel around her hips; the bottom of her bathing suit was not in view, and Flor never went in the water.

Juan Diego didn't know how Flor managed the dressing and undressing part – this would have happened in the women's locker room. Maybe she never took off the bathing suit? (It never got wet.)

'Don't worry about it,' Flor had told the boy. 'I'm not showing my junk to anyone but Señor Eduardo.'

Not in Iowa City, anyway – as Juan Diego would one day understand. It would one day also be understandable why Flor needed to get away from Iowa – not a lot, just occasionally.

If Brother Pepe had happened to see Flor in Oaxaca, he would write to Juan Diego. 'I suppose you and

Edward know she's here – "just visiting," she says. I
see her in the usual places – well, I don't mean *all* the
"usual" places!' was how Pepe would put it.

Pepe meant he'd seen Flor at La China, that gay bar
on Bustamante – the one that would become
Chinampa. Pepe also saw La Loca at La Coronita,
where the clientele was mostly gay and the transvestites were dressed to kill.

Pepe *didn't* mean that Flor showed up at the whore
hotel; it wasn't the Hotel Somega, or being a prostitute, that Flor missed. But where was a person like
Flor supposed to go in Iowa City? Flor was a party
person – at least occasionally. There was no La China
– not to mention no La Coronita – in Iowa City in the
seventies and eighties. What was the harm in Flor
going back to Oaxaca from time to time?

Brother Pepe wasn't judging her, and apparently,
Señor Eduardo had been understanding.

When Juan Diego was leaving Oaxaca, Brother
Pepe had blurted out to him: 'Don't become one of
those Mexicans who—'

Pepe had stopped himself.

'Who *what*?' Flor had asked Pepe.

'One of those Mexicans who hate Mexico,' Pepe
managed to say.

'You mean one of those *Americans*,' Flor said.

'Dear boy!' Brother Pepe had exclaimed, hugging
Juan Diego to him. 'You don't want to become one of
those Mexicans who are always coming back, either
– the ones who can't stay away,' Pepe added.

Flor just stared at Brother Pepe. 'What else *shouldn't*

he become?' she asked Pepe. 'What *other* kind of
Mexican is forbidden?'

But Pepe had ignored Flor; he'd whispered in Juan
Diego's ear. 'Dear boy, become who you want to be
– just stay in touch!' Pepe pleaded.

'You better not become *anything*, Juan Diego,' Flor
had told the fourteen-year-old, while Pepe was weeping inconsolably. 'Trust us, Pepe – Edward and I won't
let the kid amount to beans,' Flor said. 'We'll be sure
he becomes one of those Mexican *nobodies.*'

Edward Bonshaw, overhearing all this, had only
understood his name.

'Eduardo,' Edward Bonshaw had said, correcting
Flor, who'd just smiled at him understandingly.

'They were my *parents*, or they tried to be!' Juan
Diego attempted to say out loud, but the words
wouldn't come in the darkness. 'Oh,' was all he
managed to say – again. The way Miriam was moving
on top of him, he couldn't have said more than that.

PERRO MESTIZO, A.K.A. MONGREL, was quarantined and
observed for ten days – if you're looking for rabies,
this is a common procedure for biting animals that
don't look sick. (Mongrel was not rabid, but Dr.
Vargas, consistent with his giving Edward Bonshaw
rabies shots, had wanted to be sure.) For ten days, the
dog act wasn't performed at Circo de La Maravilla;
the baby-stealer's quarantine was a disruption to the
routine of the other dogs in the dump kids' troupe
tent.

Baby, the male dachshund, peed on the dirt floor

of the tent every night. Pastora, the female sheepdog, whined ceaselessly. Estrella had to sleep in the dogs' troupe tent, or Pastora would never have been quiet – and Estrella snored. The sight of Estrella sleeping on her back, her face shadowed by the visor of her baseball cap, gave Lupe nightmares, but Estrella said she couldn't sleep bareheaded because the mosquitoes would bite her bald head; then her head would itch and she couldn't scratch it without removing her wig, which upset the dogs. During Perro Mestizo's quarantine, Alemania, the female German Shepherd, stood over Juan Diego's cot at night, panting in the boy's face. Lupe blamed Vargas for 'demonizing' Mongrel; *poor* Perro Mestizo, 'always the bad guy,' was once more a victim in Lupe's eyes.

'The asshole dog bit Señor Eduardo,' Juan Diego reminded his sister. The asshole-dog idea was Rivera's. Lupe didn't believe there were asshole dogs.

'Señor Eduardo was falling in love with Flor's penis!' Lupe cried – as if this new and disturbing development had *caused* Perro Mestizo to attack the Iowan. But this meant Perro Mestizo was homophobic, and didn't that make him an asshole dog?

Yet Juan Diego was able to persuade Lupe to stay at La Maravilla – at least until after the circus had traveled to Mexico City. The trip mattered more to Lupe than it did to Juan Diego; scattering their mother's ashes (and the good gringo's ashes, *and* Dirty White's, not to mention the remains of the Virgin Mary's enormous nose) meant a lot to Lupe. She believed Our Lady of Guadalupe had been marginalized in Oaxaca's churches; Guadalupe was a second fiddle in Oaxaca.

Esperanza, whatever her faults, had been 'bumped off' by the Mary Monster, in Lupe's view. The clairvoyant child believed the wrongness of the religious world would right itself – if, and *only* if, her sinful mother's ashes were scattered at the Basílica de Nuestra Señora de Guadalupe in Mexico City. Only there did the dark-skinned virgin, la virgen morena, draw busloads of pilgrims to her shrine. Lupe longed to see the Chapel of the Well – where Guadalupe, encased in glass, lay on her deathbed.

Even with his limp, Juan Diego looked forward to the long climb – the endless stairs leading to El Cerrito de las Rosas, the temple where Guadalupe *wasn't* tucked away in a side altar. She was elevated at the front of the sacred El Cerrito, 'The Little Hill.' (Lupe, instead of saying 'El Cerrito,' liked to call the temple 'Of the Roses'; she said this sounded more sacred than 'The Little Hill.') Either there or at the dark-skinned virgin's deathbed in the Chapel of the Well, the dump kids would scatter the ashes, which they'd kept in a coffee can Rivera had found at the basurero.

The contents of the coffee can did not have Esperanza's smell. They had a nondescript odor. Flor had sniffed the ashes; she'd said it wasn't the good gringo's smell, either.

'It smells like coffee,' Edward Bonshaw had said when he'd sniffed the coffee can.

Whatever the ashes smelled like, the dogs in the

troupe tent weren't interested. Maybe there was a medicinal odor; Estrella said anything that smelled like medicine would put off the dogs. Perhaps the unidentifiable smell was the Virgin Mary's nose.

'It's definitely not Dirty White,' was all Lupe would say about the smell; she sniffed the ashes in the coffee can every night before going to bed.

Juan Diego could never read her mind – he didn't even try. Possibly Lupe liked to sniff the contents of the coffee can because she knew they would be scattering the ashes soon, and she wanted to remember the smell after the ashes were gone.

Shortly before Circus of The Wonder would travel to Mexico City – a long trip, especially in a caravan of trucks and buses – Lupe brought the coffee can to a dinner party they were invited to, at Dr. Vargas's house in Oaxaca. Lupe told Juan Diego that she wanted a 'scientific opinion' of the ashes' smell.

'But it's a dinner party, Lupe,' Juan Diego said. It was the first dinner party the dump kids had been invited to; in all likelihood, they knew, the invitation wasn't Vargas's idea.

Brother Pepe had discussed with Vargas what Pepe called Edward Bonshaw's 'test of the soul.' Dr. Vargas didn't think Flor had presented the Iowan with a *spiritual* crisis. In fact, Vargas had offended Flor by suggesting to Señor Eduardo that the only reason to worry about his relationship with a transvestite prostitute might be a medical matter.

Dr. Vargas meant sexually transmitted diseases; he meant how many partners a prostitute had, and what

Flor might have picked up from one of them. It didn't matter to Vargas that Flor had a penis – or that Edward Bonshaw had one, too, and that the Iowan would have to give up his hope of becoming a priest because of it.

That Edward Bonshaw had broken his vow of celibacy didn't matter to Dr. Vargas, either. 'I just don't want your dick to fall off – or turn green, or something,' Vargas had said to the Iowan. *That* was what offended Flor, and why she wouldn't come to the dinner party at Casa Vargas.

In Oaxaca, anyone who had an ax to grind with Vargas called his house 'Casa Vargas.' This included people who disliked him for his family wealth, or thought it was insensitive of him to have moved into his parents' mansion after they'd been killed in a plane crash. (By now, everyone in Oaxaca knew the story of how Vargas was *supposed* to have been on that plane.) And among the people who played the 'Casa Vargas' card were those who'd been offended by how *brusque* Vargas could be. He used science like a bludgeon; he was inclined to club you with a strictly medical detail – the way he'd relegated Flor to a potential sexually transmitted disease.

Well, that was Vargas – that was who he was. Brother Pepe knew him well. Pepe thought he could count on Vargas to be cynical about everything. Pepe believed the dump kids and Edward Bonshaw could benefit from some of Vargas's cynicism. This was why Pepe had prevailed upon Vargas to invite the Iowan and the dump kids to the dinner party.

Pepe knew other scholastics who'd failed their vows. There could be doubts and detours on the road to the priesthood. When the most zealous students abandoned their studies, the emotional and psychological aspects of 'reorientation,' as Pepe thought of it, could be brutal.

No doubt Edward Bonshaw had questioned whether or not he was gay, or if he was in love with this particular person who *just happened* to have breasts and a penis. No doubt Señor Eduardo had asked himself: Aren't a lot of gay men *not* attracted to transvestites? Yet Edward Bonshaw knew that some gay men *were* attracted to trannies. But did that make him, Señor Eduardo must have wondered, a sexual minority within a minority?

Brother Pepe didn't care about those distinctions within distinctions. Pepe had a lot of love in him. Pepe knew that the matter of the Iowan's sexual orientation was strictly Edward Bonshaw's business.

Brother Pepe didn't have a problem with Señor Eduardo's belatedly discovering his homosexual self (if that's what was going on), or his abandoning the quest to become a priest; it was okay with Pepe that Edward Bonshaw was smitten by a cross-dresser with a penis. And Pepe didn't dislike Flor, but Pepe had a problem with the prostitute part – not necessarily for Vargas's sexually transmitted reasons. Pepe knew that Flor had always been in trouble; she'd lived surrounded by trouble (not everything could be blamed on Houston), while Edward Bonshaw had scarcely lived at all. What would two people like that *do* together in Iowa? For Señor Eduardo, in Pepe's opinion, Flor was a step too far – Flor's world was without boundaries.

As for Flor – who knew what she was thinking? 'I think you're a very nice parrot man,' Flor had said to the Iowan. 'I should have met you when I was a kid,' she'd told him. 'We might have helped each other get through some shit.'

Well, yes – Brother Pepe would have agreed to that. But wasn't *now* too late for the two of them? As for Dr. Vargas – specifically, his 'offending' Flor – Pepe might have put Vargas up to it. Yet no litany of sexually transmitted diseases was likely to scare Edward Bonshaw away; sexual attraction isn't strictly scientific.

Brother Pepe had higher hopes of Vargas's skepticism succeeding with Juan Diego and Lupe. The dump kids were disillusioned with La Maravilla – at least Lupe was. Dr. Vargas took a dim view of reading lions' minds, as did Brother Pepe. Vargas had examined a few of the young-women acrobats; they'd been his patients, both before and after Ignacio got his hands on them. As a performer, being The Wonder – La Maravilla herself – could kill you. (No one had survived the fall from eighty feet without a net.) Dr. Vargas knew that the girl acrobats who'd had sex with Ignacio wished they were dead.

And Vargas had admitted to Pepe, somewhat defensively, that he'd first thought the circus would be a good prospect for the dump kids because he'd envisioned that Lupe, who was a mind reader, would have no contact with Ignacio. (Lupe wouldn't be one of Ignacio's girl acrobats.) Now Vargas had changed his mind; what Vargas didn't like about Lupe's reading the lions' minds was that this put the thirteen-year-old in contact with Ignacio.

Pepe had come full circle about the dump kids' prospects at the circus. Brother Pepe wanted them back at Lost Children, where they would at least be *safe*. Pepe had Vargas's support about Juan Diego's prospects as a skywalker, too. So what if the crippled foot was permanently locked in the perfect position for skywalking? Juan Diego wasn't an athlete; the boy's good foot was a liability.

He'd been practicing in the acrobats' troupe tent. The good foot had slipped out of the loops of rope in that ladder – he'd fallen a few times. And this was only the practice tent.

Lastly, there were the dump kids' expectations about Mexico City. Juan Diego and Lupe's pilgrimage to the basilica there was troubling to Pepe, who was *from* Mexico City. Pepe knew what a shock it could be to see Guadalupe's shrine for the first time, and he knew the dump kids could be finicky – they were hard kids to please when it came to public expressions of religious faith. Pepe thought the dump kids had their own religion, and it struck Pepe as unfathomably personal.

Niños Perdidos would not let Edward Bonshaw *and* Brother Pepe accompany the dump kids on their trip to Mexico City; they couldn't give their two best teachers time off together. And Señor Eduardo wanted to see the shrine to Guadalupe almost as much as the dump kids did – in Pepe's opinion, the Iowan was as likely to be overwhelmed and disgusted by the excesses of the Basílica de Nuestra Señora de Guadalupe as the dump kids were. (The throngs who flocked to the Guadalupe shrine on a Saturday morning could conceivably run roughshod over anyone's personal beliefs.)

Vargas knew the scene – the mindless, run-amok worshipers were the epitome of everything he hated. But Pepe was wrong to imagine that Dr. Vargas (or anyone else) could prepare the dump kids and Edward Bonshaw for the hordes of pilgrims approaching the Basílica de Nuestra Señora de Guadalupe on the Avenue of Mysteries – 'the Avenue of *Miseries*,' Pepe had heard Vargas call it, in the doctor's blunt English. The spectacle was one los niños de la basura and the missionary had to experience themselves.

Speaking of spectacles: a dinner party at Casa Vargas was a spectacle. The life-size statues of the Spanish conquistadors, at the top and bottom of the grand staircase (and in the hall), were more intimidating than the religious sex dolls and other statuary for sale at the virgin shop on Independencia.

The menacing Spanish soldiers were very realistic; they stood guard on two floors of Vargas's house like a conquering army. Vargas had touched nothing in his parents' mansion. He'd lived his youth at war with his parents' religion and politics, but he'd left their paintings and statues and family photos intact.

Vargas was a socialist and an atheist; he virtually gave away his medical services to the neediest. But the house he lived in was a reminder of his spurned parents' rejected values. Casa Vargas did not revere Vargas's dead parents as much as it appeared to mock them; their culture, which Vargas had rebuked, was on display, but more for the effect of ridicule than honor – or so it seemed to Pepe.

'Vargas might as well have *stuffed* his dead parents and let *them* stand guard in the family house!' Brother Pepe had forewarned Edward Bonshaw, but the Iowan was unhinged before he even arrived at the dinner party.

Señor Eduardo had not confessed his transgression with Flor to Father Alfonso or Father Octavio. The zealot persisted in seeing the people he loved as projects; they were to be reclaimed or rescued – they were never to be abandoned. Flor and Juan Diego and Lupe were the Iowan's projects; Edward Bonshaw saw them through the eyes of a born reformer, but he did not love them less for looking upon them in this fashion. (In Pepe's opinion, this was a complication in Señor Eduardo's process of 'reorientation.')

Brother Pepe still shared a bathroom with the zealot. Pepe knew that Edward Bonshaw had stopped whipping himself, but Pepe could hear the Iowan crying in the bathroom, where he whipped the toilet and the sink and the bathtub instead. Señor Eduardo cried and cried, because he didn't know how he could quit his job at Lost Children until he'd arranged to *take care of* his beloved projects.

As for Lupe, she was in no mood for a dinner party at Casa Vargas. She'd been spending all her time with Hombre and the lionesses – las señoritas, 'the young ladies,' Ignacio called the three lionesses. He'd named them, each one for a body part. Cara, 'face' (of a person); Garra, 'paw' (with claws); Oreja, 'ear' (external, the outer ear). Ignacio told Lupe he could read the lionesses' minds by these body parts. Cara scrunched up her face when she was agitated or angry; Garra looked like she was kneading bread with her paws, her claws digging into the ground; Oreja cocked one ear askew, or she flattened both her ears.

'They can't fool me – I know what they're thinking. The young ladies are obvious,' the lion tamer said to Lupe. 'I don't need a mind reader for las señoritas – it's Hombre whose thoughts are a mystery.'

Maybe not to Lupe – that's what Juan Diego was thinking. Juan Diego was in no mood for a dinner party, either; he doubted that Lupe had been entirely forthcoming to him.

'What *is* on Hombre's mind?' he'd asked her.

'Not much – typical guy,' Lupe had told her brother. 'Hombre thinks about doing it to the lionesses. To Cara, usually. Sometimes to Garra. To Oreja, hardly at all – except when he thinks of her suddenly, and then he wants to do it to her right away. Hombre thinks about sex or he doesn't think at all,' Lupe said. 'Except about eating.'

'But is Hombre dangerous?' Juan Diego asked her. (He thought it was odd that Hombre thought about sex. Juan Diego was pretty sure that Hombre didn't actually have sex, at all.)

'If you bother Hombre when he's eating – if you touch him when he's thinking about doing it to one of the lionesses. Hombre wants everything to be the same – he doesn't like change,' Lupe said. 'I don't know if the lions actually do it,' she admitted.

'But what does Hombre think about Ignacio? That's all Ignacio cares about!' Juan Diego cried.

Lupe shrugged their late mother's shrug. 'Hombre loves Ignacio, except when he hates him. It confuses Hombre when he hates Ignacio. Hombre knows he's not *supposed to* hate Ignacio,' Lupe answered.

'There's something you're not telling me,' Juan Diego said to her.

'Oh – now you read minds, do you?' Lupe asked him.

'What is it?' Juan Diego asked her.

'Ignacio thinks the lionesses are dumb twats – he's not interested in what the lionesses are thinking,' Lupe answered.

'That's it?' Juan Diego asked. Beween what Ignacio thought and the vocabulary of the girl acrobats, Lupe's language was growing filthier on a daily basis.

'Ignacio is obsessed with what Hombre thinks – it's a guy-to-guy thing.' But the next thing she said in a funny way, Juan Diego thought. 'The tamer of the *lionesses* doesn't care what the lionesses are thinking,' Lupe said. She hadn't said el domador de leones – that's what you called the lion tamer. Instead Lupe had said el domador de *leonas*.

'So what *are* the lionesses thinking, Lupe?' Juan Diego had asked her. (Not about sex, apparently.)

'The lionesses hate Ignacio – all the time,' Lupe answered. 'The lionesses *are* dumb twats – they're jealous of Ignacio because they think Hombre loves Ignacio more than the asshole lion loves them! Yet if Ignacio ever hurts Hombre, the lionesses will kill Ignacio. The lionesses are all dumber than monkey twats!' Lupe shouted. 'They *love* Hombre, even though the asshole lion never thinks about them – unless he remembers that he wants to do it, and then Hombre has trouble remembering which one he wants to do it to *more*!'

'The lionesses want to *kill* Ignacio?' Juan Diego asked Lupe.

'They *will* kill him,' she said. 'Ignacio has nothing to fear from Hombre – it's the lionesses the lion tamer should be afraid of.'

'The problem is what you tell Ignacio, or what you don't tell him,' Juan Diego told his little sister.

'That's *your* problem,' Lupe had said. 'I'm just the mind reader. You're the one the lion tamer listens to, *ceiling*-walker,' she said.

That was truly *all* he was, Juan Diego was thinking. Even Soledad had lost confidence in him as a future skywalker. The good foot gave him trouble; it slipped in the rope rungs of the ladder, and it wasn't strong enough to bear his weight in that unnatural right-angle position.

What Juan Diego saw of Dolores was often upside down. Either she was upside down or he was; in the acrobats' troupe tent, there could be only one sky-walker practicing at a time. Dolores had never had any confidence in him as a skywalker – like Ignacio, Dolores believed Juan Diego lacked the balls for it. (For balls, apparently, only the main tent – the sky-walk at eighty feet, without a net – was a true test.)

Lupe had said Hombre liked you if you were afraid of him; maybe this was why Ignacio told the girl acrobats that Hombre knew when the girls got their periods. This made the girls fear Hombre. Since Ignacio made the girls feed the lion (and the lionesses), possibly this made the girls safer?

It was sick that Hombre liked the girls *because* they were afraid of him, Juan Diego thought. But this made no sense, Lupe had said. Ignacio just wanted the girl acrobats to be afraid, *and* he wanted them to feed the lions. Ignacio thought if *he* fed the lions, they would think he was weak. The part about the girls' periods mattered only to Ignacio. Lupe said Hombre didn't think about the girls' periods – not ever.

Juan Diego was afraid of Dolores, but this didn't make Dolores like him. Dolores did say one helpful thing to him, about skywalking – not that Dolores had meant to be helpful. She was just being cruel to him, which was her nature.

'If you think you're going to fall, you will,' Dolores told Juan Diego. He was upside down in the practice tent, his feet in the first two rope rungs of the ladder. The loops of rope dug into the creases where the tops of his feet bent at his ankles.

'That's not helpful, Dolores,' Soledad had told The Wonder, but it *was* helpful to Juan Diego; at the moment, however, he'd been unable to stop thinking that he was going to fall – hence he'd fallen.

'See?' Dolores had told him, climbing up to the ladder. Upside down she seemed especially desirable.

Juan Diego had not been allowed to bring his life-size Guadalupe statue to the dogs' troupe tent. There was no room for it, and when Juan Diego tried to describe the Guadalupe figure to Estrella, the old woman had told him that the male dogs (Baby, the dachshund, and Perro Mestizo) would piss on it.

Now, when Juan Diego thought about masturbating, he thought about Dolores; she was usually upside down, when he thought of her this way. He'd said nothing to Lupe about masturbating to the image of an upside-down Dolores, but Lupe caught him thinking about it.

'Sick!' Lupe said to him. 'You imagine Dolores upside down with your penis in her mouth – what are you *thinking*?'

'Lupe, what can I say? You already *know* what I'm thinking!' Juan Diego said in exasperation, but he was also embarrassed.

It was terrible timing: their move to La Maravilla, and their respective ages at that time; it was suddenly painful to both of them – namely, that Lupe didn't want to know what her brother was thinking, and Juan Diego didn't want his little sister to know, either.

They were estranged from each other for the first time.

THUS (IN THEIR UNFAMILIAR states of mind) the dump kids arrived, with Brother Pepe and Señor Eduardo, at Casa Vargas. The statues of the Spanish conquistadors caused Edward Bonshaw to stagger on the stairs, or perhaps it was the grandeur of the foyer that unbalanced him. Brother Pepe took hold of the Iowan's arm; Pepe knew that Señor Eduardo's long list of the things he'd denied himself had shortened. In addition to having sex with Flor, Edward Bonshaw now permitted himself to drink beer – it was almost impossible to be with Flor and not drink *something* – but even a couple of beers could unbalance Edward Bonshaw.

It didn't help that Vargas's dinner-party girlfriend was there to greet them on the grand staircase. Dr. Vargas didn't have a live-in girlfriend; he lived alone, if you could call living in Casa Vargas living 'alone.' (The statues of the Spanish conquistadors amounted to an occupying force – a small army.)

For dinner parties, Vargas always came up with a girlfriend who could cook. This one was named Alejandra – a bosomy beauty whose breasts must have been a hazard around a hot stove. Lupe took an instant dislike to Alejandra; in Lupe's harsh judgment, Vargas's lustful thoughts about Dr. Gomez should have obligated Vargas to fidelity to the ENT doctor.

'Lupe, be realistic,' Juan Diego whispered to his

sullen little sister; she'd merely scowled at Alejandra, refusing to shake the young woman's hand. (Lupe didn't want to let go of the coffee can.) 'Vargas isn't *supposed to be* faithful to a woman he hasn't slept with! Vargas only *wants* to sleep with Dr. Gomez, Lupe.'

'It's the same thing,' Lupe pronounced in biblical fashion; naturally, she hated passing the Spanish army on the stairs.

'Alejandra, Alejandra,' Vargas's dinner-party girl-friend kept repeating, introducing herself to Brother Pepe and the staggering Señor Eduardo on the treacherous staircase.

'What a penis-breath,' Lupe said to her brother. She meant that Alejandra was a penis-breath – Dolores's favorite epithet. It was what The Wonder called the girl acrobats who were sleeping with, or had slept with, Ignacio. It was what Dolores called each of the lionesses, too, whenever she had to feed them. (The lionesses hated Dolores, Lupe said, but Juan Diego didn't know if that was true; he only knew for sure that Lupe hated Dolores.) Lupe called Dolores a penis-breath, or Lupe implied that Dolores was a *future* penis-breath, which (Lupe said) Dolores was too much of a dumb monkey twat to know.

Now Alejandra was a penis-breath, just because she was one of Dr. Vargas's girlfriends. Edward Bonshaw, out of breath, saw Vargas smiling at the top of the stairs – his arm around the bearded soldier in the plumed helmet. 'And who is this savage?' Señor

Eduardo asked Vargas, pointing to the soldier's sword and his breastplate.

'One of your evangelicals in armor, of course,' Vargas answered the Iowan.

Edward Bonshaw eyed the Spaniard warily. Was it only Juan Diego's anxiety for his sister that made the boy think the statue's lifeless gaze came to life when the conquistador spotted Lupe?

'Don't stare at me, rapist and pillager,' Lupe said to the Spaniard. 'I'll cut off your dick with your sword – I know some lions who would like to eat you and your Christian scum!'

'Jesus, Lupe!' Juan Diego exclaimed.

'What does Jesus matter?' Lupe asked him. 'It's the virgins who are in charge – not that they're really virgins, not that we even know who they are.'

'What?' Juan Diego said to her.

'The virgins are like the lionesses,' Lupe told her brother. 'They're the ones you have to worry about – they run the show.' Lupe's head was eye-level to the hilt of the Spaniard's sword; her small hand touched the scabbard. 'Keep it sharp, killer,' Lupe told the conquistador.

'They certainly were frightening, weren't they?' Edward Bonshaw said, still staring at the conquering soldier.

'They certainly intended to be,' Vargas told the Iowan.

They were following Alejandra's hips down a long and decorous hall. Of course they couldn't pass a portrait of Jesus without comment. 'Blessed *are*—'

Edward Bonshaw began to say; the portrait was of Jesus delivering the Sermon on the Mount.

'Oh, those endearing beatitudes!' Vargas interrupted him. 'My favorite part of the Bible – not that anyone pays attention to the beatitudes; they are not what most Church business is about. Aren't you taking these two innocents to the Guadalupe shrine? A Catholic tourist attraction, if you ask me,' Vargas went on to Señor Eduardo but for everyone's benefit. 'No evidence of the beatitudes at that unholiest of basilicas!'

'Have tolerance, Vargas,' Brother Pepe pleaded. 'You tolerate our beliefs, we'll tolerate your lack thereof—'

'The virgins rule,' Lupe interrupted them, holding tight to the coffee can. 'Nobody cares about the beatitudes. Nobody listens to Jesus – Jesus was just a baby. The virgins are the ones who pull the strings.'

'I suggest you don't translate for Lupe – whatever she said. Just *don't*,' Pepe said to Juan Diego, who was too transfixed by Alejandra's hips to have been paying attention to Lupe's mysticism – perhaps the contents of the coffee can contributed to Lupe's irritating powers.

'Tolerance is never a bad idea,' Edward Bonshaw began. Ahead of them, Juan Diego saw another Spanish soldier, this one standing at attention by a double doorway in the hall.

'This sounds like a Jesuitical trick,' Vargas said to the Iowan. 'Since when do you Catholics ever leave us nonbelievers alone?' As proof, Dr. Vargas gestured to the solemn conquistador standing guard at the doorway to the kitchen. Vargas put his hand on the soldier's breastplate, over the conquistador's heart – if the conquering Spaniard had ever had a heart. 'Try talking to this guy about free will,' Vargas said, but the Spaniard seemed not to notice the doctor's over-familiar touch; once again, Juan Diego saw the statue's distant gaze come into focus. The Spanish soldier was looking at Lupe.

Juan Diego leaned down and whispered to his sister, 'I know you're not telling me everything.'

'You wouldn't believe me,' she told him.

'Aren't they sweet – those children?' Alejandra said to Vargas.

'Oh, God – the penis-breath wants to have kids! This will ruin my appetite,' was all Lupe would say to her brother.

'Did you bring your own coffee?' Alejandra suddenly asked Lupe. 'Or is it your toys? It's—'

'It's for *him*!' Lupe said, pointing to Dr. Vargas. 'It's our mother's ashes. They have a funny smell. There's a little dog in the ashes, and a dead hippie. There's something *sacred* in the ashes, too,' Lupe added, in a whisper. 'But the smell is *different*. We can't identify it. We want a scientific opinion.' She held out the coffee can to Vargas. 'Go on – *smell* it,' Lupe said to him.

'It just smells like *coffee*,' Edward Bonshaw tried to assure Dr. Vargas. (The Iowan didn't know if Vargas had any prior knowledge of the contents of the coffee can.)

'It's Esperanza's *ashes*!' Brother Pepe blurted out.

'Your turn, translator,' Vargas said to Juan Diego; the doctor had taken the coffee can from Lupe, but he'd not yet lifted the lid.

'We burned our mother at the basurero,' Juan Diego began. 'We burned a gringo draft dodger with her – a dead one,' the fourteen-year-old struggled to explain.

'There was a dog in the mix – a small one,' Pepe pointed out.

'That must have been quite a fire,' Vargas said.

'It was already burning when we put the bodies in it,' Juan Diego explained. 'Rivera had started it – with whatever was around.'

'Just your usual dump fire, I suppose,' Vargas said; he was fingering the lid of the coffee can, but he still hadn't lifted it.

Juan Diego would always remember how Lupe was touching the tip of her nose; she held one index finger against her nose when she spoke. 'Y la nariz,' Lupe said. ('And the nose.')

Juan Diego hesitated to translate this, but Lupe kept saying it, while she touched the end of her little nose. 'Y la nariz.'

'The nose?' Vargas guessed. '*What* nose? *Whose* nose?'

'Not the *nose*, you little heathen!' Brother Pepe cried.

'*Mary*'s nose?' Edward Bonshaw exclaimed. 'You put the Virgin Mary's nose in that fire?' the Iowan asked Lupe.

'*He* did it,' Lupe said, pointing to her brother. 'It was in his pocket, though it almost didn't fit – it was a big nose.'

No one had told Alejandra, the dinner-party girlfriend, about the giant statue of the Virgin Mary losing its nose in the accident that killed the cleaning woman at the Jesuit temple. Poor Alejandra must have imagined, for a moment, the actual Virgin Mary's nose in the awful fire at the basurero.

'Help her,' was all Lupe said, pointing to Alejandra. Brother Pepe and Edward Bonshaw managed to guide the dinner-party girlfriend to the kitchen sink.

Vargas lifted the lid of the coffee can. No one spoke, though they could all hear Alejandra breathing in through her nose and out through her mouth as she tried to suppress the urge to vomit.

Dr. Vargas lowered his mouth and nose into the open coffee can. They could all hear him take a deep breath. There was no other sound but the carefully measured breathing of his dinner-party girlfriend, who was struggling not to be sick in the sink.

The first conquistador's sword was withdrawn from its scabbard and clanged against the stone floor in the foyer at the foot of the grand staircase. It was quite a loud clang, but far away from where the dinner partiers stood in the kitchen.

Brother Pepe flinched at the sound of the sword – as did Señor Eduardo and the dump kids, but not Vargas and Alejandra. The second sword clanged closer to them – the sword belonging to the Spaniard standing guard at the top of the stairs. You could not only hear the second sword clang against the stone stairs, as it slid down several steps before its descent of the staircase halted, but they had all heard the sound of the second sword being drawn from its scabbard.

'Those Spanish soldiers—' Edward Bonshaw began to say.

'It's not the conquistadors – they're just statues,' Lupe told them. (Juan Diego didn't hesitate to translate this.) 'It's your parents, isn't it? You live in their house because they're *here*, aren't they?' Lupe asked Dr. Vargas. (Juan Diego kept translating.)

'Ashes are ashes – there's little smell to ashes,' Vargas said. 'But this was a *dump* fire,' the doctor continued. 'There's paint in these ashes – maybe turpentine, too, or some kind of paint thinner. Maybe stain – something for staining wood, I mean. Something flammable.'

'Maybe gasoline?' Juan Diego said; he'd seen Rivera start more than a few dump fires with gasoline, including this one.

'Maybe gasoline,' Vargas agreed. 'Lots of chemicals,' the doctor added. 'What you smell are the chemicals.'

'The Mary Monster's nose was *chemical*,' Lupe said, but Juan Diego grabbed her hand before she could touch her nose again.

The third clang and clatter was very near to them; except for Vargas, everyone jumped.

'Let me guess,' Brother Pepe cheerfully said. 'That was the sword of our guardian conquistador by the

kitchen doorway – the one right here, in the hall,'
Pepe said, pointing.

'No – that was his helmet,' Alejandra said. 'I won't
stay here overnight. I don't know what his parents
want,' the pretty young cook said. She seemed fully
recovered.

'They just want to be here – they want Vargas to
know they're all right,' Lupe explained. 'They're glad
you weren't on the plane, you know,' Lupe said to Dr.
Vargas.

When Juan Diego translated this, Vargas just
nodded to Lupe; he knew, all right. Dr. Vargas put the
lid back on the coffee can and handed it back to Lupe.
'Just don't put your fingers in your mouth or in your
eyes, if you've touched the ashes,' he told her. 'Wash
your hands. Paint, turpentine, wood stain – they're
poisonous.'

The sword came sliding across the floor of the
kitchen, where they were standing; there wasn't much
of a clang this time – it was a wooden floor.

'*That*'s the third sword – from the nearest Spaniard,'
Alejandra said. 'They always put it in the kitchen.'

Brother Pepe and Edward Bonshaw had gone into
the long hall just to have a look around. The painting
of Jesus delivering the Sermon on the Mount was
askew on the wall; Pepe fussed with it until it hung
right.

Without looking into the hall, Vargas said: 'They
like to draw my attention to the beatitudes.'

Out in the hall, they could hear the Iowan reciting
the beatitudes. 'Blessed *are*—' and so on, and on.

'Believing in ghosts isn't the same thing as believing in God,' Dr. Vargas said to the dump kids a little defensively.

'You're okay,' Lupe told him. 'You're better than I thought,' she added. 'And you're not a penis-breath,' the girl said to Alejandra. 'The food smells good – we should eat something.' Juan Diego decided he would translate just the last part.

'"Blessed *are* the pure in heart: for they shall see God,"' Señor Eduardo was reciting. The Iowan wouldn't have agreed with Dr. Vargas. Edward Bonshaw believed that believing in ghosts amounted to the same thing as believing in God; to Señor Eduardo, the two things were at least related.

What did Juan Diego believe, then and now? He'd seen what the ghosts could do. Had he actually witnessed detectable movement from the Mary Monster, or had he only imagined it? And there was the nose trick, or whatever one called it. Some unexplainable things are real.

21

Mister Goes Swimming

'Believing in ghosts isn't the same thing as believing in God,' the former dump reader said aloud. Juan Diego spoke more confidently than Dr. Vargas ever had of his family ghosts. But Juan Diego had been dreaming that he was arguing with Clark French – though not about ghosts *or* believing in God. They were at each other's throats, again, about that Polish pope. The way John Paul II had associated both abortion and birth control with *moral decline* made Juan Diego furious – that pope was on the everlasting warpath against contraception. In the early eighties, he'd called contraception and abortion 'modern enemies of the family.'

'I'm sure there was a context you're overlooking,' Clark French had said to his former teacher many times.

'A *context*, Clark?' Juan Diego had asked (he'd also asked this when he was dreaming).

In the late eighties, Pope John Paul II had called condom use – even to prevent AIDS – 'morally illicit.'

'The *context* was the AIDS crisis, Clark!' Juan Diego had cried – not only that time but in his dream.

Yet Juan Diego woke up arguing that believing in ghosts was different from believing in God; it was disorienting, the way those transitions from dreaming to being awake can be. 'Ghosts—' Juan Diego continued, sitting up in bed, but he suddenly stopped speaking.

He was alone in his bedroom at the Encantador; this time, Miriam had truly vanished – she was not in bed beside him while (somehow) managing not to breathe. 'Miriam?' Juan Diego said, in case she was in the bathroom. But the door to the bathroom was open, and there was no answer – only the crowing of another rooster. (It had to be a different rooster; the first one had been killed mid-squawk, from the sound of it.) At least this rooster wasn't crazy; the morning light flooded the bedroom – it was the New Year in Bohol.

Through the open windows, Juan Diego could hear the children in the swimming pool. When he went to the bathroom, he was surprised to see his prescriptions scattered on the countertop surrounding the sink. Had he gotten up in the night, and – half asleep, or in a sexually sated trance – scarfed down a bunch of pills? If so, how many had he taken – and *which* pills? (Both the Viagra and Lopressor containers were open; the tablets dotted the countertop – there were some on the bathroom floor.)

Was Miriam a prescription-pill addict? Juan Diego wondered. But not even an addict would find the beta-blockers stimulating, and what would a woman want with Viagra?

Juan Diego cleaned up the mess. He took an outdoor shower, enjoying the cats who skittishly appeared on the tile roof, yowling at him. Perhaps a cat, in the cover of darkness, had killed that misguided rooster mid-squawk. Cats were born killers, weren't they?

Juan Diego was dressing when he heard the sirens, or what sounded like sirens. Maybe a body had washed ashore, he imagined – one of the perpetrators of the late-night karaoke music at the Panglao Island beach club, a night swimmer who'd danced all night and then drowned with cramps. Or the Nocturnal Monkeys had gone skinny-dipping, with disastrous results. Thus Juan Diego indulged his imagination with diabolical death scenes, the way writers will.

But when Juan Diego limped downstairs for break-fast, he saw the ambulance and the police car in the driveway of the Encantador. Clark French was officiously guarding the staircase to the second-floor library. 'I'm just trying to keep the kids away,' Clark said to his former teacher.

'Away from *what*, Clark?' Juan Diego asked.

'Josefa is up there – with the medical examiner and the police. Auntie Carmen was in the room diagonally across the hall from your woman friend. I didn't know she was leaving so soon!'

'*Who*, Clark? Who left?' Juan Diego asked him.

'Your woman friend! Who would come all this way for one night – even for New Year's Eve?' Clark asked him.

Juan Diego hadn't known Miriam was leaving; he must have looked surprised. 'She didn't *tell* you she was leaving?' Clark said. 'I thought you knew her! The desk clerk said she had an early flight; a car picked her up before dawn. Someone said *all* the doors to the second-floor rooms were wide open after your woman friend had gone. That's why they found Auntie Carmen!' Clark blathered.

'*Found* her – found her *where*, Clark?' Juan Diego asked him. The story was as chronologically challenging as one of Clark French's novels! the former writing teacher was thinking.

'On the floor of her room, between her bed and the bathroom – Auntie Carmen is *dead*!' Clark cried.

'I'm sorry, Clark. Was she sick? Had she been—' Juan Diego was asking, when Clark French pointed to the registration desk in the lobby.

'She left a letter for you – the desk clerk has it,' Clark told his former teacher.

'Auntie Carmen wrote me—'

'Your woman friend left a letter for you – *not* Auntie Carmen!' Clark cried.

'Oh.'

'Hi, Mister,' Consuelo said; the little girl with the pigtails was standing beside him. Juan Diego saw that Pedro was with her.

'No going upstairs, children,' Clark French cautioned the kids, but Pedro and Consuelo chose to follow Juan Diego as he limped through the lobby to the registration desk.

'The aunt with all the fish has died, Mister,' Pedro began.

'Yes, I heard,' Juan Diego told the boy.

'She broke her neck,' Consuelo said.

'Her *neck*!' Juan Diego exclaimed.

'How do you break your neck getting out of bed, Mister?' Pedro asked.

'No idea,' Juan Diego said.

'The lady who just appears has disappeared, Mister,' Consuelo told him.

'Yes, I heard,' Juan Diego said to the little girl with the pigtails.

The desk clerk saw Juan Diego coming; an eager-looking but anxious young man, he was already holding out the letter. 'Mrs. Miriam left this for you, sir – she had to catch an early flight.'

'Mrs. Miriam,' Juan Diego repeated. Did no one know Miriam's last name?

Clark French had followed him and the children to the registration desk. 'Is Mrs. Miriam a frequent guest at the Encantador? Is there a Mr. Miriam?' Clark asked the desk clerk. (Juan Diego knew well the tone of moral disapproval in his former student's voice; it was also a presence, a glowing heat, in Clark's *writing* voice.)

'She has stayed with us before, but not frequently. There is a daughter, sir,' the desk clerk told Clark.

'Dorothy?' Juan Diego asked.

'Yes, that's the daughter's name, sir – Dorothy,' the desk clerk said; he handed Juan Diego the letter.

'You know the mother *and* the daughter?' Clark

French asked his former teacher. (Clark's tone of voice was now in moral high-alert mode.)

'I was closer to the daughter first, Clark, but I only just met both of them – on my flight from New York to Hong Kong,' Juan Diego explained. 'They're world travelers – that's all I know about them. They—'

'They sound *worldly*, all right – at least Miriam seemed very worldly,' Clark abruptly said. (Juan Diego knew that *worldly* wasn't such a good thing – not if you were, like Clark, a serious Catholic.)

'Aren't you going to read the letter from the lady, Mister?' Consuelo asked. Remembering the contents of Dorothy's 'letter' had made Juan Diego pause before opening Miriam's message in front of the children, but how could he not open it now? They were all waiting.

'Your woman friend may have *noticed* something – I mean about Auntie Carmen,' Clark French said. Clark managed to make a *woman friend* sound like a demon in female form. Wasn't there a word for a female demon? (It sounded like something Sister Gloria would say.) A succubus – that was the word! Surely Clark French was familiar with the term. Succubi were female evil spirits, said to have sex with men who were asleep. It must come from Latin, Juan Diego was thinking, but his thoughts were interrupted by Pedro pulling on his arm.

'I've never seen anyone faster, Mister,' Pedro told Juan Diego. 'I mean your lady friend.'

'At either appearing or disappearing, Mister,' Consuelo said, pulling on her pigtails.

Since they were so interested in Miriam, Juan Diego opened her letter. *Until Manila*, Miriam had written on the envelope. *See fax from D.*, she'd also scrawled there – either hastily or impatiently, or both. Clark took the envelope from Juan Diego, reading aloud the 'Until Manila' part.

'Sounds like a title,' Clark French said. 'You're seeing Miriam in Manila?' he asked Juan Diego.

'I guess so,' Juan Diego told him; he'd mastered Lupe's shrug, which had been their mother's insouciant shrug. It made Juan Diego a little proud to believe that Clark French thought his former teacher was *worldly*, to imagine that Clark might think Juan Diego was consorting with succubi!

'I suppose D. is the daughter. It looks like a long fax,' Clark carried on.

'D. is for Dorothy, Clark – yes, she's the daughter,' Juan Diego said.

It *was* a long fax, and a little hard to follow. There was a water buffalo in the story, and stinging things; a series of mishaps had happened to children Dorothy had encountered in her travels, or so it seemed. Dorothy was inviting Juan Diego to join her at a resort called El Nido on Lagen Island – it was in another part of the Philippines, a place called Palawan. There were plane tickets in the envelope. Naturally, Clark had noticed the plane tickets. And Clark clearly knew and disapproved of El Nido. (A nido could be a nest, a den, a hole, a haunt.) Clark no doubt disapproved of D., too.

There was a sound of small wheels rolling across

the lobby of the Encantador; the sound made the hair on the back of Juan Diego's neck stand up – before he looked and saw the gurney, he had known (some-how) that it was the stretcher from the ambulance. They were wheeling it to the service elevator. Pedro and Consuelo ran after the gurney. Clark and Juan Diego saw Clark's wife, Dr. Josefa Quintana; she was coming down the stairs from the second-floor library and was with the medical examiner.

'As I told you, Clark, Auntie Carmen must have fallen awkwardly – her neck was broken,' Dr. Quintana told him.

'Maybe someone *snapped* her neck,' Clark French said; he looked at Juan Diego, as if seeking confirmation.

'They're both novelists,' Josefa said to the medical examiner. 'Big imaginations.'

'Your aunt fell hard, the floor is stone – her neck must have crumpled under her, when she fell,' the medical examiner explained to Clark.

'She also banged the top of her head,' Dr. Quintana told him.

'Or someone *banged* her, Josefa!' Clark French said.

'This hotel is—' Josefa started to say to Juan Diego. She stopped herself to watch the solemn children, Pedro and Consuelo, accompanying the gurney carrying Auntie Carmen's body. One of the EMTs was wheeling the gurney through the lobby of the Encantador.

'This hotel is *what*?' Juan Diego asked Clark's wife.

'Enchanted,' Dr. Quintana told him.

'She means *haunted*,' Clark French said.

'Casa Vargas,' was all Juan Diego said; that he'd just been dreaming about ghosts was not even a surprise. 'Ni siquiera una sorpresa,' he said in Spanish. ('Not even a surprise.')

'Juan Diego knew the daughter of his woman friend first – he only met them on the plane,' Clark was explaining to his wife. (The medical examiner had left them, following the gurney.) 'I guess you don't know them *well*,' Clark said to his former teacher.

'Not at all well,' Juan Diego admitted. 'I've slept with them both, but they're mysteries to me,' he told Clark and Dr. Quintana.

'You've slept with a mother *and* her daughter,' Clark said, as if making sure. 'Do you know what succubi are?' he then asked, but before Juan Diego could answer, Clark continued. '*Succuba* means "paramour"; a succubus is a demon in female form—'

'Said to have sex with men in their sleep!' Juan Diego hurried to interject.

'From the Latin *succubare*, "to lie beneath,"' Clark carried on.

'Miriam and Dorothy are just mysteries to me,' Juan Diego told Clark and Dr. Quintana again.

'Mysteries,' Clark repeated; he kept saying it.

'Speaking of mysteries,' Juan Diego said, 'did you hear that rooster crowing in the middle of the night – in total darkness?'

Dr. Quintana stopped her husband from repeating

the *mysteries* word. No, they'd not heard the crazy rooster, whose crowing had been cut short – perhaps forever.

'Hi, Mister,' Consuelo said; she was back beside Juan Diego. 'What are you going to do today?' she whispered to him. Before Juan Diego could answer her, Consuelo took his hand; he felt Pedro take hold of his other hand.

'I'm going to *swim*,' Juan Diego whispered to the kids. They looked surprised – all the water, which was everywhere around them, notwithstanding. The kids glanced worriedly at each other.

'What about your foot, Mister?' Consuelo whispered. Pedro was nodding gravely; both children were staring at the two-o'clock angle of Juan Diego's crooked right foot.

'I don't limp in the water,' Juan Diego whispered. 'I'm not crippled when I'm swimming.' The whispering was fun.

Why did Juan Diego feel so exhilarated at the prospect of the day ahead of him? More than the swimming beckoned him; it pleased him that the children enjoyed whispering with him. Consuelo and Pedro liked making a game of his going swimming – Juan Diego liked the kids' company.

Why was it that Juan Diego felt no urgency to pursue the usual arguing with Clark French about Clark's beloved Catholic Church? Juan Diego didn't even mind that Miriam hadn't told him she was leaving; actually, he was a little relieved she was gone.

Had he felt *afraid* of Miriam, in some unclear way?
Was it merely the simultaneity of his dreaming about
ghosts or spirits on a New Year's Eve and Miriam
having spooked him? To be honest, Juan Diego was
happy to be alone. No Miriam. ('Until Manila.')

But what about Dorothy? The sex with Dorothy,
and with Miriam, had been sublime. If so, why were
the details so difficult to remember? Miriam and
Dorothy were so entwined with his dreams that Juan
Diego was wondering if the two women existed only
in his dreams. Except that they definitely *existed* –
other people had seen them! That young Chinese
couple in the Kowloon train station: the boyfriend
had taken Juan Diego's picture *with* Miriam and
Dorothy. ('I can get one of *all* of you,' the boy had
said.) And there was no question that everyone
had seen Miriam at the New Year's Eve dinner; quite
possibly, only the unfortunate little gecko, skewered
by the salad fork, had failed to see Miriam – until it
was too late.

Yet Juan Diego wondered if he would even recognize Dorothy; in his mind's eye, he had trouble
visualizing the young woman – admittedly, Miriam
was the more striking of the two. (And, sexually
speaking, Miriam was more recent.)

'Shall we all have breakfast?' Clark French was
saying, though both Clark and his wife were distracted. Were they peeved at the whispering, or that
Juan Diego seemed inseparable from Consuelo and
Pedro?

'Consuelo, haven't you already had breakfast?' Dr.

Quintana asked the little girl. Consuelo had not let go of Juan Diego's hand.

'Yes, but I didn't eat anything – I was waiting for Mister,' Consuelo answered.

'Mr. *Guerrero*,' Clark corrected the little girl.

'Actually, Clark, I prefer just Mister – all by itself,' Juan Diego said.

'It's a two-gecko morning, Mister – so far,' Pedro told Juan Diego; the boy had been looking behind all the paintings. Juan Diego had seen Pedro lifting the corners of rugs and peering at the insides of lampshades. 'Not a sign of the big one – it's gone,' the boy said.

The *gone* word was a hard one for Juan Diego. The people he'd loved were gone – all the dear ones, the ones who'd marked him.

'I know we'll see you again in Manila,' Clark was saying to him, though Juan Diego would be in Bohol for two more days. 'I know you're seeing D., and where you're going next. We can discuss the daughter another time,' Clark French said to his former teacher – as if what there was to say about Dorothy (or what Clark felt compelled to say about her) wasn't possible to say in the company of children. Consuelo tightly held Juan Diego's hand; Pedro had lost interest in the hand-holding, but the boy wasn't going away.

'What about Dorothy?' Juan Diego asked Clark; it was hardly an innocent question. (Juan Diego knew that Clark was hot and bothered by the mother-daughter business.) 'And where is it I'm seeing her – on another island?' Before Clark could answer him, Juan Diego turned to Josefa. 'When you don't make your own plans, you never remember where you're going,' he said to the doctor.

'Those meds you're taking,' Dr. Quintana began. 'You're still taking the beta-blockers, aren't you – you haven't *stopped* taking them, have you?'

That was when Juan Diego realized that he must have stopped taking his Lopressor prescription – all those pills strewn about his bathroom had fooled him. He felt too good this morning; if he'd taken the beta-blockers, he wouldn't be feeling this good.

He lied to Dr. Quintana. 'I'm definitely taking them – you're not supposed to stop unless you do it gradually, or something.'

'You talk to your doctor before you even *think about* not taking them,' Dr. Quintana told him.

'Yes, I know,' Juan Diego said to her.

'You're going from here to Lagen Island – Palawan,' Clark French told his old teacher. 'The resort is called El Nido – it's not at all like here. It's very *fancy* there – you'll see how different it is,' Clark told him disapprovingly.

'Are there geckos on Lagen Island?' Pedro asked Clark French. 'What are the lizards like there?' the boy asked him.

'They have *monitor* lizards – they're carnivorous, as big as *dogs*,' Clark told the boy.

'Do they run or swim?' Consuelo asked Clark.

'They do both – fast,' Clark French said to the little girl with the pigtails.

'Don't give the children nightmares, Clark,' Josefa said to her husband.

'The idea of that mother *and* her daughter gives me nightmares,' Clark French began.

'Maybe not around the children, Clark,' his wife told him.

Juan Diego just shrugged. He didn't know about the monitor lizards, but seeing Dorothy on the *fancy* island would indeed be different. Juan Diego felt a little guilty – how he enjoyed his former student's disapproval, how Clark's moral condemnation was somehow gratifying.

Yet Clark and Miriam and Dorothy were, in their different ways, *manipulative*, Juan Diego thought; maybe he enjoyed manipulating the three of them a little.

Suddenly, Juan Diego was aware of Clark's wife, Josefa, holding his other hand – the one Consuelo wasn't attached to. 'You're limping less today, I think,' the doctor told him. 'You seem to have caught up on your sleep.'

Juan Diego knew he would have to be careful around Dr. Quintana; he would have to watch how he fooled around with his Lopressor prescription. When he was around the doctor, he might need to appear more diminished than he was – she was very observant.

'Oh, I feel pretty good today – pretty good for *me*, I mean,' Juan Diego told her. 'Not quite so tired, not quite so diminished,' was how Juan Diego put it to Dr. Quintana.

'Yes, I can tell,' Josefa told him, giving his hand a squeeze.

'You're going to hate El Nido – it's full of tourists, *foreign* tourists,' Clark French was saying.

'You know what I'm going to do today? It's something I *love*,' Juan Diego said to Josefa. But before he could tell Clark's wife his plans, the little girl with the pigtails was faster.

'Mister is going *swimming*!' Consuelo cried.

You could see what an effort Clark French was making – what a struggle it was for him to suppress his disapproval of *swimming*.

EDWARD BONSHAW AND THE dump kids rode in the bus with the dog lady Estrella and the dogs. The dwarf clowns, Beer Belly and his not very female-looking counterpart – Paco, the cross-dresser – were on the same bus. As soon as Señor Eduardo had fallen asleep, Paco dotted the Iowan's face (and the faces of the dump kids) with 'elephant measles.' Paco used rouge to create the measles; he dotted his own face and Beer Belly's face, too.

The Argentinian aerialists fell asleep fondling each other, but the dwarfs did not dot the lovers' faces with the rouge. (The Argentinians might have imagined the elephant measles were sexually transmitted.) The girl acrobats, who never stopped talking in the back of the bus, acted too superior to be interested in the elephant-measles prank, which Juan Diego had the feeling the dwarf clowns *always* played on unsuspecting souls on La Maravilla's road trips.

All the way to Mexico City, Pajama Man, the contortionist, slept stretched out on the floor of the bus, in the aisle between the seats. The dump kids had not seen the contortionist fully extended before; they were surprised to see that he was actually quite tall. The contortionist was also undisturbed by the dogs, who restlessly paced in the aisle, stepping on and sniffing him.

Dolores – The Wonder herself – sat apart from the less-accomplished girl acrobats. She stared out the window of the bus, or she slept with her forehead pressed against the window glass, verifying for Lupe the skywalker's status as a 'spoiled cunt' – this appellation in tandem with the 'mouse-tits' slur. Even Dolores's ankle chimes had earned her Lupe's condemnation as a 'noise-making, attention-seeking slut,' though Dolores's aloofness – from everyone, at least on the bus – made the skywalker strike Juan Diego as the opposite of 'attention-seeking.'

To Juan Diego, Dolores looked sad, even doomed; the boy didn't imagine it was falling from the sky-walk that threatened her. It was Ignacio, the lion tamer, who clouded Dolores's future, as Lupe had forewarned – 'let the lion tamer knock her up!' Lupe had cried. 'Die in childbirth, monkey twat!' It may have been something Lupe had said in passing anger, but – in Juan Diego's mind – this amounted to an unbreakable curse.

The boy not only desired Dolores; he admired her courage as a skywalker – he'd practiced the skywalk enough to know that the prospect of trying it at eighty feet was truly terrifying.

Ignacio wasn't on the bus with the dump kids; he

was in the truck transporting the big cats. (Soledad said Ignacio always traveled with his lions.) Hombre, whom Lupe had called 'the last dog, the last one,' had his own cage. Las señoritas – the young ladies, named for their most expressive body parts – were caged together. (As Flor had observed, the lionesses got along with one another.)

The circus site, in northern Mexico City – not far from Cerro Tepeyac, the hill where Juan Diego's Aztec namesake had reported seeing la virgen morena in 1531 – was some distance from downtown Mexico City, but near to the Basílica de Nuestra Señora de Guadalupe. Yet the bus carrying the dump kids and Edward Bonshaw broke free from the circus caravan of vehicles, and took an impromptu detour into downtown Mexico City, inspired by the two dwarf clowns.

Paco and Beer Belly wanted their fellow performers in La Maravilla to see the dwarfs' old neighborhood – the two clowns were from Mexico City. When the bus was slowed in city traffic, near the busy inter-section of the Calle Anillo de Circunvalación and the Calle San Pablo, Señor Eduardo woke up.

Perro Mestizo, a.k.a. Mongrel, the baby-stealer – 'the biter,' Juan Diego now called him – had been sleeping in Lupe's lap, but the little dog had managed to pee on Señor Eduardo's thigh. This made the Iowan imagine he'd peed in his own pants.

This time, Lupe had managed to read Edward Bonshaw's mind – hence she understood his confu-sion upon waking up.

'Tell the parrot man Perro Mestizo peed on him,' Lupe told Juan Diego, but by that point the Iowan had seen the elephant measles on the dump kids' faces.

'You've broken out – you've caught something dreadful!' Señor Eduardo cried.

Beer Belly and Paco were trying to organize a walking tour of the Calle San Pablo – the bus was now stopped – but Edward Bonshaw saw more elephant measles on the faces of the dwarf clowns. 'It's an epidemic!' the Iowan cried. (Lupe later said he was imagining that incontinence was an early symptom of the disease.)

Paco handed the soon-to-be-*former* scholastic a small mirror (on the inside lid of his rouge compact), which the cross-dresser carried in his purse. 'You have it, too – it's elephant measles. There are outbreaks in every circus – it's not usually fatal,' the transvestite said.

'Elephant measles!' Señor Eduardo cried. 'Not *usually* fatal—' he was saying, when Juan Diego whispered in his ear.

'They're clowns – it's a trick. It's some kind of makeup,' the dump reader told the distraught missionary.

'It's my burgundy rouge, Eduardo,' Paco said, pointing to the makeup in the little compact with the mirror.

'It made me piss my pants!' Edward Bonshaw indignantly told the transvestite dwarf, but Juan Diego was the only one who understood the Iowan's excited English.

'The mongrel pissed on your pants – the same dumb dog who bit you,' Juan Diego said to Señor Eduardo.

'This doesn't *look* like a circus site,' Edward Bonshaw was saying, as he and the dump kids followed the performers who were getting off the bus. Not everyone was interested in the walking tour of Paco and Beer Belly's old neighborhood, but it was the one look Juan Diego and Lupe would get of downtown Mexico City – the dump kids wanted to see the throngs of people.

'Vendors, protestors, whores, revolutionaries, tourists, thieves, bicycle salesmen—' Beer Belly was reciting as he led the way. Indeed, there was a bicycle shop near the corner of the Calle San Pablo and the Calle Roldán. There were prostitutes on the sidewalk in front of the bikes for sale, and more prostitutes in the courtyard of a whore hotel on the Calle Topacio, where the girls loitering in the courtyard looked only a little older than Lupe.

'I want to go back to the bus,' Lupe said. 'I want to go back to Lost Children, even if we—' The way she stopped herself from saying more made Juan Diego wonder if Lupe had changed her mind – or if she'd suddenly seen something in the future, something that made it unlikely (at least in Lupe's mind) that the dump kids would go back to Lost Children.

Whether Edward Bonshaw understood her, before Juan Diego could translate his sister's request – or if Lupe, who suddenly seized the Iowan's hand, made it sufficiently clear to Señor Eduardo what she wanted,

without words – the girl and the Jesuit went back to
the bus. (The moment had not been sufficiently clear
to Juan Diego.)

'Is there something hereditary – something in their
blood – that makes them prostitutes?' Juan Diego
asked Beer Belly. (The boy must have been thinking
of his late mother, Esperanza.)

'You don't want to think about what's in their
blood,' Beer Belly told the boy.

'*Whose* blood? What about blood?' Paco asked
them; her wig was askew, and the stubble on her face
contrasted strangely with the mauve lipstick and
matching eye shadow – not to mention the elephant
measles.

Juan Diego wanted to go back to the bus, too; going
back to Lost Children was surely also on the boy's
mind. 'Trouble isn't geographical, honey,' he'd heard
Flor say to Señor Eduardo – apropos of what, Juan
Diego wasn't sure. (Hadn't Flor's trouble in Houston
been *geographical*?)

Maybe it was the comfort of the coffee can, and its
mixed contents, that Juan Diego wanted; he and Lupe
had left the coffee can on the bus. As for going back
to Lost Children, did Juan Diego feel this would be a
defeat? (At the very least, it must have felt to him like
a form of retreat.)

'I look at you with envy,' Juan Diego had heard
Edward Bonshaw say to Dr. Vargas. 'Your ability to
heal, to change lives—' Señor Eduardo was saying,
when Vargas cut him off.

'An envious Jesuit sounds like a Jesuit in trouble.

Don't tell me you have *doubts*, parrot man,' Vargas
had said.

'Doubt is part of faith, Vargas – certainty is for you
scientists who have closed the other door,' Edward
Bonshaw told him.

'The *other* door!' Vargas had cried.

Back on the bus, Juan Diego saw who'd skipped
the walking tour. Not only the sullen Dolores – The
Wonder herself had not left her window seat – but
the other girl acrobats as well. What was the matter
with Mexico City, or this part of downtown, was at
least a little bit troubling to them – namely, the
prostitutes. Maybe the circus had saved the girl
acrobats from difficult choices; La Maravilla might
have thrust Ignacio into their future decision-making
moments, but the life of those girls selling themselves
on San Pablo and Topacio was not the life of the girl
acrobats at Circus of The Wonder – not yet.

The Argentinian aerialists had not left the bus,
either; they were cuddled together, as if frozen in the
act of fondling – their overt sex life seemed to protect
them from falling, as surely as the guy wires they
scrupulously attached to each other's safety harnesses.
The contortionist, Pajama Man, was stretching in the
aisle between the seats – his flexibility was nothing
he wanted to expose to laughter out in public. (No
one laughed at him in the circus.) And Estrella, of
course, had stayed on the bus with her dear dogs.

Lupe was asleep in two seats, her head in Edward
Bonshaw's lap. Lupe didn't mind that Perro Mestizo
had peed on the Iowan's thigh. 'I think Lupe is

frightened. I think you should both be back at Lost Children—' Señor Eduardo started to say, when he saw Juan Diego.

'But you're leaving, aren't you?' the fourteen-year-old asked him.

'Yes – with Flor,' the Iowan said softly.

'I heard your conversation with Vargas – the one about the pony on the postcard,' Juan Diego said to Edward Bonshaw.

'You shouldn't have heard that conversation, Juan Diego – I sometimes forget how good your English is,' Señor Eduardo said.

'I know what pornography is,' Juan Diego told him. 'It was a pornographic photograph, right? A postcard with a picture of a pony – a young woman has the pony's penis in her mouth. Right?' the fourteen-year-old asked the missionary. Edward Bonshaw guiltily nodded.

'I was your age when I saw it,' the Iowan said.

'I understand why it upset you,' the boy said. 'I'm sure it would upset me, too. But why does it *still* upset you?' Juan Diego asked Señor Eduardo. 'Don't grown-ups ever get over things?'

Edward Bonshaw had been at a county fair. 'County fairs weren't so *appropriate*, in those days,' Juan Diego had heard the Iowan say to Dr. Vargas.

'Yeah, yeah – horses with five legs, a cow with an extra head. Freak animals – *mutants*, right?' Vargas had asked him.

'And girlie shows, girls stripping in tents – *peep* shows, they were called,' Señor Eduardo had continued.

'In *Iowa*!' Vargas had exclaimed, laughing.

'Someone in a girlie tent sold me a pornographic postcard – it cost a dollar,' Edward Bonshaw confessed.

'The girl sucking off the pony?' Vargas had asked the Iowan.

Señor Eduardo looked shocked. 'You know that postcard?' the missionary asked.

'Everyone saw that postcard. It was made in Texas, wasn't it?' Vargas asked. 'Everyone here knew it because the girl looked Mexican—'

But Edward Bonshaw had interrupted the doctor. 'There was a man in the foreground of the postcard – you couldn't see his face, but he wore cowboy boots and he had a whip. It looked as if he had *forced* the girl—'

It was Vargas's turn to interrupt. 'Of course *someone* forced her. You didn't think it was the *girl's* idea, did you? Or the pony's,' Vargas added.

'That postcard haunted me. I couldn't stop looking at it – I *loved* that poor girl!' the Iowan said.

'Isn't that what pornography does?' Vargas asked Edward Bonshaw. 'You're not supposed to be able to stop looking at it!'

'The whip bothered me, especially,' Señor Eduardo said.

'Pepe has told me you have a thing for whips—' Vargas started to say.

'One day I took the postcard to confession,' Edward Bonshaw continued. 'I confessed my addiction to it – to the priest. He told me: "Leave the picture with me." Naturally, I thought *he* wanted it for the same reasons I'd wanted it, but the priest said: "I can destroy this, if you're strong enough to let it go. It's time that poor girl was left in peace," the priest said.'

'I doubt that poor girl ever knew *peace*,' Vargas had said.

'That's when I first wanted to be a priest,' Edward Bonshaw said. 'I wanted to do for other people what that priest did for me – he rescued me. Who knows?' Señor Eduardo said. 'Maybe that postcard destroyed that priest.'

'I presume the experience was worse for the girl,' was all Vargas said. Edward Bonshaw had stopped talking. But what Juan Diego didn't understand was why the postcard *still* bothered Señor Eduardo.

'Don't you think Dr. Vargas was right?' Juan Diego asked the Iowan on the circus bus. 'Don't you think that pornographic photo was worse for the poor girl?

'That poor girl wasn't a girl,' Señor Eduardo said; he'd glanced once at Lupe, asleep in his lap, just to be sure she was still sleeping. 'That poor girl was Flor,' the Iowan said; he was whispering now. 'That's what happened to Flor in Houston. The poor girl met a pony.'

HE'D CRIED FOR FLOR and Señor Eduardo before; Juan Diego could not stop crying for them. But Juan Diego was some distance from shore – no one could see he was crying. And didn't the salt water bring tears to everyone's eyes? You could float forever in salt water,

Juan Diego was thinking; it was so easy to tread water in the calm and tepid sea.

'Hi, Mister!' Consuelo was calling. From the beach, Juan Diego could see the little girl in pigtails – she was waving to him, and he waved back.

It took almost no effort to stay afloat; he seemed to be barely moving. Juan Diego cried as effortlessly as he swam. The tears just came.

'You see, I *always* loved her – even before I knew her!' Edward Bonshaw had told Juan Diego. The Iowan hadn't recognized Flor as the girl with the pony – not at first. And when Señor Eduardo *did* recognize Flor – when he realized she was the girl in the pony postcard, but Flor was all grown-up now – he'd been unable to tell her that he knew the pony part of her sad Texas story.

'You should tell her,' Juan Diego had told the Iowan; even at fourteen, the dump reader knew that much.

'When Flor wants to tell me about Houston, she will – it's *her* story, the poor girl,' Edward Bonshaw would say to Juan Diego for years.

'*Tell* her!' Juan Diego kept saying to Señor Eduardo, as their time together marched on. Flor's Houston story would remain hers to tell.

'*Tell* her!' Juan Diego cried in the warm Bohol Sea. He was looking offshore; he was facing the endless horizon – wasn't Mindanao somewhere out there? (Not a soul onshore could have heard him crying.)

'Hi, Mister!' Pedro was calling to him. 'Watch out for the—' (This was followed by, 'Don't step on the—';

the unheard word sounded like *gherkins*.) But Juan Diego was in deep water; he couldn't touch the bottom – he was in no danger of stepping on *pickles* or *sea cucumbers*, or whatever weird thing Pedro was warning him about.

Juan Diego could tread water a long time, but he wasn't a good swimmer. He liked to dog-paddle – that was his preferred stroke, a slow dog paddle (not that anyone could dog-paddle fast).

The dog paddle had posed a problem for the serious swimmers in the indoor pool at the old Iowa Field House. Juan Diego swam laps very slowly; he was known as the dog-paddler in the slow lane.

People were always suggesting swimming lessons for Juan Diego, but he'd *had* swimming lessons; the dog paddle was his choice. (The way dogs swam was good enough for Juan Diego; novels progressed slowly, too.)

'Leave the kid alone,' Flor once told a lifeguard at the pool. 'Have you seen this boy *walk*? His foot isn't just *crippled* – it weighs a ton. Full of metal – you try doing more than a dog paddle with an anchor attached to one leg!'

'My foot isn't full of metal,' Juan Diego told Flor, when they were on their way home from the Field House.

'It's a good story, isn't it?' was all Flor said. But she wouldn't tell *her* story. The pony on that postcard was just a glimpse of Flor's story, the only view of what happened to her in Houston that Edward Bonshaw would ever have.

'Hi, Mister!' Consuelo kept calling from the beach. Pedro had waded into the shallow water; the boy was being extra cautious. Pedro seemed to be pointing at potentially deadly things on the bottom of the sea.

'Here's one!' Pedro shouted to Consuelo. 'There's a whole bunch!' The little girl in the pigtails wouldn't venture into the water.

The Bohol Sea did not seem menacing to Juan Diego, who was slowly dog-paddling his way to shore. He wasn't worried about the killer gherkins, or whatever Pedro was worried about. Juan Diego was tired from treading water, which was the same as swimming to him, but he'd waited to come ashore until he could stop crying.

In truth, he hadn't really stopped – he was just tired of how long he'd waited for the crying to end. In the shallow water, as soon as Juan Diego could touch the bottom, he decided to walk ashore the rest of the way – even though this meant he would resume limping.

'Be careful, Mister – they're everywhere,' Pedro said, but Juan Diego didn't see the first sea urchin he stepped on (or the next one, or the one after that). The hard-shelled, spine-covered spheres were no fun to step on, even if you didn't limp.

'Too bad about the sea urchins, Mister,' Consuelo was saying, as Juan Diego came ashore on his hands and knees – both his feet were tingling from the painful spines.

Pedro had run off to fetch Dr. Quintana. 'It's okay to cry, Mister – the sea urchins really hurt,' Consuelo was saying; she sat beside him on the beach. His tears, maybe exacerbated by such a long time in the salt water, just kept coming. He could see Josefa and Pedro running toward him along the beach; Clark French lagged behind – he ran like a freight train, slow to start but steadily gaining speed.

Juan Diego's shoulders were shaking – too much treading water, perhaps; the dog paddle is a lot of work for your arms and shoulders. The little girl in pigtails put her small, thin arms around him.

'It's okay, Mister,' Consuelo tried to comfort him. 'Here comes the doctor – you're going to be okay.'

What is it with me and women doctors? Juan Diego was wondering. (He should have married one, he knew.)

'Mister has been stepping on sea urchins,' Consuelo explained to Dr. Quintana, who knelt in the sand beside Juan Diego. 'Of course, he's got other things to cry about,' the little girl in the pigtails said.

'He misses stuff – geckos, the dump,' Pedro began to enumerate to Josefa.

'Don't forget his sister,' Consuelo said to Pedro. 'A lion killed Mister's sister,' Consuelo explained to Dr. Quintana, in case the doctor hadn't heard the litany of woes Juan Diego was suffering – and now, on top of everything, he'd stepped on sea urchins!

Dr. Quintana was gently touching Juan Diego's feet. 'The trouble with sea urchins is their spines are movable – they don't get you just once,' the doctor was saying.

'It's not my feet – it's not the sea urchins,' Juan Diego tried to tell her quietly.

'What?' Josefa asked; she bent her head closer, to hear him.

'I should have married a woman doctor,' he whispered to Josefa; Clark and the children couldn't hear him.

'Why didn't you?' Dr. Quintana asked, smiling at him.

'I didn't ask her soon enough – she said yes to someone else,' Juan Diego said softly.

How could he have told Dr. Quintana more? It was impossible to tell Clark French's wife why he'd never married – why a lifetime partner, a companion till the end, was a friend he'd never made. Not even if Clark and the children hadn't been there on the beach could Juan Diego have told Josefa why he'd not dared to emulate the match Edward Bonshaw had made with Flor.

Casual acquaintances, even colleagues and close friends – including those students he'd befriended, and had seen a bit of socially (not only in class or in teacher-writer conferences) – all *presumed* that Juan Diego's adoptive parents had been a couple no one would have (or could have) sought to emulate. They'd been so *queer* – in every sense of the word! Surely, this was the commonplace version of why Juan Diego had never married anyone, why he'd not even made an effort to find that companion for life, the one so many people believed they wanted. (Surely, Juan Diego knew, this was the story Clark French would have imparted to his wife about his former teacher – an obdurate bachelor, in Clark's eyes, *and* a godless secular humanist.)

Only Dr. Stein – dear Dr. Rosemary! – understood, Juan Diego believed. Dr. Rosemary Stein didn't know everything about her friend and patient; she didn't understand dump kids – she hadn't been there when he'd been a child and a young adolescent. But Rosemary *did* know Juan Diego when he'd lost Señor Eduardo and Flor; Dr. Stein had been *their* doctor, too.

Dr. Rosemary, as Juan Diego thought of her – most fondly – knew why he'd never married. It wasn't because Flor and Edward Bonshaw had been a *queer* couple; it was because those two had loved each other so much that Juan Diego couldn't imagine ever finding a partnership as good as theirs – they'd been inimitable. And he'd loved them not only as parents, not to mention as 'adoptive' parents. He'd loved them as the best (meaning, the most unattainable) *couple* he ever knew.

'He misses stuff,' Pedro had said, citing geckos and the dump.

'Don't forget his sister,' Consuelo had said.

More than a lion had killed Lupe, Juan Diego knew, but he could no more say that – to any of them, there on the beach – than he could have become a sky-walker. Juan Diego could no more have saved his sister than he could have become The Wonder.

And if he *had* asked Dr. Rosemary Stein to marry him – that is, before she'd said yes to someone else – who knows if she would have accepted the dump reader's proposal?

'How was the swimming?' Clark French asked his former teacher. 'I mean *before* the sea urchins,' Clark needlessly explained.

'Mister likes to bob around in one place,' Consuelo answered. 'Don't you, Mister?' the little girl in pigtails asked.

'Yes, I do, Consuelo,' Juan Diego told her.

'Treading water, a little dog-paddling – it's a lot like writing a novel, Clark,' the dump reader told his former student. 'It feels like you're going a long way, because it's a lot of work, but you're basically covering old ground – you're hanging out in familiar territory.'

'I see,' Clark said cautiously. He didn't see, Juan Diego knew. Clark was a world-changer; he wrote with a mission, a positive agenda.

Clark French had no appreciation for dog-paddling or treading water; they were like living in the past, like going nowhere. Juan Diego lived there, in the past – reliving, in his imagination, the losses that had marked him.

• 22 •

Mañana

'If something in your life is wrong, or just unresolved, Mexico City is probably not the answer to your dreams,' Juan Diego had written in an early novel. 'Unless you're feeling in charge of your life, don't go there.' The female character who says this isn't Mexican, and we never learn what happens to her in Mexico City – Juan Diego's novel didn't go there.

The circus site, in northern Mexico City, was adjacent to a graveyard. The sparse grass in the stony field, where they exercised the horses and walked the elephants, was gray with soot. There was so much smog in the air, the lions' eyes were watering when Lupe fed them.

Ignacio was making Lupe feed Hombre and the lionesses; the girl acrobats – the ones who were anticipating their periods – had revolted against the lion tamer's tactics. Ignacio had convinced the girl acrobats that the lions knew when the girls got their periods, and the girls were afraid of bleeding near the big cats. (Of course, the girls were afraid of getting their periods in the first place.)

Lupe, who believed she would never get her period, was unafraid. And because she could read the lions' minds, Lupe knew that Hombre and the lionesses never thought about the girls' menstruating.

'Only Ignacio thinks about it,' Lupe had told Juan Diego. She liked feeding Hombre and the lionesses. 'You wouldn't believe how much they think about *meat*,' she'd explained to Edward Bonshaw. The Iowan wanted to watch Lupe feeding the lions – just to be sure the process was safe.

Lupe showed Señor Eduardo how the slot in the cage for the feeding tray could be locked and unlocked. The tray slid in and out, along the floor of the cage. Hombre would extend his paw through the slot, reaching for the meat Lupe put on the tray; this was more a gesture of desire on the lion's part than an actual attempt to grab the meat.

When Lupe slid the tray full of meat back inside the lion's cage, Hombre always withdrew his extended paw. The lion waited for the meat in a sitting position; like a broom, his tail swished from side to side across the floor of his cage.

The lionesses never reached through the slot for the meat Lupe was putting on the feeding tray; they sat waiting, with their tails swishing the whole time.

For cleaning, the feeding tray could be entirely removed from the slot at the floor of the cage. Even when the tray was taken out of the cage, the slot wasn't big enough for Hombre or the lionesses to escape through the opening; the slot was too small for Hombre's big head to fit through it. Not even one of the lionesses could have stuck her head through the open feeding slot.

'It's safe,' Edward Bonshaw had said to Juan Diego. 'I just wanted to be sure about the size of the opening.'

Over the long weekend when La Maravilla was performing in Mexico City, Señor Eduardo slept with the dump kids in the dogs' troupe tent. The first night – when the dump kids knew the Iowan was asleep, because he was snoring – Lupe said to her brother: 'I can fit through the slot where the feeding tray slides in and out. It's not too small an opening for *me* to fit through.'

In the darkness of the tent, Juan Diego considered what Lupe meant; what Lupe said and what she meant weren't always the same thing.

'You mean, you could climb into Hombre's cage – or the lionesses' cage – through the feeding slot?' the boy asked her.

'If the feeding tray was removed from the slot – yes, I could,' Lupe told him.

'You sound like you've *tried* it,' Juan Diego said.

'Why would I try it?' Lupe asked him.

'I don't know – why *would* you?' Juan Diego asked her.

She didn't answer him, but even in the dark he sensed her shrug, her sheer indifference to answering him. (As if Lupe couldn't be bothered to explain everything she knew, or how she knew it.)

Someone farted – one of the dogs, perhaps. 'Was that the biter?' Juan Diego asked. Perro Mestizo, a.k.a. Mongrel, slept with Lupe on her cot. Pastora slept with Juan Diego; he knew the sheepdog hadn't farted. 'It was the parrot man,' Lupe answered. The dump kids laughed. A dog's tail wagged – there was the accompanying thump-thump. One of the dogs had liked the laughter.

'Alemania,' Lupe said. It was the female German shepherd who had wagged her big tail. She slept on the dirt floor of the tent, by the tent flap, as if she were guarding (in police-dog fashion) the way in or out.

'I wonder if lions can catch rabies,' Lupe said, as if she were falling asleep, and she wouldn't remember this idea in the morning.

'Why?' Juan Diego asked her.

'Just wondering,' Lupe said, sighing. After a pause, she asked: 'Don't you think the new dog act is stupid?'

Juan Diego knew when Lupe was deliberately changing the subject, and of course Lupe knew he'd been thinking about the new dog act. It was Juan Diego's idea, but the dogs hadn't been very cooperative, and the dwarf clowns had taken over the idea; it had become Paco and Beer Belly's new act, in Lupe's opinion. (As if those two clowns needed another stupid act.)

Ah, the passage of time – one day when he'd been dog-paddling in the pool at the old Iowa Field House, Juan Diego realized that the new dog act had amounted to his first novel-in-progress, but it was a story he'd been unable to finish. (And the idea that lions could catch rabies? Didn't this amount to a story that Lupe had been unable to bring to a close?)

Like Juan Diego's actual novels, the dog act began as a *what-if* proposition. What if one of the dogs could be trained to climb to the top of a stepladder? It was that type of stepladder with a shelf at the top; the shelf was for holding a can of paint, or a workman's tools, but Juan Diego had imagined the shelf as a diving platform for a dog. What if one of the dogs climbed the stepladder and sailed into the air, off the diving platform, into an open blanket the dwarf clowns were holding out?

'The audience would love it,' Juan Diego told Estrella.

'Not Alemania – she won't do it,' Estrella had said.

'Yes – I guess a German shepherd is too big to climb a stepladder,' Juan Diego had replied.

'Alemania is too smart to do it,' was all Estrella said.

'Perro Mestizo, the biter, is a chickenshit,' Juan Diego said.

'You hate little dogs – you hated Dirty White,' Lupe had told him.

'I don't hate little dogs – Perro Mestizo isn't that little. I hate *cowardly* dogs, and dogs who bite,' Juan Diego had told his sister.

'Not Perro Mestizo – he won't do it,' was all Estrella said.

They tried Pastora, the sheepdog, first; everyone thought that a dachshund's legs were too short to climb the steps on a stepladder – surely Baby couldn't reach the steps.

Pastora could climb the ladder – those border-collie types are very agile and aggressive – but when she got to the top, she lay down on the diving platform with her nose between her forepaws. The dwarf clowns danced under the stepladder, holding out the open blanket to the sheepdog, but Pastora wouldn't even stand on the diving platform. When Paco or Beer Belly called her name, the sheepdog just wagged her tail while she was lying down.

'She's no jumper,' was all Estrella said.

'Baby has balls,' Juan Diego said. Dachshunds *do* have balls – for their size, they seem especially ferocious – and Baby was willing to try climbing the stepladder. But the short-legged dachshund needed a boost.

This would be funny – the audience will laugh, Paco and Beer Belly decided. And the sight of the two dwarf clowns pushing Baby up the stepladder was funny. As always, Paco was dressed (badly) as a woman; while Paco pushed Baby's ass, to help the dachshund up the stepladder, Beer Belly stood behind Paco – pushing her ass up the ladder.

'So far, so good,' Estrella said. But Baby, balls and all, was afraid of heights. When the dachshund got to the top of the stepladder, he froze on the diving platform; he was even afraid to lie down. The little dachshund stood so rigidly still that he began to tremble; soon the stepladder started to shake. Paco and Beer Belly pleaded with Baby as they held out the open blanket. Eventually, Baby peed on the diving platform; he was too afraid to lift his leg, the way male dogs are supposed to do.

'Baby is humiliated – he can't pee like himself,' Estrella said.

But the act was *funny*, the dwarf clowns insisted. It didn't matter that Baby wasn't a jumper, Paco and Beer Belly said.

Estrella wouldn't let Baby do it in front of an audience. She said the act was psychologically cruel. This was not what Juan Diego had intended. But that night in the darkness of the dogs' troupe tent, all Juan Diego said to Lupe was: 'The new dog act isn't *stupid*. All we need is a new dog – we need a jumper,' Juan Diego said.

It would take him years to realize how he'd been manipulated into saying this. It was so long before Lupe said something – in the snoring, farting troupe tent for the dogs – Juan Diego was almost asleep when she spoke, and Lupe sounded as if she were half asleep herself.

'The poor horse,' was all Lupe said.

'*What* horse?' Juan Diego asked in the darkness.

'The one in the graveyard,' Lupe answered him.

In the morning, the dump kids woke up to a pistol shot. One of the circus horses had bolted from the sooty field and jumped the fence into the graveyard, where it broke its leg against a gravestone. Ignacio had shot the horse; the lion tamer kept a .45-caliber revolver, in case there was any lion trouble.

'*That* poor horse,' was all Lupe said, at the sound of the shot.

La Maravilla had arrived in Mexico City on

Thursday. The roustabouts had set up the troupe tents the day they'd arrived; all day Friday, the roustabouts were raising the main tent and securing the animal barriers around the ring. The animals' concentration was affected by traveling, and they needed most of Friday to recover.

The horse had been named Mañana; he was a gelding, and a slow learner. The trainer was always saying that the horse might master a trick they'd been practicing for weeks 'tomorrow' – hence Mañana. But the trick of jumping the fence into the graveyard, and breaking his leg, was a new one for Mañana.

Ignacio put the poor horse out of his misery on Friday. Mañana had jumped a fence to get into the graveyard, but the gate to the graveyard was locked; disposing of the dead horse shouldn't have become a matter of such insurmountable difficulty. However, the gunshot had been reported; the police came to the circus site, and they were more of a hindrance than a help.

Why did the lion tamer have a big-caliber gun? the police asked. (Well, he was a *lion* tamer.) Why had Ignacio shot the horse? (Mañana's leg was broken!) And so on.

There was no permit to dispose of the dead horse in Mexico City – not on a weekend, not in the case of a horse that hadn't 'come from' Mexico City. Getting Mañana out of the locked graveyard was just the start of the difficulties.

There were performances throughout the weekend, starting with Friday night. The last was early

Sunday afternoon, and the roustabouts would collapse the main tent and dismantle the ring barriers before nightfall that day. La Maravilla would be on the road again, heading back to Oaxaca, by the middle of the day on Monday. The dump kids and Edward Bonshaw planned to go to the Guadalupe shrine on Saturday morning.

Juan Diego watched Lupe feeding the lions. A mourning dove was having a dust bath in the dirt near Hombre's cage; the lion hated birds, and maybe Hombre thought the dove was after his meat. For some reason, Hombre was more aggressive in the way he extended his paw through the slot for the feeding tray, and one of his claws nicked the back of Lupe's hand. There was only a little blood; Lupe put her hand to her mouth, and Hombre withdrew his paw – the guilty-looking lion retreated into his cage.

'Not your fault,' Lupe said to the big cat. There was a change in the lion's dark-yellow eyes – a more intense focus, but on the mourning dove or on Lupe's blood? The bird must have sensed the intensity of Hombre's calculating stare and took flight.

Hombre's eyes were instantly normal again – even bored. The two dwarf clowns were waddling past the lions' cages, on their way to the outdoor showers. They wore towels around their waists and their sandals were flapping. The lion looked at them with an utter lack of interest.

'¡Hola, Hombre!' Beer Belly called.

'¡Hola, Lupe! ¡Hola, Lupe's brother!' Paco said; the cross-dresser's breasts were so small (almost nonexistent) that Paco didn't bother to cover them when she walked to and from the outdoor showers, and her beard was at its most stubbly in the mornings. (Whatever Paco was taking for hormones, she wasn't getting her estrogens from the same source Flor got hers; Flor got her estrogens from Dr. Vargas.)

But, as Flor had said, Paco was a clown; it wasn't Paco's aim in life to make herself passable as a woman. Paco was a gay dwarf who, in real life, spent most of her time as a man.

It was as a *he* that Paco went to La China, the gay bar on Bustamante. And when Paco went to La Coronita, where the transvestites liked to dress up, Paco also went as a *he* – Paco was just another guy among the gay clientele.

Flor said that Paco picked up a lot of first-timers, those men who were having their first experiences at being with another man. (Maybe the first-timers looked at a gay dwarf as a cautious way to start?)

But when Paco was with her circus family at La Maravilla, the dwarf clown felt safe to be a *she*. She could be comfortable as a cross-dresser around Beer Belly. In the clown acts, they always acted as if they were a couple, but in real life Beer Belly was straight. He was married, and his wife wasn't a dwarf.

Beer Belly's wife was afraid of getting pregnant; she didn't want to have a dwarf for a child. She made Beer Belly wear two condoms. Everyone in La Maravilla had heard Beer Belly's stories about the perils of wearing an extra condom.

'Nobody does that – no one wears two condoms, you know,' Paco was always telling him, but Beer Belly kept using double condoms, because it was what his wife wanted.

The outdoor showers were made of flimsy, pre-fabricated plywood – they could be assembled and taken apart fairly fast. They sometimes fell down; they had even collapsed on the person taking a shower. There were as many bad stories about the outdoor showers La Maravilla used as there were about Beer Belly's extra condoms. (Lots of embarrassing accidents, in other words.)

The girl acrobats complained to Soledad about Ignacio looking at them in the outdoor showers, but Soledad couldn't stop her husband from being a lecherous pig. The morning Mañana was shot in the graveyard, Dolores was taking an outdoor shower; Paco and Beer Belly had timed their arrival at the showers – they were hoping to get a look at Dolores naked.

The two dwarf clowns were not lecherous – not in the case of the beautiful but unapproachable sky-walker, The Wonder herself. Paco was a gay guy – what did Paco care about getting a look at Dolores? And Beer Belly had all he could possibly handle with his two-condom wife; Beer Belly wasn't personally interested in seeing Dolores naked, either.

But the two dwarfs had a bet between them. Paco had said: 'My tits are bigger than Dolores's.' Beer Belly bet that Dolores's were bigger. This was why the two clowns were always trying to get a look at Dolores in the outdoor shower. Dolores had heard about the bet; she wasn't happy about it. Juan Diego had imagined the shower falling down – Dolores exposed, the dwarf clowns arguing about breast size. (Lupe, who'd used the *mouse-tits* definition for Dolores's breasts, was on Paco's side; Lupe believed Paco's tits were bigger.)

That was why Juan Diego followed Paco and Beer Belly to the outdoor showers; the fourteen-year-old hoped something might happen, and he would get to see Dolores naked. (Juan Diego didn't care that her breasts were small; he believed she was beautiful, even if her tits were tiny.)

The dwarf clowns and Juan Diego could see Dolores's head and bare shoulders above the prefabricated barrier of the outdoor shower. That was when one of the elephants appeared in the avenue of troupe tents; the elephant was dragging the dead horse, who had been chained around the neck. The police followed after Mañana's body; there were ten policemen for one dead horse. Ignacio and the policemen were arguing.

Dolores's head was thickly lathered with shampoo – her eyes were closed. You could see her ankles and her bare feet below the flimsy plywood barrier; the shampoo suds covered her feet. Juan Diego was thinking that maybe the shampoo stung the open wounds on the tops of her feet.

The lion tamer stopped talking when he saw that Dolores was in one of the outdoor showers. The policemen all looked in The Wonder's direction, too.

'Maybe now isn't such a good time,' Beer Belly said to his dwarf buddy, Paco.

'I say now's the perfect time,' Paco said, waddling faster. The dwarf clowns ran to Dolores's outdoor shower. They couldn't have seen over the prefabricated barrier without (impossibly) standing on each other's shoulders, so they looked under the plywood at the bottom of the shower – staring upward, into the falling water and shampoo. They were looking for only a second or two; their heads were wet with water (and frothy with shampoo) when they straightened up and turned away from Dolores's shower. Dolores was still washing her hair; she'd never noticed the dwarfs stealing a look at her. But then Juan Diego tried to peer over the top of the prefabricated barrier; he had to pull himself up, off his feet, with both his hands gripping the flimsy plywood.

Later, Beer Belly said that it would have been a funny clown act; the unlikeliest cast of characters were assembled on a small stage in the avenue of troupe tents. The dwarf clowns, already dappled with Dolores's shampoo, were just bystanders. (Clowns can be at their funniest when they're just standing around, doing nothing.)

Later, the elephant trainer said that what happens in the periphery of an elephant's vision can be more startling to the elephant than something the beast is looking at directly. When Dolores's outdoor shower collapsed, she screamed; she couldn't see (she was blinded by shampoo), but she surely sensed that the walls surrounding her had vanished.

Later, Juan Diego said that although he was pinned under one of the prefabricated walls of the shower, he could feel the ground shake when the elephant broke into a run mode, or a gallop mode (or whatever mode elephants break into when they panic and bolt).

The elephant trainer ran after his elephant; the chain, still attached to the neck of the dead horse, had snapped – but not before Mañana was jerked forward into a kneeling (or praying) position.

Dolores had dropped to all fours on the raised wooden platform that served as a makeshift floor to the shower; she was keeping her head under the stream of water, so she could rinse the shampoo out of her hair – she wanted to *see* again, of course. Juan Diego had crawled out from under the collapsed plywood barrier. He was trying to give Dolores her towel.

'It was me – I did it. I'm sorry,' he said to her; she took the towel from him, but Dolores seemed in no hurry to cover herself. She used the towel to dry her hair first; it was only when she saw Ignacio, and the ten policemen, that The Wonder covered herself with the towel.

'You got more balls than I thought – *some* balls, anyway,' was all Dolores said to Juan Diego.

No one realized that she'd not noticed the dead horse. All the while, the dwarf clowns just stood watching in the avenue of troupe tents – the towels around their waists. Paco's breasts were so small that not one of the ten policemen looked at her twice;

the policemen definitely thought Paco was a guy.

'I told you Dolores's are bigger,' Beer Belly said to his fellow dwarf clown.

'Are you kidding?' Paco asked him. '*Mine* are bigger!'

'Yours are smaller,' Beer Belly told her.

'Bigger!' Paco said. 'What do *you* say, Lupe's brother?' the cross-dresser asked Juan Diego. 'Are Dolores's bigger or smaller?'

'They're prettier,' the fourteen-year-old said. 'Dolores's are more beautiful,' Juan Diego said.

'You got some balls, all right,' Dolores told him; she stepped off the shower platform into the avenue of troupe tents, where she fell over the dead horse. The bullet hole was still bleeding. The wound was on the side of Mañana's face, between the ear and one of the horse's wide-open eyes.

Later, Paco would say that she disagreed with Beer Belly – not only about the relative size of Dolores's breasts, but also about the suitability of the shower episode as a clown act. 'Not the dead-horse part – that wasn't funny,' was all Paco would say about it.

Dolores, lying on the dead horse in the avenue of troupe tents, kicked her bare legs, thrashed her bare arms, and screamed. Ignacio, uncharacteristically, ignored her. He walked on with the ten policemen, but before the lion tamer continued his argument with the law-enforcement officers, he said quite a mouthful to Juan Diego.

'If you have "some balls," *ceiling*-walker, what are you waiting for?' Ignacio asked the boy. 'When are you going to try skywalking at eighty feet? I think Some Balls should be your name. Or how about Mañana? It's a free name now,' the lion tamer said, pointing to the dead horse. 'It's yours, if you want it – if you're always going to put off becoming the first male skywalker until "tomorrow." If you're going to keep putting it off – till the next mañana!'

Dolores had gotten to her feet; her towel was stained with the horse's blood. Before she walked off in the direction of the girl acrobats' troupe tent, she gave both Beer Belly and Paco a whack on the tops of their heads. 'You disgusting little creeps,' she told them.

'Bigger than yours,' was all Beer Belly said to Paco, after Dolores had left them standing there.

'Smaller than mine,' Paco told him quietly.

Ignacio and the ten policemen had walked on; they were still arguing, although the lion tamer was doing all the talking.

'If I need a permit to dispose of a dead horse, I suppose I *don't* need a permit to butcher the animal and feed the meat to my lions – do I?' the lion tamer was saying, but he wasn't waiting for an answer from the ten policemen. 'I don't suppose you expect me to drive a dead horse back to Oaxaca, do you?' Ignacio asked them. 'I could have left the horse to die in the graveyard. You wouldn't have liked that very much, would you?' the lion tamer went on, unanswered.

'Forget about skywalking, Lupe's brother,' Paco said to the fourteen-year-old.

'Lupe needs you to look after her,' Beer Belly told

Juan Diego. The two dwarf clowns waddled off; there were some outdoor showers still standing, and the two clowns started taking theirs.

Juan Diego thought that he and Mañana were alone in the avenue of troupe tents; he hadn't seen Lupe until she was standing beside him. Juan Diego guessed she'd always been there.

'Did you see—' he started to ask her.

'Everything,' Lupe told him. Juan Diego just nodded. 'About the new dog act—' Lupe began; she stopped, as if she were waiting for him to catch up to her. She was always a thought or two ahead of him.

'What about it?' Juan Diego asked her.

Lupe said: 'I know where you can get a new dog – a jumper.'

THE DREAMS OR MEMORIES he'd missed, because of the beta-blockers, had risen up and overwhelmed him; his final two days at the Encantador, Juan Diego dutifully took his Lopressor prescription – the correct dose.

Dr. Quintana must have known Juan Diego wasn't acting; his return to torpor, to a diminished level of alertness and physiological activity, was evident to everyone – he did his dog-paddling in the swimming pool (no sea urchins were lurking there) and ate his meals at the children's table. He kept company with Consuelo and Pedro, his fellow whisperers.

In the early mornings, drinking coffee by the swimming pool, Juan Diego would reread his notes (and make new notes) on *One Chance to Leave*

Lithuania; he'd gone back to Vilnius two more times since his first visit in 2008. Rasa, his publisher, had found a woman in the State Child Rights Protection and Adoption Service to talk with him; he'd brought Daiva, his translator, to the first meeting, but the woman from Child Rights spoke excellent English, and she was forthcoming. Her name was Odeta – the same name as the mystery woman on the bookstore bulletin board, the *not*-a-mail-order bride. That woman's photograph and phone number had disappeared from the bulletin board, but she still haunted Juan Diego – her suppressed but visible unhappiness, the dark circles under her late-night-reading eyes, her neglected-looking hair. Was there still no one in her life to talk with her about the wonderful novels she'd read?

One Chance to Leave Lithuania had, of course, evolved. The woman reader was not a mail-order bride. She'd put her child up for adoption, but the adoption (long a work-in-progress) had fallen through. In Juan Diego's novel, the woman wants her baby to be adopted by Americans. (She'd always dreamed of going to America; now she will give up her child, but only if she can imagine her child as happy in America.)

The Odeta in Child Rights had explained to Juan Diego that it was rare for Lithuanian children to be adopted outside Lithuania. There was quite a lengthy waiting period, allowing the birth mother a second chance to change her mind. The laws were strict: at least six months for international decisions, but the period of time (the waiting period) could take four years – hence older children were the ones most likely to be adopted by foreigners.

In *One Chance to Leave Lithuania*, the American couple waiting to adopt a Lithuanian child has a tragedy of their own – the young wife is killed on her bicycle by a hit-and-run driver; the widowed husband is in no shape to adopt a child by himself (not that Child Rights would allow him to).

In a Juan Diego Guerrero novel, everyone is a kind of outsider; Juan Diego's characters feel they are foreigners, even when they're at home. The young Lithuanian woman, who has had two chances to change her mind about putting her child up for adoption, now has a third chance to change her mind; the adoption of her child is put on hold. Another awful 'waiting period' confronts her. She puts her photo and her phone number on the bulletin board at the bookstore; she meets other women readers for coffee or beer, talking about the novels they've read – the myriad unhappiness of others.

This is a collision we should see coming, Juan Diego was thinking. The American widower takes a trip to Vilnius; he doesn't expect to see the child he and his late wife were going to adopt – Child Rights would never have let him. He doesn't even know the name of the single mother who'd put her child up for adoption. He's not expecting to meet anyone. There is an atmosphere he hopes to absorb – an essence their adopted child might have brought to America. Or is his going to Vilnius a way of reconnecting with his dead wife, a way of keeping her alive a little longer?

Yes, of course, he goes to the bookstore; maybe it's the jet lag – he thinks a novel would help him sleep. And there, on the bulletin board, he sees her photo – someone whose unhappiness is both hidden and apparent. Her lack of attention to herself draws him to her, and her favorite novelists were his *wife's* favorite novelists! Not knowing if she speaks English – of course she does – he asks the bookseller for assistance in calling her.

And *then*? The question that remained was an earlier one – namely, *whose* one chance to leave Lithuania was it? The collision course in *One Chance to Leave Lithuania* is obvious: they meet, each discovers who the other is, they become lovers. But how do they handle the crushing weight of the extreme coincidence of their meeting each other? And what do they do about their seeming fate? Do they stay together, does she keep her child, do they *all three* go to America – or does this lonely American widower remain with this mother and her child in Vilnius? (Her child has been staying with her sister – not a good situation.)

In the darkness of the single mother's tiny apartment – she is sleeping in his arms, more soundly than she's slept in years – he lies there thinking. (He has still seen only photos of the child.) If he's going to leave this woman and her child and go back to America alone, he knows he'd better leave now.

What we *shouldn't* see coming, Juan Diego thought,

is that the eponymous one chance to leave Lithuania could be the American's – *his* last chance to change his mind, to get out.

'You're writing, aren't you?' Clark French asked his former teacher. It was still early in the morning, and Clark had caught Juan Diego with one of his note-books, pen in hand, at the Encantador swimming pool.

'You know me – they're just notes about what I'm going to write,' Juan Diego answered.

'That's writing,' Clark confidently said.

It seemed natural enough for Clark to ask Juan Diego about the novel-in-progress, and Juan Diego felt comfortable telling him about *One Chance to Leave Lithuania* – where the idea came from, and how the novel had evolved.

'Another Catholic country,' Clark suddenly said. 'Dare I ask what villainous role the Church plays in this story?'

Juan Diego hadn't been talking about the role of the Church; he hadn't even been thinking about it – not yet. But, of course, Juan Diego *would* have a role for the Church in *One Chance to Leave Lithuania*. Both the teacher and his former student surely knew that. 'You know as well as I do, Clark, what role the Church plays in the case of unwanted children,' Juan Diego replied. 'In the case of what causes unwanted children to be born, in the first place—' He stopped; he saw that Clark had closed his eyes. Juan Diego closed his eyes, too.

The impasse presented by their religious differences was a familiar standoff, a depressing dead end.

When, in the past, Clark had used the *we* word, he'd never meant 'you and I'; when Clark said 'we,' he meant the Church – especially when Clark was trying to sound progressive or tolerant. 'We shouldn't be so *insistent* on issues like abortion or the use of contraceptive methods, or gay marriage. The teachings of the Church' – and here Clark *always* hesitated – 'are clear.' Clark would then continue: 'But it isn't *necessary* to talk about these issues all the time, or to sound so combative.'

Oh, sure – Clark could *sound* progressive, when he wanted to; he wasn't the absolutist about these issues that John Paul II was!

And Juan Diego, over the years, had also been insincere; he'd pulled his punches. He'd teased Clark with that old Chesterton quote too many times: 'It is the test of a good religion whether you can joke about it.' (Clark, naturally, had laughed this off.)

Juan Diego regretted that he'd wasted dear Brother Pepe's favorite prayer in more than one of his arguments with Clark. Of course Clark was incapable of recognizing himself in that prayer from Saint Teresa of Ávila, the one Pepe had faithfully repeated among his daily prayers: 'From silly devotions and sour-faced saints, good Lord, deliver us.'

But why was Juan Diego reliving his correspondence with Brother Pepe, as if Pepe had written only yesterday? Years ago, he'd written that Father Alfonso and Father Octavio had died in their sleep within days of each other. Pepe expressed his dismay to Juan Diego, regarding how the two old priests had 'slipped away'; they'd always been so dogmatic, so punitively opinionated – how had those two dared to die without a final fuss?

And Rivera's departure from this life also pissed Pepe off. El jefe hadn't been himself since the old dump had moved in 1981; there was a new dump now. Those first ten families from the colony in Guerrero were long gone.

What really undid Rivera was the no-burning policy instituted after the creation of the new dump. How could they have put an end to the *fires*? What kind of dump *didn't* burn things?

Pepe had pressed el jefe to tell him more. The end of the hellfires in the basurero hadn't bothered Brother Pepe, but it was Juan Diego's paternity that he wanted to know more about.

That woman worker in the old basurero had told Pepe that the dump boss was 'not exactly' the dump reader's father; Juan Diego himself had always believed that el jefe was 'probably not' his dad.

But Lupe had said: 'Rivera knows something – he's just not saying.'

Rivera had told the dump kids that Juan Diego's 'most likely' father had died of a *broken* heart.

'A heart attack, right?' Juan Diego had asked el jefe – because that's what Esperanza had told her children, and everyone else.

'If that's what you call a heart that's *permanently* broken,' was all Rivera had ever said to the kids.

But Brother Pepe had finally persuaded Rivera to tell him more.

Yes, the dump boss was pretty sure he was Juan Diego's biological father; Esperanza had been sleeping with no one else at the time – or so she said. But she'd later told Rivera he was too stupid to have fathered a genius like the dump reader. 'Even if you *are* his father, he should never know it,' Esperanza had said to el jefe. 'If Juan Diego knows you're his father, it will undermine his self-confidence,' she'd said. (This no doubt *undermined* what little self-confidence the dump boss ever had.)

Rivera told Pepe not to tell Juan Diego – not until the dump boss was dead. Who knew if el jefe's heart had killed him?

No one ever knew where Rivera actually lived; he died in the cab of his truck – it had always been his favorite place to sleep, and after Diablo died, Rivera missed his dog and rarely slept anywhere else.

Like Father Alfonso and Father Octavio, el jefe had also 'slipped away,' but not before he'd made his confession to Brother Pepe.

Rivera's death, including his confession, was a big part of Brother Pepe's correspondence that Juan Diego would relive – constantly.

How had Brother Pepe managed to live the epilogue to his own life so *cheerfully*? Juan Diego was wondering.

At the Encantador, no more roosters crowed in the darkness; Juan Diego slept through the night, unmindful of the karaoke music from the beach club. No woman slept (or had vanished) beside him, but he woke up one morning to discover what looked like a title – in his handwriting – on the notepad on his night table.

The Last Things, he'd written on the pad. That had been the night he'd dreamed about Pepe's last orphanage. Brother Pepe started volunteering at Hijos de la Luna ('Children of the Moon') sometime after 2001; Pepe's letters had been so positive – everything seemed to energize him, and he was then in his late seventies.

The orphanage was in Guadalupe Victoria ('Guadalupe the Victorious'). Hijos de la Luna was for children of prostitutes. Brother Pepe said the prostitutes were welcome to visit their kids. At Lost Children, Juan Diego remembered, the nuns kept the birth mothers away; this was one of the reasons that Esperanza, the dump kids' birth mother, had never been welcomed by the nuns.

At Children of the Moon, the orphans called Pepe 'Papá'; Pepe said this was 'not a big deal.' According to Pepe, the other men who volunteered at the orphanage were also called 'Papá.'

'Our dear Edward wouldn't have approved of the motorcycles parked in the classroom,' Brother Pepe had written, 'but people steal the motorcycles if you park them on the street.' (Señor Eduardo said a motorcycle was a 'death-in-progress.')

Dr. Vargas would surely have disapproved of the dogs in the orphanage – Hijos de la Luna allowed dogs: the kids liked them.

There was a large trampoline in the courtyard of Children of the Moon – dogs were *not* allowed on the trampoline, Pepe had written – and a big pomegranate tree. The upper branches of the tree were festooned with rag dolls and other toys – things the children had thrown upward, into the receptive branches. The girls' and boys' sleeping quarters were in separate buildings, but their clothes were shared – the orphans' clothes were communal property.

'I'm not driving a VW Beetle anymore,' Pepe had written. 'I don't want to kill anyone. I've got a little motorcycle, and I never drive it fast enough to kill anyone I might hit.'

That had been Brother Pepe's last letter – one of the things to be counted in *The Last Things*, the apparent title Juan Diego had written in his sleep, or when he was only half awake.

The morning he left the Encantador, only Consuelo and Pedro were awake to say goodbye to him; it was still dark outside. Juan Diego's driver was that feral-faced boy who looked too young to drive – the hornblower. But the boy was a better driver than he was a waiter, Juan Diego remembered.

'Watch out for the monitor lizards, Mister,' Pedro said.

'Don't step on any sea urchins, Mister,' Consuelo said.

Clark French had left a note for his former teacher with the desk clerk. Clark must have thought he was being funny – at least funny for Clark. *Until Manila* – that was the message.

All the way to the airport in Tagbilaran City, there was no conversation with the boy driver. Juan Diego was remembering the letter he'd received from the lady who ran Children of the Moon in Guadalupe Victoria. Brother Pepe had been killed on his little motorcycle. He'd swerved to avoid hitting a dog, and a bus had hit him. 'He had all your books – the ones you signed for him. He was very proud of you!' the lady at Hijos de la Luna had written to Juan Diego. She'd signed her name – 'Mamá.' The lady who'd written to Juan Diego was called Coco. The orphans called her 'Mamá.'

Juan Diego would wonder if there was only one 'Mamá' at Children of the Moon. As it turned out, that was the case – only one – as Dr. Vargas would write Juan Diego.

Pepe had been mistaken about the use of the *Papá* word, Vargas wrote to Juan Diego. 'Pepe's hearing wasn't so good, or he would have heard the bus,' was how Vargas had put it.

The orphans hadn't called Pepe 'Papá' – Pepe had misheard them. There was only one person the kids called 'Papá' at Hijos de la Luna – he was Coco's son, the *Mamá* lady's son.

Leave it to Vargas to straighten everything out, to give you the *scientific* answer, Juan Diego had thought.

What a long way it was to Tagbilaran City – and that was just the start of the long day's trip he was taking, Juan Diego knew. Two planes and three boats lay ahead of him – not to mention the monitor lizards, or D.

23

Neither Animal, Vegetable, nor Mineral

'The past surrounded him like faces in a crowd,' Juan Diego had written.

It was a Monday – January 3, 2011 – and the young woman seated next to Juan Diego was worried about him. Philippine Airlines 174, from Tagbilaran City to Manila, was quite a rowdy flight for a 7:30 A.M. departure; yet the woman beside Juan Diego told the flight attendant that the gentleman had instantly fallen asleep, despite the clamor of their yammering fellow travelers.

'He totally conked out,' the woman said to the stewardess. But soon after falling asleep, Juan Diego began to speak. 'At first, I thought he was speaking to *me*,' the woman told the flight attendant.

Juan Diego didn't sound as if he were talking in his sleep – his speech wasn't slurred, his thinking was incisive (albeit professorial).

'In the sixteenth century, when the Jesuits were founded, not many people could *read* – let alone learn the Latin necessary to preside at Mass,' Juan Diego began.

'What?' the young woman said.

'But there were a few exceptionally devoted souls – people who thought only of doing good – and they yearned to be part of a religious order,' Juan Diego went on.

'*Why?*' the woman asked him, before she realized his eyes were closed. Juan Diego had been a university professor; to the woman, it must have seemed like he'd been lecturing to her in his sleep.

'These dutiful men were called lay brothers, meaning they were not ordained,' Juan Diego lectured on. 'Today, they typically work as cashiers or cooks – even as writers,' he said, laughing to himself. Then, still sleeping soundly, Juan Diego started to cry. 'But Brother Pepe was dedicated to children – he was a teacher,' Juan Diego said, his voice breaking. He opened his eyes – he stared, unseeing, at the young woman beside him; she knew he was still *conked out*, as she would have put it. 'Pepe just didn't feel *called* to the priesthood, though he'd taken the same vows as a priest – thus he couldn't marry,' Juan Diego explained; his eyes were closing as the tears ran down his cheeks.

'I see,' the woman said softly to him, slipping out of her seat; that was when she went to get the flight attendant. She tried to explain to the stewardess that the man was not bothering her; he seemed like a nice man, but he was sad, she said.

'Sad?' the flight attendant asked. The stewardess had her hands full: a bunch of drunks were onboard the early-morning flight – young men who'd been carousing all night. And there was a pregnant woman; she was probably too pregnant to fly safely. (She'd told the flight attendant that she either was in labor or had eaten an inadvisable breakfast.)

'He's crying – *weeping* in his sleep,' the woman who'd been seated next to Juan Diego was trying to explain. 'But his conversation is very high-level – like he's a teacher talking to a class, or something.'

'He doesn't sound threatening,' the stewardess said. (Their conversation was clearly at cross-purposes.)

'I said he was *nice* – he's not *threatening*!' the young woman said. 'The poor man is in trouble – he's seriously unhappy!'

'Unhappy,' the flight attendant repeated – as if *unhappy* were part of her job! Yet, if only for relief from the young drunks and the pregnant idiot, the stewardess went with the woman to have a look at Juan Diego, who appeared to be sleeping peacefully in a window seat.

When he was asleep was the only time that Juan Diego looked younger than he was – his warm-brown skin, his almost all-black hair – and the flight attendant said to the young woman: 'This guy isn't "in trouble." He certainly isn't weeping – he's *asleep*!'

'What does he think he's *holding*?' the woman asked the stewardess. Indeed, Juan Diego's forearms were fixed at rigid right angles to his body – his hands apart, his fingers spread, as if he were holding something the approximate circumference of a coffee can.

'Sir?' the stewardess asked, leaning over his seat.

She gently touched his wrist, where she could feel how taut the muscles in his forearm were. 'Sir – are you all right?' the flight attendant asked, more forcefully.

'Calzada de los Misterios,' Juan Diego said loudly, as if he were trying to be heard over the din of a mob. (In his mind – in Juan Diego's memory or dream – he *was*. He was in the backseat of a taxi, creeping through the Saturday-morning traffic on the Avenue of Mysteries – in a mob.)

'Excuse me—' the stewardess said.

'You see? This is how it goes – he's not really talking to *you*,' the young woman told the flight attendant.

'Calzada, a wide road, usually cobbled or paved – very Mexican, very *formal*, from imperial times,' Juan Diego explained. '*Avenida* is less formal. Calzada de los Misterios, Avenida de los Misterios – it's the same thing. Translated into English, you wouldn't translate the article. You would just say 'Avenue of Mysteries.' Fuck the *los*,' Juan Diego added, somewhat less than professorially.

'I see,' the stewardess said.

'Ask him what he's *holding*,' the young passenger reminded the flight attendant.

'Sir?' the stewardess asked sweetly. 'What have you got in your hands?' But when she once more touched his taut forearm, Juan Diego clutched the imaginary coffee can to his chest.

'Ashes,' Juan Diego whispered.

'Ashes,' the flight attendant repeated.

'As in, "Dust to dust" – *those* kind of ashes. That's my bet,' the woman passenger guessed.

'*Whose* ashes?' the stewardess whispered in Juan Diego's ear, leaning closer to him.

'My mother's,' he answered her, 'and the dead hippie's, and a dead dog's – a puppy's.'

The two young women in the aisle of the plane were speechless; they could both see that Juan Diego was starting to cry. 'And the Virgin Mary's nose – *those* ashes,' Juan Diego whispered.

The drunken young men were singing an inappropriate song – there were children onboard Philippine Airlines 174 – and an older woman approached the flight attendant in the aisle.

'I think that very pregnant young woman is in labor,' the older woman said. 'At least *she* thinks she is. Mind you: it's her first child, so she really doesn't know what labor *is*—'

'I'm sorry, you'll have to sit down,' the stewardess said to the young woman who'd been seated next to Juan Diego. 'The sleeper with the ashes seems harmless, and it's only another thirty or forty minutes till we land in Manila.'

'Jesus Mary Joseph,' was all the young woman said. She saw that Juan Diego was weeping again. Whether he was sobbing for his mother or the dead hippie or a dead dog or the Virgin Mary's nose – well, who knew what had made him weep?

It was not a long flight from Tagbilaran City to Manila, but thirty or forty minutes is a long time to dream about ashes.

*   *   *

THE HORDES OF PILGRIMS had assembled on foot and were marching in the middle of the broad avenue, though many of them had first arrived on the Avenue of Mysteries by the busload. The taxi inched forward, then stopped, then crept cautiously ahead again. The throng of pedestrians had brought the vehicular traffic to a standstill; the pedestrians were gathered in different groups, unified and purposeful. The marchers moved relentlessly forward, both blocking and passing the overwhelmed vehicles. The marching pilgrims were making better progress along the Avenue of Mysteries than the hot and claustrophobic taxi ever could.

The dump kids' pilgrimage to Guadalupe's shrine was not a solitary one – not on a Saturday morning in Mexico City. On weekends, the dark-skinned virgin – la virgen morena – drew a mob.

In the backseat of the sweltering taxi, Juan Diego sat holding the sacred coffee can in his lap; Lupe had wanted to hold it, but her hands were small. One of the fervent pilgrims could have jostled the car, causing her to lose her grip on the ashes.

Once more, the taxi driver braked; they were halted in a sea of marchers – the broad avenue approaching the Basílica de Nuestra Señora de Guadalupe was clogged.

'All this for an Indian bitch whose name means "breeder of coyotes" – Guadalupe means "breeder of coyotes" in Nahuatl, or in one of those Indian languages,' their malevolent-looking driver said.

'You don't know what you're talking about, you rat-faced shitbreath,' Lupe said to the driver.

'What was that – is she speaking Nahuatl or something?' the driver asked; he was missing his two front teeth, among others.

'Don't give us the guidebook routine – we're not tourists. Just drive,' Juan Diego told him.

As an order of nuns marched past the stopped taxi, one of them broke her string of rosary beads, and the loose beads bounced and rolled on the hood of the cab.

'Be sure you see the painting of the baptizing of the Indians – you can't miss it,' their driver told them.

'The Indians had to give up their Indian names!' Lupe cried. 'The Indians had to take Spanish names – that's how the conversión de los indios worked, you mouse dick, you chicken-fucker sellout!'

'That's *not* Nahuatl? She sure sounds Indian—' the taxi driver started to say, but there was a masked face pressed against the windshield in front of him; he blew his horn, but the masked marchers just stared into the taxi as they passed. They were wearing the masks of barnyard animals – cows, horses or donkeys, goats, and chickens.

'Nativity pilgrims – fucking crèche crazies,' the taxi driver muttered to himself; someone had also knocked out his upper and lower canines, yet he manifested a stoned superiority.

Music was blasting songs of praise to la virgen morena; children in school uniforms were banging drums. The taxi lurched forward, then stopped again.

Blindfolded men in business suits were roped together; they were led by a priest, who made incantations. (No one could hear the priest's incantations over the music.)

In the backseat, Lupe sat scowling between her brother and Edward Bonshaw. Señor Eduardo, who could not refrain from glancing anxiously at the coffee can Juan Diego held in his lap, was no less anxious about the crazed pilgrims surrounding their taxi. And now the pilgrims were intermixed with vendors hawking cheap religious totems – Guadalupe figures, finger-size Christs (engaged in multifaceted suffering on the cross), even the hideous Coatlicue in her skirt of serpents (not to mention her fetching necklace of human hearts and hands and skulls).

Juan Diego could tell that Lupe was upset to see so many vulgar versions of the grotesque figurine the good gringo had given her. One shrill-voiced vendor must have had a hundred Coatlicue statuettes for sale – all dressed in writhing snakes, with flaccid breasts and rattlesnake-rattle nipples. Every figurine, like Lupe's, had hands and feet with ravening claws.

'Yours is still special, Lupe, because el gringo bueno gave it to you,' Juan Diego told his little sister.

'Too much mind reading,' was all Lupe said.

'I get it,' the taxi driver said. 'If she's not speaking Nahuatl, she's got something wrong with her voice – you're taking her to the "breeder of coyotes" for a cure!'

'Let us out of your asshole-smelling taxi – we can

walk faster than you drive, turtle penis,' Juan Diego said.

'I've seen you walk, chico,' the driver told him. 'You think Guadalupe is going to cure your limp – huh?'

'Are we stopping?' Edward Bonshaw asked the dump kids.

'We were never *moving*!' Lupe cried. 'Our driver has fucked so many prostitutes, his brains are smaller than his balls!'

Señor Eduardo was paying the taxi fare when Juan Diego told him, in English, not to tip the driver.

'¡Hijo de la chingada!' the taxi driver said to Juan Diego. This was something Sister Gloria might have thought to herself about Juan Diego; Juan Diego thought the taxi driver had called him a 'whore's son' – Lupe doubted this translation. She'd heard the girl acrobats use the *chingada* word; she thought it meant 'motherfucker.'

'¡Pinche pendejo chimuelo!' Lupe shouted at the driver.

'What did the Indian say?' the driver asked Juan Diego.

'She said you are a "miserable toothless asshole" – it's obvious someone beat the shit out of you before,' Juan Diego said.

'What a beautiful language!' Edward Bonshaw remarked with a sigh – he was always saying this. 'I wish I could learn it, but I don't seem to be making much progress.'

After that, the dump kids and the Iowan were caught up in the pressing crowd. First they were stuck behind a slowly moving order of nuns who were walking on their knees – their habits were hiked half-way up their thighs, their knees bleeding on the cobblestones. Then the dump kids and the lapsed missionary were slowed down by a bunch of monks from an obscure monastery who were whipping themselves. (If they were bleeding, their brown robes hid the blood, but the lashing of their whips made Señor Eduardo cringe.) There were many more drum-banging children in school uniforms.

'Dear God,' was all Edward Bonshaw managed to say; he'd stopped giving anxious looks at the coffee can Juan Diego was carrying – there were too many other appalling things to see, and they hadn't even reached the shrine.

In the Chapel of the Well, Señor Eduardo and the dump kids had to fight their way through the self-abusing pilgrims, who made a sickening display of themselves. One woman kept gouging at her face with fingernail clippers. A man had pockmarked his forehead with the point of a pen; the blood and ink had commingled, running into his eyes. Naturally, he couldn't stop blinking his eyes – he appeared to be crying purple tears.

Edward Bonshaw put Lupe on his shoulders, so she could see over the men in business suits; they'd taken their blindfolds off, so they could see Our Lady of Guadalupe on her deathbed. The dark-skinned virgin lay encased in glass, but the roped-together men in business suits would not move on – they wouldn't allow anyone else to see her.

The priest who'd led the blindfolded businessmen to this spectacle continued his incantations. The priest also held all the blindfolds; he resembled a badly dressed waiter who'd foolishly gathered the used napkins in an evacuated restaurant during a bomb scare.

Juan Diego had decided it was better when the blasting music made it impossible to hear the priest's incantations, because the priest seemed stuck in a groove of the most simplistic repetition. Didn't everyone who knew *anything* about Guadalupe already know by heart her most famous utterance?

'¿No estoy aquí, que soy tu madre?' the priest holding the wrinkled blindfolds kept repeating. 'Am I not here, for I am your mother?' It was truly a senseless thing for a man holding a dozen (or more) blindfolds to be saying.

'Put me down – I don't want to see this,' Lupe said, but the Iowan couldn't understand her; Juan Diego had to translate for his sister.

'The banker-brained dickheads don't need blindfolds – they're blind *without* the blindfolds,' Lupe also said, but Juan Diego didn't translate this. (The circus roustabouts called tent poles 'dream dicks'; Juan Diego thought it was only a matter of time before Lupe's language lowered itself to the dream-dick level.)

What waited ahead for Señor Eduardo and the dump kids were the endless stairs leading to El Cerrito de las Rosas – truly an ordeal of devotion *and* endurance. Edward Bonshaw bravely began the ascent of the stairs with the crippled boy now on his shoulders, but there were too many stairs – the climb was too long and steep. 'I can walk, you know,' Juan Diego tried to tell the Iowan. 'It doesn't matter that I limp – limping is my thing!'

But Señor Eduardo struggled onward; he gasped for breath, the bottom of the coffee can bumping against the top of his bobbing head. Of course no one would have guessed that the failed scholastic was carrying a cripple up the stairs; the flailing Jesuit looked like any other self-abusing pilgrim – he might as well have been carrying cinder blocks or sandbags on his shoulders.

'Do you understand what happens if the parrot man drops dead?' Lupe asked her brother. 'There goes your chance to get out of this mess, and this crazy country!'

The dump kids had seen for themselves the complications that could arise when a horse died – Mañana had been a horse from out of town, right? If Edward Bonshaw keeled over, climbing the stairs to El Cerrito – well, the Iowan was from out of town, wasn't he? What would Juan Diego and Lupe do *then*? Juan Diego was thinking.

Naturally, Lupe had an answer for his thoughts. 'We will have to rob Señor Eduardo's dead body – just to get enough money to pay a taxi to take us back to the circus site – or we will be kidnapped and sold to the brothels for child prostitutes!'

'Okay, okay,' Juan Diego told her. To the panting, sweating Señor Eduardo, Juan Diego said: 'Put me down – let me limp. I can *crawl* faster than you're carrying me. If you die, I'll have to sell Lupe to a children's brothel just to have money to eat. If you die, we'll never get back to Oaxaca.'

'Merciful Jesus!' Edward Bonshaw prayed, kneeling on the stairs. He wasn't really praying; he knelt because he lacked the strength to lift Juan Diego off his shoulders – he dropped to his knees because he would have fallen if he'd tried to take another step.

The dump kids stood beside the gasping, kneeling Señor Eduardo while the Iowan strained to catch his breath. A TV crew climbed past them on the stairs. (Years later, when Edward Bonshaw was dying – when the dear man was similarly straining to breathe – Juan Diego would remember that moment when the television crew passed them on the stairs to the temple Lupe liked to call 'Of the Roses.')

The on-camera TV journalist – a young woman, pretty but professional – was giving a cut-and-dried account of the miracle. It could have been a travel show, or a television documentary – neither high-brow nor sensational.

'In 1531, when the virgin first appeared to Juan Diego – an Aztec nobleman *or* peasant, according to conflicting accounts – the bishop didn't believe Juan Diego and asked him for proof,' the pretty TV journalist was saying. She stopped her narration when she saw the foreigner on his knees; maybe the Hawaiian shirt had caught her eye, if not the worried-looking children attending to the apparently praying man. And it was here the cameraman shifted his attention: the cameraman clearly liked the image of Edward Bonshaw kneeling on the stairs, and the two children waiting with him. They drew the television camera to them, the three of them.

It was not the first time Juan Diego had heard of the 'conflicting accounts,' though he preferred thinking of himself as being named for a famous *peasant*; Juan Diego found it a little disturbing to think that he might have been named for an Aztec *nobleman*. That word didn't jibe with the prevailing image Juan Diego had of himself – namely, a standard-bearer for dump readers.

Señor Eduardo had caught his breath; now he was able to stand and to move unsteadily forward up the stairs. But the cameraman had zeroed in on the image of a crippled boy climbing to El Cerrito de las Rosas. Hence the TV crew moved slowly in step with the Iowan and the dump kids; they ascended the stairs together.

'When Juan Diego went back to the hill, the virgin reappeared and told him to pick some roses and carry them to the bishop,' the TV journalist continued.

Behind the limping boy, as he and his sister reached the top of the hill, was a spectacular view of Mexico City; the TV camera captured the view, but neither Edward Bonshaw nor the dump kids ever turned around to see it. Juan Diego carefully held the coffee can in front of him, as if the ashes were a sacred offering he was bringing to the temple called 'The Little Hill,' which marked the spot where the miraculous roses grew.

'This time, the bishop believed him – the image of the virgin was imprinted on Juan Diego's cloak,' the pretty TV journalist went on, but the cameraman had lost interest in Señor Eduardo and the dump kids; his attention had been seized by a group of Japanese honeymoon couples – their tour guide was using a megaphone to explain the Guadalupe miracle in Japanese.

Lupe was upset that the Japanese honeymooners were wearing surgical masks over their mouths and noses; she imagined the young Japanese couples were dying of some dread disease – she thought they'd come to Of the Roses to beg Our Lady of Guadalupe to save them.

'But aren't they *contagious*?' Lupe asked. 'How many people have they infected between here and Japan?'

How much of Juan Diego's translation and Edward Bonshaw's explanation to Lupe was lost in the crowd noise? The proclivity of the Japanese to be 'precautionary,' to wear surgical masks to protect themselves from bad air or disease – well, it was unclear if Lupe ever understood what that was about.

More distracting, the nearby tourists and worshipers who'd heard Lupe speak had raised their own cries of faith-based excitement. One earnest believer pointed to Lupe and announced she'd been speaking in tongues; this had upset Lupe – to be accused of the ecstatic, unintelligible utterances of a messianic child.

A Mass was in progress inside the temple, but the

rabble entering El Cerrito didn't seem conducive to the atmosphere for a Mass: the armies of nuns and uniformed children, the whipped monks and roped-together men in business suits – the latter were blindfolded again, which had caused them to trip and fall ascending the stairs (their pants were torn or scuffed at the knees, and two or three of the business-men limped, if not as noticeably as Juan Diego).

Not that Juan Diego was the only cripple: the maimed had come – the amputees, too. (They'd come to be cured.) They were all there – the deaf, the blind, the poor – together with the sightseeing nobodies and the masked Japanese honeymooners.

At the threshold to the temple, the dump kids heard the pretty TV journalist say: 'A German chemist actually analyzed the red and yellow fibers of Juan Diego's cloak. The chemist determined, scientifically, that the colors of the cloak were neither animal, vegetable, nor mineral.'

'What do the *Germans* have to do with it?' Lupe asked. 'Either Guadalupe is a miracle or she isn't. It's not about the *cloak*!'

The Basílica de Nuestra Señora de Guadalupe was, in fact, a group of churches, chapels, and shrines all gathered on the rocky hillside where the miracle supposedly occurred. As it would turn out, Edward Bonshaw and the dump kids saw only the Chapel of the Well, where Guadalupe lay under glass on her deathbed, and El Cerrito de las Rosas. (They would never see the enshrined cloak.)

Inside El Cerrito, it's true that the Virgin of

Guadalupe isn't tucked away in a side altar; she is elevated at the front of the chapel. But so what if they'd made her the main attraction? They had made Guadalupe at one with the Virgin Mary; they'd made them the same. The Catholic hocus-pocus was complete: the sacred Of the Roses was a zoo. The crazies far outnumbered the worshipers who were trying to follow the Mass-in-progress. The priests were performing by rote. While the megaphone was not permitted inside the temple, the tour guide continued in Japanese to the honeymooners in their surgical masks. The roped-together men in business suits – their blindfolds were once more removed – stared unseeing at the dark-skinned virgin, the way Juan Diego stared when he was dreaming.

'Don't touch those ashes,' Lupe said to him, but Juan Diego was holding the lid tightly in place. 'Not a speck gets sprinkled here,' Lupe told him.

'I know—' Juan Diego started to say.

'Our mother would rather burn in Hell than have her ashes scattered here,' Lupe said. 'El gringo bueno would never sleep in El Cerrito – he was so beautiful when he slept,' she said, remembering. It wasn't lost on Juan Diego that his sister had stopped calling the temple 'Of the Roses.' Lupe was content to call the temple 'The Little Hill'; it wasn't so sacred to her anymore.

'I don't need a translation,' Señor Eduardo told the dump kids. 'This chapel is not holy. This whole place is not right – it's all wrong, it's not the way it was meant to be.'

'Meant to be,' Juan Diego repeated.

'It's neither animal, vegetable, nor mineral – it's like the German said!' Lupe cried. Juan Diego thought he should translate this for Edward Bonshaw – it had a disturbing ring of truth to it.

'*What* German?' the Iowan asked, as they were descending the stairs. (Years later, Señor Eduardo would say to Juan Diego: 'I feel I am still leaving The Little Hill of the Roses. The disillusion, the dis-enchantment I felt when I was descending those stairs, is ongoing; I am still *descending*,' Edward Bonshaw would say.)

As the Iowan and the dump kids descended, more sweaty pilgrims pressed and bumped against them, climbing to the hilltop site of the miracle. Juan Diego stepped on something; it felt a little soft and a little crunchy at the same time. He stopped to look at it – then he picked it up.

The totem, slightly larger than the finger-size suf-fering Christs that were everywhere for sale, was not as thick as Lupe's rat-size Coatlicue figurine – also everywhere for sale in the compound of buildings comprising the vast Basílica de Nuestra Señora de Guadalupe. The toy figure Juan Diego had stepped on was of Guadalupe herself – the subdued, passive body language, the downcast eyes, the no-breasts chest, the slight bulge where her lower abdomen was. The statuette radiated the virgin's humble origins – she looked as if she spoke only Nahuatl, if she spoke at all.

'Someone threw it away,' Lupe said to Juan Diego.

'Someone as disgusted as we are,' she said. But Juan Diego put the hard-rubber religious figure in his pocket. (It wasn't as big as the Virgin Mary's nose, but it still made his pocket bulge.)

At the bottom of the stairs, they passed through a gauntlet of snack and soft-drink salesmen. And there was a group of nuns, selling postcards to raise money for their convent's relief of the poor. Edward Bonshaw bought one.

Juan Diego was wondering if Señor Eduardo was still thinking about the postcard of Flor with the pony, but this postcard was just another Guadalupe photo – la virgen morena on her deathbed, encased in glass, in the Chapel of the Well.

'A souvenir,' the Iowan said a little guiltily, show-ing the postcard to Lupe and Juan Diego.

Lupe looked only briefly at the photo of the dark-skinned virgin on her deathbed; then she looked away. 'The way I feel right now, I would like her *better* with a pony's penis in her mouth,' Lupe said. 'I mean *dead*, but also with the pony's penis,' Lupe added.

Yes, she'd been asleep – with her head in Señor Eduardo's lap – when the Iowan told Juan Diego the story of that terrible postcard, but Juan Diego had always known that Lupe could nonetheless read minds when she was asleep.

'What did Lupe say?' Edward Bonshaw asked.

Juan Diego was looking for the best way to escape from the enormous flagstoned plaza; he was wonder-ing where the taxis were.

'Lupe said she's glad Guadalupe is dead – she

thinks that's the best part of the postcard,' was all Juan Diego said.

'You haven't asked me about the new dog act,' Lupe said to her brother. She stopped, as she had before, waiting for him to catch up to her. But Juan Diego would never catch up to Lupe.

'Right now, Lupe, I'm just trying to get us out of here,' Juan Diego told her irritably.

Lupe patted the bulge in his pocket, where he'd put the lost or discarded Guadalupe figure. 'Just don't ask *her* for help,' was all Lupe said.

'Behind every journey is a reason,' Juan Diego would one day write. It had been forty years since the dump kids' journey to the Guadalupe shrine in Mexico City, but – as Señor Eduardo would one day put it – Juan Diego felt he was still *descending*.

24

Poor Leslie

'I'm always meeting people in airports,' was the innocent-sounding way Dorothy began her fax to Juan Diego. 'And, boy, did this young mother need help! No husband – the husband had already dumped her. And then the nanny abandoned her and the kids at the start of their trip – the nanny just disappeared at the airport!' was how Dorothy set the story in motion.

The long-suffering young mother sounds *familiar*, Juan Diego was thinking as he read and reread Dorothy's fax. As a writer, Juan Diego knew there was a lot in Dorothy's story; he suspected there might be more that was missing. Such as: how 'one thing led to another,' as Dorothy would put it, and why she'd gone to El Nido with 'poor Leslie,' and with Leslie's little kids.

The *poor Leslie* part rang a bell with Juan Diego, even the first time he read Dorothy's fax. Hadn't he heard about a poor Leslie before? Oh, yes, he had, and Juan Diego didn't need to read much more of Dorothy's fax before he was reminded of what he'd heard about poor Leslie, and from whom.

'Don't worry, darling – she's not another writer!' Dorothy had written. 'She's just a writing student – she's *trying* to be a writer. In fact, she knows your friend Clark – Leslie was in some sort of workshop at a writers' conference where Clark French was her teacher.'

So she was *that* poor Leslie! Juan Diego had realized. This poor Leslie had met Clark before she'd taken a writing workshop with him. Clark had met her at a fund-raising event – as Clark had put it, one of several Catholic charities he and poor Leslie supported. Her husband had just left her; she had two little boys who were 'a bit wild'; she thought the 'mounting disillusionments' in her young life deserved to be written about.

Juan Diego remembered thinking that Clark's advice to Leslie was most unlike Clark, who hated memoirs *and* autobiographical fiction. Clark despised what he called 'writing as therapy'; he thought the memoir-novel 'dumbed down fiction and traduced the imagination.' Yet Clark had encouraged poor Leslie to pour out her heart on the page! 'Leslie has a good heart,' Clark had insisted, when he'd told Juan Diego about her. 'Poor Leslie has just had some bad luck with *men*!'

'Poor Leslie,' Clark's wife had repeated; there'd been a pause. Then Dr. Josefa Quintana said: 'I think Leslie likes women, Clark.'

'I don't think Leslie's a lesbian, Josefa – I think she's just *confused*,' Clark French had said.

'Poor Leslie,' Josefa had repeated; it was the lack of conviction in the way she said it that Juan Diego would remember best.

'Is Leslie pretty?' Juan Diego had asked.

Clark's expression was the model of indifference, as if he hadn't noticed if Leslie were pretty or not.

'Yes,' was all Dr. Quintana said.

According to Dorothy, it was entirely Leslie's idea that Dorothy come with her and the wild boys to El Nido.

'I'm not exactly nanny material,' Dorothy had written to Juan Diego. But Leslie was pretty, Juan Diego was thinking. And if Leslie liked women – whether or not Leslie was a lesbian, or just *confused* – Juan Diego didn't doubt that Dorothy would have figured her out. Whatever Dorothy was, she wasn't confused about it.

Naturally, Juan Diego didn't tell Clark and Josefa that Dorothy had hooked up with poor Leslie – if, indeed, Dorothy had. (In her fax, Dorothy wasn't exactly *saying* if she had.)

Given the disparaging way Clark had called Dorothy 'D.' – not to mention with what disgust he'd referred to Dorothy as 'the daughter,' or how turned off Clark had been by the whole mother-daughter business – well, why would Juan Diego have made Clark more miserable by suggesting that poor Leslie had hooked up with 'D.'?

'What happened to those children wasn't *my* fault,' Dorothy had written. As a writer, Juan Diego usually sensed when a storyteller was purposely changing the subject; he knew Dorothy hadn't gone to El Nido out of her desire to be a *nanny*.

He also knew that Dorothy was very *direct* – when she wanted to be, she could be very specific. Yet the details of exactly what happened to Leslie's little boys were vague – perhaps purposely so?

This was what Juan Diego was thinking when his flight from Bohol landed in Manila, jolting him awake.

He couldn't understand, of course, why the young woman seated beside him – she was in the aisle seat – was holding his hand. 'I'm so sorry,' she said to him earnestly. Juan Diego waited, smiling at her. He hoped she would explain what she meant, or at least let go of his hand. 'Your mother—' the young woman started to say, but she stopped, covering her face with both hands. 'The dead hippie, a dead dog – a *puppy* – and all the rest!' she suddenly blurted out. (In lieu of saying 'the Virgin Mary's nose,' the young woman seated beside him touched the nose on her own face.)

'I see,' was all Juan Diego said.

Was he losing his mind? Juan Diego wondered. Had he talked the whole way to the stranger next to him? Was he somehow destined to meet mind readers?

The young woman was now scrutinizing her cell phone, which reminded Juan Diego to turn on his cell phone and stare at it. The little phone rewarded him by vibrating in his hand. He liked the vibration mode best. He disliked all the 'tones,' as they called them. Juan Diego saw he had a text message from Clark French – not a short one.

Novelists aren't at their best in the truncated world of text messages, but Clark was a persevering type – he was dogged, especially when he was indignant about something. Text messages were not meant for moral indignation, Juan Diego thought. 'My friend Leslie has been seduced by your friend D. – the daughter!' Clark's message began; he'd heard from poor Leslie, alas.

Leslie's little boys were nine and ten – or seven and eight. Juan Diego was trying to remember. (Their names were impossible for him to remember.)

The boys had German-sounding names, Juan Diego thought; he was right about that. The boys' father, Leslie's ex-husband, was German – an international hotelier. Juan Diego couldn't remember (or no one had told him) the German hotel magnate's name, but that was what Leslie's ex *did*: he owned hotels, and he bought out blue-ribbon hotels that were in financial straits. And Manila was a base of the German hotelier's Asian operations – or so Clark had implied. Leslie had lived everywhere, the Philippines included; her little boys had lived all over the world.

Juan Diego read Clark's text message on the runway, following his flight from Bohol. A kind of Catholic umbrage – a feeling of pique – emanated from it, on Leslie's behalf. After all, poor Leslie was a person of faith – a fellow Catholic – and Clark sensed that she'd been wronged, yet again.

Clark had texted the following message: 'Watch out for the water buffalo at the airport – not as docile as it appears! Werner was trampled, but not seriously injured. Little Dieter says neither he nor Werner did anything to incite charge. (Poor Leslie says Werner and Dieter are "innocent of provoking buffalo.") And then little Dieter was stung by swimming things – the resort called them "plankton." Your friend D. says stinging things were the size of human thumbnails – D., swimming with Dieter, says so-called plankton resembled "condoms for three-year-olds," hundreds of them! No allergic reaction to miniature stinging condoms yet. "Definitely not plankton," D. says.'

D. says, Juan Diego thought to himself; Clark's account of the water buffalo and the stinging things differed only slightly from Dorothy's. The image of those 'condoms for three-year-olds' was consistent, but Dorothy – in her vague way – had implied the water buffalo was provoked. She didn't say how.

There was no water buffalo to be wary of at the airport in Manila, where Juan Diego changed planes for his connecting flight to Palawan. The new plane was a twin-engine prop – cigar-shaped, with only one seat on either side of the aisle. (Juan Diego would be in no danger of telling a total stranger the story of the ashes he and Lupe *didn't* scatter at the Guadalupe shrine in Mexico City.)

But before the propeller plane taxied away from their gate, Juan Diego felt his cell phone vibrate again. Clark's text message seemed hastier or more hysterical than before: 'Werner, still sore from

buffalo trampling, stung by pink jellyfish swimming
vertically (like sea horses). D. says they were "semi-
transparent and the size of index fingers." Necessary
for poor Leslie and her boys to evacuate the island
posthaste, due to Werner's immediate allergic reaction to see-through finger things – swelling of lips,
tongue, his poor penis. You will be alone with D. She
is staying behind to settle cancellations of room
reservations – poor Leslie's, not yours! Avoid
swimming. See you in Manila, I hope. Watch yourself around D.'

The prop plane had begun to move; Juan Diego
turned off his cell phone. Regarding the second stinging episode – the pink jellyfish swimming vertically
– Dorothy had sounded more like herself. 'Who
needs this shit? Fuck the South China Sea!' Dorothy
had faxed Juan Diego, who was trying to imagine
being alone with Dorothy on an isolated island,
where he wouldn't dare to swim. Why would he want
to risk the stinging condoms for three-year-olds
or the pink, penis-swelling jellyfish? (Not to mention
the monitor lizards the size of dogs! How had Leslie's
wild boys managed to escape an encounter with the
giant lizards?)

Wouldn't he be happier returning to Manila? Juan
Diego mused. But there was an in-flight brochure to
look at; he looked longest at the map, with disquieting results. Palawan was the farthest westward of the
Philippine islands. El Nido, the resort on Lagen Island
– off the northwestern tip of Palawan – was the same
latitude as Ho Chi Minh City and the mouths of the

Mekong. Vietnam was due west across the South China Sea from the Philippines.

The Vietnam War was why the good gringo had run away to Mexico; el gringo bueno's father had fallen in an earlier war – he lay buried not far from where his son could have died. Were these connections coincidental or predetermined? 'Now *there's* a question!' Juan Diego could hear Señor Eduardo saying – though, in his lifetime, the Iowan hadn't answered the question himself.

When Edward Bonshaw and Flor died, Juan Diego would pursue the same subject with Dr. Vargas. Juan Diego told Vargas what Señor Eduardo had revealed to him about recognizing Flor in the postcard. 'How about *that* connection?' Juan Diego would ask Dr. Vargas. 'Would you call that coincidence or fate?' was how the dump reader put it to the atheist.

'What would you say to somewhere in between?' Vargas asked him.

'I would call that copping out,' Juan Diego answered. But he'd been angry; Flor and Señor Eduardo had just died – fucking doctors had failed to save them.

Maybe now Juan Diego would say what Vargas had said: the way the world worked was 'somewhere in between' coincidence and fate. There were mysteries, Juan Diego knew; not everything came with a scientific explanation.

It was a bumpy landing at Lio Airport, Palawan – the runway was unpaved, a dirt landing strip. Upon leaving the plane, the passengers were greeted by native singers; standing aloof from the singers, as if bored by them, was a weary-looking water buffalo. It was hard to imagine this sad water buffalo charging or trampling anyone, but only God (or Dorothy) really knew what Leslie's wild boys (or one of them) may have done to provoke the beast.

Three boats were required the rest of the way, though the El Nido resort on Lagen Island wasn't a long way from Palawan. What you saw of Lagen from the sea were the cliffs – the island was a mountain. The lagoon was hidden; the buildings of the resort circled the lagoon.

There was a friendly young spokesman for the resort to greet Juan Diego upon his arrival at El Nido. Consideration had been given to his limp; his room, with a view of the lagoon, was only a short walk to the dining hall. The misfortunes leading to poor Leslie's sudden departure were discussed. 'Those boys were a bit wild,' the young spokesman said tactfully, when he showed Juan Diego his room.

'But the *stingings* – surely those stinging things were not the result of any wildness on the boys' part?' Juan Diego asked.

'Our guests who swim are not usually stung,' the young man said. 'Those boys were seen stalking a monitor lizard – this is asking for trouble.'

'Stalking!' Juan Diego said; he tried to imagine the wild boys, armed with spears made from mangrove roots.

'Ms. Leslie's friend was swimming with those boys

– *she* wasn't stung,' the young spokesman for the resort pointed out.

'Ah, yes – her *friend*. Is she—' Juan Diego started to ask.

'She's here, sir – I take it you mean Ms. Dorothy,' the young man said.

'Yes, of course – Ms. Dorothy,' was all Juan Diego could say. Had last names gone out of style? Juan Diego would wonder, albeit briefly. He was surprised how pleasing a place El Nido was – remote but beautiful, he thought. He would have time to unpack, and perhaps limp around the perimeter of the lagoon, before dinner. Dorothy had arranged everything for him: she'd paid for his room and all his meals, the young spokesman for the resort had said. (Or had poor Leslie paid for everything? Juan Diego wondered, also briefly.)

Juan Diego didn't know what he would do at El Nido; he was definitely questioning the idea that he truly liked the prospect of being alone with Dorothy.

He'd just finished unpacking – he had showered and shaved – when he heard the knock on his door. As knocks go, this one wasn't tentative.

That would be her, Juan Diego thought; without looking in the peephole, he opened the door.

'I guess you were expecting me, huh?' Dorothy asked. Smiling, she pushed past him, bringing her bags into his room.

Hadn't he figured out what kind of trip he was taking? Juan Diego was thinking. Wasn't there something about this trip that felt preternaturally arranged? On this journey, didn't the connections seem more predetermined than coincidental? (Or was he thinking too much like a writer?)

Dorothy sat on the bed; slipping off her sandals, she wiggled her toes. Juan Diego thought her legs were darker than he remembered – maybe she'd been in the sun since he'd last seen her.

'How did you and Leslie meet?' Juan Diego asked her.

The way Dorothy shrugged seemed so familiar; it was as if she'd watched Esperanza and Lupe shrug, and Dorothy was imitating them. 'You meet so many people in airports, you know,' was all she said.

'What happened with the water buffalo?' Juan Diego asked.

'Oh, those boys!' Dorothy said, sighing. 'I'm so glad you don't have kids,' she told him with a smile.

'The water buffalo was provoked?' Juan Diego asked her.

'The boys found a live caterpillar – it was green and yellow, with dark-brown eyebrows,' Dorothy said. 'Werner put the caterpillar up the water buffalo's nose – he stuck it all the way up one nostril, as far as it would go.'

'Much tossing of the head and horns, I imagine,' Juan Diego said. 'And those hooves – they must have made the ground shake.'

'You would snort, too, if you were trying to blow a caterpillar out of your nose,' Dorothy told him; it was clear she took the water buffalo's side. 'Werner wasn't that badly trampled, considering.'

'Yes, but what about the stinging condoms and the transparent fingers that swam vertically?' Juan Diego asked her.

'Yeah, they were creepy. They didn't sting *me*, but that kid's penis was nothing anyone could be prepared for,' Dorothy said. 'You just never know who's going to be allergic to what – and *how*!'

'You just never know,' Juan Diego repeated; he sat down on the bed beside her. She smelled like coconut – maybe it was her sunscreen.

'I'll bet you've missed me, huh?' Dorothy asked him.

'Yes,' he told her. Juan Diego had missed her, but until now he'd not realized how much Dorothy reminded him of the sex-doll statue of Guadalupe – the one the good gringo had given him, the statue Sister Gloria had disapproved of from the start.

It had been a long day, but was that why Juan Diego felt so exhausted? He was too tired to ask Dorothy if she'd had sex with poor Leslie. (Knowing Dorothy, of course she had.)

'You look sad,' Dorothy was whispering. Juan Diego tried to speak, but the words wouldn't come. 'Maybe you should eat something – the food is good here,' she told him.

'Vietnam,' was all Juan Diego managed to say. He wanted to tell her that he'd been a new American once. He was too young for the draft, and when the draft ended, the lottery drawings didn't matter. He was crippled; they would never have taken him. But because he'd known the good gringo, who had died trying not to go to Vietnam, Juan Diego would feel guilty for not going – or for not having to maim himself or run away in order not to go.

Juan Diego wanted to tell Dorothy that it troubled him to be so geographically close to Vietnam – on the same South China Sea – because he'd not been sent there, and how it bothered him that el gringo bueno was dead because the luckless boy had tried to run away from that misbegotten war.

But Dorothy said suddenly: 'Your American soldiers came here, you know – I don't mean *here*, not to this resort, not to Lagen Island or Palawan. I mean when they were on leave, you know – for what they called R and R from the Vietnam War.'

'What do you know about that?' Juan Diego found the words to ask her. (To himself, he sounded as incomprehensible as Lupe.)

There was Dorothy's familiar shrug, again – she'd understood him. 'Those frightened soldiers – some of them were only nineteen-year-olds, you know,' Dorothy said, as if she were remembering them, though she couldn't have *remembered* any of those young men.

Dorothy wasn't that much older than those boys had been during the war; Dorothy couldn't have been *born* when the Vietnam War ended – it was thirty-five years ago! Surely, she'd been speaking *historically* about those frightened nineteen-year-olds.

They'd been frightened of dying, Juan Diego

imagined – why wouldn't young boys in a war be frightened? But, again, his words wouldn't come, and Dorothy said: 'Those boys were afraid of being captured, of being tortured. The United States suppressed information about the degree of torture the North Vietnamese practiced on captured American soldiers. You should go to Laoag – the northernmost part of Luzon. Laoag, Vigan – those places. That's where the young soldiers on leave from Vietnam went for R and R. We could go there, you know – I know a place,' Dorothy told him. 'El Nido is just a resort – it's nice, but it's not real.'

All Juan Diego managed to say was: 'Ho Chi Minh City is due west from here.'

'It was Saigon then,' Dorothy reminded him. 'Da Nang and the Gulf of Tonkin are due west of Vigan. Hanoi is due west of Laoag. Everyone in Luzon knows how the North Vietnamese were into torturing your young Americans – that's what those poor boys were afraid of. The North Vietnamese were "unsurpassed" in torture – that's what they say in Laoag and Vigan. We could go there,' Dorothy repeated.

'Okay,' Juan Diego told her; it was the easiest thing to say. He'd thought of mentioning a Vietnam vet – Juan Diego had met him in Iowa. The war veteran told some stories about R&R in the Philippines.

There'd been talk about Olongapo and Baguio, or maybe it was Baguio City. Were they cities in Luzon? Juan Diego wondered. The vet had mentioned bars, nightlife, prostitutes. There'd been no talk of torture, or of the North Vietnamese as experts in the field, and no mention of Laoag or Vigan – not that Juan Diego could recall.

'How are your pills? Should you be taking something?' Dorothy asked him. 'Let's go look at your pills,' she said, taking his hand.

'Okay,' he repeated. As tired as he was, he had the impression that he didn't limp when he walked with her to the bathroom to look at the Lopressor and the Viagra tablets.

'I like this one, don't you?' Dorothy was asking him. (She was holding a Viagra.) 'It's so perfect the way it is. Why would anyone cut it in half ? I think a whole one is better than a half – don't you?'

'Okay,' Juan Diego whispered.

'Don't worry – don't be sad,' Dorothy told him; she gave him the Viagra and a glass of water. 'Everything's going to be okay.'

Yet what Juan Diego suddenly remembered was not *okay*. He was remembering what Dorothy and Miriam had cried out, together – as if they were a chorus.

'*Spare me* God's will!' Miriam and Dorothy had spontaneously cried. Had Clark French heard this, Juan Diego had little doubt, Clark would have thought this was a *succubi* kind of thing to say.

Did Miriam and Dorothy have an ax to grind with God's will? Juan Diego wondered. Then he suddenly thought: Did Dorothy and Miriam resent God's will because *they* were the ones who carried it out? What a crazy idea! The thought of Miriam and Dorothy as messengers who carried out God's will didn't jibe with Clark's impression of those two as demons in female form – not that Clark could have persuaded Juan Diego to believe that this mother and daughter were evil spirits. In his desire for them, surely Juan Diego felt that Miriam and Dorothy were bodily attached to the corporeal world; they were flesh and blood, not shades or spirits. As for the unholy two of them actually being the ones who carried out God's will – well, why even think about it? Who could imagine it?

Naturally, Juan Diego would never express such a crazy idea – certainly not in the context of the moment, not when Dorothy was giving him the Viagra tablet and a glass of water.

'Did you and Leslie—' Juan Diego started to ask.

'Poor Leslie is confused – I just tried to *help* her,' Dorothy said.

'You tried to *help* her,' was all Juan Diego could say. The way he said it didn't sound like a question, though he was thinking that if he were confused, being with Dorothy wouldn't exactly *help*.

25

Act 5, Scene 3

The way you remember or dream about your loved ones – the ones who are gone – you can't stop their endings from jumping ahead of the rest of their stories. You don't get to choose the chronology of what you dream, or the order of events in which you remember someone. In your mind – in your dreams, in your memories – sometimes the story begins with the epilogue.

In Iowa City, the first centralized HIV clinic – with nursing, social services, and teaching components – opened in June 1988. The clinic was held in Boyd Tower – it was called a tower, but it wasn't. So-called Boyd Tower was a new five-story building tacked onto the old hospital. The Boyd Tower building was part of the University of Iowa Hospitals and Clinics, and the HIV/AIDS clinic was on the first floor. It was called the Virology Clinic. At the time, there was some concern about advertising an HIV/AIDS clinic; there was a legitimate fear that both the patients and the hospital would be discriminated against.

HIV/AIDS was associated with sex and drugs; the

disease was uncommon enough in Iowa that many locals thought of it as an 'urban' problem. Among rural Iowans, some patients were exposed to both homophobia and xenophobia.

Juan Diego could remember when the Boyd Tower building was under construction, in the early seventies; there was (there still is) an actual tower, the Gothic tower on the north side of the old General Hospital. When Juan Diego first moved to Iowa City with Señor Eduardo and Flor, they lived in a duplex apartment in an overelaborate wedding cake of a Victorian house with a dilapidated front porch. Juan Diego's bedroom and bathroom, and Señor Eduardo's study, were on the second floor.

The rickety front porch was of little use to Edward Bonshaw or Flor, but Juan Diego remembered how he'd once loved it. From the porch, he could see the Iowa Field House (where the indoor pool was) and Kinnick Stadium. That decaying front porch on Melrose Avenue was a great location for student-watching, especially on those autumn Saturdays when the Iowa football team had a home game. (Señor Eduardo referred to Kinnick Stadium as the Roman Colosseum.)

Juan Diego wasn't interested in American football. Out of curiosity, at first – and, later, to be with his friends – Juan Diego would occasionally go to the games in Kinnick Stadium, but what he really liked was sitting on the front porch of that old wooden house on Melrose, just watching all the young people go by. ('I suppose I like the sound of the band, from a distance – and imagining the cheerleaders, up close,' Flor would say, in her hard-to-read way.)

Juan Diego would be finishing his undergraduate studies at Iowa when the Boyd Tower building was completed; from their Melrose Avenue neighborhood, the distinctively different family of three could see the Gothic tower on the old General Hospital. (Flor later said she'd lost her fondness for that old tower.)

Flor was the first to have symptoms; when she was diagnosed, of course Edward Bonshaw would be tested. Flor and Señor Eduardo tested positive for HIV in 1989. That insidious pneumonia *Pneumocystis carinii*, PCP, was the earliest presentation of AIDS for both of them. That cough, the shortness of breath, the fever – Flor and the Iowan were put on Bactrim. (Edward Bonshaw would develop a rash from the Bactrim.)

Flor had been almost beautiful, but her face would be disfigured with Kaposi's sarcoma lesions. A violet-colored lesion dangled from one of Flor's eyebrows; another purplish lesion drooped from her nose. The latter was so prominent that Flor chose to hide it behind a bandanna. La Bandida, she called herself – 'The Bandit.' But, hardest for her, Flor would lose the *la* (the feminine) in herself.

The estrogens she was taking had side effects – in particular, on her liver. Estrogens can cause a kind of hepatitis; the bile stagnates and builds. The itching that occurred with this condition drove Flor crazy. She had to stop the hormones, and her beard came back.

It seemed unfair to Juan Diego that Flor, who'd

worked so hard to feminize herself, was not only dying of AIDS, but dying as a man. When Señor Eduardo's hands were no longer steady enough to shave Flor's face every day, Juan Diego did it. Yet, when he kissed her, Juan Diego could feel the beard on Flor's cheek, and he could always see the shadow of a beard – even on her clean-shaven face.

Because they were an unconventional couple, Edward Bonshaw and Flor had wanted a young doctor for their primary care physician, and Flor had wanted a woman. Their pretty GP was Rosemary Stein; she'd insisted they be tested for HIV. In 1989, Dr. Stein was only thirty-three. 'Dr. Rosemary' – as Flor was the first to call her – was Juan Diego's age. At the Virology Clinic, Flor called the infectious disease doctors by their first names – their last names were a nightmare for a Mexican to say. Juan Diego and Edward Bonshaw – *their* English was perfect – also called the infectious disease doctors 'Dr. Jack' and 'Dr. Abraham,' just to make Flor feel like less of a foreigner.

The waiting room in the Virology Clinic was very bland – very 1960s. The carpets were brown; the chairs were single or two-person seats with dark, vinyl-coated cushions – Naugahyde, almost certainly. The check-in desk was a burnt-orange color with a light-colored Formica top. The wall facing the check-in desk was brick. Flor said she wished the Boyd Tower building had been nothing but brick, inside and out; it upset her to think that 'shit like Naugahyde and Formica' would outlive her and her dear Eduardo.

Flor had infected the Iowan, everyone supposed, though only Flor ever said so. Edward Bonshaw never accused her; he would say nothing to incriminate her. They'd taken no official vows, but they had promised each other the usual. 'In sickness and in health, for as long as we both shall live,' Señor Eduardo would devotedly recite to her, when Flor would accuse herself, confessing her occasional infidelities (those return trips to Oaxaca, the partying – if only for old times' sake).

'What about "forsaking all others" – I agreed to that, didn't I?' Flor would ask her dear Eduardo; she was intent on blaming herself.

But you couldn't take the lawlessness out of Flor. Edward Bonshaw would remain true to her – Flor was the love of his life, he always said – as he remained true to his Scottish oath, the insane one about 'yielding under no winds,' which, idiotically, he couldn't refrain from repeating in the original Latin: haud ullis labentia ventis. (This was the same lunacy he'd proclaimed to Brother Pepe, the chicken feathers heralding his arrival in Oaxaca.)

In the Virology Clinic, the blood-drawing room was next to the waiting room, which the HIV-positive patients shared, most of the time, with the diabetics. The two groups of patients sat on opposite sides of the room. In the late eighties and early nineties, the number of AIDS patients grew, and many of the dying were visibly marked by their disease – and not only by their wasted bodies, or the Kaposi's sarcoma lesions.

Edward Bonshaw was marked in his own way: he suffered from a seborrheic dermatitis; it was flaky and greasy-looking – mostly on his eyebrows and scalp, and on the sides of his nose. There were cheesy patches of *Candida* in Señor Eduardo's mouth, coating his tongue white. The *Candida* would eventually go down the Iowan's throat, into his esophagus; he had difficulty swallowing, and his lips were crusted white and fissured. In the end, Señor Eduardo could scarcely breathe, but he refused to go on a ventilator; he and Flor wanted to die together – at home, not in a hospital.

In the end, they fed Edward Bonshaw through a Hickman catheter; they told Juan Diego that the intravenous feeding was necessary for patients who couldn't feed themselves. With the *Candida*, and the difficulty he had swallowing, Señor Eduardo was starving. A nurse – an older woman whose name was Mrs. Dodge – moved into what had been Juan Diego's bedroom on the second floor of that duplex apartment on Melrose. For the most part, the nurse was there to take care of the catheter – Mrs. Dodge was the one who flushed out the Hickman with heparin solution.

'Otherwise, it will clot off,' Mrs. Dodge told Juan Diego, who had no idea what she meant; he didn't ask her to explain.

The Hickman catheter dangled from the right side of Edward Bonshaw's chest, where it had been inserted under his clavicle; it tunneled under the skin a few inches above his nipple, and entered the subclavian vein below the collarbone. Juan Diego couldn't get used to seeing it; he would write about the Hickman catheter in one of his novels, where a number of his characters died of AIDS – some of them with the AIDS-associated, opportunistic illnesses that had afflicted Señor Eduardo and Flor. But the AIDS victims in that novel were not even remotely 'based on' the Iowan or La Loca, The Queen – La Bandida, as Flor called herself.

In his own way, Juan Diego wrote about what happened to Flor and Edward Bonshaw, but he would not once write *about them*. The dump reader was self-taught, and had taught himself how to imagine, too. Maybe the self-taught part was where the dump reader got the idea that a fiction writer *created* characters, and that you *made up* a story – you didn't just write about the people you knew, or tell your own story, and call it a novel.

There were too many contradictions and unknowns about the real people in Juan Diego's life – real people were too incomplete to work as characters in a novel, Juan Diego thought. And he could make up a better story than what had happened to him; the dump reader believed his own story was 'too incomplete' for a novel.

When he'd taught creative writing, Juan Diego had not once told his students how they should write; he would never have suggested to his fiction-writing students that they should write a novel the way he wrote his. The dump reader wasn't a proselytizer. The problem is that many young writers are searching for a method; young writers are vulnerable to picking up a writing process and believing there is a one-and-only way to write. (Write what you know! Only imagine! It's all about the language!)

Take Clark French. Some students stay students all their lives: they seek and find generalizations they can live by; as writers, they want the way they write to be established as a universal and ironclad code. (Using autobiography as the basis for fiction produces drivel! Using your imagination is faking it!) Clark maintained that Juan Diego was 'on the anti-autobiographical side.'

Juan Diego had tried not to be drawn into taking sides.

Clark insisted that Juan Diego was 'on the imagination's side'; Juan Diego was a 'fabler, not a memoirist,' Clark said.

Maybe so, Juan Diego thought, but he didn't want to be on anyone's *side*. Clark French had turned writing fiction into a polemical competition.

Juan Diego had tried to *de*-polemicize the conversation; he'd attempted to talk about the literature he loved, the writers who'd made him wish he could be a writer – not because he saw these writers as standard-bearers of a *way* to write, but simply because he loved what they'd written.

No surprise: the library of English-language literature at Lost Children was limited and generally not newer than the nineteenth-century models of the form, including the novels Father Alfonso and Father Octavio had designated for destruction in the hellfires of the basurero and those essential novels Brother Pepe or Edward Bonshaw had saved for the library's small collection of fiction. These novels were what had inspired Juan Diego to be a novelist.

That life was not fair to dogs had prepared the dump reader for Hawthorne's *The Scarlet Letter*. Those matronly churchwomen gossiping about what *they* would do to Hester – brand her forehead with a hot iron, or kill her, rather than merely mark her clothes – helped prepare Juan Diego for what vestiges of American Puritanism he would encounter after moving to Iowa.

Melville's *Moby-Dick* – most notably, Queequeg's 'coffin life-buoy' – would teach Juan Diego that foreshadowing is the storytelling companion of fate.

As for fate, and how you can't escape yours, there was Hardy's *The Mayor of Casterbridge*. Michael Henchard, drunk, sells his wife and daughter to a sailor in the first chapter. Henchard can never atone for what he does; in his will, Henchard requests 'that no man remember me.' (Not exactly a redemption story. Clark French hated Hardy.)

And then there was Dickens – Juan Diego would cite the 'Tempest' chapter from *David Copperfield*. At the end of that chapter, Steerforth's body washes ashore and Copperfield is confronted with the remains of his former childhood idol and sly tormentor – the quintessential older boy you meet at school, your predestined abuser. Nothing more was necessary to say about Steerforth's body on the beach, where he lies 'among the ruins of the home he had wronged.' But Dickens, being Dickens, gives Copperfield more to say: 'I saw him lying with his head upon his arm, as I had often seen him lie at school.'

'What more did I need to know about writing novels than what I learned from those four?' Juan Diego had asked his writing students – Clark French included.

And when Juan Diego presented those four nineteenth-century novelists to his writing students – 'my *teachers*,' he called Hawthorne, Melville, Hardy, and Dickens – he never failed to mention Shakespeare, too. Señor Eduardo had shown Juan Diego that long before anyone wrote a novel, Shakespeare understood and appreciated the importance of *plot*.

Shakespeare was a mistake to mention around Clark French; Clark was the Bard of Avon's self-appointed bodyguard. Coming, as Clark did, from the only-imagine school of thought – well, you can imagine how Clark had a bug up his ass about those infidels who believed *someone else* wrote Shakespeare.

And any thoughts of Shakespeare brought Juan Diego back to Edward Bonshaw and what had happened to him and Flor.

AT THE BEGINNING, WHEN Señor Eduardo and Flor were still strong enough – when they could carry things and deal with stairs, and Flor was still driving – they made their own way to the first-floor clinic in the Boyd Tower building; it was only a third of a mile

from their house on Melrose. When everything
became more difficult, Juan Diego (or Mrs. Dodge)
would take Flor and Edward Bonshaw across Melrose
Avenue; Flor was still walking, but Señor Eduardo
was in a wheelchair.

In the early to mid-1990s – before the number of
deaths from AIDS plummeted (due to the new meds)
and the number of HIV-positive patients in the
Virology Clinic began to increase – the number of
patients visiting the clinic stabilized, at about two
hundred a year. Many of the patients sat in their
partners' laps in the waiting room; there was the
occasional conversation about gay bars and drag
shows, and there were a few flamboyant dressers –
flamboyant for Iowa.

Not Flor – not anymore. Flor would lose most of
her womanly appearance, and though she continued
to dress as a woman, she dressed modestly; she was
aware that her allure had dimmed, if not in Señor
Eduardo's adoring eyes. They held hands in the
waiting room. In Iowa City, at least in Juan Diego's
memory, the only place Flor and Edward Bonshaw
were publicly demonstrative of their affection for
each other was in the waiting room of the HIV/AIDS
clinic in the Boyd Tower building.

One of the AIDS patients was a young man from a
Mennonite family who'd originally disowned him;
they would later reclaim him. He brought vegetables
from his garden to the waiting room; he handed out
tomatoes to the clinic staff. The young Mennonite
wore cowboy boots and a pink cowboy hat.

One of the times when Mrs. Dodge took Flor and Edward Bonshaw to the clinic, Flor said something funny to the young gardener in the pink cowboy hat.

Flor always wore her bandanna in public. La Bandida said: 'You know what, cowboy? If you've got a couple of horses, you and I could rob a train or stick up a bank.'

Mrs. Dodge told Juan Diego that 'the whole waiting room laughed' – even she laughed, she said. And the Mennonite in the pink cowboy hat went right along with the joke.

'I know North Liberty pretty well,' the cowboy said. 'There's a library that sure would be easy to knock off. You know North Liberty?' the cowboy asked Flor.

'No, I don't,' Flor told him, 'and I'm not interested in sticking up a library – I don't read.'

This was true: Flor didn't read. Her spoken vocabulary was very sharp – she was an excellent listener – but her Mexican accent hadn't changed since 1970, and she never read anything. (Edward Bonshaw or Juan Diego would read aloud to her.)

It had been a comic interlude in the HIV/AIDS clinic, according to Mrs. Dodge, but Señor Eduardo was upset by Flor's flirting with the cowboy gardener.

'I wasn't flirting – I was making a joke,' Flor said.

Mrs. Dodge didn't think that Flor had been flirting with the farmer. Later, when Juan Diego asked her about the episode, Mrs. Dodge said: 'I think Flor is done with flirting.'

Mrs. Dodge was from Coralville. Dr. Rosemary had recommended her. The first time Edward Bonshaw said to the nurse, 'In case you were wondering about my scar—' well, Mrs. Dodge knew all about it.

'Everyone in Coralville – that is, everyone of a certain age – knows that story,' Mrs. Dodge told Señor Eduardo. 'The Bonshaw family was famous, because of what your father did to that poor dog.'

Señor Eduardo was relieved to hear that the Bonshaw family had not escaped scrutiny in Coralville – you can't get away with shooting your dog in the driveway. 'Of course,' Mrs. Dodge went on, 'I was still a young girl when I heard the story, and it wasn't about you *or* your scar,' she told Señor Eduardo. 'The story was about *Beatrice*.'

'That's entirely as it should be – she was the one who got shot. The story is about Beatrice,' Edward Bonshaw declared.

'Not to me – not to anyone who loves you, Eduardo,' Flor said to him.

'You were flirting with that farmer in the pink cowboy hat!' Señor Eduardo had exclaimed.

'I wasn't flirting,' Flor had insisted. Later, Juan Diego would think that these accusations concerning Flor's flirtation with the young Mennonite cowboy in the clinic came the closest to recriminations that Edward Bonshaw would ever make about Flor's return trips to Oaxaca – and what one could only imagine were the nature of Flor's *flirtations* there.

Of course, and not only because she was pretty,

this was when Juan Diego made friends with Rosemary Stein. She was Señor Eduardo's doctor, and Flor's doctor. Why wouldn't Dr. Rosemary become Juan Diego's doctor, too?

Flor told Juan Diego that he should ask Dr. Rosemary to marry him, but Juan Diego would ask her to be his doctor first. It would be embarrassing to Juan Diego to remember, later, that his first visit to Dr. Stein's office as a patient was driven by his imagination. He wasn't sick; there was nothing the matter with him. But Juan Diego's exposure to seeing those AIDS-associated, opportunistic illnesses had convinced him that he should be tested for HIV.

Dr. Stein assured him that he'd done nothing to contract the virus. Juan Diego had some difficulty remembering when he'd last had sex – he couldn't even be sure about the *year* – but he knew it was with a woman and he'd used a condom.

'And you're not an intravenous drug user?' Dr. Rosemary had asked him.

'No – never!'

Yet he'd imagined the white plaques of *Candida* encroaching on his teeth. (Juan Diego admitted to Rosemary that he'd woken up at night and peered into his mouth and looked down his throat with a handheld mirror and a flashlight.) In the Virology Clinic, Juan Diego had heard about those patients with cryptococcal meningitis. Dr. Abraham told him the meningitis was diagnosed by a lumbar puncture – it presented with fever and headache and confusion.

Juan Diego dreamed of these things incessantly; he woke up at night with the fully imagined symptoms. 'Let Mrs. Dodge take Flor and Edward to the clinic. That's why I found her for you – let Mrs. Dodge do it,' Dr. Stein said to Juan Diego. 'You're the one with an imagination – you're a *writer*, aren't you?' Dr. Rosemary had asked him. 'Your imagination isn't a water faucet; you can't turn it off at the end of the day, when you stop writing. Your imagination just keeps going, doesn't it?' Rosemary asked.

He should have asked her to marry him *then*, before someone else asked her. But by the time Juan Diego finally knew he should ask Rosemary to marry him, she'd already said yes to someone else.

If Flor had been alive, Juan Diego could hear what she would have told him. 'Shit, you're slow – I always forget how slow you are,' Flor would have said. (It would have been just like Flor to mention his dog-paddling.)

In the end, Dr. Abraham and Dr. Jack would experiment with sublingual morphine versus morphine elixir – Edward Bonshaw and Flor were willing guinea pigs. But, by then, Juan Diego was letting Mrs. Dodge do everything; he'd listened to Dr. Rosemary and yielded the nursing to the nurse.

It would soon be 1991; both Juan Diego and Rosemary would be thirty-five when Flor and Señor Eduardo died – Flor first, Edward Bonshaw following her in just a few days.

That area of Melrose Avenue would keep changing; those over-the-top, extravagant Victorian houses with the grand front porches had already begun to disappear. Like Flor, Juan Diego had once loved the view of the Gothic tower from the front porch of that wooden house on Melrose, but what was there to love about that old tower after you'd seen the Virology Clinic on the first floor of the Boyd Tower building – after you'd seen what was going on below that tower?

LONG BEFORE THE AIDS epidemic, when Juan Diego was in his high school years, he was starting to feel slightly less enthusiasm for his Melrose Avenue neighborhood in Iowa City. For a limper, for example, West High was a long walk west on Melrose; it was more than a mile and a half. And just past the golf course, near the intersection with Mormon Trek Boulevard, there was a bad dog. There were also bullies at the high school. They weren't the sort of bullies Flor had told him to expect. Juan Diego was a black-haired, brown-skinned, Mexican-looking boy; yet racist types weren't very prevalent in Iowa City – they *were* represented (in small numbers, in a few incidences) at West High, but they weren't the worst of the bullies Juan Diego would be exposed to there.

Mostly, the juvenile slings and arrows aimed at Juan Diego were about Flor and Señor Eduardo – his not-a-real-woman mother and his 'fag' father. 'A couple of queer lovebirds,' one kid at West High had called Juan Diego's adoptive parents. The boy baiting him was blond, with a pink face; Juan Diego didn't know the kid's name.

So the lion's share of the bigotry Juan Diego would be exposed to was sexual, not racial, but he didn't dare tell Flor or Edward Bonshaw about it. When the lovebirds could discern that Juan Diego was troubled, when Flor and Señor Eduardo would ask what was bothering him, Juan Diego didn't want them to know that they were the problem. It was easier to say he'd had some anti-Mexican stuff to deal with – one of those south-of-the-border insinuations, or an outright slur of the kind Flor had warned him about.

As for the long limp to and from West High – all along Melrose – Juan Diego didn't complain. It would have been worse to have Flor drive him; her dropping him off and picking him up would have inspired more sexual bullying. Besides, Juan Diego was already a grind in his high school years; he was one of those nonstop students with downcast eyes – a silent male who stoically endured high school, but who had every intention of thriving in his university years, which he did. (When a dump reader's only job is going to school, he can be reasonably happy, not to mention successful.)

And Juan Diego didn't drive – he never would. His right foot was at an awkward angle for stepping on the gas or the brake. Juan Diego would get his driving permit, but the first time he tried driving, with Flor beside him in the passenger seat – Flor was the only licensed driver in the family; Edward Bonshaw refused to drive – Juan Diego had managed to step on both the brake and the accelerator at the same time. (This was natural to do if your right foot was pointed toward two o'clock.)

'That's it – we're done,' Flor had told him. 'Now there are two non-drivers in our family.'

And, of course, there'd been a kid or two at West High who thought it was intolerable that Juan Diego didn't have a driver's license; the not-driving part was more isolating than the limp or the Mexican-looking factor. His not being a driver marked Juan Diego as queer – *queer* in the same way that some of the kids at West High had identified Juan Diego's adoptive parents.

'Does your mom, or whatever she calls herself, shave? I mean her face – her fucking upper lip,' the blond, pink-faced kid had said to Juan Diego.

Flor had the softest-looking trace of a mustache – not that this was the most masculine-looking thing about Flor, but it was apparent. In high school, most teenagers don't want to stand out; they don't want their parents to stand out, either. But, to his credit, Juan Diego was never embarrassed by Señor Eduardo and Flor. 'It's the best the hormones can do. You may have noticed that her breasts are pretty small. That's the hormones, too – there's a limit to what the estrogens can accomplish. That's what I know,' Juan Diego told the blond boy.

The pink-faced kid wasn't expecting the frankness of Juan Diego's reply. It seemed that Juan Diego had won the moment, but bullies don't take losing well.

The blond boy wasn't done. 'Here's what I know,' he said. 'Your so-called mom and dad are *guys*. One of them, the big one, dresses as a woman, but they both have dicks – that's what I know.'

'They adopted me – they love me,' Juan Diego told the kid, because Señor Eduardo had told him he should always tell the truth. 'And I love them – that's what I know,' Juan Diego added.

You don't ever exactly win these bullying episodes in high school, but if you survive them, you can win in the end – that was what Flor had always told Juan Diego, who would regret that he'd not been entirely honest with Flor or Señor Eduardo about *how* he'd been bullied, or *why*.

'She shaves her face – she doesn't do such a good job on her fucking upper lip – whoever or *whatever* she is,' the pink-faced prick of a blond boy said to Juan Diego.

'She *doesn't* shave,' Juan Diego said to him. He traced his finger over the contours of his own upper lip the way he'd seen Lupe do it when she'd been bugging Rivera. 'The hint of a mustache is just always there. It's the best the estrogens can accomplish – like I told you.'

Years later – when Flor got sick and she had to stop the estrogens, and her beard came back – when Juan Diego was shaving Flor's face for her, he thought of that blond bully with the pink face. Maybe I'll see him again one day, Juan Diego had thought to himself.

'See *who* again?' Flor had asked him. Flor was no mind reader; Juan Diego realized that he must have spoken his thoughts out loud.

'Oh, no one you know – I don't even know his name. Just a kid I remember from high school,' Juan Diego had told her.

'There's no one I ever want to see again – definitely not from high school,' Flor said to him. (Definitely not from *Houston*, either, Juan Diego would remember thinking as he shaved her, being careful not to say *that* thought out loud.)

When Flor and Señor Eduardo died, Juan Diego was teaching at the Iowa Writers' Workshop – in the MFA program, where he'd once been a student. After he left his second-floor bedroom in the Melrose Avenue duplex apartment, Juan Diego didn't live on that side of the Iowa River again.

He'd had a number of boring apartments on his own, near the main campus and the Old Capitol – always close to downtown Iowa City, because he wasn't a driver. He was a walker – well, better said, a *limper*. His friends – his colleagues and his students – all recognized that limp; they had no trouble spotting Juan Diego from a distance, or from a passing car.

Like most nondrivers, Juan Diego didn't know the exact whereabouts of those places he'd been driven; if he hadn't *limped* there, if he'd been only a passenger in someone else's car, Juan Diego never could have told you where the place was, or how to get there.

Such was the case with the Bonshaw family plot, where Flor and Señor Eduardo would be buried – together, as they'd requested, *and with* Beatrice's ashes, which Edward Bonshaw's mother had kept for him. (Señor Eduardo had saved his dear dog's ashes in a safe-deposit box in a bank in Iowa City.)

Mrs. Dodge, with her Coralville connections, had known exactly where the Bonshaw burial plot was – the cemetery wasn't in Coralville, but it was 'somewhere else on the outskirts of Iowa City.' (This was the way Edward Bonshaw himself had described it; Señor Eduardo wasn't a driver, either.)

If it hadn't been for Mrs. Dodge, Juan Diego wouldn't have discovered where his beloved adoptive parents wanted to be buried. And after Mrs. Dodge died, it was always Dr. Rosemary who drove Juan Diego to the mystery cemetery. As they'd wished, Edward Bonshaw and Flor had shared one headstone, inscribed with the last speech in Shakespeare's *Romeo and Juliet*, which Señor Eduardo had loved. Tragedies affecting young people were those that had moved the Iowan the most. (Flor would profess to having been less affected. Yet Flor had yielded to her dear Eduardo on the matter of their common-law name and the gravestone's inscription.)

FLOR & EDWARD
BONSHAW

'A GLOOMING PEACE THIS
MORNING WITH IT BRINGS.'
ACT 5, SCENE 3

That was the way the headstone was marked. Juan Diego would question Señor Eduardo's request.

'Don't you want, at least, to say 'Shakespeare,' if not *which* Shakespeare?' the dump reader had asked the Iowan.

'I don't think it's necessary. Those who know Shakespeare will know; those who don't – well, they won't,' Edward Bonshaw mused, as the Hickman catheter rose and fell on his bare chest. 'And no one has to know that Beatrice's ashes are buried with us, do they?'

Well, Juan Diego would know, wouldn't he? As would Dr. Rosemary, who also knew where her writer friend's standoffishness – concerning the commitment required in permanent relationships – came from. In Juan Diego's writing, which Rosemary also knew, where everything *came from* truly mattered.

It's true that Dr. Rosemary Stein didn't really know the boy from Guerrero – not the dump-kid part, not the dump-reader tenacity inside him. But she had seen Juan Diego be tenacious; the first time, it had surprised her – he was such a small man, so slightly built, and there was his identifying limp.

They were having dinner in that restaurant they went to all the time; it was near the corner of Clinton and Burlington. Just Rosemary and her husband, Pete – who was also a doctor – and Juan Diego was with one of his writer colleagues. Was it Roy? Rosemary couldn't remember. Maybe it was Ralph, not Roy. One of the visiting writers who drank a lot; he either said nothing or he never shut up. One of those passing-through writers-in-residence; Rosemary believed they were the most badly behaved.

It was 2000 – no, it was *2001*, because Rosemary had just said, 'I can't believe it's been ten years, but they've been gone ten years. My God – that's how long they've been gone.' (Dr. Rosemary had been talking about Flor and Edward Bonshaw.) Rosemary was a little drunk, Juan Diego thought, but that was okay – she wasn't on call, and Pete was always the driver when they went anywhere together.

That was when Juan Diego had heard a man say something at another table; it was not what the man said that was special – it was the way he said it. 'That's what I know,' the man had said. There was something memorable about the intonation. The man's voice was both familiar and confrontational – he was sounding a little defensive, too. He sounded like a last-word kind of guy.

He was a blond, red-faced man who was having dinner with his family; it seemed he'd been having an argument with his daughter, a girl about sixteen or seventeen, Juan Diego would have guessed. There was a son, too – he was only a little older than the daughter. The son looked to be about eighteen, tops; the boy was still in high school – Juan Diego would have bet on it.

'It's one of the O'Donnells,' Pete said. 'They're all a little loud.'

'It's Hugh O'Donnell,' Rosemary said. 'He's on the zoning board. He always wants to know when we're building another hospital, so he can be opposed to it.'

But Juan Diego was watching the daughter. He knew and understood the beleaguered look on the young girl's face. She'd been trying to defend the sweater she was wearing. Juan Diego had heard her say to her father: 'It's not 'slutty-looking' – it's what kids wear today!'

This was what had prompted the dismissive 'That's what I know' from her red-faced father. The blond man hadn't changed much since high school, when he'd said those hurtful things to Juan Diego. When was it – twenty-eight or twenty-nine, almost thirty, years ago?

'Hugh, *please*—' Mrs. O'Donnell was saying.

'It's not "slutty-looking," is it?' the girl asked her brother. She turned in her chair, trying to give the smirking boy a better look at her sweater. But the boy reminded Juan Diego of what Hugh O'Donnell *used to* look like – thinner, flaxen-blond with more pink in his face. (Hugh's face was much redder now.) The boy's smirk was the same as his dad's; the girl knew better than to continue modeling her sweater for him – she turned away. Anyone could see that the smirking brother lacked the courage to take his sister's side. The look he gave her was one Juan Diego had seen before – it was a no-sympathy look, as if the brother thought his sister would be slutty-looking in *any* sweater. In the boy's condescending gaze, his sister looked like a slut, no matter what the poor girl wore.

'Please, *both* of you—' the wife and mother started to say, but Juan Diego got up from the table. Naturally, Hugh O'Donnell recognized the limp, though he'd not seen it – or Juan Diego – for almost thirty years.

'Hi – I'm Juan Diego Guerrero. I'm a writer – I went

to school with your dad,' he said to the O'Donnell children.

'Hi—' the daughter started to say, but the son didn't say anything, and when the girl glanced at her father, she stopped speaking.

Mrs. O'Donnell blurted out something, but she didn't finish what she was going to say – she just stopped. 'Oh, I know who you are. I've read—' was as far as she got. There must have been more than a little of that dump-reader tenacity in Juan Diego's expression, enough to alert Mrs. O'Donnell to the fact that Juan Diego wasn't interested in talking about his books – or to her. Not right now.

'I was your age,' Juan Diego said to Hugh O'Donnell's son. 'Maybe your dad and I were between your ages,' he said to the daughter. 'He wasn't very nice to me, either,' Juan Diego added to the girl, who seemed to be increasingly self-conscious – not necessarily about her much-maligned sweater.

'Hey, look here—' Hugh O'Donnell started to say, but Juan Diego just pointed to Hugh, not bothering to look at him.

'I'm not talking to you – I've heard what you have to say,' Juan Diego told him, looking only at the children. 'I was adopted by two gay men,' Juan Diego continued – after all, he did know how to tell a story. 'They were partners – they couldn't be married, not here or in Mexico, where I came from. But they loved each other, and they loved me – they were my guardians, my adoptive parents. And I loved them, of course – the way kids are supposed to love their parents. You know how that is, don't you?' Juan Diego asked Hugh O'Donnell's kids, but the kids couldn't answer him, and only the girl nodded her head – just a little. The boy was absolutely frozen.

'Anyway,' Juan Diego went on, 'your dad was a bully. He said my mom shaved – he meant her face. He thought she did a poor job shaving her upper lip, but she *didn't* shave. She was a *man*, of course – she dressed as a woman, and she took hormones. The hormones helped her to look a little more like a woman. Her breasts were kind of small, but she had breasts, and her beard had stopped growing, though she still had the faintest, softest-looking trace of a mustache on her upper lip. I told your dad it was the best the hormones could do – I said it was all the estrogens could accomplish – but your dad just kept being a bully.'

Hugh O'Donnell had stood up from the table, but he didn't speak – he just stood there.

'You know what your dad said to me?' Juan Diego asked the O'Donnell kids. 'He said: "Your so-called mom and dad are *guys* – they both have dicks." That's what he said; I guess he's just a "That's what I know" kind of guy. Isn't that right, Hugh?' Juan Diego asked. It was the first time Juan Diego had looked at him. 'Isn't that what you said to me?'

Hugh O'Donnell went on standing there, not speaking. Juan Diego turned his attention back to the kids.

'They died of AIDS, ten years ago – they died here, in Iowa City,' Juan Diego told the children. 'The one who wanted to be a woman – I had to shave her when she was dying, because she couldn't take the estrogens and her beard grew back, and I could tell she was sad about how much she looked like a man. She died first. My "so-called dad" died a few days later.'

Juan Diego paused. He knew, without looking at her, that Mrs. O'Donnell was crying; the daughter was crying, too. Juan Diego had always known that women were the real *readers* – women were the ones with the capacity to be affected by a story.

Looking at the implacable, red-faced father and his frozen, pink-faced son, Juan Diego would pause to wonder what *did* affect most men. What the fuck would ever affect most men? Juan Diego wondered.

'And *that's* what I know,' Juan Diego told the O'Donnell kids. This time, they both nodded – albeit barely. When Juan Diego turned and limped his way back to his table, where he could see that Rosemary and Pete – and even that drunken writer – had been hanging on his every word, Juan Diego was aware that his limp was a little more pronounced than usual, as if he were consciously (or unconsciously) trying to draw more attention to it. It was almost as if Señor Eduardo and Flor were watching him – some-how, from somewhere – and they'd also been hanging on his every word.

In the car, with Pete behind the wheel, and the drunken writer in the passenger seat – because Roy or Ralph was a big guy, and a clumsy drunk, and they'd all agreed he needed the legroom – Juan Diego had sat in the backseat with Dr. Rosemary. Juan

Diego had been prepared to limp home – he lived close enough to the corner of Clinton and Burlington to have walked – but Roy or Ralph needed a ride, and Rosemary had insisted that she and Pete drive Juan Diego where he was going.

'Well, that was a pretty good story – what I could understand of it,' the drunken writer said from the front seat.

'Yes, it was – very *interesting*,' was all Pete said.

'I got a little confused during the AIDS part,' Ralph or Roy soldiered on. 'There were two guys – I got that, all right. One of them was a cross-dresser. Now that I think of it, it was the shaving part that was confusing – I got the AIDS part, I think,' Roy or Ralph went on.

'They're dead – it was ten years ago. That's all that matters,' Juan Diego said from the backseat.

'No, that's not all,' Rosemary said. (He'd been right, Juan Diego would remember thinking: Rosemary was a little drunk – maybe more than a little, he thought.) In the backseat, Dr. Rosemary suddenly seized Juan Diego's face in both her hands. 'If I'd heard you say what you said to that asshole Hugh O'Donnell – I mean *before* I agreed to marry Pete – I would have asked you to marry me, Juan Diego,' Rosemary said.

Pete drove down Dubuque Street for a while; no one spoke. Roy or Ralph lived somewhere east of Dubuque Street, maybe on Bloomington or on Davenport – he couldn't remember. To be kind: Roy or Ralph was distracted; he was trying to locate Dr.

Rosemary in the backseat – he was fumbling around with the rearview mirror. Finally, he found her.

'Wow – I didn't see *that* coming,' Roy or Ralph said to her. 'I mean your asking Juan Diego to marry you!'

'I did – I saw it coming,' Pete said.

But Juan Diego, who was struck silent in the backseat, was as taken aback as Roy or Ralph – or whoever that itinerant writer was. (Juan Diego hadn't seen *that* coming, either.)

'Here we are – I think we're here. I wish I knew where I fucking *lived*,' Roy or Ralph was saying.

'I don't really mean I *would* have married you,' Rosemary tried to say, revising herself – either for Pete's benefit or for Juan Diego's; perhaps she meant it for both of them. 'I just meant I *might* have asked you,' she said. This seemed more reasonable.

Without looking at her, Juan Diego knew that Rosemary was crying – the way he'd known Hugh O'Donnell's wife and daughter had been crying.

But so much had happened. All Juan Diego could say from the backseat was: 'Women are the readers.' What he also knew, even then, would have been unsayable – namely, sometimes the story begins with the epilogue. But, really, how could he have said anything like *that*? It needed a context.

Sometimes Juan Diego would feel he was still sitting with Rosemary Stein in the semidarkness of the car's backseat, the two of them not looking at each other, and not talking. And wasn't this what that line from Shakespeare meant, and why Edward

Bonshaw had been so attached to it? 'A glooming peace this morning with it brings' – well, yes, and why would such darkness ever depart? Who can happily think of what else happened to Juliet and her Romeo, and *not* dwell on what happened to them at the end of their story?

26

The Scattering

The dislocations of travel had been a familiar theme in Juan Diego's early novels. Now the demons of dislocation were besetting him again; he was having trouble remembering how many days and nights he and Dorothy had stayed at El Nido.

He remembered the sex with Dorothy – not only her screaming orgasms, which were in what sounded like Nahuatl, but how she'd repeatedly called his penis 'this guy,' as if Juan Diego's penis were a non-speaking but otherwise obtrusive presence at a noisy party. Dorothy was definitely noisy, a veritable earthquake in the world of orgasms; their near neighbors at the resort had phoned their room to inquire if everyone was all right. (But no one had used the *asswheel* word, or the more common *asshole* appellation.)

As Dorothy had told Juan Diego, the food at El Nido was good: rice noodles with shrimp sauce; spring rolls with pork or mushrooms or duck; serrano ham with pickled green mango; spicy sardines. There was also a condiment made from fermented fish, which Juan Diego had learned to be on the lookout for; he thought it gave him indigestion or heartburn. And there was flan for dessert – Juan Diego liked custard – but Dorothy told him to avoid anything with milk in it. She said she didn't trust the milk on the 'outer islands.'

Juan Diego didn't know if only a *little* island constituted an *outer* island, or if all the islands in the Palawan group were (in Dorothy's estimation) of the *outer* kind. When he asked her, Dorothy just shrugged. She had a killer shrug.

It was strange how being with Dorothy had made him forget Miriam, but he'd forgotten that being with Miriam (even *wanting* to be with Miriam) had once made him forget about being with Dorothy. Very strange: how he could, simultaneously, obsess about these women and forget about them.

The coffee at the resort was overstrong, or perhaps it seemed strong because Juan Diego was drinking it black. 'Have the green tea,' Dorothy told him. But the green tea was very bitter; he tried putting a little honey in it. He saw that the honey was from Australia.

'Australia is nearby, isn't it?' Juan Diego asked Dorothy. 'I'm sure the honey is safe.'

'They dilute it with something – it's too watery,' Dorothy said. 'And where's the water come from?' she asked him. (It was her outer-islands theme, again.) 'Is it bottled water, or do they boil it? I say fuck the honey,' Dorothy told him.

'Okay,' Juan Diego said. Dorothy seemed to know

a lot. Juan Diego was beginning to realize that, increasingly, when he was with Dorothy or her mother, he acquiesced.

He was allowing Dorothy to give him his pills; she'd simply taken over his prescriptions. Dorothy not only decided when he should take the Viagra – always a whole tablet, not a half – but she told him when to take the beta-blockers, and when *not* to take them.

At low tide, it was Dorothy who insisted they sit overlooking the lagoon; low tide was when the reef egrets came to search the mudflats. 'What are the egrets looking for?' Juan Diego had asked her.

'It doesn't matter – they're awesome-looking birds, aren't they?' was all Dorothy had said.

At high tide, Dorothy held his arm as they ventured onto the beach in the horseshoe-shaped cove. The monitor lizards liked to lie in the sand; some of them were as long as an adult human arm. 'You don't want to get too close to them – they can bite, and they smell like carrion,' Dorothy had warned him. 'They look like penises, don't they? Unfriendly-looking penises,' Dorothy said.

Juan Diego had no idea what unfriendly-looking penises resembled; how any penis could or might look like a monitor lizard was beyond him. Juan Diego had enough trouble understanding his own penis. When Dorothy took him snorkeling in the deep water outside the lagoon, his penis stung a little.

'It's just the salt water, and because you've been

having a lot of sex,' Dorothy told him. She seemed to know more about his penis than Juan Diego did. And the stinging soon stopped. (It was more like *tingling* than stinging, truthfully.) Juan Diego wasn't under attack from those stinging things – the plankton that looked like condoms for three-year-olds. There were no upright-swimming index fingers – those stinging pink things, swimming vertically, like sea horses, the jellyfish he'd heard about only from Dorothy and Clark.

As for Clark, Juan Diego started getting inquiring text messages from his former student before he and Dorothy left El Nido and Lagen Island.

'D. is STILL with you, isn't she?' the first such text message from Clark inquired.

'What should I tell him?' Juan Diego asked Dorothy.

'Oh, Leslie is texting Clark, too – is she?' Dorothy had asked. 'I'm just not answering her. You would think Leslie and I had been going steady, or something.'

But Clark French kept texting his former teacher. 'As far as poor Leslie knows, D. has just DISAPPEARED. Leslie was expecting D. to meet her in Manila. But poor Leslie is suspicious – she knows you know D. What do I tell her?'

'Tell Clark we're leaving for Laoag. Leslie will know where that is. Everyone knows where Laoag is. Don't get more specific,' Dorothy told Juan Diego.

But when Juan Diego did exactly that – when he sent Clark a text that he was 'off to Laoag with D.' – he heard back from his former student almost immediately.

'D. is fucking you, isn't she? You understand: I'm not the one who wants to know!' Clark texted him. 'Poor Leslie is asking ME. What do I tell her?'

Dorothy saw his consternation as he stared at his cell phone. 'Leslie is a very possessive person,' Dorothy said to Juan Diego, without needing to ask him if the text was from Clark. 'We have to let Leslie know she doesn't *own* us. This is all because your former student is too uptight to fuck her, and Leslie knows her tits won't stay perky forever, or something.'

'You want me to blow off your bossy girlfriend?' Juan Diego asked Dorothy.

'I guess you've never had to blow off a bossy girl-friend,' Dorothy said; without waiting for Juan Diego to admit that he hadn't *had* a bossy girlfriend – or many other kinds of girlfriends – Dorothy told him how he should handle the situation.

'We have to show Leslie that she doesn't have an emotional ball-and-chain effect on us,' Dorothy began. 'Here's what you say to Clark – he'll tell Leslie everything. One: Why shouldn't D. and I do it? Two: Leslie and D. did it, didn't they? Three: How are those boys doing – that one kid's poor penis, especially? Four: Want us to say hi to the water buffalo for the whole family?'

'That's what I should say?' Juan Diego asked Dorothy. She really *did* know a lot, he was thinking.

'Just send it,' Dorothy told him. 'Leslie needs to be

blown off – she's begging for it. *Now* you can say you've had a bossy girlfriend. Fun, huh?' Dorothy asked him.

He sent the text, per Dorothy's instructions. Juan Diego was aware he was blowing off Clark, too. He was having fun, all right; in fact, he couldn't remember when he'd had this much fun – the quickly passing stinging sensation in his penis notwithstanding.

'How is *this guy* doing?' Dorothy then asked him, touching his penis. 'Still stinging? Still *tingling* a tiny bit, maybe? Want to make this guy tingle some more?' Dorothy asked him.

He could barely manage to nod his head, he was so tired. Juan Diego was still staring at his cell phone, thinking about the uncharacteristic text message he'd sent to Clark.

'Don't worry,' Dorothy was whispering to him; she kept touching his penis. 'You look a little tired, but not *this guy*,' she whispered. '*He* doesn't get tired.'

Dorothy now took his phone away from him. 'Don't worry, darling,' she said to him in a more commanding fashion than before – the *darling* word impossibly sounding the way it had when Miriam had said it. 'Leslie won't bother us again. Trust me: she'll get the message. Your friend Clark French does everything she wants – except fuck her.'

Juan Diego wanted to ask Dorothy about their trip to Laoag and Vigan, but he couldn't form the words. He couldn't possibly have expressed to Dorothy his doubts about going there. Dorothy had decided – *because* Juan Diego was an American, and one of the

Vietnam generation – that he should at least see where those young Americans, those frightened nineteen-year-olds who were so afraid of being *tortured*, went to get away from the war (when, or if, they could manage to get away from it).

Juan Diego had meant to ask Dorothy, too, where exactly the doctrinaire certainty of her opinions came from – you know how Juan Diego was always wondering where everything *came from* – but he'd been unable to summon the strength to question the autocratic young woman.

Dorothy disapproved of the Japanese tourists at El Nido; she disliked how the resort catered to the Japanese, pointing out that there was Japanese food on the menu.

'But we're very near to Japan,' Juan Diego reminded her. 'And other people like Japanese food—'

'After what Japan *did* to the Philippines?' Dorothy asked him.

'Well, the war—' Juan Diego had started to say.

'Wait till you see the Manila American Cemetery and Memorial – if you actually end up seeing it,' Dorothy said dismissively. 'The Japanese shouldn't come to the Philippines.'

And Dorothy pointed out that the Australians out-numbered all the other white people in the dining hall at El Nido. 'Wherever they go, they go as a group – they're a gang,' she said.

'You don't like Australians?' Juan Diego asked her. 'They're so friendly – they're just naturally gregarious.' This was greeted by Dorothy's Lupe-like shrug.

Dorothy might as well have said: If you don't *understand*, I couldn't possibly have any success in *explaining* it to you.

There were two Russian families at El Nido, and some Germans, too. 'There are Germans *everywhere*,' was all Dorothy said.

'They're big travelers, aren't they?' Juan Diego had asked her.

'They're big *conquerors*,' Dorothy had said, rolling her dark eyes.

'But you like the food here – at El Nido. You said the food is good,' Juan Diego reminded her.

'Rice is rice,' was all Dorothy would say – as if she'd never said the food was good. Yet, when Dorothy was in a *this-guy* mood, her focus was impressive.

Their last night at El Nido, Juan Diego woke with the moonlight reflecting off the lagoon; their earlier, intense attention to 'this guy' must have distracted them from closing the curtains. The way the silvery light fell across the bed and illuminated Dorothy's face was a little eerie. Asleep, there was something as lifeless as a statue about her – as if Dorothy were a mannequin who, only occasionally, sprang to life.

Juan Diego leaned over her in the moonlight, putting his ear close to her lips. He could not feel the breath escaping her mouth and nose, nor did her breasts – lightly covered by the sheets – appear to rise and fall.

For a moment, Juan Diego imagined he could hear Sister Gloria saying, as she once had: 'I don't want to hear another word about Our Lady of Guadalupe *lying down.*' For a moment, it was as if Juan Diego were lying next to the sex-doll likeness of Our Lady of Guadalupe – the gift the good gringo had given him, from that virgin shop in Oaxaca – and Juan Diego had finally managed to saw the pedestal off the mannequin's imprisoned feet.

'Is there something you're expecting me to say?' Dorothy whispered in his ear, startling him. 'Or maybe you were thinking of going down on me, and waking me up that way,' the young woman indifferently said.

'Who are you?' Juan Diego asked her. But he could see in the silvery moonlight that Dorothy had fallen back to sleep, or she was pretending to be asleep – or else he'd only imagined her speaking to him, *and* what he'd asked her.

THE SUN WAS SETTING; it lingered long enough to cast a coppery glow over the South China Sea. Their little plane from Palawan flew on, toward Manila. Juan Diego was remembering the goodbye look Dorothy gave to that tourist-weary water buffalo at the airport, as they were leaving.

'That's a water buffalo on beta-blockers,' Juan Diego had remarked. 'The poor thing.'

'Yeah, well – you should see him when there's a caterpillar up his nose,' Dorothy had said, once more giving the water buffalo the evil eye.

The sun was gone. The sky was the color of a bruise. By the far-apart, twinkling lights onshore, Juan Diego could tell they were flying over ground – the sea was now behind them. Juan Diego was staring out the plane's little window when he felt Dorothy's heavy head make contact with his shoulder and the side of his neck; her head felt as solid as a cannonball.

'What you will see, in about fifteen minutes, are the city lights,' Dorothy told him. 'What comes first is an unlit darkness.'

'An unlit darkness?' Juan Diego asked her; his voice sounded alarmed.

'Except for the occasional ship,' she answered him. 'The darkness is Manila Bay,' Dorothy explained. 'First the bay, then the lights.'

Was it Dorothy's voice or the weight of her head that was putting him to sleep? Or did Juan Diego feel the unlit darkness beckoning?

The head that rested on him was Lupe's, not Dorothy's; he was on a bus, not a plane; the mountain road that snaked by in the darkness was somewhere in the Sierra Madre – the circus was returning to Oaxaca from Mexico City. Lupe slept as heavily against him as an undreaming dog; her little fingers had loosened their grip on the two religious totems she'd been playing with, before she fell asleep.

Juan Diego was holding the coffee can with the ashes – he didn't let Lupe pinch it between her knees when she was sleeping. With her hideous Coatlicue statuette and the Guadalupe figurine – the one Juan Diego had found on the stairs, descending from El Cerrito – Lupe had been waging a war between super-heroes. Lupe made the two action figures knock heads, exchange kicks, have sex; the serene-looking

Guadalupe seemed an unlikely winner, and one look at Coatlicue's rattlesnake-rattle nipples (or her skirt of serpents) left little doubt that, between the two combatants, she was the representative from the Underworld.

Juan Diego had let his sister act out the religious war within her in this childish superhero battle. The saintly-looking Guadalupe figurine at first appeared overmatched; she held her hands in a prayerful position, above the small but discernible swell of her belly. Guadalupe didn't have a fighter's stance, whereas Coatlicue looked as poised to strike as one of her writhing snakes, and Coatlicue's flaccid breasts were scary. (Even a starving infant would have been turned off by those rattlesnake-rattle nipples!)

Yet Lupe engaged the two action figures in a variety of emotionally charged activities: the fighting and fucking were equally intermixed, and there were moments of apparent tenderness between the two warriors – even kissing.

When Juan Diego observed Guadalupe and Coatlicue *kissing*, he asked Lupe if this represented a kind of truce between the fighters – a putting aside of their religious differences. After all, couldn't kissing mean making up?

'They're just taking a break,' was all Lupe said, recommencing the more violent, nonstop action between the two totems – more fighting and fucking – until Lupe was exhausted and fell asleep.

As far as Juan Diego could tell, looking at Guadalupe

and Coatlicue in the loosening fingers of Lupe's small hands, nothing had been settled between the two bitches. How could a violent mother-earth goddess coexist with one of those know-it-all, do-nothing virgins? Juan Diego was thinking. He didn't know that, across the aisle of the darkened bus, Edward Bonshaw was watching him when he gently took the two religious figurines from his sleeping sister's hands.

Someone on the bus had been farting – one of the dogs, maybe; the parrot man, perhaps; Paco and Beer Belly, definitely. (The two dwarf clowns drank a lot of beer.) Juan Diego had already opened the bus window beside him, just a crack. The gap was sufficient for him to slip the two superheroes through the opening. Somewhere, one everlasting night – on a winding road through the Sierra Madre – two formidable religious figures were left to fend for themselves in the unlit darkness.

What now – what *next*? Juan Diego was thinking, when Señor Eduardo spoke to him from across the aisle.

'You are not alone, Juan Diego,' the Iowan said. 'If you reject one belief and then another, still you aren't alone – the universe isn't a godless place.'

'What now – what *next*?' Juan Diego asked him.

A dog with an inquiring look walked between them in the aisle of the circus bus; it was Pastora, the sheepdog – she wagged her tail, as if Juan Diego had spoken to her, and walked on.

Edward Bonshaw began babbling about the Temple

of the Society of Jesus – he meant the one in Oaxaca. Señor Eduardo wanted Juan Diego to consider scattering Esperanza's ashes at the feet of the giant Virgin Mary there.

'The Mary Monster—' Juan Diego started to say.

'Okay – maybe not *all* the ashes, and only at her *feet!*' the Iowan quickly said. 'I know you and Lupe have *issues* with the Virgin Mary, but your mother *adored* her.'

'The Mary Monster *killed* our mother,' Juan Diego reminded Señor Eduardo.

'I think you're interpreting an accident in a dogmatic fashion,' Edward Bonshaw cautioned him. 'Perhaps Lupe is more open to revisiting the Virgin Mary – the Mary Monster, as you call her.'

Pastora, pacing, passed between them in the aisle again. The restless dog reminded Juan Diego of himself, and of the way Lupe had been behaving lately – uncharacteristically unsure of herself, perhaps, but also secretive.

'Lie down, Pastora,' Juan Diego said, but those border-collie types are furtive; the sheepdog continued to roam.

Juan Diego didn't know what to believe; except for skywalking, everything was a hoax. He knew that Lupe was also confused – not that she would admit it. And what if Esperanza had been right to worship the Mary Monster? Clutching the coffee can between his thighs, Juan Diego knew that scattering his mother's ashes – and all the rest – was not necessarily a rational decision, no matter where the ashes were deposited. Why *wouldn't* their mother have wanted her ashes scattered at the feet of the enormous Virgin Mary in the Jesuit temple, where Esperanza had made a good name for herself? (If only as a cleaning woman.)

Edward Bonshaw and Juan Diego were asleep when the dawn broke – as the caravan of circus trucks and buses came into the valley between the Sierra Madre de Oaxaca and the Sierra Madre del Sur. The caravan was passing through Oaxaca when Lupe woke up her brother. 'The parrot man is right – we should scatter the ashes all over the Mary Monster,' Lupe told Juan Diego.

'He said "only at her *feet*," Lupe,' Juan Diego cautioned his little sister. Maybe Lupe had misread the Iowan's thoughts – either when she was asleep or when Señor Eduardo was sleeping, or during some combination of the two.

'I say the ashes go all over the Mary Monster – make the bitch prove herself to us,' Lupe told her brother.

'Señor Eduardo said "maybe not *all* the ashes," Lupe,' Juan Diego warned her.

'I say all of them, all over her,' Lupe said. 'Tell the bus driver to let us and the parrot man out at the temple.'

'Jesus Mary Joseph,' Juan Diego muttered. He saw that all the dogs were awake; they were pacing in the aisle with Pastora.

'Rivera should be there – he's a Mary worshiper,' Lupe was saying, as if she were talking to herself.

Juan Diego knew that, in the early morning, Rivera might be at the shack in Guerrero or sleeping in the cab of his truck; probably he would already have started the hellfires in the basurero. The dump kids would be getting to the Jesuit temple before the early-morning Mass; maybe Brother Pepe would have lit the candles, or he would still be lighting them. It was unlikely that anyone else would be around.

The bus driver had to make a detour; there was a dead dog blocking the narrow street. 'I know where you can get a new dog – a jumper,' Lupe had said to Juan Diego. She hadn't meant a *dead* dog. She'd meant a rooftop dog – one used to jumping, one who hadn't fallen.

'A rooftop dog,' was all the driver said, about the dead dog in the street, but Juan Diego knew this was what Lupe had meant.

'You can't train a rooftop dog to climb a step-ladder, Lupe,' Juan Diego told his sister. 'And Vargas said the rooftop dogs have rabies – they're like perros del basurero. Dump dogs and rooftop dogs are rabid. Vargas said—'

'I have to talk to Vargas about something else. Forget the jumper,' Lupe said. 'The stupid stepladder trick isn't worth worrying about. The rooftop dog was just an idea – they jump, don't they?' Lupe asked him.

'They die, they definitely *bite*—' Juan Diego started to say.

'The rooftop dogs don't matter,' Lupe said impatiently. 'The bigger question is *lions*. Do they get rabies? Vargas will know,' she said, her voice trailing off.

The bus had navigated the dead-dog detour; they were approaching the corner of Flores Magón and Valerio Trujano. They could see the Templo de la Compañía de Jesús.

'Vargas isn't a *lion* doctor,' Juan Diego said to his little sister.

'You have the ashes, right?' was all Lupe said; she'd picked up Baby, the cowardly male dachshund, and had poked the dog's nose into Señor Eduardo's ear, waking him up. The cold-nose method brought the startled Iowan to his feet in the aisle of the bus, the dogs milling around him. Edward Bonshaw saw how tightly the coffee can was held in the cripple's hands; he knew the boy meant business.

'I see – we're *scattering*, are we?' the Iowan asked, but no one answered him.

'We're covering the bitch from head to toe – the Mary Monster will have ashes in her eyes!' Lupe raved incoherently. But Juan Diego didn't translate his sister's outburst.

At the entrance to the temple, only Edward Bonshaw paused at the fountain of holy water; he touched it and then his forehead, under the portrait of Saint Ignatius looking to Heaven (forever) for guidance.

Pepe had already lit the candles. The dump kids didn't pause for even a small splash of holy agua. In the nook after the fountain, they found Brother Pepe praying at the Guadalupe inscription – the 'Guadalupe bullshit,' as Lupe was now calling it.

'¿No estoy aquí, que soy tu madre?' (Lupe meant *that* bullshit.)

'No, you are *not* here,' Lupe said to the smaller-than-life-size likeness of Guadalupe. 'And you're *not* my mother.' When Lupe saw Pepe on his knees, she said to her brother: 'Tell Pepe to go find Rivera – the dump boss should be here. El jefe will want to see this.'

Juan Diego told Pepe they were scattering the ashes at the feet of the big Virgin Mary, and that Lupe wanted Rivera to be present.

'This is different,' Pepe said. 'This represents quite a change in thinking. I'm guessing the Guadalupe shrine was a watershed. Maybe Mexico City marks a turning point?' Pepe asked the Iowan, whose forehead was wet with holy water.

'Things have never felt so uncertain,' Señor Eduardo said; this sounded to Pepe like the beginning of a long confession – Pepe hurried on his way, with scant apology to the Iowan.

'I have to find Rivera – those are my instructions,' Pepe said, though he was full of sympathy for how Edward Bonshaw's reorientation was progressing. 'By the way, I heard about the *horse*!' Pepe called to Juan Diego, who was hurrying to catch up to Lupe; she was already standing at the base of the pedestal (the ghastly frozen angels in the pedestal of Heavenly clouds), staring up at the Mary Monster.

'You see?' Lupe said to Juan Diego. 'You can't

scatter the ashes at her feet – look who's already *lying* at her feet!'

Well, it had been a while since the dump kids had stood in front of the Mary Monster; they'd forgotten the diminutive, shrunken-looking Jesus, who was suffering on the cross and bleeding at the Virgin Mary's feet. 'We're not scattering Mother's ashes on *him*,' Lupe said.

'Okay – *where*, then?' Juan Diego asked her.

'I really think this is the right decision,' Edward Bonshaw was saying. 'I don't think you two have given the Virgin Mary a fair chance.'

'You should get on the parrot man's shoulders. You can throw the ashes higher if *you're* higher,' Lupe said to Juan Diego.

Lupe held the coffee can while Juan Diego got on Edward Bonshaw's shoulders. The Iowan needed to grasp hold of the Communion railing to rise, unsteadily, to his full height. Lupe took the lid off the coffee can before handing the ashes to her brother. (Only God knows what Lupe did with the lid.)

Even from his elevated position, Juan Diego was barely eye-level with the Virgin Mary's knees; the top of his head was only thigh-high to the giantess.

'I'm not sure how you can sprinkle the ashes in an upward fashion,' Señor Eduardo tactfully observed.

'Forget about *sprinkling*,' Lupe said to her brother. 'Grab a handful, and start throwing.'

But the first handful of ashes flew no higher than the Mary Monster's formidable breasts; naturally, most of the ashes fell on Juan Diego's and the Iowan's uplifted faces. Señor Eduardo coughed and sneezed; Juan Diego had ashes in his eyes. 'This isn't working very well,' Juan Diego said.

'It's the *idea* that counts,' Edward Bonshaw said, choking.

'Throw the whole can – throw it at her head!' Lupe cried.

'Is she praying?' the Iowan asked Juan Diego, but the boy was concentrating on his aim. He hurled the coffee can, which was three-quarters full – the way he'd seen soldiers in the movies lob a grenade.

'Not the whole can!' the dump kids heard Señor Eduardo cry.

'Good shot,' Lupe said. The coffee can had struck the Virgin Mary in her domineering forehead. (Juan Diego was sure he saw the Mary Monster blink.) The ashes rained down, dispersing everywhere. There were ashes falling through the shafts of morning light and on every inch of the Mary Monster. The ashes kept falling.

'It was as if the ashes fell from a superior height – from an unseen source, but a *high* one,' Edward Bonshaw would later describe what happened. 'And the ashes went on falling – as if there were more ashes than could possibly have been contained in that coffee can.' At this point, the Iowan always paused before saying: 'I hesitate to say this. I truly do. But the way those ashes wouldn't stop falling made the moment seem to last forever. Time – time itself, all sense of time – stopped.'

In the ensuing weeks – for *months*, Brother Pepe

would maintain – those worshipers who'd arrived early for the first morning Mass continued to call the ashes falling in the shafts of light 'an event.' Yet those ashes that appeared to *bathe* the towering Virgin Mary in a radiant but gray-brown cloud were not heralded as a *divine* occurrence by everyone arriving at the Jesuit temple for morning Mass.

The two old priests Father Alfonso and Father Octavio were annoyed by what a mess the ashes had made: the first ten rows of pews were coated with ashes; a film of ash clung to the Communion railing, which was curiously sticky to touch. The big Virgin Mary looked soiled; she was definitely darkened, as if by soot. The dirt-brown, death-gray ashes were everywhere.

'The children wanted to scatter their mother's ashes,' Edward Bonshaw started to explain.

'In the *temple*, Edward?' Father Alfonso asked the Iowan.

'All this was a *scattering*!' Father Octavio exclaimed. He tripped on something, unintentionally kicking it – the empty coffee can, which was rattling around underfoot. Señor Eduardo picked up the can.

'I didn't know they were going to scatter the entire contents,' the Iowan admitted.

'That coffee can was *full*?' Father Alfonso asked.

'It was not just our mother's ashes,' Juan Diego told the two old priests.

'Do tell,' Father Octavio said. Edward Bonshaw stared into the empty can, as if he hoped it possessed oracular powers.

'The good gringo – may he rest in peace,' Lupe began. 'My dog – a small one.' She stopped, as if waiting for Juan Diego to translate this much, before she continued. Or else Lupe stopped because she was wondering if she should tell the two priests about the Mary Monster's missing nose.

'You remember the American hippie – the draft dodger, the boy who died,' Juan Diego said to Father Alfonso and Father Octavio.

'Yes, yes – of course,' Father Alfonso said. 'A lost soul – a tragically self-destructive one.'

'A terrible tragedy – such a waste,' Father Octavio said.

'And my sister's little dog died – the dog was in the fire,' Juan Diego went on. 'And the dead hippie.'

'It's all coming back – we did know this,' Father Alfonso said. Father Octavio nodded grimly.

'Yes, please stop – that's enough. Most distasteful. We remember, Juan Diego,' Father Octavio said.

Lupe didn't speak; the two priests wouldn't have understood her, anyway. Lupe just cleared her throat, as if she were going to say something.

'Don't,' Juan Diego said, but it was too late. Lupe pointed to the noseless face of the giant Virgin Mary, touching her little nose with the index finger of her other hand.

It took Father Alfonso and Father Octavio a few seconds to catch on: the Mary Monster was still without a nose; the incomprehensible child from the dump was indicating that her own small nose was intact; there'd been a fire at the basurero, an infernal burning of human and canine bodies.

'The Virgin Mary's *nose* was in that hellish fire?' Father Alfonso asked Lupe; she vigorously nodded her head, as if she were trying to dislodge her teeth or make her eyes fall out.

'Merciful Mother of—' Father Octavio started to say.

The falling coffee can made a startling clatter. It's not likely that Edward Bonshaw had intentionally dropped the coffee can, which he quickly retrieved. Señor Eduardo may have lost his grip; he might have realized that the news he was continuing to withhold from Father Alfonso and Father Octavio (namely, his vow-ending love for Flor) would soon come as a greater shock to those two old priests than the burning of an inanimate statue's nose.

Because he'd seen the Mary Monster cast a most disapproving glance at his mother's cleavage – because Juan Diego was aware of how *animated* the Virgin Mary could be, at least in the area of condemning looks and withering glares – Juan Diego would have questioned anyone's supposition that the towering statue (or her lost nose) was *inanimate*. Hadn't the Mary Monster's nose made a spitting sound, and hadn't a blue flame erupted from the funeral pyre? Hadn't Juan Diego seen the Virgin Mary blink when the coffee can had struck her forehead?

And when Edward Bonshaw clumsily dropped and retrieved the coffee can, hadn't the resounding clatter drawn a fiery flash of frightful loathing from the all-seeing eyes of the menacing Virgin Mary?

Juan Diego wasn't a Mary worshiper, but he knew better than to treat the dirtied giantess with less than the utmost respect. 'Lo siento, Mother,' Juan Diego quietly said to the big Virgin Mary, pointing to his forehead. 'I didn't mean to hit you with the can. I was just trying to reach you.'

'These ashes have a foreign smell – I would like to know what else was in that can,' Father Alfonso said.

'Dump stuff, I suppose, but here comes the dump boss – we should ask him,' Father Octavio said.

Speaking of Mary worshipers, Rivera strode down the center aisle toward the towering statue; it was as if the dump boss had his own business to attend to with the Mary Monster; Pepe's mission, to go fetch el jefe from Guerrero, may have been merely coincidental. Yet it was clear that Pepe had interrupted Rivera in the middle of something – 'a small project, the fine-tuning part,' was all the dump boss would say about it.

Rivera must have left Guerrero with some sense of urgency – who knows how Pepe might have announced the scattering to him? – because the dump boss was still wearing his woodworking apron.

The apron had many pockets and was as long as an unflattering, matronly-looking skirt. One pocket was for chisels, of varying sizes; another was for different patches of sandpaper, coarse and fine; a third pocket was for the glue tube and the rag Rivera used to wipe the residue of glue from the nozzle of the tube. There was no telling what was in the other pockets – the pockets were what Rivera said he liked about his woodworking apron. The old leather apron held many secrets – or so Juan Diego, as a child, had once believed.

'I don't know what we're waiting for – for *you*, maybe,' Juan Diego said to el jefe. 'I think the giantess is unlikely to *do* anything,' the boy added, nodding to the Mary Monster.

The temple was filling up, though there was still time before the Mass, at the moment when Brother Pepe and Rivera arrived. Juan Diego would remember, later, that Lupe paid more attention to the dump boss than she usually did; as for el jefe, he was even warier around Lupe than he usually was.

Rivera had his left hand thrust deep inside a mystery pocket of his woodworking apron; with the fingertips of his right hand, the dump boss touched the film of ash on the Communion railing.

'The ashes smell a little funny – not an over-powering smell,' Father Alfonso said to el jefe.

'There's something sticky in these ashes – a foreign substance,' Father Octavio said.

Rivera sniffed his fingertips, then wiped them on his leather apron.

'You've got a lot of stuff in your pockets, jefe,' Lupe said to the dump boss, but Juan Diego didn't translate this; the dump reader was miffed that Rivera hadn't responded to the giantess joke – namely, Juan Diego's prediction that the Virgin Mary was unlikely to *do* anything.

'You should snuff the candles, Pepe,' the dump

boss said; pointing to his beloved Virgin Mary, Rivera then spoke to the two old priests. 'She's highly flammable,' el jefe said.

'Flammable!' Father Alfonso cried.

Rivera recited the same litany of the coffee can's contents that the dump kids had heard from Dr. Vargas – a scientific, strictly *chemical* analysis. 'Paint, turpentine – or some kind of paint thinner. Gasoline, definitely,' Rivera told the two old priests. 'And probably stuff for staining wood.'

'The Holy Mother won't be stained, will she?' Father Octavio asked the dump boss.

'You better let me clean her up,' the dump boss said. 'If I could have a little time alone with her – I mean before the first morning Mass tomorrow. The best would be after the evening Mass tonight. You don't want to mix water with some of these *foreign substances*,' Rivera said, as if he were an alchemist who couldn't be refuted – not your usual dump boss, in any case.

Brother Pepe, on tiptoe, was at work extinguishing the candles with the long gold candle snuffer; naturally, the falling ashes had already snuffed out those candles nearest to the Virgin Mary.

'Does your hand hurt, jefe – where you cut yourself ?' Lupe asked Rivera. He was a hard one to read, even for a mind reader.

Juan Diego would later speculate that Lupe may have read *everything* on Rivera's mind – not only el jefe's thoughts about his cutting himself, and how much he was bleeding. Lupe might have known all about whatever 'small project' Pepe had interrupted Rivera in the middle of, including what Rivera had called 'the fine-tuning part' – namely, what exactly the dump boss was working on when he slashed the thumb and index finger of his left hand. But Lupe never said what she knew, or *if* she knew, and Rivera – like the pockets of his woodworking apron – held many secrets.

'Lupe wants to know if your hand hurts, jefe – where you cut yourself,' Juan Diego said.

'I just need a couple of stitches,' Rivera said; he kept his left hand hidden in the pocket of the leather apron.

Brother Pepe had thought Rivera shouldn't drive; they'd taken Pepe's VW from the shack in Guerrero. Pepe wanted to drive the dump boss to Dr. Vargas right away for the stitches, but Rivera had wanted to see the results of the scattering first.

'The *results*!' Father Alfonso repeated, after Pepe's account.

'The results amount to a species of vandalism,' Father Octavio said, looking at Juan Diego and Lupe when he spoke.

'I need to see Vargas, too – let's go,' Lupe said to her brother. The dump kids weren't even looking at the Mary Monster; they weren't expecting much in the area of *results* from her. But Rivera looked up at the Virgin Mary's noseless face – as if, her darkened visage notwithstanding, the dump boss expected to see a sign, something bordering on instructions.

'Come on, jefe – you're hurting, you're still

bleeding,' Lupe said, taking Rivera's good right hand. The dump boss was unused to such affection from the ever-critical girl. El jefe gave Lupe his hand and let her lead him up the center aisle.

'We'll see that you have the temple to yourself, before closing time tonight!' Father Alfonso called after the dump boss.

'Pepe – you'll lock up after him, I presume,' Father Octavio said to Brother Pepe, who'd returned the candle snuffer to its sacred place; Pepe was hurrying after Rivera and the niños de la basura.

'¡Sí, sí!' Pepe called to the two old priests.

Edward Bonshaw was left holding the empty coffee can. Now was not the time for Señor Eduardo to say what he knew he needed to say to Father Alfonso or Father Octavio; now was not the time to confess – there was a Mass upcoming, and the lid to the coffee can was missing. It had simply (or not so simply) disappeared; it might as well have gone up in smoke, like the Virgin Mary's nose, Señor Eduardo was thinking. But the lid to that secular coffee can – last touched by Lupe – had vanished without a flaming blue hiss.

The dump kids and the dump boss had left the temple with Brother Pepe, leaving Edward Bonshaw and the two old priests to face the noseless Virgin Mary and their uncertain future. Perhaps Pepe understood this best: Pepe knew that the process of reorientation was never easy.

27

A Nose for a Nose

The nighttime flight from Manila to Laoag was packed with crying children. They weren't in the air for more than an hour and a quarter, but the wailing kids made the flying time seem longer.

'Is it a weekend?' Juan Diego asked Dorothy, but she told him it was a Thursday night. 'A school night!' Juan Diego declared; he was dumbfounded. 'Don't these kids go to school?' (He knew, before she did it, that Dorothy was going to shrug.)

Even the nonchalance of Dorothy's shrug – it was such a slight gesture – was sufficient to dislocate Juan Diego from the present time. Not even the crying children could keep him in the moment. Why was he so easily (and repeatedly) carried back to the past? Juan Diego wondered.

Was it all to do with the beta-blocker business, or was his footing in the Philippines of an insubstantial or transient nature?

Dorothy was saying something about her inclination to talk more when there were children around – 'I would rather listen to myself than the kids, you know?' – but Juan Diego found it difficult to listen to Dorothy. Though it had happened forty years ago, the conversation with Dr. Vargas at Cruz Roja – on the occasion of Vargas's stitching the thumb and index finger of Rivera's left hand – was more *present* in Juan Diego's mind than Dorothy's monologue en route to Laoag.

'You don't like children?' was all Juan Diego had asked her. After that, he didn't say a word for the rest of the flight. He'd *listened* to more of what Vargas and Rivera and Lupe were saying – over the stitches, that long-ago morning at the Red Cross hospital – than he actually heard (or would remember) of Dorothy's discursive soliloquy.

'I'm okay if people have children – I mean *other* people. If other adults want kids, that's fine with me,' Dorothy stated. Not quite in chronological order, she began her lecture on local history; Dorothy must have wanted Juan Diego to know at least a little about where they were going. But Juan Diego missed most of what Dorothy would tell him; he was paying closer attention to a conversation at Cruz Roja, one he should have listened to more closely forty years ago.

'Jesus, jefe – were you in a sword fight?' Vargas was asking the dump boss.

'It was just a chisel,' Rivera told Vargas. 'I tried the bevel chisel first – it has a cutting edge that makes an oblique angle – but it wasn't working.'

'So you changed chisels,' Lupe prompted el jefe. Juan Diego translated this.

'Yeah, I changed chisels,' Rivera said. 'The problem

was the object I was working on – it doesn't lie flat. It's hard to hold at the base – the object doesn't really *have* a base.'

'It's hard to stabilize the object with one hand while you cut, or chip away, with the chisel in your other hand,' Lupe explained. Juan Diego translated this clarifying point, too.

'Yeah – the object is hard to stabilize, all right,' the dump boss agreed.

'What kind of object is it, jefe?' Juan Diego asked.

'Think of a doorknob – or the latch to a door, or to a window,' the dump boss answered him. 'Kind of like that.'

'Tricky business,' Lupe said. Juan Diego also translated this.

'Yeah,' was all Rivera said.

'You cut the shit out of yourself, jefe,' Vargas told the dump boss. 'Maybe you should stick to the basurero business.'

At the time, everyone had laughed – Juan Diego could still hear their laughter, as Dorothy rambled on and on. She was saying something about the north-western coast of Luzon. Laoag was a trading port and a fishing site in the tenth and eleventh centuries – 'one sees the Chinese influence,' Dorothy was saying. 'Then Spain invaded, with their Mary-Jesus business – your old friends,' Dorothy said to Juan Diego. (The Spanish came in the 1500s; they were in the Philippines for more than three hundred years.)

But Juan Diego wasn't listening. There was other dialogue that weighed on him, a moment when he might have (could have, should have) seen something coming – a moment when he might have diverted the course of things to come.

Lupe stood near enough to touch the stitches, watching Vargas close the wounds in Rivera's thumb and index finger; Vargas told Lupe he was in danger of attaching her inquisitive little face to el jefe's hand. That was when Lupe asked Vargas what he knew about lions and rabies. 'Can lions get rabies? Let's start with that,' Lupe began. Juan Diego translated, but Vargas was the kind of guy who wouldn't readily admit there was something he didn't know.

'An infected dog can transmit rabies when the virus reaches the dog's salivary glands, which is about a week – or less – before the dog dies from rabies,' Vargas replied.

'Lupe wants to know about a *lion*,' Juan Diego told him.

'The incubation period in an infected human is usually about three to seven weeks, but I've had patients who developed the disease in ten days,' Vargas was saying, when Lupe interrupted him.

'Let's say a rabid dog bites a lion – you know, like a rooftop dog, or like one of those perros del basurero. Does the lion get sick? What happens to the *lion*?' Lupe asked Vargas.

'I'm sure there have been studies – I'll have to look at what research has been done on rabies in lions,' Dr. Vargas said, sighing. 'Most people who get bitten by lions probably aren't worried about rabies. That wouldn't be the first worry you would have, in the case of a lion bite,' he told Lupe.

Juan Diego knew there was no translation for Lupe's shrug.

Dr. Vargas was bandaging the thumb and index finger of Rivera's left hand. 'You have to keep this clean and dry, jefe,' Vargas was telling the dump boss. But Rivera was looking at Lupe, who looked away from him; el jefe knew when Lupe was keeping something to herself.

And Juan Diego was anxious to get back to Cinco Señores, where La Maravilla would be setting up the tents and quieting down the animals. At the time, Juan Diego believed he had more important business to attend to than what was on Lupe's mind. As a fourteen-year-old boy will, Juan Diego was dreaming about himself as a hero – he had *skywalking* aspirations on his mind. (And of course Lupe knew what her brother was thinking; she could read his thoughts.)

The four of them fit into Pepe's VW Beetle; Pepe drove the dump kids to Cinco Señores before he took Rivera back to the shack in Guerrero. (El jefe had said he wanted to take a nap before the local anesthetic wore off.)

In the car, Pepe told the dump kids they were welcome to come back to Lost Children. 'Your old room is ready for you, anytime,' was the way Pepe put it. But Sister Gloria had returned Juan Diego's life-size sex doll of the Guadalupe virgin to the Christmas-parties place – Lost Children would never be the same, Juan Diego was thinking. And why would you leave an orphanage, and then go back? If you leave, you leave, Juan Diego thought – you move *on*, not back.

When they got to the circus, Rivera was crying; the dump kids knew the local anesthetic had not worn off, but the dump boss was too upset to speak.

'We *know* we would be welcome to come back to Guerrero, jefe,' Lupe said. 'Tell Rivera we know the shack is *our* shack, if we ever need to go home,' Lupe told Juan Diego. 'Tell him we miss him, too,' Lupe said. Juan Diego said all that, while Rivera kept crying – his big shoulders were shaking in the passenger seat.

It is simply amazing, at that age, when you're thirteen or fourteen, how you can take being loved for granted, how (even when you are *wanted*) you can feel utterly alone. The dump kids were *not* abandoned at Circo de La Maravilla; yet they'd stopped confiding in each other, and they were confiding in no one else.

'Good luck with that object you're working on,' Juan Diego told Rivera, when the dump boss was leaving Cinco Señores to go back to Guerrero.

'Tricky business,' Lupe repeated, as if she were talking to herself. (After Pepe's VW Beetle drove off, only Juan Diego could have heard her, and he wasn't really listening.) Juan Diego was thinking about his own tricky business. When it came to having balls, apparently, only the main tent – the skywalk at eighty feet, without a net – was a true test. Or so Dolores had said, and Juan Diego believed her. Soledad had coached him, teaching him how to skywalk in the troupe tent for the young-women acrobats, but Dolores said that didn't count.

Juan Diego remembered that he'd dreamed about skywalking – before he knew what skywalking was, when he and Lupe were still living in Rivera's shack in Guerrero. And when Juan Diego had asked his sister what she thought of his dream about walking upside down in the heavens, she'd been typically mysterious. All he'd said about the dream to Lupe was: 'There comes a moment in every life when you must let go with your hands – with *both* hands.'

'It's a dream about the future,' Lupe had said. 'It's a death dream,' was how she'd put it.

Dolores had defined the crucial moment, the one when you must let go with your hands – with *both* hands. 'I never know whose hands I am in then, at that moment,' Dolores had told him. 'Maybe those miraculous virgins have magic hands? Maybe I'm in *their* hands, at that moment. I don't think you should think about it. That's when you have to concentrate on your *feet* – one step at a time. In every life, I think there's always a moment when you must decide where you *belong*. At that moment, you're in no one's hands,' Dolores had said to Juan Diego. 'At that moment, everyone walks on the sky. Maybe all great decisions are made without a net,' The Wonder herself had told him. 'There comes a time, in every life, when you must let go.'

The morning after a road trip, Circo de La Maravilla slept late – 'late' for a circus, anyway. Juan Diego was counting on getting an early start, but it's difficult to get up earlier than dogs. Juan Diego tried to sneak out of the dogs' troupe tent without causing suspicion; naturally, any dog who was awake would want to go with him.

Juan Diego got up so early, only Pastora heard him; she was already awake, already pacing. Of course the sheepdog didn't understand why Juan Diego wouldn't take her with him when he left the tent. It was probably Pastora who woke up Lupe, after Juan Diego had left.

In the avenue of troupe tents, there was no one around. Juan Diego was on the lookout for Dolores; she got up early, to run. Lately, it seemed, she was running too much or too hard; some mornings, she made herself sick. Though he liked Dolores's long legs, Juan Diego had no appreciation for her insane running. What boy with a limp likes to run? And even if you *loved* to run, why would you run until you threw up?

But Dolores took her training seriously. She ran, and she drank a lot of water. She believed both were essential for not getting muscle cramps in her legs. In the rope loops of the skywalk, Dolores said, you didn't want to get a cramp in your weight-bearing leg – not at eighty feet, not when the foot attached to that leg was all that held you to the ladder.

Juan Diego had comforted himself with the thought that none of the girls in the acrobats' troupe tent was ready to replace Dolores as The Wonder; Juan Diego knew that, next to Dolores, he was the best skywalker at La Maravilla – if only at twelve feet.

The main tent was another story. The knotted rope was what all the aerialists used to climb to the top of the tent. The knots were spaced on the thick rope to accommodate the hands and feet of the trapeze artists – the knots were within Dolores's reach, and within the reach of the sexually overactive Argentinian flyers.

For Juan Diego, the knots were not a problem; his grip was strong (he probably weighed about the same as Dolores), his hands could easily reach the next knot above him, and his good foot could securely feel the knot at his feet. He pulled himself up and up; climbing a rope is a workout, but Juan Diego looked fixedly ahead – he looked only up. Above him, he could see the ladder with the rope loops at the top of the main tent – with every pull of his arms, he saw the ladder inch nearer.

But eighty feet is a long climb, only an arm's length at a time, and the problem was that Juan Diego didn't dare look down. He kept the rope rungs of the ladder for the skywalk in view above him; his only focus was the top of the main tent, which was inching closer – one tug at a time.

'You have another future!' he heard Lupe call to him, as she'd said to him before. Juan Diego knew that looking down wasn't an option – he kept climbing. He was almost at the top; he'd already passed the platforms for the trapeze artists. He could have reached out and touched the trapezes, but that would have meant letting go of the rope, and he wouldn't let go – not even with one hand.

He had passed the spotlights, too – almost without noticing them, because the lights were off. But he was marginally aware of the unlit bulbs – the spotlights were pointed in an upward direction. They were meant to illuminate the skywalker, but they also lit the rope rungs of the skywalking ladder with the brightest possible light.

'Don't look down – *never* look down,' Juan Diego heard Dolores say. She must have finished her run, because he could hear her retching. Juan Diego didn't look down, yet Dolores's voice had made him pause; the muscles in his arms were burning, but he felt strong. And he didn't have far to go.

'Another future! Another future! Another future!' Lupe called to him. Dolores went on throwing up. Juan Diego guessed they were his only audience.

'You shouldn't have stopped,' Dolores managed to tell him. 'You have to get from the climbing rope to the skywalking ladder without thinking about it, because you have to let go of the rope before you can grab hold of the ladder.' This meant he had to let go *twice*.

No one had told him about this part. Neither Soledad nor Dolores had thought he was ready for this part. Juan Diego realized that he couldn't let go *once* – not even with one hand. He just froze; holding still, he could feel the thick rope sway.

'Come down,' Dolores said to him. 'Not everyone

has the balls for this part. I'm sure you're going to have the balls for lots of other stuff.'

'You have another future,' Lupe repeated, more calmly.

Juan Diego came down the rope without once looking down. When his feet touched the ground, he was surprised to see that he and Lupe were alone in the vast tent.

'Where did Dolores go?' Juan Diego asked.

Lupe had said some terrible things about Dolores – 'let the lion tamer knock her up!' Lupe had said. (In fact, Ignacio *had* knocked Dolores up.) 'That's her only future!' Lupe had said, but now she was sorry she'd said those things. Dolores had gotten her first period a while ago; maybe the lions didn't know when Dolores started bleeding, but Ignacio did.

Dolores had been running to lose the baby – she wasn't having her period anymore – but she couldn't run hard enough to make herself miscarry. It was morning sickness that made Dolores throw up.

When Lupe told all this to Juan Diego, he asked Lupe if Dolores had talked about it, but Dolores hadn't told Lupe about her condition. Lupe had just read what was on Dolores's mind.

Dolores did say one thing to Lupe that morning when The Wonder left the main tent – once Dolores knew Juan Diego was coming down the climbing rope. 'I'll tell you what I don't have the balls for – because you're such a little know-it-all, you probably know already,' Dolores said to Lupe. 'I don't have the balls for the next part of my life,' the skywalker said.

Then Dolores left the main tent – she wouldn't be back. La Maravilla wouldn't have a skywalker.

The last person to see Dolores in Oaxaca was Dr. Vargas, in the ER at Cruz Roja. Vargas said Dolores died of a peritoneal infection – from a botched abortion in Guadalajara. Vargas said: 'The asshole lion tamer knows some amateur he sends his pregnant skywalkers to see.' By the time Dolores got to Cruz Roja, the infection was too advanced for Vargas to save her.

'Die in childbirth, monkey twat!' Lupe had once said to The Wonder. In a way, Dolores would; like Juan Diego, she was only fourteen. Circo de La Maravilla lost La Maravilla.

The chain of events, the links in our lives – what leads us where we're going, the courses we follow to our ends, what we don't see coming, and what we do – all this can be mysterious, or simply unseen, or even obvious.

Vargas was a good doctor, and a smart man. One look at Dolores, and Vargas had known everything: the abortion in Guadalajara (Vargas had seen the results before); the amateur who'd botched the job (Vargas knew the butcher was Ignacio's pal); the fourteen-year-old who'd gotten her first period fairly recently (Vargas was aware of the weird connection between skywalking and menstruating, though he'd not known the lion tamer had told the girls that the *lions* knew when the girls were bleeding).

But not even Vargas knew everything. For the rest of his life, Dr. Vargas would be interested in lions and rabies; he would continue to send Juan Diego details of the existent research. Yet when Lupe had asked the question – when Lupe was looking for answers – Vargas never followed up with any lion information.

True to his nature, Vargas had a scientific mind – he couldn't stop speculating. He wasn't *really* interested in lions and rabies, but long after Lupe's death, Vargas would wonder why Lupe had wanted to know.

Señor Eduardo and Flor had died of AIDS and Lupe was long gone when Vargas wrote to Juan Diego about some incomprehensible 'studies' in Tanzania. Research on rabies in lions in the Serengeti raised these 'significant' points, which Vargas had highlighted.

Rabies in lions originated in domestic dogs; it was thought to spread from dogs to hyenas, and from hyenas to lions. Rabies in lions could cause disease, but it could also be 'silent.' (There had been epidemics of rabies in lions in 1976 and 1981, but no disease occurred – they were called silent epidemics.) Presence of a certain parasite, which had been likened to malaria, was thought to determine whether the disease from rabies did or didn't occur – in other words, a lion could spread rabies while not being sick, and never getting sick; whereas a lion could get the same rabies virus and die, depending on coinfection with the parasite.

'This has to do with the effects on the immune system caused by the parasite,' Vargas had written to Juan Diego. There had been 'killer' epidemics of rabies in lions in the Serengeti – these occurred in periods of drought, which killed off the Cape buffalo. (The buffalo carcasses were infested with ticks, which carried the parasite.)

It wasn't that Vargas thought these Tanzanian 'studies' would ever have helped Lupe. She'd been interested in whether or not *Hombre* could get rabies, and if the rabies would make Hombre sick. But *why*? That's what Vargas wished he knew. (What was the point of knowing it *now*? Juan Diego thought. It was too late to know what Lupe had been thinking.)

For a lion to get sick with rabies was a long shot, even in the Serengeti, but what crazy idea had Lupe considered, before she changed her mind and thought of her next crazy idea?

Why would Hombre's getting sick with rabies have mattered? That must have been where the rooftop-dog idea came from, before Lupe abandoned it. A rabid dog bites Hombre, or Hombre kills and eats a rabid dog, but *then* what? So Hombre gets sick – then Hombre bites Ignacio, but what happens *next*?

'It was all about what the lionesses thought,' Juan Diego had explained to Vargas a hundred times. 'Lupe could read the lions' minds – she knew that Hombre would never harm Ignacio. And the girls at La Maravilla would never be safe – not as long as the lion tamer lived. Lupe knew that, too, because she could read *Ignacio's* mind.'

Naturally, this fanciful logic was not in the language of the scientific *studies* Dr. Vargas found convincing.

'You're saying Lupe somehow *knew* that the lion-esses would kill Ignacio, but only if the lion tamer

killed Hombre?' Vargas (always incredulous) asked
Juan Diego.

'I heard her say it,' Juan Diego had told Vargas repeatedly. 'Lupe *didn't* say the lionesses "would" kill Ignacio
– she said they "*will*" kill him. Lupe said the lionesses
hated Ignacio. She said the lionesses were all dumber
than monkey twats – because the lionesses were jealous
of Ignacio, and thought Hombre loved the lion tamer
more than the lion loved them! Ignacio had nothing to
fear from Hombre – it was the *lionesses* the lion tamer
should have been afraid of, Lupe always said.'

'Lupe knew all that? How did she know all that?'
Dr. Vargas always asked Juan Diego. The doctor's
studies of rabies in lions would continue. (It was not
a very popular field of study.)

THE SAME DAY THAT Juan Diego chickened out of skywalking would be known (for a while) in Oaxaca as
'The Day of the Nose.' It would never be called 'El Día
de la Nariz' on a church calendar; it wouldn't become
a national holiday, or even a local saint's day. The
Day of the Nose would soon pass from memory –
even from local lore – but, for a while, it would
amount to a *small* big deal.

In the avenue of troupe tents, Lupe and Juan Diego
were alone; it was still early in the morning, before
the first morning Mass, and Circo de La Maravilla
was still sleeping in.

There was some commotion coming from the dogs'
troupe tent – clearly Estrella and the dogs weren't
sleeping in – and the dump kids hurried to see what

the cause of the commotion was. It was unusual to see Brother Pepe's VW Beetle in the avenue of troupe tents – the little car was empty, but Pepe had left the engine running – and the kids could hear Perro Mestizo, the mongrel, barking his brains out. At the open flaps of the dogs' troupe tent, Alemania, the female German shepherd, was growling – she was holding Edward Bonshaw at bay.

'*There* they are!' Pepe cried, when he saw the dump kids.

'Uh-oh,' Lupe said. (Obviously, she knew what was on the Jesuits' minds.)

'Have you seen Rivera?' Brother Pepe asked Juan Diego.

'Not since you saw him,' Juan Diego answered.

'The dump boss was thinking about going to the first morning Mass,' Lupe said; she waited for her brother to translate this, before she told Juan Diego the rest. Since Lupe knew everything Pepe and Señor Eduardo were thinking, she *didn't* wait for them to tell Juan Diego what was going on. 'The Mary Monster has grown a new nose,' Lupe said. 'Or the Virgin Mary has sprouted someone else's nose. As you might expect, there's a debate.'

'About what?' Juan Diego asked her.

'About the miracle business – there are two schools of thought,' Lupe told him. 'We scattered the *old* nose's ashes – now the Mary Monster has a new nose. Is it a miracle, or is it just a nose job? As you might imagine, Father Alfonso and Father Octavio don't like to hear the *milagro* word used loosely,' Lupe reported. Naturally, Señor Eduardo had heard and understood the *milagro* word.

'Does Lupe say it's a *miracle*?' the Iowan asked Juan Diego.

'Lupe says that's one school of thought,' Juan Diego told him.

'And what does Lupe say about the change in the Virgin Mary's *color*?' Brother Pepe asked. 'Rivera cleaned up the ashes, but the statue is much darker-skinned than she used to be.'

'Father Alfonso and Father Octavio say she's not our old Mary, with the white-as-chalk skin,' Lupe reported. 'The priests think the Mary Monster looks more like Guadalupe than like Mary – Father Alfonso and Father Octavio think the Virgin Mary has become a giant *dark-skinned* virgin.'

But when Juan Diego translated this, Edward Bonshaw became quite animated – or as animated as he dared to be, with Alemania growling at him. 'Aren't we – I mean *we*, the *Church* – always claiming that, in a sense, the Virgin Mary and Our Lady of Guadalupe are one and the same?' the Iowan asked. 'Well, if the virgins are *one*, surely the color of this one's skin doesn't *matter*, right?'

'That's one school of thought,' Lupe pointed out to Juan Diego. 'The color of the Mary Monster's skin is also a matter of debate.'

'Rivera was alone with the statue – he *asked* to be alone with her,' Brother Pepe reminded the dump kids. 'You niños don't suppose the dump boss *did* anything, do you?'

As you might imagine, the issue of whether or not Rivera did anything had already been a matter of debate.

'El jefe said the object he was working on didn't lie flat, and it was hard to hold at the base – the dump boss said the object didn't really *have* a base,' Lupe pointed out. 'Sounds like a nose,' she said.

'Think of a doorknob – or the latch to a door, or to a window. Kind of like that,' el jefe had said. (Kind of like a nose, Juan Diego was thinking.)

'Tricky business,' Lupe had called what the dump boss was working on. But Lupe would never say if she *knew* Rivera had made a new nose for the Mary Monster, and – long before the dump kids drove back to the Temple of the Society of Jesus, with Brother Pepe and Señor Eduardo in the VW Beetle – Lupe and Juan Diego had adequate experience to know that el jefe had harbored secrets before.

From Cinco Señores into the center of Oaxaca, they were driving with the rush-hour traffic. They got to the Jesuit temple after the Mass. Some of the new-nose devotees were still hanging around, gawking at the darker-skinned Mary Monster; in cleaning up the statue, Rivera had managed to remove some of the staining elements from the chemical contents of the ash assault on the Virgin Mary. (It appeared that the giant virgin's clothes hadn't been darkened – at least her clothes weren't as noticeably darkened as her skin.)

Rivera had attended the Mass, but he'd separated himself from the nose-gawkers; the dump boss was quietly praying to himself on a kneeling pad, at some distance from the front rows of pews. El jefe's stolid temperament had been an impenetrable barrier against the insinuations of the two old priests.

As for the new darkness of the Virgin Mary's skin, Rivera spoke only of paint and turpentine – or of 'some kind of paint thinner' and 'stuff for staining wood.' Naturally, the dump boss also mentioned the possibly harsh effects of gasoline, his favorite fire starter.

As for the new nose, Rivera claimed that the statue had still been noseless when he had finished the cleaning job. (Pepe said he hadn't noticed the new nose when he locked up for the night.)

Lupe was smiling at the darker-skinned Mary Monster – the giant Virgin Mary was definitely more *indigenous*-looking. Lupe liked the new nose, too. 'It's less perfect, more human,' Lupe said. Father Alfonso and Father Octavio, who were unused to seeing Lupe smile, asked Juan Diego for a translation.

'It looks like a boxer's nose,' Father Alfonso said, in response to Lupe's assessment.

'One that's been broken, certainly,' Father Octavio said, staring at Lupe. (No doubt he believed that *less perfect, more human* was an inappropriate look for the Virgin Mary.)

The two old priests had asked Dr. Vargas to come and give them his scientific opinion. It wasn't that they liked (or believed in) science, Brother Pepe knew, but Vargas was not one to use the *milagro* word loosely; Vargas wasn't inclined to use the *miracle* word at all, and Father Alfonso and Father Octavio were very much in favor of downplaying the miraculous interpretation of the Mary Monster's darker skin and new nose. (The two old priests must have known they were taking a risk in seeking Vargas's opinion.)

Edward Bonshaw's beliefs had been newly shaken, his vows, not to mention his 'yielding-under-no-winds' resolve, having been broken; he had his own reasons for seeking a liberal acceptance of the altered but no less all-important Virgin Mary before them.

As for Brother Pepe, he was ever the one to embrace change – and tolerance, always tolerance. Pepe's English had been much improved by his contact with Juan Diego and the Iowan. But in his enthusiasm to accept the darker-skinned virgin with her different nose, Pepe declared that the transformed Mary Monster was a 'mixed blessing.'

Pepe must not have realized that the *mixed* word carried pro and con meanings, and Father Alfonso and Father Octavio failed to see how an *indigenous-*looking Virgin Mary (with a fighter's nose) could be anything resembling a 'blessing.'

'I think you mean a "mixed bag," Pepe,' Señor Eduardo helpfully said, but this was not well received by the two old priests, either.

Father Alfonso and Father Octavio did not want to think of the Virgin Mary as anything resembling a 'bag.'

'This Mary is what she is,' Lupe said. 'She's already done more than I expected her to do,' Lupe told them. 'At least she's done *something*, hasn't she?' Lupe asked the two old priests. 'Who cares where her nose came from? Why does her nose have to be a miracle? Or why *can't* it be a miracle? Why do you have to interpret *everything*?' she asked the two old priests. 'Does anyone know what the *real* Virgin Mary looked like?' Lupe asked all of them. 'Do we know the color of the real virgin's skin, or what kind of nose she had?' Lupe asked; she was on a roll. Juan Diego translated every word she said.

Even the new-nose devotees had stopped gawking at the Mary Monster; they'd turned their attention to the babbling girl. The dump boss had looked up from his silent prayers. And they all saw that Vargas had been there the whole time. Dr. Vargas was standing at some distance from the towering statue. He'd been looking at the Virgin Mary's new nose through a pair of binoculars; Vargas had already asked the new cleaning woman to bring him the long ladder.

'I would like to add one thing Shakespeare wrote,' Edward Bonshaw – ever the teacher – said. (It was that familiar passage from the Iowan's beloved *Romeo and Juliet*.) '"What's in a name?"' Señor Eduardo recited to them – the scholastic changed the *rose* word to *nose*, naturally. '"That which we call a nose / By any other word would smell as sweet,"' Edward Bonshaw orated in a booming voice.

Father Alfonso and Father Octavio had been speechless upon hearing Juan Diego's translation of Lupe's inspired utterances, but Shakespeare hadn't impressed the two old priests – they'd heard Shakespeare before, very secular stuff.

'It's a question of *materials*, Vargas – her face, the new nose, are they the same material?' Father Alfonso asked the doctor, who was still examining the nose in question through his all-seeing binoculars.

'And we're wondering if there's a visible seam or crack where the nose attaches to her face,' Father Octavio added.

The cleaning woman (this sturdy roughneck *looked* like a cleaning woman) was dragging the ladder down the center aisle; Esperanza could not have dragged that long ladder (she certainly couldn't have *carried* it) by herself. Vargas helped the cleaning woman set up the ladder, leaning it against the giantess.

'I'm not remembering how the Mary Monster reacts to *ladders*,' Lupe said to Juan Diego.

'I'm not remembering with you,' was all Juan Diego told her.

The dump kids didn't know, for sure, if the Mary Monster's former nose had been made of wood or stone; both Lupe and Juan Diego believed it was wood, *painted* wood. But, years later, when Brother Pepe wrote to Juan Diego about the 'interior restoration' of the Templo de la Compañía de Jesús, Pepe had mentioned the 'new limestone.'

'Did you know,' Pepe had asked Juan Diego, 'that limestone yields lime when burned?' Juan Diego didn't know that, nor did he understand if Pepe meant the Mary Monster herself had been restored. Was the giant virgin included in what Pepe had called the temple's 'interior restoration' – and, if so, did the restored statue (now made of 'new limestone') imply that the *former* Virgin Mary had been made of another kind of stone?

As Vargas climbed the ladder to get a closer look at the Mary Monster's face – inscrutable, for the moment; the indigenous-looking virgin's eyes betrayed no potential for animation, so far – Lupe read Juan Diego's mind.

'Yes, I'm also thinking wood – not stone,' Lupe said to Juan Diego. 'On the other hand, if Rivera was using woodworking chisels for cutting and shaping *stone* – well, that might explain why he cut himself. I've never seen him cut himself before, have you?' Lupe asked her brother.

'No,' Juan Diego said. He was thinking that both noses were made of wood, but that Vargas would probably find a way to sound scientific without saying too much about the *material* composition of the miraculous (or unmiraculous) new nose.

The two old priests were watching Vargas intently, though the doctor was a long way up the ladder; it was hard to see what Vargas was doing, exactly.

'Is that a knife? You're not *cutting* her, are you?' Father Alfonso called up the long ladder.

'That's a Swiss Army knife. I used to have one, but—' Edward Bonshaw began, before Father Octavio interrupted him.

'We're not asking you to draw blood, Vargas!' Father Octavio calld up the long ladder.

Lupe and Juan Diego didn't care about the Swiss Army knife; they watched the Virgin Mary's unresponsive eyes.

'I must say, this is a pretty seamless nose job,' Dr. Vargas reported from near the top of the precarious-looking ladder. 'As surgery goes, there's often quite a distinction between the amateur and the sublime.'

'Are you saying this surgery is in the sublime category, but a surgery nonetheless?' Father Alfonso called up the ladder.

'There's a slight blemish on the side of one nostril, like a birthmark – you would never see it from down there,' Vargas said to Father Alfonso.

The so-called birthmark could have been a blood-stain, Juan Diego was thinking.

'Yes, it could be blood,' Lupe said to her brother. 'El jefe must have bled a lot.'

'The Virgin Mary has a *birthmark*?' Father Octavio asked indignantly.

'It's not a flaw – it's actually intriguing,' Vargas said.

'And the *materials*, Vargas – her face, the new nose?' Father Octavio reminded the scientist.

'Oh, there is more of the *world* about this lady than I detect of *Heaven*,' Vargas said; he was having fun with the two old priests, and they knew it. 'More of the *basurero* in her perfume than I can smell of the sweet *Hereafter*.'

'Stick to science, Vargas,' Father Alfonso said.

'If we want poetry, we'll read Shakespeare,' Father Octavio said, glaring at the parrot man, who understood from Father Octavio's expression not to recite more passages from *Romeo and Juliet*.

The dump boss was done praying; he was no longer

on his knees. Whether the new nose was his doing or not, el jefe wasn't saying; he was keeping his bandage clean and dry, and he was keeping quiet.

Rivera would have left the temple, leaving Vargas high on the ladder and the two old priests feeling mocked, but Lupe must have wanted all of them to be there when she spoke. Only later would Juan Diego realize why she'd wanted all of them to hear her.

The last of the idiot nose-gawkers had left the temple; maybe they'd been miracle-seekers, but they knew enough about the real world to know they weren't likely to hear the *milagro* word from a doctor with binoculars and a Swiss Army knife on a ladder.

'It's a nose for a nose – that's good enough for me. Translate everything I say,' Lupe said to Juan Diego. 'When I die, *don't* burn me. Give me the whole hocus-pocus,' Lupe said, looking straight at Father Alfonso and Father Octavio. 'If you want to burn something,' she said to Rivera and Juan Diego, 'you can burn my clothes – my few things. If a new puppy has died – well, sure, you can burn the puppy with my stuff. But don't burn *me*. Give me what *she* would want me to have,' Lupe told them all – pointing to the Mary Monster with the boxer's nose. 'And sprinkle – *just* sprinkle, don't throw – the ashes at the Virgin Mary's feet. Like you said the first time,' Lupe said to the parrot man, 'maybe not *all* the ashes, and only at her *feet*!'

As he translated her, word for word, Juan Diego could see that the two old priests were captivated by

Lupe's speech. 'Be careful of the little Jesus – don't get the ashes in his eyes,' Lupe told her brother. (She was even being considerate of the shrunken Christ, suffering on the diminutive cross, bleeding at the big Virgin Mary's feet.)

Juan Diego didn't have to be a mind reader to know Brother Pepe's thoughts. Could this be a conversion, in Lupe's case? As Pepe had said on the occasion of the first scattering: 'This is different. This represents quite a change in thinking.'

This is what we think about in a monument to the spiritual world, such as the Temple of the Society of Jesus. In such a place – in the towering presence of a giant Virgin Mary – we have religious (or irreligious) thoughts. We hear a speech like Lupe's, and we think of our religious differences or similarities; we hear only what we imagine are Lupe's *religious* beliefs, or her *religious* feelings, and we weigh her beliefs or feelings against our own.

Vargas, the atheist – the doctor who'd brought his own binoculars and a knife to investigate a miracle, or to examine an unmiraculous nose – would have said that, for a thirteen-year-old, Lupe's spiritual sophistication was 'pretty impressive.'

Rivera, who knew Lupe was special – in fact, the dump boss, who was a Mary worshiper and *very* superstitious, was afraid of Lupe – well, what can one say of el jefe's thoughts? (Rivera was probably relieved to hear that Lupe's religious beliefs were sounding less radical than those he'd heard her express before.)

And those two old priests, Father Alfonso and Father Octavio – surely they were congratulating themselves, and the staff at Lost Children, for having made such apparent progress in the case of a challenging and incomprehensible child.

The good Brother Pepe may have been praying there was hope for Lupe, after all; maybe she wasn't as 'lost' as he'd first assumed she was – maybe, if only in translation, Lupe could make sense, or at least make sense *religiously*. To Pepe, Lupe sounded converted.

No burning – that was probably all that mattered to dear Señor Eduardo. Certainly, no burning was a step in the right direction.

This must have been what they all thought, respectively. And even Juan Diego, who knew his little sister best – even Juan Diego missed hearing what he should have heard.

Why was a thirteen-year-old girl thinking of *dying*? Why was this the time for Lupe to be making last requests? Lupe was a girl who could read what others were thinking – even lions, even *lionesses*. Why had none of them been able to read Lupe's mind?

28

Those Gathering Yellow Eyes

This time, Juan Diego was so deeply immersed in the past – or he was so removed from the present moment – that the sound of the landing gear dropping down, or even the jolt of their landing in Laoag, didn't instantly bring him back to Dorothy's conversation.

'This is where Marcos is from,' Dorothy was saying.

'Who?' Juan Diego asked her.

'Marcos. You know Mrs. Marcos, right?' Dorothy asked him. 'Imelda – she of the million shoes, *that* Imelda. She's still a member of the House of Representatives from this district,' Dorothy told him.

'Mrs. Marcos must be in her eighties now,' Juan Diego said.

'Yeah – she's really old, anyway,' Dorothy concluded.

There was an hour's drive ahead of them, Dorothy had forewarned him – another dark road, another night, with quickly passing glimpses of foreignness. (Thatched huts; churches with Spanish architecture;

dogs, or only their eyes.) And, befitting of the darkness surrounding them in their car – their innkeeper had arranged the driver and the limo – Dorothy described the unspeakable suffering of the American prisoners of war in North Vietnam. She seemed to know the terrible details of the torture sessions in the Hanoi Hilton (as the Hoa Lo prison in the North Vietnamese capital was called); she said the most brutal torture methods were used on the U.S. military pilots who'd been shot down and captured.

More politics – *old* politics, Juan Diego was thinking – in the passing darkness. It wasn't that Juan Diego *wasn't* political, but, as a fiction writer, he was wary of people who presumed they knew what his politics were (or should be). It happened all the time.

Why else would Dorothy have brought Juan Diego *here*? Just because he was an American, and Dorothy thought he should see where those aforementioned 'frightened nineteen-year-olds,' as she'd called them, came for their R&R – *fearfully*, as Dorothy had emphasized, in terror of the torture they anticipated if they were ever captured by the North Vietnamese.

Dorothy was sounding like those reviewers and interviewers who thought Juan Diego should somehow be more Mexican-American *as a writer*. Because he was a Mexican American, was he *supposed* to write like one? Or was it that he was supposed to write about *being* one? (Weren't his critics essentially telling him what his subject should be?)

'Don't become one of those Mexicans who—' Pepe

had blurted out to Juan Diego, before stopping himself.

'Who *what*?' Flor had asked Pepe.

'One of those Mexicans who hate Mexico,' Pepe had dared to say, before hugging Juan Diego to him. 'You don't want to become one of those Mexicans who are always coming back, either – the ones who can't stay away,' Pepe had added.

Flor had just stared at poor Pepe; she'd given him a withering look. 'What else *shouldn't* he become?' she'd asked Pepe. 'What *other* kind of Mexican is forbidden?'

Flor had never understood the *writing* part of it: how there would be expectations of what a Mexican-American writer should (or shouldn't) write about – how what was *forbidden* (in the minds of many reviewers and interviewers) was a Mexican-American writer who *didn't* write about the Mexican-American 'experience.'

If you accept the Mexican-American label, Juan Diego believed, then you accept performing to those expectations.

And compared to what had happened to Juan Diego in Mexico – compared to his childhood and early adolescence in Oaxaca – nothing had happened to Juan Diego since he'd moved to the United States that he felt was worth writing about.

Yes, he had an exciting younger lover, but her politics – better said, what Dorothy imagined his politics *should* be – drove her to explain the importance of where they were to him. She didn't understand.

Juan Diego didn't need to be in northwestern Luzon, or see it, in order to imagine those 'frightened nineteen-year-olds.'

Perhaps it was the reflection of the headlights from a passing car, but a glint of a lighter color flashed in Dorothy's dark eyes and for just a second or two, they turned a tawny yellow – like a lion's eyes – and, in that instant, the past reclaimed Juan Diego.

It was as if he'd never left Oaxaca; in the predawn darkness of the dogs' troupe tent, redolent of the dogs' breath, no other future awaited him but his life as his sister's interpreter at La Maravilla. Juan Diego didn't have the balls for skywalking. Circus of The Wonder had no use for a *ceiling*-walker. (Juan Diego hadn't yet realized there would be no skywalker after Dolores.) When you're fourteen and you're depressed, grasping the idea that you could have another future is like trying to see in the dark. 'In every life,' Dolores had said, 'I think there's always a moment when you must decide where you *belong*.'

IN THE DOGS' TROUPE tent, the darkness before dawn was impenetrable. When Juan Diego couldn't sleep, he tried to identify everyone's breathing. If he couldn't hear Estrella's snoring, he figured she was dead or sleeping in another tent. (This morning, Juan Diego remembered what he'd known beforehand: Estrella was taking one of her nights off from sleeping with the dogs.)

Alemania slept the most soundly of the dogs; her breathing was the deepest, the least disturbed.

(Her waking life as a policewoman probably tired her out.)

Baby was the most active dreamer of the dogs; his short legs ran in his sleep, or he was digging with his forepaws. (Baby woofed when he was closing in on an imaginary kill.)

As Lupe had complained, Perro Mestizo was 'always the bad guy.' To judge the mongrel strictly by his farting – well, he was definitely the bad guy in the dogs' troupe tent (unless the parrot man was also sleeping there).

As for Pastora, she was like Juan Diego – a worrier, an insomniac. When Pastora was awake, she panted and paced; she whined in her sleep, as if happiness were as fleeting for her as a good night's rest.

'Lie down, Pastora,' Juan Diego said as quietly as he could – he didn't want to wake the other dogs.

This morning, he'd easily singled out the breathing of each dog. Lupe was always the hardest to hear; she slept so quietly, she seemed to breathe scarcely at all. Juan Diego was straining to hear Lupe when his hand touched something under his pillow. He needed to grope around for the flashlight under his cot before he could see what his under-the-pillow hand had found.

The missing lid to the once-sacred coffee can of ashes was like any other plastic lid, except for its smell; there'd been more *chemicals* in those ashes than there were traces of Esperanza or the good gringo or Dirty White. And whatever magic might have been contained in the Virgin Mary's old nose, it wasn't something you could smell. There was more of the basurero on that coffee-can lid than there was anything *otherworldly* about it; yet Lupe had saved it – she'd wanted Juan Diego to have it.

Also tucked under Juan Diego's pillow was the lanyard with the keys to the feeding-tray slots in the lion cages. There were two keys, of course – one for Hombre's cage and the other for the lionesses'.

The bandmaster's wife enjoyed weaving lanyards; she'd made one for her husband's whistle when he was conducting the circus band. And the band-master's wife had made another lanyard for Lupe. The strands of Lupe's lanyard were crimson and white; Lupe wore the lanyard around her neck when she carried the keys to the lion cages at feeding time.

'Lupe?' Juan Diego asked, more quietly than he'd told Pastora to lie down. No one heard him – not even one of the dogs. 'Lupe!' Juan Diego said sharply, shining the flashlight on her empty cot.

'I am where I always am,' Lupe was always saying. Not this time. This time, just as the dawn was break-ing, Juan Diego found Lupe in Hombre's cage.

Even when the feeding tray was removed from the slot at the floor of the cage, the slot wasn't big enough for Hombre to escape through the opening.

'It's safe,' Edward Bonshaw had told Juan Diego, when the Iowan first observed how Lupe fed the lions. 'I just wanted to be sure about the size of the opening.'

But on their first night in Mexico City, Lupe had said to her brother: 'I can fit through the slot where the feeding tray slides in and out. It's not too small an opening for *me* to fit through.'

'You sound like you've *tried* it,' Juan Diego had said.

'Why would I try it?' Lupe asked him.

'I don't know – why *would* you?' Juan Diego asked her.

Lupe hadn't answered him – not that night in Mexico City, not ever. Juan Diego had always known that Lupe was usually right about the past; it was the future she didn't do accurately. Mind readers aren't necessarily any good at fortune-telling, but Lupe must have believed she'd seen the future. Was it *her* future she imagined she saw, or was it Juan Diego's future she was trying to change? Did Lupe believe she'd envisioned what their future would be if they stayed at the circus, and if things remained as they were at La Maravilla?

Lupe had always been isolated – as if being a thirteen-year-old girl isn't isolating enough! We'll never know what Lupe believed, but it must have been a terrifying burden at thirteen. (She knew her breasts weren't going to grow any bigger; she knew she wouldn't get her period.)

More broadly, Lupe had foreseen a future that frightened her, and she seized an opportunity to change it – dramatically. More than her brother's future would be altered by what Lupe did. What she did would make Juan Diego live the rest of his life in his imagination, and what happened to Lupe (and to Dolores) would mark the beginning of the end of La Maravilla.

In Oaxaca, long after everyone had stopped talking about The Day of the Nose, the more talkative citizens of the city still gossiped over the lurid dissolution – the sensational demise – of their Circus of The Wonder. It is unquestionable that what Lupe did would have an *effect*, but that isn't the question. What Lupe did was also terrible. Brother Pepe, who knew and loved orphans, said later it was the kind of thing that only an extremely distraught thirteen-year-old would have thought of. (Well, yes, but there's not much anyone can do about what thirteen-year-olds *think of*, is there?)

Lupe must have unlocked the slot for the feeding tray in Hombre's cage the night before – that way, she could leave the lanyard with the keys to the lion cages under Juan Diego's pillow.

Maybe Hombre was agitated because Lupe had shown up to feed him when it was still dark outside – that was unusual. And Lupe had slid the feeding tray entirely out of the cage; furthermore, she didn't put the meat on the tray for Hombre.

What happened next is anyone's guess; Ignacio speculated that Lupe must have brought the meat to Hombre by crawling inside his cage. Juan Diego believed that Lupe may have pretended to eat Hombre's meat, or at least she would have tried to keep the meat away from him. (As Lupe had explained the lion-feeding process to Señor Eduardo, you wouldn't believe how much lions think about *meat*.)

And, from the first time she met him, hadn't Lupe called Hombre 'the last dog' – *'the last one,'* hadn't she repeated? 'El último perro,' she'd distinctly said of the lion. 'El último.' (As if Hombre were the king of the rooftop dogs, the king of *biters* – the *last* biter.)

'It'll be all right,' Lupe had repeated to Hombre, from the beginning. 'Nothing's your fault,' she'd told the lion.

That was not how the lion looked, when Juan Diego saw him sitting in a corner at the back of his cage. Hombre looked guilty. Hombre was sitting at the farthest possible distance from where Lupe lay curled in a ball – in the diagonally opposite corner of the lion's cage. Lupe was curled up in the corner nearest the open slot for the feeding tray; her face was turned away from Juan Diego. At the time, he was grateful he'd been spared seeing Lupe's expression. Later, Juan Diego would wish he'd seen her face – it might have spared him from imagining her expression for the rest of his life.

Hombre had killed Lupe with one bite – 'a crushing bite to the back of the neck,' as Dr. Vargas would describe it after examining her body. There were no other wounds on Lupe's body – not even a claw mark. There were scant traces of blood in the area of the bite marks on Lupe's neck, and not a drop of Lupe's blood anywhere in the lion's cage. (Ignacio later said that Hombre would have licked up any blood – the lion had finished eating all the meat, too.)

After Ignacio shot Hombre – twice, in his big head – there was quite a lot of the lion's blood in that corner of his cage, where Hombre had banished himself. Looking remorseful wouldn't save the confused and sorrowful lion. Ignacio had taken a quick look at the placement of Lupe's body near the open slot for the feeding tray, and at the diagonally opposite (almost submissive) position Hombre had chosen in the farthest corner of the lion's cage. And when Juan Diego had come limping, on the run, to the lion tamer's tent, Ignacio had brought his gun with him to the scene of the crime.

Ignacio shot Mañana because the horse had a broken leg. In Juan Diego's opinion, Ignacio wasn't justified in shooting Hombre. Lupe had been right: what happened wasn't the lion's fault. What motivated Ignacio to shoot Hombre was twofold. The lion tamer was a coward; he didn't dare go inside Hombre's cage after the lion had killed Lupe – not when Hombre was alive. (The tension in the lion's cage, after Lupe was killed, was unknown territory.) And Ignacio was assuredly motivated by some macho bullshit of the 'man-eater' mentality – namely, the lion tamer needed to believe that instances of humans falling victim to lions were *always* the lions' fault.

And of course, however misguided Lupe's thinking was, she'd been right about everything that *would* happen if Hombre killed her. Lupe knew Ignacio would shoot Hombre – she must have known what would happen as a result of that, too.

As it turned out, Juan Diego wouldn't fully appreciate Lupe's foresight (her superhuman, if not divine, omniscience) until the following morning.

The day Lupe was killed, Circo de La Maravilla was

overrun by those types Ignacio thought of as the 'authorities.' Because the lion tamer had always seen himself as *the* authority, Ignacio did not function very well in the presence of *other* authorities – the police, and people with similarly official roles to play.

The lion tamer was curt with Juan Diego when the boy told him that Lupe had fed the lionesses before she fed Hombre. Juan Diego knew this, because he figured that Lupe would have thought *no one* would feed the lionesses that day if she didn't.

Juan Diego also knew this because he'd gone to have a look at the lionesses after Lupe and Hombre were killed. The night before, Lupe had unlocked the slot for the feeding tray in the cage for the lionesses, too. She must have fed the lionesses the usual way; then she'd pulled the feeding tray entirely out, leaving it leaning against the outside of the lionesses' cage, exactly the way she'd left the feeding tray to Hombre's cage.

Besides, the lionesses *looked* as if they'd been fed; 'las señoritas,' as Ignacio called them, were just lying around at the back of their cage and had simply stared at Juan Diego in their unreadable way.

Ignacio's response to Juan Diego made the boy feel it didn't matter to the lion tamer whether Lupe had fed the lionesses before she died, or not, but it *did* matter, as things would turn out. It mattered a lot. It meant that no one else had to feed the lionesses on the day Lupe and Hombre were killed.

Juan Diego even tried to give Ignacio the two keys

to the slots in the lion cages for the feeding trays, but Ignacio didn't want the keys. 'Keep them – I got my own keys,' the lion tamer told him.

Naturally, Brother Pepe and Edward Bonshaw hadn't allowed Juan Diego to spend another night in the dogs' troupe tent. Pepe and Señor Eduardo had helped Juan Diego pack his things, together with Lupe's few things – namely, her clothes. (Lupe had no keepsakes; she didn't miss her Coatlicue figurine, not since Mary's new nose.)

In the hasty move from La Maravilla to Lost Children, Juan Diego would lose the lid to the coffee can that had held the nose-inspiring ashes, but that night he slept in his old room at Lost Children, and he went to bed with Lupe's lanyard around his neck. He could feel the two keys to the lion cages; in the dark, he squeezed the keys between his thumb and index finger before he fell asleep. Next to him, in the small bed Lupe used to sleep in, the parrot man watched over him – that is, when the Iowan wasn't snoring.

Boys dream of being heroes; after Juan Diego lost Lupe, he wouldn't have those dreams. He knew his sister had sought to save him; he knew he'd failed to save her. An aura of fate had marked him – even at fourteen, Juan Diego knew this, too.

The morning after he lost Lupe, Juan Diego woke to the sound of children chanting – the kindergartners were repeating Sister Gloria's responsive prayer. 'Ahora y siempre,' the kindergartners recited. 'Now and forever' – not this, not for the rest of my life, Juan Diego was thinking; he was awake, but he kept his eyes closed. Juan Diego didn't want to see his old room at Lost Children; he didn't want to see Lupe's small bed, with no one (or perhaps the parrot man) in it.

That next morning, Lupe's body would have been with Dr. Vargas. Father Alfonso and Father Octavio had already asked Vargas for a viewing of the child's body; the two old priests wanted to bring one of the nuns from Lost Children with them to Cruz Roja. There were questions about how Lupe's body should be dressed, and – given the lion bite – whether or not an open casket was advisable. (Brother Pepe had said he couldn't do it – that is, *view* Lupe's body. That was why the two old priests asked Vargas for a viewing.)

That morning, as far as anyone at La Maravilla knew – except for Ignacio, who knew differently – Dolores had simply run away. It was the talk of the circus, how The Wonder herself had just disappeared; it seemed so unlikely that no one had seen her in Oaxaca. A pretty girl like that, with long legs like hers, couldn't just vanish from sight, could she?

Maybe only Ignacio knew that Dolores was in Guadalajara; maybe the amateur abortion had already occurred, and the peritoneal infection was just developing. Perhaps Dolores believed she would recover soon, and she'd started her return trip to Oaxaca.

That morning, at Lost Children, Edward Bonshaw must have had a lot on his mind. He had a huge confession to make to Father Alfonso and Father Octavio – not the kind of confession the two old priests were used to. And Señor Eduardo knew he needed the Church's help. The scholastic had not only forsaken his vows; the Iowan was a gay man in love with a transvestite.

How could two such people hope to adopt an orphan? Why would anyone allow Edward Bonshaw and Flor to be legal guardians of Juan Diego? (Señor Eduardo didn't just need the Church's *help*; he needed the Church to bend the rules, more than a little.)

That morning, at La Maravilla, Ignacio knew he had to feed the lionesses himself. Who could the lion tamer have persuaded to do it for him? Soledad wasn't speaking to him, and Ignacio had managed to make the girl acrobats afraid of the lions; his bullshit about the lions sensing when the girls got their periods had scared the young acrobats away. Even before Hombre killed Lupe, the girls were frightened – even of the lionesses.

'It's the lionesses the lion tamer should be afraid of,' Lupe had predicted.

That morning, the day after Ignacio shot and killed Hombre, the lion tamer must have made a mistake when he was feeding the lionesses. 'They can't fool me – I know what they're thinking,' Ignacio had bragged about the lionesses. 'The young ladies are obvious,' the lion tamer had told Lupe. 'I don't need a mind reader for las señoritas.'

Ignacio had told Lupe he could read the lionesses' minds by the body parts they were named for.

That morning, the lionesses must not have been as

easy to read as the lion tamer once thought. According to studies of lions in the Serengeti, as Vargas would later impart to Juan Diego, lionesses are responsible for the majority of the kills. Lionesses know how to hunt as a team; when stalking a herd of wildebeest or zebra, they encircle the herd, cutting off any escape routes, before they attack.

When the dump kids had just met Hombre for the first time, Flor whispered to Edward Bonshaw: 'If you think you just saw the king of beasts, think again. You're about to meet him now. Ignacio is the king of beasts.'

'The king of *pigs*,' Lupe had suddenly said.

As for those statistics from the Serengeti, or other studies of lions, the only part the king of *pigs* might have understood was what took place in the wild after the lionesses had killed their prey. That was when the male lions asserted their dominance – they ate their fill before the lionesses were allowed to eat their share. Juan Diego was sure the king of *pigs* would have been okay with that.

That morning, no one saw what happened to Ignacio when he was feeding the lionesses, but lionesses know how to be patient; lionesses have learned to wait their turn. Las señoritas – Ignacio's young ladies – would have their turn. That morning, the beginning of the end of La Maravilla would be complete.

Paco and Beer Belly were the first to find the lion tamer's body; the dwarf clowns were waddling along the avenue of troupe tents, on their way to the outdoor showers. They must have wondered how it was possible that the lionesses could have killed Ignacio when his mangled body was outside their cage. But anyone familiar with how lionesses work could figure it out, and Dr. Vargas (naturally, Vargas was the one who examined Ignacio's body) had little difficulty reconstructing a likely sequence of events.

As a novelist, when Juan Diego talked about plot – specifically, how he approached plotting a novel – he liked to talk about the 'teamwork of lionesses' as 'an early model.' In interviews, Juan Diego would begin by saying that no one saw what happened to the lion tamer; he would then say that he never tired of reconstructing a likely sequence of events, which was at least partially responsible for his becoming a novelist. And if you add together what happened to Ignacio with what Lupe might have been thinking – well, you can see what could have fueled the dump reader's imagination, can't you?

Ignacio put the meat for the lionesses on the feeding tray, as usual. He slid the feeding tray into the open slot in the cage, as usual. Then something unusual must have happened.

Vargas couldn't restrain himself from describing the extraordinary number of claw wounds on Ignacio's arms, his shoulders, the back of his neck; one of the lionesses had grabbed him first – then other paws, with claws, took hold of him. The lionesses must have hugged him close to the bars of their cage.

Vargas said the lion tamer's nose was gone, as were

his ears, both cheeks, his chin; Vargas said the fingers of both hands were gone – the lionesses had overlooked one thumb. What killed Ignacio, Vargas said, was a suffocating throat bite – what the doctor described as a 'messy one.'

'This was no clean kill,' as Vargas would put it. He explained that a lioness could kill a wildebeest or a zebra with a single suffocating throat bite, but the bars of the cage were too close together; the lioness who eventually killed Ignacio with a suffocating throat bite couldn't fit her head between the bars – she didn't get to open her jaws as widely as she wanted to before she got a good grip on the lion tamer's throat. (This was why Vargas used the *messy* word to describe the lethal bite.)

After the fact, the 'authorities' (as Ignacio thought of them) would investigate the wrongdoings at La Maravilla. That was what always happened after a fatal accident at a circus – the experts arrived and told you what you were doing wrong. (The experts said the amount of meat that Ignacio was feeding the lions was wrong; the number of times the lions were fed was also wrong.)

Who cares? Juan Diego would think; he couldn't remember what the experts said would have been the *correct* number of times or the *right* amount. What was wrong with La Maravilla had been what was wrong with Ignacio himself. The *lion tamer* had been wrong! In the end, no one at La Maravilla needed experts to tell them that.

In the end, Juan Diego would think, what Ignacio

saw were those gathering yellow eyes – the final looks, less than fond, from his señoritas – the unforgiving eyes of the lion tamer's last young ladies.

THERE'S A POSTSCRIPT TO every circus that goes under. Where do the performers go when a circus goes out of business? The Wonder herself, we know, went out of business fairly soon. But we also know, don't we, that the other performers at La Maravilla couldn't do what Dolores did? As Juan Diego had discovered, not everyone could be a skywalker.

Estrella would find homes for the dogs. Well, no one wanted the mongrel; Estrella had to take him. As Lupe had said, Perro Mestizo was always the bad guy.

And no other circus had wanted Pajama Man; his vanity preceded him. For a while, on the weekends, the contortionist could be seen contorting himself for the tourists in the zócalo.

Dr. Vargas would later say he was sorry the medical school had moved. The new medical school, which is opposite a public hospital, away from the center of town, is nowhere near the morgue and the Red Cross hospital, Vargas's old stomping grounds – where the old medical school was, when Vargas still taught there.

That was the last place Vargas saw Pajama Man – at the old medical school. The contortionist's cadaver was hoisted from the acid bath to a corrugated metal gurney; the fluid in Pajama Man's cadaver drained into a pail through a hole in the gurney, near the contortionist's head. On the sloped steel autopsy slab – with a deep groove running down the middle to a draining hole, also at Pajama Man's head – the cadaver was opened. Stretched out, forever uncontorted, Pajama Man was not recognizable to the medical students, but Vargas knew the onetime contortionist.

'There is no vacancy, no absence, like the expression on a cadaver's face,' Vargas would write to Juan Diego after the boy had moved to Iowa. 'The human dreams are gone,' Vargas wrote, 'but not the pain. And traces of a living person's vanity remain. You will remember Pajama Man's attention to sculpting his beard and trimming his mustache, which betrays the time the contortionist spent looking into a mirror – either admiring or seeking to improve his looks.'

'Sic transit gloria mundi,' as Father Alfonso and Father Octavio were fond of intoning, with solemnity.

'Thus passes the glory of this world,' as Sister Gloria was always reminding the orphans at Lost Children.

The Argentinian flyers were too good at their job, and too happy with each other, not to find work at another circus. Fairly recently (anything after 2001, the new century, struck Juan Diego as *recently*), Brother Pepe had heard from someone who saw them; Pepe said the Argentinian flyers were flying for a little circus in the mountains, about an hour's drive from Mexico City. They may have since retired.

After La Maravilla went out of business, Paco and

Beer Belly went to Mexico City – it was where those two dwarf clowns were from, and (according to Pepe) Beer Belly had stayed there. Beer Belly went into a different business, though Juan Diego couldn't remember what it was – Juan Diego didn't know if Beer Belly was still alive – and Juan Diego had a hard time imagining Beer Belly *not* being a clown. (Of course, Beer Belly would always be a dwarf.)

Paco, Juan Diego knew, had died. Like Flor, Paco couldn't stay away from Oaxaca. Like Flor, Paco loved to hang out at the old hanging-out places. Paco had always been a regular at La China, that gay bar on Bustamante, the place that would later become Chinampa. And Paco was also a regular at La Coronita – the cross-dressers' party place that closed, for a while, in the 1990s (when La Coronita's owner, who was gay, died). Like Edward Bonshaw and Flor, both La Coronita's owner and Paco would die of AIDS.

Soledad, who'd once called Juan Diego 'Boy Wonder,' would long outlive La Maravilla. She was still Vargas's patient. There'd been stress on her joints, no doubt – as Dr. Vargas had observed of the former trapeze artist – but these joint injuries notwithstanding, Soledad was still strong. Juan Diego would remember that she'd ended her career as a catcher, which was unusual for a woman. She'd had strong enough arms and a strong enough grip for catching men who were flying through the air.

Pepe would tell Juan Diego (around the time of the dissolution of the orphanage at Lost Children) how Vargas had been one of several people Soledad mentioned as a reference when she'd adopted two of Lost Children's orphans, a boy and a girl.

Soledad had been a wonderful mother, Pepe reported. No one was surprised. Soledad was an impressive woman – well, she could be a little *cold*, Juan Diego remembered, but he'd always admired her.

There'd been a brief scandal, but this was after Soledad's adopted kids had grown up and left home. Soledad had found herself with a bad boyfriend; neither Pepe nor Vargas would elaborate on the *bad* word, which they'd both used to describe Soledad's boyfriend, but Juan Diego took the word to mean *abusive*.

After Ignacio, Juan Diego was surprised to hear that Soledad would have had any patience for a bad boyfriend; she didn't strike him as the type of woman who would tolerate abuse.

As it turned out, Soledad didn't have to put up with the bad boyfriend for very long. She came home from shopping one morning, and there he was, dead, with his head on his arms, still sitting at the kitchen table. Soledad said he'd been sitting where he was when she'd left that morning.

'He must have had a heart attack, or something,' was all Brother Pepe ever said.

Naturally, Vargas was the examining physician. 'It may have been an intruder,' Vargas said. 'Someone who had an ax to grind – someone with strong hands,' Dr. Vargas surmised. The bad boyfriend had been strangled while sitting at the kitchen table.

The doctor said Soledad couldn't possibly have strangled her boyfriend. 'Her hands are a wreck,' Vargas had testified. 'She couldn't squeeze the juice out of a lemon!' was how Vargas had put it.

Vargas offered the prescription painkillers Soledad was taking as evidence that the 'damaged' woman couldn't have strangled anyone. The medication was for joint pain – it was mostly for the pain in Soledad's fingers and hands.

'Lots of damage – lots of pain,' the doctor had said.

Juan Diego didn't doubt it – not the damage and pain part. But, looking back – remembering Soledad in the lion tamer's tent, and the occasional glances Soledad sent in Ignacio's direction – Juan Diego had seen something in the former trapeze artist's eyes. There'd been nothing in Soledad's dark eyes resembling the yellow in a lion's eyes, but there'd definitely been something of a lioness's unreadable intentions.

29

One Single Journey

'Cockfighting is legal here, and very popular,' Dorothy was saying. 'The psycho roosters are up all night, crowing. The stupid gamecocks are psyching themselves up for their next fight.'

Well, Juan Diego thought, that might explain the psycho rooster who'd crowed before dawn that New Year's Eve at the Encantador, but not the subsequent squawk of the rooster's sudden and violent-sounding death – as if Miriam, by merely wishing the annoying rooster were dead, had made it happen.

At least he'd been forewarned, Juan Diego was thinking: there would be gamecocks crowing all night at the inn near Vigan. Juan Diego was interested to see what Dorothy would do about it.

'Someone should kill that rooster,' Miriam had said in her low, husky voice that night at the Encantador. Then, when the deranged rooster crowed a third time and his crowing was cut off mid-squawk, Miriam had said, 'There, that does it. No more heralding of a false dawn, no more untruthful messengers.'

'And because the cocks crow all night, the dogs never stop barking,' Dorothy told him.

'It sounds very restful,' Juan Diego said. The inn was a compound of buildings, all old. The Spanish architecture was obvious; maybe the inn had once been a mission, Juan Diego was thinking – there was a church among the half-dozen guesthouses.

El Escondrijo, the inn was called – 'The Hiding Place.' It was hard to discern what kind of place it was, arriving after ten o'clock at night, as they did. The other guests (if there were any) had gone to bed. The dining room was outdoors under a thatched roof, but it was open-sided, exposed to the elements, though Dorothy promised him there were no mosquitoes.

'What kills the mosquitoes?' Juan Diego asked her.

'Bats, maybe – or the ghosts,' Dorothy answered him indifferently. The bats, Juan Diego guessed, were also up all night – neither crowing nor barking, just silently killing things. Juan Diego was somewhat accustomed to ghosts, or so he thought.

The unlikely lovers were staying on the sea; there was a breeze. Juan Diego and Dorothy were not in Vigan, or in any other town, but the lights they could see were from Vigan, and there were two or three freighters anchored offshore. They could see the lights from the freighters, and when the wind was right, they could occasionally hear the ships' radios.

'There's a small swimming pool – a kids' pool, I guess you would call it,' Dorothy was saying. 'You have to be careful you don't fall in the pool at night, because they don't light it,' she warned.

There was no air-conditioning, but Dorothy said the nights were cool enough not to need it, and there was a ceiling fan in their room; the fan made a ticking sound, but given the crowing gamecocks and barking dogs, what did a ticking fan matter? The Hiding Place was not what you would call a resort.

'The local beach is adjacent to a fishing village and an elementary school, but you hear the children's voices only from a distance – with kids, hearing them from a distance is okay,' Dorothy was saying, as they were going to bed. 'The dogs in the fishing village are territorial about the beach, but you're safe if you walk on the wet sand – just stay close to the water,' Dorothy advised him.

What sort of people stay at El Escondrijo? Juan Diego was wondering. The Hiding Place made him think of fugitives or revolutionaries, not a touristy place. But Juan Diego was falling asleep; he was half asleep when Dorothy's cell phone (in the vibrate mode) made a humming sound on the night table.

'What a surprise, Mother,' he heard Dorothy say sarcastically in the dark. There was a long pause, while cocks crowed and dogs barked, before Dorothy said, 'Uh-huh,' a couple of times; she said, 'Okay,' once or twice, too, before Juan Diego heard her say, 'You're kidding, right?' And these familiar *Dorothyisms* were followed by the way the less-than-dutiful-sounding daughter ended the call. Juan

Diego heard Dorothy tell Miriam: 'You don't want to hear what I dream about – believe me, Mother.'

Juan Diego lay awake in the darkness, thinking about this mother and her daughter; he was retracing how he'd met them – he was considering how dependent on them he'd become.

'Go to sleep, darling,' Juan Diego heard Dorothy say; it was almost exactly the way Miriam would have said the *darling* word. And the young woman's hand, unerringly, reached for and found his penis, which she gave an ambivalent squeeze.

'Okay,' Juan Diego was trying to say, but the word wouldn't come. Sleep overcame him, as if on Dorothy's command.

'When I die, *don't* burn me. Give me the whole hocus-pocus,' Lupe had said, looking straight at Father Alfonso and Father Octavio. That was what Juan Diego heard in his sleep – Lupe's voice, instructing them.

Juan Diego didn't hear the crowing cocks and the barking dogs; he didn't hear the two cats fighting or fucking (or both) on the thatched roof of the outdoor shower. Juan Diego didn't hear Dorothy get up in the night, not to pee but to open the door to the outdoor shower, where she snapped on the shower light.

'Fuck off or die,' Dorothy said sharply to the cats – they stopped yowling. She spoke more softly to the ghost she saw standing in the outdoor shower, as if the water were running – it wasn't – and as if he were naked, though he was wearing clothes.

'I'm sorry, I didn't mean *you* – I was speaking to

those cats,' Dorothy told him, but the young ghost had vanished.

Juan Diego hadn't heard Dorothy's apology to the quickly disappearing prisoner of war – he was one of the ghost guests. The emaciated young man was gray-skinned and dressed in prison-gray garb – one of the tortured captives of the North Vietnamese. And by his haunted, guilty-looking expression – as Dorothy would later explain to Juan Diego – she'd surmised he was one of the ones who'd broken down under torture. Maybe the young P.O.W. had capitulated under pain. Perhaps he'd signed letters that said he did things he never did. Some of the young Americans had made broadcasts, reciting Communist propaganda.

It wasn't their fault; they shouldn't blame themselves, Dorothy always tried to tell the ghost guests at El Escondrijo, but the ghosts had a way of vanishing before you could tell them anything.

'I just want them to know they're forgiven for whatever they did, or were forced to do,' was how Dorothy would put it to Juan Diego. 'But these young ghosts keep their own hours. They don't listen to us – they don't interact with us at all.'

Dorothy would also tell Juan Diego that the captured Americans who'd died in North Vietnam didn't always dress in their gray prison garb; some of the younger ones wore their fatigues. 'I don't know if they have a choice regarding what they wear – I've seen them in sportswear, Hawaiian shirts and shit like that,' was the way Dorothy would put it to Juan Diego. 'Nobody knows the rules for ghosts.'

Juan Diego hoped he would be spared seeing the tortured P.O.W. ghosts in their Hawaiian shirts, but his first night at the old inn on the outskirts of Vigan, the ghostly appearances of the long-dead R&R clientele at El Escondrijo were as yet unseen by Juan Diego; he slept in the contentious company of his own ghosts. Juan Diego was dreaming – in this case, it was a loud dream. (It's no wonder Juan Diego didn't hear Dorothy speaking to those cats or apologizing to that ghost.)

Lupe had asked for the 'whole hocus-pocus,' and the Temple of the Society of Jesus had not held back. Brother Pepe did his best; he tried to persuade the two old priests to keep the service simple, but Pepe should have known there would be no restraining them. This was the Church's bread and butter, the death of innocents – the death of children didn't call for restraint. Lupe would get a no-holds-barred service – nothing simple about it.

Father Alfonso and Father Octavio had insisted on the open casket. Lupe was in a white dress, with a white scarf snug around her neck – hence no bite marks, no swelling, showed. (You were forced to imagine what the back of her neck must have looked like.) And there was so much incense-swinging, the unfamiliar-looking face of the broken-nosed Virgin Mary was obscured in a pungent haze. Rivera was worried about the smoke – as if Lupe were being consumed by the hellfires of the basurero, as she once would have wanted.

'Don't worry – we'll burn something later, like she said,' Juan Diego whispered to el jefe.

'I've got my eye out for a dead puppy – I'll find one,' the dump boss answered him.

They were both disconcerted by the Hijas del Calvario – the 'Daughters of Calvary,' the wailing nuns for hire.

'The professional weepers,' as Pepe called them, seemed excessive. It was enough to have Sister Gloria leading the orphaned kindergartners in their oft-rehearsed responsive prayer.

'¡Madre! Ahora y siempre,' the children repeated, after Sister Gloria. 'Mother! Now and forever, you will be my guide.' But even to this repetitive plea, and to all else – to the cry-on-command Daughters of Calvary, to the incense wreathing the Mary Monster's towering presence – the darker-skinned Virgin Mary, with her boxer's nose, made no response (not that Juan Diego could see her clearly in the rising clouds of sacred smoke).

Dr. Vargas came to Lupe's service; he rarely took his eyes from the untrustworthy statue of the Virgin Mary, nor did he join the procession of mourners (and curious tourists, or other sightseers) who filed to the front of the Jesuit temple for a look at the lion girl in her open casket. That was what they were calling Lupe, in and around Oaxaca: the 'lion girl.'

Vargas had come to Lupe's service with Alejandra; these days, she seemed to be more than a dinner-party girlfriend, and Alejandra had liked Lupe, but Vargas wouldn't join his girlfriend for a look at Lupe in the open casket.

Juan Diego and Rivera couldn't help overhearing

their conversation. 'You're not looking?' Alejandra had asked Vargas.

'I know what Lupe looks like – I've seen her,' was all Vargas said.

After that, Juan Diego and the dump boss didn't want to see Lupe all in white in the open casket. Juan Diego and el jefe had hoped that their memories of Lupe, when she was alive, would be how they always saw her. They sat unmoving in their pew, next to Vargas, thinking the way a dump kid and a dump boss think: of things to burn, of the ashes they would sprinkle at the Mary Monster's feet – '*just* sprinkle, don't throw,' as Lupe had instructed them – 'maybe not *all* the ashes, and only at her *feet*!' as Lupe had distinctly said.

The curious tourists and the other sightseers who'd seen the lion girl in her open casket rudely left the temple before the recession; apparently, they were disappointed not to see signs of the lion attack on Lupe's lifeless body. (There would be no open-casket viewing of Ignacio's body – as Dr. Vargas, who'd seen the lion tamer's remains, fully understood.)

The recessional hymn was 'Ave Maria,' unfortunately sung by an ill-chosen children's choir – also for hire, like the Daughters of Calvary. These were brats in uniforms from a superior-sounding school of music; their parents were taking snapshots during the departing procession of the clergy and the choir.

At this point, discordantly, the 'Hail Mary' choir was met by the circus band. Father Alfonso and Father Octavio had insisted that the circus band remain *outside* the Templo de la Compañía de Jesús, but La Maravilla's brass-and-drum version of 'Streets of Laredo' was difficult to suppress; their moribund and dirgelike distortion of the cowboy's lament was loud enough for Lupe herself to have heard it.

The music-school children's voices, straining to make their 'Ave Maria' heard, were no match for the uproarious blare and percussion of the circus band. You could hear the piteous lamenting of La Maravilla's 'Streets of Laredo' in the zócalo. Flor's friends – those prostitutes at work in the Hotel Somega – said the cowboy's histrionic death song reached them as far away from the Jesuit temple as Zaragoza Street.

'Perhaps the sprinkling of the ashes will be *simpler*,' Brother Pepe said hopefully to Juan Diego, as they were leaving Lupe's service – the unholy hocus-pocus, the flat-out mumbo jumbo of a Catholic kind, which was exactly what Lupe had wanted.

'Yes – more *spiritual*, perhaps,' Edward Bonshaw had chimed in.

He'd not at first understood the English translation of Hijas del Calvario, which indeed did mean 'Daughters of Calvary,' though in the pocket dictionary Señor Eduardo consulted, the Iowan seized upon the informal meaning of *Calvario* or *Calvary*, which could mean 'a series of disasters.'

Edward Bonshaw, whose life would be a series of disasters, had mistakenly imagined that the nuns who wept for hire were *called* 'Daughters of a Series of Disasters.' Given the lives of those orphans left at Lost Children, and given the awful circumstances of

Lupe's death – well, one can appreciate the parrot man's misunderstanding of the Hijas del Calvario.

And one could sympathize with Flor – her appreciation of the parrot man was wearing a little thin. Not to put too fine a point on it, but Flor had been waiting for Edward Bonshaw to shit or get off the pot. Upon Señor Eduardo's confusing the Daughters of Calvary with an order of nuns dedicated to a series of disasters – well, Flor had just rolled her eyes.

When, if ever, would Edward Bonshaw find the balls to confess his love for her to the two old priests?

'The main thing is *tolerance*, right?' Señor Eduardo was saying, as they were leaving the Temple of the Society of Jesus; they passed the portrait of Saint Ignatius, who was ignoring them but looking to Heaven for guidance. Pajama Man was splashing his face in the fountain of holy water, and Soledad and the young-women acrobats bowed their heads there as Juan Diego limped by.

Paco and Beer Belly were standing outside the temple, where the brass-and-drum bombardment of the circus band was loudest.

'¡Qué triste!' Beer Belly shouted, when he saw Juan Diego.

'Sí, sí, Lupe's brother – how sad, how sad,' Paco repeated, giving Juan Diego a hug.

Now, amid the dirgelike din of 'Streets of Laredo,' was not the time for Señor Eduardo to confess his love for Flor to Father Alfonso and Father Octavio – whether or not the Iowan would ever find the balls for such a formidable confession.

As Dolores had said to Juan Diego, when The Wonder herself was talking him down from the top of the main tent: 'I'm sure you're going to have the balls for lots of other stuff.' But *when*, and *what* other stuff? Juan Diego was wondering, while the circus band played on and on – it seemed the dirge would never end.

The way 'Streets of Laredo' was reverberating, the corner of las calles de Trujano y Flores Magón was shaking. Rivera might have felt it was safe to shout; the dump boss may have thought no one would hear him. He was wrong – not even the brass-and-drum version of the cowboy's lament could conceal what Rivera shouted.

The dump boss had turned to face the entrance to the Jesuit temple, off Flores Magón; he'd shaken his fist in the direction of the Mary Monster – he was so angry. 'We'll be back, with more ashes for you!' el jefe had shouted.

'You mean the *sprinkling*, I assume,' Brother Pepe said to the dump boss, as if Pepe were speaking conspiratorially.

'Ah, yes – the *sprinkling*,' Dr. Vargas joined in. 'Be sure you tell me when that's happening – I don't want to miss it,' he told Rivera.

'There's stuff to burn – decisions to be made,' the dump boss mumbled.

'And we don't want too many ashes – just the right amount this time,' Juan Diego added.

'And only at the Virgin Mary's *feet*!' the parrot man reminded them.

'Sí, sí – these things take time,' el jefe cautioned them.

But not always in dreams – sometimes dreams go fast. Time can be compressed in dreams.

IN REAL LIFE, IT took a few days for Dolores to show up at Cruz Roja, presenting Vargas, as she did, with her fatal peritoneal infection. (In his dream, Juan Diego would skip that part.)

In real life, el hombre papagayo – the dear parrot man – would take a few days to find the balls to say what he had to say to Father Alfonso and Father Octavio, and Juan Diego would discover that he *did* have the balls for 'lots of other stuff,' as Dolores had tried to assure him when he just froze at eighty feet. (In his dream, of course, Juan Diego would skip how many days it took him and the Iowan to discover their balls.)

And, in real life, Brother Pepe spent a couple of days doing the necessary research: the rules regarding legal guardianship, pertaining (in particular) to orphans; the role the Church could play, and had played, in appointing or recommending legal guardians for kids in the care of Lost Children. Pepe had a good head for this kind of paperwork; constructing Jesuitical arguments from history was a procedure he understood well.

It was unremarkable, in Pepe's opinion, how often Father Alfonso and Father Octavio were on record for saying, 'We are a Church of rules'; yet Pepe discovered that the two old priests were not once on record for saying they could or would *bend* the rules. What was remarkable was how frequently Father Alfonso and Father Octavio *had* bent the rules – some orphans weren't very adoptable; not every potential guardian was indisputably suitable. And, not surprisingly, Pepe's precisionist preparation and presentation regarding *why* Edward Bonshaw and Flor were (in Juan Diego's difficult case) the dump reader's *most* suitable guardians imaginable – well, you can understand why these academic disputations weren't dream material. (When it came to dreaming, Juan Diego would skip Pepe's Jesuitical arguments, too.)

Last but not least, in real life, it would take a few days for Rivera and Juan Diego to sort out the burning business – not only what went into the fire at the basurero, but how long to let it burn and how many ashes to take out. This time, the container for the ashes would be small – not a coffee can but just a coffee cup. It was a cup Lupe had liked for her hot chocolate; she'd left it in the shack in Guerrero, where el jefe had kept it for her.

There was, importantly, a second part to Lupe's last requests – the sprinkling-of-the-ashes part – but the preparation of those interesting ashes would also be absent from Juan Diego's dream. (Dreams not only can go fast; they can be very selective.)

His first night at El Escondrijo, Juan Diego got up to pee – he wouldn't remember what happened, because he was still dreaming. He sat down to pee; he could pee more quietly sitting down, and he didn't want to wake up Dorothy, but there was a second reason for his sitting down. He'd seen his cell phone – it was on the countertop next to the toilet.

Because he was dreaming, Juan Diego probably didn't remember that the bathroom was the only place he could find to plug in his cell phone; there was only one outlet next to the night table in the bedroom, and Dorothy had beaten him to it – she was such an aware young woman, technologically speaking.

Juan Diego wasn't at all aware. He still didn't understand how his cell phone worked, nor could he access the things on (or not on) his cell phone's irritating menu – those things other people found so easily and stared at with such transfixed fascination. Juan Diego didn't find his cell phone very interesting – not to the degree that other people did. In his routine life in Iowa City, there had been no younger person to show him how to use his mysterious phone. (It was one of those already-old-fashioned cell phones that flipped open.)

It irked him – even half asleep, and dreaming, and peeing while he was sitting down – that he *still* couldn't find the photo the young Chinese man had taken in the underground of Kowloon Station.

They could all hear the train coming – the boy had to hurry. The photo caught Juan Diego, and Miriam and Dorothy, by surprise. The Chinese couple seemed to think it was a disappointing picture – perhaps out of focus? – but then the train was there. It was Miriam who'd snatched the cell phone away from the couple, and Dorothy who – even more quickly – had taken it from her mom. When Dorothy gave him back his phone, it was no longer in the camera mode.

'We don't photograph well,' was all Miriam had said to the Chinese couple, who'd seemed unduly disturbed by the incident. (Perhaps the pictures they took usually turned out better.)

And now, sitting on the toilet in his bathroom at El Escondrijo, Juan Diego discovered – completely by accident, and probably because he was half asleep and dreaming – that there was an easier way to find that photo taken at Kowloon Station. Juan Diego wouldn't even remember how he found the picture the young Chinese man took. He'd unintentionally touched a button on the side of his cell phone; suddenly his screen said, 'Starting Camera.' He could have taken a photo of his bare knees, extending from the toilet seat, but he must have seen the 'My Pics' option – that was how he saw the photo taken at Kowloon Station, not that he would remember doing this.

In fact, in the morning, Juan Diego would think he'd only *dreamed* about the photograph, because what he'd seen when he was sitting on the toilet – what he'd seen in the actual photo – couldn't have been real, or so he thought.

In the photo Juan Diego had seen, he was alone on the train platform at Kowloon Station – as Miriam had said, she and Dorothy truly *didn't* 'photograph well.' No wonder Miriam had said that she and Dorothy couldn't stand the way they looked in photographs – they didn't show up in photos, at all!

No wonder the young Chinese couple, who'd seen the picture, seemed *unduly disturbed*.

But Juan Diego wasn't really awake in the present moment; he was in the grip of the most important dream and memory in his life – the sprinkling part. Besides, Juan Diego couldn't have accepted (not yet) that Miriam and Dorothy hadn't been captured in the photo at Kowloon Station – the one that caught all three of them by surprise.

And when Juan Diego, as quietly as possible, flushed the toilet in his bathroom at The Hiding Place, he failed to see the young ghost standing anxiously under the outdoor shower. This was a different ghost from the one Dorothy saw; this one was wearing his fatigues – he looked too young to have started shaving. (Dorothy must have left the shower light on.)

In the split second before this young ghost could vanish, forever missing in action, Juan Diego had limped back into the bedroom; he would have no memory of seeing himself alone on the train platform at Kowloon Station. Knowing that he *hadn't* been alone on that platform was sufficient to make Juan Diego believe he'd merely dreamed he was making this journey without Miriam and Dorothy.

As he lay down beside Dorothy – at least it seemed to Juan Diego that Dorothy was really there – perhaps the *journey* word reminded him of something before he could fall back to sleep and fully return to the past. Where had he put that round-trip ticket to

Kowloon Station? He knew he'd saved it, for some reason; he'd written something on the ticket with his ever-present pen. The title for a future novel, perhaps? *One Single Journey* – was that it?

Yes, that was it! But his thoughts (like his dreams) were so disjointed, it was hard for him to focus. Maybe it was a night when Dorothy had dispensed a double dose of the beta-blockers – not a night to have sex, in other words, but one of those nights to make up for the beta-blockers he'd skipped? If so – if he'd taken a double dose of his Lopressor prescription – would it have mattered if Juan Diego had seen the young ghost standing anxiously under the outdoor shower? Wouldn't Juan Diego have believed he was only dreaming he saw the soldier's ghost?

One Single Journey – it almost sounded like the title for a novel he'd already written, Juan Diego was thinking as he drifted back to sleep, more deeply into his lifelong dream. He thought of 'single' in the sense of unaccompanied by others – in the sense of *lone* or *sole* – but also 'single' in the sense of having no equal (in the sense of *singular*, Juan Diego supposed).

Then, as suddenly as he'd gotten up and gone back to bed, Juan Diego wasn't thinking anymore. Once again, the past had reclaimed him.

30

The Sprinkling

The sprinkling part of Lupe's last requests did not have a very spiritual start. Brother Pepe had been talking to an American immigration lawyer – this was in addition to Pepe's talks with the authorities in Mexico. The *legal guardian* words weren't the only ones in play; it would be necessary for Edward Bonshaw to 'sponsor' Flor for 'permanent residency,' Pepe was saying as discreetly as possible. Only Señor Eduardo and Flor could hear him.

Naturally, Flor objected to Pepe's saying she had a criminal record. (This would call for more bending of the rules.) 'I haven't done anything *criminal*!' Flor protested. She'd had a run-in or two – the Oaxaca police had busted her once or twice.

According to police records, there'd been a couple of beatings at the Hotel Somega, but Flor said she'd 'only' beaten up Garza – 'that thug-pimp had it coming!' – and, another night, she'd kicked the shit out of César, Garza's slave boy. These weren't *criminal* beatings, Flor had maintained. As for what had happened to Flor in Houston, the American immigration lawyer told Pepe that nothing had turned up. (The pony in the postcard, which Señor Eduardo would forever keep secret, in his heart, didn't amount to a matter of criminal record – not in Texas.)

And before the sprinkling got started in the Jesuit temple, some unspiritual attention was paid to the contents of the ashes.

'Exactly what was burned, if we may ask?' Father Alfonso began with the dump boss.

'We hope there are no *foreign substances* this time,' was the way Father Octavio put it to Rivera.

'Lupe's clothes, a lanyard she wore around her neck, a couple of keys – plus an odd this or that from Guerrero,' Juan Diego told the two old priests.

'Mostly *circus* things?' Father Alfonso asked.

'Well, the burning was done at the basurero – burning is a dump thing,' el jefe answered warily.

'Yes, yes – we know,' Father Octavio quickly said. 'But the *contents* of these ashes are mostly from Lupe's life at the circus – is that true?' the priest asked the dump boss.

'*Mostly* circus things,' Rivera mumbled; he was being careful not to mention Lupe's puppy place, where she'd found Dirty White. The puppy place was near the shack in Guerrero, where el jefe had found a new dead puppy for Lupe's fire.

Because they'd asked to be included at the sprinkling, Vargas and Alejandra were there. It had already been a bad day for Vargas; the business with Dolores's lethal infection had forced the doctor to deal with various authorities, not a satisfying process.

Father Alfonso and Father Octavio had chosen the siesta time of day for the sprinkling, but some of the homeless types – drunks and hippies, who hung out in the zócalo – liked churches for their afternoon naps. The hindmost pews of the Jesuit temple were temporary resting places for these undesirables; therefore, the two old priests wanted the sprinkling to proceed *quietly*. The sprinkling of ashes, if only at the Virgin Mary's *feet*, was an irregular request. Father Alfonso and Father Octavio didn't want the public to get the idea that *anyone* could sprinkle ashes in the Temple of the Society of Jesus.

'Be careful of the little Jesus – don't get the ashes in his eyes,' Lupe had told her brother.

Juan Diego, holding the coffee cup Lupe once liked for her hot chocolate, approached the unreadable Mary Monster respectfully.

'The ashes seemed to affect you – I mean the last time,' Juan Diego began cautiously; it was difficult to know how to speak to such a towering presence. 'I'm not trying to trick you. These ashes are not *her* – they're just her clothes, and a few things she liked. I hope that's okay,' he said to the giant virgin, sprinkling a few ashes on the three-tiered pedestal where the Mary Monster stood – her big feet standing in an essentially meaningless motif, an unnatural configuration of angels frozen in clouds. (It was impossible to sprinkle ashes at the Virgin Mary's feet without the ashes getting in the angels' eyes, but Lupe had said nothing about being careful of the angels.)

Juan Diego went on sprinkling, ever mindful that

the ashes went nowhere near the agonizing face of the shrunken, suffering Christ – there weren't many ashes left in the little cup.

'May I say something?' Brother Pepe suddenly asked.

'Of course, Pepe,' Father Alfonso said.

'Speak up, Pepe,' Father Octavio urged him.

But Pepe wasn't asking the two old priests; he'd dropped to his knees before the giantess – he was asking *her.* 'One of us, our beloved Edward – our dear Eduardo – has something to ask you, Mother Mary,' Pepe said. 'Don't you, Eduardo?' Brother Pepe asked the Iowan.

Edward Bonshaw had more balls than, heretofore, Flor had thought. 'I'm sorry if I disappoint you,' Señor Eduardo said to the impassive-looking Mary Monster, 'but I have forsaken my vows – I am in love. With *her,*' the Iowan added; he'd glanced at Flor, his voice trembling as he bowed his head at the Virgin Mary's big feet. 'I'm sorry if I disappoint you, too,' Edward Bonshaw said, looking over his shoulder at the two old priests. 'Please let us go – please *help* us,' Señor Eduardo asked Father Alfonso and Father Octavio. 'I want to take Juan Diego with me – I am dedicated to this boy,' the Iowan told the two old priests. 'I'll look after him properly – I promise you,' Edward Bonshaw implored the giant virgin.

'I love you,' Flor told the Iowan, who began to sob, his shoulders shaking in his Hawaiian shirt, in those trees ablaze with parrots riotously represented there. 'I've done questionable things,' Flor said suddenly to the Virgin Mary. 'I've not had many opportunities to meet what you would call good people. Please help us,' Flor said, turning to the two old priests.

'I want another future!' Juan Diego cried – at first to the Mary Monster, but he had no more ashes to sprinkle at the feet of the unresponsive giantess. He turned to Father Alfonso and Father Octavio instead. 'Let me go with them, please. I've tried it here – let me try Iowa,' the boy beseeched them.

'This is shameful, Edward—' Father Alfonso started to say.

'The two of you – the very idea! That you two should raise a *child*—' Father Octavio sputtered.

'You're not a *couple*!' Father Alfonso said to Señor Eduardo.

'You're not even a *woman*!' Father Octavio said to Flor.

'Only a married couple can—' Father Alfonso started to say.

'This boy can't—' Father Octavio blurted out, before Dr. Vargas interrupted him.

'What are this boy's chances *here*?' Vargas asked the two old priests. 'What are Juan Diego's prospects in Oaxaca, after he leaves Lost Children?' Vargas asked, more loudly. 'I just saw the star of La Maravilla – The Wonder herself!' Vargas cried. 'If Dolores didn't have a chance, what are the dump kid's chances? If the boy goes with *them*, he's got a shot!' Vargas shouted, pointing at the parrot man and Flor.

This was not the *quiet* sprinkling the two old priests once had in mind. Vargas woke up the homeless types with his shouting; from the hindmost pews of the temple, the drunks and hippies had risen – well, except for one hippie; he'd fallen asleep under a pew. They could all see his scuffed, forlorn-looking sandals where the hippie's dirty feet extended into the center aisle.

'We didn't ask for your *scientific opinion*, Vargas,' Father Alfonso said sarcastically.

'Please keep your voice down—' Father Octavio started to say to the doctor.

'My *voice*!' Vargas screamed. 'What if Alejandra and I wanted to adopt Juan Diego—' he started to ask, but Father Alfonso was faster.

'You're not married, Vargas,' Father Alfonso said calmly.

'Your rules! What do your rules have to do with the way people actually live?' Vargas asked him.

'This is our Church – these are our rules, Vargas,' Father Alfonso told him quietly.

'We are a Church of rules—' Father Octavio started to say. (It was the hundredth time Pepe had heard it.)

'We make the rules,' Pepe pointed out, 'but don't we, *can't* we, also bend them? I thought we believed in charity.'

'You do favors for the "authorities" all the time – they owe you favors in return, don't they?' Vargas asked the two old priests. 'This boy has no better chance than these two—' Vargas had started to say, but Father Octavio suddenly decided to shoo the homeless types out of the temple; he was distracted. Only Father Alfonso was listening to Vargas – hence

Vargas interrupted himself, though it seemed pointless (even to Vargas) to continue. It was hopeless to think the two old priests could be persuaded.

Juan Diego, for one, was through asking them. 'Please just *do* something,' the boy said despairingly to the giant virgin. 'You're supposed to be somebody, but you don't do anything!' Juan Diego cried to the Mary Monster. 'If you can't help me – okay, okay – but can't you do *anything*? Just *do* something, if you can,' the boy said to the towering statue, but his voice trailed off. His heart wasn't in it; what small belief he'd had was gone.

Juan Diego turned away from the Mary Monster – he couldn't look at her. Flor had already turned her back on the giant virgin; Flor was no Mary worshiper, to begin with. Even Edward Bonshaw had turned his face away from the Virgin Mary, though the Iowan's hand lingered on the pedestal, just below the virgin's big feet.

The homeless types had straggled their aimless way out of the temple; Father Octavio was returning to the unhappy gathering at the main attraction. Father Alfonso and Brother Pepe exchanged glances, but they quickly looked away from each other. Vargas had not been paying much attention to the Virgin Mary, not this time – all the doctor's efforts were directed to the two old priests. And Alejandra was in her own world, whatever world that was: an unmarried young woman with a solitary-minded young doctor. (*That* world, whatever you call it – if there's a name for it.)

No one was asking the giant virgin for anything –
not anymore – and only one of the attendees at the
sprinkling, the one who hadn't said a word, was
watching the Virgin Mary. Rivera was watching her
very closely; he'd been watching her, and only
her, from the start.

'Look at her,' the dump boss told all of them. 'Don't
you see? You have to come closer – her face is so far
away. Her head is so high – up there.' They could all
see where el jefe was pointing, but they had to come
closer to see the Virgin Mary's eyes. The statue was
very tall.

The first of the Mary Monster's tears fell on the
back of Edward Bonshaw's hand; her tears fell from
such a height, they made quite an impact, quite a
splash.

'Don't you see?' the dump boss asked them again.
'She's crying. See her eyes? See her tears?'

Pepe had come close enough; he was staring
straight up, at the Virgin Mary's crooked nose, when
a giant teardrop hit him like a hailstone, landing
smack between his eyes. More of the Mary Monster's
tears were striking the uplifted palms of the parrot
man's hands. Flor refused to reach out her hand for
falling tears, but she stood near enough to Señor
Eduardo to feel the tears hitting him, and Flor could
see the broken-nosed virgin's tear-streaked face.

Vargas and Alejandra had a different kind of
curiosity concerning the giant virgin's falling tears.
Alejandra tentatively held out her hand – she sniffed
a teardrop in the palm of her hand before wiping her

hand on her hip. Vargas, of course, went so far as to taste the tears; he was also straining to see far above the Mary Monster – Vargas wanted to be sure the roof wasn't leaking.

'It's not raining outside, Vargas,' Pepe told him.

'Just checking,' was all Vargas said.

'When people die, Vargas – I mean the people you will always remember, the ones who changed your life – they never really go away,' Pepe told the young doctor.

'I know that, Pepe – I live with ghosts, too,' Vargas answered him.

The two old priests were the last to approach the towering virgin; this sprinkling had been irregular enough – those few things that had mattered to Lupe, reduced to ashes – and now there was more disruption, the oversize tears from the not-so-inanimate Mary. Father Alfonso touched a tear that Juan Diego held out to him – a glistening, crystal-bright teardrop in the cupped palm of the dump reader's small hand. 'Yes, I see,' Father Alfonso said, as solemnly as possible.

'I don't think a pipe has burst – there are no pipes in the ceiling, are there?' Vargas not-so-innocently asked the two old priests.

'No pipes – that's correct, Vargas,' Father Octavio curtly said.

'It's a miracle, isn't it?' Edward Bonshaw, his face streaked with his own tears, asked Father Alfonso. 'Un milagro – isn't that what you call it?' the Iowan asked Father Octavio.

'No, no – not the *milagro* word, please,' Father Alfonso said to the parrot man.

'It's much too soon to mention *that* word – these things take time. This is, as yet, an uninvestigated event – or a series of events, some might say,' Father Octavio intoned, as if he were talking to himself or rehearsing his preliminary report to the bishop.

'To begin with, the bishop must be told—' Father Alfonso speculated, before Father Octavio cut him off.

'Yes, yes – of course – but the bishop is just the beginning. There is a *process*,' Father Octavio stated. 'It could take years.'

'We follow a procedure, in these cases—' Father Alfonso started to say, but he stopped; he was looking at Lupe's hot-chocolate cup. Juan Diego was holding the empty cup in his small hands. 'If you're done with the sprinkling, Juan Diego, I would like to have that cup – for the records,' Father Alfonso said.

It took two hundred years for the Church to declare that Our Lady of Guadalupe was Mary, Juan Diego was thinking. (In 1754, Pope Benedict XIV declared Guadalupe patron of what was then called New Spain.) But Juan Diego wasn't the one who said it. The parrot man was the one who said it, at the moment Juan Diego handed Lupe's cup to Father Alfonso.

'Are you talking about two hundred years?' Edward Bonshaw asked the two old priests. 'Are you pulling a Pope Benedict the Fourteenth on us? It was two hundred years after the fact when Benedict declared that *your* Virgin of Guadalupe was Mary. Is that the kind of *process* you have in mind?' Señor Eduardo asked Father Octavio. 'Are you following a procedure, as you put it, that will take two hundred years?' the Iowan asked Father Alfonso.

'That way, all of us who saw the Virgin Mary cry will be dead, right?' Juan Diego asked the two old priests. 'No witnesses, right?' the boy asked them. (Now Juan Diego knew that Dolores hadn't been kidding; now he knew he would have the balls for other stuff.)

'I thought we believed in miracles,' Brother Pepe said to Father Alfonso and Father Octavio.

'Not *this* miracle, Pepe,' Vargas said. 'It's the same old Church-of-rules business, isn't it?' Vargas asked the two old priests. 'Your Church isn't about the miracles – it's about your *rules*, isn't it?'

'I know what I saw,' Rivera told the two old priests. 'You didn't do anything – *she* did,' the dump boss said to them. Rivera was pointing *up there*, at the Mary Monster's face, wet with tears. 'I don't come here for you – I come for *her*,' el jefe said.

'It's not your various virgins who are full of shit,' Flor said to Father Alfonso. 'It's you and your rules – your rules for the rest of us,' Flor told Father Octavio. 'They won't help us,' Flor said to Señor Eduardo. 'They won't help us because you disappoint them, and because they disapprove of me,' she told the Iowan.

'I think the big girl has stopped crying – I think she's out of tears,' Dr. Vargas observed.

'You could help us, if you wanted to,' Juan Diego told the two old priests.

'I told you the kid had balls, didn't I?' Flor asked Señor Eduardo.

'Yes, I believe the tears have stopped,' Father Alfonso said; he sounded relieved.

'I see no new tears,' Father Octavio joined in; he sounded hopeful.

'These three,' Brother Pepe said suddenly, his arms surprisingly encompassing the two unlikely lovers and the crippled boy – it was as if Pepe were herding them together. 'You can, you *could*, resolve the plight of these three – I've looked into what has to be done, and how you can do it. You could resolve this,' Brother Pepe told the two old priests. 'Quid pro quo – am I saying it correctly?' Pepe asked the Iowan. Pepe knew that Edward Bonshaw was proud of his Latin.

'Quid pro quo,' the parrot man repeated. 'Something given or received for something else,' Señor Eduardo said to Father Alfonso. 'A deal, in other words,' was the way Edward Bonshaw put it to Father Octavio.

'We know what it means, Edward,' Father Alfonso said peevishly.

'These three are bound for Iowa, with your help,' was the way Brother Pepe put it to the two old priests. 'Whereas you – that is, *we*, in the sense of the Church – have a miracle, or not a miracle, to soft-pedal or *suppress*.'

'No one has said the *suppress* word, Pepe,' Father Alfonso rebuked him.

'It's simply premature to say the *milagro* word, Pepe – we have to wait and see,' Father Octavio reprimanded him.

'Just help us get to Iowa,' Juan Diego said, 'and we'll wait and see for another two hundred years.'

'That sounds like a good deal for everybody,' the Iowan chimed in. 'Actually, Juan Diego,' Señor Eduardo told the dump reader, 'Guadalupe waited two hundred and twenty-three years to be officially *declared*.'

'It doesn't matter how long we wait for them to tell us that a milagro is a milagro – it doesn't even matter what the milagro is,' Rivera told them all. The Mary Monster's tears had stopped; the dump boss was on his way out. 'We don't need to *declare* what a miracle is or isn't – we *saw* it,' el jefe reminded them, as he was leaving. 'Of course Father Alfonso and Father Octavio *will* help you – you don't need to be a mind reader to know that, do you?' the dump boss asked the dump kid.

'Lupe knew *these two* were a necessary part of it, didn't she?' Rivera asked Juan Diego, pointing to the parrot man and Flor. 'Don't you think your sister also knew they would be part of your getting away?' El jefe pointed to the two old priests.

The dump boss paused only long enough at the fountain of holy water to think twice about touching it. He didn't touch the holy water on his way out – apparently, the Mary Monster's tears had been enough.

'You better come say goodbye to me before you go

to Iowa,' Rivera told the dump reader; it was clear that the dump boss was through talking to anyone else.

'Come see me in a day or two, jefe – I'll take those stitches out!' Vargas called after Rivera.

Juan Diego didn't doubt what the dump boss had said; he knew that the two old priests would comply, and he also knew that Lupe had known they would. One look at Father Alfonso and Father Octavio told Juan Diego that the two old priests knew they would comply, too.

'What's that Latin shit again?' Flor asked Señor Eduardo.

'Quid pro quo,' the Iowan said softly; he didn't want to rub it in.

Now it was Brother Pepe's turn to cry – his tears were not a miracle, of course, but crying was a big deal to Pepe, who couldn't stop himself. His tears just kept coming.

'I'm going to miss you, my dear reader,' Brother Pepe told Juan Diego. 'I think I'm already missing you!' Pepe cried.

THE CATS DIDN'T WAKE up Juan Diego – Dorothy did. Dorothy was a jackhammer in the superior position; with her heavy breasts swaying just above his face, and her hips rocking back and forth as she sat on him, the young woman took Juan Diego's breath away.

'I'm going to miss you, too!' he'd cried out, when he was still asleep and dreaming. The next thing he knew, he was coming – Juan Diego had no memory of her slipping the condom on him – and Dorothy was coming, too. Un terremoto, an earthquake, Juan Diego thought.

If there were any cats on the thatched roof over the outdoor shower, surely Dorothy's screams dispersed them; her screaming momentarily silenced the crowing gamecocks, too. Those dogs who'd been barking all night recommenced barking.

There were no telephones in the rooms at The Hiding Place, or some asswheel in a nearby room would have called to complain. As for those ghosts of the young Americans who'd died in Vietnam, now and forever on R&R at El Escondrijo, Dorothy's explosive-sounding cries must have made their unbeating hearts twitch for a beat or two.

It wasn't until Juan Diego limped to the bathroom that he saw the open container of his Viagra prescription; the pills were beside his plugged-in cell phone on the countertop. Juan Diego didn't remember taking the Viagra, but he must have taken a whole tablet, not a half – whether he took it himself when he'd been half awake, or whether Dorothy had given him the 100-milligram dose when he'd been sound asleep and dreaming about the sprinkling. (Did it matter how he'd taken it? He definitely took it.)

It's hard to say what surprised Juan Diego more. Was it the young ghost himself or the lost soldier's Hawaiian shirt? Most surprising was the way the American casualty of that distant war stared searchingly for a trace of himself in the mirror above the bathroom sink; the young victim was not reflected in the mirror at all. (Some ghosts do appear in mirrors – not this one. It's not easy to compartmentalize ghosts.) And the sight of Juan Diego in that same mirror, above the bathroom sink, caused this ghost to vanish.

The ghost who wasn't reflected in the bathroom mirror reminded Juan Diego of the weird dream he'd had about the photograph the young Chinese man took at Kowloon Station. Why weren't Miriam and Dorothy in that photo? What was it Consuelo had called Miriam? 'The lady who just appears' – wasn't that what the little girl in pigtails said?

But how had Miriam and Dorothy *disappeared* from a photograph? Juan Diego was wondering. Or had the cell-phone camera failed to capture Miriam and Dorothy in the first place?

That thought, that *connection* – not the young ghost himself, and not his Hawaiian shirt – was what spooked Juan Diego the most. When Dorothy found him standing stock-still in the bathroom, where he was staring into the little mirror above the sink, she guessed he'd seen one of the ghosts.

'You saw one of them, didn't you?' Dorothy asked him; she quickly kissed the back of his neck, before gliding behind him, naked, on her way to the out-door shower.

'One of them – yes,' was all Juan Diego said. He'd never taken his eyes from the bathroom mirror. He felt Dorothy kiss his neck; he felt her brush against his back as she glided behind him. But Dorothy didn't appear in the bathroom mirror – like the ghost in the Hawaiian shirt, she wasn't reflected there. *Un*like the ghost of that young American captive, Dorothy didn't bother searching for herself in the mirror; she'd passed so unnoticeably behind Juan Diego that he didn't see she was naked – not until he saw her standing in the outdoor shower.

For a while, he watched her wash her hair. Juan Diego thought Dorothy was a very attractive young woman, and if she were a specter – or, in some sense, not of this world – it seemed more believable to Juan Diego that she would want to be with him, even if her being with him was of an unreal or illusory nature.

'Who are you?' Juan Diego had asked Dorothy at El Nido, but she'd been asleep, or she was pretending to be asleep – or else Juan Diego only imagined that he'd asked her.

He felt all right about not asking her who she was anymore. It was a great relief to Juan Diego to imagine that Dorothy and Miriam might be spectral. The world he'd imagined had brought him more satisfaction and less pain than the real world ever had.

'You want to take a shower with me?' Dorothy was asking him. 'That would be fun. Only the cats and dogs can see us, or the ghosts, and what do they care?' she said.

'Yes, that would be fun,' Juan Diego answered her. He was still staring at the bathroom mirror when the little gecko came out from behind the mirror and stared back at him with its bright, unblinking eyes.

There was no question that the gecko saw him, but, just to be sure, Juan Diego shrugged his shoulders and moved his head from side to side. The gecko darted behind the bathroom mirror; the little lizard hid itself in half a second.

'I'll be right there!' Juan Diego called to Dorothy; the outdoor shower (not to mention, Dorothy in it) looked very inviting. And the gecko had absolutely seen him – Juan Diego knew he was still alive, or at least visible. He was not some kind of ghost – not yet.

'I'm coming!' Juan Diego called to her.

'Promises, promises,' Dorothy called back to him from the outdoor shower.

She liked to make his cock slippery with shampoo and rub herself against him under the water. Juan Diego wondered why he'd not known any girlfriends like Dorothy, but even as a younger man, he supposed there'd been a bookishness to his conversation, a seeming seriousness that had driven the good-time girls away. And was this why, in his imagination, Juan Diego would have been prone to *make up* a young woman like Dorothy?

'Don't worry about the ghosts – I just thought you should see them,' Dorothy was telling him in the shower. 'They don't expect anything, from you – they're just sad, and there's nothing you can do about their sadness. You're an American. What they went through is part of you, or you're part of what they went through – or something.' Dorothy went on and on.

But what part of them was truly part of him? Juan

Diego wondered. People – even ghosts, if Dorothy was a kind of ghost – were always trying to make him 'part of' something!

You cannot take the scavenging out of scavengers; los pepenadores will be foreigners wherever they go. What was Juan Diego *part of*? A kind of universal foreignness traveled with him; it was who he was, not only *as a writer*. Even his name was fictitious – not 'Rivera' but 'Guerrero.' The American immigration lawyer had objected to Juan Diego's having Rivera's name. It didn't suffice that Rivera was 'probably not' Juan Diego's father. Rivera was alive; it didn't look good that the adopted boy had Rivera's name.

Pepe had to explain this awkwardness to the dump boss; Juan Diego would have had trouble telling el jefe that the 'adopted boy' needed a new name.

'How about "Guerrero"?' Rivera had suggested, looking only at Pepe, not at Juan Diego.

'Are you okay with "Guerrero," jefe?' Juan Diego had asked the dump boss.

'Sure,' Rivera said; he now allowed himself to look at Juan Diego, just a little. 'Even a dump kid should know where he comes from,' el jefe had said.

'I won't forget where I come from, jefe,' was all Juan Diego said, his name already becoming something *imagined*.

Nine people had seen a miracle in the Templo de la Compañía de Jesús in Oaxaca – tears had fallen from a statue's eyes. This was no less than a statue of the Virgin Mary, but the miracle was never recorded, and six of the nine witnesses had died. Upon the deaths of the surviving three – Vargas, Alejandra, and Juan Diego – the miracle itself would die, wouldn't it?

If Lupe were alive, she would have told Juan Diego that this crying statue wasn't the major miracle in his life. 'We're the miraculous ones,' Lupe had told him. And wasn't Lupe herself the major miracle? What she had known, what she had risked – how she had *willed* another future for him! These mysteries were what Juan Diego was *part of.* Next to these mysteries, his other experiences paled.

Dorothy was talking about something; she was still going on and on.

'About the ghosts,' Juan Diego interrupted her, as casually as he could. 'I guess there are ways to tell them apart from the other guests.'

'The way they vanish when you look at them makes it pretty clear,' Dorothy said.

At breakfast, Dorothy and Juan Diego would discover that El Escondrijo wasn't very crowded; there weren't many other guests. The ones who came to breakfast at the outdoor dining tables didn't vanish when you looked at them, but they did seem a little old and tired-looking to Juan Diego. Of course, he'd looked at himself in a mirror this morning – a little longer than he was used to doing – and he would have said that he seemed a little old and tired-looking, too.

After breakfast, Dorothy wanted Juan Diego to see the little church or chapel among the compound of old buildings; she thought the architecture might remind Juan Diego of the Spanish style he'd been accustomed to in Oaxaca. (Oh, those Spaniards – they really got around! Juan Diego was thinking.)

The interior of the chapel was very basic, not at all ornate or fancy. There was an altar like a small café table, one for two customers. There was a Christ on the Cross – this Jesus didn't appear to be suffering too greatly – and a Virgin Mary, not a towering but a merely life-size presence. The two of them could almost have been having a conversation with each other. But these familiar two, this mother and son, were not the two most commanding presences – this Mary and her Jesus weren't the two who got Juan Diego's immediate interest.

It was the two young ghosts in the foremost pew of the chapel who seized all of Juan Diego's attention. The young men were holding hands, and one of them rested his head on the other's shoulder. They seemed somehow more than former comrades-in-arms, though they were both wearing their fatigues. It was not that the long-dead American captives were (or had been) lovers that took Juan Diego by surprise. These ghosts had not seen Dorothy and Juan Diego enter the little church; not only did these two not vanish, but they continued to look beseechingly at Mary and Jesus – as if they believed they were alone and unobserved in the chapel.

Juan Diego would have thought that, when you were dead and you were a ghost, your countenance – especially in a church – would be different. Wouldn't you no longer be seeking guidance? Wouldn't you, somehow, know the answers?

But these two ghosts looked as clueless as any two troubled lovers who had ever stared uncomprehendingly at Mary and Jesus. These two, Juan Diego knew, didn't know anything. These two dead soldiers were no better informed than anyone living; these two young ghosts were still looking for answers.

'No more ghosts – I've seen enough ghosts,' Juan Diego said to Dorothy, at which point the two former comrades-in-arms vanished.

Juan Diego and Dorothy would stay at The Hiding Place that day and night – a Friday. They would leave Vigan on a Saturday; they took another night flight from Laoag to Manila. Once more – except for the occasional ship – they flew over the unlit darkness, which was Manila Bay.

31

Adrenaline

Another nighttime arrival in another hotel, Juan Diego was thinking, but he'd seen the lobby of this one before – the Ascott, in Makati City, where Miriam had said he should stay when he returned to Manila. How strange: to be checking in with Dorothy, where he'd once imagined Miriam's attention-getting entrance.

As Juan Diego remembered, it was a long walk to the registration desk from where the elevators opened into the lobby. 'I'm a little surprised my mother isn't—' Dorothy started to say; she was looking all around the lobby when Miriam just appeared. It was no surprise to Juan Diego how the security guards never took their eyes off Miriam, all the way from the elevators to the registration desk. 'What a surprise, Mother,' Dorothy laconically said, but Miriam ignored her.

'You poor man!' Miriam exclaimed to Juan Diego. 'I would guess you've seen enough of Dorothy's ghosts – frightened nineteen-year-olds aren't everyone's shot of tequila.'

'Are you saying it's your turn, Mother?' Dorothy asked her.

'Don't be crude, Dorothy – it's never as much about sex as you seem to think it is,' her mother told her.

'You're kidding, right?' Dorothy asked her.

'It's that time – it's Manila, Dorothy,' Miriam reminded her.

'I know what time it is – I know where we are, Mother,' Dorothy said to her.

'Enough sex, Dorothy,' Miriam repeated.

'Don't people still have sex?' Dorothy asked her, but Miriam once again ignored her.

'Darling, you look tired – I'm worried about how tired you look,' Miriam was saying to Juan Diego.

He watched Dorothy as she was leaving the lobby. She had an irresistibly coarse allure; the security guards watched Dorothy coming toward them, all the way to the elevators, but they didn't look at her in quite the same way they had looked at Miriam.

'For Christ's sake, Dorothy,' Miriam muttered to herself, when she saw that her daughter had left in a huff. Only Juan Diego heard her. 'Honestly, Dorothy!' Miriam called after her, but Dorothy didn't appear to have heard; the elevator doors were already closing.

At Miriam's request, the Ascott had upgraded Juan Diego to a suite with a full kitchen, on one of the uppermost floors. Juan Diego certainly didn't need a kitchen.

'After El Escondrijo, which is about as sea-level and depressing as it gets, I thought you deserved a more *high-up* view,' Miriam told him.

The *high-up* part notwithstanding, the view from the Ascott of Makati City – the Wall Street of Manila, the business and financial center of the Philippines – was like many high-rise cityscapes at night: the variations on subdued lighting or the darkened windows of daytime offices were offset by the brightly lit windows of hotels and apartment buildings. Juan Diego didn't want to sound unappreciative of Miriam's efforts on behalf of his view, but there was a universal sameness (a void of national identity) to the cityscape he saw.

And where Miriam took him to dinner – very near the hotel, in the Ayala Center – the atmosphere of the shops and restaurants was refined but fast-paced (a shopping mall relocated to an international airport, or the other way around). Yet it may have been the anonymity of the restaurant in the Ayala Center, or the traveling-businessman atmosphere of the Ascott, that compelled Juan Diego to tell Miriam such a personal story: what had happened to the good gringo – not only the burning at the basurero but every verse of 'Streets of Laredo,' the lyrics spoken in a morbid monotone. (Unlike the good gringo, Juan Diego couldn't sing.) Don't forget, Juan Diego had been with Dorothy for days. He must have thought that Miriam was a better listener than her daughter.

'Wouldn't you cry if you never forgot how *your* sister was killed by a lion?' Miriam had asked the children at the Encantador. And then Pedro had fallen asleep with his head against Miriam's breast, as if he had been bewitched.

Juan Diego decided he should talk to Miriam non-stop; if he never let her talk, maybe she wouldn't bewitch *him*.

He went on and on about el gringo bueno – not only how the doomed hippie had befriended Lupe and Juan Diego, but the embarrassing business of Juan Diego's not knowing the good gringo's name. The Manila American Cemetery and Memorial had beckoned Juan Diego to the Philippines, but Juan Diego told Miriam he had no expectations that he would ever be able to locate the missing father's actual grave – not among the eleven burial plots, not without knowing the dead father's name.

'Yet a promise is a promise,' was the way Juan Diego put it to Miriam at the restaurant in the Ayala Center. 'I promised the good gringo I would pay his respects to his dad. I imagine the cemetery is pretty overwhelming, but I *have* to go there – I should at least *see* it.'

'Don't see it tomorrow, darling – tomorrow is a Sunday, and not just *any* Sunday,' Miriam said. (You can see how easily Juan Diego's decision to talk non-stop was derailed; as so often happened with Miriam and Dorothy, these women knew something he didn't know.)

Tomorrow, Sunday, was the annual procession known as the Feast of the Black Nazarene. 'The thing came from Mexico – a Spanish galleon carried it to Manila from Acapulco. Early 1600s, I'm guessing – I think a bunch of Augustinian friars brought the thing,' Miriam told him.

'A *black* Nazarene?' Juan Diego asked her.

'Not racially black,' Miriam explained. 'It's a wooden, life-size figure of Jesus Christ, frozen in the act of bearing his cross to Calvary. Maybe it was made from some kind of dark wood, but it wasn't supposed to be black – it was burned in a fire.'

'It was *charred*, you mean?' Juan Diego asked her.

'It was burned at least three times, the first time in a fire on board the Spanish galleon. The thing *arrived* charred, but there were two more fires after the Black Nazarene got to Manila. Quiapo Church was twice destroyed by fire – in the eighteenth century and in the 1920s,' Miriam said. 'And there were two earthquakes in Manila – one in the seventeenth century, one in the nineteenth. The Church makes a big deal about the Black Nazarene's 'surviving' three fires and two earthquakes, *and* the thing survived the Liberation of Manila in 1945 – one of the worst bombings in the Pacific Theater of World War Two, by the way. But what's the big deal about a wooden figure that "survives" – a wooden figure can't die, can it? The thing just got burned a few times, and it turned blacker!' was the way Miriam put it. 'The Black Nazarene was shot once, too – in the cheek, I think. The gun incident was fairly recent – in the 1990s,' Miriam said. 'As if Christ didn't suffer enough, on the way to Calvary, the Black Nazarene has "survived" six catastrophes – both the natural and the unnatural kind. Believe me,' Miriam said suddenly to Juan Diego, 'you don't want to leave the hotel tomorrow. Manila is a mess when the Black Nazarene's devotees are having their crazy procession.'

'There are thousands of marchers?' Juan Diego asked Miriam.

'No, *millions*,' Miriam told him. 'And many of them believe that *touching* the Black Nazarene will heal them of whatever ails them. Lots of people get hurt in the procession. There are male devotees of the Black Nazarene who call themselves Hijos del Señor Nazareno – "Sons of the Lord Nazarene" – and their devotion to the Catholic faith causes them to "identify," as they put it, with the Passion of Christ. Maybe the morons want to suffer as much as Jesus suffered,' Miriam said; the way she shrugged gave Juan Diego a chill. 'Who knows what true believers like that want?'

'Maybe I'll go to the cemetery on *Monday*,' Juan Diego suggested.

'Manila will be a mess on Monday – it takes them a day to clean up the streets, and all the hospitals are still dealing with the injured,' Miriam said. 'Go Tuesday – the afternoon is best. The most fanatical people do everything as early in the morning as they're allowed – don't go in the morning,' Miriam told him.

'Okay,' Juan Diego said. Just listening to Miriam made him feel as tired as he might have felt if he'd marched in the Black Nazarene procession, suffering the inevitable crowd injuries and dehydration. Yet as tired as he was, Juan Diego doubted what Miriam had told him. Her voice was always so authoritative, but this time what she said seemed exaggerated, even untrue. It was Juan Diego's impression that Manila was huge. Could a religious procession in Quiapo really affect the Makati area?

Juan Diego drank too much San Miguel beer and ate something curious; any number of things could have been the cause of his not feeling well. He suspected the Peking duck lumpia. (Why did they put duck in a spring roll?) And Juan Diego didn't know that lechon kawali was deep-fried pork belly, not until Miriam informed him; the sausage served with bagoong mayonnaise took him by surprise, too. Later, Miriam told him the mayonnaise was made with that fermented-fish condiment – the stuff Juan Diego thought gave him indigestion or heartburn.

In truth, it may not have been the Filipino food (or too much San Miguel beer) that upset his stomach and made him feel sick. The all-too-familiar craziness of the fervent followers of the Black Nazarene upset him. *Of course* the burned Jesus and his charred-black cross had come from *Mexico*! Juan Diego was thinking, as he and Miriam navigated the escalators in the vast mall of the Ayala Center – as they rode the elevator, up and up, to their suite in the Ascott.

Once again, Juan Diego almost didn't notice how his limp seemed to go away when he was walking anywhere with Miriam or Dorothy. And Clark French was assailing him with one text message after another. Poor Leslie had been texting Clark; she'd wanted Clark to know his former teacher was 'in the clutches of a literary stalker.'

Juan Diego didn't know there *were* literary stalkers; he doubted that Leslie (a writing *student*) was besieged by them, but she'd told Clark that Juan Diego had been seduced by a 'groupie who preys on writers.' (Clark persisted in calling Dorothy just plain 'D.') Leslie had told Clark that Dorothy was a 'woman of possibly satanic intentions.' The *satanic* word never failed to excite Clark.

The reason there were so many text messages from Clark was that Juan Diego had turned off his cell phone before the flight from Laoag to Manila; not until he was leaving the restaurant with Miriam did he remember to turn it back on. By then, Clark French's imagination had taken a fearful and protective turn.

'Are you all right?' Clark's most recent text message began. 'What if D. *is* satanic? I've met Miriam – I thought *she* was satanic!'

Juan Diego saw he'd missed a text message from Bienvenido, too. It was true that Clark French had made most of the arrangements for Juan Diego in Manila, but Bienvenido knew that Mr. French's former teacher was back in town and that he had changed hotels. Bienvenido didn't exactly contradict Miriam's warnings about Sunday, but he wasn't as adamant.

'Best to lie low tomorrow, due to crowds attending the Black Nazarene event – at least avoid any proximity to the procession routes,' Bienvenido texted him. 'I'll be your driver Monday, for the onstage interview with Mr. French and the dinner afterward.'

'WHAT onstage interview with you Monday, Clark – WHAT dinner afterward?' Juan Diego immediately texted Clark French, before addressing the *satanic* situation that had so excited his former writing student.

Clark called to explain. There was a small theater in Makati City, very near Juan Diego's hotel – 'small but pleasant,' Clark described it. On Monday nights, when the theater was dark, the company hosted on-stage interviews with authors. A local bookstore provided copies of the authors' books, for signing; Clark was often the interviewer. There was a dinner afterward for patrons of the writers' onstage series – 'not a lot of people,' Clark assured him, 'but a way for you to have some contact with your Filipino readers.'

Clark French was the only writer Juan Diego knew who sounded like a publicist. And, like a publicist, Clark mentioned the media last. There would be a journalist or two, at the onstage event *and* the dinner, but Clark said he would warn Juan Diego about the ones to watch out for. (Clark should just stay home and *write*! Juan Diego thought.)

'And your friends will be there,' Clark suddenly said.

'Who, Clark?' Juan Diego asked.

'Miriam and her daughter. I saw the guest list for dinner – it just says "Miriam and her daughter, friends of the author." I thought you would know they were coming,' Clark told him.

Juan Diego looked carefully around his hotel suite. Miriam was in the bathroom; it was almost midnight – she was probably getting ready for bed. Limping his way to the kitchen area of the suite, Juan Diego lowered his voice when he spoke on his cell phone to Clark.

'D. is for *Dorothy*, Clark – Dorothy is Miriam's daughter. I slept with Dorothy before I slept with Miriam,' Juan Diego reminded his former writing student. 'I slept with Dorothy before she met Leslie, Clark.'

'You admitted you didn't know Miriam and her daughter *well*,' Clark reminded his old teacher.

'As I told you, they're mysteries to me, but your friend Leslie has her own issues – Leslie is just jealous, Clark.'

'I don't deny that poor Leslie has *issues*—' Clark started to say.

'One of her boys was trampled by a water buffalo – the same boy was later stung by pink jellyfish swimming vertically,' Juan Diego whispered into his cell phone. 'The other boy was stung by plankton resembling condoms for three-year-olds.'

'Stinging condoms – don't remind me!' Clark cried.

'Not condoms – the stinging plankton *looked like* condoms, Clark.'

'Why are you whispering?' Clark asked his old writing teacher.

'I'm with Miriam,' Juan Diego whispered; he was limping around the kitchen area, trying to keep an eye on the closed bathroom door.

'I'll let you go,' Clark whispered. 'I thought Tuesday would be a good day for the American Cemetery—'

'Yes, in the afternoon,' Juan Diego interrupted him.

'I've booked Bienvenido for Tuesday morning, too,' Clark told him. 'I thought maybe you would like to see the National Shrine of Our Lady of Guadalupe – the one here, in Manila. There are only a couple of buildings, just an old church and monastery – nothing as grand as your Mexico City version. The church and monastery are in a slum, Guadalupe Viejo – the slum is on a hill above the Pasig River,' Clark carried on.

'Guadalupe Viejo – a slum,' was all Juan Diego managed to say.

'You sound tired. We'll decide this later,' Clark abruptly said.

'Guadalupe, sí—' Juan Diego started to say. The bathroom door was open; he saw Miriam in the bedroom – she had only a towel around her, and she was closing the bedroom curtains.

'That's a "yes" to Guadalupe Viejo – you want to go there?' Clark French was asking.

'Yes, Clark,' Juan Diego told him.

Guadalupe Viejo didn't sound like a slum – to a dump kid, Guadalupe Viejo sounded more like a destination. It seemed to Juan Diego that the very existence of the National Shrine of Our Lady of Guadalupe in Manila was more of a reason for his taking this trip to the Philippines than the sentimental promise he'd made to the good gringo. More than the Manila American Cemetery and Memorial, Guadalupe Viejo sounded like where a dump reader from Oaxaca would *end up* – to use Dorothy's blunt way of putting it. And if it was true that an aura of fate had marked him, didn't Guadalupe Viejo sound like Juan Diego Guerrero's kind of place?

'You're shivering, darling – do you have a chill?' Miriam asked him when he came into the bedroom.

'No, I was just talking to Clark French,' Juan Diego told her. 'There's an onstage event Clark and I are doing – an interview together. I hear you and Dorothy are coming.'

'We don't get to go to a lot of literary events,' Miriam said, smiling. She'd spread the towel for her feet on the carpet, on her side of the bed. She was already under the covers. 'I put out your pills,' she said matter-of-factly. 'I didn't know if it was a Lopressor or a Viagra night,' Miriam told him in that insouciant way of hers.

Juan Diego was aware he'd been alternating nights: he chose the nights when he wanted to feel adrenalized; he resigned himself to those other nights, when he knew he would feel diminished. He was aware that his skipping a dose of the beta-blockers – specifically, to unblock the adrenaline receptors in his body, to give himself an adrenaline release – was dangerous. But Juan Diego didn't remember when it became routine for him to have *either* 'a Lopressor or a Viagra night,' as Miriam had put it – a while ago, he imagined.

Juan Diego was struck by what was the same about Miriam and Dorothy; this had nothing to do with how they looked, or their sexual behavior. What was the same about these two women was how they were able to manipulate him – not to mention that whenever he was with one of them, he was inclined to forget about the other one. (Yet he forgot and obsessed about both of them!)

There was a word for how he was behaving, Juan Diego thought – not only with these women but with his beta-blockers. He was behaving *childishly*, Juan Diego was thinking – not unlike the way he and Lupe had behaved about the virgins, at first preferring Guadalupe to the Mary Monster, until Guadalupe disappointed them. And then the Virgin Mary actually had done something – enough to get the dump kids' attention, not only with her nose-for-a-nose trick but with her unambiguous tears.

The Ascott was not El Escondrijo – no ghosts, unless Miriam was one, and any number of outlets where Juan Diego could have plugged in and charged his cell phone. Yet he chose an outlet in the area of the bathroom sink, because the bathroom was private. And Juan Diego hoped that – whether she was a ghost or not – Miriam might have fallen asleep before he was finished using the bathroom.

'Enough sex, Dorothy,' he'd heard Miriam say – that oft-repeated line – and, more recently, 'it's never as much about sex as you seem to think it is.'

Tomorrow was Sunday. Juan Diego would be flying home to the United States on Wednesday. He'd not only had enough sex, Juan Diego was thinking – he'd had enough of these two mysterious women, whoever they were. One way to stop obsessing about them was to stop having sex with them, Juan Diego thought. He used the pill-cutting device to slice one of the oblong Lopressor tablets in half; he took his prescribed dose of the beta-blockers, plus this additional half.

Bienvenido had said it was 'best to lie low' on Sunday; Juan Diego would *lie low*, all right – he would miss most of Sunday in a diminished state. And it wasn't the crowds or the religious insanity of the Black Nazarene procession Juan Diego was intentionally missing. He wished Miriam and Dorothy would just disappear; it was feeling diminished, as usual, that he wanted.

Juan Diego was making an effort to be normal again – not to mention that he was trying, albeit belatedly, to follow his doctor's orders. (Dr. Rosemary Stein was often on his mind, if not always as his doctor.)

'Dear Dr. Rosemary,' he began his text to her – once again sitting with his hard-to-understand cell phone on the bathroom toilet. Juan Diego wanted to tell her he'd taken some liberties with his Lopressor prescription; he wanted to explain about the unusual circumstances, the two interesting (or at least interested) women. Yet Juan Diego wanted to assure Rosemary that he wasn't lonely, or pathetic; he also wanted to promise her that he would stop fooling around with the required dose of his beta-blockers, but it seemed to take him *hours* just to write 'Dear Dr. Rosemary' – the stupid cell phone was an insult to any writer! Juan Diego could never remember which stupid key you pushed to capitalize a letter.

That was when a simpler solution occurred to Juan Diego: he could send Rosemary the photograph of him with Miriam and Dorothy at Kowloon Station; that way, his message could be both shorter and funnier. 'I met these two women, who caused me to diddle around with my Lopressor prescription. Fear not! Am back on track and abstinent again. Love—'

That would be the briefest way to confess to Dr. Rosemary, wouldn't it? And the tone wasn't self-pitying – no hint of the longing or lost opportunity attached to that night in the car on Dubuque Street, when Rosemary had seized Juan Diego's face and said, 'I would have asked you to marry me.'

Poor Pete was driving. Poor Rosemary tried to revise what she'd said; 'I just meant I *might* have asked you,' was the way Rosemary said it. And, without looking at her, Juan Diego had known she was crying.

Ah, well – it was best for Juan Diego *and* his dear Dr. Rosemary not to dwell on that night in the car on Dubuque Street. And how could he send her that photo taken at Kowloon Station? Juan Diego didn't know how to find the photo on his stupid cell phone – not to mention how to attach the photo to a text. On the infuriating keypad of his little phone, even the key for 'clear' wasn't spelled out. The correct key for 'clear' was marked CLR – there was room on the keypad for two more letters, in Juan Diego's opinion. He angrily cleared his text message to Rosemary, one letter at a time.

Clark French would know how to find the photo that young Chinese man took at Kowloon Station; he could show Juan Diego how to send the photo with a text message to Dr. Rosemary. Clark knew how to do everything, except what to do with poor Leslie, Juan Diego was thinking as he limped to bed.

No dogs were barking, no gamecocks were crowing, but – not unlike New Year's Eve at the Encantador – Juan Diego could discern no detectable breathing from Miriam.

Miriam was asleep on her left side, with her back turned toward him. Juan Diego thought he could lie on his left side and put his arm around her; he wanted to put his hand on her heart, not on her breast. He wanted to feel if her heart was beating or not.

Dr. Rosemary Stein could have told him that you can feel a pulse better in other places. Naturally, Juan Diego felt Miriam – all over her chest! – but he couldn't feel her heartbeat.

While he was groping all around, his feet touched her feet; if Miriam was alive, and not a spectral presence, surely she must have felt him touching her. Nevertheless, Juan Diego was bravely trying to assert his familiarity with the spiritual world.

The boy who'd been born in Guerrero was no stranger to spirits; Oaxaca was a town full of holy virgins. Even that Christmas-parties place, the virgin shop on Independencia – even one of those sex-doll replicas of the city's famous virgins – was a *little* holy. And Juan Diego was a Lost Children kid; surely the nuns, and the two old priests at the Temple of the

Society of Jesus, had exposed the dump reader to the spiritual world. Even the dump boss was a believer; Rivera had been a Mary worshiper. Juan Diego wasn't afraid of Miriam or Dorothy – whoever, or whatever, they were. As el jefe had said: 'We don't need to *declare* what a miracle is or isn't – we *saw* it.'

It didn't matter who or what Miriam was. If Miriam and Dorothy were Juan Diego's personal angels of death, he was unimpressed. They wouldn't be his first or his only miracle. As Lupe had told him: 'We're the miraculous ones.' All this was what Juan Diego believed, or what he tried to believe – what he sincerely *wanted* to believe – while he went on touching Miriam.

The sudden, sharp intake of Miriam's breath nonetheless startled him. 'It's a Lopressor night, I'm guessing,' she said to him in her low, husky voice.

He tried to reply to her nonchalantly. 'How did you know?' Juan Diego asked her.

'Your hands and feet, darling,' Miriam told him. 'Your extremities are already turning colder.'

It's true that beta-blockers reduce blood circulation to the extremities. Juan Diego didn't wake up until noon on Sunday, and his hands and feet were freezing. He wasn't surprised that Miriam was gone, or that she hadn't left him a note.

Women know when men don't desire them: ghosts and witches, deities and demons, angels of death – even virgins, even ordinary women. They always know; women can tell when you have stopped desiring them.

Juan Diego felt so diminished; he wouldn't remember how that Sunday, and Sunday night, slipped away. Even that extra half of a Lopressor tablet had been too much. On Sunday night, he flushed the unused half of the pill down the toilet; he took only the required dose of his Lopressor prescription. Juan Diego would still sleep till noon on Monday. If there was any news that weekend, he missed it.

The writing students at Iowa had called Clark French a 'do-gooder Catholic,' an 'übernerd,' and Clark had been busy with Leslie while Juan Diego slept. 'I believe poor Leslie's foremost concern is your well-being,' Clark's first text message to Juan Diego began. There were more messages from Clark, of course – mostly to do with their onstage interview. 'Don't worry: I won't ask you who wrote Shakespeare, and we'll skirt the issue of autobiographical fiction as best we can!'

There was more about poor Leslie, too. 'Leslie says she's NOT jealous – she wants nothing to do with D.,' Clark's text message declared. 'I'm sure that Leslie is strictly concerned with what witchcraft, what violent sorcery, D. may unleash on you. Werner told his mom the water buffalo was INCITED to charge and trample – Werner said D. stuck a caterpillar up the buffalo's nose!'

Someone is lying, Juan Diego was thinking. He didn't put it past Dorothy to have stuck the caterpillar all the way up one nostril, as far as it would go. Juan Diego didn't put it past young Werner, either.

'Was it a green and yellow caterpillar, with dark-brown eyebrows?' Juan Diego texted Clark.

'It WAS!' Clark answered him. I guess Werner got a good look at the caterpillar, Juan Diego was thinking.

'Definitely witchcraft,' Juan Diego texted Clark. 'I'm not sleeping with Dorothy or her mother anymore,' he added.

'Poor Leslie will be at our onstage event tonight,' was Clark's reply. 'Will D. be there? With her MOTHER? Leslie says she's surprised D. has a mother, living.'

'Yes, Dorothy and her mother will be there,' was Juan Diego's last text message to Clark. It gave him some small pleasure to send it. Juan Diego was noticing it was less stressful to do mindless things when you were a little low on adrenaline.

Was this why retired men were content to putter around their backyards, or play golf, or do shit like that – like sending text messages, one tedious letter at a time? Juan Diego was wondering. Was trivia more tolerable when you were already feeling diminished?

He'd not anticipated that the news on TV, and in the newspaper the hotel delivered to his room, would be *all* about the Black Nazarene procession in Manila. The only news was local. He'd been so out of it on Sunday, he hadn't noticed there was a drizzling rain all day – 'a northeast monsoon,' the newspaper called it. Despite the weather, an estimated 1.7 million Filipino Catholics (many of them barefoot) turned out for the procession; the devotees were joined by 3,500 police officers. As in previous years, several hundred injuries were reported. Three devotees fell or jumped off the Quezon Bridge, the Coast Guard reported; the Coast Guard also said they'd deployed several intelligence teams in inflatable boats to patrol the Pasig River – 'not only to provide security for the devotees, but to be on the lookout for any outsiders who might create an unusual scenario.'

What 'unusual scenario'? Juan Diego had wondered.

The procession always ended up back at Quiapo Church, where the practice called *pahalik* was performed – the act of kissing the statue of the Black Nazarene. Mobs of people waited in line, crowding the altar area, waiting for a chance to kiss the statue.

And now a doctor was on TV, speaking dismissively of the 'minor injuries' suffered by 560 devotees at this year's Black Nazarene procession. The doctor strongly suggested that all the lacerations were to be expected. 'Typical crowd-type injuries, such as tripping – the bare feet are just asking for trouble,' the doctor said. He was young and impatient-looking. And the abdominal issues? the young doctor was asked. 'Brought on by bad food choices,' the doctor said. What about all the sprains? 'More crowd-type injuries – falls, from all the pushing and shoving,' the doctor answered, sighing. And all the headaches? 'Dehydration – people don't drink enough water,' the doctor said, with rising contempt. Hundreds of marchers had been treated for dizziness and difficulty breathing – some fainted, the doctor was told. 'Unfamiliarity with marching!' the doctor cried, throwing up his hands; he reminded Juan Diego of

Dr. Vargas. (The young doctor seemed on the verge of crying out, 'The problem is *religion*!')

How about the incidences of back pain? 'Could be caused by anything – definitely exacerbated by all the pushing and shoving,' the doctor replied; he had closed his eyes. And hypertension? 'Could be caused by *anything*,' the doctor repeated – he kept his eyes closed. 'More marching-related business is a likely cause.' His voice had all but trailed away when the young doctor suddenly opened his eyes and spoke directly to the camera. 'I'll tell you what the Black Nazarene procession is *good* for,' he said. 'The procession is good for scavengers.'

Naturally, a dump kid would be sensitive to this derogatory-sounding use of the *scavengers* word. Juan Diego wasn't only imagining los pepenadores from the basurero; in addition to the *professional* trash collectors of the dump-kid kind, Juan Diego was thinking sympathetically of dogs and seagulls. But the young doctor wasn't speaking derogatorily; he was being very derogatory about the Black Nazarene procession, but in saying the procession was *good* for 'scavengers,' he meant it was good for poor people – the ones who followed after the devotees, cashing in on all the discarded water bottles and plastic food containers.

Ah, well – *poor people*, Juan Diego thought. There was certainly a history that linked the Catholic Church to poor people. Juan Diego usually fought with Clark French about that.

Of course the Church was 'genuine' in its love for

poor people, as Clark always argued – Juan Diego didn't dispute this. Why *wouldn't* the Church love poor people? Juan Diego was in the habit of asking Clark. But what about birth control? What about abortion? It was the 'social agenda' of the Catholic Church that made Juan Diego mad. The Church's policies – in opposition to abortion, even in opposition to contraception! – not only *subjected* women to the 'enslavement of childbirth,' as Juan Diego had put it to Clark; the Church's policies kept the poor poor, or made them poorer. Poor people kept reproducing, didn't they? Juan Diego kept asking Clark.

Juan Diego and Clark French had fought on and on about this. If the subject of the Church didn't come up when the two of them were onstage tonight, or when they were out to dinner afterward, how could it not come up when they were together in a Roman Catholic church tomorrow morning? How could Clark and Juan Diego coexist in the Our Lady of Guadalupe church in Manila without a recurrence of their oh-so-familiar Catholic conversation?

Just thinking about this conversation made Juan Diego aware of his adrenaline – namely, needing it. It wasn't only for sex that Juan Diego wanted the adrenaline release he'd been missing since he'd started the beta-blockers. The dump reader had first encountered a little Catholic history on the singed pages of books saved from burning; as a Lost Children kid, he thought he understood the difference between those unanswerable religious mysteries and the man-made rules of the Church.

If he was going to the Our Lady of Guadalupe church with Clark French in the morning, Juan Diego was thinking, maybe skipping a dose of his Lopressor prescription tonight wasn't a bad idea. Given who Juan Diego Guerrero was, and where he came from – well, if you were Juan Diego, and you were going to Guadalupe Viejo with Clark French, wouldn't you want as much adrenaline as you could get?

And there was the ordeal onstage, and the dinner afterward – there was tonight *and* tomorrow to get through, Juan Diego considered. To take, or not to take, the beta-blockers – that is the question, he was thinking.

The text message from Clark French was short but would suffice. 'On second thought,' Clark had written, 'let's begin with my asking you who wrote Shakespeare – we know we agree about that. This will put the issue of personal experience as the only valid basis for fiction writing behind us – we know we agree about this, too. As for the types who believe Shakespeare was someone else: they underestimate the imagination, or they overesteem personal experience – their rationale for autobiographical fiction, don't you think?' Clark French wrote to his former writing teacher. Poor Clark – still theoretical, forever juvenile, always picking fights.

Give me the adrenaline, all I can get, Juan Diego thought – once more not taking his beta-blockers.

32

Not Manila Bay

From Juan Diego's point of view, the good thing about being interviewed by Clark French was that Clark did most of the talking. The difficult part was listening to Clark; he was such a pontificator. And if Clark was on your side, he could be more embarrassing.

Juan Diego and Clark had recently read James Shapiro's *Contested Will: Who Wrote Shakespeare?* Both Clark and Juan Diego had admired the book; they'd been persuaded by Mr. Shapiro's arguments – they believed that Shakespeare of Stratford was the one and only Shakespeare; they agreed that the plays attributed to William Shakespeare were not written collaboratively, or by someone else.

Yet why, Juan Diego wondered, didn't Clark French begin by quoting Mr. Shapiro's most compelling statement – the one made in the book's epilogue? (Shapiro writes, 'What I find most disheartening about the claim that Shakespeare of Stratford lacked the life experience to have written the plays is that it diminishes the very thing that makes him so exceptional: his imagination.')

Why did Clark begin by attacking Mark Twain? An assignment to read *Life on the Mississippi*, in Clark's high school years, had caused 'an almost lethal injury to my imagination' – or so Clark complained. Twain's autobiography had nearly ended Clark's aspirations to become a writer. And according to Clark, *The Adventures of Tom Sawyer* and *The Adventures of Huckleberry Finn* should have been one novel – 'a short one,' Clark railed.

The audience, Juan Diego could tell, didn't understand the point of this rant – no mention had been made of the *other* writer onstage (namely, Juan Diego). And Juan Diego, unlike the audience, knew what was coming; he knew that the connection between Twain and Shakespeare had not yet been made.

Mark Twain was one of the culprits who believed that Shakespeare couldn't have written the plays attributed to him. Twain had stated that his own books were 'simply autobiographies'; as Mr. Shapiro wrote, Twain believed 'great fiction, including his own, was necessarily autobiographical.'

But Clark hadn't *connected* this to the who-wrote-Shakespeare debate, which Juan Diego knew was Clark's point. Instead, Clark was going on and on about Twain's lack of imagination. 'Writers who have no imagination – writers who can *only* write about their own life experiences – simply can't imagine that other writers can imagine *anything*!' Clark cried. Juan Diego wished he could disappear.

'But who wrote Shakespeare, Clark?' Juan Diego

asked his former student, trying to steer him to the point.

'*Shakespeare* wrote Shakespeare!' Clark sputtered.

'Well, that settles it,' Juan Diego said. There was a small sound from the audience, a titter or two. Clark seemed surprised by the tittering, faint though it was – as if he'd forgotten there was an audience.

Before Clark could continue – venting about the other culprits in the camp of unimaginative scoundrels who subscribed to the heresy that Shakespeare's plays had been written by someone else – Juan Diego tried to say a little about James Shapiro's excellent book: how, as Shapiro put it, 'Shakespeare did not live, as we do, in an age of memoir'; how, as Mr. Shapiro further said, 'in his own day, and for more than a century and a half after his death, nobody treated Shakespeare's works as autobiographical.'

'Lucky Shakespeare!' Clark French shouted.

A slender arm waved from the stupefied audience – a woman who was almost too small to be seen from the stage, except that her prettiness stood out (even seated, as she was, between Miriam and Dorothy). And (even from afar) the bracelets on her skinny arm were of the expensive-looking and attention-getting kind that a woman with a rich ex-husband would wear.

'Do you think Mr. Shapiro's book defames Henry James?' Leslie timidly asked from the audience. (This was, without a doubt, *poor* Leslie.)

'Henry James!' Clark cried, as if James had caused

Clark's imagination another unspeakable wound in those vulnerable high school years. Poor Leslie, small as she was, seemed to grow smaller in her seat. And was it only Juan Diego who noticed, or did Clark also see, that Leslie and Dorothy were holding hands? (So much for Leslie's *saying* she wanted nothing to do with D.!)

'Pinning down Henry James's skepticism about Shakespeare's authorship isn't easy,' Shapiro writes. 'Unlike Twain, James wasn't willing to confront the issue publicly or directly.' (Not exactly *defamatory*, Juan Diego was thinking – though he'd agreed with Shapiro's description of 'James's maddeningly elliptical and evasive style.')

'And do you think Shapiro *defames* Freud?' Clark asked his adoring writing student, but poor Leslie was now afraid of him; she looked too small to speak.

Juan Diego would have sworn that was Miriam's long arm wrapped around poor Leslie's shaking shoulders.

'Self-analysis had enabled Freud, by extension, to analyze Shakespeare,' Shapiro had written.

No one but Freud could imagine Freud's lust for his mother, or Freud's jealousy of his father, Clark was saying – and how, from *self-analysis*, Freud had concluded this was (as Freud put it) 'a universal event in early childhood.'

Oh, those universal events in early childhood! Juan Diego was thinking; he'd hoped Clark French would leave Freud out of the discussion. Juan Diego didn't want to hear what Clark French thought of the Freudian theory of penis envy.

'Just *don't*, Clark,' said a stronger-sounding female voice in the audience – not Leslie's timid voice this time. It was Clark's wife, Dr. Josefa Quintana, a most impressive woman. She stopped Clark from telling the audience his impressions of Freud – the saga of the untold damage done to literature *and* to young Clark's vulnerable imagination at a formative age.

With a beginning of this oppressive kind, how could the onstage interview hope to achieve a spontaneous liftoff? It was a wonder that the audience didn't leave – except for Leslie, whose early exit was very visible. It was a mild success that the interview got a little better. There was some mention of Juan Diego's novels, and it registered as a small triumph that the issue of Juan Diego's being, or his not being, a Mexican-American writer was discussed without further reference to Freud, James, or Twain.

But poor Leslie hadn't left alone, not entirely. If not everyone's idea of a mother and her daughter, those two women with Leslie were certainly competent-looking, and the way they'd escorted Leslie up the aisle and out of the theater suggested they were used to taking charge. In fact, how Miriam and Dorothy had taken hold of the small, pretty woman might have caused some concern among the more observant members of the audience – if anyone even noticed, or had been paying attention. The unshakable grip Miriam and Dorothy had on poor Leslie could have meant they were comforting her or *abducting* her. It was hard to tell.

And where had Miriam and Dorothy gone? Juan Diego kept wondering. Why should he care? Hadn't he wished they would just disappear? Yet what did it mean when your angels of death departed – when your personal phantasms stopped haunting you?

THE DINNER AFTER THE onstage event was in the labyrinth of the Ayala Center. To an out-of-towner, the dinner guests were not discernible from one another. Juan Diego knew who his readers were – they announced themselves by their familiarity with the details of his novels – but the dinner guests Clark identified as 'patrons of the arts' were aloof; their sympathies toward Juan Diego were unreadable.

You shouldn't generalize about those people who are patrons of the arts. Some of them have read nothing; they're often the ones who appear to have read everything. The other ones have an out-of-it expression; they seem disinclined to speak or, if they talk at all, it's only to make an offhand remark about the salad or the seating plan – and they're usually the ones who've read everything you've written, and everyone else you've ever read.

'You have to be careful around patron-des-arts types,' Clark whispered in Juan Diego's ear. 'They are not what they seem.'

Clark was wearing thin on Juan Diego – Clark could grate on anyone. There were those known things Clark and Juan Diego disagreed about, but it was when Juan Diego most agreed with Clark that Clark grated on him *more*.

To be fair: Clark had prepared him to expect 'a journalist or two' at the dinner party; Clark had also said he would warn Juan Diego about 'the ones to watch out for.' But Clark didn't know all the journalists.

One of the unknown journalists asked Juan Diego if the beer he was drinking was his first one, or his second.

'You want to know how many beers he's had?' Clark asked the young man aggressively. 'Do you know how many *novels* this author has written?' Clark further asked the journalist, who was wearing an untucked white shirt. It was a dress shirt, but one that had known fresher days. By its bedraggled appearance and a mélange of stains, the shirt – and the young man wearing it – signified, if only to Clark, a life of unclean disarray.

'Do you like San Miguel?' the journalist asked Juan Diego, pointing to the beer; he was deliberately ignoring Clark.

'Name two titles of novels this author has written – just two,' Clark told the journalist. 'Of the novels Juan Diego Guerrero has written, name one you've read – just one,' Clark said.

Juan Diego could never (*would* never) behave like Clark, but Clark was redeeming himself with each passing second; Juan Diego was remembering what he liked best about Clark French – notwithstanding all the other ways in which Clark could be Clark.

'Yes, I like San Miguel,' Juan Diego told the

journalist, holding up his beer as if he were toasting the unread young man. 'And I believe this is my second one.'

'You don't have to talk to him – he hasn't done his *homework*,' Clark said to his former teacher.

Juan Diego was thinking that his nice-guy assessment of Clark French was not quite correct; Clark *is* a nice guy, Juan Diego thought, provided you're not a journalist who hasn't done your homework.

As for the unprepared journalist, the young man who was not a reader, he had wandered off. 'I don't know who he is,' Clark muttered; he was disappointed in himself. 'But I know *that one* – I know *her*,' Clark told Juan Diego, pointing to a middle-aged woman who'd been eyeing them from afar. (She'd been waiting for the younger journalist to drift away.) 'She is a horror of insincerity – imagine a venomous hamster,' Clark hissed to Juan Diego.

'One of the ones to watch out for, I guess,' Juan Diego said; he smiled knowingly at his former student. 'I feel safe with you, Clark,' Juan Diego suddenly said. This was verily spontaneous and heartfelt, but until he said it, Juan Diego hadn't realized how unsafe he *had* felt – and for how long! (Dump kids don't take feeling safe for granted; circus kids don't assume a safety net is there.)

For his part, Clark felt moved to wrap his big, strong arm around his former teacher's slender shoulders. 'But I don't think you need my protection from *this one*,' Clark whispered in Juan Diego's ear. 'She's just a gossip.'

Clark was talking about the middle-aged woman journalist, who was now approaching – the 'venomous hamster.' Had he meant her mind ran in place, making repetitive rotations on the going-nowhere wheel? But what was *venomous* about her? 'All of her questions will be recycled – stuff she saw on the Internet, the reiteration of every stupid question you were ever asked,' Clark was whispering in his former teacher's ear. 'She will not have read a single novel you've written, but she'll have read everything *about* you. I'm sure you know the type,' Clark added.

'I *know*, Clark – thank you,' Juan Diego gently said, smiling at his former student. Mercifully, Josefa was there – the good Dr. Quintana was dragging her husband away. Juan Diego had not realized he'd been standing in the food line until he saw the buffet table; it was dead ahead.

'You should have the fish,' the woman journalist told him. Juan Diego saw that she'd inserted herself in the food line beside him, possibly the way venomous hamsters do.

'That looks like a cheese sauce, on the fish,' was all Juan Diego said; he helped himself to the Korean glass noodles with vegetables, and to something called Vietnamese beef.

'I don't think I've seen anyone actually eat the mangled beef here,' the journalist said. She must have meant to say 'shredded,' Juan Diego was thinking, but he didn't say anything. (Maybe the Vietnamese *mangled* their beef; Juan Diego didn't know.)

'The small, pretty woman – the one who was there tonight,' the middle-aged woman said, helping herself to the fish. 'She left early,' she added, after a long pause.

'Yes, I know who you mean – Leslie someone. I don't know her,' was all Juan Diego said.

'Leslie someone told me to tell you something,' the middle-aged woman told him, in a confiding (not quite motherly) tone.

Juan Diego waited; he didn't want to appear too interested. And he was looking everywhere for Clark and Josefa; he realized he wouldn't object if Clark bullied this woman journalist, just a little.

'Leslie said to tell you that the woman with Dorothy can't be Dorothy's mother. Leslie said the older woman isn't old enough to be Dorothy's mother – besides, they look nothing alike,' the journalist said.

'Do you know Miriam and Dorothy?' Juan Diego asked the frumpy-looking woman. She was wearing a peasant-style blouse – the kind of loose shirt the American hippie women wore in Oaxaca, those women who didn't wear bras and put flowers in their hair.

'Well, I don't *know* them – I just saw they were very much *with* Leslie,' the woman journalist said. 'And they left early, too, with Leslie. For what it's worth, I thought the older of the two women *wasn't* old enough to be the younger one's mother. And they *didn't* look anything alike – not to me,' she added.

'I saw them, too,' was all Juan Diego said. It was hard to imagine why Miriam and Dorothy were *with*

Leslie, Juan Diego thought. Perhaps harder to imagine was why poor Leslie was with them.

Clark must have gone to the men's room, Juan Diego was thinking; he was nowhere in sight. Yet an unlikely-looking savior was headed Juan Diego's way; she was dressed badly enough to be another journalist, but there was the recognizable glint of unexpressed intimacies in her eager eyes – as if reading him had changed her life. She had stories to share, of how he'd rescued her: maybe she'd been contemplating suicide; or she was pregnant with her first child, at sixteen; or she'd lost a child when she happened to read – well, these were the kind of intimacies glinting in her I-was-saved-by-reading-you eyes. Juan Diego loved his diehard readers. The details they'd cherished in his novels seemed to sparkle in their eyes.

The woman journalist saw the diehard reader coming. Was there some partial recognition between them? Juan Diego couldn't tell. They were women of a similar age.

'I *like* Mark Twain,' the journalist said to Juan Diego – her parting shot, as she was leaving. Was that all she had for *venom*? Juan Diego wondered.

'Be sure to tell Clark,' he told her, but she might not have heard him – she seemed to be leaving in a hurry.

'Go away!' Juan Diego's avid reader called after the woman journalist. 'She hasn't read anything,' the new arrival announced to Juan Diego. 'I'm your biggest fan.'

To tell the truth, she was a big woman, easily 170

or 180 pounds. She wore baggy blue jeans, torn at both knees, and a black T-shirt with a fierce-looking tiger between her breasts. It was a protest T-shirt, expressing anger on behalf of an endangered species. Juan Diego was so out of it, he didn't know tigers were in trouble.

'Look at you – you're having the beef, too!' his new biggest fan cried, wrapping an arm as seemingly strong as Clark's around Juan Diego's smaller shoulders. 'I'll tell you something,' the big woman told Juan Diego, leading him to her table. 'You know that scene with the duck hunters? When the idiot forgets to take off the condom, and he goes home and starts peeing in front of his wife? I *love* that scene!' the woman who loved tigers told him, pushing him ahead of her.

'Not everyone was fond of that scene,' Juan Diego tried to point out to her. He was remembering a review or two.

'Shakespeare wrote Shakespeare, right?' the big woman asked him, pushing him toward a seat.

'Yes, I think so,' Juan Diego said warily. He was still looking all around for Clark and Josefa; he *did* love his diehard readers, but they could be a little overwhelming.

It was Josefa who found him, and took him to the table where she and Clark had been waiting. 'The save-the-tiger woman is a journalist, too – one of the good ones,' Clark told him. 'One who actually reads novels.'

'I saw Miriam and Dorothy at the onstage event,'

Juan Diego told Clark. 'Your friend Leslie was with them.'

'Oh, I saw Miriam with someone I didn't know,' Josefa said.

'Her daughter, Dorothy,' Juan Diego told the doctor.

'D.,' Clark explained. (It was obvious Clark and Josefa had discussed Dorothy as *D*.)

'The woman I saw didn't look like Miriam's *daughter*,' Dr. Quintana said. 'She wasn't beautiful enough.'

'I'm very disappointed in Leslie,' Clark told his former teacher and his wife. Josefa said nothing.

'Very disappointed,' was all Juan Diego could say. But all he could think about was Leslie *someone*. Why would she have gone anywhere with Dorothy and Miriam? Why would she even be with them? Poor Leslie wouldn't have been with them, Juan Diego thought – not unless she'd been *bewitched*.

IT WAS A TUESDAY morning in Manila – January 11, 2011 – and the weekend news from Juan Diego's adopted country wasn't good. This had happened on Saturday: Representative Gabrielle Giffords, an Arizona Democrat, had been shot in the head; she was given a fair chance to survive, if not with all her brain function. Six people were dead in the shooting rampage, including a nine-year-old girl.

The Arizona shooter was a twenty-two-year-old; he'd been firing a Glock semiautomatic pistol with a high-capacity magazine that held thirty rounds. The shooter's reported utterances made him sound illogical and incoherent – was he another whack-job anarchist? Juan Diego wondered.

Here I am in the faraway Philippines, Juan Diego was thinking, but my adopted country's home-grown hatreds and vigilante-minded divisiveness are never that far away.

As for the local news – at his breakfast table at the Ascott, Juan Diego was reading a Manila newspaper – he saw that the good journalist, his diehard reader, had done him no damage. The profile of Juan Diego Guerrero was informed and complimentary about his novels; the big journalist Clark had called the 'save-the-tiger woman' was a good reader, and she'd been very respectful of Juan Diego. The photo the newspaper ran wasn't her fault, Juan Diego knew; an asswheel photo editor doubtlessly chose the photograph; nor could the woman who loved tigers be blamed for the caption.

In the photo of the visiting author – at the dinner table, with his beer and his *mangled* beef – Juan Diego's eyes were closed. He looked worse than asleep; he appeared to have passed out in an inebriated stupor. The caption read: HE LIKES SAN MIGUEL BEER.

Juan Diego's irritation at the caption might have been an early indication to him that his adrenaline was raring to go, but he didn't think twice about it. And whatever slight indigestion he'd been sensing – maybe his heartburn was acting up again – Juan Diego paid no attention to it. In a foreign country, it was easy to eat something that disagreed with your stomach. What he'd had for breakfast, or last night's Vietnamese beef, could have been the cause – or so Juan Diego assumed as he crossed the long lobby of the Ascott to the elevators, where he saw that Clark French was waiting.

'Well, I'm relieved to see your eyes are open this morning!' Clark greeted his former teacher. Clearly, Clark had seen the photo of Juan Diego with his eyes closed in the newspaper. Clark had a gift for conversation stoppers.

Unsurprisingly, Clark and Juan Diego didn't know what else to say to each other when they were descending in the elevator at the Ascott. The car, with Bienvenido in the driver's seat, was waiting for them at street level, where Juan Diego trustingly held out his hand to one of the bomb-sniffing dogs. Clark French, who'd never failed to do his homework, began lecturing as soon as they had gotten under way to Guadalupe Viejo.

The Guadalupe district of Makati City had been formed into a barrio and was named after the 'patroness' of the first Spanish settlers – 'friends of your old friends, and mine, from the Society of Jesus,' was the way Clark put it to his former teacher.

'Oh, those Jesuits – how they get around,' Juan Diego said; it was not a lot to say, but he was surprised by how hard it was to talk and breathe at the same time. Juan Diego was aware that his breathing no longer felt like a natural process. Something was sitting, most intractably, in his stomach; yet it weighed very heavily on his chest. It must have been the beef – definitely *mangled*, Juan Diego was thinking. His face felt flushed; he'd started to sweat. For someone who hated air-conditioning, Juan Diego was about to ask Bienvenido to make the car a little colder, but he stopped himself from asking – suddenly, with the effort it took to breathe, he doubted he could speak.

During World War II, the Guadalupe district had been the hardest-hit barrio in Makati City, Clark French was lecturing.

'Men, women, and children were massacred by the Japanese soldiers,' Bienvenido had chimed in.

Of course Juan Diego could see where this was going – leave it to Our Lady of Guadalupe to *protect* everyone! Juan Diego knew how the so-called pro-life advocates had appropriated Guadalupe. 'From the womb to the tomb,' various prelates of the Church were ceaselessly intoning.

And what were the solemn-sounding lines from Jeremiah they were always quoting? Idiots held up signs in the end-zone seats at football games: JEREMIAH 1:5. How did it go? Juan Diego wanted to ask Clark. He knew Clark would know it by heart: 'Before I formed you in the womb I knew you; before you were born I set you apart.' (It was something like that.) Juan Diego tried to tell Clark his thoughts, but the words wouldn't come; only his breathing mattered. His sweat now poured forth; his clothes clung to him. If he'd tried to speak, Juan Diego knew he would get no further than 'Before I formed you in the womb—' at the *womb* word, he suspected he would vomit.

Maybe the car was making him sick – a kind of motion sickness? Juan Diego was wondering, as Bienvenido drove them slowly through the narrow streets of the slum on the hill above the Pasig River. In the soot-stained courtyard of the old church and monastery was a sign with a warning: BEWARE OF DOGS.

'Of *all* dogs?' Juan Diego gasped, but Bienvenido was parking the car. Clark, of course, was talking. No one had heard Juan Diego try to speak.

There was a green bush next to the Jesus figure at the entrance of the monasterio; the bush was decorated with gaudy stars, like a tacky Christmas tree.

'Christmas here goes on for fucking forever,' Juan Diego could hear Dorothy saying – or he imagined that this was what Dorothy would say, if she were standing beside him in the courtyard of the Our Lady of Guadalupe church. But, of course, Dorothy wasn't there – only her voice. Was he hearing things? Juan Diego wondered. What he heard most of all – what he'd not noticed hearing before – was the wild, ramped-up beating of his heart.

The blue-cloaked statue of Santa Maria de Guadalupe, half obscured by the palm trees shading the soot-darkened walls of the monastery, had an unreadably calm expression for someone who had endured such a calamitous history – Clark, of course, was reciting the history, his professorial tone in

seeming rhythm with the percussive pounding of
Juan Diego's heart.

For no known reason, the monasterio was closed,
but Clark led his former teacher into the Guadalupe
church – it was officially called Nuestra Señora de
Gracia, Clark was explaining. Not *another* Our Lady
– enough of the 'Our Lady' business! Juan Diego was
thinking, but he said nothing, trying to save his
breath.

The image of Our Lady of Guadalupe had been
brought from Spain in 1604; in 1629, the buildings
of the church and monastery were completed. Sixty
thousand Chinese rose in arms in 1639, Clark was
telling Juan Diego – no explanation was given as to
why! But the Spaniards brought the image of Our
Lady of Guadalupe to the battlefield; miraculously,
there were peaceful negotiations and bloodshed was
averted. (Maybe not *miraculously* – who said this was
a miracle? Juan Diego was thinking.)

There'd been more trouble, of course: in 1763, the
occupation of the church and monastery by British
troops – burning and destruction ensued. The image
of the Lady of Guadalupe was saved by an Irish
Catholic 'official.' (What kind of *official* came to the
rescue? Juan Diego was wondering.)

Bienvenido had waited with the car. Clark and
Juan Diego were alone inside the old church, except
for what appeared to be two mourners; they knelt in
the foremost pew, before the tasteful, almost delicate-
looking altar table and the not-imposing Guadalupe
portrait. Two women, all in black – they wore veils,

their heads completely covered. Clark kept his voice low, respecting the deceased.

Earthquakes had nearly leveled Manila in 1850; the vault of the church collapsed amid the tremors. In 1882, the monastery was turned into an orphanage for the children of cholera victims. In 1898, Pío del Pilar – a revolutionary general of the Philippines – occupied the church and monastery with his rebels. Pío was forced to retreat from the Americans in 1899, setting the church on fire as he fled – furniture, documents, and books were burned.

Jesus, Clark – can't you see there's something wrong with me? Juan Diego was thinking. Juan Diego knew something was wrong, but Clark wasn't looking at him.

In 1935, Clark suddenly announced, Pope Pius XI declared that Our Lady of Guadalupe was 'patroness of the Philippines.' In 1941, the American bombers came – they shelled the shit out of the Japanese soldiers who were hiding in the ruins of the Guadalupe church. In 1995, the restoration of the church altar and sacristy was completed – thus Clark concluded his recitation. The silent mourners had not moved; the two women in black, their heads bowed, were as motionless as statues.

Juan Diego was still struggling to breathe, but the sharpening pain now made him alternately hold his breath, then gasp for air, then hold his breath. Clark French – as always, consumed by his own way with words – had failed to notice his former teacher's distress.

Juan Diego believed he couldn't possibly say all of Jeremiah 1:5; that was too much to say with how little breath he had left. He decided to say only the last part; Juan Diego knew that Clark would understand what he was saying. Juan Diego struggled to say it – just the 'before you were born I set you apart.'

'I prefer saying "I sanctified you" to your saying "I set you apart" – though both are correct,' Clark told his former teacher, before turning to look at him. Clark caught Juan Diego under both arms, or Juan Diego would have fallen.

In the commotion that followed in the old church, neither Clark nor Juan Diego would have noticed the silent mourners – the two kneeling women had only slightly turned their heads. They'd lifted their veils, no more than enough to allow them to observe the comings and goings at the rear of the church – Clark ran out to fetch Bienvenido; the two men then carried Juan Diego from where Clark had left his former teacher, lying in the hindmost pew. In such obvious emergency circumstances – and kneeling, as the two women were, in the forefront of the dimly lit old church – no one would have recognized Miriam or Dorothy (not all in black, and not with their scarves still covering their heads).

Juan Diego was a novelist who paid attention to the chronology of a story; in his case, as a writer, the choice of where to begin or end a story was always a conscious one. But was Juan Diego conscious that he'd begun to die? He must have known that the effort to breathe and the pain of breathing could not have been the Vietnamese beef, but what Clark and Bienvenido were saying seemed of little importance to Juan Diego. Bienvenido would have vented his opinion of the 'dirty government hospitals'; of course Clark would have wanted Juan Diego to go to the hospital where his wife worked – where surely everyone would know Dr. Josefa Quintana, where Clark's former teacher would receive the best possible care.

'As luck would have it,' Juan Diego may have heard his former student say to Bienvenido. Clark said this in response to Bienvenido's telling him that the nearest Catholic hospital to the Guadalupe church was in San Juan City; part of metropolitan Manila, San Juan was the town next to Makati, only twenty minutes away. What Clark meant by 'luck' was that this was the hospital where his wife worked – the Cardinal Santos Medical Center.

From Juan Diego's point of view, the twenty-minute drive was dreamlike but a blur; nothing that was real registered with him. Not the Greenhills Shopping Center, which was fairly close to the hospital – not even the oddly named Wack Wack Golf & Country Club, adjacent to the medical center. Clark was worried about his dear former teacher, because Juan Diego didn't respond to Clark's comment about the spelling of Wack. 'Surely one *whacks* a golf ball – there's an *h* in *whack*, or there should be,' Clark said. 'I've always thought golfers were wasting their time – it's no surprise they can't spell.'

But Juan Diego didn't respond; Clark's former

teacher didn't even react to the crucifixes in the emergency room at Cardinal Santos – this really worried Clark. Nor did Juan Diego seem to notice the nuns, making their regular rounds. (At Cardinal Santos, Clark knew, there was always a priest or two on hand in the mornings; they were giving Communion to those patients who wanted it.)

'Mister is going swimming!' Juan Diego imagined he heard Consuelo cry, but the little girl in pigtails was not among the upturned faces in the enveloping crowd. No Filipinos were watching, and Juan Diego wasn't swimming; he was walking without a limp, at last. He was walking upside down, of course; he was skywalking, at eighty feet – he'd taken the first two of those death-daring steps. (And then another two, and then two more.) Once again, the past surrounded him – like those upturned faces in the watchful crowd.

Juan Diego imagined Dolores was there; she was saying, 'When you skywalk for the virgins, they let you do it forever.' But skywalking wasn't a big deal for a dump reader. Juan Diego had snatched the first books he read from the hellfires of the basurero; he'd burned his hands saving books from burning. What were sixteen steps at eighty feet for a dump reader? Wasn't this the life he might have had, if he'd been brave enough to seize it? But you don't see the future clearly when you're only fourteen.

'We're the miraculous ones,' Lupe had tried to tell him. 'You have another future!' she'd correctly predicted. And, really, for how long could he have kept himself and his little sister alive – even if he'd become a skywalker?

There were just ten more steps, Juan Diego thought; he'd been silently counting the steps to himself. (Of course, no one in the emergency room at Cardinal Santos knew he was counting.)

The ER nurse knew she was losing him. She'd already called for a cardiologist; Clark had insisted that his wife be paged – naturally, he'd been texting her, too. 'Dr. Quintana is coming, isn't she?' the ER nurse asked Clark; in the nurse's opinion, this didn't matter, but she thought it was wise to keep Clark distracted.

'Yes, yes – she's coming,' Clark muttered. He was texting Josefa again – it was something to do. It suddenly irritated him that the old nun who'd admitted them to the ER was still there, still hovering near them. And now the old nun crossed herself, her lips moving inaudibly. What was she doing? Clark wondered – was she *praying*? Even her praying irritated him.

'Perhaps a *priest*—' the old nun started to say, but Clark stopped her.

'No – no priest!' Clark told her. 'Juan Diego wouldn't want a priest.'

'No, indeed – he most definitely *wouldn't*,' Clark heard someone say. It was a woman's voice, very authoritative, a voice he'd heard before – but when, but where? Clark was wondering.

When Clark looked up from his cell phone, Juan Diego had silently counted two more steps – then

two more, and then another two. (There were only
four more steps to go! Juan Diego was thinking.)

Clark French saw no one with his former teacher
in the emergency room – no one except the ER nurse
and the old nun. The latter lady had moved away; she
was now standing at a respectful distance from where
Juan Diego lay fighting for his life. But two women –
all in black, their heads completely covered – were
passing in the hall, just gliding by, and Clark caught
only a glimpse of them before they vanished. Clark
didn't really get a good look at them. He'd distinctly
heard Miriam say, 'No, indeed – he most definitely
wouldn't.' But Clark would never connect the voice
he'd heard with that woman who'd stabbed the gecko
with a salad fork at the Encantador.

In all probability – even if Clark French had gotten
a good look at those women gliding by in the hall –
he wouldn't have said the two women in black
resembled a mother and her daughter. The way the
women's heads were covered, and how they weren't
speaking to each other, made Clark French think the
women were nuns – from an order whose all-black
habits seemed standard to him. (As for Miriam and
Dorothy, they'd just disappeared – in that way they
had. Those two were always just appearing, or disappearing, weren't they?)

'I'll go find Josefa myself,' Clark said helplessly to
the ER nurse. (Good riddance – you're of no use here!
she might have thought, if she thought anything.)
'No priest!' Clark repeated, almost angrily, to the old
nun. The nun said nothing; she'd seen dying of all

kinds – she was familiar with the process, and with all sorts of desperate, last-minute behavior (such as Clark's).

The ER nurse knew when a heart was finished; neither an OB-GYN nor a cardiologist would jump-start this one, the nurse knew, but – even so – she went looking for *someone*.

Juan Diego was looking like he'd lost count of something. Isn't it only two more steps, or is it still four more? Juan Diego was thinking. He hesitated to take the next step. Skywalkers (real skywalkers) know better than to hesitate, but Juan Diego just stopped skywalking. That was when he knew he wasn't *really* skywalking; that was when Juan Diego understood that he was just imagining.

It was what he was truly good at – just imagining. Juan Diego knew then that he was dying – the dying wasn't imaginary. And he realized that this, exactly this, was what people did when they died; this was what people wanted when they passed away – well, it was what Juan Diego wanted, anyway. Not necessarily the life everlasting, not a so-called life after death, but the actual life he *wished* he'd had – the hero's life he once imagined for himself.

So this is death – this is all death is, Juan Diego thought. It made him feel a little better about Lupe. Death was not even a surprise. 'Ni siquiera una sorpresa,' the old nun heard Juan Diego say. ('Not even a surprise.')

Now there was no chance to leave Lithuania. Now there was no light – there was only the unlit darkness. That was what Dorothy had called the view from the plane of Manila Bay, when you were approaching Manila at night: an unlit darkness. 'Except for the occasional ship,' she'd told him. 'The darkness is Manila Bay,' Dorothy had explained. Not this time, Juan Diego knew – not this darkness. There were no lights, no ships – this unlit darkness was not Manila Bay.

In her shriveled left hand, the old nun clutched the crucifix around her neck; making a fist, she held the crucified Christ against her beating heart. No one – least of all, Juan Diego, who was dead – heard her say, in Latin, 'Sic transit gloria mundi.' ('Thus passes the glory of this world.') Not that anyone would have doubted such a venerable-looking nun, and she was right; not even Clark French, had he been there, would have uttered a qualifying word. Not every collision course comes as a surprise.

• Acknowledgments •

- Julia Arvin
- Martin Bell
- David Calicchio
- Nina Cochran
- Emily Copeland
- Nicole Dancel
- Rick Dancel
- Daiva Daugirdienė
- John DiBlasio
- Minnie Domingo
- Rodrigo Fresán
- Gail Godwin
- Dave Gould
- Ron Hansen
- Everett Irving
- Janet Irving
- Stephanie Irving
- Bronwen Jervis
- Karina Juárez
- Delia Louzán
- Mary Ellen Mark

- José Antonio Martínez
- Anna von Planta
- Benjamin Alire Sáenz
- Marty Schwartz
- Nick Spengler
- Jack Stapleton
- Abraham Verghese
- Ana Isabel Villaseñor

A Prayer for Owen Meany

John Irving

Eleven-year-old Owen Meany, playing in a Little League baseball game in Gravesend, New Hampshire, hits a foul ball and kills his best friend's mother. Owen doesn't believe in accidents; he believes he is God's instrument. What happens to Owen after that 1953 foul is both extraordinary and terrifying. At moments a comic, self-deluded victim, but in the end the principal, tragic actor in a divine plan, Owen Meany is the most heartbreaking hero John Irving has yet created.

'Marvellously funny . . . the author's wit is an intrinsic part of the book . . . What better entertainment is there than a serious book which makes you laugh?'
PHILIP GLAZEBROOK, *SPECTATOR*

'I believe it to be a work of genius . . . Because of its absolutely irrepressible flow of invention and suggestion, expressed in some of the most fascinating prose written in fiction today. Originality has distinguished all Mr Irving's books, but in *A Prayer for Owen Meany* it achieves a new pitch and a new profundity'
JAN MORRIS, *INDEPENDENT*

The Cider House Rules

John Irving

Set among the apple orchards of rural Maine, it is a perverse world in which Homer Wells' odyssey begins. As the oldest unadopted offspring at St Cloud's orphanage, he learns about the skills which, one way or another, help young and not-so-young women, from Wilbur Larch, the orphanage's founder, a man of rare compassion and with an addiction to ether.

Dr Larch loves all his orphans, especially Homer Wells. It is Homer's story we follow, from his early apprenticeship in the orphanage surgery, to his adult life running a cider-making factory and his strange relationship with the wife of his closest friend.

'John Irving has been compared with Kurt Vonnegut and J.D. Salinger, but is arguably more inventive than either. Wry, laconic, he sketches his characters with an economy that springs from a feeling for words and mastery over his craft. This superbly original book is one to be read and remembered'
THE TIMES

'*The Cider House Rules* is difficult to define and impossible not to admire'
DAILY TELEGRAPH